I0760845

Reden Books Collector's Edition Volume 2

The Phantom Series

Laura C. Reden

Reden Books Collector's Edition Vol. 2:

The Phantom Series

Hardback: ISBN 978-1-954587-36-6

eBook: ISBN 978-1-954587-28-1

Laura's Book Count 8-11

Edited by:

Maxwell Anderson

Sandusky Editorial Services

Cover designed by Laura C. Reden

Cover Images:

© Adobe Stock / fran_kie

© Adobe Stock / kromkrathog

© Adobe Stock / Deleon 8211

© Envato Elements / helga_helga

© Envato Elements / Kateryna_Maksymenko

© Envato Elements / JRChild

Dream Big . . .

Contents

Phantom Reality
Volume 1

Dark Reflections
Volume 2

Haunted Waters
Volume 3

Beautiful Poison
Volume 4

Phantom Reality

Volume 1

PHANTOM
REALITY

Prologue

I always wanted a scar. Nothing revolting. Just a gash. A sexy one that said I was dangerous . . . or that I could be. Like, you didn't know what you were getting into when you met me. I'd be mysterious, and often, I'd be known as "that girl." But as the tires lifted off the highway and the sky fell sideways through the windshield of my car, all I could think was, *Not like this. Not now*.

1

The loons let out their long, mournful wails across Baylor Lake, serenading us with their haunting symphony. The water was deep with deceit, and the summer air was warm and thick with secrets that kicked up like the dust when the light breeze blew. The dusk-lit sky illuminated the water's glassy surface, but there was no way of telling what lay below.

But all I could see now was the silhouette of Noah and the wide grin on his face that screamed of freedom and the beginning of our independence. It was too dim to see his blue eyes or the sandy golden hues of his hair. Too dark to see the fine lines around his eyes that I knew were there with that smile he wore. The one that had brought butterflies to my stomach for the past two years. And it was far too dark to see my dead grandmother standing by the water's edge.

"No way!" Asher exclaimed, admiring the view from the back porch. He stretched across the railing, taking in the lake's serenity. Yeah, he was excited. We all were.

"We get to stay here all summer?" Kimber asked in disbelief, as she wrapped her hand around the crook of Asher's elbow.

"This place is amazing, Kins! Why haven't we been here before?" Noah poked me in the side playfully, and I smirked, biting the inside of my cheek as I basked in his attention. The cabin had been left to my great uncle Tanner when his parents passed. My family had visited every summer since. But this summer was different. The twelve of us were here for two months, celebrating our high school graduation. Some of us were here to say goodbye before moving away for college, others were here for the memories, and I had my suspicions that at least one of us was here to hook up. *Levi.* But it was probably more than just him. We were a rowdy bunch, and we were young and full of promise.

That wasn't why I was here, though, and that's not why I'd invited the group to come with me. While it's true I'd wished for Noah's heart while blowing out my eighteenth birthday candles, I was here to celebrate my independence. I'd been planning the trip with Lainey our entire senior year, and nothing was going to change that. *Nothing.*

It was the first time we'd be away from our parents for an extended length of time. This summer, we hung in the balance between needing to be looked after by our parents and being fully capable adults, living on our own. Come fall, most of us would set off to realize our full potential. But this summer? This summer, we had each other. We would be a safety net for each other if one of us fell. We would look out for one another. We would be our own family of misfits.

"I'm going in!" Mason yelled. He ripped his T-shirt off and threw it to the floor. Scarlett May threw her hands up in the air and hollered before taking off her top. Her bra was a sweet baby blue, full of intricate eyelet lace. Emma's eyes grew large as she watched Scarlett May strip down to a matching lace thong. It sent the boys into a frenzy of adrenaline and testosterone, and before I knew it, they were all taking their clothes off. I felt it too. The heat flushed my cheeks and rolled down to my belly, making me want to do something crazy—something stupid.

Luggage was dropped and backpacks tossed. Shoes were kicked off and flew through the air, some rolling down the hill toward the lake. I was transfixed by the shadow of Noah's obliques, my eyes traveling further down. My breath quickened.

"Last one in's a rotten egg!" Asher yelled in a full run. Kimber threw her duffel bag to the ground, and I shrugged off my backpack onto the wooden planked deck and shimmied out of my jeans. Every single one of us stripped and ran down to the dock, even Emma in her plain cotton bralette. The grass was dry, and the pine needles were sharp beneath my feet. My heart raced with excitement as I ran side by side with my best friends to the old wooden dock to begin what promised to be the best summer of our lives.

I had the faintest memory of running past my gran. It wasn't that I saw her there in the flesh; it was more like I felt her presence. I knew she was watching. Always watching. She'd died of cancer just three days shy of my eighteenth birthday, and ever since, I'd been having dreams about her. Realistic dreams. Lasting dreams. The kind that stuck with you long after you woke. Her presence haunted me when nobody was there and my mind fell quiet. Losing her was harder than anything I'd ever gone through in my short life. But her presence thereafter, terrified me.

I loved my late gran—more than anything—but that didn't mean I wanted her looming over me. Watching me from the shadows. Her passing had been painful enough. So much so, I could barely acknowledge it. I'd rather forget. Push it away and never look at it again. But she wouldn't let that happen. And to my surprise, she'd apparently followed me to Baylor Lake. I didn't know why, but I knew it made me feel legitimately nuts.

There was a part of me that thought I could hide all that crazy behind my friends. Bury it in my feelings for Noah and forget all about the pain of losing somebody I'd loved while I busied myself at the Water's Edge Concert, the Fourth of July Baylor Parade, and Summerfield State Fair. It was going to be the best summer yet, and I was sure by the end of it, I'd no longer be haunted by dreams of my late gran. And I'd no longer feel the hollow ache in my heart when I was reminded of her. I'd leave this lake house a woman, no longer a girl afraid of the things she couldn't see. I was ready to put the childish fears to bed.

It was no surprise that Mason Fry was the first one in the water. He flipped off the dock and landed with a heavy splash. We were all a little crazy here, but Mason was known for it. In a world of impulsivity, Mason was the one you could count on to do something outrageous. Seconds later, Asher dove in. His body was like that of a Greek god, and his goddess was Kimber, who stood at the edge of the dock with her arms wrapped around her tiny waist.

"Come on!" Asher yelled, slapping the water. Kimber plugged her nose and took the leap with much trepidation and a small squeal. Ethan Patrick pushed Emma in, and I laughed at her as I leaped onto Noah's back, wrapping my legs around his tight core. He grabbed the backs of my knees and took off running down the dock. I held my breath as he launched into the air, and for just a moment, it was like I was flying.

I had my whole life ahead of me . . . and my legs wrapped around Noah's waist. Something in me felt different. Like I was on the brink of a new life. And I had the power to make of it whatever I wanted. Whatever I longed for. Change was just around the corner, and it was mine for the taking.

I tightened my grip across his chest as we plunged into the lake. The water was chilly and invigorating. Just what we needed after a long idle plane ride. I let go of Noah's sleek body and dared to open my eyes underwater. My eyes stung as I searched for him, but the water was far too dark to see anything. I kicked to the surface and filled my lungs. As I did, Trinity dove in next to us, and I turned just in time to see Lainey jump in. Her dog, Gunner, was barking at the end of the dock, pacing back and forth. It didn't take long before he dove in after her, and his brown head popped out of the water as he swam to her side.

Lainey was my best friend. She was cautious and timid, and she suffered from anxiety. I had always thought it was a trait passed down from her mother. Her mom had barely let her come to the lake house. We'd begged and begged for the better part of our senior year, and bringing the dog was one of her conditions, among many others. Call every night, don't stay out late, don't take drinks from strangers, don't walk alone. The list went on and on. The dog was her comfort, though, and we'd all agreed he would be our group's mascot. Everyone cheered when Gunner leaped into the water.

Noah grabbed my waist, and while his hands fumbled around on my bare skin, I splashed water in his face, an oversized goofy smile on my face. I reached out for him, but Trinity got to him first. She dunked his head under the water, stealing the bits of attention that kept me fed. But I was hungry for more, and she was getting on my nerves. I swam away so I wouldn't have to see him flirting with her. It was easier to deal with when I closed my eyes to it.

Trinity was bold, but more than that, she was malicious. She didn't really want Noah. I knew that. She only wanted me to know that she could have him if she wanted. I couldn't stand it, always being trumped by her, but she was a part of our group, and whether I liked it or not, I was the one who'd invited her. I hadn't been able to stand the thought of being socially uncomfortable all senior year as we planned a trip for the group but excluded her. So, against my better judgment, I'd invited everybody. And I can't say I was surprised when she continued her hunt for Noah. Just because it was my cabin we were staying at didn't mean she'd back off from my crush. And if anything, she had more to prove now.

"The water is so refreshing!" Lainey said, swimming up to me.

"Isn't it?" I asked, reaching for Gunner as he swam laps around us. He was a strong swimmer, and after a long day on the plane, this was exactly what he needed before a good night's sleep. The dog required lots of exercise, and if he didn't get it, he'd tear up the yard, digging holes by the dozen; I'd seen him do it. "Swim boy, swim!" I called out, laughing at the way his head bobbed.

I glanced at Noah as he wrestled with Trinity in the water. I tried not to imagine all the things I couldn't see below the water's surface. Like an iceberg, I knew only a fraction was visible.

It was everything I wanted in that moment—to switch places with Trinity. Whatever power I thought I had over Noah paled in comparison to hers. I dipped under the water, letting the air leave my lungs slowly in little air bubbles as I sank into a pocket of warm water. It was peaceful there—the voices muted and the buoyancy suspending my arms. I wanted to stay there forever, but I needed to breathe. I kicked, bringing myself back up to the surface. And when I opened my eyes, I saw a dark figure standing on the dock. The dusk sky had nearly given way to nightfall, and I couldn't tell who had gotten out of the water. But when Noah left Trinity for me, none of it mattered anymore.

"Kins! You've got to save me!" he called out, his long strides propelling himself toward me.

"Oh yeah? Or what?" I teased, backpedaling. *Come and get me.*

"Or what? Or what!? You just wait right there because I'm gonna get you!" he said, picking up speed. He swam past Asher and Kimber, who were locked in an embrace, and I licked my lips in anticipation.

"Give it your best shot," I said. I weaved my hands back and forth, treading the cool water and slightly pushing away from the group. I wanted to get Noah alone. The smile on my face faded when I peeked above Noah's head and saw the figure still watching, waiting. An unsettled feeling spawned in my stomach. But when Noah reached me and grabbed my hand, I screamed with delight, splashed him in the face, and turned away from him, swimming deeper into the lake where perhaps a kiss could be stolen.

"You're going to get it now!" He swam after me. I didn't know what *it* was, but I wanted it. I wanted it really bad. Though I still intended to make him to work for it. I kicked hard, swimming as fast as I could. But Noah Hampton was a swim captain—and football player—and he closed the distance between us with a few powerful strokes. I felt him grab my foot, and I screamed out, slowing intentionally to get caught. *Catch me.*

I ached for him to grab more than just my toes, but when he grasped my thigh, the thrill I felt was short-lived. The lust turned to panic in a matter of seconds. I was pulled under the water violently with such force, I barely had time to grab a breath of air. It didn't feel like the hands of a lover or the touch leading to a first kiss. I didn't know what had a hold of my thigh, but I knew it was too strong and too fast to be human. I opened my eyes to see the surface disappear in a flurry of white bubbles.

My heart pounded against my chest as I tried to free my leg from the jaws of . . . Hand! It was a *hand*! Somebody's hand had a death grip around my leg. I clawed and scraped at flesh as I thrashed around in the water, fighting with every ounce of my strength. For a moment, I thought I was gaining momentum, and when my hand broke the surface, I splashed wildly. But there was nothing within my reach to take hold of. Nobody there to help me. No safety net.

My lips breached the surface, and I let out a guttural scream for help before I was pulled back under the water. I took one tiny gulp of air with me. It wasn't enough. The pressure built as I plunged into the depths of the dark lake. I gave it everything I had, but when the pockets of warm water surrounded me, I knew it was too late. I was too deep. And too weak.

A calmness came over me as the fight fled from my veins, and I gave in to the threat. A butterfly caught in a web, the fangs sinking in, spreading the venom and slowly paralyzing it. *So, this is it? This is how I die?* I had no other choice, ensnared deep within the malevolent grip. I watched my life pass before me as I searched the water for answers. And when all I saw was blackness, I closed my eyes in preparation for sleep. There were no answers for me to claim that night, only fear.

Sparks of light flashed behind my eyelids—brainwaves firing off their last sparks. Images flashed of a red door, crows by the hundreds, and a tall stone tower. A large circle dazzled me with lights and drew me in. A Ferris wheel rotated in my mind's eye. It was so welcoming, and I was thankful that, as death was upon me, I could conjure one last beautiful sight. Something to take the focus off my last fleeting moments. And for the first time, I was comforted that my gran's ghost was nearby to take me home.

I watched the Ferris wheel sparkle with magic in the summer air until I abruptly felt the release of my pinched thigh. It hardly registered at first. I remained paralyzed as I began floating toward the surface. The pocket of warm water moved down my body as I rose, free of my attacker. I didn't wake until a breath of air filled my lungs, and then a crash of adrenaline coursed through my veins. I screamed instinctively, hammering the water as I spun around looking for help. But there was no one there.

Disoriented, I looked out into the open water and back again to find the dock. But the dock was nowhere to be seen. The lake was quiet, the water still. The loons sang their haunting calls, cutting through the blanket of darkness. I was alone.

Where was I? Where did everybody go? How had I gotten into the middle of the lake? And how was I going to get back? I feared the depths of the water. Was that thing still down there? Would it grab me again? I had no idea how much I was bleeding into the water, and I feared the scent would attract the predator again, and it would come to finish me off. I began to swim, only to stop after a few strokes. Which direction? I couldn't see anything. Even the blackened night sky was barely discernible from the lake's surface.

My heartbeat echoed in my ears, and the sensory deprivation threatened to swallow me whole. I didn't know right from left and could barely tell up from down had I not felt the water.

"Are you okay?" A guy's voice called out from the void and echoed all around me.

"H-Hello?" I called back in a breathy tone, spinning around in search of help.

"Hello there. Are you okay?" The voice rang out again.

"No! No! I need help! Please!" I said in a voice that didn't belong to me but to a young girl not yet ready to be on her own. A girl who was still afraid of the dark.

"I'm right here. Give me your hand." The water lapped against the canoe that appeared beside me, seemingly out of nowhere. I reached my hand out and took hold of safety. Warm, dry hands plucked me from the lake of nightmares, and I spilled across the bottom of the canoe, panting. My body was too heavy to move, and I moaned in relief and tried my hardest not to cry.

"Are you all right?" the guy asked.

I opened my eyes to find his face looming over me. I blinked several times, trying to grasp what had just happened. It was dark as a moonless midnight, and I'd just had a near-death experience, but there was something in this guy's barely visible face that brought me comfort in my time of need. I let my eyes wander across the shadows of his face as I tried to swallow the rising lump in my throat. I didn't want him to see me cry.

His outline was etched in the deepest shade of coal, his jaw sharp and dimples piercing. His face was unshaven, and his stubble glimmered in the starlight. I couldn't tell the color of his hair or the shade of his eyes, but I knew they were kind, and I could tell he was worried. I said nothing—only blinked over and over again, trying to regain my composure.

"Hello?" His voice soothed my trembling bones.

His words were fleeting. I looked past him. When had the stars come out? I was certain that we'd just arrived at the cabin and it was still dusk. How much time had I been under the water? How had I survived? The stars twinkled in a hypnotizing manner, and I watched them as my breath slowed and my heart returned to a normal rhythm.

"Hello?" he asked again, his worry growing.

"Ya-yeah. Yes," I stammered, drawing my attention back to the guy in front of me.

His dimples disappeared. "What the hell are you doing all the way out here? We must be miles from the nearest shore."

I raised myself on my elbows. "I . . . I don't know. I don't know how I got out here." And the second the words left my lips, I regretted them. I sounded like a lunatic. And judging by this guy's body language, that was precisely how he perceived me. "I, um, I live at Rock Creek Cove, if you could take me there?" I pointed behind me with a shaky, wet finger.

The guy frowned and pointed behind his shoulder in the opposite direction. I arched my back and craned my neck, looking in every direction. There was no way for me to tell where we were, and I had no idea how he knew. He then spun the canoe in the opposite direction and began paddling.

"You really don't know how you got out here?" he asked, his voice a little softer.

"I'm sorry. I—"

"Don't be sorry. I just want to make sure you're okay. Did you hit your head?" he asked.

I reached my hand into my hair and rubbed my scalp. There were no lumps and, as far as I could tell, no evidence of an injury. My head did hurt, though, now that he mentioned it. "What did you say your name was?" I asked, sitting up and trying to get a look at my thigh.

"I didn't. It's Walker. And you are?" he asked, paddling the canoe effortlessly.

"I'm Kinsley Wilde. It's nice to meet you, Walker," I said, extending my hand.

He held the paddle in one hand and reached for my hand with the other. "Walker St. James. And it's nice to save you. Here, take this. You're shaking like a leaf." He shrugged out of his flannel, and my eyes trailed his silhouette.

"Thank you," I said, taking the shirt and pulling it on. His warm beachy scent lingered on the flannel. It reminded me of the summer I had spent by the sea with my family learning to surf. My stomach clenched, and I shivered, pulling it tightly across my chest.

Slowly, I ran my hand down the length of my thigh, feeling for damage. The flesh ripped to the bone . . . the exposed muscle numbed by my fear. But my skin was smooth. Not even an indentation where I had been pierced. And the wetness trickling down my calf that I had been sure was blood, was no more than water.

The lake was still and quiet except for the rhythmic sound of the paddle as it propelled us through the water. It was late, and the two of us were in the middle of nowhere, but I still felt oddly safe in his presence. Being alone with a stranger paled in comparison to the thing in the water's depths that had nearly taken my life. Or maybe it was his cologne that took me back to better times. Times when the worst thing imaginable was failing to stand up on the surfboard by the end of the day. Or my favorite flavor of Icee selling out . . . again. Either way, the lump in my throat had dissipated and my heartbeat finally slowed to normal.

"Wow, what a beautiful night," I said, surprising myself. As the canoe glided through the water, I crashed from the height of terror to a low and tranquil state. A pendulum swinging from one extreme to the next. Baylor Lake was a beautiful spot for stargazing, but tonight was extraordinary. And it was calling to me. I couldn't remember it ever being so remarkable. The Milky Way was tinged pink and teal, and the stars twinkled like golden embers. I lowered my gaze to find Walker smiling at me.

"It's quite something," he said, looking up into the sky. He didn't say much, and neither did I. We spent the rest of the trip stealing glances at each other and admiring the Milky Way. Rock Creek Cove came out of nowhere, and Walker eased the canoe alongside the dock. He dropped the paddle and tied a small rope to the dock cleat. He offered his hand as I climbed out of the boat. His touch was so warm and strong that I wasn't ready to leave it.

"Thank you for the lift," I said, fiddling with the cuff of his flannel. That wasn't all I wanted to say, but it was all that came out.

"Anytime," he replied, climbing out after me. We stood eye to eye as my words failed me. I didn't know how to thank this guy for saving my life. And a part of me didn't want to say goodbye at all. So I said nothing. I gave him an awkward half-wave, turned on my heels, and started for the cabin. I walked down the dock barefoot, my bra and thong still wet and my long brown hair dripping down the back of his flannel. But my lack of words and indecency were the least of my worries. There was something evil in that water, and I feared it was only the beginning.

2

Every light in the house was on, and I could hear the music from the water's edge. They were all there. Safe and warm. Partying. Why had nobody been in the cove searching for me? Where was the ambulance? Where were the police? My friends? Had my absence gone unnoticed by everybody? Even Noah? Who had been swimming after me? Or Lainey and Emma, my best friends? Nobody was out searching? I stared at the cabin—my cabin—as an outsider looking in, and my stomach sank. Something was terribly wrong.

As I stepped off the dock, I looked back toward Walker. He'd been standing there, waiting to make sure I got home safely. He'd been the only person who cared about my safety, and he was a complete stranger. Did he think it was sad that nobody was out looking for me? Did he pity me? I looked away, embarrassed, as I rubbed the nape of my neck and hobbled up the grassy hill to the cabin. The pine needles poked at my bare feet. As I came closer to the cabin, I could hear the boys arguing over something stupid and meaningless. It only hurt me more. My life was a minuscule dot on their radar.

"Good afternoon, dear! It's so good to see you," my neighbor called from his back yard, startling me. Mr. Vandal stood at the edge of his property holding a shovel. He didn't seem to notice that anything was wrong. That I was in my bra and underwear. Wet. My face probably as pale as a ghost and drawn down with sheer sadness. But how could he? It was too dark for him to see that I'd been through the wringer or that I'd been dropped off at the dock by a stranger. He couldn't have known that I was one of twelve, and I was all alone because nobody cared about me. That I was shut out of my own cabin as my best friends celebrated the beginning of summer without me. It was only the beginning, but still, I found his chipper temperament peculiar. And it was far from afternoon; it was sometime late in the night. Perhaps even early morning. I didn't know.

"Hello Mr. Vandal, how are you?" I asked with a sigh.

"Are you here with the whole family?" he called out.

"No, actually I'm here with a group of friends for the summer." I nodded toward the cabin, hitching my thumb over my shoulder at the bright lights and bass pumping through the cabin walls. I smiled apologetically.

"All right then," he said. Mr. Vandal wrestled with his shovel before disappearing into his house.

"All right then," I whispered under my breath. The Vandals had always been a little weird, but that had been odd, even by their standards. I frowned, examining their house briefly before turning back to mine. Why was he gardening at this hour?

The bugs swarmed around the light bulb on the back porch, and I stood there with my hand on the door's cold knob for a moment, feeling overwhelmed and alone. I looked back toward the dock one last time, but if Walker was still there, I never would have known it. I squinted into the night but couldn't see past the glow of the porch light and the buzzing bugs. I wondered if I'd ever see him again.

When I entered the cabin, Levi and Mason were arguing about who could chug a beer faster. Asher and Kimber were making out on the sofa, and Noah and Kai were playing pool. Nobody had seen me come in, and nobody seemed to care that I'd been gone. Life had resumed in my absence, and even though I was back now, I might as well have still been missing. I closed the back door softly as I searched the kitchen and game room for Emma and Lainey. Surely they would be upset that I had been gone. The music blared and my head pounded. I reached up to my temple, squinting against the brightness. Maybe I *had* hit my head.

"Okay, go!" Scarlett May yelled, as she held her phone and the timer ran. Her hair was dried and waved. Her makeup was freshly applied. She'd had time for makeup? A chill crept over my skin, leaving goosebumps in its wake. They were all dressed for a night out. A night to be remembered. And I felt ill thinking of Scarlett May applying her lipstick as I sank to the bottom of the lake on my last breath.

Levi and Mason threw their heads back and chugged their beers. Suds dribbled down Mason's chin and onto his shirt. They were clothed, and I was standing in nothing but my wet underwear and a stranger's soaked flannel. I pulled it tight, not realizing I'd taken it with me but thankful that I had. It was like a bad dream. The kind where you're in public and look down to realize you're naked. Exposed. Different. I was different. Too different. I wanted to run away. And not just from the insecurity that clung to me like the wet hair did to the sides of my cheeks, but I wanted to run from the feeling that I wasn't worthy of being noticed in my absence. I could have died out there. I nearly had. And this is what it would have looked like afterward. A party.

"Wow, watch it!" Ethan said as he bumped into me, holding his beer high in the sky so it wouldn't spill a single drop. Because that would be devastating. His eyes trailed down the opening of Walker's flannel to my wet belly and his cheeks flushed. The strong stench of tequila permeated the air and trailed after him in his wake. I grabbed hold of the kitchen countertop behind me as he staggered away. The flannel parted, exposing me further, and I quickly covered back up.

"Done!" Mason declared. I whipped my head around to see him throw his can to the floor. My floor. The one I helped my mom clean every summer. She'd be so mad if she only knew.

"No, dude! I finished first!" Levi shoved Mason's chest, and Mason shoved him back. I sidestepped out of their way, afraid to get knocked over. But even more afraid to be noticed. Because even though I'd started out as a strong pillar of this group when we'd arrived, something had changed. The Earth had spun on its axis and I found myself an outsider.

"Nooo! Mason won by a nanosecond. Like, just a nanosecond. But, hey! Hey! Hey, now. It's my turn! I race the winner! Loser fetches the beer," Scarlett May said, her words slurring together.

"No—" Levi started.

"Just go! And hold the timer—" she said, thrusting her phone into his chest.

I took a step toward the game room where Noah had been playing pool, but Trinity came out of nowhere. She slid her hands up his back and rubbed his shoulders. It stopped me in my tracks. He smiled back at her, and she took his pool cue in her hands. I was unable to look away as I watched him wrap his arms around her waist. She leaned over the pool table, and her body pressed against his, not a breath of air between them. My hair dripped lake water on the kitchen floor as I watched my long-time crush flirt with another girl. It was hard enough to watch him do it when I was around, but even more difficult to know he'd done it in my absence. Especially at a time when my life was threatened. Lainey was standing near Kai, but her eyes were glued to Ethan. Tears pricked the corners of my eyes as I bolted for the stairs. Not even Lainey cared.

I took the stairs two at a time. I passed Emma, whose hair was curled and makeup done, and I couldn't bear to stop and talk with her. I ran right past her.

"Where are you going?" she called out. "Hey! Kinsley! Did you go for another swim?" But I kept going, and I didn't stop until I reached the confines of the master bedroom. I slammed the door behind me and locked it.

I shut my eyes tightly, but the tears escaped and spilled over my cheeks. I lowered my forehead to the door, my lip curling as I sucked in uneven pockets of air. I almost died. I almost died! I thought I had! My knees buckled underneath me, and I fell to the floor, hunched over and drowning in my feelings of inadequacy. I almost died . . .

What would have happened if that thing hadn't let me go? If I'd succumbed to the darkness in the way I thought I had? If there were no more days of summer? No more life left to live? How long would it have taken my friends to notice I was missing? And how was it that the only person who cared at all was an utter and complete stranger? Was this what it all came down to? Was I worth so little that my thrashing arms, my hysteric screams for help, my drowning before their very eyes, went completely unnoticed by all eleven of them? Eleven chances to be looked after, cared for, and loved . . . all failed. The dog. Not even him, with his natural senses, had noticed me. The air left my lungs and my chest froze. I needed air but couldn't breathe. I didn't deserve to.

Long after I knew my face had turned purple, air finally rushed into my lungs, and I let out a long, somber wail. I knew I wasn't as popular as Kimber or Trinity. I didn't rule the school with my beauty. I didn't have Kimber's modelesque figure or Trinity's sex appeal. I wasn't as loud and gregarious as Scarlett May Marks, who was everyone's party favorite. I wasn't as smart as Emma or as kind as Lainey. I was plain. Maybe even a little forgettable, sure. But never would I have imagined that I was so . . . so . . . so *insignificant*, that I could just disappear—vanish—without ever being noticed.

I cried for a long time. I cried so hard, I thought I might die all over again. But it wasn't that easy. Nothing was. I soaked the borrowed flannel sleeves in my tears as the party raged on without me. *So, this is adulthood*, I thought. It wasn't quite the celebration of independence I'd had in mind. Never had I wanted to be this alone. I picked my limp body off the floor and started the shower. I let the hot water wash over my skin as my eyes remained unfocused on the white tiles and beige grout. The steam rose, and I slowly tilted my head back under the waterspout.

In a flash, behind my closed eyelids, I saw the bubbles escape my mouth and the water's surface disappear. I felt the tug on my leg, and I jerked and gasped for air. I reached out and pressed the palms of my hands against the cool, wet tile, and I breathed through my rising anxiety before it closed my throat. Would I ever be able to close my eyes in the shower again? I worried about closing my eyes in bed later that night. I knew I'd never be the same. What nightmares would I see?

After combing my fingers through my hair, I realized I'd left my suitcase in the kitchen and my backpack on the deck. I couldn't put myself through the pain of seeing everybody downstairs again. I looked through my mom's dresser until I found some of her pajamas. They still smelled of her, and it brought me some comfort to be wrapped in something of hers. I wasn't one to get homesick, but after the night I'd had, I wanted nothing more than for her to hold me. I was an adult now but wished this wasn't the case. The lump in my throat grew as I longed to be back in my twin-sized bed down the hall from Mom and Dad.

I lay in bed, afraid to call. I didn't want my parents to hear the fear in my voice, but I couldn't imagine going to bed without saying goodnight. I'd told them I would call when we got to the cabin. That was before the lake had swallowed me whole. I picked up the telephone, an old-school rotary dial phone my mom loved too much to get rid of. I used to play with it as a child. What once had been cream was now yellowed by time. As my finger circled the dial on the last digit, I hesitated. I was a terrible liar.

The phone rang only once before my dad picked up. "Hello?"

"Hi, Dad."

"Honey! You made it!" He was chipper, and I could almost hear the smile lines around his eyes through the phone.

I smiled, and the sting of tears threatened again. "Yeah! We did." My voice weakened, and I tightened my grip around the receiver. *Be strong.*

"Clara? Kinsley is on the phone!" Dad called out, his voice seeming so far away.

"Oh, oh, I want to talk to her!" my mom said.

"Okay, okay. Hold on. Kins? Your mother wants to talk to you. Just a sec."

"Kinsley? Is that you?"

"Hi, Mom. It's me." My voice was so meek, and I willed myself to be stronger.

"Is everything okay?" she asked immediately. *Shit . . .*

I paused for a second too long. "I—I . . ." It was the fatal flaw. Honesty. She knew me too well. I loved her too much. Lying had never been my strong suit.

"Oh no. What's the matter?" Mom's tone filled with worry, but I didn't want her to panic. I was old enough to deal with this on my own. I couldn't go running back to my mom. I was eighteen now and out of high school.

All the emotions from before my shower came swelling back. I bit my lip, attempting to feel the pinch above all else. "Nothing!" I said, but my pitch was too high. She sighed heavily into the receiver. I knew if I didn't make this about something else—something small—she would worry all night and possibly all summer. "It's just that . . ."

"Yes? I'm listening . . ."

"It's just that I don't think Noah likes me as much as I like him," I said. It wasn't a lie, unfortunately, but it wasn't the whole truth.

"Oh, honey." *She bought it.*

"What? What's the matter?" my dad asked.

"It's just boy problems," she whispered back. I could hear a door click shut, and I imagined she was taking the phone into the bedroom for more privacy. Just boy problems . . . I wished. "Well, dear, you just got there. Maybe it's too early to tell?"

"I think Trinity likes him. And it looks like he's interested in her, too. It's fine. It's fine. I just wish I didn't have to spend my summer vacation watching the two of them flirt in front of me," I said, dispelling the image of Noah swimming after me. His hand wrapped around my foot. I pulled a throw pillow into my lap and played with the tassels.

"Well, if he can't see how special you are, then he's not worth your time," Mom said. I rolled my eyes.

"You have to say that," I replied.

"What? No, I don't!"

"Yes, you do! All moms say that!" And it was true. They did.

"And what do you have to compare to?"

I smiled. "All the other moms I've had," I joked.

"So, what's first on the agenda? Are you guys going to the Water's Edge Concert?" she asked, changing the subject.

"Yeah, I think we'll go."

"Do you know who's playing this year?"

"Um, no. It's some band I've never heard of. But Scarlett May said that she's heard of them before and they're good."

"Oh, good!"

"Yeah. And I think I'll just unpack, get some grocery shopping in, and stuff like that," I said.

"Okay. Well, you've got a full-time job ahead of you keeping all those boys fed. I foresee a lot of pizza in your future," she said to lighten the mood, and it worked.

"Yeah. Probably." I looked down at the pillow tassel and the line fell quiet. "I love you, Mom," I said, my heart hitching like it might be the last time I ever told her.

"I love you, too, Kins."

"I know you do. Tell Dad I love him, too." I bit my lip. *Be strong.*

"Okay, honey. I will. Have a good night. Get some rest."

"I will. Oh! And Mr. Vandal said hi . . . sort of."

My mom laughed, and I chuckled. "I'm sure he did," she said.

"Goodnight," I said, happy that I heard her voice.

"Goodnight dear."

I listened to the click of the line being severed before I hung up the telephone, and then I chucked the throw pillow to the floor. I looked around the empty room, wishing that I had the company of someone. Anyone. I listened to the party rage on without me and sighed heavily. I just wanted to go to sleep. I wanted to forget today had ever happened. I reached over to the bedside lamp and pulled the string. The room went dark, and I lay my head down on the pillow. I was ready to be done with the day but not yet ready for tomorrow to come.

I didn't know how to face my friends. *Friends?* Were they still my friends? I tried to convince myself that there was a perfectly good explanation for it all and that I would find out come morning. I told myself that if I could only fall asleep, the nightmare I'd experienced in the lake would be nothing but a dream. But no matter what I told myself or how much of it I believed, I was still afraid to close my eyes.

I knew the second I dropped my lids I would fall victim to the cold depths of Baylor Lake. I'd re-live the torture of the attack all over again. I couldn't do it. I wouldn't. I forced my eyes to stay open. I forced my mind to be anywhere except for that lake. But my mind couldn't process the negative, and the more I tried not to think of it, the more I failed. Instead, I tried to detect what the voices were saying through the walls. The baritone of the boys' debates, the high-pitched hollers from . . . Scarlett May. It had to be Scarlett May. She was the only one obnoxious enough to literally scream for attention.

Eventually, my eyes closed, and I was so tired from the accident and so exhausted from the crying that I didn't even notice when I fell asleep. There was no terrifying lake or nefarious creature of the deep. No near-death drowning or house of fake friends. But there was my sweet gran . . . because not even the dreamwork of the night would keep her at bay.

Gran stood with me under the overpass. We held hands, her skin thin and cold, while a car flew through the air, spinning before our very eyes. And in slow motion, we watched it turn over, again and again. The blue four-door sedan with tinted windows spun like a ballerina twirling on stage, while shards of glass scintillated alongside it. The front bumper hit the road first. The front end smashed like an accordion, and the car momentarily stood perpendicular on the road before teetering over. It landed flat on its roof. The top of the car compressed under the force of the impact. The windows burst as the frame bent. The fog lights flickered into the distance, lighting up the condensation that hung like heavy weights in the night sky. Light-yellow fabric pressed against what was left of the driver's side window.

Gran turned to me slowly. Her droopy eyes showed no emotion. Her cheeks hung like those of a marionette, and though she'd once had the most stunning green eyes, they were no more than a silver fog of cataracts. "We should go," she said, leading me under the bridge. We walked away from the accident, and I never looked back. We walked until the road disappeared and there was no sky above and no ground below.

We walked until a rocking chair appeared near a roaring wood burning fire. Somehow, it did nothing to heat the frigid air. I shivered, rubbing my arms while looking around. There was no sky, no ceiling—nothing but a gray void beyond the cozy reading nook that sat before us. A stack of half a dozen books sat on top of a side table. Gran let go of my hand and took a seat. There was only room for one. She cracked the spine of a children's book and began to read. And though I saw her mouth moving rhythmically, I couldn't hear her words.

I had an odd feeling as I stood there watching her read. She looked different. Not better and not worse—just different. I couldn't tell what it was. Her hair was still stark white and brittle due to her age and the cancer. Her body was frail and bony. She rocked slowly back and forth as she read, and she didn't seem to notice when I began to slip away.

I woke with a jerk and a gasp for air, my hands full of bedsheets and my eyes wide with fear. It had happened again. The visit from my gran. I was positive that I'd have nightmares of the lake, but it was she who'd prevailed. I didn't know if I should thank her or look for a deeper meaning. Was it an omen of bad things to come? It was probably just repressed feelings. Something I should have said to her before she passed but didn't. She'd probably hang around until I was ready to say goodbye. But I wasn't ready, and I doubted I ever would be. But the more I thought about it, the more I wondered if she had been hanging around to take me home. But I'd survived the near-drowning in the lake, so why was she still here?

I'd been waking to dreams of her for nearly a week. And there was nothing like it. Nothing like seeing someone in a dream, only to wake and remember that they were gone. Really gone. That your reality is one they no longer live in. It's worse than any nightmare there ever was, because at the end of the dream . . . it's real, and your nightmare begins as your day does.

Gran and I had a special relationship. She had been close to my mom, but since I was the first grandchild, I'd had the privilege of spending lots of time with her. Undivided time. She loved to read me stories. All kinds of stories. But for the longest time, she had only read fairy tales. The classics. She'd read them so many times when I was young that she could nearly recite them from memory. Sometimes she did.

It was three days before my birthday when she'd passed. I'd never known anybody who'd passed before. I guess I was lucky. But it didn't feel like luck. Here one moment, gone the next. I didn't understand . . . and I still didn't. And I think that was the reason I was seeing her in my dreams, and sensing her when I was sure nobody was there. I think I simply wasn't ready to let go. And since I hid away the sorrow when I was awake, it haunted me while I slept.

3

I woke to a headache that refused to let me rest. The music was still playing through the walls, though I was positive nobody was awake. I didn't know what to expect when I went downstairs, but I imagined they would be riddled with hangovers, regret, and, if I were lucky, a spotty memory. I myself wasn't so lucky. I remembered everything. Enough to make me not want to be here. Enough to consider catching the first flight out of Baylor. But I hadn't run. Not yet.

Barefoot, I padded down the stairs, and when I reached the stereo in the game room, I carefully leaned over Noah, where he lay sleeping on a plush velvet cream chair, and turned the music off. His shaggy, dirty-blond hair was swept over his eyes. I wanted to reach down and brush his locks out of his face, even though his behavior had hurt me deeply. How could he have been swimming after me and just lost interest so quickly? By the time I'd resurfaced, he'd moved on. They all had. I straightened my back, looking around the room. I was only mildly relieved that Trinity wasn't wrapped up in Noah's arms, but that still didn't erase the memory I had of them the night before. I passed by a red bra strewn across the pool table and cringed, thinking of what had happened the night I'd been forgotten by all.

Ethan twitched on the sofa, and I tiptoed away, careful not to wake him. I wasn't ready to face any of my friends. And if they slept all day, I'd have some time to collect myself away from their disloyal, watchful eyes.

The kitchen was a wreck, even worse than I'd imagined it would be. Empty cans were everywhere, pretzels smashed on the tile floor, and a shot of amber liquid had been spilled across the countertop. Somebody's swim trunks sat in a pool of water where the carpet met the tile, and wet towels were draped over every surface of the kitchen. I sighed when my eyes fell upon a vase I'd made my freshman year of high school in ceramics class, broken into several pieces on the floor. Nobody had even bothered to pick it up. I'd loved that vase. I closed my eyes. Had this trip been a mistake? Had these people never been my real friends? The sour feeling of regret settled in my stomach, and I felt like there wasn't enough oxygen in the air. I needed to get away.

I opened the door to the back porch, hungry for a breath of fresh air. Everyone's belongings had been taken inside last night except mine. I found my shoes and backpack lying across the wooden planks. I picked them up and slung the bag over my shoulder. The heaviness weighed me down as I took my belongings upstairs, closing my eyes to the mess as I passed. I got dressed for a hike. I needed to get out into the open air to clear my head. Sort the facts from the painful feelings. What I knew to be true may very well have been a lie. I did that sometimes. I'd get so caught up in my own insecurities that I'd fail to see what was actually true. Maybe there was a good explanation for all of it. I just needed time to think.

When I snuck outside, ready for my hike, I was surprised to find Lainey awake, clipping a leash onto Gunner's collar on the back porch.

"Kinsley! You're up early!" she said, startled.

"I was thinking the same about you," I said in a weak voice. *She doesn't care . . .*

"Ugh, yeah. Crazy night, huh? I bet they'll sleep all day."

"Yeah . . . it was," I replied. I watched her intently as she pulled her medium-length brown hair into a low ponytail. There was no indication that she knew about my accident last night. Not a single hint of concern anywhere to be found. No time-lapse, no empathy behind her eyes, not so much as a furrowed brow. Lainey was her natural happy-go-lucky self. She may have been a little tired from staying up late the night before, but she harbored no guilt about leaving me to die alone in the dark, malignant waters.

"Are you going out for a run? Because I was going to take Gunner on a walk, but I don't know the trails around here. And we'd just run with you, but honestly, I don't think my body will allow me any type of cardio right now. It's a struggle just to take Gunner out. And I wouldn't have gotten up at all, except he wouldn't stop pushing his wet nose against my cheek this morning. And the last thing I want is for him to pee inside the cabin." Lainey rolled her eyes, exhausted by the responsibility of her dog not twenty-four hours into the trip. I could see this was going to have to be a team effort. Which was okay—we all loved him. Gunner's eyes squinted and he looked like he was smiling.

"I was just going to walk," I said, exhausted myself.

"Can we join you?" she asked, although it was really more of a statement.

She had no reason to believe I wouldn't want her to join me. And the entire conversation made me question if last night had been real at all.

"Okay. I guess you can fill me in on what happened last night," I said, stepping off the back porch. The morning was warm already, and I could tell it was going to be a particularly hot day. I might have even thought it to be beautiful, if my life hadn't been turned upside down. I took the ponytail holder off my wrist and tied my long, dark, chestnut locks into a messy bun on top of my head.

"Well, you know. I mean, you were there," Lainey said, tight-lipped. "Oh, you mean because you went to bed early? You didn't miss anything. It really just went downhill after the pool tournament." I looked at my best friend's face. The freckles dusting her cheeks gave her an air of innocence, and I could tell that she wasn't being malicious—not in the least. She didn't have a mean bone in her body. So it must have been me. I was the one who was faltering.

"What pool tournament?" I asked, looking for clues.

"The pool tournament. You don't remember?" she asked, trying to read my face. "Oh, man! You don't remember? And I thought I drank too much!" Lainey laughed, shaking her head.

I frowned down at the path, which was wide enough here for us to walk side by side. All of the paths weren't this wide, though. Many of them had offshoots that wound tightly through the forest. Had I been drugged? I hated that my immediate thought turned to Trinity. But she was the only one who had a motive. I shook my head, dispelling the thought that one of my friends could actually drug me. It wasn't like that.

I'd lost a good amount of time last night between dusk and nightfall. Perhaps I had hit my head, and that was the reason I couldn't remember. I felt . . . off. My stomach was a little queasy now that I thought about it. And I knew that concussions could make you feel like that for days after. Weeks even. Maybe Lainey was right and I'd been there all along. I reached up to the back of my head, checking for bumps and lumps—anything that would prove the theory—but found nothing.

"Honestly, I don't remember anything after we dove into the lake. I mean, there was this one bit when Mason won a beer-drinking contest . . . And Trinity hitting on Noah." I shrugged, shaking the thought from my memory. Out of all the things that could have happened last night, it was Trinity that I remembered. The way she'd slipped her hands around Noah's shoulders. The way he'd smiled at her over his shoulder.

"Oh yeah! I think Levi and Mason had a chug fest. And then at some point, Ethan joined." Lainey nodded and her cheeks turned the soft pink of embarrassment. "Don't get me started on Trinity! She only wants Noah because she knows you like him! She gets a rise out of seeing you fume. I think she's jealous of you because this is your cabin and she feels inferior being on your trip. Sometimes I even see her flirt with Asher just to get Kimber all riled up. And it works, you know. Kimber gets weird and stops eating for like a week. I don't know why Trinity gets such a high out of it. Why did you even invite her?" Lainey looked at me with one brow raised.

"I had to! I couldn't invite the entire group and conspicuously not invite her. Especially since we've been talking about it for nearly a year now. She would have found out and ended up coming anyway. Then she would have made my life a living hell!" I said in a low, weary tone. I couldn't imagine if she'd actually had a real reason to hate me. She was conniving enough as it was.

"Isn't that what she's doing now? Making your life a living hell? God, Kins, sometimes I think you're your own worst enemy," Lainey said, her head tilted in sympathy. I sighed, knowing that I had nobody to blame but myself.

"I guess so," I said. No matter what I did, though, if I was up against Trinity, I'd lose. Lainey and I exchanged a look of mutual defeat. She understood where I was coming from because she, too, had been the victim of Trinity Myers once before. Back in the day, when Trinity was the new girl at school, she'd quickly climbed the social ranks by spreading rumors. She'd told everyone that she was in a commercial for kids' swimsuits. But the lies didn't stop there. After she became popular, she started rumors about other girls, Lainey being one of them. I'd never believed that Lainey Summers had a crush on old Wigg, the overweight fifth-grade PE teacher rumored to wear a toupee, but many did, and it had stuck with her for some time.

"Hey, is it okay if I let Gunner off the leash?" she asked, looking around. I stretched my eyes as far as they could see. Not a soul in sight. We were approaching what I called the wall. The cabin sat in a clearing in the cove, surrounded by a wall of trees. A thick forest with winding pathways, blackberry bushes, and a rumored graveyard. I'd never seen it.

"Yeah, I think that's fine. Will he come back?" I asked, looking forward to the shade the trees would cast over us.

"Yes, he's a good boy! Isn't that right? He's such a good boy!" Lainey scratched Gunner's head as she unhooked the leash. He took off, sprinting down the path, hunting for birds, squirrels, and anything else that moved. His brown head and white speckled body disappeared in no time, but Lainey didn't seem worried, so neither was I.

"So, did I miss anything? From last night I mean?" I asked in all honesty, the feeling of deceit leaving my system. Bewilderment was the only thing I felt now, and it was stronger than ever.

"You really don't remember anything?" asked Lainey, studying me.

"Really." I looked down at my shoes kicking up dust on the trail and I winced at the pain I'd felt behind the locked door of the master bedroom. "Actually, can I tell you something?"

"Of course." Lainey wound the untethered leash around her hand.

"I have this one memory . . ." I didn't want to say it aloud. But I always told Lainey everything, and I feared what it would do to me if I kept it inside.

"Oh, yeah?" she asked.

"I have a memory of . . . drowning. I drowned last night in the lake." I refused to look at her. Clearly, I hadn't drowned. I was right here, at her side.

Lainey took a moment. "Are you serious?"

"I didn't die, though," I muttered.

"Well, obviously!" she laughed. But I wasn't laughing. I felt ashamed. Like something bad had happened, and I didn't want anybody to know about it. They hadn't known.

"I mean, I was about to. But this guy . . . he saved me."

"A guy?" she asked, surprised. This wasn't a story she'd heard before. I looked at Lainey and she was both intrigued and concerned for my well-being. I was concerned too.

"Don't look at me like that! It was real! I swear it was," I said, doubting myself. Heat crept into my cheeks. Not from embarrassment, but from anger. I knew it was true, but somebody had been playing a trick on me.

Lainey sucked in a deep breath, and we both whipped our heads to the left as Gunner came bounding out of the bushes. He flew past us, breaking the tension, and she burst into laughter. I cracked a small smile, but it didn't reach my eyes. "Okay, Kins. So tell me about this mystery guy." She wiggled her brows and nudged my side.

"I don't know. He was just a guy. He came out of nowhere in a canoe—"

"A man in a canoe? That's hot—"

"It wasn't like that. He gave me a ride back to the dock. We didn't say much. But I felt like he was kind . . . and caring." I looked at Lainey. Her eyebrows were raised expectantly. I knew she wanted more, and a part of me did too. "I don't know. The whole thing was weird," I said, shrugging. I glanced down at my thigh, but there wasn't so much as a scrape from being pulled into the canoe, let alone bone-deep claw marks. I'd definitely hit my head last night. There was no other way around it.

"Well, it sounds like Noah better watch his back, because a local Baylor boy is ready to take his spot!" Lainey said, picking up the pace in her excitement.

"Stop that! It's not like that. I don't even know the guy! And he was . . . older."

"Like how much older?"

"I don't know. It was dark. But maybe, like, a few years. Five years?" It was hard to tell his age, but he was no boy. He wasn't like the other high schoolers I'd known and dated. It wasn't something that I could see in his face, but more of a feeling. He was an old soul. Responsible . . . like he had the weight of the world on his shoulders, and plucking a damsel in distress from the midnight lake was all in a day's work. He'd made me feel protected in a way that no other guy ever had. I only assumed it came from a few extra years of independence. The very thing I had expected to gain this summer but had already regressed from.

Lainey bumped my shoulder and made a low humming sound. "Stop!" I shoved Lainey lightly. She stumbled just off the trail into a clump of bushes.

"Do you see that?" Lainey pointed to the purple flowering bush beneath her feet.

"What? The flowers?" I asked, taking a step closer.

"Yes. That little purple flower is called rampion bellflower, also known as rapunzel. It's one of my favorites, but I don't see it too often. I love that it grows rampant out here." I looked at the bushes covering the forest floor, and most of them had the little purple flowers she spoke of. I hadn't noticed them before, but now that I looked, they were beautiful in their own right.

We hiked to the water's edge and let Gunner cool off in the lake for a few minutes before turning around. Lainey pointed out several species of plants and trees, telling me which berries were edible and which to avoid. We spotted a few birds along the way, of which my favorite was the downy woodpecker. She described how the males have a beautiful stripe of red across the back of their heads. It kept me looking high into the trees as we walked back to the cabin. And I felt lighter with my face up to the sun, the filtered light gleaming into my eyes. There was nothing a good friend couldn't help by just being close by. The morning air had warmed significantly by the time we returned. And from the smell of bacon that permeated the air, I knew the rest of our friends had finally woken up. At least I was less afraid to greet them. But by all means, it was only a *little* less.

My stomach clenched as I followed Lainey in through the back door, Gunner by our sides. He collapsed immediately upon entry into the living room. Scarlett May stood in the kitchen, whisking eggs and wearing sky-high pajama shorts. Her hair, blonde and blunt, was still wavy from the night before. She glanced over at us as we came in, but it was clear that I was the only one who remembered the neglect. I wrapped my arms around my waist, trying to support myself. Her strength only made me feel small and weak. Forgotten. I scanned the room for Noah, but he was nowhere to be found.

"Thanks for making coffee," I said, pulling a mug out of the cabinet. It was another one of my ceramic creations. Not good enough to keep at home, but good enough not to throw away. I liked how the thumb imprint was fitted for my hand specifically. I also liked how nobody had broken it. Yet. I filled my cup with coffee and creamer and then drew in a long, medicinal sip.

"I hope you don't mind, but I had to make eggs and bacon. It's a tradition for my family every time we come to Baylor Lake. Us kids are woken up by the smell of a bacon-and-egg breakfast. And when I saw that nobody else was going to do it this morning, I figured, if you want something done right, you've got to do it yourself," Scarlett May said.

"Oh, no, I don't mind. I actually appreciate the cooking. So make yourself at home. Now . . . if I could just get someone to help clean up, because this place is a mess," I said, looking around the kitchen.

"I didn't realize you've been to Baylor Lake before," Lainey said, as she placed a bowl of water on the kitchen floor for Gunner.

"I have an aunt who lives in Baylor. My family usually visits here once a year. Normally, we go in the winter, so I'm not familiar with this heat. But I know the town pretty well," Scarlett May said.

"Oh, nice," Lainey said.

"Oh yeah! I grew up on the Baylor Lake ghost stories. They were the only ones my dad ever told us. We used to go to the farmers' market on the weekends if it wasn't rained out. And we know all the locals. I have a really good friend who lives here, and he throws the best lakeside parties. You'll love him. I actually have plans to go visit my aunt later today, but it looks like she'll have to pick me up because I don't see a car in your driveway." Scarlett May looked at me inquisitively.

"Right. We don't keep a car here. We usually only come for the summer, and most often we stay at the cabin. There *is* a golf cart, but that won't take you into town," I said.

"Wait, did you say Baylor Lake ghost stories?" Emma asked, stretching. Her shirt was oversized and her hair a mess. Kimber stumbled into the kitchen after her. She looked like she hadn't slept a wink; her eyes were puffy and red. She opened the refrigerator door and pulled out a bottle of water. I glanced at Kimber briefly, looking for clues that she remembered last night's events, but she paid me no attention. Typical. I looked at Emma, but she was enthralled with the idea of hearing a morning ghost story. She loved her stories. Emma was the only person I knew who could read for eight hours straight.

"Everybody's heard the Baylor Lake ghost stories. Right, Kinsley?" Scarlett May looked to me briefly before flipping the bacon with tongs.

"I don't think I've ever heard them," I said, scratching my head, my fingers still searching for hidden battle wounds.

"Are you sure this is even your cabin? Everybody knows about the Baylor Butcher." Scarlett May had a way of making you feel small with her sharp, lashing tongue. My cheeks flushed, and I gave a small shrug.

"What's the story?" Kimber asked, her voice groggy. Asher came to her side, taking the water out of her hands and guzzling the rest of the bottle.

"Yeah, tell us." Emma pulled up a seat like an eager child ready for story time.

"Long, long ago—I can't believe you guys haven't heard this—there was this man who was a serial killer. He used to go on dates with women all the time because he was ruggedly handsome, and on the third date or so, he would kill them, chop them up into tiny pieces, and spread their bodies into the lake at night." Scarlett May spun around with a butcher knife in her hand for theatrics. I flinched, my nervous system still reeling from the night before.

"Eww!" cried Lainey, scowling.

"Gross." Kimber clutched her stomach and looked like she might be sick.

I felt a bit nauseous myself, remembering the feeling of my nails clawing at the hand under the water. Did that hand have a body? A breath? A soul? Or was the hand no more than a haunted dismemberment of a Baylor Butcher victim seeking vengeance? Or, perhaps I had heard the ghost stories before and forgotten them. And last night was no more than a reflection—a distant memory. Maybe it was a dream? Or, more likely, a nightmare.

I looked down at my fingernails and imagined that they'd been packed with scrapings of something dank and dingy. Fleshy bits of evidence of my frantic attempts to free myself. I spun to the sink, washing my nails vigorously. *It was just a dream. Just a dream.*

Asher stole a handful of bacon from Scarlett May's platter, and she slapped his hand with the back of the spatula. "One day," Scarlett May scowled at Asher as she continued.

"Bacon!" Mason yelled, reaching for a handful.

"Wait until I'm done," Scarlett May snapped and swatted the spatula about. "One day, when the Baylor Butcher had come to his third date with a beautiful girl who had made him yearn for more time, he stalled. He chose not to kill her. Instead, he finished his date, a canoe ride across the lake during sunset. He thought that maybe she'd be the one to stop him in his tracks. To turn his life around. He'd gotten away with murder, and he'd never kill again. But when he tried to set up a fourth date, the woman had escaped, never to be found again."

I dried my hands, running the dishtowel under my nails. I hadn't heard this story before.

"What happened next?" Emma asked.

Ethan waltzed into the kitchen and went straight for the coffeepot. "Seriously, guys?" He held up the empty pot. I smiled at him apologetically. I had always liked Ethan. Not romantically, but in the sense that I could tell he was good to his core. Still, he hadn't noticed when I'd gone missing either. My smile faded.

"I'll make more," I said curtly, taking the empty pot from Ethan's hand.

"So, the butcher haunted the lake and the woods every night from dusk till dawn, searching for the one who got away," Scarlett May said, finally placing a platter of eggs and bacon on the kitchen island. In a blink of an eye, the food was gone. Everyone awake, except for Kimber and I, inhaled it.

"I guess I'm done swimming in that lake!" Kimber said.

"At least after dusk," Lainey replied.

"What? Are you afraid of a little ghost story? Afraid that the lake turns into poison and the woods into a web of nightmares as soon as the sun goes down?" Scarlett May laughed at the absurdity of it all.

But my stomach knotted, because that's exactly what I was afraid of. A web of nightmares.

4

It had been a lazy morning. With the exception of myself, everyone else had been hungover. Most of them slept until while I busied myself cleaning up after their mass destruction from the night before. And although everyone was tired and lacked the energy to contribute to the cabin, they were all raring to go again come nightfall.

It was an endless loop of celebrating our freedom. After all, we deserved it. Eighteen years of being under somebody's thumb at all times. No more parents, teachers, or coaches. We'd made it, and now nobody could tell us what to do. We would go to college because it was our choice. But when it came to cleaning up after ourselves . . . well, needless to say, it wasn't happening. Nobody would help. At first, the idea of a constant party and lack of responsibility and structure exhausted me, but somewhere along the way, I desired it. I grew sick of looking at my friends as an outsider. I didn't want to be the only one who cared anymore. I needed to let go. Just one night. No responsibility, worry, or skepticism. I didn't want to think of it. I wanted to turn my mind off and act on pure instinct, chasing the joy and adrenaline wherever it might be found.

It was somewhere between my first and third drink that I stopped seeing the messes made, the spills on the carpet, and the wasteful byproduct of half-eaten bags of chips and near-full soda cans abandoned. I stopped fretting over the ceramic pieces I'd made and how I could never replace them if they were broken. I turned off the nagging voice in my head by drowning it, and I narrowed my focus to Noah Hampton. It was more fun this way. He was messing with the stereo, trying to find the perfect song. I'd convinced myself that nobody had abandoned me the first night at the cabin. That it was all in my head. And every time I saw Walker's flannel, I'd just look away. It was the only way I could heal. The only way I could move on. And I needed that.

I quickly glanced around the room. Trinity was out front with Kimber and Scarlett May, so I had some uninterrupted time with Noah.

"Are you looking for a particular song?" I asked, peeking over his shoulder.

Noah smirked at me, his dark-blue denim eyes peering out from beneath his shaggy, sandy hair. "I might be," he said, inviting me in. A low hum escaped my chest.

I felt my cheeks heat as laugh lines appeared around his eyes. His face was so close to mine. My gaze trailed from his eyes to the crevices around his mouth and then to his lips. I wanted to kiss him, but it was that exact thought that made me lose my confidence. I faltered for just a second, and I looked down to the floor, shattering the moment. Disappointment washed over me. I always did that.

"I might be able to help," I suggested.

"Oh yeah? Here. Find me the perfect song." Noah handed me his phone. My fingers grazed his as I took the cell phone. Noah and I had flirted before—on many occasions—but that didn't mean it wasn't like the first time every time. I smiled, the butterflies fluttering up and down in my stomach, looking for a way out. It was hard to pry my eyes off him, but I did so in search of the perfect song. One that would describe everything I felt inside, not only in that moment, but for him in general. I had known Noah since I was a kid, but it had only been in the last two years that my feelings for him had grown into something more. I was pretty sure he felt the same way. I scrolled through many songs, but none of them were perfect. It was a tall order. I felt his gaze on me as I scrolled through the songs, my thumb hovering over each and every one that confessed feelings of love or lust. But as I recited the words in my head, I decided against them all. Nervously, I peeked up at him.

Noah placed his hand against the wall, his body stretching out around me. I leaned into him, scrolling through songs as he lowered his head close to mine. This song was too angry, this one too mushy, this one was too old. I bit the inside of my cheek and craned my neck, looking up at him. It wasn't the perfect moment for our first kiss, but it could do. I was positive that any first kiss with Noah would be romantic, regardless of timing. Our eyes would be closed either way. He looked down at me, smiling, and leaned in just a hint, right when Mason and Asher stumbled into the room. Our connection was severed by the commotion.

"Are you going to put some music on? Or are you just going to stand there?" Asher complained, his stance wide, his presence imposing. Asher was the quarterback of the football team and arguably the most popular guy at our school. He and Kimber had been prom king and queen, and the rest of us were living in their shadow.

"I am! I'm working on it. It's a hard decision, you know?" I said. Noah pulled away, his warmth leaving my side. I frowned, returning Noah's cell phone, and he took it with little thought. Our hands didn't graze each other this time. The moment was squashed, thanks to Asher's demand. *Music now, peasants!*

"Just pick something!" Asher yelled as he grew impatient.

"There!" Noah called back, selecting a random song. One that in no way, shape, or form was a confession of love. Asher took a seat on the couch, and Noah followed. I paused for a moment, surveying the room, before sitting to Noah's right.

"This guy says he's eaten glass before. Can you believe that?" Asher asked as he gripped Mason's shoulders. Lainey came into the room, picking up the TV remote.

"You've eaten glass?" Lainey said, flipping through the channels. Her thumb hovered briefly over the channel button as a reporter spoke at the scene of a car accident. Our hometown of Clover scrolled in bold letters on a bright red banner across the screen. My attention piqued just as she flipped the channel, landing on a documentary about large cats. I peeled my eyes away from the screen as she turned the volume down and split her attention between the cheetahs and Mason's speculative diet of glass. I frowned.

"I've got a stomach of steel. I can eat anything you put in front of me. I'm a machine!" Mason howled and beat his chest. I chuckled, and Lainey leaned into me, giggling. Mason Fry was a true rebel. His hair hung to his shoulders and was a mess. He always looked like he'd just woken up—or perhaps had an early morning surf session. He was dangerously daring and brave. More fun than anybody I'd ever known. And at his core, I believed he was a pretty great guy. Had he not been so obnoxious, I might have gone for him. But his need for attention was insatiable, and it often had the rest of us rolling our eyes.

"It's true. I've seen him do it before," Noah said as he leaned back, extending his arm around the back of the sofa, encapsulating my shoulders. I pretended not to notice but slouched a little deeper into the plush sofa and his side.

"You've seen him eat glass before?" I asked.

"Oh yeah! He used to do it all the time freshman year. It was our favorite trick. Somewhere along the line, I thought maybe he'd grow up, but no such luck. He really does have an iron stomach, though."

"What did you say?" Mason asked Noah.

Noah leaned into me and whispered in my ear, "We can't egg him on, or we'll have no light bulbs left, and we might have to spend the night in the ER!"

I raised my eyebrows and chuckled. I had no intention of watching Mason eat glass, and I wanted to keep what lighting fixtures we had intact. So when Lainey changed the subject, I was glad.

"Did you know the cheetah can run sixty miles per hour?" she asked, eyes trained on the TV.

"I can run sixty miles per hour!" Mason argued. I threw my head back on Noah's arm and moaned. Noah and Lainey laughed, and Asher just stared at Mason, seeming to consider if it was possible.

"No, you can't!" said Asher flatly.

"I can run sixty miles per hour. I can do it right now. And I'll do it naked!" he said. The entire room erupted in laughter. It wouldn't be the first time I'd seen Mason naked. He was a fan of streaking and often gathered huge followings. One time, he'd led a pack of sixteen naked sophomores across the football field at halftime.

"Want to make a bet?" Asher asked, knowing very well that Mason would strip and run, but not at sixty miles per hour.

"No! Don't egg him on!" I said, leaning over Noah's lap and swatting at Asher.

"I'll take that bet! I want to see this!" Noah said. Lainey laughed and shrugged as if she didn't care one way or another, but I knew she wanted to see it too. I slapped my forehead. Who were these people?

"See what?" Kimber asked as she, Scarlett May, and Trinity walked in from outside. The moment Trinity walked in, Noah's arm pulled back to his lap and he leaned forward, casting me into his shadow. My side turned cold, and my heart sank with disappointment. Had it been a coincidence? I didn't know, but it crushed me all the same.

"Mason is going to run sixty miles per hour with his pecker out," Asher said, laughing.

"Wow, okay. We're doing this?" Kimber asked, looking around the room.

"Sixty bucks. Sixty miles per hour. My body is just the cherry on top for all you ladies." Mason seductively traced his hand down his torso to his groin.

"Eww!" I groaned.

"I've got twenty on this," Asher said.

"Same," Noah replied.

"I'll throw in twenty," Lainey said, with a coy smile and a shrug.

"Lainey!" I shoved her shoulder, and she laughed out loud. I questioned her motive. If she liked Mason, I might have understood. But I happened to know that Lainey Summers liked nobody like she liked Ethan. She'd never *admitted* that she liked Ethan, but a best friend knows. She couldn't hide the blush under her freckled cheeks every time she said his name.

"What? He can't run sixty miles per hour, you guys. Honestly? You're letting him do this?" Kimber asked.

"True story. He can't do it," I said and shrugged. Noah stood up and walked to neutral ground. My eyes flicked to Trinity's and hers to mine. I tried to hide my disappointment. Mason took off his shirt and beat his chest like a gorilla one more time. All the girls in the room laughed, and the boys shoved each other around, getting excited. This was the stupidest thing I had ever seen, and I had seen some ridiculous stuff before. I stood up and looked for Emma, because this wasn't something she would want to miss.

"Emma! Mason is going to attempt to run sixty miles per hour, and he's going to do it naked! You have to come see this!" I yelled.

"Mason is going streaking? Again?" Levi asked.

"Yes!"

"I'll go streaking!" Levi jumped at the chance to take his clothes off. Emma and I laughed and followed Levi to the front of the cabin. Mason was unbuckling his belt when we came out to the driveway. His shoes were kicked off and socks already cast aside. Levi wasted no time joining in. He took his baseball cap off and placed it on Emma's head, then started unbuttoning his shirt. Emma turned toward me with a small squeal.

"What are you doing, man?" Mason asked Levi.

"We're going streaking!" he said.

"I'm getting paid sixty bucks. I'm not sharing that with you."

"I'll do it for free. I can't make these ladies watch your ass run down the street when they can have the pleasure of watching mine. That's just cruel," Levi said.

Levi kicked off his shoes and hopped as he peeled the socks off his feet. He threw his dirty socks at Scarlett May's face, and she screamed, batting them down to the ground. We all laughed at her. I hadn't laughed this hard in a long time. Who knew all I needed was a naked nighttime race to feel so alive? My summer was officially back on track. Mason and Levi stood side by side, naked, on the road that stretched before the cabin. The air had cooled from the hot day, but not as much as the boys claimed as they cupped themselves in their hands. The gravel was sharp, but I doubted they would feel the pain under the rush of adrenaline.

"All right, are you guys ready?" Scarlett May asked, holding her arm high in the air.

"Wait!" Asher said, ripping his shirt off and tossing it to Kimber.

"What are you doing? Babe?" she asked in a whiny tone.

"What? I can't watch a race without entering, I've got to compete. It's in my blood," he replied. I grabbed Emma's arm and squeezed just above her elbow. Her eyes grew to saucers as Asher pulled his clothes off. He had a nice strong build that made us giggle like schoolgirls.

"You sure you don't want to get in on this Noah?" I called out, hoping. Praying. But he shook his head like it was a terrible idea.

"I can't believe this!" Lainey said, the whites of her eyes bright in the night.

"On your mark. Get set. Go!" Scarlett May yelled.

Levi, Mason, and Asher took off, running full speed down the street. Their arms outstretched, pushing and pulling each other as they ran. I laughed so hard I folded in two, fearing I'd pee my pants right there in the street. But it wasn't until Emma grabbed my shoulder and pointed to my neighbor, Mrs. Vandal, as she walked out to the end of her driveway to take out the trash that I stopped breathing altogether and then really lost it. Tears squeezed from my eyes as I staggered, nearly falling to the ground. Emma wasn't as strong. She *did* fall, taking Lainey down with her. I nearly tripped over the two of them, laughing even harder. Harder than I had in my entire life. I missed the race, I laughed so hard.

I heard the boys yelling a laundry list of profanity as their voices became smaller the more distant they became. It could have been my imagination, but I thought I heard Mrs. Vandal mutter in disbelief, and when I did, my knees became so weak they buckled. Emma tried to help herself up, but she only pulled me down with her. The three of us sprawled in the street, the boys' voices echoing in the cove.

"Look at them! And they thought they could run sixty miles per hour! They couldn't even get to the end of the street," Lainey said in hysterics.

"Quick! Grab their clothes!" Trinity hissed. Trinity Myers was usually the reason for the sour taste in my mouth or the cold chip on my shoulder, but at that moment, she was my hero.

"Yes! Oh my god, yes!" I bounded to my feet, stumbling and scooped up various boxers, T-shirts, socks, and pants. Emma held Levi's hat on top of her head and took off running to the cabin. Trinity and I bumped into one another, hands full of stolen clothes, and I all but forgot that she was the closest thing I had to an enemy.

It was for this very reason that Trinity was so popular; she was mean . . . in the most entertaining of ways. It was always at somebody's expense. But tonight, when I wasn't the target of her entertainment, I easily hopped on board. I became her partner because the fun was too great to pass up, and the boys—they'd done it to themselves, really.

All of us except Kimber ran into the house and locked the doors behind us. Kai took it upon himself to close the windows and lock them too. And

Scarlett May took out her cell phone, ready to document the three naked cheetahs by way of video and, regrettably, social media.

It wasn't long before Mason and Levi came pounding on the door. Asher and Kimber were attempting to sneak into the garage, but Kai had locked that too. When I thought I couldn't laugh anymore, I did. Levi stood in front of the window, hiding his bits behind his hands while Scarlett May snapped picture after picture. The others filled the house with hooting and hollering while running to check the locks at every entry. Mason ran wild throughout the yard, doing cartwheels on the grass and making us all laugh even harder. He ate it up. We all did. They endured a rough ten minutes in the "cold" before Trinity had a new idea. The perfect sequel to her first.

"Let's throw their clothes in the lake! That way, they have to jump in to get them!" she said.

"That one's on you!" Kai said, holding up his hands. He didn't want to be responsible for taking it a step further, but I did.

I helped Trinity scoop up the clothes. We peered out the windows, making sure we wouldn't be caught. And when the coast was clear, we unlocked the door. Slowly and quietly, we stepped off the porch. My heart was pounding in my chest. Once we made our way to the grassy knoll, we took off running in a sprint for the dock, laughing the whole way. Ethan tripped and went down, somersaulting several times before coming to a full stop. The rest of us, on our feet, continued running down the dock. Once we reached the end, Trinity threw handfuls of clothing into the lake. But I stood, frozen. The black water did its mesmerizing dance. Hypnotizing me. Reminding me. Drawing me in.

"What are you doing? Throw them in!" Trinity yelled. I stood motionless, feeling the phantom hand reach up my thigh and yank me under the water. My gaze fell unfocused. I went somewhere else—a world I didn't want to know existed.

"Give me that!" Trinity grabbed the boxers and jeans out of my hands, snapping me back to the present, and threw them into the water just as Levi yelled.

"Hey!" he yelled. "Hey, over here! They have our clothes!" I watched the water ripple out from the clothing until the heavier jeans had been swallowed whole. I was paralyzed. I felt like somebody was watching me. But from where? For how long? I scoured the shore, looking for eyes in the dark.

"No!" Asher came out of nowhere, running down the dock. Kimber stood in the grass, hiding behind her muffled laughter.

"Look at those cheeks!" She giggled. Mason was nowhere to be found.

We hung around long enough to see the two of them jump in after their clothes, and a part of me knew they would never surface again. In that moment, I felt the sobering effects of fear. This wasn't fun any longer. Something was wrong. Something was terribly wrong. I watched for what felt like minutes strung out in slow motion until their heads breached the water. Relief washed over me, making me dizzy.

I reached down to help Levi out of the water, and Noah came up behind me, grabbing my waist and startling me. I nearly leapt into the water in shock. I screamed louder than I would have liked, and an image of a cold, gray, dismembered hand reaching out of the black water flashed through my head. I felt the blood drain from my face. I turned around and slapped Noah on the shoulder, and he laughed. I still felt the eyes on me.

"Where's my money? Pay up," Asher said to Noah. We all laughed at Asher's ridiculous request. Nobody had agreed to pay him—only Mason, and Mason was still running naked in the woods.

"Do you think he really believes he ran sixty miles per hour?" Lainey asked, leaning into me.

I looked at her and smiled. "Actually . . . probably," I said, and we both laughed. The group walked slowly up the hill and back to the cabin, recalling elements of the race. Emma told everyone how the next-door neighbor had seen it all too. The group laughed hysterically as Asher tied Kimber's tiny sweater around his waist. Levi wrung out his clothes.

It was in these memorable times that I always felt like somebody was watching me. I tried to brush it off, but it picked away at me until striking a nerve. An owl called out, and I gave in and peeked back over my shoulder. Just one look to tell myself I was crazy. One look to confirm that nobody was there. But somebody *was* there. A dark figure stood at the edge of the dock. We had just been down there moments ago, and nobody had been around. I stopped and squinted into the night, stretching my sight as far as it would take me. I saw a large shadow cast on the water. A canoe? Was that Walker?

I stood frozen, split between emotions. On one end, I was excited to see him again. I'd been curious about him. And I'd felt safe by his side. A part of me wanted to explore that under more normal circumstances. And I'd be lying if I completely ignored how handsome he was. But there was another part of me—an even larger part, perhaps—that worried about his presence looming down by the dock. If he was there now, then I really had been in the middle of the lake on our first night, and it wasn't something I could sweep under the rug as a false memory or twisted dream. If I really had almost drowned, then I had never hit my head. And all the friends who had left me in that lake to drown weren't really my friends at all.

I looked back to Noah, Emma, and Ethan, who trailed behind the group, and it was clear that nobody would miss me if I slipped away. It had already happened. A pattern being painted before my very eyes. And for the first time in a long time, I was pleased by that. I wanted to see Walker again—to thank him for saving my life. But also to give him back his flannel. But I didn't grab his flannel when I headed out to the dock. I only grabbed Gunner's leash and told Lainey that I was taking him to go to the bathroom. She hardly blinked an eye, happy for the help.

I gripped the leash tightly in my hand as I made my way down the hill. There was a heat in my cheeks that told me I was flushed. Hopefully it would be hidden in the dark of the night. Was he waiting there for me? Had he come here to check up on me? What was I going to say to him? And the one question in my head I wouldn't allow myself to ask: why hadn't I brought his flannel?

5

The red leash was wrapped around my hand so tightly it nearly cut off the circulation to my fingers. I squeezed it tighter still. I wanted to see Walker again. Only I hadn't imagined it would be this soon . . . or ever at all. I hoped I would have more time to think of something clever to say, to gather my wits. But I had nothing. I had no idea how to thank him. And at this point, I didn't know if he had really saved my life, or if I had made up the whole thing. But the fact that he was there at the edge of the dock and his flannel had been lying across the foot of my bed for days could only mean one thing. Whatever had happened to me the first night we got to Baylor, it was real.

I reached the dock, my shoes padding over the wood planks and Gunner prancing happily at my side. Walker stood with his hands balled deep in his pockets, his stance wide. He'd come here looking for me. And it was more than any of my friends had done. A smile crept up my cheeks, and I lowered my head so my hair spilled over my face.

"I didn't expect to see you here so soon," I said, closing the distance between us.

"I came to check on you. It looks like you're doing just fine," Walker said, motioning to the raging party going on inside the cabin on top of the hill. Rock Creek Cove consisted of the Vandal's cabin and ours within a large clearing. The party was hard to miss. I looked back, a bit embarrassed at my friends' antics. There was no courage left from the drinks I'd had before the races started. The flashes of nightmare had sobered me up and dried me out.

"Oh, yeah . . . *that*. I have a group of friends staying the summer with me. They can get a little . . . rowdy," I said, shrugging. I studied his face. His dimples were deep, his face scruffy, and his eyes . . . I still couldn't discern what color they were. It was dark tonight, but not as ominous as the night we'd met. I could see a little more of his face in the shadows, and every bit was a welcome surprise. He was handsome, even more so than I remembered.

Walker sat down on the dock with a small groan, hanging his legs over the edge. Gunner came over to investigate, and Walker reached out to pet him before leaning back on the palms of his hands and looking up at me with his dark, mysterious eyes. I looked nervously back at the cabin. The lights were on, and the music was loud, even in the distance. I bent down and unhooked Gunner's leash, letting him run off to relieve himself and give us some privacy. Lainey said that he would come back, and I assumed this was true even when she wasn't around. I watched him race off and then loosened the leash around my hand. I took a seat next to Walker, but I didn't dare hang my legs over the edge.

"Is that your dog?" he asked. His warm, beachy scent brought up images of a sunny day. A frisbee. A dog galloping into the surf.

"Oh, no. That's my friend Lainey's dog. His name is Gunner. He's a really sweet dog. He just needs a lot of exercise. He'll come back," I said. We watched the dog disappear into the night, and I questioned my better judgment in letting him go. But it didn't last long, because right then, a pair of boxers surfaced in the lake before us.

"Oh . . ." I gasped.

"Do you see that?" Walker asked, his brows furrowed. It wasn't how I'd expected the conversation to go. I wanted to minimize our immaturity, not highlight it.

"So, there's this thing called The Naked Cheetah Races," I began.

"Really?" he asked, amused. I felt myself shrink just a little.

"It's where you race naked down the street as fast as you can. It's not really popular yet, but I think it will catch on." My eyes were trained on the boxers until they drifted underneath the dock and out of sight.

"Does that underwear belong to one of contestants?" he asked.

"Well, yes. We just figured that, after the naked races had finished, we would throw all the contestants' clothes in the lake, so they would have to jump in the lake . . . naked." It sounded so much more malicious out loud than it did in my head.

"And this is a tradition?" he asked.

"It might be the first annual race. Only time will tell."

He chuckled, and a relieved smile spread across my lips.

"Hey, I never got a chance to say thank you," I said. Walker looked at me, and in that moment, I knew that everything I had experienced that night was no lie. No charade. And no devious dream. I had thought maybe I was crazy, that I had made the whole thing up, or had an injury, but the look on Walker's face said it all. This was very real. Which made it very dangerous. I owed him everything.

"I don't know how to thank you for saving my life, but I do know that if you hadn't been there in the middle of the lake, I may never have gotten back alive. And I can't imagine what that would have done to my family. I just can't thank you enough. Honestly." My eyes watered, and I wiped a tear away before it had a chance to spill over my cheek.

Walker nodded, looking down at his feet dangling over the dock's edge. He gave me a moment of silence, and I tried to clear my throat of emotion. "I'm just grateful I was there, too," he said. A wash of relief came over me because, even though I knew from looking into his eyes that the night had been real, I hadn't known if we were on the same page until he'd said it out loud. And it felt good to finally be in sync with someone. Anyone.

"So, you're here for the summer with a group of friends?" he asked, looking back at me.

"Yeah. Eleven of my friends, one dog, and me. We've been planning it all senior year."

"High school?" Walker raised his eyebrows. I'd assumed he was older than I was, but not by much. Clearly, he was taken aback.

"We just finished high school. We flew here right after high school graduation. It's our summer of freedom. How . . . How old are you?" I asked and immediately regretted it. *So rude.*

"Twenty-four."

I looked at Walker. It wasn't too much of a difference. I smiled, trying to read his face, but I detected some sadness there. He looked out over the lake, and I watched his pensive gaze deepen. Was he upset that I was only eighteen? That was stupid. It's not like we were dating. I shook my head, dispelling yet another thought.

"After this summer, I'll be going away to college. For many of us, this is our last true break. Then come the bills, the rent, the jobs," I said.

"What are you going to college for?"

"Art history." I shrugged. Art history was never something I was passionate about, but it would have to do. I liked art enough. It just wasn't my first choice. "I just left an internship at a small art gallery in town. It was okay. The husband and wife that owned it were a little peculiar though." A frown spread across my face as I remembered all the times I had walked in on something that seemed fishy. I'm not sure if they were cooking the books or laundering drug money through art sales, but I knew something didn't add up. I'd been thankful my internship was only a matter of months. And I learned quite a few things, regardless.

"You don't sound too excited."

I twisted the leash in my hand and scanned the grounds for Gunner.

"I don't know. I like art enough, but if I was being honest with myself, I would have chosen something else. I think I'm really good at art. Not like painting or sculpting, not even drawing, but I'm good at selling it. I'm good at looking at the brushstrokes and knowing what technique was used, or even what era the art had come from. I really excelled at it in school. At first, it was just an easy grade, but then I thought, maybe it was an easy living, too. It's an odd talent, and I figured I should just run with it."

"Well, if you have a talent, I think it's great you're furthering your abilities. But why do you say you like it . . . *enough*?"

"I just like other aspects of art better, but I'm not good at them. I can't make a living off them. And I figured it would be smart to choose the option I thought would be most lucrative," I said.

"So you choose art?" he laughed.

I shook my head with a sheepish smile. He was right. I'd probably make a better living being a waitress, and I wouldn't have to go to college for it. Sometimes I thought I had it all figured out, and other times I knew I was a mess.

"Where does your *passion* lie?" he asked, his smile not yet fading.

"Um, nooo . . ." I said, tucking my hair behind my ears. But he just waited expectantly. The silence ate at me, and I finally caved.

"It's kind of embarrassing, but I really love movies. I can play movies in my head, anywhere, anytime. I fall asleep at night playing movies in my head. Daydream all day. I can imagine the best of times, and I can imagine the most tragic of them. I know where the music should start and how it should build. It's like a symphony, and I want to create that more than anything. So when you ask where my passion lies, if I were being honest, I'd have to say screenwriting." I ran my free hand through my hair nervously and didn't dare look at him. I didn't want him to ask the million-dollar question. Because the embarrassing part wasn't *what* I was passionate about but more the fact that I could never do it justice. Being dyslexic was like a hand that always held me down, held me back, and I knew not to go up against it. For I would lose, every time.

"What do you do?" I asked, not giving him any time to ruminate over my dream.

"Well, you talk about what's lucrative, and for me right now, it's bartending. You wouldn't believe the amount of money I make bartending. But it's taxing. Most nights, I go home feeling lonely—so lonely. It's really hard when you're in a room full of people and it only makes you feel more alone." He sighed, long and heavy. "But when everybody is drinking, and everyone is on a date or with friends, and you're the only person there who is sober, responsible, and alone, it can be mentally and emotionally taxing."

Walker looked into my eyes for a long moment, and I could almost feel his pain. I didn't know a thing about him other than that he was lonely, and it was enough to break my heart. He had saved my life. The least I could do was be a friend to him.

"So, if bartending is lucrative for you—if it pays your bills—then what is it that *you're* passionate about but can't squeeze a penny out of?" I asked.

"Most nights, I work air traffic control at the airport. I love it. And it actually does pay the bills. But I'm still learning, and I have a little way to go before I climb the ranks. And so, I bartend on the weekends."

"Do you mean you tell the planes where to go?" I asked.

"Yes. I watch the skies. I talk to everybody in the air and tell them when the coast is clear. I'm like a traffic light for the sky." He looked up at the stars, and I followed his gaze. I imagined planes flying through the sky and stopping at his command. Stoplights made from twinkling stars.

"Why do you bartend if you're making money doing what you love?" It made little sense to me.

"Like I said before, nights can be lonely. And since I spend nights doing air traffic control, I'm awake while the rest of the world is asleep. It only made sense for me to get another job during the nighttime hours. At first, I imagined being around a lively group of people would cure the emptiness, but what I didn't realize until months into the job was that it only made it worse."

Walker steepled his fingers under his chin, and I imagined what his stubble would feel like on the palm of my hand if I caressed his face. I took a deep breath, prying my eyes from his jawline. *Emptiness. So sad.* "I get that," I said, looking back at the cabin.

"You do?" he asked.

I inhaled, looking away from him, out over the water. When somebody saves your life, all other boundaries seem to prove nebulous. No topic was off limits.

"I do. I'm in this cabin with eleven of my closest friends, and I've never felt as alone as I did that night. The night of the . . . the night we met."

"The other night? You felt alone?" he asked.

"I don't think anybody even noticed I was gone," I said, my voice choking up a bit. I bowed my chin to my chest and fiddled with the leash in my hands, turning it over again and again.

"That's impossible," he said.

I smiled because that's exactly what I had thought. I shrugged, trying not to cry. Looking away, I caught a glimpse of something in the distance. At first, I thought it was Gunner running through the woods, but then I realized it was much taller. As if the dog had stood upright and run on his back two legs. I arched my back, craning my neck to get a better look.

Walker followed my gaze, looking into the woods himself. "What in the . . ." he mumbled.

The blur came at lightning speed, and when it breached the wall of pines into the clearing, it was clear that it was no dog. Mason was running full speed, buck naked. A wash of disbelief poured over me, and I burst into laughter. I covered my mouth with both hands, suppressing what I could. Walker started to laugh too, and we sat on the dock watching a naked guy running through the clearing at top speed. Sixty miles per hour? No, but pretty darn close. He kept looking behind him as if something was chasing him. As if he were running for his life. Not far behind him was Gunner.

"Ahhh!" Mason yelled as Gunner closed in on him. I looked at Walker, tears filling my eyes once more. This was far more embarrassing than the underwear floating in the water or my top-secret dream to be a screenwriter.

"That must be a contestant?" Walker asked.

"Clearly, he came in last!" I said.

Mason slammed the door behind him as he rushed into the cabin, locking Gunner outside. I watched the dog sniff around the grassy knoll after his prey had fled, and I was happy that he'd returned home. The hazing going on inside the cabin was audible from the dock, and it made me smile. I could only imagine what they were saying to Mason, but I was positive that Scarlett May had videotaped it all, and I could watch it later.

"So, the races are every Friday night. Sign-ups are inside . . ." I said as our laughter died down. I peeked at Walker when the air between us fell silent, and he had a small smile on his face as he stared out over the water. It was a far better look than the pensive, lonely gaze he'd been wearing when we'd first sat down.

"So, do you live around here?" I asked.

Walker shook his head. "No. I'm just here visiting, like you." My eyes locked onto his canoe, tied to the end of the dock.

"Where are you staying?" I asked.

"I'm staying at the Williams' cabin. It's across the lake. They rent it out as often as they can. I stay there sometimes when work becomes too much and I need a break from all of it." Walker's voice was ragged now.

"You mean, when you need a break from being lonely, you come to the lake to get away from everyone?" I teased. Apparently, it was something we both did. Walker smiled at me, and I felt the warmth creep into my cheeks once more. He caught me staring at his lips, and I looked away, thankful he couldn't see my swarthy hue betray me.

"Now you're getting it," he said with a full smile. He wore it well, but something told me he didn't wear it often.

"Actually, I do," I said.

The cabin door opened and slammed closed, stealing my attention. Out came Lainey and Kimber, arms interlocked. They leaned against each other, swerving from side to side. I knew my time with Walker was coming to an end, and I'd have to say goodbye.

"I still have your flannel!" I blurted out in an attempt to make further plans with him.

"Oh, you can keep it," he said, swiping a hand through the air.

I'd like that very much, but I still needed a reason to see him again. It's not like I was old enough to keep him company at the bar where he worked.

"No, I'll get it back to you." I insisted. "Will I see you again?" I asked. Hopeful.

"Yeah, of course. I'll be here for a while."

Lainey and Kimber barely made it to the dock without tumbling to the ground. Squeals and screams were heard as they slipped on the wet grass—and once again when Gunner pushed up beside them. I watched as they swerved dangerously close to the dock's edge. I stood up anxiously, the leash wrapped around my hand. Walker stood too, and I gave him an awkward shrug of apology. I knew he was lonely, and I could have sat there all night talking to him if he'd let me. If we weren't interrupted. But there were naked men running from ferocious beasts in the woods and inebriated girls in stitches stumbling down the dock. An entire night to connect might be in our future, but it wasn't tonight.

"Okay, so I'll see you again then?" I asked worriedly.

"You sure will," he said, stuffing his hands into his pockets. I started toward my friends, saving them from walking the plank that they'd inevitably tumble over. And even though the water was shallow, I knew it was the home of something nefarious.

"Where'd Gunner go?" Lainey asked, slurring her words. I searched the hilltop. Gunner was digging a hole just beyond the cabin. I sighed. It was my fault.

"He's right over there. He didn't go far."

"What are you doing out here?" Kimber asked, eyes searching. I looked behind me. Walker stood, assessing the situation. I smiled, turning back to Kimber and Lainey.

"Nothing!" I reached out to grab Kimber's arm as she stumbled over her own two feet. "Easy there. Or you're going to fall into the lake," I said.

"I'll be careful. I can do it. Watch this. Watch." Kimber closed her eyes and tilted her head back, trying to touch each pointer finger to her nose. She failed miserably, stuffing her right finger into her eye and her left into her cheek. I cringed inside.

"Oh yeah, I can see that," I said.

"Gunner! Gunner? Come'er boy!" Lainey yelled. Gunner came running down the hill, abandoning his hole. When he reached us, I clipped the leash onto his collar, thankful he'd come back. We reached the end of the dock, and Lainey wrapped her arm in mine, her weight making me stagger too.

"But seriously, who were you talking to?" she asked.

I turned back, looking at Walker. Like a gentleman, he was still there, waiting to make sure I got back into the cabin safely. I smiled, butterflies fluttering in my stomach, and said, "Nobody!" in a coy tone, denying myself the truth.

6

The room was dark and empty. Not a thing could be seen except for Gran's chair lit by a blazing fire, though I felt no heat. Goosebumps prickled the nape of my neck, and a shiver spilled down my spine, quaking deep in my bones. I'd been to this place before; that much I was sure of. I felt a sense of familiarity as I looked around me. Gran's chair was empty, and a book lay open with a bookmark nestled between the pages. I looked into the void, as far as my eyes could stretch, but there was nothing there . . . there never was.

I'd been here before, but I couldn't remember when, or why. A dream? Was I dreaming? I looked down at my hands, opening and closing them. They moved in slow motion. I turned them over, examining them closely. Something was off, but I couldn't pinpoint what. It was like I had been peeking behind the curtain during a magic show.

I pressed my fingers against my palm, slowly and steadily, until something odd happened. My fingertips disappeared as they sank into my flesh. I couldn't feel it. I couldn't feel anything but cold. I watched as they poked out the backside of my hand.

I did it again in disbelief—this time faster . . . harder. My fingers drove through the meaty part of my palm and jutted out the other side. A small sound escaped my throat as I pulled my hands apart and whipped my head around, looking again to see if anything was out there in the void. But I was alone. Just me and the thudding of my heart like a caged animal driven mad.

Hypnotized, I grabbed at my arm fast and fierce, but it was different. I was able to hold my arm with a firm grip. What was happening? *Am I here? Am I not here?* I concentrated on doing it again. I tried to prove to myself that I saw it. My head hurt as my hand glitched through my arm. I was no more than a figment of my own imagination. A ghost. I wasn't supposed to be here. I swallowed the lump of anxiety building in my throat. I was in some state of subconsciousness. A higher level of awareness. But why? How?

With a creak of the rocking chair, I whipped my head up. Gran was there, as if she had been sitting there the whole time. She looked at me and smiled, though I felt no peace in her pleasure. No love in her eyes.

"This is a dream," I heard myself say.

Gran slowly turned the page, as if my presence meant nothing to her, and continued to read. "This isn't real," I said, repeating myself.

"This is as real as you make it, my dear," she said, eyes still transfixed on the page.

"No, this is just a dream. Only a dream." I looked back at my hands and realized why they looked so weird. There weren't any wrinkles where my knuckles should have been. It was smooth skin, like it had been manipulated by a computer-generated image. I ran my hand over my face, feeling my features. My lips, the bridge of my nose, my icy breath.

"Oh dear, you have so much to learn. And so little time," she said.

"What do you mean, Gran? Is there something you need to tell me? Is that why you're here?" I asked. I didn't think she was supposed to be here. I *knew* that *I* wasn't.

Gran slowly closed the book and placed it on the table before her. "In fact, I have something to tell you. You see, there are answers to the questions you seek. There are answers out there, waiting for you to find them. If only you would find them, dear," she said, in a dark, mysterious tone. It wasn't the voice I'd grown up listening to.

"What do you mean, answers?" I asked.

"Dear, there is a girl out there who needs your help. A girl who's lost and lonely. Even more lost than you are now. And there's no way out." She motioned to the black void. "You're the only one who can find her and bring her home safely. You need to find her."

"A girl?" I didn't care about a girl. I only wanted to know where I was. And why I was so cold.

"A girl. You must find her," she insisted.

"Well, how? How do I do that?"

"Find her!" Gran bellowed. I didn't hear her voice with my ears; instead, I felt it throughout my body, shaking my bones and echoing into the distant emptiness of the void. The fire faded out, the orange flames shrinking down to glowing red coals before disappearing in a trail of smoke. As impossible as it would seem, the place grew colder. The chills raked through me until I was frozen. I turned to stone, unable to move an inch except for my eyes. My skin was tight and dry, and I felt as if I might crack in half and shatter against the floor. Gran grew dim as the shadows spread across her face, and she began to disappear. I knew my time was closing in.

"Gran? Where do I find her?" I asked without ever moving my lips. The thought echoed far away and went unanswered. The room had turned dark as coal and Gran was no longer there. Nothing was. No chair. No fireplace. No books.

"Gran! Gran! What does she look like? How will I know?" I yelled into the darkness. My voice called out for miles but reached no one.

I used all my strength to break out of the stone—to escape the fixation that encapsulated me. I jolted awake, covered in a blanket of sweat and gasping for air. I gripped the sheets in my hands, panting, and looked around, taking in my surroundings. I was in the cabin, the master bedroom. And though it was the middle of the night, it wasn't as dark as the void, nor as cold. My head pounded, and I brought my hands up to my forehead, squinting. It wasn't a fight I could manage alone. I threw the blanket off me and swung my knees over the edge of the bed, my toes touching down on the soft plush carpet. I slipped on some shorts and tiptoed downstairs in search of pain medicine.

I didn't know if my headache was from the few drinks I'd had the night before or the recurring dreams of my gran that tormented me, but I knew I would no longer be able to sleep with the throbbing between my ears. The stairs creaked as I made my way to the kitchen. The air hit the sweat on my shirt, leaving me chilled. A green sleeping bag was sprawled on the living room floor, a body stuffed inside. I figured it was Mason, who had been known for his unconventional sleeping habits.

There were only three bedrooms in the cabin—all of them upstairs. Asher and Kimber were sharing a room, since they were the only couple in the group. Emma and Lainey shared the third bedroom because they were my closest friends. And I, of course, had the master. Everyone else slept wherever. On various sofas, recliners, and sometimes, I'd come to learn, the back porch.

"What the hell?" A small moan came from a sleeping bag when I turned the kitchen lights on. I quickly turned them off again, trying not to disturb the sleeper. I fumbled around, thankful it was my cabin and I knew where the first aid kit was kept. By the light of the refrigerator, I managed to take out a couple of pain killers and pour myself a glass of water.

Before I had finished my water, Noah surprised me in the kitchen, wearing only a pair of boxer shorts. His sandy hair was a mess, and his face pink from sleep. "Hey," I whispered, my shirt wet and clinging to my chest.

"Hey," he replied. His eyes traveled down and back up lazily.

"What are you doing up?" I asked.

"I've got this headache that won't quit. Do you have ibuprofen?" he asked.

"Yeah, I just took some, too. I've got a raging headache also. Right here," I said, rubbing the top of my forehead.

"Mine's in the back," he said, rubbing the back of his head.

As Noah and I stood in the kitchen, both rubbing our heads, I flashed back to a memory of when we were young. "Do you remember that one time, when we were at your house and our moms were hosting a book club meeting?" I asked with a coy smile.

"I remember her book clubs, but which time?"

"The time we hit our heads together on your trampoline, and we were too embarrassed to go inside and interrupt the meeting," I said, still rubbing my head.

"Oh, that time. How could I forget? I thought I was going to die!" Noah whispered, cracking a smile. I stifled my laughter as I tried not to wake up whoever was wrapped in the sleeping bag in the living room.

"I thought we were dying too. It hurt so bad."

Noah and I had grown up together. Our moms were friends and often hosted random parties together—book club once a month and the occasional Tupperware party or Bunco night. Basically, any reason to get together and uncork the wine. Often, I would go with my mom, and Noah and I would play in the yard while our moms got toasted.

We grew up as good friends, but somewhere along the way, when puberty had struck and our feelings began to develop for the opposite sex, things between us grew awkward. Many years passed where we wouldn't speak to one another, and I no longer went to his house for our mothers' meetings. Eventually, in high school, we started talking again. We picked up right where we'd left off and became fast friends again. Our groups combined—his the athletic, popular group and my threesome of Lainey, Emma, and me. It wasn't until the last couple of years that I had developed feelings for him. I believed those feelings were mutual, but I couldn't be sure. I knew staying at my cabin all summer would either flush out our feelings or chase them away.

"Hey, do you still get those nightmares? The ones about your shed?" I asked.

"No, not often. But every once in a while, one will resurface." Noah seemed embarrassed, but I wasn't judging him, just trying to connect. He'd had a rough time with nightmares when he was a kid. Something about the shed in his back yard always seemed to scare him. I was never sure where the fear stemmed from. And every now and then, I would think about it and try to figure out what the missing piece of the puzzle was. But as far as I could tell, it was just his mother's potting shed and nothing more.

"That's good," I said, finishing my water. The room fell quiet, but neither Noah nor I made a move to leave the kitchen. Neither one of us wanted the conversation to end. And presumably, neither one of us could sleep with our headaches. I kept the conversation going with the only thing I knew about nightmares. Mine.

"I've been having nightmares myself," I confessed, as I recalled the one that had woken me up. I tugged at the hem of my shirt, and it peeled away from my chest.

"You've been having nightmares? What about?" he asked, no longer embarrassed about his own.

"I don't know. They're kind of weird. It's always this empty dark place. My gran is there, and it's as if she never died. Like she thinks she is still alive. Only I know better. I know she shouldn't be there with me, and a part of me wonders if she's trying to get a message through. But that's stupid."

"That's not stupid. That's awesome," he said. I looked up from the countertop into his denim-blue eyes. They were compassionate, and I knew he only wanted the best for me.

"You think so?" I asked, wrinkling my nose.

"Yeah. I've heard enough stories like that to believe that maybe there's some truth in them. What does she say?" he asked with honest curiosity.

"Well, the one I just woke up from . . . she was there in this room of . . . of . . . nothingness. She told me I needed to find a girl," I said, thinking about it for the first time since waking up.

"A girl?"

"Yeah, a girl. But that's pretty much it. She didn't say where I would find her, or what she would look like. She only said that I needed to find her. Bring her home."

"That's all? Do you have any idea what it means?"

"No, but she said that the girl needed my help." I shook my head, dispelling the stupid idea that my grandmother was talking to me from beyond the grave. A large part of me didn't believe it myself, but there was a small part that wouldn't let it go—an itty-bitty part that believed that maybe she was alive somewhere. That I was special enough for her to cross worlds beyond ours, just to talk to me. Maybe she had gone through all of this effort to reach through the veil of the living to get some special message to me. I didn't know who this girl was, and I didn't intend to go find her. But the riddle would keep me up at night. That much, I was sure of.

"How are you doing with your grandma and all? I meant to reach out earlier, but honestly, I didn't know what to say. I know you two were close," he said, biting his lip the way he did when he was nervous.

I could feel the warmth of emotion heating my skin. Gran and I had been close. I missed her deeply, but I knew my mom missed her more, and for that reason, I felt invalidated in my hardship. I brushed it off like I was stronger than I was. "I'm doing all right," I lied.

"You know you can talk to me, right? We've been friends forever," he said. *Friends? But was that all?* I looked at him but saw nothing behind his eyes—other than a well of sympathy for my pain. It could have been the love you had for someone because they grew up with you, like family, or it could have been more.

"I know I can talk to you. It's just hard. It's hard to think that somebody so significant in your life can be there one minute and gone the next. If I'm being honest with you, it's turned my universe upside down. All the things I thought were important before just aren't anymore. And I don't know if it's some sort of depression from her passing or a simple change of perspective. But everything I see and everything I think . . . it's different now." I looked down at my fingers interlocking with one another as I fidgeted. A part of me focused on the resistance of my fingers against my hand, and I remembered what it had been like in my dream when I was fluid.

"I get that. Do you feel like these new perspectives on life are better than before?" he asked.

"Better?" I thought back to all the times I'd questioned the loyalty of my friendships or the motives behind their actions. I thought about all the times I'd sat on the edge of my bed alone, wondering what the point was. If I should even bother with college if it couldn't buy me happiness. "Not better. Just different," I lied again, as a movement caught the corner of my eye.

Mason staggered into the kitchen, his sleeping bag still around his lower half as he clutched it tight around his waist. Both Noah and I stared at him curiously. Was he sleepwalking? Was he still drunk? He slid his feet along the kitchen floor as he moseyed toward the refrigerator. He didn't notice either of us as he opened the door and pulled out a cold beer. He cracked it open with one hand and guzzled back what I could only assume to be half the can, if not more. He was about to close the fridge when he saw something else and opened it back up. It felt like Noah and I were watching a National Geographic documentary.

Mason reached into the refrigerator with his other hand, and his sleeping bag dropped to the floor, exposing his bare butt. I sucked in a quick gasp, and Mason spun around to see Noah and me standing behind him with large, watchful eyes.

"Oh shit! Oh . . . It's just you guys," he said, somewhat disappointed. My eyes dropped below his waistline, and Mason turned back to the fridge and pulled out a slice of pizza. He set everything down on the kitchen counter before pulling up his sleeping bag once again. I forced my gaze away, but my eyes were still wide with surprise.

"You sleep naked, man?" Noah asked.

"My clothes are wet, douche bag."

Noah and I snickered. He had more clothes in a bag somewhere. He totally slept naked.

"Because somebody threw them in the lake. Whose bright idea was that anyway?" Mason asked through a mouthful of cold pizza.

"Don't look at me!" I said, holding up my hands.

"I don't know, but it was brilliant," Noah said.

"Brilliant? I should throw your clothes in the lake and see how you feel, asshole," Mason said, taking another bite. My eyes dropped from Mason's face down to his leftover pizza, and my stomach growled.

"Is there any more?" I asked.

"Yeah, there's a bunch in there." Mason turned to open the refrigerator and dropped his sleeping bag once again, only this time he bent over, giving us a view of his undercarriage.

"Eww, stop that!" I hissed. Mason tossed a Ziploc bag full of pizza onto the kitchen counter.

"There's the pizza, but I already gave you what you *really* wanted," he said with a hip thrust.

"You wish," Noah said.

The three of us stood in the kitchen chatting quietly while we ate our midnight snack and Noah and I waited for the ibuprofen to kick in. When my pain was no more than a memory, I told the boys I was going to try to get some sleep. I swiped my hand across Noah's back as I passed to say good night. My fingers kept contact as long as they could. Noah gave me a look that said he'd much prefer my company over Mason's, and I smiled before turning away.

I tiptoed up the stairs with a full belly and a smile on my face, hoping for a more restful night. But when I crawled into bed, all I could see was the framed photograph of my gran sitting on top of my parents' dresser. Ornate golden corners and a grainy old photo. She'd had the most beautiful eyes—green like emeralds—but as she'd aged, they'd turned cloudy and gray. She was like that in my dreams. And that's how I knew they were nightmares. Because she was still hindered by her cataracts and cancer.

I closed my eyes to sleep, but I couldn't think of anything other than the mystery girl. The most haunting thing that wracked my mind wasn't the girl, but the part where my gran had said there was no way out.

As I waited for sleep to take me, I imagined Noah in the kitchen. His sleep-mussed sandy hair and boxer shorts. But this time, a very different scenario. One where we didn't talk about my gran or nightmares. One where I had the courage to kiss him instead. One where the kiss was so passionate, it led to much, much more. But somewhere along the way, Noah turned into Walker. And I couldn't tell if that was the reason for the increased passion or not. I fell asleep before I could figure out what it all meant. And when the sun rose, all that really mattered was the fact that I rose with a smile.

7

I sipped on my coffee as I pondered my dream from the night before. I wasn't planning on looking for a girl, but if I did . . . if I did, who would it be? A slow chill crawled down the nape of my neck, inching its way to my spine. There was something at the edge of my mind trying to get in. But I couldn't quite recall what it might be. I picked at it. Something Scarlett May had said. A story. It began to fester, and before I knew it, there was no more coffee left in my mug. I poured myself another and stared off into the distance. My eyes dry as I remembered the Baylor Butcher and the girl who had gotten away.

The girl had escaped her own death by just one date. She'd followed her instincts to safety. And had she seen him just one night later, she might not have been alive. She probably went into hiding. *Hiding*. A girl who was hiding needed to be found. Had the girl my gran spoke of been the same girl that had escaped the Baylor Butcher? No. I was stretching.

But *if* the girl I was supposed to find had been the girl from the stories, then how was I to help? I had nothing in common with a stranger who had dated a monster long, long ago. At least, nothing that I knew of. It was then that curiosity lit inside me. A small flame at first, but it was being fed, and growing brighter and hotter. I needed to find out who this girl was to see if we had a connection. I hesitated to ask Scarlett May any more questions for fear of her sharp tongue, but she was the obvious place to start.

I looked around the living room at the slow-moving zombies before me. Several people were awake, but none of them alert. Many of them were like me, a mug in their hand and a distant gaze on their face. It was time I started taking matters into my *own* hands. I had a mission. A mission that wasn't driven by my late gran, but one that had been ignited by my own curiosity. Who was she?

"Hey, Emma? I'm going to run to the grocery store in a little bit. Is there anything in particular that you want me to pick up for you?" Emma rubbed the sleep from her eyes while she thought about it.

"Some yogurt would be good. I like to eat that for breakfast," she said.

"Yogurt. No problem," I said, writing it down.

"Do you want me to go with you?"

"I don't think that'll be necessary," I said, looking away. I had much more than grocery shopping to do. I wanted to talk to some of the locals about the Baylor ghost stories, and I couldn't exactly do that if I had a friend tagging along. Not without follow-up questions, that is.

I took my notes and went to find Lainey, who was a vegetarian and surely had a long list of specialty items for me to gather at the grocery store. I found her upstairs brushing her hair in the bathroom.

"Good morning," I said, leaning against the doorjamb.

"Morning."

"I'm going to the grocery store. What kinds of things should I pick up for you?" I asked, tapping the pen on the pad.

"Oh, I can just go with you," she said, fumbling around in her bag for toothpaste and a toothbrush.

"No, that's all right. Why don't you stay here and enjoy the lake? It's going to be a nice day," I said.

"I don't mind at all. Plus, I have a lot of weird things to pick up that you're probably unfamiliar with." Lainey shoved her toothbrush into her mouth and looked at me sideways.

"You like those vegetarian sausage patties, right?" I asked, jotting it down.

"Yeah, but it has to be the brand with the green box. They have another one that comes in a blue box and they are gross. But seriously, I'll just go with you!" Suds ran down her chin, and she leaned over the sink.

"Actually, I was just going to run some errands and then hit the grocery store on the way back home. I'll probably be gone most of the day," I said.

"Okay, why don't I write it down for you then," Lainey said. I waited patiently for her to finish brushing her teeth and write out her list.

Lainey had been an animal lover from the time she was a young child. She'd stopped eating meat after watching a documentary about how farm-raised fish made it to the market. A long time ago, I'd asked her if she missed it, and she'd said that she didn't.

"Thank you. I'll just call if I have any questions," I said.

"Yeah, and if you change your mind, I'm happy to go with." Lainey turned back to the mirror for one last look.

I ventured downstairs in search of Scarlett May. I found her on the back porch talking on the phone. The way she spoke made me think she was talking to a crush. There was a smirk on her face, her cheek lifted, and a sparkle brightened her eyes. She was dressed to impress in studded jean shorts and red cowgirl boots. Everyone else in the house was still in pajamas, with the exception of Mason, who I assumed was still naked in his sleeping bag. Scarlett May hung up the phone and looked at me with raised brows but didn't say anything.

"Are you going somewhere?" I asked, checking her out.

"I'm meeting my friend Sampson today." Jack Sampson was a family friend of hers. Whenever she came to visit the lake, she and Sampson would get into all sorts of mischief. She'd been planning for the group to meet up with him and his friends for a bonfire. I wondered if they were more than just friends by the way she was dressed and the light in her eyes when she spoke to him.

"I'm running to the grocery store. Is there anything that you need?" I asked.

"Yeah, get eggs and bacon. Probably coffee too." Scarlett May stuffed her cell phone into the back pocket of her shorts and started to head for the door.

"Oh, I just had a question real quick. You know how you were telling us about the Baylor ghost stories? I was wondering if you had any more details on the girl who got away? Like a name, or perhaps—"

"You're not serious, are you?" she interrupted.

"What do you mean?" I felt the shrinking of my presence, like a reprimanded dog shaking before its owner. She cocked her head to the side, looking at me as if I were stupid. Was I? Stupid?

"You don't really think she has a name, do you? For me to have a name would mean that the ghost stories were real. And ghost stories aren't real. They're no more than fables meant to scare the living daylights out of young children. And last time I checked, you're not a young child." Scarlett May stared at me with her head still cocked. "Well, are you?" she asked.

"What? Am I what?"

"A child?"

"No, I—"

"That's what I thought. So don't get spooked by the kiddie story." She spun on her heels and then peered over her shoulder and whispered, "It's not real . . ." Then she left me on the back patio, stewing in my humiliation. The door slammed shut, making me jump.

It was going to be a beautiful day. The sky was clear, and the green grass was glistening with morning dew. The lake itself was like glass, with not a soul in sight. Nobody except Mrs. Vandal. She watched me as she watered her rose bushes. I gave her a curt wave, and she looked away, ignoring me. Yup, it was going to be a beautiful day in Baylor, but that wouldn't clear the gloom I felt building inside me.

I found Ethan with Asher in the game room. They were using the pool table as a dining table, their breakfast plates on top of the green felt; my dad would be furious. "Do you guys want anything from the grocery store?" Ethan Patrick was Asher's biggest fan. I think he liked him even more than Kimber did. Both of them had dark hair, but only Ethan's was sun-kissed, shining red under the sun's rays. Ethan styled his hair much like Asher did, and he even dressed like him. I sometimes thought of Ethan as Asher's shadow, and I wasn't the only one.

"You're running to the grocery store?" Ethan asked. "Why don't I come along and give you a hand? That's a lot of people to shop for," he said, blushing. I'd known Ethan had a crush on me since second grade, the same way I'd known when somebody had been watching me, even if there was nobody there. Typically, he took failure well, but there was something about this trip that was different. I imagined he had goals of his own to achieve this summer. His last chance to make a move. It's how I felt about Noah.

"I appreciate it, but I'm going alone. I have a bunch of errands to do in town, and grocery shopping is only my last stop. But I'm happy to pick up whatever you need." I tapped the pen on the pad that was nearly full of special requests. Lainey didn't talk much about Ethan, probably because she felt he liked me too. But I knew she had feelings for him, which made it difficult for me. I usually tried to minimize my time with Ethan so she would feel more comfortable.

"Just make sure you get lots of meat. I think I went through the sandwich meat in one sitting yesterday," Asher said.

"Lots of real meat, and lots of fake meat. Got it," I said.

I called a cab to get into town. It was too far away for the golf cart to handle. Most of the visitors around the lake needed temporary transportation, so cabs were crawling around all the local attractions. With the list stuffed in my back pocket, I had the cab drop me off on the main street, just before the grocery store. There was only one store in Baylor, and it was slim pickings. The floors were scuffed and in desperate need of renovation. The shelves were stocked, but mostly with off-brand products. I wasn't sure if I would be able to find anything that Lainey wanted. Especially the green-boxed sausages.

I grabbed a cart and strolled through the aisles, slowly looking for not only the items on my list but locals who looked like they'd heard a story or two before. The air was frigid, and the wheel on my grocery cart squeaked every time it rotated. I didn't know which was worse, the squeak or the elevator music that piped through the speakers. If I had chosen the grocery store to start my research on the Baylor ghost stories, then I had chosen the wrong place. There wasn't a soul in sight.

By the third aisle, I passed a mother with a young child. Young enough to have nightmares about the questions I had planned to ask. I smiled at them politely as I passed by.

I came upon a store clerk. A young man—probably in his twenties—with a face full of acne. He was stocking shelves and pretended not to notice me. "Excuse me? Do you know where the lunchmeat is?" I asked. Even though I had already walked past it three times, looking for people to start my investigation.

"Aisle twelve," he said, eyes fixed on the cans of corn before him. I tightened my grip on the shopping cart, but I didn't move.

"I have a really weird question that maybe you can help me with? I'm in town for the summer, and I've recently heard of an old tale about a butcher. Something about a man who haunts Baylor Lake. Have you ever heard of something like that before?" I asked.

"I'm sorry ma'am, I don't know of any ghost stories." The store clerk stood up and abandoned his cans. I watched his tall thin figure walk away. I scratched my head, looking up and down the empty aisle.

I had just about finished my shopping when I found a large man, both tall and wide, taking a bag of trash out back. I seized the opportunity. "Excuse me! Excuse me!" I yelled as I pushed my cart, squeaky wheel and all, as fast as I could. When I approached the store clerk, he was much more intimidating up close than from afar. He was an older gentleman and quite rough around the edges. And there was a smell. Putrid in its own right.

"You talkin' to me?" he asked, with a furrowed brow.

"I was curious if you had a moment? I'm doing a little research on some town gossip, and I was wondering if you've heard any Baylor ghost stories before?" I asked, my heart beating a little faster than normal.

"Which Baylor ghost story? There are several. Which one you wanna know about?"

"You've heard them!" I was so excited that I finally had someone to ask my questions that when he walked out the back of the grocery store, I didn't hesitate to follow him. I left my cart inside and stepped into the back alley. It was an unsightly place, filled with dumpsters and a few parked cars. Trash lined the curb, and the cars looked like they'd been there for months. Spider webs stretched from the tires to the street. Slightly uneasy, I looked at the man's nametag. Jim.

"My friend recently told me of a story about a man who used to, um, kill his dates. She said that one lady got away, and since then, he's haunted the lake. But that's all that she told me, and I was curious enough about it to start doing some research," I said hopefully.

"Why are you so curious?" he asked, throwing the trash bag into the dumpster.

"Oh, I don't know. I was just intrigued by the history of it all. Is it real?" Jim walked straight toward me, and I feared he wouldn't stop. He was uncomfortably close, and I had to take several steps back.

"It's real, all right. The man. The ghost. The one who got away," he said, stepping forward. I stepped backward.

His blue button-down shirt gaped between buttons, exposing the skin beneath his navel. He reeked of something sour. And I imagined it was the smell of not bathing for days on end. The sense that I had done something foolish washed over me. My eyes flicked to the door and back.

"Do you know any of their names?" I asked, my voice quivering as I took another step back.

"I don't know their names, but I know how he did it. He got the women to go on dates. And then he loaded them into a boat. He went out to the middle of the lake where nobody could hear their screams." He began to whisper. "Then, he took a saw, and he—"

"I was only looking for names," I said, "but thank you." With that, I turned to the door, quickly grabbing the handle. It was locked. I tried the handle again, pulling it down with force, only it didn't budge. I heard the jingle of keys behind me.

"Piece by piece, he threw their bodies into the lake. Using their flesh as fish chum. A hand here. A head there. They say he was a fisherman. Best damn one around. Fish love human blood," he said in a deep, breathy tone, spit gathering at the corners of his lips.

"Oh, thanks for your time. But I have to get going now." A tremble began inside me and worked its way out.

"Do you know what happens when little girls go looking for the one who got away?" he asked, dangling the keys to the locked door. I spun around, my heart starting to hammer in my chest.

"No," I said in a whimper.

"They become fish chum. And there's a tournament coming up, don't you know?"

"I'm sorry I took up so much of your time. I really have to be going now," I jiggled the door handle, but it wouldn't budge.

"The butcher haunts the lake until he finds her. If he gets her, he comes back to life with renewed power. Is that what you want?" he spat.

"No! No, I don't want that! I'm sorry," I pled.

"Then don't go poking your nose where it don't belong!" His belly pressed up against me and I was suffocated by his odor. I feared it would be the last thing I remembered. He pushed me against the door, grabbing my shoulders, his fingers squeezing into my bones as I screamed. The door pushed open and I was shoved forward, grabbing a hold of Jim to steady myself.

Just then, the acne-riddled store clerk appeared out of nowhere and barked at Jim in an authoritative tone I hadn't imagined he had in him.

"Jimmy! Get back to work! You're not allowed to talk to the customers! Do you want to be suspended again?"

Jim released me and spat on the floor before ridding me of his death stare. I gasped, throwing my hand across my chest. I could feel my heartbeat steady under my hand.

"Ma'am, are you okay? Jimmy's a little crazy. He's not supposed to talk to people. That's why he's on trash duty. We try to keep him in the back. I don't even know how you got out here." The clerk was upset. With Jimmy *and* with me.

"I'm okay! I'm okay."

"Shit!" hissed the clerk under his breath as I gathered myself. The store clerk unlocked the door, and we both went back inside. He strode away, leaving me alone. I looked frantically for Jim, but he was nowhere in sight.

I gathered my abandoned cart and hurried to the front of the store. The squeak of my loose wheel was sharp in my ears and even more unnerving than before. The elevator music was hauntingly calm.

A woman began checking me out, scanning multiple packs of lunchmeat. She looked nice enough, possibly like she might have grown up in Baylor. I was sure that she was the one I should have asked about the stories from the very beginning. But I was far too frightened to ask her about the fables now. I paid with a shaky hand and continued to look over my shoulder as I left the store, wishing I'd let Ethan come with me.

As I waited for my cab, there were two things I was sure of. First, the Baylor Butcher was real. Dangerous even. And there was a story there to be unearthed. Second, I had no business uncovering it. I was an out-of-towner and didn't belong to this world. I never wanted to see Jim or smell the stench of his unwashed folds again. And if he said not to look for the girl who got away, I wasn't about to.

8

Ethan met me at the front door and helped carry the grocery bags inside. We set them on the countertops, and Emma and Lainey dug through the loot. It was like Christmas morning in June.

"You'll never believe what happened to me!" I said, placing the yogurt in the refrigerator.

"What happened? Ethan asked.

"So, I randomly asked this guy who worked at the grocery store if he knew anything about the Baylor Butch—"

"What? Why would you do that?" Lainey asked.

"I . . . I . . . I overheard him talking about it, and I was curious. Anyway, that's not the point. The point is, I followed him outside into the back alley—"

"You did what?" Ethan asked, head cocked to the side.

"It was an accident. I didn't mean to. It just sort of happened that way," I said.

"Okay. So, what happened next?" Emma asked.

"Once we were out there all alone, the door locked behind us, and I was trapped with this big scary guy!" I said, holding my hands high above my head to show that he'd been roughly the size of a yeti.

"I knew I should have gone with you!" said Ethan. Lainey's eyes flicked from me to Ethan and back again.

"No, it all turned out fine. But he ended up grabbing me and shaking me violently."

"What? He touched you?" Ethan hissed.

"Yeah. He grabbed my shoulders and shook me! He towered over me, and he smelled so bad. And we were all alone! I don't know what would've happened if the other store clerk—who turned out to be the manager—hadn't come out and saved me," I said, taking out several loaves of bread for sandwiches and piling them in the bread box.

"Geez, Kinsley, you shouldn't be following creepy guys into back alleys. Didn't your mom ever teach you that?" Emma asked.

I sighed, knowing it had been a stupid idea. But the truth was, I hadn't been thinking much at the time. I'd become so consumed with the idea of finding this mystery girl that I'd lost my senses. It wouldn't happen again.

Kimber came into the kitchen and took several snacks out of the bags and began reading the labels.

"It was stupid all right. I'm just glad I made it out of there," I said, shaking my head in disbelief.

"Next time, Kinsley, I'm going with you," Ethan said. I smiled at him and nodded. I was careful not to lead him on, but I really wished I'd had somebody by my side when I was out there today, even if that meant making Lainey jealous.

We had just finished putting the groceries away when Scarlett May came in and told us about the plans she'd secured for the night. Sampson was going to have a bonfire at his place across the lake, and he'd invited everyone. Maybe a night out was exactly what I needed. I put away the part of me that was still wanting to find the missing girl—the compulsion I felt to uncover a name, at the least. A simple name. It couldn't be *that* hard to find.

It was well after dinner when everybody was getting ready to go to Sampson's house. Several of us girls packed into the bathroom, fighting for real estate in the mirror. Scarlett May had changed her blouse but stayed in the short-shorts and cowgirl boots. Kimber tied her hair up in a top bun. Maybe it was her hair, or maybe it was her impossibly thin, lanky build, but I would've bet money that she could leap into the air with the elegance of a professional ballerina.

"Sampson is so cool. You're going to love him. He's a mechanic and can fix anything. Maybe we should give him Kinsley's golf cart to fix," Scarlett May suggested.

"What's wrong with my golf cart?" I asked, swiping a smoky shade of eyeshadow across my lids.

"Nothing . . . if you have nowhere to be. It's just a little slow. He can put a turbo engine in there, and we can zip around the lake in half the time," she said.

Trinity tied a braid in her long, dark, ominous hair. Her light hazel eyes popped like those of a rattlesnake—alluring, but poisonous. It was no wonder she was so popular. She was drop-dead gorgeous . . . when her mouth was closed. I did what I could with my makeup. I had to try and keep up with all of my beautiful friends. But no amount of makeup would make my brown eyes shine. There was a small fleck of green at the bottom of the left one—a memento from my gran—but my eyes were still a muddy brown, and no amount of eyeliner would change that. My mom used to say they were full of wonder, but I always thought it was her motherly way of saying they were round and slightly oversized. At some point in my life, I'd looked in the mirror and recognized that I was plain. I'd never be as pretty as Trinity, and I'd accepted that long ago.

I left the girls in the bathroom to change my top one last time. I wore a white blouse that I'd loved fifteen minutes ago, but after seeing Kimber in her white tank, I knew I needed to change. I stood in my closet flipping through the few shirts I'd brought when I heard something behind me. I looked to my left, where I thought I heard a whisper tickle my ear. There was nothing there. Not so much as an open window. Slowly, I turned back to my closet and yanked a black T-shirt off the hanger. It was more casual than I wanted, but it would have to do.

As I slipped the T-shirt over my head, my eyes were covered for a split second, and I heard the whisper again. I pulled the shirt down, and I spun around, whipping my head from side to side. A small light shone on the bedside table. The windows remained closed. An old antique wooden table sat in the bedroom's corner, the paint on its legs chipped. There was nobody there. My heart thumped in my chest as I felt eyes spying on me. My instincts told me to leave. To *run.* And that's what I intended to do. I grabbed the door handle, eager to join the girls in the bathroom across the hall. But when the whisper touched my ear again, I heard it, and I heard it clear as day. *Find the girl.*

I couldn't tell if it was my gran from the breathy voice. It was only a whisper. But I gathered it was her from the demand she had given me the night before as she sat in her rocking chair. It was the first time that I'd heard her voice—as quiet as it had been—outside of my dreams. I'd sensed that she was watching me before, but I had never heard her speak. With my hand glued to the doorknob, I stood frozen—not in fear, but bewilderment. A knock came from the other side.

"Kinsley? Are you in there? We're getting ready to leave," Lainey said.

"One second," I said, gathering myself.

I was caught between the fear that big Jim had instilled in me in that dingy back alley and the not-so-subtle urgency that my gran had pushed down on me. To find the girl or not. It might be a dangerous road to travel, but my loyalty lay with my grandmother. I'd do just about anything to make her proud, and if she wanted me to uncover something hidden—something lost—then I'd do it. Or I'd at least try. Even if it scared me a little. At that moment, I decided to stay behind.

I desperately needed another night to take my mind off all the craziness swirling inside my head, but if my gran had come back from the dead to tell me this one thing, could I really ignore it? I opened the door and joined the girls down the hall. "I think I'm going to stay back tonight. I'm just not feeling that well," I lied.

"What!? You have to come," Lainey said. Her face was a mixture of disappointment and confusion.

"Suit yourself," Trinity said.

"Sorry. I just got this headache out of nowhere. I think I'm going to just lie in bed and maybe read a book." I rubbed the side of my head for dramatic effect, squinting my eyes as if the pain were too much to bear. I followed the group of girls downstairs to see them out.

"Damn, I'm going to miss you. I'll text you updates," Emma said.

"I've never seen you read a book . . ." Lainey called me out. My eyes widened.

"It's her loss," Scarlett May said, her boots clacking on the kitchen floor. I forced a smile. It *was* my loss. I knew that. I didn't want to be home alone researching an old ghost story. I didn't want visits from my dead grandmother. I wanted to go to the bonfire, to see all the guys, and to whisper in my friends' ears. I wanted to have a drink, let loose, and be present. It was a loss.

Noah came into the kitchen, his shaggy hair styled, and his denim-blue eyes trained on me. "What's this I hear about you not going to the bonfire?" he asked.

"I have a headache," I lied, rubbing my head again.

"Why don't you take some pain medicine and come along? I'm sure it will fade soon."

"Maybe. I think I'm just going to stay here. I've got a book to keep me company. I'll go next time," I said, regretting my choice already. Lainey shot me a glare that I chose to ignore. Noah's eyes looked sad, like he'd miss me at the party. I already missed him as it was. I wanted to continue our conversation from the night before—the conversation we'd been sharing before Mason had joined us in his birthday suit.

"Well . . ." Noah looked around the room, his hands stuffed into his jacket pockets. "I could stay here with you?" he asked. And it was more than a question. It was an invitation to spend one-on-one time with him. A vision flashed through my head of me lying in bed with his head across my lap. The cabin quiet and still and my hand in his hair. I shook my head, dispelling the thought.

"Oh, you don't have to do that." I felt my cheeks flush. It was then that Trinity took notice. Like a dog catching sight of a rodent scampering by.

"Do what?" she asked, looking between Noah and me.

"Are you sure? I don't mind," Noah said. A part of me wanted to agree, just so that Trinity couldn't have him.

"Do what?" she asked again.

I looked at her nervously and then back at Noah and nodded my head. I wanted him to stay more than anything, but Gran's whisper echoed through my head. A haunting reminder I had work to do.

"Nothing. Kinsley just isn't feeling well, so I said I could stay back with her," Noah said to Trinity. Her face hardened, and her jaw flexed.

"You're not going to miss the bonfire to sit in this musty old cabin all night, right?" she asked, a deep crevice forming between her eyebrows. Noah looked at me once more, just to make sure.

"No, I guess not," he said. Something in his voice told me he was disappointed. Perhaps, as much as I was.

"Great! Then you can be my date!" Trinity slipped her arm in his and pulled him away. He stole a look at me one last time before the door closed on his way out. And when the cabin fell quiet, I groaned with regret. If I ever lost my chance with Noah, it was because of this moment. This choice. And that damn ghost story.

I listened to cab doors slam closed and the tires turn over on the asphalt as I stood, unsure of what to do with myself. I gathered up a pen and paper and fired up my laptop. But before I could focus, my stomach growled. I remembered there was some pasta in the refrigerator that Kai had made for lunch but hadn't finished. I knew he wouldn't mind if I finished it. Kai was a gentle soul. Gifted athletically. Book smart too. He would always come up with inventions late at night. Some unrealistic, some quite good. I had no doubt that he would change the world, one small gadget at a time.

I ate the pasta cold, too lazy to heat it in the microwave. Gunner came to my side, asking for scraps, and I fed him a noodle here and there. He wagged his tail, excited for more, and I was grateful that I wasn't completely alone. I was still a little rattled by what had happened at the grocery store.

When the pasta was gone, and Gunner wouldn't leave my side, I opened the back door to let him outside. I sat down with my laptop and opened a browser. I started with "The Baylor Butcher," but only local butcheries populated the search. I tried searching "local ghost stories of Baylor Lake," but local tourist spots like bed-and-breakfasts, the Crumpet Café, and the Summerfield State Fair were all I got. I spent a good hour exhausting the search engine, to no avail. I sighed, thinking that my sacrifice to stay home had been pointless.

Gunner scratched at the back door, startling me. But as I turned to let him in, I heard a noise upstairs. It sounded as if something had been knocked over, falling on the carpet with a thud. I swung the door open, eager to let Gunner inside. He came in, nose in the air. Had he smelled an intruder? I watched him carefully. He looked as if he were hunting something unfamiliar. He froze mid-step, one paw in the air, and my body went rigid. I scanned the kitchen for anything I could use as a weapon. I drew a thick, sharp meat cleaver from a wooden block and gripped it tightly in my hand. Gunner slowly put his paw down and stalked toward the stairs. I followed in his wake.

Another thud came from upstairs . . . but this time it was louder. There was something up there all right. My every instinct told me to run straight out the front door. But I didn't listen. Not because I didn't want to, but because the fear kept me rooted in place. My legs were heavy and the floor was like molasses. Gunner growled, and I raised my cleaver high in the air.

I looked up the staircase, and it seemed to stretch for miles. My cell phone buzzed in my back pocket, and I screamed aloud, dropping the cleaver and leaping backward. The knife stuck to the floor and stood on end. I knew if it had landed on my foot, it would have meant a severed toe. The thud of the knife striking the floor sent Gunner barking ferociously—something I had never seen him do before. I took my phone out of my pocket, and as luck would have it, it was Lainey on the other end.

"Hello?" I answered, breathy.

"Hello? Kinsley, hello?" Lainey said on the other end. I could barely hear her through the commotion.

"Lainey! Your dog is going nuts! He won't stop barking at something upstairs! I think somebody is up there!" I hurried to get it out.

"H—hello? H—home . . ." The phone broke up, and I could only make out pieces of what Lainey was saying.

"Lainey? Can you hear me?" I said frantically. A door slammed shut upstairs, unleashing Gunner from his pointing stance. He bounded up the stairs at full force, skipping several stairs at a time. A growl ripped through his chest. My breath stalled. I dropped the phone and it clattered to the floor. I yanked the cleaver out of the floor, and I stumbled backward until the front door pressed against my back.

I heard Gunner rip into something. *Somebody.* A body fell to the floor. I could hear the wrestling through the floorboards as the cabin creaked and moaned.

Thoughts raced through my head. Was I being robbed? Was the butcher here to get me? Chop me into pieces? Use me as fish chum? How had they gotten in? How long had they been there? I felt the whisper in my ear, and I had the frightening thought that they'd been up there when I was changing. When the cabin was full and I'd felt safe.

I imagined Jim, the store clerk, hiding in a closet upstairs, and it was enough to send me running. I turned to bolt out the front door, but I heard something just then that broke through the deafening adrenaline.

"Kinsley? Where are you going?" somebody asked.

I whipped my head around to find Ethan standing at the bottom of the stairs, calm and collected. I gasped and ran into his arms.

"Wow! Are you okay?" he asked, almost seductively in my ear. I gasped for air. I looked up the stairs and realized everything had fallen quiet. Gunner was no longer barking, and the wrestling had stopped.

"There's somebody here!" I hissed, my eyes snapping from Ethan's face to the upstairs landing.

Ethan turned slowly to follow my gaze. "Somebody's here?" he asked, brow furrowed.

"Yes! Gunner ran up there and attacked them!" I said. Ethan drew in a long, deep breath, studying my face. Slowly, his eyes left mine and landed on the cleaver gripped in my hands.

Embarrassment ripped through me. It was so quiet. Like there had been no threat. And Ethan was looking at me like he wasn't sure if I'd imagined the whole thing.

"Is he up there now?"

"Yes!"

"Stay behind me," he said, taking my hand in his and treading quietly.

My hand, slick with sweat, gripped his as I followed him step by step. Everything in my body screamed not to go upstairs. Why were we going upstairs? I was afraid of what we might find. Was Gunner okay? Was that intruder still there? I didn't think there was a safe way to jump out the second-story window. I looked down the hall, afraid of what I might see. It scared me to find nothing.

Ethan looked back at me and I pointed to the master bedroom, breathing laboriously. He nodded before continuing. "I, I think it was in there," I stammered, our backs pressed against the wall.

My heart was thumping in my chest like a rabbit caught in a snare. I pulled my sweaty hand from his and reached for my cell phone. I patted my back pockets, then remembered that I'd dropped it. Ethan took the cleaver from my sweat-slick hand. He had a better chance of defending us with the kitchen knife than I did. He wiped his palms on his pants before raising the cleaver above his head. I placed my hand on his back and cowered behind him. We slowly turned the corner into the master bedroom.

Expecting to find a massacre, broken lamps, and bloodshed, I was taken aback by the stillness of the dark room. I flipped the lights on, and there was no sign of a struggle. I looked around the room. My abandoned white blouse lay on the floor just before the closet. Everything else was perfectly in its place. Ethan turned to me questioningly.

"Maybe it was in Asher and Kimber's room?" I whispered, pointing across the hall. Ethan shrugged, and we turned to check out the other rooms. I hid in his shadow as we trekked down the hall. Every single bedroom was clear. Ethan began to relax, but I became more and more unnerved.

As we went downstairs, a chill ripped down my spine when we found Gunner sleeping on his dog bed. I wasn't the only one who'd noticed him. Ethan looked back at me, pointing to the dog fast asleep.

"I swear, he fought off the intruder. I heard the whole thing!" I said as Ethan returned the cleaver to the butcher block. Fear shifted to anger. "What are you even doing here?" I snapped. It was a mixture of terror and embarrassment; it wasn't something I was proud of.

"When I heard that you had stayed back because you weren't feeling well, I thought about the trouble you got into at the grocery store and how I wished I'd gone with you. I took a cab back from the party so I could check on you. And clearly, my instincts were right. You shouldn't be alone," he said sternly.

I hated everything about that. I hated that Lainey liked Ethan and that I needed him. I hated that I felt like I was leading him on or that I owed him for saving me. And I hated he was the one who had come back and not Noah. His words echoed in my head. I shouldn't be left alone. I was eighteen years old—an adult. But if I couldn't go to the grocery store alone, or even be in a cabin alone, then I was still only a child. A helpless child afraid of her own shadow. One with a wild imagination that would get her into trouble.

9

I looked around the room restlessly. I couldn't stay here. Not because it was only Ethan and me—and he was looking for something more than I could give him—but because something inside had stirred, telling me I wasn't safe. I looked at Ethan, wondering when he had arrived and if he'd ever left for the party in the first place.

"I want to go to the party. Only, I'm not sure how to get there. Could you take me? You can drive the golf cart." I looked toward Ethan, anxiously awaiting his response. I knew it wasn't what he wanted. He wanted to stay in the cabin, alone with me. He wanted to bond. And he wanted me to look at him as my knight in shining armor. But how far would he take it? Had he staged the whole thing so that I'd go running into his arms? *Impossible.*

I could never look at Ethan like he wanted me to. Not because of Lainey, but because of Noah. Because I only had eyes for the boy I had grown up with. The boy who'd been my friend long before I developed feelings for him. My heart resided with Noah Hampton.

"Are you sure you feel good enough to go to the party? I thought you had a headache? And you look pretty upset. We could just stay here and watch a movie or something?" Ethan suggested. I swallowed down the lump in my throat and shook my head. It's what he'd wanted the whole time. For me to be scared and seek his comfort. I couldn't stay in this cabin one more second. I grabbed my phone from the floor where I had dropped it in the heat of the attack and stuffed it in my back pocket.

"Well, I'm going to go, and you can either come or not. But I don't want to stay here." Before I could get out the door, Ethan was on my heels.

"No, I'll come. Plus, you don't know how to get there. And I've always wanted to drive a golf cart." He was standing closer than I was comfortable with, but I was thankful that I didn't need to drive through the woods at night alone. I was too rattled as it was. We fired up the golf cart, and Ethan's face lit up. He came to life behind the wheel like a young boy excited to play with a new toy. I taught him what little he needed to know in a few quick seconds, and before I knew it, we were pulling out of the driveway. At first, the ride was a little touch and go, but he quickly got the hang of it.

I pointed to a trail that ran parallel to the main road around the lake. It weaved in and around the massive pine trees through the dark forest. I gripped the handle above my head. The night was cool and the wind on my face refreshing. I closed my eyes, breathing in deeply and exhaling the fear that had coiled inside the pit of my stomach. The panic from the break-in paled in comparison to the worry and horror I felt wondering if my mind might be slipping from me. I was too young and too healthy to have a mind that was deteriorating into a false reality. But something was off. Something didn't add up. And I was the only common denominator.

My eyes flew open as the golf cart launched over a large rock and my seat lifted off the bench. Ethan laughed, a little embarrassed about the rough ride. I gave him a small smile back. The trail was uneven and the ride bumpy; it was to be expected. But Ethan took my smile as something else entirely. He reached over and grabbed my hand. I quickly recoiled. His smile dropped, and even in the dark, I could see the shame spread across his features. I was mortified that I had made him feel that way. Guilt overcame me.

"Ethan . . ." I began.

"No, you don't have to do that," he started, too embarrassed to hear what was about to come next. His hands gripped the steering wheel tightly, and he refused to look at me.

"Ethan, I'm sorry—"

"You don't need to be sorry. I know. It's not you, it's me, blah blah blah. I've heard it all before."

I bit the inside of my cheek, rolling the flesh between my teeth. The golf cart launched over another molehill and I accidentally bit down, drawing blood. "Ah!" I called out, cupping my mouth. The taste of copper spread throughout my mouth and dressed my lips.

"Are you okay?" he asked, letting off the gas. I leaned over the edge of the golf cart and spat out a mouthful of blood.

"Ahh, I just bit my cheek." I spat once more. I looked at my hand, unsure of what to do with the crimson on my fingertips.

"Here," Ethan held out his sleeve.

"I can't use that! It will stain," I said.

"It's okay, it's black," he insisted. Thankfully, I found a small rag tucked inside a pocket near the center console and spared his sleeve.

"Ethan, I really like you. Just not the way I think you might want." I ran my tongue over the wound and found that it had begun to swell.

Ethan sighed, looking away and tightening his grip on the steering wheel.

"It's complicated. If things were different, if I didn't have feelings for somebody else . . ." I shrugged.

"It's Noah, isn't it?" I didn't have to say anything. He already knew. I nodded, and he did too.

"And Lainey?" he asked.

"You know?"

The sounds of the forest came alive as his disappointment silenced us both. "It's okay. I'm fine." Ethan started the ignition again and our bumpy ride continued. I reached out to his forearm and gave it a squeeze. A gesture he would have adored ten minutes prior. But now, I knew it pained him. I looked out at the passing trees as we drove the rest of the way in the dead of night, and the cool breeze washed away the awkward conversation. The harsh feelings wafted in a trail behind us for the forest to feed on.

I knew we had reached Sampson's cabin by the volume of the bass bouncing from one tree to the next. An orange halo glowed around the bonfire by the water's edge where a group huddled. Ethan handed me the keys to the golf cart and, without a word, disappeared into the crowd. I was the worst person alive to have hurt him. And after he'd saved me, no less. I knew I wouldn't be able to talk to anyone about it either, because Lainey would be crushed if she caught wind of it. Alone, I ventured into the cabin in search of my friends. A small group of girls hung around the kitchen island, pouring drinks and talking about guys.

"Did you see the one with the sandy hair? He's wearing that jacket with a red patch," one girl said, pointing to her shoulder where a patch would reside. Immediately, I knew she was talking about Noah. The red patch was our high school mascot. I knew the jacket well because I'd borrowed it one time and hadn't given it back for a week.

"Oh yeah! He's cute! But I think he has a girlfriend," the girl responded. I frowned, approaching the island. It wasn't true.

"Can I get one of those drinks?" I asked.

"Yeah, sure!"

"He has a girlfriend?"

"It's that really pretty girl with the long dark hair and light eyes. You couldn't have missed her," the girl said. *Trinity*. Something came over me.

"That's not his girlfriend!" I blurted out. The group of girls stopped and stared at me blankly. "Sorry! I just . . . I just overheard, I'm sorry." I stammered and felt the urge to flee without my drink.

"So he doesn't have a girlfriend then?" the inquisitive one asked. I'd shot myself in the foot. That's exactly what I did.

"Um, no, he doesn't," I said, taking my drink and excusing myself.

"You should totally go for him then." I heard on my way out the back door. I spotted Lainey and Emma, only they were talking with Ethan, and I wanted to get as far away from that situation as possible. I pressed on through the crowd until I found Noah. Trinity was wrapped around his arm. I took a step back, hiding behind a couple of guys in line for the keg, and I watched for a moment.

Trinity whispered something in his ear, and whatever it was, it stole his attention. His brows lifted, and I could tell that he was intrigued. I didn't have to know what the proposition was to know how it made me feel. My stomach dropped with jealousy. I could tell why the other girls had thought that Trinity was his girlfriend. If I hadn't known any better, I would've thought the same thing. It was then that she grabbed his hand, pulling him away from the crowd. He followed . . . hesitantly, but he followed nonetheless.

I watched him look around the crowd, searching for faces, presumably mine. And when he didn't see me, or whomever it was that he was looking for, he went with her. Trinity shrugged off her burgundy leather jacket and threw it over her shoulder. Her hips swayed from side to side in a way that reminded me of a leopard stalking its prey through tall blades of grass. I took several steps back, watching as long as I could. I followed them inside the house. I peeked around the corner from the kitchen down into a hallway and watched her lead him into a back bedroom. My heart broke, and a wave of nausea passed through me.

"Hey, do you know where that guy went?" It was the girl who had made me the drink.

I looked back toward the bedroom, and the door was now closed. "No, I haven't seen him. Sorry." I said. I crossed my arms over my chest, tapping my fingers on my red plastic cup, fuming inside. My face was hot with betrayal, and I stared blindly off into the sea of people. I acknowledged the pain and deceit and then quickly tucked it away into a dark corner of my mind. It's what I did best. I only let it sting for a second, and then I drowned the discomfort with my drink. I got another on my way outside. And since I couldn't join my two best friends, and my crush had been stolen from me, I joined the group down by the bonfire.

I took the only open seat, a blue camping chair with cigarette burns in the arms. I ran my tongue across the sore in my cheek, using the sharp pain of the cut to cover the ache in my chest over Noah and Trinity. I wished I had never invited Trinity to the cabin. Before, I'd thought it was unavoidable, but knowing what I did now, I wished I had put my foot down. I wished I would have said straight to her face that she couldn't come. That she wasn't invited because she wasn't my friend.

I briefly wondered if I should stand up for myself now—barge into that room and declare that she get off him. But the truth was that Noah was just as guilty as Trinity was . . . though *guilty* wasn't really fair. He was in that room because that's where he wanted to be, and he didn't owe me anything. We weren't a couple. And I had never once told him how I felt about him. I was a coward, and this was what I got. I accepted in that moment that it was my fault and my fault alone for whatever happened. What was happening right now behind that locked door. Because it was I who allowed her to walk all over me. And it was I who wasn't brave enough to have told Noah to stay back at the cabin with me. It was my fault. And whether Noah liked me or not didn't really matter anymore, because it was clear that I wasn't the only one he had eyes for.

"Guys, this is Kinsley Wilde. She's the one who owns the cabin where we're staying. Kinsley, this is everyone. That's Sampson, Skid, Tina, Pat, and Lola," Scarlett May said. I looked around the bonfire and waved meekly. Everyone was warm enough. Tina sat on top of one guy's lap, who Scarlett May had called Skid. I presumed they were dating. But after seeing Trinity and Noah together, I couldn't be sure.

"This is the girl I was telling you guys got attacked by Big Jimmy today," Scarlett May continued.

"Oh gosh, yeah, that happened today," I said, nodding. I could feel the warmth spread across my cheeks. It wasn't from the heat of the fire.

"Big Jimmy is dangerous. You have to stay away from him! Everybody in Baylor knows that!" a guy with a backward hat said—Pat, I think.

"This one time, Big Jimmy slept in his car in the middle of the forest for a month straight. Nobody knew where he had gone, but they knew he was off his medication," Sampson shared. "The hounds found him, and he had to stay in the loony bin until he was right again."

Makes sense, I thought.

"He's legit crazy," said a girl—Tina, I think. "And if he goes off his medication, he gets mean. He's gone to jail for assaulting a woman before, and they just let him off because he has mental health issues or whatever. And I heard the grocery store can't fire him because his instability is a disability."

"Makes sense to me. He seemed pretty crazy in the alley. I'm pretty sure he hadn't showered in quite some time, and he was angry. He snapped for no reason," I said.

"How did you find yourself with him in the back alley, anyway?" Tina asked.

"It's kind of embarrassing, but I was asking him about the Baylor Butcher."

I shrank a little at Scarlett May's glare. *You're not a child, are you?* I tried to ignore how her look made me feel small and insignificant. "I overheard him talking about it, and since Scarlett May had shared the story with us a little while ago, I was just curious. He started talking as he was taking the trash out back, and I just sort of followed him without thinking. The door closed, and we were trapped. *I* was trapped." The story was embellished, but only a little.

"The Baylor Butcher! I haven't heard that story in a long time!" Skid said with amusement.

"Skid?" I asked, pointing a finger. What kind of name was that?

"Adam Skid. It's my last name," he said.

"Oh, okay," I said and nodded. "Well, it was my first time hearing the story. So, I guess I'm a little late to the party."

"You've never heard it before? I love that story!" Tina said.

"What? You love it?" Scarlett May admonished.

"It's such a beautiful story," Tina said with a shy shrug. Her hoodie was covering most of her face, but I could tell that there was something more than a morbid sense of beauty in her mind's eye.

"I think we're thinking about different stories here. The one we're talking about is the one where the guy butchered all his dates and threw pieces of their bodies into the lake," Scarlett May clarified in a dry, cutting tone.

"What? No! That's not the Baylor Butcher ghost story!" Tina argued. My ears perked and my back straightened. Was there a different side to the story? Of course there was. There were two sides to every story.

"What—" I began.

"Yes, it is! That's the one I grew up with," Scarlett May argued.

"Is there a different version?" I asked Tina. The fire crackled when Sampson threw another log in the pit.

"Yeah, I can't believe you guys haven't heard this one before. It's a love story."

"Tell the story, babe," Skid said, patting her leg.

"You guys want to hear a love story?" she asked everyone.

"I do!" I said, almost too enthusiastically.

"Oh, here we go. Kinsley and her wild obsession with ghost stories," Scarlett May muttered loud enough for me to hear on the other side of the fire. I ignored her.

Tina sat up from her boyfriend's chest and leaned forward. "Long, long ago, there was a butcher. See? Same story. Only he didn't butcher people; he worked as an actual butcher. I swear things get so mixed up, the more mouths they get passed through. But I swear this is the true story."

"It's not, but continue," Scarlett May said, and Sampson laughed. My eyes were trained on Tina, waiting for more. I was vaguely aware that my interest in the story was helping to cover the gnawing ache that I was losing my chance with Noah.

"The butcher was so in love with this girl—more in love than anybody had ever been with another. Their love was known across many towns, traveling nearly statewide. They were a pretty big deal. One day, when the butcher was taking her out to propose, they got in a terrible accident. His car crashed alongside the lake and tumbled down into the water. He survived, but his girlfriend didn't. He was so distraught that, after a year of grief, he took his own life in hopes to be with her. But that didn't happen. It's said that he haunts the lake looking for her because he can't move on without her. But she's not here because she left to go to heaven. And he's trapped here because he damned himself by taking his own life. Now, he's in his own personal hell, here in Baylor. He looks for her every evening around the lake and in the forest. But he'll never find her, and he'll never move on," Tina said.

My heart sank. Hearing the story brought me deep sorrow. It was just an old story, but I felt the pain as if it were my own. I slipped my hand over my heart, rubbing the ache. "That's so sad," I said.

"It is! It's so sad, but it's so beautiful. He still looks for her every evening. And he'll keep looking for her for the rest of eternity because he loves her that much. Some people call him The Phantom of the Lake," said Tina, turning to Skid. "Would you look for me, for the rest of eternity, babe?" she asked.

"Yeah, I would!" Skid said, thrusting his pelvis into her. Tina slapped his shoulder, and Lola laughed. I smiled, wishing that I had had somebody to joke with. But Noah was—a flash of Trinity straddling him in bed crossed my mind —occupied . . .

"I heard they're buried next to each other in the Baylor Cemetery," Lola added.

"I know! It's so cute!" Tina said, leaning back against her boyfriend.

"I still think he was a murderer," Scarlett May said.

"Who hurt you?" Sampson said, laughing. We all joined him.

The conversation moved effortlessly away from the ghost story and fell upon my deaf ears. I watched the orange flames dance in the fire and listened to the crackling logs. If it had been a love story, then what was in the depths of the lake that had tried to take my soul?

If it had been a love story, then why had Big Jimmy become so violent over it? I pictured the lake in the evening when the fog bank would settle in and the loons would call out to one another. It had always been haunting, but in a soothing, eerie way. In a way that spread a sense of serenity throughout my body and mind but still managed to raise a few hairs on the nape of my neck. I imagined that the fog carried within it an epic love searching for its soulmate. And a small smile crept across my face.

I wanted more than anything to think that the Baylor ghost story was a hopeful one. That true love did exist. That there was one person out there meant to find another. And when they did, nothing could break their bond. Like souls that were fated to belong to one another. It made me hopeful that I'd find my soulmate one day. If I hadn't already.

But as I imagined the fog bank of low-hanging clouds, I also imagined the dismembered hands reaching out of the water, grasping for one last chance at survival. It soured my stomach, giving me heartburn. I shook my head, in limbo between the darkest horror and the greatest love story. Only, I couldn't decipher which of them was right. The truth was on that nebulous line between fact and fiction. Reality and illusion.

10

The bulk of us came home that night, but it didn't escape me that Trinity hadn't returned. I was thankful she'd stayed back because I wasn't ready to look her in the face. Neither was I ready to look at Noah, but I wasn't as lucky on that front. Many times, I saw him stealing glances in my direction, and every time, it turned his cheeks a swarthy red of regret. I didn't know how far he had gone with Trinity, but the details didn't matter. He'd made his choice when he'd closed that door, and it hadn't been with me. I hated that I still had feelings for him, even though I knew he lacked the loyalty I so deserved. We were friends long before we grew feelings for each other, and I knew friends wouldn't treat each other the way he'd treated me tonight.

"Did Scarlett May come home?" Lainey asked.

"No, I think she's staying at Sampson's tonight," I said.

"She must be staying there with Trinity," she said, shrugging. At the sound of Trinity's name, my eyes met Noah's, and he all but fled the room. I sighed, throwing my head back. The tension in the room was suffocating.

"Who knows? She can stay there for the rest of the summer for all I care," I said to Lainey. She raised her brows and nodded. She understood that like no one else here. "I'm exhausted. I'm going to bed," I said.

"Yeah, me too."

As Lainey and I headed for the stairs, I overheard Mason's booming voice.

"Did you get with Trinity tonight?" he asked. And I knew instantly that he was talking to Noah. Lainey wrapped her arm around me as she watched the disappointment spread across my face. We hovered on the staircase, eavesdropping.

"No man," said Noah, his voice low and disgruntled.

"Yeah, you did!"

"No, seriously."

"You're such a liar, man."

I rolled my eyes and stomped up the stairs. Lainey followed. He was such a liar. I'd seen him go into the back bedroom and shut the door behind him. Even the girls at Sampson's cabin thought that he and Trinity had been together. It was clear for everyone to see.

"I'm sorry, Kins. That really sucks," Lainey said, hovering in the doorjamb.

"No, it's fine. I can't help who Noah likes, and it's my fault for inviting her. I knew she was like this, and I really just wish I hadn't let her come."

"That doesn't mean it's your fault," she argued.

"I guess it really wouldn't have changed anything. I just don't want to spend my summer watching them hook up. It's cruel and unusual punishment." I frowned. "Sometimes I think I do it to myself. Like I don't deserve happiness, so I invite people like Trinity to rain down on me. Or I let myself fall for someone who can't give me what I need." I rolled my tongue over the inside of my cheek, still swollen from me biting down on it in the golf cart.

"Don't say that. You had nothing to do with this. And you deserve all the happiness in the world. I really do think that Noah likes you. I mean, does Noah even know that you like him? Because on the one hand, he has Trinity, who is a sure thing. And on the other hand, he has you, and he probably doesn't even know you like him. You guys have been flirty for years, and nothing has ever come of it. He probably just assumes that's the nature of your relationship."

I took a moment to think about what she said. She was right. I'd never told Noah how I felt about him. How could I expect him to know it?

"You're right, Lainey. And that's just another reason it's my fault. I never told him."

"Well, it's never too late," she said with a hopeful smile.

"Oh yeah? Are you going to tell Ethan you like him?" I asked, hand on hip.

Lainey's cheeks turned red. "I don't like Ethan," she hissed. But both of us knew that wasn't true. And I was being an ass.

"Sorry, I'm just irritated. And I'm super tired. I think I need to go to bed."

"Well, try to get some sleep." Lainey headed for her room.

"Good night," I said before closing my door.

Once alone in the master bedroom, I took a deep cleansing breath; it was anything but refreshing. I inhaled the memory of Gunner fighting off the intruder on this very floor. In this very room. And for a brief moment, I saw it. I saw the man in black, a ski mask covering his face, and Gunner at his throat. I saw the broken lamp and the tipped-over nightstand. The commotion of them rolling around on the carpet and the snarling of the dog. I jumped back, my back hit the door behind me, and it all disappeared.

My heart pounded as I opened the door and ran out into the hall. I heard Noah and Mason talking in the stairwell, and everything seemed normal. It was only a daydream. A vision. Slowly, I crept back into the master bedroom, where I had seen the attack that never happened. I checked the bathroom and closet multiple times before crawling into bed. And even then, I felt the room spinning with the presence of an intruder. I hesitated before turning out the light, my fingers on the pull string as I stared at the lamp; I was sure it had broken. I forced myself to be brave enough to close my eyes. And I prayed for sleep to overtake me.

When morning came and I realized I'd survived the night without the torment of a nightmare, I was only mildly relieved. I'd need much more than a single night without a nightmare to feel all right. Nothing was okay. Noah had chosen Trinity over me. He chose a girl who didn't even like him over a long-standing friendship that had blossomed into so much more. And that was just the tip of the iceberg.

I decided to throw myself into finding this girl—though I was sure it was nothing but a ghost story. Still, though, if my current reality had nightmares coming to life before my very eyes, then maybe there was more to finding this girl than anybody realized. Maybe there was a reason for it all, and like my gran had said, the girl needed me.

I'd overheard Lola speak of the cemetery last night, where supposedly the butcher and his girlfriend were buried next to one another. And the best part about cemeteries? Headstones. That was where I'd find the names. It was as good a place as any to start my research, and therein lay my mission. Find the cemetery . . . find the name.

I got dressed and headed downstairs, somewhat surprised that I had slept in. Kai and Ethan were making breakfast when I entered the kitchen, and Mason lay in his sleeping bag telling stories from the night before. Lainey and Emma were on the back porch drinking coffee, and it appeared that Trinity and Scarlett May hadn't come home last night.

"Good morning," I said to everyone. Kai greeted me, but Ethan shied away. Guilt sat like a heavy brick in the pit of my stomach. I walked past Mason, kicking him gently as any good friend would, and then went to the back porch.

"Morning," I said.

"Good morning. You slept in," Emma said.

"First time in a long time," I said. I looked out at the lake. The fog bank was clearing. I remembered the love story I'd heard the night before, and in that moment, it seemed so clear to me which side of the ghost story was the prevailing truth. In all the beauty that lay before us, there was no question that this ghost story was rooted in love.

"Hey, Lainey, can I take Gunner for a walk?" I asked.

"That would be great! Because I caught him digging a hole in your yard again." Lainey shook her head, annoyed.

"I'm going to have to pick up some grass seed before the summer is over," I said, and Lainey nodded.

"Don't worry, I'll make sure everything is taken care of; your mom will never know," she said.

I tucked my phone into my back pocket and set out on a hike with Gunner. He was just as eager as I was. He pulled against the leash, and I quickened my step to keep up. I didn't know where I was going, but I had heard a long time ago that the cemetery was hidden within the forest. I had a faint memory of passing it when I was a child. And there was only one hiking trail I didn't frequent.

As I entered the wall of trees, the shadows from the pines offered welcome shade, and I let Gunner off his leash. He took off, galloping down the path for a moment before bounding into the bushes. I let my eyes wander through the forest in search of clues. It was about a two-mile hike that I had planned, ending with a giant boulder that was a popular place for locals to jump into the lake. I was sure there was a small trail off the beaten path that led to the cemetery. I couldn't remember exactly where it had been, but I was confident that I would remember when we came across it.

"Gunner?" I called out, hoping to see his little brown head bobbing above the bushes. But I caught no sight of him hunting. Still, I figured I'd run into him before getting off the main trail. After some time walking alone in the forest, I finally felt at ease. I even spotted the downy woodpecker that Lainey had told me about the last time we'd walked. I craned my neck to watch as the bird pecked a hole into the tree. He had a distinctive red spot on the back of his head, but I couldn't remember if Lainey had told me that meant it was male or female. I enjoyed the view either way. The sound of his pecking echoed throughout the forest, bouncing from tree to tree.

When I came across an opening, a hint of a trail off the beaten path, I knew it was the one I had been looking for. The bushes had overgrown most of the trail, and it looked like nobody had hiked it in some time. I regretted wearing shorts, because I knew my legs would get cut up from the thorns in the bushes. But it wouldn't deter me. Nor would the fact that I couldn't find Gunner. I took one last look around, scanning the tops of all the bushes for a little brown head, and when he couldn't be found, I trudged on, taking the overgrown path. At first, the thorns were really irritating, scratching the flesh just enough to break the skin. But the farther I got, the more terrain I recognized, and the less I cared about my legs.

When I came upon the clearing where I recalled the cemetery had been located, it shocked me to see something else entirely. A large stone tower, nearly three stories high. It looked like it had come straight from a medieval fairy tale. The only things missing were the fire-breathing dragons and a spellbound princess. I knew I had never seen the tower before. But that was suspicious in itself, because the tower appeared to be so old. It looked like it had been built ages ago, and I was surprised that I had never heard stories about it when I was young. I looked around the grounds, but there wasn't a headstone in sight. Disoriented, I worried that I had gotten myself lost. I pulled out my phone, and as luck would have it, I had no service.

While I was here, lost in the middle of the forest, I might as well relieve my itching curiosity. I had to know what was inside. And this chance might never come along again. I walked up to it, placing my hands on the stones, and it surprised me that they felt warm to the touch.

"Hello? Is anybody there?" I called out. I don't know what I thought—maybe that somebody had inhabited it. But as I walked around the base of the tower, it was clear that there was no way in. The tower had been sealed up, stone by stone. But I couldn't imagine the point of a structure with no way in. Or no way out. I took several steps back, looking toward the top, and on one side of the tower was a window. I scratched my head, staring and waiting for a way inside to magically appear. But when it didn't come, I got the odd sense that I should be on my way. That I might not be safe all the way out here.

As soon as I made the decision to leave, I felt it. The same sense I'd had when my friends and I had run down the dock to jump into the lake. I felt the eyes watching me. I looked around, my breaths becoming more frequent and shallow. No movement but the subtle rise and fall of tree branches swaying in the breeze. I turned back the way I came, quickening my pace through the angry bushes. If I could only get to the main trail, I thought. Twigs snapped several feet behind me, as if there was something closing in on me. But when I looked back, dizzy and breathless, there was nothing. Nothing my eyes could see—nothing from this world. My legs were painted red by the time I got back to the main trail. It was there that I thought the chase would be over. But the feeling of something closing in on me only grew more keen.

I whipped my head from side to side, totally disoriented. My breath became jagged as I jogged down the trail. Slowed down by the frequent backward glances. Time I didn't have to spare. I quickened my step from a jog to a run the moment I heard the gravel stir behind me. When I looked, I thought I saw a subtle shift in the air. A density suspended over the main trail. But I couldn't be sure and wasn't about to stop to investigate. I felt it though. I felt the predator hunting me. I felt the adrenaline rush through my veins, and I knew I had been singled out as prey.

"Gunner! Gunner!" I yelled. The voice that escaped me wasn't my own but a husky cry for help.

I glimpsed something in motion close upon my flank. I couldn't tell what it was, but I knew it was after me. My run turned into a sprint. My legs thrust as fast as they could to save my life. My heart rate redlined. "Gunner!" I screamed.

Each time I looked behind me, I saw the thing closing in at an impossible speed. And each time, I found it within myself to run even faster than before. I let out a scream with a breath I couldn't hold onto. And then, out of nowhere, the trail ended, and a cabin appeared in a peaceful clearing.

"Help! Help!" I screamed, tripping over my own feet. The gravel gouged into my wrists and forearms as I sprawled onto my stomach. I rolled onto my back just as the figure leaped for me, snatching its prey. I shut my eyes and threw my arms over my face, cowering in anticipation.

"Help!" I screamed one last time.

Time stilled as I waited for claws to pull me apart, slash by deadly slash. Teeth to rip the limbs from my body. My life to end before it had begun. But the attack never came. Instead, a hand grabbed my shoulder, and I screamed, kicking out on instinct. My foot made contact with a very hard mass, and I heard a disgruntled groan. My eyes sprung open to see Asher grabbing his thigh. Mason stood there too, breathless and confused. I looked from the boys back to the woods. The trail was still, the air reminiscent of a light summer day.

I couldn't see the vile thing that had chased me, and from the looks of both Mason and Asher, they hadn't seen it either.

"What the hell, Kinsley?" Asher said.

"What—" I gasped breathlessly, looking all around me, my hands on the warm sandy pathway. "What happened?" I asked.

"You're asking me? You screamed for help and then kicked the shit out of me!" Asher said.

"Did you see? The thing?" I gasped, dusting my hands. Kai and Noah had just reached us, and they, too, were breathless, their faces red from running out to the forest.

"Are you okay?" Noah asked.

The truth was, I didn't know. My legs were bloodied, but I was positive that was from walking through the overgrown bushes. My hands and forearms were shredded, but that was road rash. The real threat . . . That had been invisible. A figment of my imagination. So, I guess the answer was no; I wasn't all right. Far from it. My mind was the most dangerous predator in those woods. And I was out to get me.

"I . . . I . . . I don't know," I said, as he helped me to my feet. My body ached, and my lungs burned.

"What happened to your legs?" Mason asked.

"Why did you kick me?" Asher asked.

My eyes dropped to Asher's thigh, and there was a dusty footprint from my shoe painted on his shorts.

"I'm sorry I . . . I was being chased, I thought you were the . . . the thing," I said, looking between the guys.

"What was chasing you?" Asher and Kai looked into the woods, and I looked too, following their gaze. The woods were quiet, not so much as a breeze to lift a branch.

"I don't know. I couldn't see it. But it was big, and it was fast."

"How do you know it was big if you didn't see it?" Kai asked.

"She just got scared—that's all," Mason said, batting a hand through the air.

"Damn, Kinsley! You really scared us!" Asher said.

I dusted off my butt, and I began the walk of shame back to the cabin where the rest of my friends stood on pins and needles, watching and waiting to see if I was okay. On one hand, I was mortified that I had cried wolf. But given the choice to have them run to my side and be disappointed or to fight my demons alone and have nobody notice, I'd choose the former. Because nothing hurt more than being forgotten.

"What happened?" Lainey asked, as soon as we were in earshot. The girls stood on the back porch, faces etched with worry. I looked at the boys. What they had seen differed greatly from what I had experienced. Two sides of the same story.

"It was like a wolf or something," I said. I caught the alarming glare that passed between Asher and Kai, and I looked down at my feet before I could see the look on Noah's face.

"What *really* happened?" Lainey whispered, as I got closer and the guys dispersed. I ran a hand through my hair, picking out a single twig. I watched the guys go back to their mundane activities. "Are you okay?" Lainey looked down at my legs. It looked like I had been mauled by a raccoon that tried to climb me like a tree trunk.

"It was a wolf, I think. A wolf was chasing me. And I lost Gunner," I said, worried.

"You lost Gunner?" she asked, trying to hide her dismay. My mouth fell open, but no words came out. I'd lost much more than her dog in those woods. And I didn't know how to tell her the truth.

11

Late into the morning, when Scarlett May had returned home and Trinity had not, we began to worry. Scarlett May had had a life in Baylor long before we came up for the summer. She'd spent time here with her family and friends outside of our little world. But Trinity was different. She didn't know anybody in town, and she was part of our core team. It had been easy to think that maybe she'd stayed at Sampson's house because she was there with Scarlett May. But now that we knew she hadn't, the alarm went off. Something was wrong. And I hated the part of me that was glad it was her. The part of me that thought maybe she had gotten what she deserved.

"So, you're telling me that Trinity wasn't with you last night?" I asked Scarlett May.

"No, was she supposed to be?" she asked.

"Well, no, but we haven't seen her. We figured she was with you last night."

"She was with Noah last night," Mason said. My stomach clenched. Scarlett May's brow lifted.

"And you haven't seen her this morning?" I asked one more time.

"I haven't seen her since you guys left last night."

I looked to Kimber, who was pulling on her bottom lip, eyes unfocused in front of her as she tried to recall the night before. They weren't the best of friends, but Trinity was to Kimber what Ethan was to Asher. She was her shadow—and a mean one at that, but it didn't stop them from being friends. Kimber, Trinity, and Scarlett May had always ruled the school. Kimber was the most popular, but that was because she had some kindness in her. She was the total package, minus the mental instability, but most never saw that part. Scarlett May was the outgoing one . . . and the one I liked to think of as obnoxious. She often spat cruel comments where they didn't belong. And Trinity was the mean one disguised in dark beauty. Many of the boys liked her, but it was the girls who could see through her long locks, bright hazel eyes, and wicked smile. It was her actions that always spoke volumes about her integrity.

I felt bad for Kimber, but there was that deep part inside of me—that smoldering ember—that was glad it hadn't been Emma or Lainey who'd turned up missing. Surely if it were one of them, something tragic would've happened. But Trinity? Trinity was most likely on some grand adventure. She'd probably found the band crew who were set to play at the Water's Edge Concert in a couple of weeks and had been partying all night long. She'd come home with some epic story to tell that would make everyone jealous. Especially Noah. I wasn't worried.

"Have you called her?" Asher asked from the kitchen. Kai ran his hands through his hair and walked outside. Levi nodded as if it were as easy as that.

"Yeah, have you called her phone?" Levi repeated, as if it had been his own idea.

I pointed my finger to my chest, surprised as I looked between the wandering eyes in the room. I certainly hadn't called her. What would I have to say to Trinity? Other than asking her if she'd slept with Noah with the intent to crush his heart or mine. But I wasn't about to do that. *Why not, though?* Maybe I *should* confront her.

"I've called her a dozen times. Sent two dozen texts. And somewhere along the way, her phone stopped ringing. It's unlike her. Normally, she'd answer. She'd call me back or text immediately," Kimber said. Her blue eyes glistened with worry as she wrapped her pale blonde hair around her finger, twisting until it was strung tight.

"This is stupid. I'm calling her right now," Scarlett May said, with the phone pressed to her ear. We watched and waited as her eyes drifted slowly to the floor and she slipped the phone into her back pocket. "It went straight to voicemail," she murmured.

"Well, I think I'm going to go back over to Sampson's house and see if anybody has heard anything. Many people are still there, just barely waking up. Does anybody want to go with me?" Scarlett May asked.

"Yeah, I'll go," Asher said.

"Me too," Levi said.

"I was just about to run into town and tape flyers up for Gunner. I'll keep my eyes open," Lainey said.

"I'm going with her, so call us if you need anything," Emma said.

Kimber looked at me with worried eyes, and I knew I needed to satisfy her in some way or another. "Kimber, do you want to go drive through the woods in the golf cart? I know of some trails back there that she could have gotten lost on."

Kimber nodded, and we gathered our things as everyone but Kai and Mason headed out. Ethan and Noah were down the street, and nobody bothered to fill them in on the hunt for Trinity. Which was ironic, because Noah was probably the last person to see her. We split up, making plans to check in with one another in an hour or so. I wasn't expecting to find Trinity out in the woods. I was really only taking the trip to keep Kimber busy.

My distaste for Trinity grew as I watched the group pull together as a team. Unity in their worry for one of the members. But where had the search team been when *I* was missing? When I'd nearly drowned in the middle of the lake. And here Trinity was, sucking up all the love. Even though she'd burned down most of the authentic relationships she'd ever had. I stewed inside. Why hadn't I tried to talk to her before? I'd always run from my truth, but for the first time, I felt the need to say it. When she stumbled back from her epic night with the band, she and I were going to have a little talk.

I started the golf cart, and we pulled out of the driveway. Kimber grabbed hold of the overhead handle and cursed me for taking sharp turns. Had she not already been on edge, she may have enjoyed the ride. We dipped into the forest, and a sense of foreboding crashed down upon me. I was out here alone, and I was being hunted. The air shifted as the shadows enveloped us. The temperature dropped as we left the sunny clearing. I couldn't think of that now, and I knew I'd be safe as long as Kimber was by my side. My eyes wandered deep into the shrubs, jumping from treetop to treetop and whipping back and forth down the trail. I punched the gas.

Kimber was so worried about Trinity that she hadn't even realized how paranoid I was. I tried to take my mind off it by asking her questions that would force her to open up. It was good for the both of us. "When was the last time you spoke with Trinity?" I asked.

"I think she found me last night after she . . ." the words hung in the air between us, and the gentle breeze did little to lift them away. *After she slept with Noah?*

"I know she was with him last night. I saw them go into the back bedroom," I said, clearing the air of unspoken words.

"Yeah, okay, so you know. She came to talk to me after that, but it wasn't long, and she didn't say much. She staggered off to talk to Kai about something, and that was the last time I saw her."

Kimber gathered her hair and pulled it over one shoulder, trying to fight the few tresses that were blowing in the wind. We came upon a fork in the road where I could stay near the main road or travel deeper into the forest where I thought the cemetery had been. And even though I'd been hunted like an animal of prey the last time I was there, I still chose to venture into the depths of the shadows.

"She went to talk to Kai? He never said anything . . ." I said.

I parked the golf cart by the boulder that many of the locals used as a platform to jump into the lake. There was also a rope swing, but I thought that to be far more dangerous. There were a few teenagers perched on the rock who didn't look too happy to have the company. We looked around briefly, and when there was no sign of Trinity, I started the engine again just as a dog barked. I looked over my shoulder to find Gunner eating scraps from somebody's bagged lunch.

"Gunner!" His ears perked up, and he barked once more. "Come here, boy!" I yelled, slapping my leg. He came running and jumped into the golf cart, smothering Kimber. "Thank god I found him. Lainey is going to be so happy," I said, feeling a sense of relief wash over me. I'd think twice next time before letting him off the leash. I stepped on the gas, and we continued down the trail.

"I just feel terrible because I was fighting with Asher and I probably didn't give Trinity the attention she needed. What if this was my fault? What if she needed me and I wasn't there for her?" Kimber asked, her voice cracking as if she might cry. She pushed Gunner's face away, and I ended up with a face full of his dog breath.

I wanted to tell her that was stupid and that Trinity was probably just partying with a random group from Sampson's house, but the strain behind Kimber's eyes told me she was more than worried. I felt the compunction settle in my chest, for I had been far too guilty of not caring as much as I should.

"Don't do that to yourself, Kimber. Trinity is going to be just fine. Now, why don't you tell me about this fight that you and Asher had? What was it about?" I asked, taking a turn toward the mysterious tower that I had found earlier. Who knew? Maybe Trinity was there now.

"It was stupid, really. I don't even know how it started. I wanted to go back to the cabin, but he wanted to stay. It was a simple disagreement, but it ended with him calling me names. Sometimes we have these fights, and I wonder why he's with me in the first place. I see the way he looks at other girls, and I look nothing like them. They all seem so perfect, you know?" she asked through a veil of insecurity. She had no idea how beautiful she was. And I bet that when she looked in the mirror, she was blind to it.

"Did you want to go back to the cabin because he was looking at other girls?"

"Well, yeah! Why would I want to stay when my boyfriend is being tempted by the lake locals?" she said defensively. "Where are we even going?" Kimber looked out into the forest and not a single soul was in sight. "I doubt that Trinity is out here," she said.

"You know? I came across something the other day, and I thought it was a cool hiding spot. It was this enormous stone tower. Maybe she's out there. I'm sure people party there all the time," I said, shrugging to hide my own self-interest. The guilt crept in again. What if Trinity really was in danger, and I was wasting precious minutes? But as we came upon the overgrown trail that led to my mysterious tower, fear pricked the nape of my neck and coiled in my stomach, and Kimber got a text from Scarlett May.

"They said to meet back at the cabin. They're heading there now. Oh no. That doesn't sound good, does it?" she asked.

"I'm sure it's fine. Totally fine." I pulled away from the haunted trail and felt the eyes watching as we motored away.

When we got back to the cabin, it was clear that it was anything but fine. The boys paced back and forth with nervous energy, and Sampson had followed Scarlett May and the others back to the cabin. Gunner leapt out of the golf cart, greeting everybody one by one, but nobody seemed to notice. Before we reached the back deck, Asher approached us with news of a found cell phone.

"Is that hers?" I asked Kimber, but she didn't need to say anything. The tears in her eyes were enough for me to realize that maybe this was more serious than I'd originally thought. The wishes of ill-will I'd made upon her last night crept into my mind.

"Where did you find that?" Kimber asked, her voice strained. I looked between Asher and Scarlett May as unspoken worry passed between them. "What? Just tell me!" she said.

"We found it in the back bedroom. It was just lying on the floor," Sampson said.

"She'd never go anywhere without her phone. Something is definitely wrong," Scarlett May said, summing up what we were all thinking.

"We need to talk to Noah. He was the one with her in that bedroom last night. Where is he?" Levi asked. Unwanted images of Noah and Trinity together floated through my mind. Noah's smile in response to Trinity's kisses. His hands, sliding down the small of her back and beneath her jeans. I suddenly realized everyone was looking at me. Everybody relied on me to know Noah's whereabouts. Was it really that obvious? It made the whole situation worse. As if I were nothing more than a doormat he stepped over. I wanted to tell them all to shove it—that I didn't know where he was . . . and why would I? But the truth was, I did know where he'd gone because my eyes were trained to follow him. And everybody in that room knew it.

"Noah and Ethan rented a boat earlier. I saw them out front with fishing poles while we were heading back," I said. As if on cue, I looked out the kitchen window and saw them tying the boat to the dock upon their return. I nodded in their direction, and Asher strode outside and down the hill. We all followed, and I was afraid of what I might see. Or more so, what I might hear.

"Hey, man, Trinity is still missing. What the hell happened between you two last night in that bedroom?" Asher demanded. I turned away briefly, but who was I fooling? I wanted to know as much as the rest of them. We all walked down the grassy knoll to the dock. This was a conversation that involved all of us.

"What are you talking about, man? We didn't do anything!" Noah said, his eyes flickered toward me.

"Then where is she? She never came home last night, and she left her phone in that room. What happened?"

"I'm telling you! Nothing happened! She was drunk, and she wanted to hook up, but I stopped her. That's it. That's all. Nothing more," Noah said. *Lies . . .*

Kimber turned away crying, and I stared at Noah in red-hot anger. He looked far too guilty for nothing to have happened. And I had known him a long time—long enough to know what his guilty conscience looked like. He was wearing it now. His darkening complexion. The crevices in his forehead. The sweat beading in his hairline.

"Why was her phone left in the bedroom?" Mason asked. All of our eyes flicked back to Noah for his response.

Only Ethan hadn't taken his eyes off me. He was probably wondering if we had a chance now that Noah had been with Trinity. But the fact that Noah had deceived me didn't make Ethan any more appealing.

"I don't know why her phone was left in the bedroom. She was really drunk, staggering all over the room. It probably fell out when she . . ." Noah said, before stopping. His eyes trained on me, and my mistrust was visible for all to see. "When she tried undressing," he said, in a softer voice, one filled with regret. I imagined he wouldn't have found himself in this situation had he known I had been at the party.

"I'm going to call the local hospital and see if she's there. Who knows? Maybe there was an accident we didn't hear about?" Emma said. She turned away, walking back toward the cabin.

The boys argued a bit longer about what specifically had happened in that bedroom, but I couldn't listen to it anymore. I turned away, and it was Ethan who ran after me. I couldn't deal with both my emotions and his. Not only was I hurt by Noah, but I felt terrible for wishing for Trinity's demise on the same night that she'd vanished. And worse, I hadn't cared come morning, when I knew that something could be wrong. I was a terrible person, and I had no room in my heart to let Ethan down softly for a second time.

"Hey, Kins, do you think Noah has something to do with Trinity going missing?" Ethan asked, checking behind him. I stopped halfway to the cabin and looked at Ethan and then down toward Noah and the group. A flash of Noah's smile turned violent and feral, but I stopped it there. That wasn't him, and I couldn't let it play out in my head.

"What do you mean? Like did he . . . harm her?" I asked, confused about where he was going with this.

"I don't know. I mean, you know him better than anyone. Right? You guys grew up together. Do you think he could have hurt her?" he asked, his hair shining red under the sunlight. I wasn't sure if it was Asher's conspiracy coming through his shadow or if Ethan had conjured up this theory to make Noah look even worse, but I was thoroughly disgusted.

"Noah would never hurt anybody! Is that what you guys think? Do you seriously think he hurt her?" I snapped. Ethan took a step back, absorbing my anger like a punch to the gut. He shrugged, seemingly unsure of how to respond. I trudged off without him.

The clocks raced forward as the tension grew. Emma said there was no record of her at any of the local hospitals. Kimber wanted to call the police and make a missing person's report, but most of the boys strongly disagreed—Kai in particular. They argued to give it one more day for fear of looking guilty themselves. I understood not wanting cops involved, but I believed it was time. Lainey had mentioned calling Trinity's mom first, to let her know what happened. She said it would be worse if she heard it from the cops, and I agreed with that, but nobody wanted to be the one to call her. I suggested it was Kimber or Scarlett May, as they were better friends, but neither one of them wanted to step up to the plate. As the owner of the cabin, the responsibility fell on me.

I got the phone number and stepped outside, away from the argument, to make the call. But when I did, I found I wasn't alone. Kai rested his forearms on the back porch railing as he looked out toward the vast black lake. All the light had drained from the sky, and had I not heard the water lapping against the shore below, I would've never believed there to be a lake beyond the porch.

"Are you okay, Kai?" I asked, joining him.

"I saw Trinity." His stare was pensive, and his pain, palpable.

"What do you mean? You saw her *when*?" I asked.

"I saw her last night. After . . . she was with Noah. I think I was the last one to see her," he said in a soft voice, as if even he didn't want to hear himself say it out loud.

"Kai, you have to tell me what happened. You have to tell everybody what happened. We need to find her, and if you're holding information back, that's not going to help anybody."

"But I'm not proud of myself, Kins. I'm really damn ashamed, to be honest. And I don't want to admit it."

I ran a hand through my hair, sighing. "You can tell me," I said, placing a hand on his forearm and giving him an encouraging squeeze.

"Trinity was drunk. She went to hook up with Noah, but he turned her down. I wasn't so strong. God . . ." Kai hung his head. It seemed as if all the guys had fallen for Trinity's wicked good looks at one time or another.

"So, you guys hooked up then?" I asked.

"No. Actually, we didn't. We were going to. We were about to, when she realized she'd left her phone in the bedroom. She pulled me far into the woods where nobody would see. She pushed me up against a tree, and even though I knew it was wrong and that she was using me to make Noah upset, I let her do it." Kai steepled his fingers beneath his chin, pausing for a moment.

"She unbuttoned my shirt and kissed my neck. But when she realized her phone was missing, she told me to stay put. She said she would be right back. She ran off through the woods, and she never returned. I waited out there like a fool. It must have been an hour. I looked for her on my way back, but I didn't see her. By the time I realized she'd stood me up, I was too embarrassed to say anything. I didn't want to see her then, and when a cab showed up to take Asher and Kimber back to the cabin, I jumped in with them."

I took in a deep, steadying breath and let my eyes wander through the darkness. I imagined Trinity running back for her phone and getting snatched in the middle of the forest. Presumably by the thing that had chased me. She must have been so scared. And if I hadn't been worried about Trinity before, I certainly was now. I looked down at the cell phone in my hands and knew it was time to call Trinity's mother . . . but how? How would I tell her mom that eleven of us had lost her daughter to the dark woods?

"I'm so sorry, Kinsley. I'm such an ass. It was unlike me, and I regret it so much. And now I'm afraid that the cops are going to think I did it," Kai said, his eyes misty.

"No, nobody is going to think you did anything. But we have to tell the cops, and we have to tell everybody inside, too. Because if you hide this information, you're going to look far more suspicious when they find out. And they will."

We looked back into the house, which had fallen quiet, and my stomach sank when I saw two cops standing inside my living room. They were already there. The red and blue lights were flashing against the side of the house as Kai and I shared a look of dread for what was to come.

12

After the cops left that night, every conversation devolved into an argument. Somewhere along the way, it had been flushed out that Mason already had a strike against him for battery, and he was afraid of what a missing girl tied to his file might look like for him in the future. Levi had unpaid parking tickets, and anytime a cop would come close, he'd break into a sweat. But one thing the group had agreed on unanimously was that nobody wanted to talk. Noah hadn't said a word to the cops about his time in the back bedroom, and Kai hadn't told them about his time with Trinity in the woods. In fact, he hadn't told anybody at all. I didn't know if the group could see it, but it was clear as day to me, when Kai's face was painted red and his lips pursed closed into a thin, straight line, that he was hiding something.

You never know how a group of people are going to deal with a missing girl, but I never thought the group would fall apart. They turned inward as all their skeletons were flushed out. Secrets were billowing into the open air like a poisonous gas. Their knowledge of the event at hand was simply tucked away. Trinity missing was no more our fault than the weather shift, a summer storm blowing in from the east. Yet everybody had their own reasons for hiding, and it only made us, as a group, look more suspicious. I, myself, had motive. And that scared the hell out of me.

When morning came, I asked Lainey if she wanted to take Gunner on a walk. I told her I wanted to vent, and she didn't need any convincing after that. It was a lot for anybody to handle, and time alone to straighten our thoughts had become a necessity. But I didn't just want to talk about Trinity; I wanted to talk about what had happened to me in the woods. I wanted to take

Lainey back to the tower, and I needed to understand how my mind was playing tricks on me. I had to face my fear to get past it.

We set out on the trail, and our conversation went from zero to sixty a few steps in. Lainey dove in deep the second we stepped off the back porch.

"I have something to confess, but you can't tell anybody," Lainey said, her eyes full of worry and her brows scrunched to match. Honestly, knowing that I wasn't the only one with secrets hidden inside felt like a blessing. It only made me feel like I was normal, and that was the best of feelings for me. I hadn't felt normal since my gran died, and I had never yearned for something so mediocre in my life.

"I won't tell anybody," I said.

Lainey reached down and let the dog off the leash. She took a deep breath as she watched him run into the woods. I looked behind us at the cabin, and nobody was outside to hear Lainey's deep, dark secret.

"I was the one who called the cops. I know everybody said not to. To give it time. But I just felt like I had to. I had to file a missing person's report. It was the right thing to do," she said, staring at me as if asking for forgiveness. It pained me to think that this had eaten at her all night long.

"Oh, Lainey, I honestly would have done the same thing if I was brave enough. I'm glad you called the cops. It was something that needed to be done." Voices could be heard in the distance, and they grew louder as we walked down the main path. An older couple was headed our way.

"Yeah, but everybody is so mad. Everyone is going to hate me when they find out," she said, hanging her head.

"No, they won't. And hey, nobody even needs to know. Maybe it was somebody at Sampson's house. They don't know."

"You think?" she asked hopefully.

"Of course! Do you know what I did?" I asked. "I called her mom last night."

"You did?"

We fell silent while the couple passed us, giving them a small curt wave hello.

"Yeah. I didn't know how to tell her mom that we lost her or, worse, that something terrible had happened. I was sweating bullets outside on the back porch while everybody was inside talking to the cops. The phone rang four miserable times before it went to voicemail. I've never been so conflicted in my life. On the one hand, I was relieved that I didn't have to speak to her. But on the other hand . . . I knew I would have to do it again. But this morning, when I told myself that I should call her, I couldn't bring myself to do it. I faltered, thinking that maybe the cops had done it, and it was no longer my job."

I stared down the trail before us, knowing that I should have made that call. I could do it now, right? But the cell service was spotty in the woods. Lainey didn't have much to say about that as we walked deeper into the forest, the dirt crunching under our shoes as our feet fell in step with one another.

"I have a secret to tell you. Promise not to say anything to anybody?" I asked, looking behind me. I knew the forest had eyes and ears, and I didn't want it hearing what I was about to say.

"Kins, of course. This is confidential, like always."

"You know how Trinity hooked up with Noah at the party?" I asked.

"Or, so we think. He says he didn't. You don't believe him?" she asked.

"No, do you?" I asked, taken aback. Our pace slowed.

"Well, why would he lie?"

It felt like a dig. Like I wasn't reason enough to lie. Like a potential relationship with me wasn't worth covering his tracks for.

"I don't know. Maybe because he wasn't proud of it?" I said, omitting the truth. Lainey shrugged, and I felt like I had made the whole thing up. Like Noah had never had feelings for me like I thought he had.

"Do you still like him?" she asked, her question hanging in the crisp morning air. It was a question I'd asked myself over and over since I saw him close that bedroom door. I knew I still had feelings for Noah, but I was ashamed of it now. Those feelings were tainted with the guilt of knowing that I deserved more and I wasn't giving it to myself.

"So, what's the secret?" Lainey asked, pointing to Gunner as he flushed out a covey of birds. I took a moment to watch them fly away, noting the low drum of their wings. I loved birds in flight, and I wished my insecurities could be taken away with them. When the birds disappeared into the treetops, my eyes fell back to the forest floor, and the hidden trail of thorns appeared.

"It's this way. The thorns are pretty bad, so just be careful where you step." We took the turn, and Lainey called Gunner back to make sure he followed us. I mused over the fact that he came running when she called because he did no such thing when I needed him.

"So, it turns out that Noah wasn't the only one spending special one-on-one time with Trinity that night." It spilled from my lips like a hot, sweet syrup, thick with gossip.

Lainey's pants snagged on a thorn, and she cursed as it ripped a small hole in her pant leg. "Nooo!" she gasped.

"Apparently, after Noah, she turned to Kai. And Kai took the bait. She led him deep into the woods where nobody would see, and then she left him there. She never came back."

We stepped over a fallen tree trunk, and Lainey turned to me. "She never came back?"

"No. He said that she headed into the woods because she left her phone back in the bedroom, and that was the last time he saw her." I looked up from the trail, trying to find the tall, arcane stone tower that I'd stumbled upon before, but there was nothing there.

"And he hasn't told anybody?" she asked.

"He . . ." I stopped and stared at the clearing. A multitude of trees freshly cut. A dozen stumps two feet tall, exposing their pale heartwood. I was sure that we were in the right spot. How could a tower the size of a lighthouse be there one day and gone the next? "He didn't want to tell anybody. I don't know why he mentioned it to me," I said, looking for the tower in every direction.

As we approached the clearing and my eyes traveled down to the ground where the base of the tower should've been, I was surprised to find the old, historical cemetery, hidden in plain sight.

Both large and small headstones sank into the overgrown forest floor. The stones were crooked, and many had crumbled as if they'd been here since the beginning of time. Letters had been etched into the rock as if one by one, each symbol drastic in variation. A small picket fence lined the cemetery's perimeter, and I imagined that it had been painted white long ago. But as it stood today, it was splintered, brown, and dilapidated. Multiple posts were missing, and the ones that still stood had been damaged by the weather or chewed on by the wildlife.

"Did you know this was here?" Lainey asked as we approached the memorial grounds.

I looked behind me as Gunner flushed out a new covey of birds, jumping at the sound, afraid I was being attacked again. I laughed along with Lainey, though it was nothing more than nervous energy. I didn't enjoy being there one bit, and Lainey only brought me a small sense of comfort. Much less than I imagined she would. "No. I knew the cemetery was out here in the woods, but I was here the other day, and I swear, it wasn't."

"You were here?" Lainey asked, her voice trailing off, as did my attention.

I looked around the grounds, my eyes following the beaten trail of thorny bushes, and without a shadow of a doubt, I knew this was exactly where I had stood. I wasn't the best with directions, I admit, but I knew this. I knew my mind was playing tricks on me.

I bit my tongue, refusing to sound like an eighteen-year-old suffering from psychosis. I might be worried about that, but I stuffed it deep down inside, where I was sure nobody would find it. The only problem was, *I* still knew it was there. I placed my hand on the first headstone I came upon and felt the rough texture under my fingertips as they trailed over the arc of the weathered stone. It was cool to the touch, and I imagined that at one time this stone had a lot of attention. At one time, there were loved ones crowded around it, mourning their loved one. "Jack Timmerman," I read.

"Adaline Stems," Lainey read.

I walked around each and every headstone, careful to step over the spaces where the bodies were buried. Many of the headstones only had a last name and the date, some with first and last names, and rarer yet, the date they were born. I didn't know what I was looking for, but I knew I hadn't found it yet. I searched for the name of the butcher, and I looked for signs of his lover. There were no indications that a famous love story had been buried here in the Baylor cemetery.

"You have to find her," Lainey mumbled, some three headstones away. I raised my head and looked over to her as she kneeled by a particularly short headstone.

"What did you say?" I asked. A pocket of cold air passed like a low-hanging cloud. The temperature dropped, and goosebumps covered my arms, sending a chill down the nape of my neck. I wasn't sure if Lainey heard me or not, but she said nothing. I watched her read the headstone as Gunner leaned into her side, tail wagging. I looked away, searching the forest for answers, but there were none to be found.

Lainey stood and moved to the next headstone. "I just love all of these purple shrubs, don't you?" she asked. I hadn't even noticed them until she said something. She was always keen on foliage. The purple popped, covering the ground. How could I have not noticed so many flowers? Then again, how could I have not seen an entire cemetery until I was upon it?

"You have to find her," she said, again, the moment my eyes wandered to the next headstone. I whipped my head back, absolutely positive this time of what I had heard.

"What?" I hissed.

"What?" she asked.

"You said something."

"Oh! I just love these purple flowers."

"No . . . after that."

"I didn't say anything after that," she said, confused. I stared at her, rolling my teeth over my bottom lip. She frowned, not liking the way I was staring at her. Like I was mad.

"You did," I said, digging my heels in.

She let out a small uncomfortable laugh and shook her head. "Kinsley, I didn't say anything!"

"I think it's time we go back," I said, feeling the chill seep into my bones. I checked back behind me, and the trees began to swirl as my head lightened. I stumbled forward, grabbing a headstone, feeling like I might faint.

"Are you okay?" Lainey and Gunner came to my side.

"Just a little dizzy," I said, gripping the top of the rotting headstone for balance.

"Kinsley, she needs your help!" Lainey said, gripping my shoulder with force.

"Why? How?" I labored with breath I didn't have to spare.

"Because she can't get out. Nobody can," she said.

"Get out of where?" I asked. The trees and the stones returned to their singular form as the spinning slowed to a crawl. Lainey's eyes only grew more concerned as the threat of me fainting dissipated.

"Get out of where?" Lainey looked at me, just as confused as I was. "What are you even talking about?" she asked.

I let go of the stone and grabbed her forearm. She steadied me as I stood to my full height. "You were talking about the girl and how I needed to help her," I said.

"Kinsley, you're starting to scare me. I haven't said *anything*. I don't know what you're talking about," she said. Crows called out from the treetops, and the sound echoed, bouncing between the pines. There was a warning in their calls. The leaves rustled in the wind with a distant static sound. As the sounds of nature became deafening, I knew it was time to go home. The forest no longer welcomed us. Lainey pulled a drink from her backpack, and I guzzled down the sweet syrupy punch. I felt the sugar tantalizing every cell in my body, and I wondered if my crazy had been a simple dip in blood sugar. By the time I handed her the half-empty bottle, I felt like my normal self.

"I'm sorry, Lainey. I didn't mean to scare you. I feel much better now. Thank you," I said, the heat from my embarrassment warming my flesh. As we walked back to the main trail, I felt lonelier than I ever had in my entire life. My best of friends didn't understand. And worst of all, I couldn't even trust myself. I didn't know who I was anymore. All the things I'd seen—the things I'd heard and felt. They were no more than a figment of my imagination. My reality was no longer real. And as I floundered in this phantom reality, I desperately needed something or someone to grasp onto. I needed to steady myself.

It was in that moment when I needed grounding that I smelled the cologne of Walker St. James. I remembered how safe I'd felt in his flannel. The way he'd made me feel. He'd been the only one in this world who cared, in a time when my friends had abandoned me. In my most dire of times, it was Walker who'd stood by my side. It was the beautiful stranger in the canoe who'd saved my life. I didn't know what was so special about this guy that I'd only met a couple of times, but I knew I needed him now. Like a drug, he drew me to him—seeking peace when I felt the sting of instability.

13

I waited till evening before I slipped out of the cabin—unnoticed. It was an easy feat with all the commotion over Trinity still in full swing. The battle of moral obligation that took place in that cabin had no end in sight, and I couldn't take it any longer. I needed a break, but that made me feel guilty. Especially knowing that Trinity didn't have time to rest. So why should I? At least, I assumed she didn't. But I stuffed that speculation deep down, and I turned outward as I decided to take the night off from worry and despair. Like a weighted vest, I slipped it off, knowing I'd need to come back to carry the load again. But not tonight. Tonight was a break that I'd take for myself. And hopefully, by the end, I'd come away feeling renewed. Strong. Clear-minded. Sane.

I didn't know how to find Walker St. James, and I kicked myself for never getting his cell phone number. I wore his flannel tied around my waist and hoped my desire would be enough to summon him. I needed him now, and prayed that he felt it too. Call it fate or call it the stars—whatever you want—but I felt deep down that there was something between Walker and me that tied us together. A tether. Maybe it was the fact that he'd saved my life, and maybe I owed him mine in return . . . but I didn't think that it stopped there. When he'd saved my life, it had felt like the beginning.

I walked out to the end of the dock as the twilight sky continued to darken. The air was heavy with humidity. It was going to be a particularly misty night. One of those nights where the fog banks rolled in, thick and opaque. They were my favorite nights and made for the most beautiful of mornings. The loons would be calling out to one another through the poor visibility, and the whole lake would be haunted by their calls.

I paced the dock until my feet were tired and my nervous energy had finally subsided. When it did, I sat at the end of the dock with my legs crossed so that they wouldn't dangle over the dark water. I let my eyes wander in search of the guy who'd saved my life—and could possibly save me now—and they fell upon my neighbors in their back yard. I couldn't tell from where I was, but it looked as if they were gardening. I thought it was far too dark to garden, but who was I to say? I'd killed every plant I'd ever looked at. A "black thumb," my gran would say. I leaned back, my palms pressed against the wooden planks as I waited for my destiny to arrive.

Find the boy, I thought. *Find the boy . . . find the girl. Help the girl . . .* It all sounded so easy.

The first loon called out from the cool mist. Like a wolf, howling at the moon. I inhaled, releasing the tension I'd been carrying with me. *Help the girl.* Was she trapped? Was she stuck? Was she the girl from the ghost stories? How old would that make her? Regardless, I didn't know what I had to do with any of it. If there was one person who could help, it certainly wouldn't be me. Emma maybe, or Kai, but not me.

I closed my eyes, tipped my head to the sky, and I willed Walker to come find me. I imagined him paddling his canoe up to the dock. A smile on his face, his dimples piercing his cheeks. I imagined he'd ask for his flannel, and I'd untie it from my hips and hand it to him. Our fingertips would touch, and the exchange would send butterflies through my chest. He'd take me for a ride in his canoe, and all my worries would remain onshore as we drifted away. I needed him so I could feel sane. I wasn't sure what I was doing—if it was some kind of meditation or a simple daydream—but when I opened my eyes, Walker's canoe was tied to the end of the dock.

My back stiffened as I whipped my head back and forth, searching for him. I hadn't heard the canoe hit the dock, and I certainly hadn't heard Walker step out. I climbed to my feet and peered inside the belly of the canoe. There were no signs that it had been occupied. It was clear that he wasn't on the dock. The visibility was poor, but I could see to the end of it. I felt the urge to climb inside and paddle away. I needed to get out of here so desperately. I was losing my mind, and I felt it slipping further the longer I stayed.

I glanced back to the cabin. They'd never notice my absence. And the lake was calling me. I steadied myself with one hand on the dock post as I pulled the canoe closer. I nearly fell in the water when a figure approached me, materializing out of thin air. I gasped and whipped my head around to find Noah standing with his hands tucked deep into his pockets and a guilty sadness in his eyes. The last person I wanted to see right now was him, and yet here he stood. The only thing stopping me from running away. Slowly, begrudgingly, I let go of the canoe and stood, wiping my hands on my jeans.

"What are you doing down here?" he asked.

"I was about to ask you the same thing," I said.

"I was just out for a breather. I saw you down here all alone, and I thought maybe we should talk." Thankful for the dim sky, I rolled my eyes and immediately hoped that he hadn't seen. I crossed my arms over my chest and leaned a hip against the dock post, waiting for him to clear his conscience. "Is that okay with you?" he asked.

"If you have something to say, Noah, just say it." I knew I had been upset with him for breaking a bond that neither of us was brave enough to secure, but I was surprised by the sharpness in my tone.

"Nothing happened between Trinity and me. I swear it."

"Okay," I said.

"You have to believe me, Kins."

"And why is that? You don't owe me anything." And that was the truth. We weren't boyfriend-girlfriend—only longtime friends who had longed for something more.

Noah bowed his head, then nodded. "That may be true, but I wanted you to know."

"You wanted me to know what, Noah? That you didn't sleep with her? Why do you care what I think?" Because, clearly, his actions proved he didn't care. So why was he pretending now?

"You know I care about you, right? We . . . We're . . ." he stuttered.

"You can't finish that sentence, can you? You know what?" I asked, pausing. Did I really want this? "I can't either, and there's a reason for that. It's because we're nothing. We're just two people who used to be neighbors. Friends along the way. And I thought that maybe there was something more between us—"

"There is!" he blurted out.

"No, there's not!" I said.

Noah took a step forward and reached for my hand. A week ago, I would have given anything for this moment. I would have closed my eyes and leaned forward for a kiss. But as I stood here now, on a dock over evil waters, I knew I'd made a mistake when I blew out my birthday candles.

"There can be. If you wanted . . ."

I stared into his denim blue eyes and thought they looked black. His hand was clammy in mine. And I honestly didn't know what to say. I didn't know if I wanted him any longer. I knew I shouldn't. I knew I didn't in this moment. But I had no idea how I'd feel tomorrow or a week from now. I had pined after Noah for a long time. I'd known him better than I knew some of my girlfriends. I cared deeply about him, and as much as I hated it, I was attracted to him. Could I ignore the fact that I'd been hurt at Sampson's house and begin a relationship with him, hoping that maybe I'd get over it? But what if I didn't? What about Trinity? Where was she, and what if she came back? . . . What if she didn't? And . . . what about Walker? As I thought about my flannel stranger, the canoe bumped against the dock, summoning me.

"Is that what you want?" I asked in a softer tone, and I wished it hadn't come out sounding so breathy and needy. I was stronger than this.

He didn't say anything, but he nodded and took a step closer. As the gap closed between us, I instinctively took a step back. I tried not to think about what it meant, but in that moment, all I could think was one step away from Noah was one step closer to the canoe. I wanted to get away. And Noah was one of the things I wanted to get away from. And as soon as I realized it, I couldn't keep it in any longer.

"I can't do this right now. I need some time to think. I need to go," I said, dropping his hand and turning away. It wasn't that easy though. He reached for my arm and pulled me close.

"Kinsley, come on."

My jaw dropped as I stared at him, appalled by the abrupt action. The tension between us was palpable. I waited for the electricity. For the tension to bleed into lust. But it never came. Noah's knife was still lodged in my back. His whole body slumped in sadness as I slowly pulled my arm out of his grasp. I stepped into the canoe, untied it from the dock, and never looked back.

I probably shouldn't have followed my instincts, because they hadn't been a friend of mine in recent weeks, but I picked up the paddle and began to row. I paddled through the heavy water until my arms burned. It was just beginning. I never looked back, my heart galloping as I abandoned the mess that had unraveled at the cabin.

I wondered if I was making a mistake with Noah. But I couldn't think clearly with the emotions that clouded my thoughts. The sadness was twisted inside me in tangled knots. Something was off. Something was *very* off. But I couldn't tell what. I didn't know if it was me or him . . . our relationship or this lake. But I couldn't breathe. And the farther I paddled, the more my lungs expanded. The shackles unlocked, and I was finally unbound.

The night grew cool, but I didn't need Walker's flannel to cover my shoulders. I was hot from paddling and nearly out of breath. I didn't stop until my arms grew numb, and I lacked control over their mobility. But as soon as I let my heavy limbs rest, I felt the canoe ease forward, despite the end of my paddle dragging through the thick secrets of the lake water. I took in a deep breath as the canoe propelled itself into the middle of the expansive lake. And as if the sky had been painted just for me, an array of stars glinted in the night sky. An amber Milky Way splashed the horizon, making for a brilliant view. The lake was quiet except for the water lapping at the canoe, and the sense of being exactly where I was meant to be, screaming loud and clear between my ears. I felt all the tension roll off me in sheets like hail in the eye of a storm. And as the seconds ticked by, the more I began to feel like my old self.

Maybe it was the fear of losing my mind or the guilt from wishing Trinity away the night she'd vanished, but a lump in my throat rose until tears dripped from my eyes. It wasn't until I'd put some distance between myself and that cabin that I let myself wash away all of the hurt and deceit that I had felt since coming up here for the summer. I cried and cried in the middle of the lake, under the majestic sky, until my body was spent and my mind had quieted from pure exhaustion. When I finally calmed down, I started to feel the cold. I untied Walker's flannel from my waist and slipped my arms into the sleeves, thankful for him once again.

I tipped my head back to the sky, enjoying it from a different perspective, when I heard quiet breathing behind me. I startled. Turning my head slowly, afraid of what might be in the boat with me, my heart pounded against my chest. But when I saw those dimples piercing Walker's cheeks, my heart swelled like a balloon too big for its cavity.

I wasn't even surprised that he'd appeared out of thin air—that was on par with the rest of my experience at Baylor Lake—but I *was* taken aback by the butterflies that spread throughout my belly. My feelings for this stranger were growing at an alarming rate.

I couldn't ask him how he'd come to be in the canoe or how long he'd been there without admitting my deepest, darkest fear. The fear that I no longer knew myself. The fear that perhaps something or someone else lived within me. And the fear that I could no longer trust myself or my senses.

So I started out simple. I didn't talk about the weather or the stars, but I pretended that he'd been there with me all evening. I pretended I was sane and sound, like he probably assumed I was. "Thanks again for letting me borrow your flannel," I said, turning around on the seat so that I faced him.

"It looks better on you than it ever did on me. Keep it," he said. The sound of his voice made me hunger for more. This was the feeling I was supposed to have when Noah grabbed my hand on the dock. But I had it with another guy. Not the one I had grown to love, but the one I knew nothing about.

14

I couldn't keep my feet from wobbling back and forth in the belly of the canoe. My nerves were at an all-time high, and I wouldn't have had it any other way. These nerves were the *good* kind. The kind that hung on every word, doted on every movement and gesture. I listened not only to what Walker said but to what he didn't say. I did my best to fill in the blanks. Because everything inside this canoe mattered, and everything outside it meant nothing as I sat opposite of Walker St. James.

"Where are we going?" I asked, trying to see the horizon through the darkness.

"I'm taking you to a special finger of the lake. It's quite remote. Not many people know it's there," he said.

I smiled and nodded, curious to see a part of the lake I'd never known before. "I've been coming here for many years now. I thought I knew the entire lake. I don't recognize this part, though."

"I'm not sure if you've noticed it or not, but this lake can be quite mysterious," he said, his eyes settling on mine. I let myself linger there for just a moment, then redirected my attention. Every time I'd seen Walker, it had been so dark that I couldn't tell what color his eyes were. It was something I wanted to know, but I was too afraid to ask. I was becoming accustomed to the shade they were at night, and I liked the warmth that I felt behind them and their dark hue.

"It's funny you say that. I've noticed some . . . rather odd things since coming to the lake this summer. I mean, little things, like maybe I wouldn't have even noticed if you hadn't said anything . . ." I lied. Such a terrible lie.

Especially since he was the one who had rescued me from the middle of the lake that mind-bending night we'd met.

"Many do. It wouldn't be uncommon."

"Really?" I leaned forward.

"Oh yeah. I told you, I come up here sometimes when I need a break from it all. And sometimes while I'm here, things get so upside down, I can't wait to get home to the mess I left. Things at Baylor can become so weird that it has a way of making you feel lucky for your past life. It's called the Baylor phenomenon. It's known well among the locals. Many people come here to run away from their day-to-day grind. But two weeks later, they're packing their bags, running back to whatever they fled from in the first place. And they do so with a smile on their faces."

"That's so weird that you just said that. I think I've been feeling that exact same thing. Although I wasn't running from anything when I came to Baylor Lake; I was just looking for a great summer." *Had* I been running from something, though? "Then again, maybe I was running from my childhood. I was so eager to move out. Move on." Most definitely, I was running from the death of my gran. From having to mourn properly. I didn't like what that realization did to my body—it was making my skin crawl. I pushed the thought away.

"Did you have a rough childhood?"

"No." I smiled. My childhood memories were filled with warm beginnings and loving ends. "But, since we've been here, things have become so twisted that I can't seem to get them right in my head. It's almost as if time is missing. Like memories are fleeting. Not specific memories—just lapses. As if I jump from one to the next and sometimes it's like . . ." I locked my jaw and shook my head. I wasn't making any sense. I couldn't possibly put this into words that he could understand. Especially if I couldn't even understand myself.

"This one time, years ago," said Walker, "I was up here with some friends. We were having the time of our lives, and out of nowhere, it ended. We were back home as if nothing had ever happened. None of us could remember when we got home or how. And to this day, some of my friends can't even remember the trip at all. I would've thought I was crazy if I didn't have the pictures to prove it. You should have seen the looks on their faces when I got the film developed. Those that didn't remember thought it was a prank. And the few that partially recall the trip still question where the rest of our time went. I don't bother with it anymore. Now I know that's just Baylor Lake."

"Huh, I should get a Polaroid camera or something. Just in case my summer becomes a trip like yours. Forgotten."

"Yes, take it from me. Document everything." His face softened into a smile, but there was a sadness that lingered.

"Do you have any more tips? I've been coming to this lake a long time, but this is the first time I've felt the phenomenon. My friends are starting to think I've lost it." Maybe that wasn't true, but *I* was starting to think so.

"I have all sorts of tips. But they're not free. Stick with me, and you'll learn a thing or two," he said, with a wink and an alluring smile that pulled me in like a moth to the flame.

I floundered there in his gaze for some time before he looked away with a shy smile. I could stay there forever, swimming in his gaze, basking in the light that he cast on me. It was in that moment that I gave up fighting my feelings for him. I threw caution to the wind, and I relished them. They were so blatantly obvious, and I had nothing left to lose. I liked the guy. And I thought I liked him a lot.

I tried not to compare, but my feelings for Noah were based on years of friendship. And what I felt for Walker was far different. It was more about a burning, yearning need for safety and sanity. And lust. I didn't only like him, but I liked how he made me feel. And it wasn't just something I wanted, but something I needed. I needed to feel understood, and if I could do it while looking into his beautiful deep eyes, then why the hell wouldn't I?

"It's like a black hole, that phenomenon. Sometimes I feel like anything is possible here," he said in a way that made me feel almost hopeful. Like maybe it wasn't a curse but a gift.

I rolled my lip between my teeth and hesitated before opening up to him. I didn't want to scare him away, but I desperately wanted to talk to him about all of it. And it seemed as if maybe he was the only person who could understand. Maybe he had the same stories to tell. Maybe I wasn't alone.

"This girl, Trinity—she's one of our friends, and she just went missing the other night. I figured she was staying with a friend or some guy that she had just met, but she never came home the next morning, and we found her phone left behind. My other friend called the cops and filed a missing person's report. We've all been pretty worried about her. And since she's gone missing, everybody in the house has been fighting. That's probably what they're all doing now, back at the cabin. I felt like I needed to get away from it all and just breathe, you know?"

"That's scary. Have you looked for her?"

"Yes, we all have. We retraced our steps from the night before. My friends and I were at a party across the lake. She wasn't there the next morning, and last she was seen was somewhere in the woods. I drove our golf cart looking for her in the forest near my cabin, but it's huge, and she could be anywhere. I'm sure the cops are waiting a certain amount of days before sending search and rescue. But it all just seems impossible. Like it can't be real." I shook my head, staring off into the distance. It couldn't be real. I'd heard of kidnappings when

I was a child, but it never seemed like something that could happen to one of your friends at eighteen.

"So, you've got cops stopping by for reports and such?" he asked, brows furrowed.

"They stopped by the other night. But I was outside for most of it, trying to call Trinity's mother. She never answered." Silence stretched between us, and it was just the tip of the iceberg. I went on, diving deeper.

"I was taking the dog for a walk in the woods, and I swear I was being chased." It all tumbled out. "I don't know what it was, but it was big, and it was fast. My whole body screamed to run, and I barely made it out alive. But then when I saw my friends, they all looked at me like I was crazy. Nobody had seen the thing that was chasing me. Nobody except for me. And it was just a shift in the density of the air. Barely noticeable. Is that . . . is that the Baylor phenomenon?" I asked, squinting in fear that I had just exposed my true colors as a lunatic. But relief washed over me as soon as Walker nodded.

"Yes. That's exactly the phenomenon. Pretty much anything that would make you feel insane and send you packing. A mysterious sound, a repeating symbol, or if you have it real bad, haunting images and life-like phantoms. Sounds like you have a particularly bad case. Most don't. Most will just feel a little forgetful and have a sense of being homesick." His eyes were locked on mine, and I couldn't believe what I was hearing. I wouldn't have weeks ago.

"Huh . . ." I shuddered.

"It's almost as if your fear became a projection, which became your reality. You were out there in the woods all alone, and you felt . . . afraid? So, the thing you were worried about became a reality. It chased you because in your head you felt like prey."

I shook my head in disbelief. How could he know me so well? Walker rested the paddle on the side of the canoe, and we bumped onto the shore. I looked around at the grounds I'd never seen before. It was an entirely new shoreline. I'd scoured the perimeter of this lake before, but I'd never seen this.

"Actually, it can be a gift if you let it . . ." he said, pondering.

"Wait. You think I conjured up that animal—that thing?" I asked.

"Were you afraid *before* you were chased?" He smiled. He knew.

"Yes." I remembered the sounds of snapping twigs behind me and the goosebumps breaking out across my arms.

"Then you conjured it." I sighed as soon as the words left his lips. I should have been more afraid, but I wasn't. I felt relief. It was just silly old me. Letting my mind play tricks on me. A dark forest, a deep lake—it could scare anyone. These fears could get into anybody's head and run away with them.

"Do you think it could have hurt me? I mean, if it wasn't real," I asked, shaking my head as if I already knew the answer.

"Oh, it was *real,* all right. I'm sure that whatever was chasing you could have, in fact, taken your soul," Walker said, stepping out of the canoe and pulling it farther up on the sand.

Taken my soul?

And just like that, my sense of relief disappeared. Here one moment, gone the next. I stood and placed my hand in his. As I crawled out of the canoe onto the shore, I couldn't help but compare holding his hand with holding Noah's. Walker's hand was not only dry but warm—and strong. I felt protected there in the dark with him. We let go of each other as soon as I was safely onshore.

"So that thing was deadly even though *I* made it come after me. That's . . . just . . . awesome."

"You have to be careful, for sure. Especially in those woods. It sounds like something about the trees and the water amplifies your fears. Just keep a clear mind, and you'll do just fine," Walker said, taking a seat on a large piece of driftwood. I sat next to him, enjoying the warmth that radiated from his body, and I didn't mind so much that the wood was sharp against my butt.

"It almost makes you feel crazy, doesn't it?" he asked.

"It does." I never thought I could feel understood by somebody else when I couldn't understand myself. But there he was. My other half.

"The funny thing is, all your friends in the cabin probably feel just the same way. They're probably missing memories too, and they're too afraid to say something," he said.

"Now, that would be funny, but I don't think that's the case. They seem pretty sure of themselves," I said, thinking back to how they'd made me feel so small and insecure.

"I guess the Baylor phenomenon doesn't affect everybody. Typically, it's people like you and me that it has an effect on. Just means you're special," Walker said with a wink and a piercing smile. I felt the heat spread across my cheeks, and I wanted to believe it. When I couldn't hide the smile of embarrassment, I bumped his shoulder with mine and he chuckled.

"So this may sound really weird, but I've been having dreams about my grandmother who recently passed. Do you think that maybe I'm conjuring her as well?" I asked, digging the heels of my shoes into the sand.

"That's something, isn't it? I wouldn't sweep it under the rug."

"I had a dream about her, and she told me to find this girl. She didn't tell me anything about the girl or where I'd find her. She only said that she needs my help," I said with a chuckle. Was I trying to send him running? Why was I still talking? I sounded mad. I ran my hand through my hair and peered up at him.

"A girl?" Walker asked, intrigued. His eyes narrowed on mine, and I felt embarrassed for bringing it up.

"I don't know," I said with a laugh, shaking my head. I must have sounded so stupid. "Hey speaking of, have you ever heard of the Baylor Butcher ghost story?" I asked, as if this topic was a better argument for my sanity. Why did I let myself keep talking to him?

"I have," he said, leaning in. His gaze was pensive, like every last drop of his focus was trained on me. He was intrigued, just like I had been the first time I'd heard about it.

"I don't know much about the story, other than I have heard two entirely different sides of it. I was thinking about doing some research and learning more about it. I'm wondering if the girl in the ghost story was who my grandmother wanted me to find. Oh, my god. It sounds so ridiculous when I say it out loud," I said, laughing at myself. It wasn't funny up until now. Until I was sitting on a piece of driftwood next to a handsome stranger. The one that I was sure had been plucked from the heavens and gifted to me alone.

"The elusive Layla Barns! The girl who got away," he said, in a haunting tone. Goosebumps prickled the nape of my neck.

"Layla Barns?" I asked.

"Yeah, that was the girl the butcher fell in love with," he said. There was a pain in his voice that I could feel somewhere inside my chest. How could I be so in tune with this guy that I could already share his hurt? I searched his face, looking for answers as he stared at the water lapping against the shore.

"Do you know anything else about her?" I asked.

"Just a few things I've heard over the years as the story changes hands. I've never researched it, though, so I couldn't tell you for sure." He picked up a pebble from the sand and chucked it into the water with too much force for such a tiny object.

"Maybe it's just the memory of my gran, but I've grown really curious about their story. I think I'm going to look into it while I'm here. I've asked around a little bit, but all I've heard are tall tales."

"If you want some help, I'll look into it with you. I've been curious about what happened to Layla too. And it's not like I have much else going on. I'm just here for the summer, waiting until I have an itch to go back to my monotonous life. Air traffic control and bartending. Man, when I say it like that, I need to get a dog or something," he said with a chuckle of embarrassment.

I laughed at him. He didn't need a dog. He just needed someone special in his life. I kicked myself for thinking I could be that person.

"Let's do it. You and me. Let's crack the cold case of Layla Barns. Maybe it will bring us some peace?" I joked.

"I'm in. I'm *all* in. We should start at the library tomorrow. You won't find anything on the internet," he said, eagerly.

"Actually, you're right. I've tried." I wasn't sure what was happening between us, but we had formed some sort of alliance. A club of two. Two amateurs trying to crack a cold case like we were super sleuths. But I didn't care. I so desperately wanted something to take my mind off the weird Baylor phenomenon that made me feel unstable. And there was something that Walker was running away from, too. Maybe we could help each other.

"Well, I hate to go, but it's probably time I get you back." Walker patted the top of my hand and I leaned into him with a sad smile.

"You're probably right."

"Always am," he said, standing. I reached for the hand that he offered and pulled myself up. This time, he didn't let go until I was inside the canoe. I watched his strong arms use the paddle to push us off the shore and begin moving us across the lake. I knew how hard it had been on my puny arms to get as far as I did, and I admired his strength as he effortlessly pulled the paddle through the heavy water.

Unfortunately, the ride back to the cabin took only a fraction of the time we'd spent getting to the secretive side of the lake. And although I wasn't surprised, I was filled with disappointment. We'd spent most of the ride stealing glances at each other and smiling when we'd get caught. I was pretty sure that whatever I was feeling was mutual.

We confirmed our plans to meet at the library before I climbed out of the canoe. And it was hard to say good night, but I held on to the plan we had to meet the following day. I'd see his eyes for the first time in the day's light. And I'd better be able to dream about him after knowing what they looked like. I snuggled into Walker's flannel as I walked down the dock toward the cabin.

I peeked over my shoulder to smile at Walker one last time before climbing the grassy knoll. But he wasn't there at all. He'd vanished. My smile faded. I searched the lake for his canoe, and I prayed that I hadn't imagined the entire night. I was hesitant to turn my back, because that would mean another night of torture inside my head. My reality clashing with some other world I didn't belong to. I hung my head and climbed the hill, wondering if I'd see him tomorrow or not. And I hated the fact that I was unsure if one of the best nights of my life had been real or not.

15

It didn't matter how many cups of coffee I had that morning, the caffeine couldn't bring me to life after the sleepless night I'd had. With a mug resting on my lips and my eyes focused in the distance, I noticed that Emma was studying me. I vaguely felt her eyes looking me over, but I couldn't pull myself into the moment. I was lost somewhere out there on the lake with Walker. I'd spent the night dreaming of him and wondering what it would be like if my days were filled with his presence. He'd be the cane that supported me. The crutch I needed so that I could stand up straight. And, no longer hobbled, we would become a pair. A perfect fit.

I weighed my options between Noah and Walker, and I imagined what it would be like to kiss his lips. I'd already spent significant time wondering what color his eyes would be in the daylight. I had been so impatient that the thought of seeing them for the first time today at the library was enough to keep me awake for most of the night. That and the fear that he wouldn't show.

It was early still, but since I had barely slept, I was up. And so was Emma. Although it was unlike her to be up so early, I welcomed her company on the back deck.

"Do you think Lainey is afraid of ghosts?" I mumbled while looking out over the foggy lake. The paint was peeling on the deck, and tiny white flakes had fallen from the railing.

"I think Lainey is afraid of a lot of things. Why do you ask?" Emma asked.

"She didn't seem interested at all when I tried to talk to her about the Baylor ghost stories. And when I talk to her about that stuff, she seems . . . I don't know. *Weird.* She just kind of shuts down. I think she might be afraid of it."

"Maybe. I love that stuff, though."

"You like ghost stories?" I asked.

"I've only read about a hundred haunted mansion books. You're not very observant." Emma chuckled, but I knew that it stung.

Emma was a big-time reader, but I'd never bothered to look at the book covers. I was dyslexic, and reading wasn't a strength of mine. I wanted it to be. I wanted to dive into stories and live in that fictional world while cuddled up on the sofa, wrapped in a throw blanket. I'd have a raging fire and a cup of hot cocoa by my side. It sounded fantastic. It just wasn't for me. The same way that being an athlete wasn't.

"I'm sorry I didn't realize that. I always figured you were reading steamy romances." I winked at her, and Emma laughed.

"Well, I read those too," she said. This time, her laugh was a little higher-pitched than normal.

"Can I tell you a secret?" I asked.

"It's a little early for secrets, but I think I can handle it. Lay it on me." Emma set her coffee down on the side table and leaned in.

"I met this guy. He's a local here. He and I are going to the library today to do some research on the Baylor ghost story. I told him I was interested in it, and he said he was too. And I'm not sure, but I kind of feel like it's a date," I said, pursing my lips and trying not to smile.

"What! I thought you liked *Noah*."

"SHHH, keep your voice down," I said, looking back into the kitchen windows. It was still early, and I didn't think anybody was up, but I couldn't be too sure. "I don't know what I think of Noah now. But I do know what I think of Walker. And he's so cute! And he's nice! And he listens to me . . ." I said, my head in the clouds.

"Walker?"

"Walker St. James . . ." I said, feeling giddy inside. I wrapped my hands in the long sleeves of my shirt and covered the ever-growing smile on my face.

"Oh my god. You've got it bad!" Emma laughed again. We talked a little more as I finished my coffee, and then I laced my shoes up for a morning hike. I was tired from not sleeping, yet I still had excess nervous energy that I needed to get rid of before I saw Walker that afternoon. Maybe I would crash later—take a little nap—but for right now, I needed to get out. I knew I liked the guy, but admitting it to Emma felt like a new level. It made it real. And that scared me, since I didn't know if our time last night had been real or not. He'd vanished as quickly as he'd appeared. I tried not to think about it.

I tightened Gunner's collar and secured the leash by wrapping it around my hand several times. I wasn't going to let him run this time. Not just because I didn't want to lose him again—I didn't—but because I needed him by my side for protection. I wasn't going off-trail this time either. The main trail in the forest was popular enough that I should be safe. And I couldn't live my summer in fear of going into the woods. As I set off, I thought about what Walker had said about manifesting my fears. I was in a different mindset now than I had been the times before, and I wondered if I'd have a different experience because of it.

The way the light filtered through the trees and danced softly on the trail was hypnotizing. Peaceful even. If I were to conjure this feeling into something outside of myself, what would it be? *Something beautiful*, I thought. I listened to the birds sing and was hyperaware of the rhythmic panting from Gunner. I concentrated on my breathing and tried to slow it down. Walker had been right about the Baylor phenomenon; it was a special force if you learned how to control it.

Was it as easy as thinking good thoughts? Pulling up good memories and seeing them unfold before you in the forest? I was sure that the shadows on the trail hadn't danced before. No, before they had jumped; they had struck out like snakes. And I hadn't heard the birds singing before—only the woodpeckers hammering the trees like a drum.

The entire experience was different, and the more I thought about how I had the power to change it, the more I felt the worry and the dark seep back into the woods. I was the last person who should be in control. I wasn't the most reliable person I knew. Not now. Not ever.

I saw a splash of color and a blur of long, dark, ominous hair disappear into the woods. *Trinity*. It had to have been her. I pulled Gunner back and stiffened, searching for the motion that I'd caught in the corner of my eye.

"Trinity?" I called out, my voice bouncing from tree to tree. It sounded as if a thousand of us were out here searching for her.

I whipped my head around, looking in every direction, but I was the only one on the trail. I began walking again. Gunner was pulling on the leash. But this time, I wasn't as sure of myself as I had been seconds prior. A morsel of fear had broken the seal, and I was sure that the small crack would widen over time. A lump formed in my throat, and I had trouble swallowing it down. *It's just a manifestation.*

I brought a shaky hand to the bridge of my nose and closed my eyes, briefly wishing they would open with a sense of confidence that I didn't possess. It was too much to ask for. I should have never asked for that much. By the time I opened my eyes, I'd been thrown into a full-blown nightmare.

Fog surrounded me—so thick, I could hardly see halfway down the leash. A red tether to god knew what. I felt Gunner pull on the other side. His presence brought me little comfort as I looked around the fog, trying to discern up from down. My heart fluttered in my chest, and my breathing quickened. I knew my panting matched Gunner's when my mouth fell open and my tongue grew dry.

I pulled on the leash, attempting to turn around. We hadn't been walking long, and I was certain I could find the clearing of Rock Creek quickly. I took a step, and twigs snapped under my feet. I froze for a moment. *It's not real.*

I took slow and steady steps forward with a hand stretched out until I slammed into something that had no place being in the middle of the trail. "Ah!" I called out, grabbing my knee. A large curved stone stood between me and my way out. A headstone. I gasped. The fog was thick and white as the dozens of headstones came into view. *It's just my fear.*

I knew I had been on the main trail when I closed my eyes, and I hadn't even taken a step before I opened them to the cemetery. It wasn't real. It couldn't be. I knew that now, after talking to Walker. I only wished the knowledge was enough to take away the fear that coursed through my veins. I tried to remain calm, but everything inside me told me to run.

Don't run. It will only make it worse.

I forced my legs to stay still. I didn't know how to get out of there anyway. *Don't run.* The fog was so thick I couldn't see my feet. I closed my eyes once again and tried to calm myself. *I'm conjuring all of this myself. It's just my imagination. It's only fear.*

I told myself that when I opened my eyes I'd be back on the main trail and the fog would be receding. I imagined clear skies, warm air, and Gunner wagging his tail happily at the end of the red leash. But something stronger than my will intruded on my thoughts at the last second.

I peeked through squinted eyes. At the end of the leash was a skinless, grotesque monster. With its hind legs crouched and ready to vault. Its fangs dripping with saliva, and its jowls hanging flaccid and free. I sucked in a breath, my blood curdling as my eyes sprung wide open and I fell backward. The phantom disappeared as I hit the ground.

Gunner went ballistic, growling furiously like he had in the cabin with the ghostly intruder. I held on as tightly as I could to the leash. It dug into the palms of my hands. He was my lifeline, and I wasn't going to let him go if it was the last thing I did.

Gunner snarled, whipping his head from side to side. His hair stood up on the ridge of his back, and I began to slide on my butt as he pulled me forward. Through the fog, a figure appeared. *It very well could have taken your soul.* Walker's words streamed through my head.

Gunner was unbelievably strong, and I dug my heels into the dirt, trying to gain traction. The figure stood still, assessing the threat as I heaved all my weight into holding Gunner back. But slowly, I was being delivered to the soul eater. One inch at a time.

The figure took a step forward, and the gray shadow turned black. A face appeared—devilishly handsome and rugged. Walker St. James. A sense of relief washed over me, causing me to slacken my grip. The slight release allowed Gunner to rip the leash from my hands, burning my flesh. Gunner snarled as he ran full speed at Walker.

"No!" I screamed.

Walker did nothing to protect himself. He didn't even flinch. And Gunner barreled toward him at lightning speed. My eyes went wide with horror. I couldn't bear to see the attack, but I didn't have to. Gunner snarled as he ran mere inches past Walker, never slowing down. I could hear his growling rip through the fog as he continued to run into the distance. *What the hell was he chasing?*

My heart was pounding like a wrecking ball, swinging back and forth in my chest, breaking my bones until there was nothing but a heaping pile of dust inside me. *Why wasn't he afraid?* I pulled my eyes from Walker down to the palms of my hands, which were bloodied and burned from the leash. Stinging intensely, they trembled with pain. I scrambled to my feet, cradling my wounded hands.

I'd lost Gunner. Again.

Walker approached me slowly, with the same fear in his eyes that I'd held in mine. But something was off, and I couldn't be sure what. He came closer, stopping to place his hand on top of the headstone I'd run into. I strained to see his eyes. They surprised me. A bright luster of molten gold. He had a scar I'd never noticed before on the tail end of his right eyebrow. A jagged inch of freshly-healed skin. His hair was a dark brown and his stubble had shades of amber under the sunlight. He was even more beautiful in the sun than when he was under the stars, and all I could do was stare into his eyes.

He tapped his hand ever so slightly on the headstone, drawing my attention away from his gorgeous face. *Layla Barns.*

He'd found her. I labored to stand without the use of my hands, staggering backward to get a better view of the headstone.

"You found her!" I gasped, knowing that this stone hadn't been here before. I would have remembered this one.

"Your hands. Are you okay?" Walker asked, looking behind him for the dog.

My hands were pink and swollen, and blood dripped from one of my palms. Parts of the meaty flesh were missing, and my hands trembled, even though I tried to brace them. "I think I need to get this cleaned up."

"We should go back to the cabin. I can help," he suggested.

"Yeah, thanks." I looked down at the elusive headstone in awe one more time. "Layla Barns . . ." I whispered as I passed by.

She was dead. I'd heard that her body lay resting beside her lover's, but I think there was some part of me that had hoped she was still alive. Some part of me that had wondered if I could speak to her. How was I supposed to help her if she was lying six feet under the ground? I looked from left to right and found a headstone beside hers with no inscription. No name to go by. Just a blank stone. I looked up at Walker with disappointment, though I knew it was the butcher's.

"I was kind of hoping she'd still be alive," I said in a somber tone.

"This was long ago. She's been dead for some time now." He leaned forward, placing a hand on my shoulder, and I looked up at him with a smile. I was so thankful that he had shown up when he did. Who knows what my imagination would have done to me if he hadn't appeared.

"I couldn't sleep. I was up all night. I found out where she was buried—where she crashed—"

"Where she crashed?"

"Apparently, they were in a car crash. On the opposite side of the lake. It's a long drive, but if we leave soon, I think we could make it there and back with plenty of light. We could look around and see if there are any clues as to what else happened there. I heard there were markings on a tree and some sort of shrine. We can't miss it," Walker said.

"Okay, yeah, let's do it." I looked just beyond Walker, hoping to find Gunner before returning to the cabin. "But I should probably find the dog first. He ran right past you. I don't know what he was after," I said.

"I'm sure he'll turn up. Let's get that hand looked at, and then we can take a drive around the lake," Walker said, putting his arm around my shoulder.

I told him about how the fog had taken over and I'd appeared in the middle of the cemetery without taking a step off the trail. He assured me it was all normal practice for the Baylor phenomenon and, even though it didn't make sense, I accepted it. Because he accepted me. By the time we stepped onto the trail, we spotted both Emma and Lainey walking Gunner.

"You found him!" I called out.

"Found him?" Lainey asked. An uncomfortable silence grew between the four of us as my eyes bounced from Lainey to Emma to Walker. Only he knew that we had lost the dog, and I watched his face as he realized what was happening. I noticed the red leash in Lainey's hand, the one that had been ripped from my death grip. It didn't look like it had been dragged through miles of dirt.

The girls eyed Walker suspiciously, and I could tell immediately that they didn't like him. Lainey's brows furrowed as Gunner sniffed at his pant leg. "Hey, Kinsley. We're looking for Trinity, and I think you should come with us," she said, gesturing toward Emma.

"Yeah, you should probably help. We need all the eyes we can get," Emma agreed. I couldn't argue with that. They needed as much help as they could get, but I was pretty sure they were disingenuous in their request by the way their eyes kept flickering to Walker.

I looked up toward Walker, who was calm and collected. "Actually, Walker and I were going to take a drive around the lake. We might have better visibility there. And we could look for her on the other side of the lake, since you guys have this part covered."

"Um, the cops are coming back to the house today, and they said they need to speak with everybody. That includes you. So I really think you should join us for that. Plus, you won't have time to get to the other side of the lake and back, and it looks like you need to bandage your hand first anyway," Lainey said, fidgeting with the leash. I looked down at Gunner, who was happy as a clam. A stark difference from before.

"I guess I can't make it to the crash scene today. But we can reschedule?" I asked, turning to Walker.

He nodded, his disappointment etched in his forehead. I took in his golden eyes one last time before I left him there in the middle of the woods. I wasn't sure why Emma and Lainey were so insistent, but the tension that spread between the three of us as we walked away was palpable. I didn't like the way they were looking at one another, and I could tell that they were wary of Walker. I looked over my shoulder as the distance between us grew. He watched us walk away with his arms folded across his chest.

16

I looked over my shoulder to see Walker watching the three of us walk away. The separation between us felt like much more than a simple redirection. For some reason I couldn't yet understand, it felt like saying goodbye. An invisible string tugged my heart with every step I took in the opposite direction, and I looked at Emma and Lainey for answers. But whatever answers they had, they weren't keen on sharing. The looks exchanged between the two of them were burdened. They were hiding something from me.

"Is somebody going to tell me what's going on?" I asked.

The stuttering blame pushed off from one to the other was difficult to watch, and I became more upset with each second that ticked by. "W—well you said that you had just met this guy. And I was leery. I was leery before I did research on the butcher, but the second you left, I hopped on my computer, and I couldn't think of anything other than your safety. Out here, alone, in the woods. Meeting some man you don't even know. He's just a stranger. I mean, really, who is this guy? And how old is he? Do you even know anything about him?" Emma rambled like a freight train barreling down the rail.

"That's ridiculous, Emma. I know him. Actually, the guy saved my life when you didn't!"

"Oh, here we go . . ." Lainey said.

"What are you even talking about?" Emma asked.

I sighed, knowing I'd said too much. But it wasn't something I couldn't come back from. "I'm sorry, that's not what I meant. He's just a really nice guy. And he's not old; he's only twenty-four."

"That's six years older than us," Emma said.

"That's not that much older!" I looked between the two of them. It wasn't *that* much older. We weren't in school anymore, talking about what grade our boyfriend was in.

"And what do you mean, he saved your life?"

"It was nothing. There was an incident where I thought I was drowning. He came out of nowhere and helped me onto his canoe." I tried rubbing away the stress on my forehead with the back of my bloodied hand. It hurt. Defending my relationship with Walker was making my head hurt. They should just be happy for me. Why weren't they?

"When?" Emma asked. I glimpsed Lainey shaking her head, and I knew she thought I'd gone mad. It made me question myself.

"It was some time ago," I said, vaguely. The truth was, I wasn't entirely sure when it had happened, or if it even had. Lainey thought it was an outright lie. Maybe she thought I was trying to get attention? That was the last thing I wanted.

"Look, as soon as you left for your walk, I learned about all sorts of creepy things the butcher did to lure in women and make them fall for him. It was gaslighting at its best. He manipulated their minds, making them believe that he was the only one that made sense in a life that seemed crazy. He was a master manipulator, and I just don't want that to happen to you. You've seemed a little . . ." Emma frowned, glancing at me sideways. "A little off lately," she said gently. I tipped my head back, soaking in the truth. I knew I'd been acting crazy, but I'd hoped that nobody could see it. It was stupid to think they hadn't.

"I appreciate you looking out for me," I said. I didn't want their help, but I knew it was coming from a good place, and I had to stop and acknowledge that. Appreciate it.

We walked back to the cabin, the crunching of gravel beneath our feet filling the awkward silence between us. Lainey halfheartedly told us about different species of bushes here and there, but mostly, we kept to ourselves. Her attempts at normalcy were unwanted and awkward. Every now and then, I would check over my shoulder, but Walker was long gone. And I was thankful he hadn't heard the conversation we'd had about him.

The house was lively when we got back. The kitchen was bustling with four guys trying to make an epic breakfast. A cure for their hangovers. Kimber was lying in Asher's lap on the sofa, and Scarlett May was wrapped in a blanket on the carpet drinking coffee. Everyone seemed to be working together this morning, and I could barely remember that one of us was still out there. Missing. I briefly thought about the night I'd met Walker. How I'd come into the cabin, and nobody had noticed I was gone. Is this what was happening now?

It was hard to think about Trinity when I felt eyes on me. I tried to pretend I hadn't noticed Noah, but the tension was searing. I went to wash my wounded hands in the sink, but as I ran my hands under the water, and the blood circled the drain, I noticed that the flesh underneath was perfectly intact. I scrubbed furiously, and then examined my perfect hands. They didn't even hurt. I felt a wave of dizziness and went to grab a glass from the cabinet to pour myself some orange juice, when Noah reached for the cabinet at the same time. We both pulled back, allowing the other to go first. And then both reached at the same time again, our hands barely bumping into each other.

We both obviously felt the awkwardness after our conversation on the dock. I'd left him wondering, and our relationship had been hanging in the balance ever since. But somewhere in the night, while Walker paddled and I gazed out at the night sky, I'd realized I had feelings for him, and they unequivocally trumped my feelings for Noah.

I tried not to look at him directly, but it was unavoidable. When our eyes caught, I knew that my feelings for Noah had died. There was something in the way he held himself that told me he knew where I stood. His shoulders slackened, and the corners of his mouth drew downward. The light from his eyes was gone. I poured my orange juice, feeling guilty for the pain that I'd caused him. And even though the exchange had gone unspoken, I knew I'd have to say it aloud at some point in the near future. It wasn't a conversation I was looking forward to having.

Ironically, I bumped into Ethan on my way out of the kitchen, spilling my orange juice all over my chest. I deserved it. I deserved a lot more than a spill for making these two feel inadequate in any way, shape, or form. I wasn't good enough for either of them, and I *definitely* wasn't good enough for Walker. The thought of making them feel small made me feel sick to my stomach. And now, Ethan felt bad about my shirt, too. I assured him it was okay and rushed out of the kitchen, not because the stain was about to set, but because I couldn't wait to get away from the claws of compunction that were threatening to tear me apart.

Emma and Lainey followed me upstairs, and they closed the door behind us when we reached the master bedroom. "What was all that?" Lainey asked.

"Oh, I didn't tell you? Noah asked if we could have a relationship last night, and I told him I didn't know what I wanted." I pulled my shirt over my head and tossed it into the sink. Lainey and Emma sat on the edge of the bed while I dug through the dresser for another T-shirt.

"No!" Emma said.

"Wait, I thought you liked him?" Lainey asked.

"I did. Until . . ."

"Until Walker," Emma mumbled. Lainey and I looked at her, and when their eyes fell back on me, I nodded, confirming. The air in the room shifted and became uncomfortable.

"Yeah, I don't know when it happened, but I really like this guy. I've been thinking about him constantly." I pulled on an old but comfortable T-shirt.

"I wanted to show you an article I found. Will you at least read it?" Emma asked. She turned her laptop toward me, and I sighed.

"Well, that's my cue. I'll leave you guys to it," Lainey said, standing up.

"You don't like the ghost stories, do you?" I asked.

"I just prefer to think none of it ever happened. The thought of murder makes my skin crawl. Why would I ever want to dive into that world? Why do *you*? It just makes little sense. Why you guys are interested in this is beyond me. I just can't." Lainey spun toward the door and paused. "You do remember I had to have an emotional support dog accompany me here, right? This whole thing about Trinity . . . and now a ghost story—it's too much." Lainey waved her hand through the air dismissively. She closed the door behind her, and neither Emma nor I found the words to reply to her.

"I guess it's just us then," I said to Emma. I felt terrible that Lainey had been upset about all of this. We all were, but she was the most fragile of the group.

"Guess so."

"Thanks for helping me do research. I know it's kind of weird and all, but I appreciate it. I haven't gotten too far on my own, yet," I said.

"Just read this, and we can start from there. But I wanted you to at least be aware of this killer's tactics." Emma pushed the laptop toward me, urging me to read. I sat on the edge of the bed, placed her laptop in front of me, and glanced over the document. The words blurred together, and I felt the anxiety boil in my chest. The font seemed too tiny, and the concentration needed too vast. I shut down before even trying.

"Just tell me what it says," I said, shrugging, pushing the laptop across the bedsheets.

"Just read it!"

"I can't! I don't want to!" I felt my voice hitch in my throat.

"Why are you being so weird?" Emma asked.

"I'm dyslexic, Emma. You know that!" I hated repeating it. Like admitting I'd done something wrong. It was like wearing a scarlet letter across my chest. I'd told her before in passing, but I guess it never really sank in.

Emma stared at me blankly, and I felt my face heat with frustration. "I know that. But you *can* read . . ." she said.

"Yeah, I can. It's just frustrating as hell. Do you know what I see when I look at that screen? I see the white space between the letters and words. I search for patterns that aren't there. I see a lot of little marks that tend to blur together. I see an uphill battle. And I'm exhausted just by looking at it. If you want me to read this article, I'm going to need full concentration and dedication. And I just don't have that in me right now."

I wasn't going to pretend to read it either. I did that sometimes. When the stakes were high and somebody was waiting for me to read a meme or a funny joke. They'd hold their phone up to my face, and I'd just freeze up, worried I wouldn't finish reading in time, and it would get weird. They would wonder what was taking so long, and I'd choke. So, I'd just gaze at the passage, try to pick what a normal speed would be, and then smile at the end, hoping it was the reaction they were looking for.

It's not that I didn't read. I did. But it had to be on my own terms. It had to be interesting, and it had to be quiet. No distractions. And I'd use my finger to help keep my eyes from jumping from line to line. It was the little words that tripped me up the most. They could be here or there and then back again. Nobody understood because they were all good at reading. And there is a real segregation in the younger years when reading is cool and you still struggle.

Dumb. It was one of my first identity markers. I had cool light-up shoes. I had friends. But I was dumb. And that stuck with me. The trends came and went. Hell, the friends did too. Most of them. But it was stupidity that stuck with me. It burrowed its way into my subconscious, and I believed it.

"So, if you could just tell me the key parts of this article that you want me to know, then we can move past this fairly quickly." The tightness in my chest wasn't from the explanation I needed to give to one of my best friends but the tension I felt from just looking at the screen. And the expectation that I'd read it. The disappointment that would follow when I wouldn't.

I hated admitting that I had dyslexia or that I needed help. It was like telling somebody that you had been faking your whole life. Like you pretended to be somebody you weren't. An intellect. Sure, I got good grades. And none were the wiser. But what they hadn't seen was that I had spent countless hours every single night at my parents' dining table with tears in my eyes as I tried to wade through the homework and studying. I had never read a full book before, but that didn't stop me from finding the answers I needed. Call it cheating, call it making do, but I had the grit that kept me in the game.

I'd gotten by, but it was only by the skin of my teeth. I had barely hung on in every single class, but I was the only one to ever know how much I struggled. Even my parents weren't fully aware. I should have just been a terrible student. It would have been so much easier. But for some reason, getting good grades meant a lot to me. And at some point along the way, I'd come to realize that effort was just as important as intellect. There were many kids that never had to study and could get A's on all their tests. And then there were kids like me, who studied for hours upon hours to only grasp the lower end of the B.

"Okay. Sorry." Emma shrugged. I sat down on the bed, avoiding eye contact as she filled me in on the twisted ways of the Butcher of Baylor. It wasn't anything I hadn't figured out myself. A murderer must have done some pretty awful things if he was killing in the first place. But the part that concerned me the most was that Emma related these nefarious acts to Walker. I didn't understand how he had anything to do with this or why she felt like my life may be in danger when I was alone with him.

"How did this remind you of Walker?" I asked. I watched Emma flounder and immediately concluded that her argument was unfounded. Dogmatic.

"Well, it doesn't sound very safe for you to be gallivanting around the lake with some guy we never met before. He could be dangerous," she said in a motherly tone.

"He could be. And Noah could be Trinity's killer!" I said, regretting it the moment it came out of my mouth. Emma stared at me in shock. "I didn't mean that."

"You think Trinity is dead?" Emma stammered.

"No . . ." I shook my head.

"And you think Noah did it?" Emma said beneath her breath.

"No," I said, as I considered the possibility. "No, I didn't say that. That's not what I meant."

"But that's what you said."

"I know. I'm just under a lot of stress. I think we all are. I don't know why that came out, but it's not what I meant. I swear." I turned away from her and looked out the window.

"Then what did you mean by it?" she asked. I spun around to face her. She was a little paler, now that she'd been considering that one of our own did something to Trinity.

"I mean, I really like Walker. And I don't think he's dangerous. He's a really nice guy. And just because I don't know him as well as I know Noah, I don't think we should judge him because one of our friends went missing. I mean, we shouldn't judge Noah because he was the last to see Trinity, right? Why does this have to be so complicated? This was supposed to be the best summer of our lives, and now Trinity is missing! And I'm falling for a complete stranger who my friends think is a murderer!" I threw myself backward onto the bed, draping an arm over my eyes. I listened to Emma sigh.

"He *is* pretty cute," she said. A small smile crept across my face as I glanced at her from beneath my arm. She tried to hide her blush behind her hair, but I could still see it.

"Emma Olsen! Did you just say that he was, and I quote, *pretty cute*?"

Emma was fairly introverted as it was, but when it came to guys, she was incredibly shy. She never talked about them, and even though I knew she liked Levi, I'd never spoken to her about it.

"I mean, for you. He's cute for you. You guys are cute together—"

I laughed in the face of her lie. And I was glad that we had finally broken the ice.

We stayed in the master bedroom for most of the day, pulling up articles on the twenty-year-old accident and scouring the local high school's old yearbooks. Most of them had been scanned and uploaded to the internet, and we had a good laugh about the past styles that were now long gone. We researched Layla Barns until we were confident we had found everything the internet had to offer. I had a pretty good idea of where the accident had occurred, but that wasn't very exciting, because Walker had already gathered that information. It seemed both sides of the ghost story had some truth to them. And at the end of the day, I hadn't learned anything new other than where she had gone to school and that she was a local here. Born and raised.

It wasn't until the air shifted in the bedroom—Emma had frozen rigid and the blood had drained from her face—that I considered our research to have uncovered anything meaningful. I knew we were on the verge of something big when she looked like she had seen a ghost. I waited for her to speak, but it was clear she was unable. I grew impatient, my breath catching in my throat. Emma's eyes flickered toward mine and then back again to her laptop. Her back was as straight as a board, and her fingertips hovered over the keys.

"What'd you find?" I asked, unable to keep it in any longer. I figured it was some sort of grotesque picture of a victim pulled from the lake, so I didn't try to look at her screen. I didn't need to see that.

"Read it," she said. But when I glared at her, she nodded and pulled her computer back to her lap. "Right. Sorry. I'll read it. It says, 'The accident that took the life of two haunts Baylor Lake until we can uncover answers as to what caused this terrible wreckage. Residents gather on the side of the road with candles in honor of the two young lives lost. The car carrying Barns and boyfriend—'" Emma paused, her eyes slowly tracking back to mine.

The anticipation was killing me.

"'Boyfriend . . . St. James, skidded down the embankment, crashing into multiple trees and landing upside down by the water's edge. Police are still investigating, as there were no witnesses.'"

"St. James? What a coincidence . . ."

Emma's forehead creased with worry, and she continued to read. "'High school best friend, Chelsea Sims, says, *I know they're together again, and that their love will last an eternity.*'" Emma continued to read, but I stopped listening.

My eyes trailed off into the distance, finding the glow of the window. As I tried to place the generations of potential St. James, I wondered why he had mentioned nothing to me before—other than the fact that he, too, was interested in the story. Of course, he was interested in the story. He was related to the deceased. His family probably had questions of their own.

"How many St. James do you think live in Baylor?" I asked.

But there was no answer from Emma. She sat still and cold as a rock, and I wondered where her emotion had gone. She wasn't giving me anything to go on. Her face was as blank as if she were sleeping with her eyes open, and I feared for just a moment she really *had* seen a ghost. Was it behind me? I whipped my head around to find nobody at all. Though the room *was* oddly frigid. In the silence, I could hear the TV on downstairs, and I listened to the rumbling of the voices. I looked back at Emma, who finally formulated an answer for me.

"One . . ."

17

I tried to fall asleep several times that night. None of them were successful. My head pounded with stress, and I had dry eyes from staring at the ceiling. I couldn't understand how the one person who'd made me feel safe this summer carried the same name as the Baylor Butcher. I didn't know his relationship, but it was obvious that he was tied to the story somehow, some way. Talk about family drama . . .

He was either tangled in the web of the greatest love story ever told or the most heinous killing spree Baylor has ever seen. And based on the feelings I had for Walker St. James, I had to imagine that it was the former. Maybe, just maybe, I was the next love story. I pondered how the best love stories always ended in tragedy. Anxiety settled in my stomach like bricks; heavy, with sharp corners. Maybe I didn't want to have an epic love story after all. On the other hand, mediocrity was pretty terrible too. I got out of bed and flipped on the lights, unable to sleep.

My grandparents had had a beautiful love story. The only tragic part was that my grandpa now had to live without his best friend. But knowing what pain that would cause him in the end, he'd still go all in. Their love was worth every sharp edge that came with watching her wither away. My parents had a good relationship, too. They had fun together. Even my great uncle Tanner and his new wife Brooklyn proved it was never too late for love. If true love was genetic, I was destined for greatness.

I opened my laptop, and seeing that it was nearly out of battery, I dug out the charger and plugged it in. I wasn't as good as Emma with research; I didn't read the articles the way she did, scouring every word. But I was able to get the gist of it. I pulled out keywords here and there. Usually, the words that were longer or in bold at the top of the pages. Sometimes, I'd scan with my finger until a certain word or phrase would jump out at me. Often, there would be too much jumping and too little comprehending. But Walker St. James stuck out like a sore thumb against the black text. His high school wasn't difficult to find, and before I knew it, I was looking at a high school photo in the online yearbooks.

My breath quickened when I finally spied Walker's picture. He was a handsome teenager. My cheeks tightened into a smile. I stared at the thumbnail picture until the pixels slowly came to life before me. The eyes shifting ever so slightly to look directly into mine. *What the hell?* I slammed the laptop shut, feeling like I had just gotten caught snooping. My heart pounded as I sat frozen, one hand on top of the laptop, just in case it sprang to life. None of it made sense. But that was normal for around here.

I needed to talk to Walker, but a part of me was afraid. Afraid of what I might find out. What if Emma and Lainey were right? What if Walker was dangerous? I couldn't stop the thought from creeping in; what if *Noah* was dangerous? I tried not to compare the two, but it was proving to be more difficult than I would have imagined. Until recently, I'd been all-in on one of my best friends. But my feelings for Noah had changed when he'd chosen Trinity on the night he thought I'd never see. Had I run straight into the hands of a cold-blooded killer? If one thing was clear through all of this, it was that I couldn't trust my judgment.

It was already night, and my eyes were burning like they'd been set on fire, and my head hung heavy as I fought the sleep I needed. Suddenly a small *tick-tick-tick* sound came from outside the window. The first time was easily dismissed, but by the second and third times, I could no longer ignore it. I listened for the TV downstairs, but it was quiet. Everyone in the house must have been asleep, as they often were when I needed them most. A spatter of stones hit my window, and I ripped the sheets off my bare legs and crawled out of bed. In nothing more than a large T-shirt and a pair of underwear, I padded to the bedroom window. My heart raced as I placed my hands on the cold glass and slowly slid the window open. The cold air rushed in and awakened my senses. I peered out the window to see a dark figure down below.

"Is that you Wilde?" a man's voice called out in a raspy whisper.

"Who is that?" I asked, straining my tired eyes.

"It's me. Walker. We need to talk," he said. My stomach dropped both in fear and excitement. The stakes were sky-high. I would either live out the ultimate love story . . . or die trying.

I shouldn't have gone to him. But I was drawn to him like a moth to a flame. He was my friend, at the least, and he was on my back porch calling for me. Was I supposed to shut my window and go to sleep? That wasn't possible. And the truth was, I wanted to see him. I liked the guy. Regardless of the confusion stirred up by the articles.

"One second," I said, closing the window and rushing to slip on a pair of pajama shorts. I bounded down the stairs quickly and quietly. The last thing I wanted to do was wake up anybody in the house—especially Noah. But as I passed through the living room, it was clear that I wasn't the only one awake. Quiet whispers escaped a lump underneath the large comforter on the floor where the peak of the blanket had flattened and stilled. I only briefly wondered who I was interrupting, and I was thankful that I no longer felt the sickening twist in my stomach when I walked up to something I wasn't supposed to see in the cabin. There was nobody here for me any longer, and if Noah was under that blanket with somebody else, it wasn't any of my business.

I unlocked the back door and crouched with the clicking of the lock sliding open. My eyes wandered around the room and a sleeping bag stirred. I was pretty sure it was Ethan's sleeping bag. He was another one that I particularly didn't want to wake up. Although I could have used his help back in the grocery store, I didn't want his protective presence looming over my conversation with Walker now.

I opened the door slowly and slipped out, careful to close it quietly behind me. The back porch light turned on as I stepped out. Immediately, I fell for his deep dimples under the scruff of his face. His eyes were hidden under the shadow of a ball cap, making him only more mysterious and drawing me in for a deeper stare. He stepped closer, reaching out for a quick hug. And I should have run, but I did no such thing. I wrapped my arms around his waist and indulged myself. A guilty pleasure. His core was strong, and I clung to it like a child would their favorite blanket. A blanket that brought comfort throughout the dark, lonely nights. It pained me to let go, my heart was like a butterfly trying to escape its cage, but I couldn't hang onto him forever.

"What are you doing here?" I asked, suddenly embarrassed at the thought that he could tell I was stalking him over the internet.

"I had to see you," he said, adjusting the bill on his hat. His eyes twinkled, but I caught a glimpse of something dark around his brows. "You left in such a hurry, and it had me worried. I know you said that you've had trouble sleeping lately, and I have too. I figured you'd be awake." Walker shrugged, hiding his hands deep in his pockets.

"Are you . . . bleeding?" I asked, pointing to his brow. I leaned in closer.

"Oh! That's nothing," he said, pulling the bill of his hat down again.

"What's wrong?" I asked, reaching for his hat. He took a step back, flinching away from my grasp.

"It's nothing."

It was hard for me to let it go, but he obviously didn't want to talk about it. I wondered if he had come to me for help, and I looked for clues to tell me as much. "Well, you were right. I haven't been able to sleep. And I'm sorry about earlier. Something came up, and my friends needed me." A partial truth.

"Did the cops come?"

"No. They never showed," I said. He shifted from one foot to the other.

"Are you sure I can't get you anything? Like a bandage?" I asked. "I can clean that up for you?"

Walker shook his head but ultimately caved with a little pressing on my end. "It's just a scab, but if you want to bandage me up, I guess that would be all right." I nodded, looking back to the quiet cabin.

"Everyone is sleeping, so we have to be quiet. There's a first aid kit in the downstairs bathroom. Just follow me," I said, leading the way. I opened the door as my gaze fell on Ethan's sleeping bag. I pretended not to notice when he lifted his head to see me sneaking a stranger in. And while I wanted privacy, I couldn't help but notice a small part of me that felt relief to have watchful eyes.

Somewhere deep inside, there must have been a hint of doubt. Falling for a guy felt like a lot of things. A racing heart. Butterflies tickling your stomach. Nervous energy. It sounded a whole lot like fear. A pounding heart. A churning stomach. Adrenaline. It was very possible that I was afraid of Walker, even as his rugged good looks and intoxicating smell drew me in. But I had no reason to doubt Walker other than the stupid article Emma had read to me earlier that day. I wished I had never seen it. Because now, I couldn't unsee it.

Walker followed me into the tiny bathroom, and I closed the door behind us. Trapping us inside together made my heart sing and the hairs on my neck stand on end. I couldn't tell if I was falling in love or fearing for my life, but whatever it was, it was more intense than anything else I'd felt before.

Walker lifted his hat from his head, and his dark hair flopped to the side. His brow was cut open, and the gash looked fairly deep. Blood had dripped and dried near the corner of his golden eye. My breath hitched in my throat at our close proximity as I met his direct stare. "Oh," I muttered. "What happened?"

"It's nothing. Just a little scrape." But it was more than a scrape. He probably needed stitches. His scar had been ripped right open, and the surrounding flesh was puffy and tinted blue. Whatever he had done, he was going to get a giant black eye. I looked under the cabinet for our first aid kit. I pulled out the red tin and placed it on the countertop with a clatter, only vaguely concerned about the noise I was making.

"It's more than just a scrape. I'll do my best to clean it, but you probably need to get checked out at the doctor," I said, my back turned to him.

"I don't need to go to the doctor," he said, his breath warming the back of my neck. The warmth ran down into the depths of my stomach, and I turned around, only to drop the peroxide bottle on the floor.

"Shit!" I hissed, kneeling down to pick it up. I looked to the door, listening for the sound of anyone stirring at the noise, but all I could hear was the beating of my own heart. I set the bottle upright and yanked a towel down to soak up the mess. I rose again with the bottle and a swab. My hands shook as I dampened the cotton. "This might sting a little." I reached up to Walker's eye and lightly dabbed the wound.

He winced, and I felt his pain as if it were my own. "Sorry!"

He smiled. One dimple kissing the side of his cheek, his eyes never leaving mine as I slowly continued to dab his brow. I didn't know if it was our proximity to one another, the small bathroom with the closed door, or taking care of him when he was in need, but there was something in the moment that felt extremely intimate. Our shared breath was intoxicating, and I wanted to lift onto my tippy-toes and taste his lips. My hand trembled on the side of his face as I steadied my palm against his cheek. I couldn't keep my eyes on the dried blood any longer. His lips were slightly parted, and my heart was about to leap out of my chest. Pure instinct took over, and I lifted to kiss him.

Walker placed his hands on my shoulders, bracing me from coming any closer, our lips a mere inch from meeting. I felt the burn of rejection in my eyes first. Then it spread to my throat. Rejection felt a lot like dying inside. Like ice crystallizing in my veins until everything was frozen solid. I wanted to die right there. Shrink until I no longer existed. I looked to him for answers as I lowered onto my heels.

"I'm sorry," he whispered.

"No—"

"I can't," he said. I shook my head, trying to brush off the humiliation. I spun around, reaching for another cotton ball to drench, and he caught my wrist. Dropping the bloodied cotton swab down the sink, I refused to look at him. "It's . . . It's not you," he said.

I sucked in an uneven breath. It was almost worse than not hearing anything at all.

"Do you want to tell me what's really going on here?" I asked.

"What are you talking about?"

"I read your name in an article tied to Layla Barns." My eyes scanned the contents of the first aid kit as I waited for answers. Answers I didn't want to come.

"I wanted to tell you. I was going to. I was only waiting for the right time. I didn't want you to find out this way," he said.

I spun around and continued to clean his brow like nothing had ever happened between us. "Tell me now then," I said, devoid of emotion. I dabbed aggressively, even though Walker winced. I was now numb to his pain.

"I . . . It's a long family history that I don't want to get into. A tragic death that everyone knew about. I was given this name out of love—for he who couldn't pass it on himself," Walker said, pain dripping off every word.

And this I felt. I paused, pulling the swab back. Then who was the butcher? A relative?

"It's a curse. Passed down from generation to generation. A love that cannot be." Walker leaned against the sink, his head hanging in sorrow. Was that why he wouldn't kiss me? Because he thought our fate was cursed?

"But that's not going to happen to you," I assured him.

He lifted his gaze to meet mine. His eyes were like spun honey when he said, "It already did."

I didn't understand. I was right here. And nothing was standing in our way. "I don't understand, I—"

"I have a girlfriend," he said.

My face fell. *Girlfriend?* How had I misread this?

"*Had* a girlfriend," he corrected himself.

"Had?" I asked.

"She passed away."

"Oh," I whispered. I knew what that felt like. To lose somebody.

I could see the longing behind every fiber of his being, and even though it hurt to know he felt like this for another, I wanted to take away his pain. I didn't want him to feel this way. I knew all too well what it felt like. Having Walker express his heartache for another girl was like dropping my heart, then watching it shatter into a million tiny pieces.

Wasn't this ironic? I'd put all my eggs in this basket—this handsome basket—and all the while it had a hole in it. A discrete hole at the bottom, one I could never have seen coming. I felt like the one who was cursed, not Walker. I wondered if there was ever a chance for us somewhere down the road. A chance for him to turn his fate around and fall for me instead. Was I crazy? I already knew the answer.

18

The next morning, Ethan made several attempts to get a word with me. I avoided the first few, but there was only so much I could do. He cornered me on the stairs. "Are we going to talk about what happened last night?" he asked with worry in his eyes.

"I don't think there's anything we need to talk about, Ethan," I said, shaking my head, one hand still on the banister. I took a step up the stairs, but he willed me to stop and talk.

"Who was that guy?"

"That was just a friend of mine. You don't need to worry about it. I won't be seeing him again," I said, only a part of me hoping it was true. The better part. The part that knew what was good for me. It was a part that was becoming more and more unfamiliar to me by the day.

"Did he hurt you?" he asked. He took another step toward me, and I leaned back on my heels.

"What? No. Why?"

Ethan scowled. "Because you ran out of the bathroom after the crash, holding your head and wincing."

"What? No, I didn't," I said, just as confused as he was. "No, he didn't hurt me. We were just . . . he was just hurt. He hurt himself, and I was fixing him up."

Ethan obviously didn't buy it. He looked at me sideways and pressed on. "He hurt himself? How?"

I opened my mouth and then closed it again when I realized I had no idea what he had done to himself. I didn't know how he'd split his brow open, and he'd been very vague about it. Perhaps for good reason. "He slipped. No big deal."

"Okay. Then why were you guys fighting? Then why did you storm off? And why did I have to fight him off last night?" he asked. Ethan's patience was running thin, and I could tell by the way his elevens had deepened between his eyes.

"I don't know what argument you're talking about, Ethan."

"Who are you?" he said, using air quotes. "No . . . Kinsley, you have to listen to me," Ethan continued. It was a conversation that had never happened. I wasn't the only one losing my mind.

"Look, I don't need you looming over me all the time. I don't need to be saved!" I said, my hands in the air. But it was a lie. I needed somebody to save me. I hated that I was so weak and mentally inept. I needed to try harder. Be better.

I spun around, grabbing the banister and pulling myself up the stairs and away from Ethan. Away from the *truth*. That I was incapable of taking care of myself. I knew I wasn't the best self-advocate, but Ethan's words solidified that. A part of me wondered if I should run back home to my mom and dad where I could be looked after like the child I was.

The day crawled on as everybody prepared for an epic party. It was the last thing on my mind, and I stayed under the covers of my bed, wallowing in self-pity. Both Emma and Lainey came to talk to me, but I didn't speak a single word. They already didn't like Walker, and I didn't need to give them another reason. Plus, I didn't want to know what they thought of me now. I was two for two. I was the girl who would give her heart to anyone . . . just as long as they promised to break it.

A storm rolled in that evening that matched my bleak, edgy mood. While the rain fell and the music blared, I took a drink from Kimber and nursed it cautiously. I needed the fruity cocktail to knock back my woes, but I couldn't tolerate any more mental dysfunction beyond what I had already experienced. I needed my senses intact. Because I was on the edge. I'd been battling the idea of going home all day. And as I looked around the room at all my friends and their carefree, self-absorbed entertainment, I inched ever closer toward the idea of packing my bags.

I looked down into my pink drink and swirled the ice cubes around with my finger. I should leave now. The thought came on repeat.

"I think Mason is about to do something stupid again!" Emma slurred.

"Oh no! Like what?" I looked around the room for the first naked guy I could find. And I swore to myself, if he took his clothes off and ran through the cabin one more time, I'd march upstairs and grab my things.

I was already on the verge of giving up on the best summer ever. Trinity was gone. Simply gone. Things were happening in the woods that I couldn't explain, and there was a real danger in that water. I didn't want to hang around watching everyone pretend that life was good. Normal. Because it wasn't. There was something seriously off about this place.

"I don't know, but he's unscrewing all the light bulbs in the den. Must be up to something, huh?" Emma asked.

"Jesus . . . I can't deal with him right now." I sighed, burying my forehead in the heel of my palm.

Sampson chose that minute to come through the front door with a gaggle of girls and a few of his buddies from the bonfire. Scarlett May ran to greet him at the door. They were all wet, tracking mud through the house as the storm raged on. I didn't want to look at the footprints that littered the carpet, so I drowned myself in my pink drink instead. It wasn't long before Kimber brought me another, and if it had been stronger than the first, I never would have known. My head was swimming.

I was squished between Kai and Noah on the sofa when I thought I saw somebody tall, dark, and handsome in the crowd. A navy-blue flannel, dark hair, and a baseball cap disappeared into the sea of people. I straightened my back as I watched for a reappearance. Noah continued to babble in my ear about second chances when I stood up mid-sentence and followed the apparition.

I rested my hand on the bare shoulder of a girl wearing a tube top. Her shoulder was still wet from the rain as I lightly moved her out of my way. She stumbled forward with a giggle. I moved through the crowd, peering into each and every room of the cabin. But the handsome mirage was nowhere to be found. I walked into the den, peering into the shadows. I felt the presence of somebody or something else breathing. A dark figure emerged from the corner.

I backed up against the wall and fumbled for the light switch. My fingers frantically scrabbled across the wall to turn the light on, but when I found the switch and flipped it, the room remained pitch black. "Dammit, Mason!" I hissed.

"It's me," Walker said.

"What are you doing here?" I asked.

"We need to talk. There are a lot of things you don't understand."

I smelled his warm beachy cologne before my eyes adjusted to the dark. I might as well get the closure before saying goodbye. "What about this curse?" I asked. But I didn't want to know about his ex. I only wanted to know if the door was truly closed between us.

"I come from a long string of epic love stories. All of them tragic. I loved her then, and I love her now. She has my heart and always will." Walker's golden eyes burned with bottomless desire and longing. But all I could hear was one word. *Always.*

"Always?" I asked, my voice hitching. Walker winced, and I tried to take a step back. His heart had been claimed, and there wasn't a chance for him and me. Ever. And every minute I spent falling for him was another minute I let my heartache grow deeper.

I had just lost my gran. I had come to the lake in hopes that my friends and a fun summer would take my mind off that pain. But all I did was chase after guys who were unavailable. I traded one pain for another. I couldn't keep digging this hole. I needed to love myself more than that.

"So, are you related to the butcher then?" I asked, looking for reasons to leave. Because my own heartache wasn't enough to keep me from him.

Suddenly, my headache came back with a vengeance. I reached up, grabbing the side of my head, but I never once took my eyes off of him. I watched as his eyes shifted from sorrow to something else. Something I feared. Uncertainty swirled inside my chest.

I blinked once. That's all it took, and we were back in the bathroom. The lights hurt my eyes, and I squinted through the pain of my migraine. Walker's brow was bleeding, and I was helping him clean it. I'd gone back exactly twenty-four hours to the night before. Walker never broke character.

"Who are you?" I asked, not wanting to know the answer. I took a step backward, but my back hit the towel rack against the wall. Suddenly, I didn't want to be trapped in a tiny bathroom with him. What had once felt intimate felt dangerous now.

"Wilde, you have to listen to me," he said, taking a step forward.

"No!" I snapped.

"Wilde," he said, reaching out. I dropped the bottle of peroxide and shrieked. The door burst open, and Ethan barged in between us. I ran out of the bathroom, leaving the two of them together, and I heard Ethan and Walker get into it as I ran up the stairs.

"I'm not here to hurt you, Wilde," Walker said.

I gasped. The room was dark, and my back was up against the wall of the den. I was back. The party was raging in the cabin. The storm was raging outside.

What had just happened? The bathroom. It was like a flash. A moment in time that had slipped through the cracks. Glitched in and out of the present. Had Ethan had a premonition about the fight? Or had I simply forgotten about it? It didn't feel like a memory. I could have sworn it was real. It felt more like an alternate ending. Like I could have chosen how the night had ended with Walker in the bathroom. My first alternate ending was the reason for my sadness. Walker was in love, just not with me. And the second ending, the one I'd just seen, was the reason for my chilling fear. The darkness in his eyes. A fear I could feel, but not remember why I'd ever felt it. I was afraid now, my hands trembled.

He stared deep into my eyes, and I knew I had fallen for the wrong guy. Not just any guy, but a direct descendent of the Baylor Butcher.

"I'm feeling misunderstood by you. There are some things you need to know before you draw your conclusions about me. I'm not a monster," he said, and I didn't need the light to see the pain in his eyes because I could hear it dripping from his voice.

"What just happened?" I asked, breathless. I looked out into the dark den, wondering where the bathroom had come from, and where it had gone now.

"Ignore that. Focus, Kinsley." Walker placed his hands on either side of my face, and our eyes locked. Our souls intertwined. I hated myself for feeling empathy toward him.

"Have you killed people? Did you throw their bodies in the lake?" I asked, my voice breaking.

"What!?" He flinched backward.

"You heard me. Answer me! If you didn't do it, who did? And did you help them? Were you an accomplice? How many St. Jameses are there?" I shook with anger, not about his past but my own present. How'd I ever let myself get here? I was falling for somebody who had killer written in their DNA. Somebody I wanted to be close to but was equally afraid of. If he wasn't directly guilty, he was guilty by association. I ripped his hands off me.

"Of course not! What are you talking about? You think I am the killer? The Baylor Butcher? That's nothing but an old wives' tale. Are you serious?"

My heart thudded. Slow and strong.

"Yes, I'm serious. I've heard two stories now about the Baylor Butcher. One is a love story, and one is a horror story. So, which one is it? Which one are you?" I asked, trembling with fear.

"Don't forget who saved you from that lake." He reached out to touch my arm, and I jerked it away from him. "Wilde . . . I'm not a murderer. I would never hurt anybody. At least, not on purpose. This place is messing with you. You have to believe me?" he pled. And I couldn't help but hear Emma's voice ring through my head, *Essentially, he gaslights girls into thinking they're crazy.*

"There's a lot more to this story than I can tell you right now, right here, in this dark den. And if I answer these questions in their simplest form . . . I'd never see you again. And that's not a chance I'm willing to take." He spoke hastily until it came in a whisper. "I need you, Wilde. I need your help. I'm begging," he whispered, sounding like a tortured soul. A victim himself. Regardless of his past, he was just as afraid as I was.

I couldn't grasp why he needed me. Why would anybody need me? My sanity was nonexistent. I was a complete and utter wreck. I had no control over my life, and some days I lacked the will to try. And on the darkest days, I wondered if I should have drowned in that lake. Maybe it had been my time. And maybe I'd escaped but shouldn't have.

I looked up to the dark figure before me, and with all my fears, insecurities, and inadequacies, I did what I did best—I ran from what I couldn't understand. I felt his fingertips slide off my waist as I escaped the den. I vaguely noticed Mason chewing something with blood running down his chin and a small crowd gathered around him in the living room. Cheering him on like he was about to crush a world record. I was pretty sure the only thing he was crushing was the lightbulb from the den.

I ran up the stairs and locked myself in the master bedroom, but Walker was close on my heels. As soon as I took my first breath behind the locked door, he knocked on the other side. "Kinsley, let me in?" he asked softly.

"Go away, Walker!" I yelled.

"Who's Walker?" the voice asked.

I froze; my ears perked.

"It's Noah. Can I come in?" I felt a rush of disappointment. My shoulders dropped, and I was done. I pulled out my suitcase.

"Wilde, let me in!" I perked up. Freezing in the silence. I was sure it was Walker this time.

"Who are you, man?"

"Who are *you*?"

I rolled my eyes and sat on the edge of my bed. I picked up the old telephone on the nightstand and called my mom, ignoring everything on the other side of that door. The phone rang three times, and I thought she would never answer. But when I heard her voice on the other end, all the other voices from the party seemed to fade away.

"Mom?" I asked.

"Kinsley, is that you?" Her voice sounded weary on the other end of the line.

"Yeah, Mom, it's me. How are you?" I asked.

"I'm doing well. How are you?"

"I'm doing all right, I guess. I've been better. Actually, I'm thinking of sending everybody home and coming back early."

"What? Why? Is everything all right?" she asked.

"I didn't know how to say this earlier, but we sort of . . . *lost* . . . Trinity." I bit the corner of my lip. The knocking on the door continued, and it stole my attention for a moment before my mom could answer.

"What do you mean, *lost?*"

"Well, we were at a party, and she sort of disappeared. We haven't seen her since. It's been about a week, and nobody has heard from her. I tried to call her mom, but she didn't answer."

"Did you call the cops?" she asked.

"Of course, we called the cops! It was the first thing we did! They barely opened up a missing person case. They haven't been doing squat!" I said, thinking back to the one time they'd shown up and asked a few questions, jotting down the answers on a notepad.

"I'm going to call Trinity's mom," she said.

"Wait! Mom? I'm worried. What if something happened to her?" I asked, sitting on the edge of the bed and staring at the open suitcase.

"You *should* be worried! It wouldn't be the first time..." She stopped, and I could hear her breath hitch at the other end of the line.

"What do you mean, it wouldn't be the first time?" I asked, a knot forming in the depths of my stomach.

"Dear, I've gotta go now. I've already said too much."

I frowned. How could she have possibly said too much? If anything, she'd said way too little. What was she talking about? "Wait! Mom?" But her response never came. "Mom!?" The dial tone hummed through the receiver. An icy shiver ran down my back. Something was going on—something strange. But one thing I would never have guessed was that my own mother would be in on it.

A thump at my bedroom door told me that somebody was still waiting for me on the other side. But if I hadn't known who I could trust before, I certainly didn't know now.

19

It was when the knocking stopped that I noticed the party had fallen silent, too. I finished stuffing my laptop into my backpack and crossed the room quietly. I placed my ear against the door and listened for signs of life. There was a rumbling downstairs, and I could hear sounds coming from outside by the lake rather than inside the house. I couldn't wrap my head around why everyone would be outside in the storm.

At first, I was glad. Happy to have the party leave for another spot. I'd have some peace and quiet so I could pack alone and not be bombarded by boy problems and, worse yet, phantom problems. But my curiosity was piqued. It was like a buzzing in my ears that continued to grow louder, and I couldn't ignore it. I looked outside my window, and what I saw was more concerning than anything from before. A large group of partygoers stood by the water's edge in a small circle looking at something.

I gripped the doorknob, confident that neither of the guys were waiting on the other side, but I still opened it cautiously. I poked my head into the hall and was greeted by silence. A part of me screamed, *trap*, but a larger part of me couldn't help but wonder what was so fascinating to these people. What could pull them away from free booze, free food, and shelter?

A fight? A fight would pull them away. I wasn't sure why, and I'd never understood it, but people loved to see a fight. I imagined two of our friends rolling around and bloodying the shallow waters. I imagined punches thrown and broken noses. The crowd surrounding them, taking pictures and videos to share with their friends. Seconds crawled by as I wondered who it was. And I just knew. I just knew that it was Walker. My stomach twisted. But who would fight him? And why? Was it Ethan? Ethan was jealous all right, but he wasn't the fighting type. He was a follower at best. Was it Noah? Would Noah fight Walker because of me? Or had this not been about me at all? I liked that thought, but deep down, I had a sick feeling about Walker, and I was worried.

I made my way downstairs and out the back, passing not a single soul. There were no stragglers making out on the sofa, and nobody was passed out on the living room floor. No stoned friends loitering in front of the open refrigerator, and no line for the restroom. The house was eerily quiet, and I hated every second of it. The anticipation was deafening, and I feared what I was about to find. I knew in the moment I crossed the kitchen and saw nothing but empty cups that tonight's party wouldn't be like any other. Tonight's party was going to be a night to remember. The way fire burns the skin, leaving a mark to last a lifetime.

When I stepped off the back porch, I could feel the tension thicken in the damp air. Gasps bounced from one end of the crowd to the next, and whispers carried through the air like the storm's wind. The rain was just a mist now, but it clung to my cheeks as I hurried down the grassy knoll to the water's edge. I threw my arms in the air, nearly slipping on the slick blades of grass. Several flashes went off through the crowd as various people took pictures of whatever lay in the center of the group.

I wondered where the ruckus had gone. There was no yelling, no grunting, and no commotion of people trying to break up a fight. Everyone was oddly quiet, and they were suspiciously still. I had no idea what I was getting myself into when I penetrated that crowd, but I fought tooth and nail to find out, pushing and squeezing my way into the center.

When I'd cleared the thick crowd of hungry eyes, I found not a fight but a body—a dead body. It had washed up on shore and lay mangled in the sand with water lapping at the legs.

The skin was a cool gray, which told me that there was no longer any blood pumping through the veins and probably hadn't been for quite some time. It was face down, with long exposed legs and bare feet. It was a girl. Tattered clothes covered bits of her body, but she needed far more to be considered decent. Long, dark, ominous hair lay matted across her face. Her mouth was partially open. My stomach wrenched as the bile rose in my throat.

I had never seen a dead body like this before. I'd seen my grandmother recently. But she'd been covered in makeup and dressed in her best, tucked away in a casket with folded hands. She hadn't looked like herself, but it was a peaceful illusion. Everyone said that it would help with the mourning process. I didn't believe that to be true. Maybe if it had been my grandmother that lay in that casket—but it wasn't. It was no more than a shell of a person I used to know. The part that I loved so dearly was gone. And that was the part I longed to see one last time. This . . . this, on the other hand, was anything but peaceful. This was a girl who had struggled. A girl who had fought for her last breath and lost. This was a tragedy. A nightmare.

I scanned the crowd as they all watched the body lying on the sandy shore, the water pushing and pulling at the dingy remnants of clothing. Everyone's eyes were glued to the girl except for one pair. Walker stood on the opposite side of the small clearing, his eyes fixed on mine. My breath hitched in my throat as I caught his gaze. I didn't know what it meant, but for that short period of time, I felt relieved that it wasn't him lying in the center of the crowd. My eyes watered as they lowered from Walker's, back to the girl whose soul had left her some time ago.

Walker was safe.

Asher crouched down next to the girl and lifted the scraggly hair off her face with a stick. I recognized her instantly. It was Trinity. Her eyes were fixed open with a vacant stare. They were no longer the alluring, hazel snake eyes, but a foggy, opalescent blue that swallowed her whole. Her face was frozen in an expression of fear like a time capsule of her last breath.

Asher dropped the stick and lurched backward, falling onto his butt and causing a small ripple of fumbling throughout the crowd. Kimber screamed a wretched cry, and strangers took her into their arms. With wide eyes, I searched the crowd for answers. All these people and no answers.

Everyone was watching and waiting for an authoritative figure to take action. It wasn't any of us. Nobody knew what to do. We were only eighteen. Most of us anyway. And while eighteen had seemed like an adult just a few weeks ago, when we were graduating from high school, now it seemed like we were no more than children. None of us knew how to handle the death of a friend. And none of us had ever dealt with a murder. The killer still lurking in the woods.

Were they out there now? I looked into the faces that surrounded me. Was it him, or him? Or maybe that girl who showed no empathy while Trinity lay lifeless at our feet? Was it Noah or Kai who had seen her last? There was something in my chest that told me it wasn't Walker, and I had to believe that.

As of late, my mind had been playing tricks on me. My grasp on reality was dwindling, so when my gut told me something, I knew it was an unreliable source. For all I knew, *I* had been the one to kill Trinity. I still had questions for Walker, and I still wondered if he was dangerous—though I believed he wasn't a threat to me—but as I looked down at the cold, gray body lying face down before us, I was positive that she hadn't died by the hands of Walker St. James.

I didn't know who the killer was, and judging by the speculative stares dripping with paranoia all around me, it was clear that nobody else did either.

But that wasn't my focus now, though maybe it should have been. Right now, there was only one question racing through my head: *who would be next?*

I'd never thought anybody would die. But if I had to guess who'd be the first, I would have said Trinity. Or maybe Scarlett May. They were the kind of girls who'd get themselves into trouble. The kind to make secret enemies. But as I looked around the crowd now, if I had to guess who was next, I'd guess . . .

My stomach dropped, and my mouth ran dry. It was *me*. My guess would be me.

I couldn't pry my eyes off her dead body, and I wasn't the only one. All of us stood, staring silently. A few were crying, but most of us were paralyzed. I didn't know who had done it, how it had happened, or who was next, and I imagined that the same string of questions was going through everyone's head at the same moment. These were the questions I saw in the faces of not only my friends but Sampson's group of locals, too.

Movement in a far-off corner caught my eye, and I arched my back to see who it was. It had been Noah who'd pulled away from the group. I watched him walk away, wondering what he was up to, until I saw him lurch forward and puke into the bushes. A few people dispersed, and I wondered where they would go and what they would do next. Were they all going home? Was the party over now that a life had been stolen?

I heard an authoritative voice call out to me over the crowd. "Kinsley, what's your address?" Lainey asked, her phone pressed to her ear.

I made my way to her as she gave my address to the police. The crowd started to back up, presumably not wanting to be associated with the incident. It was clear that the police were on their way as Lainey's voice cut through the silence. It was enough to send three-quarters of the party home. All of our friends stayed, and some of Sampson's close buddies did, too. But most went home.

Home. My home was calling me too. I felt deep inside that this wasn't the place for me any longer. I'd made a terrible mistake in coming to Baylor this summer. I needed to get out of here, and I needed to do it now. If I wanted to survive this summer, I needed to go home. I thought about my backpack half-stuffed upstairs on the bed, and I slipped out of the crowd to go grab it and make my silent departure.

From the corner of my eye, I glimpsed a baseball cap, flannel, and dark jeans disappear into the woods, and to my surprising sorrow, I was pretty sure I'd never see Walker again. I knew it was for the best, but there was a part of my heart that ached for him. He'd tried to talk to me earlier, and at this point in the night, he'd given up. Gone home with the rest of them. I didn't blame him. Sometimes, I gave up on myself too.

Still, there was a tightness in my chest, knowing I had made the decision to run. Because staying and fighting wasn't an option for me. I wanted to live. And I was in over my head. I couldn't even find a missing girl, and the more I looked, the more trouble I wound up in. I couldn't stay now that I knew this threat was real. Now that Trinity was gone. Really gone.

I snuck upstairs to grab a few of my most precious belongings. Cell phone. Laptop. Keys. All the rest could stay in the cabin for me to grab at another time. A safer time. A time when I wasn't being hunted by a cold-blooded killer. A mist in the night. I slung my backpack over my shoulder and grabbed a baseball cap on the way out the door.

I wasn't going to tell anybody of my plan to flee, but when I bumped into Emma on my way out, I couldn't not say goodbye. "Where are you going?" Emma asked. I looked around the room, thankful nobody was watching us.

"I've gotta get out of here. I'm going home."

"What?" Her head cocked to the side, and her voice hitched.

"Look, weird things have been happening, and I'd be lying if I said that Trinity was the worst of it," I whispered, pulling her away from a few stragglers entering the cabin.

"What are you talking about? What else is going on? Is this about the ghost story? You're going to leave because of a damn ghost story?" Her voice was growing rough.

"No. There are a lot of things that have happened since we came to the lake that I can't talk about right now." I looked over my shoulder to see who was watching. I didn't see anybody, but I felt their eyes nonetheless. "I'm not safe here! And honestly, neither are you. Come with me." She closed her eyes and dropped her head.

"Kinsley, we're here for the summer. The entire summer. I'm going away to college, and I won't see you for—I don't know—years. Are you really going to leave when we all need you? We need to stick together. That's how we're going to survive this. I mean, Trinity is gone. You can't leave too." Emma's eyes begged me to stay, and while she had a point that we should all stick together, there was urgency boiling inside of me that screamed that I should flee.

"I can't. I can't do it. I have to go. I'm so sorry." I hugged her quickly, pinning her arms to her sides. She was stiff as a board. "I love you. Be safe," I said hastily as I ran out the door into the rain.

"Kinsley, wait! You can't go!" she called out behind me, but I never looked back.

I ran up the driveway and onto the main road. I ran past my neighbors' house. The curtains pulled back as they peeked out, and a warm yellow glow was cast into the night. The police cars came into sight down the street. The red and blue lights illuminated the pines like searchlights as they drove in. I vaguely wondered if my fleeing the scene would make me a suspect. But I'd rather be a suspect than a victim.

And I believed that. I believed that if I stayed just one more night, I'd be next. Death would find me one way or another. At the hands of the killer or by way of nightmare. I knew I wouldn't last through the night. So, I ran from my fear. I ran into the woods and down the stormy street. I ran until I had to stop to catch my breath.

I found myself a couple of miles down the road, my shoes rain-soaked and my lungs burning. I realized then that I hadn't really thought this through. I couldn't walk in the rain all the way to the airport. It was a good hour and a half away, and I needed a plan. I needed more than a plan. I needed tickets. One thing at a time. First and foremost, I needed a ride. I needed to get out of this rain. I pulled out my phone to call a cab.

I wasn't sure if it was the thick forest cover or the summer storm, but I had not an ounce of service to call for a ride. For the first time, I looked behind me. It was nothing but blackness and the sound of rain hitting the pavement. The night was chilly, and my feet were blistered, but I felt none of that. The will to survive took precedence over comfort.

I continued to walk forward because there was no chance that I was going back. I wasn't afraid of the animals lurking out in the woods. But I was afraid of the killer. I was afraid of the evil that lived inside that lake. And I was afraid of *myself*. Something I couldn't run from.

It was my mind that I feared. Walker had said the Baylor phenomenon fed on my imagination. He said that I had a particularly bad case compared to others. And I worried I had put myself in a compromised position being alone in the woods at night. A state of mind where I could be killed by my own shadow. And if the killer didn't find me here, the Baylor phenomenon would.

I wished Emma had come with me. I tightened my arms around my waist. And as a branch cracked in the woods, I even wished that Ethan was by my side, there to protect me once more. Another branch cracked . . . this time closer. I quickened my pace. It was my fear that I needed to control the most. Otherwise, things would get out of hand. I braced myself as I tried to be strong and brave. I forced myself to slow down. I tried to imagine a protective bubble all the way around me—a bubble filled with light and strength. And I wasn't sure whether it was my conjuring or just a coincidence, but just then, the forest lit up with the warm headlights of a big rig.

As the headlights approached, I felt it was fate drawing the truck in. I'd never hitchhiked before, but at this moment, on this particular night, where I was sure my life was on the line, I took my chances. I stepped out into the street, my arm outstretched and my thumb up. The truck plowed through the storm, coming closer and closer. I didn't think it was going to slow down. But my luck had turned around, and the big rig slammed on its brakes, screeching to a halt.

My heart pounded as the large white cab pulled up alongside me. The heat from the engine radiated in the frosty night air, giving me temporary warmth and filling my lungs with gasoline fumes. I bit my lip, questioning my decision as I read the words on the side of the truck. Decker Transports. I wasn't sure what I was getting myself into, and I wasn't sure what they were transporting, but I had to imagine that anything was safer than staying at the cabin for one more night. Believing that the threat was behind me, I took a step forward, accepting my ride. My fate.

20

With no other options, I slipped my hand around the door handle and pulled it open. I didn't look at the driver as I crawled into the cab. There was a heavy stench permeating the air. The smell of cigarettes and something else. Beef jerky? Pork rinds? I shut the door behind me and secured my seatbelt. Then, and only then, I let my eyes wander. The open beer can in the cup holder was my first warning sign, but I feared that whatever was out there in the woods was far worse. Through the glow of the radio, I could see the grime that had built up on the console—most likely over years. I placed my hands on my lap and forced a smile. "Thanks for the ride."

"Pretty little girl like yourself shouldn't be out here in the woods all alone at night," he said. His voice was a low grumble. A warning or a threat, I didn't know.

I lifted my eyes to the driver. He was large and gruff. A scraggly beard hung down to the middle of his chest, and a putrid smell escaped his mouth when he spoke. He was wearing a red plaid flannel, but unlike those that Walker wore, it wasn't attractive. Far from it.

"I didn't have service to call for a ride," I said.

"What's your name?" he asked. I looked around, wondering why we weren't driving. Why were we just sitting in the middle of the road? And why did he want to know my name?

"K—Kansas . . ." I lied. As if it would do anything to protect me. But I had seen too many shows, and my mom had warned me too many times not to let a stranger know your name. Because they would weaponize it against you. Although I couldn't see how in this particular situation. I was already in the man's truck in the middle of the forest.

"Well, Kansas, you're all wet." I didn't like the way he articulated the word. I shifted in my seat. I peered down at my lap, my hair dripping all over the seat.

"I'm sorry. I—"

"That's all right." I felt his eyes trailing down my body, and a sick feeling came over me. I looked at the door handle and questioned whether I should get out and run straight into the night. But as soon as the thought entered my mind, he put his foot on the gas and the truck lurched forward. *It's too late now.*

"I, um, I'm going to the airport. Are you headed in that direction?" I rubbed my forearm, wishing I had spoken with more conviction.

"Sure . . ." His jaw was tense, eyes unblinking.

Sure? Generally, it was a yes or no question. But he made it sound like he'd go anywhere—or more like he would *say* he would go anywhere—that I wanted. I pinched the bridge of my nose and closed my eyes. I took in a deep breath of old cigarette smoke, and it did nothing to calm my nerves. I didn't know how I'd ended up in this situation, and now that I was in the cab of a locked truck, driving down the windy, wet roads of the forest with this gruff stranger, I wondered if I had made the wrong decision. Possibly a decision that would cost me my life. But there wasn't time for that now. I was moving forward with the plan either way. The wheels were turning and the pines passing by. I tapped my finger on my thigh as I accepted my fate, looking out the foggy window.

The trees blurred together as we picked up speed, turning into one dark brush stroke. And it was in that stroke of trees that I saw something that didn't belong. Something that stuck out—not like a sore thumb—but like an ethereal glowing light upon a dark stormy background. It was there on the side of the road that we passed my gran. Her full-body apparition stood just a few feet into the woods, watching me pass by in the Freightliner's window. I straightened and craned my neck, trying to watch her as long as I could. She disappeared by the next bend in the road.

My stomach was queasy. It could have been the powerful stench of jerky or knowing that my time was coming to an end, but I thought it was more likely from seeing my dead grandmother on the side of the road. She'd come to me frequently in my dreams, but never once had I seen her when I was awake. I thought she'd been near a time or two. That eerie feeling of somebody watching you from a distance was hard to miss . . . and I'd always figured that it was her. But this time . . . this time, I knew. I *saw* her with my own two eyes.

What did it mean? Had she come back because I found myself barreling down the wrong path? Was I not supposed to come to the lake with all my friends? Maybe if I hadn't, Trinity would still be alive. Although there was a part of me that believed in fate, and that part believed that when it was somebody's time to go, how they went didn't really matter. Their time would find them one way or another. Was my gran telling me it was *my* time? I peeked at the gruff driver beside me, and hot acid boiled up my throat and splashed into my mouth, sending a shiver down my spine.

I sat rigid in the deflated seat. I must have sunk a foot deep, as the padding had been worn thin. The dashboard reminded me of the cockpit of a plane with all of its buttons and levers. It looked nothing like being in the front seat of a normal truck. Old-school rock played softly in the background, but it wasn't enough to deafen the silence between us or cut through the tension.

"Where are you heading?" I asked.

"Oh, don't you worry about that, pretty little thing. I'm heading where you're heading," he said. I held my breath. His comment dripped with disturbing thoughts.

"You're headed to the airport, too?" I asked. He didn't answer, and he didn't need to. All he needed to say was in the smirk hidden beneath his beard. He wasn't going to the airport. *And neither was I.*

"So, what's your boyfriend think about you walking out here all by your lonesome?" he asked, peering at me from the side of his eye. I looked behind me and was shocked to see two twin-size bunk beds. No sheets, no pillowcases —only a pair of ratty old mattresses. It looked like there was a sleeping bag shoved in the corner, and a large black trash bag was draped over the bottom bunk. I didn't want to know what was on the top bunk. I swallowed the lump in my throat and spun a lie.

"My boyfriend is meeting me at the airport. My whole family is meeting me there. They're all waiting for me. I was supposed to get a ride, but the storm was too thick with cloud cover and I couldn't get a callout. I didn't want to be late and miss my plane, so I started walking. It was a stupid idea, but I figured I could at least get somewhere. I have service now. I could probably just call a cab so that you don't have to drive me," I said, looking at my phone, which had no service.

"No! No, I'm going that way anyhow. I'll drive you," he said, forcing a carefree tone, but it sounded foreign in his mouth. I sucked in a broken breath and nodded.

"Well, if it's not too much of a hassle, I suppose it helps me out. Thank you." Kindness. It wasn't a weapon by any means, but it was all I had. My backpack only had a laptop, my wallet, and a worthless cell phone. I was sure that if I dug to the bottom I could find a pen or two, but would it be enough? I looked at his large meaty hands and dismissed the idea that a pen could save me. It was utterly stupid.

I directed my gaze out the window and once again saw the familiar glowing figure amid the dark blur of the forest. We plowed by, giving me a close-up of my gran's face. It was stolid and still as stone. Her hair lay motionless in the passing wind of the Freightliner, and she was dry in the midst of the storm. I couldn't believe my eyes. She looked right at me.

"I don't get passengers often. So it's a treat for me. I get someone to talk to. Someone to—look at . . ." he said in a gravelly tone. And I hoped he wasn't looking at me then, because he would've seen the disturbance that had been pulsing through my veins and was surely written all over my face.

We drove into town, and I was thankful the moment I saw streetlights again. We passed a gas station, and I told him I could get out there, but he refused to drop me off. When the service returned on my phone, I got a text message to Emma detailing my whereabouts. I told her what Freightliner had picked me up and described the scruffy man sitting next to me.

It didn't bring me any comfort knowing that he had a better chance of being found if I didn't survive this trip because I'd still die. And then, would I even care what happened to him? Probably not. I'd be more interested in haunting him the way my gran did me. I imagined the ways I would do it. I'd probably make him think he was going crazy one day at a time—a slow burn, the way I had suffered through my summer thus far. I couldn't think of anything worse.

But on the fifth time I asked to hop out of the cab early, he let me, and I had a renewed faith that I might just survive the night. When I stepped out of the truck and slammed the door behind me, my knees nearly buckled beneath me, and I let out a long, heavy breath. I watched the Freightliner disappear into the storm. I had a second chance. And I couldn't help but think my gran had something to do with it.

I stood under the roof of the gas station, shivering in the rain as I called a cab. I texted Emma my update and refused to read the long string of texts that she had written me back in response. It wasn't a time to be lectured. I was well aware of all the things I had done wrong. I was just lucky I had survived to learn the lesson. When my cab arrived to take me the rest of the way, I melted into the back seat. My body was like Jell-O after being rigid for so long.

Some thirty minutes later, I finally arrived at the airport. I slung my backpack over my shoulder and stepped into the rain, running to the grand entry overhang. Large glass sliding doors opened, and the bright neon lights welcomed me in from the storm outside. I couldn't be more thankful to be surrounded by all these people. I was safe now, and I'd be home in no time.

I couldn't wait to see my mom and dad. To sleep in my own bed. Did I feel guilty for leaving my friends to fend for themselves? Yes. I did. But what was stopping them from leaving? Why hadn't any of them gone home the second

Trinity went missing? Were they all taking this adult thing so seriously that they wouldn't run back to the safety of their parents' homes? I didn't care if it made me immature. I'd be a coward by night if it meant survival.

"Hello. I'm looking for the next flight out to Decord City," I said, tapping my fingers rhythmically on the high counter.

A pretty uniformed woman with a tight, slick bun typed away on her computer. She cocked her head to the side. "I have a flight leaving in forty-five minutes," she said, her eyebrows raised questioningly.

"Really?"

She looked at me and, with a warm smile, typed a little more. "And there is an open seat in first class with your name on it! I'd be happy to upgrade you for free," she said. Her voice was like a bell. It was the best thing I'd heard all night.

I must have looked pretty distressed for her to bend over backward for me. "Oh my god! Thank you so much! I've never sat in first class," I said, tugging on the bottom of my jacket and brushing the hair out of my eyes.

"My pleasure. You'll have to hurry, though. The security line has quite the wait right now."

"I'll run!" I said, pulling out my wallet.

The sound of her laughter brought a genuine smile to my face. My luck was finally turning around. Maybe that Baylor phenomenon had lifted since we were out of town? She handed me the ticket and stilled as she looked into my eyes.

"Get home safe," she said in a hushed tone. I couldn't pull my gaze from her cool chocolate eyes. Her comment pulsed like a warning. Had I told her I was going home? I hadn't. The intensity broke as she welcomed the next customer. Chipper yet again.

The man's oversized duffle bag bumped into me, and I stumbled backward. Perhaps she knew I was going home because of my ID. Of course. I was only being paranoid. I had to shake it off. I was safe now. I hurried to the security line, and it was backed up, just like she'd said. I stood impatiently at the back of the line, checking the time on my phone. With my luck, I'd probably miss my flight. The only flight I'd ever have a first-class seat in.

Security walked by, taking a special interest in me. I probably looked guilty of something. It was the same look that had gotten me a first-class upgrade that was going to get me a full-body pat-down. If I looked like I'd just seen a ghost, there was nothing I could do about it now.

"Hello, Miss. What flight are you on tonight?" the security guard asked. His brown eyes shone warm against his dark skin.

"I'm heading to Decord City on flight 351," I said.

"351? That leaves in half an hour. You're never going to make it in this line!" he said, stepping back and looking the line over.

I clenched my jaw. It was the very thing I'd feared. "I know . . . How long do you think it will take to get through the line?" I asked, my eyes scanning the crowd.

The woman in front of me turned around and chimed in. "I swear, I've been in this line for twenty minutes and I've only taken two steps forward," she said, her face like stone and brows pinched.

"Oh, no." I'd miss my flight for sure. I was going to have to sleep in the airport until the next flight out.

"Tell you what—follow me," said the guard, lifting the yellow barrier for me to pass. I hesitated only for a second.

"What about me?" the woman asked, throwing up her hand.

"Sorry. Only for flight 351," he replied.

"I'm flight 351!" someone called out from the middle of the line, but the security guard paid no attention. My cheeks heated as I hurried to keep up with his long, quick strides. He lifted the barrier in the front of the line and waved me forward. I blushed as I ducked under his arm.

"Sorry," I said with a wince, stepping in front of a family. The mother groaned, and the father shook his head. The little girl clasped her book of fairy tales to her chest, and she glared at me too. Thankfully, I was called forward quickly. I placed my backpack on the conveyer belt and walked through the metal detector. No pat-down.

"Is this a laptop, hun?" a lady asked as she pointed to the x-ray of my backpack.

"Oh, shoot. Sorry, I forgot to take it out."

"It's okay. No need to re-scan it. Have you found the girl yet?" she asked, staring at the screen.

"What?" My stomach dropped.

"I said, have a safe flight! Next!" she called out, waving the family forward.

I stood frozen, searching for answers in her expression. But, just like at the cemetery, the woman had no idea what she had said. It was much more likely that I was the one hearing things. The little girl's book bumped into my backpack, and her pink roller suitcase nearly plowed over it. I snapped back to the present and took my belongings from the conveyer belt.

I found a seat by my gate with time to spare, and I watched the people pass by in the airport. Such an eclectic crowd. I watched wholesome families pass by. Religious groups. Teens dressed in black from head to toe. The best part was they were all under one roof. Everyone had at least one thing in common, no matter what they looked like. They were headed somewhere. On an adventure, a much-needed vacation, a work opportunity. Some of them might be off to spread the ashes of a loved one. No matter where they were headed, they were waiting, and like me, probably filled with anticipation.

21

I shivered now and then, my clothes still wet from my trek in the storm. The air conditioning pumped throughout the airport, and I wished I had packed a change of clothes in a small bag to take with me. It wasn't long before someone over the speaker called flight 351. And as a first-class ticket holder, I was able to board first. I slung my backpack over my shoulder and hurried to the end of the short line.

I heard a familiar little voice behind me, and I didn't need to look back to know it was the girl that I cut in front of in the security line. She wasn't angry with me now, though, as she chatted with her little brother about how excited she was to ride on a plane for the first time. I listened to her shrill voice, and I remembered a time when soaring high in the sky seemed like a dream come true. Now I would snap my fingers and be home if I could.

"Do you think we're going to see all the people that live in the clouds? All the people with their unicorns? I get the window seat," the little girl babbled.

"No, I get the window seat!" her brother said.

"No! Remember, I gave you half my cookie last night, and you gave me the window seat."

"Mom!" he yelled out. I smiled, remembering that time too. The time when everything turned into a fight and all could be settled with a cookie. I took a step forward as the line moved swiftly.

"Your sister gets the window because she has a very special job to do. She has to find the girl. And she'll be looking out the window for her . . ."

My jaw clenched. I couldn't help but turn around and look at her, and when I did, it was clear that she found my glare intrusive. What girl was she talking about? A girl with a unicorn that lived in the clouds? *I must be losing my mind.*

I stepped forward. My turn was next. I slapped my plane ticket across the palm of my hand as nervous energy sprang to life in my hands. When it was my turn, I stepped up to the lady in uniform, who reached for my ticket.

"Did you find the girl?" she asked absentmindedly.

"What?" I barked, and she snatched the ticket out of my hand, her eyes bulging momentarily before blinking rapidly.

"I said good evening," she muttered, scanning my ticket.

"Oh, I'm sorry I just—"

"Seat A6," she said hastily, eager to move me along. She handed me my ticket, and I trudged down the corridor, checking over my shoulder often. Things were becoming weirder and weirder by the minute, and I couldn't wait to get into the air and leave it all behind me.

When I reached the plane, there was a small gap where the corridor met the plane, and I could see the tarmac below. The cold air rushed in through the gap, and somehow, taking the step over that gaping hole felt like a much larger step than it was. I felt like I was making a decision, choosing a path where there had been a fork in the road.

"Good evening. Your seat is A6 to the left." The flight attendant waved me on to my seat.

The moment I saw my seat, I all but forgot about the fork in the road. The decision I'd made to run. Leave my friends behind. Leave Walker behind. I'd never sat in such luxury on a plane before. The seat was wide and plush. I wondered what kinds of goodies they'd give me for being in first class. All I really wanted was one of those little blankets they hand out during long overnight flights. I reached above my head and twisted the air conditioning nozzle closed.

The family filed in after me and surprisingly took up the first-class seating to my left. I vaguely wondered what the parents did to make enough money to buy such expensive tickets. The boy and girl fought over the window again, and I turned my head and looked out at the workers below. They were hustling and bustling despite the stormy weather. I knew how cold it was outside, but at least these workers were properly dressed.

I took out my cell phone to switch it to airplane mode and was surprised by the numerous text messages I'd received. Not just from Emma, but Noah too. I looked around at all the people filing in and slouched in my seat to read the texts. I opened Emma's long messages and skimmed through them. They started off mad. Angry that I would leave her at such a desperate time. Then it continued to build. She was angry with me for my brash decision to leave. She even went so far as to accuse me of having a death wish myself. I knew that getting in the stranger's truck had been a stupid idea—especially after we knew a killer was on the loose—but I didn't need to hear it from Emma.

It was pure instinct. Something was seriously off at that cabin. Call it the Baylor phenomenon, call it pure evil, but I didn't want to stick around to see just how far it would go. I'd already been dragged underwater by the claws of some malevolent monster, and I didn't want to know what would happen when I met that monster face to face the way Trinity had. I didn't want to be the next girl to wash up on shore. And I refused to feel guilty about that.

Emma had asked several questions about the guy driving, and when I hadn't answered, she'd threatened to tell the cops, who were currently at the cabin writing up reports and collecting the body. She talked about how they questioned everybody who had stayed behind, which hadn't been many. She also mentioned that Kai had had some sort of breakdown, but she didn't know why. And that Kimber had been throwing up in the bathroom for nearly an hour.

It was these texts that made me feel like my instinct to survive had triumphed over the loyalty that I had—should have—given my friends.

Guilt started to spread throughout my chest. Not just about Emma, but Kimber and Kai too. I'd left them in a time of need, and for what? So I could feel safe and toasty in my childhood bed? So my mother could tuck me in at night? I knew the reason I'd fled the cabin was based on fear. But at what cost? I'd already lost one friend. Had I just lost the other ten? Had I given them all a reason to lose trust in me? I wasn't the kind of friend they needed by their side when times turned rough. I was a coward.

I was just about the worst friend anybody could have. And I hadn't even gotten to Noah's texts yet. With some of Emma's messages left unread—I couldn't bear to know what else she had thought about me or what else had happened in the cabin after I'd left—I texted her one last time that I was on the plane and was safe. Then I switched my phone to airplane mode. I couldn't read anymore. The decision had been made. And I'd have to live with myself for that. I tucked my phone away in my damp backpack, and I closed my eyes, leaning my head against the window.

I drifted off to a familiar place, the plane's engine thrumming in my ears and lulling me to sleep. It was the void again. A roaring fire that cast no warmth. A rocking chair that rocked ever so slowly, even though nobody occupied it. I could still hear the kids arguing beside me and briefly thought about how my mind was in two places at once—split between my world and one beyond. I couldn't tell if I was awake or asleep as I explored the empty space.

"Gran?" I called out. Was she here? Or was she still in the woods where I had last seen her? The fire crackled, and the air shifted like it had made space for another soul. Gran sat in the rocking chair like she'd been there the whole time. A book of fairy tales was open in front of her face, a tall stone tower with a small window on the front cover. Long, yellow locks that bound down to the ground. It sparked a memory that I couldn't quite grasp.

"Gran?" I asked, and she lowered the book.

"Oh, dear. What are you doing here?" she asked. Her eyes grew as she took me in. I ran forward, kneeling beside her and grabbing her hands.

"Oh, Gran!" I gripped her hands so tight, surprised that I could feel the flesh of her feeble bony hands in mine. The tears welled in my eyes, as she had never been more real to me since her passing. I looked up into her cloudy eyes, and even through the cataracts, I could see the empathy she held for me.

"Dear. You're not supposed to be here," she said. The book folded closed and lay across her lap.

"I know, Gran! I know! I think I made a mistake. I think I was supposed to stay at the lake. But I was afraid. I don't want to find the girl. I want to go home!" My voice cracked while I pled with her as if she were my gatekeeper.

Gran pried a hand from my grasp and stroked my head gently. Her hands didn't tremble a bit; they hadn't been that way in years. She'd passed just three days before my eighteenth birthday, but it seemed like forever since she'd last run her shaky hands down the back of my head. With everything going on at the cabin, I'd forgotten just how much I missed her. And I knew that, somewhere along the way, that had been my plan. To forget. I thought if I could just put it behind me, the pain of losing her would subside. It didn't though. It only manifested in different ways. Sleepless nights. An emptiness inside. And now guilt for trying to forget.

I vowed to myself that I wouldn't sweep her memory away any longer. That I'd let it come, and that I'd welcome it. I'd share it. And maybe that way, the pain of losing her wouldn't be a secret burden that only I knew I carried. Even though I couldn't feel the warmth from the fire, I could smell her perfume, and it did weird things to my chest. A tightness spread across my throat as I gripped her hand. I knew our time was running short. I couldn't break down now, though. I didn't want her to see me like that.

"I know you're scared, dear. So am I. But you have to help the girl. It's the only way." Gran's features softened as she held my gaze steadily. Her mouth wasn't moving now, but somehow, I still received the message crystal clear.

"Layla Barns? Is she the girl?" I asked.

"The girl." Gran nodded with encouragement.

I didn't know what she was talking about. She never gave me any details—only this one demand. Was I supposed to know how to do this myself? I knew from looking into her eyes that she'd believed in me when I hadn't believed in myself. And if she needed me to do this one thing, then I must do it for her. I must find a way. Essentially, it was my gran's dying wish. One so very important that she had come back from the dead for it. I wanted to ask why, and how, but the most important thing to me in that moment was that she knew she could count on me.

"Okay, Gran. I'm going to do it. I'm going to find her. I want to make you proud. I promise. I promise I'll do it." I said it hastily, but I meant it. I was going to be brave. I was going to face my fears—the thing that had killed Trinity, and the mind-bending phenomenon of the lake that threatened my sanity—and I was going to find that damn girl and help her get home if it was the last thing I did. I stood up, holding onto Gran's hands as long as I could.

"Oh, dear, there's just one more thing. Go easy on that dear boy . . ." Gran's head tilted as she looked up at me.

"Noah?" I asked. My head flinched backward.

"Not that one, dear. The other one." Gran winked a cloudy eye as she became fuzzy and distant.

"Walker? Are you talking about Walker?" I asked. But it was her time to go, and there was nothing I could do to stop it.

I watched her disintegrate into thin air, and all that was left were little particles that shimmered before turning to dust. The fire fizzled out, and the smoke rose into the air, taking the chair and children's book with it. The last to go was a thirteen-day calendar on her wall. A wall that didn't exist. It hung on nothing but thin air, and one day was crossed off in red. Watching the last bit of the red-marked calendar flutter away was like watching my heart leave me. I was hollow without it. And I knew that I had a long road ahead of me if I wanted to get it back.

I lurched when the flight attendant's voice came over the loudspeaker. My eyes opened to the bright cabin and the whining kids. My heart galloped in my chest as I felt the air thin around me. I gasped, hungry for oxygen as I grabbed the seat in front of me. I lowered my forehead to rest on the hard tray folded up before me, and I closed my eyes. That thirteen-day calendar was something I'd seen before. And I couldn't help but think that there were only twelve of us in that cabin. Thirteen if you counted Gunner. That was before Trinity died. It was only after she went missing that the first day had been crossed off. A sickening pit formed in my stomach as I concluded that all my friends in that cabin had a mark on their back. Me included.

I knew how fate worked. I knew how it would bend and twist but never break. Fate was inescapable. It was impervious to change. And people who had escaped their own fate had a funny way of falling back to where they belonged, sooner or later. And oftentimes in a worse situation than they should have been in. No, you couldn't outrun your destiny. And only the desperate tried. If I had a mark on my back, it was going to follow me whether

I was home under my parents' roof or in that cold, haunted cabin. And if I was going to die either way, I'd rather not do it being a rotten friend. I had to get back there. *Now.*

I had to get off the plane, and I had to go back to Baylor Lake. Abruptly, I jumped out of my seat, startling even myself. My legs had a mind of their own, and they strode right up to the flight attendant as she was delivering the safety instructions to the passengers over the loudspeaker. I interrupted without a second thought, and I pled fiercely. She held her microphone down to her chest and glared at me with a slackened jaw.

"I'm sorry. I'm so sorry. I have to get off the plane. I have to get off!" I said hastily, my eyes darting around, looking for signs in her face. I could hear my pleas echo over the loudspeaker from the bits and pieces getting picked up on the microphone. My eyes burned as I tried to hold back tears of regret. I'd made a terrible mistake, and if she could be so kind to let me off the plane and make it right, I'd be forever in her debt.

"Ma'am. Ma'am, you have to sit down. You can't be up here." She patted my shoulder forcefully, trying to calm me and put some distance between us; but there was no stopping me now. I stepped closer, and her eyes filled with alarm.

"I'm sorry. I have to get off. You have to open the door!"

"Ma'am, you need to sit down. We can't open the doors after they've been shut. You can't get off the plane." Her tone was direct and growing louder.

I tried to push past her and get to the door myself, but another flight attendant blocked the way. I was vaguely aware that I was making a scene, but my instincts took over, much like they had when I'd fled the cabin.

"Something's wrong! I've got to go!" I said louder. After hearing my own voice that sounded nothing like me over the loudspeaker, and the several gasps and stirring of chatter that erupted from the passengers, I suddenly realized what I had just done.

"Something's wrong? What's wrong?" a man yelled from a few seats back.

"What's wrong?" somebody echoed from farther still.

A male flight attendant grabbed me firmly across the shoulders and shoved me back to my seat. He forced me down, and I popped back up, relentless. This time, he used more of his strength and I found myself at a crossroads. I was either going to fight this man, probably unsuccessfully, or I was going to comply. I gritted my teeth. It took everything inside me to comply. I would have to get off in Decord City and turn around and fly back. It would take me all night long or longer, and I wasn't sure how long my friends had before their marks would catch up to them. A whole night seemed like an eternity.

Many passengers watched as I settled back down. The little girl beside me was one of them. I glared back at her as she was trying to pull her fairytale book away from her little brother. I couldn't help but notice the cover. It stuck out like a red flag. A tall stone tower with locks of gold flowing down to the bottom. It was the same book my gran had been reading, and I couldn't help but notice that it looked similar to the tower I'd seen in the forest.

It was then that I remembered something. Déjà vu swirled in my head. It had seemed so insignificant at the time. Lainey had pointed out the rapunzel plant. The little purple flowers that covered all the shrubs. It had been right there before me the whole time. The tower. It was everywhere. Even my gran had been showing me the clues along the way. I had tried to find that tower for a second time, and it had disappeared. But somehow, I knew that if I went back into that forest, knowing what I knew now, I'd find it. And when I did? I'd find Layla right along with it.

I still wasn't sure how I could help her. I wasn't worried about it, though. As long as I found the girl, the task would be complete. My mission. Maybe then my friends would be saved, and no more marks would be made. It was a heavy burden to carry, and I wasn't sure I'd be able to do it alone. But I had to try.

The plane's engines got louder, and I could feel the rumble beneath my seat. The flight attendant walked by and handed me a couple of shots of alcohol. It was clear by the look she gave me that she knew I was underage, but she didn't want any trouble, and neither did I. I nodded apologetically and took the two glass bottles from her hand. One of the perks of being in first class, I supposed.

The plane started to roll down the tarmac, and I fixed my eyes on the tiny people waving their lights in their glowing vests down below. The rain was lit by the lights on the plane's wing. I told myself I'd be back that very night. I tried not to fret over the things I couldn't control, but as the plane took off, throwing me back into my seat, I knew I was in for a ride.

22

There wasn't enough oxygen. And what little there was, it was much too thin. Tiny gray spots floated at the rim of my vision, and my head was light as air. I reached for the white bag before me. I wasn't going to throw up, but I was on the verge of hyperventilating. I shouldn't have run. My friends were back there now, and they needed me. I put the bag up to my mouth and took deep breaths as I cowered in the corner of my seat. I didn't want anyone to see me. I already had a target on my back from the stunt I'd pulled with the flight attendant, so I didn't need to draw any more attention to myself than I already had. But as I breathed in the recycled air, hating the way the bag crinkled so loudly, I thought about how I'd let Walker down most of all.

I was ashamed that I'd had to fight my feelings for Walker, even after finding out that he was in love with someone else. As if that was the worst part. As if I hadn't accused him of being the Butcher of Baylor Lake.

The fact that I could still long for the moments we'd spent locked in the bathroom together in the middle of the night . . . the proximity of his breath on my neck . . . it worried me. It worried me because I wasn't thinking clearly. Baylor was like a black hole, stealing my wits and leaving me utterly defenseless.

But what did the curse upon his family even mean? That Walker had had the greatest love story of all time? Did it mean he had no room in his heart for me? Ever? His love story was all dried up?

It was hard to wrap my head around the fact that the one person who made me feel safe, normal, and sane was the one person who I couldn't keep by my side. And what did that mean for me? I thought of the weird things that had been happening to me that made me question my reality, and I placed Walker at the end of a growing list of abnormalities.

Walker had been nothing but kind to me, though. He'd been there for me in a time of need. A lonesome stranger who was looking for a friend. I shouldn't have turned my back on him the way I had. He didn't owe me anything, and just because his heart was spoken for didn't mean I couldn't be loyal to him. He'd saved my life, after all. And it's not that I owed him anything; I *wanted* to be there for him. And I'd let him down.

His golden eyes seemed to shimmer in the sunlight. His dimples hidden beneath his scruff. I even adored the scar through his eyebrow. I thought about it for a second. Hadn't the scar been there before he'd injured himself? I recalled seeing him for the first time in daylight. I'd noticed the scar on his eyebrow then. It must have been a freak accident to have reopened it sometime later. I could have thought all night about Walker's face—every inch of detail—but the turbulence was doing nothing to calm my anxiety. I gave up on the hyperventilation bag and stuffed it in the pocket of the seat in front of me.

I was going to turn around the second this plane landed, and I was going to tell Walker that I was sorry for the way I had acted. And everything I'd accused him of. Did I have to tell him the truth? The truth that I was afraid? Jealous? No, I didn't have to tell him I had feelings for him. I only had to show up. Be there. Loyalty wasn't about being honest a hundred percent of the time; it was about not turning your back on someone in their time of need. Which was exactly what I'd done. I hung my head.

If I hadn't been such a coward, maybe I could have been a good friend. But I was never going to be anything other than a work in progress. I was never going to be anything but the scaredy-cat, the loner, the invisible, the illiterate. I would never get a guy like Walker. Even with his mangled past. Hell, I couldn't even attract Noah until my competition literally dropped dead. And he had been my friend and neighbor since I was a kid. You'd think I would have had time to grow on him. I shook my head and looked out the window, wondering what was wrong with me.

It was black outside, and had it not been for the flashing lights on the wing of the plane, I'd never have known that it was still raining. When the lights flashed, I saw just how torrential the storm had become. I saw the wings flexing under the fierce wind, and I felt the blood drain from my face. Like all these passengers here, I was at the mercy of the storm. A plastic bag caught in the wind. Turbulence shook the plane, and I grabbed my armrests tight, my knuckles turning white as I reminded myself just how safe planes really were. I looked over at the little kids beside me, and they were oblivious. Too young to know a thing about reality. The plane dipped, and I lost my stomach. A shudder from a few rows back. And then I flinched when a woman stole the open seat next to me. She buckled up quickly.

She was rough-looking, kind of like she belonged in the mountains. Which wasn't unusual, since we were flying out of Baylor. But it didn't look like she belonged in first class. Then again, neither did I. I was still wet from the storm and lacking dry clothes. The woman squeezed her eyes shut. Her face was sweaty and flushed. She pulled the seatbelt strap tight against her belly. "Hope you don't mind! I sure would like a seat in first class, and after seeing you flip out earlier, I thought you could use a companion during the rough patches. You think the turbulence is bad now, just wait," she said, her eyes fixed ahead.

I looked the woman over from head to toe. She had auburn hair flecked with gray. I couldn't tell if the creases in her forehead were from time itself or a life full of stress, but I would have guessed she was in her forties. I didn't know a thing about her, but it felt like she was running from something. I looked back to the coach seating and none were the wiser.

"I don't mind." The thought of having someone next to me was a welcome distraction. I only wished that her panic was odorless.

"Oh, good. Because I'm not going back there," she said, hooking a thumb over her shoulder.

"Have you ever been in first class before?" I asked.

"It's my first time."

"Well, then it looks like we have something in common." I offered a small smile and closed my eyes as the plane shook vigorously.

"What's your name?" she asked.

"My name's Kinsley," I said, holding my hand out.

"Name's Mary," she said, taking my hand. "So, you want to tell me why you wanted to get off the plane? You're not some psychic, are you? We're not gonna crash, right?" she said with a breathy chuckle.

"Sorry! No. I'm not a psychic. Far from it. I can't even tell what's going on in the present, let alone predict the future," I said, mimicking her laughter. But it was nervous laughter. I was still uneasy about being in the wrong place at the wrong time. About my poor decisions and lack of foresight. The cabin lights flickered on and off, and I looked around at all the worried faces. I turned to my window for answers, but Mary drew me back in.

"That's normal." Mary's lips were pursed into a thin, straight line.

"Right. I know. I'm just a little jumpy, I guess."

"Are you afraid of flying?" she asked.

"Not particularly. But I've never flown in a storm. And it looks to be a bad one," I said, peeking out the window one more time. Lightning lit the sky, and the wings flexed up and down.

"We're safe up here in the air. These planes are built to withstand a lot. Now, why did you want to get off the plane?"

I cocked my head. It was a lot to unpack. But I guess I had time, being that I was stuck on a wrong way flight. "I only wanted to get off because I made a mistake by coming. I ran from something I shouldn't have. And now, I think I'm ready to face it head-on. Only, they wouldn't let me off the plane."

"So, just to be clear, no predictions of the future?" Mary's eyes seemed to burrow into me, and I laughed, looking down at my lap.

"No. Why? Do *you* have a prediction?" I asked, more curious than ever.

"Me? No! But, I'd have to imagine a girl such as yourself, pleading to get off the plane before it lifts into the air, is a bad omen. Do you believe in bad omens?" The deep crevices of her forehead deepened. My eyes wandered around the cabin as I pondered her question.

"I guess I do."

And then, like a bad omen itself, the plane dropped. Several screams were unleashed throughout the cabin, and for a brief moment, the lights went out. As quickly as it happened, it was over, but the adrenaline remained, coursing through my veins. I was sure my face was as white as a ghost, but Mary looked worse. A sheen of sweat beaded her upper lip. I looked out the window, and as the lights flashed, I could see several panels on the wing were now missing in the severity of the storm.

"See, the thing about bad omens is . . . they precede a terrible event."

Something sickening churned in my chest as I looked at Mary for answers. I wasn't psychic, but it seemed like maybe she had some opinions about the future that she was holding back. And I didn't like where this was heading. Originally, I thought Mary had sat next to me to calm my anxiety. Maybe even for the upgraded seat. But now, I questioned why she was really here.

"You see, I've been watching that storm out there. It's been ebbing and flowing alongside your anxiety. It was pretty bad when you tried to get off the plane, but we were safe on the tarmac. And it seemed to have calmed when I sat down. But when I spoke of bad omens, it took a turn for the worse. You didn't like that, did you? So, why don't you tell me what you really are?" Mary said in a deep secretive tone. What I really was? I wanted to know who *she* really was. She seemed to know more about what was going on than I did.

"I don't know what you're talking about," I said, shaking my head. But just then, the plane dipped again, and the same voices from before called out in fear. I tightened my grip on the armrest, my fingernails bending against the plastic.

"See! You're doing that, aren't you?" She leaned in, her face jutting toward mine.

"No! I'm not doing anything!" I said. Mary's distraction was no longer welcome, and I couldn't get away as I was trapped in my seat, pressed against the window.

The flight attendant's voice came over the loudspeaker as Mary and I were locked in an uncomfortable stare. "Please remain seated with your seatbelts securely fastened. There is turbulence now, and we expect it to get worse before it gets better. We're going to climb in altitude to look for smoother patches of air. Please bear with us."

I pried my eyes from Mary's and pulled on my seatbelt strap. It was already tight against my hips.

"You better make sure we climb to smoother air," Mary said, pressing the back of her head against her headrest and closing her eyes. The plane rumbled, and my head bobbed up and down, but my gaze never left her face.

"Stop that!" she hissed under her breath. Her eyes remained closed, and a bead of sweat dripped down her temple.

The plane dove, and several more people screamed. My heart lurched in my chest as I stared at Mary, questioning if she had foreseen this bad omen.

"I said *stop that*! Control it!" she hissed through her grinding teeth. Perhaps *she* was the bad omen. Perhaps *she* was the one responsible for all of this. And then I remembered the Baylor phenomenon. The manifestation of fear itself. But surely not; we weren't in Baylor any longer. Mary's eyes watered with panic and were flanked red with fear. I wasn't afraid of flying, but clearly, she was. She'd sought me out because she couldn't stop thinking about a crash. She thought I had the answers when I tried to get off the plane. But she was crazy. And she was sitting right next to me, her negative energy radiating off her in waves and filling the cabin.

"I'm not doing anything!" I snapped at her. The plane shook, along with my anger.

"Stop it! Make it stop!" she seethed. The storm was angry, both inside and outside of the cabin.

"I'm not doing it!" I yelled, snapping as the anger boiled inside me, clashing with the fear and anxiety to make for one giant force.

"I. Said. St—"

Mary pulsed. And just as the threat reached the back of my throat, an explosion ignited the tension that had been building inside me all summer long. A lightning bolt flashed outside the window, and the cabin plunged vertically.

The flight attendant in the aisle lifted into the air, her back slamming against the ceiling of the plane and then plummeting to the floor with a thud. The screams sounded distant with the whoosh of blood hammering through my ears. The turbulence was so violent my head shook wildly, making my vision no more than a blur. I whipped my head from side to side, looking out my window. It wasn't until another lightning bolt lit the air that my eyes beheld the blurry truth. The wing was glowing red and missing the last three-quarters.

I stopped breathing the moment I saw the wreckage. My stomach was in a perpetual state of free-fall. I was frozen in fear as my mind raced to understand. Was this it? Was I dying now? The turbulence was bad. Terrible. But we couldn't survive with only one wing. I was going to die a disloyal friend. It had been my latest fear, and it was coming true. I knew my time was limited.

A hand gripped mine, the strength bone-crushing. It was just enough to grab my attention. But when I looked over expecting to see Mary blazing with rage, I saw my gran sitting in the seat instead. I wasn't sure if she'd possessed Mary, or if Mary had simply vanished. But it was my gran sitting next to me, her hand on mine. My heart kicked as my eyes took her in.

One last comfort. Like an angel here to collect me. She was as real as anything could be. She was blood and flesh, and she was right next to me. In that moment of bewilderment and wonder, I forgot my life was ending. I guess that's how it was meant to be. Your mind conjures up something so unimaginable that it protects you from the tragedy at hand. I remembered the stunning Ferris wheel glowing in the dark waters the night I'd almost drowned.

"Gran?" My breath left me as the lights flickered on and off. Gran was the only vision I had that was clear and unwavering. The screams were never-ending, but they had faded further in the distance.

"Why are you doing this?" she asked, her voice not her own but Mary's deep threatening tone. Her forehead was creased and pulled tight.

Why am I doing this? I wasn't doing anything. I'd already told Mary that. I couldn't control this any more than I could control the storm outside.

"Gran?" I asked, not knowing if it was crazy Mary or my late grandmother. My eyes searched the cabin frantically, and my stomach was reaching its upper limit of motion sickness. It swirled up to my chest and was approaching my throat. I didn't know where the flight attendant who had hit the ceiling had gone, but there were several empty seats now. Missing passengers. Was I doing this? Was *I* the bad omen? Was it the mark of fate that I had brought onto this plane?

I looked at the kids beside me, and the dread on their little faces made me even sicker. I wanted to help them. I wanted to save them. And if I thought for just one minute that this was my fault? I'd surely die from a broken heart. I didn't deserve to live if this was my doing. I felt my face turn cold with mortification as the plane spun in circles, spiraling down toward the ground. I sucked in a deep broken breath.

"Gran? Help! Help!"

"You can do this," Gran said, her sweet voice encouraging as it broke through Mary's rage.

"No! No—" I pled. I couldn't do it. I couldn't do anything. I could barely get into college. What made her think I could save a one-winged plane from crashing?

"*Wake. Up!*" Gran pled, her pale green eyes glistening. There one second and gone the next.

"You did this!" screeched Mary, her voice crude and vile. She was back with a vengeance. Gran's face bled into the auburn hair with its gray flecks. "You did this!" She crushed my hand, and pain shot up my arm. My gran was long gone.

I took a blow to the face. It was a dull pain that sank into my cheek and spread beneath my eye. The lights flickered, and I saw the children's book with the tower and the long blonde locks that flowed to the ground sprawled across my lap. Only, this time, it wasn't a cartoon drawing but the exact haunted tower I'd seen in the woods.

Something sparked in my mind, and I knew what I had to do. But did I have enough time? The lights went out and didn't come back on. Through the darkness, I saw the city lights outside my window fast approaching—a blur of undeniable speed.

We were going to crash all right. I wasn't sure if it was the free fall or the spinning, but my head felt light . . . as if I were flying. I had the urge to run. Flee. But I was so disoriented, I didn't know up from down. It didn't stop me though. It couldn't stop me from wanting to survive. Nothing could. The instinct I had to save my life was pure and raw, and it took hold of me now.

I unbuckled myself and was immediately lifted into the air. Mary's grip on my hand was painful but grounding. I felt my sweaty hand pull out of hers, and I slammed into a seat, my shoulder smashing into a corner, my arm bending until it broke like a twig, and my legs plunging into passengers on my way to the back of the plane.

My head slammed against the back wall. The pain was intense. Like submerging my head in ice-cold water. It trickled down to my neck and out through my shoulder blades. I didn't know if it was blood, and I didn't care.

I was pressed against several bodies that were no longer living—the lucky ones—and a few that were. Those that were broken and battered still felt the crippling fear of the last few seconds before the plane crashed.

I wished the blow had taken me out, but I had survived to watch the end. It was unlike anything I had ever seen.

It happened in slow motion. The city lights lit the cabin from the outside in. The nose of the plane impacted the ground, and suddenly there were flames everywhere. The stark bright light of the explosion illuminated every single soul as it took their lives.

The family up front, Mary, the newlyweds, the elderly, the kids, the pregnant, the men, the women. I saw it all. I saw every last breath. And I couldn't help the guilt that spread throughout my body, from my fingertips to my toes, knowing that I was the one who had created it all. That it was my mark that had taken their lives. I deserved to watch every face suffer.

Moments after the light reached me, I felt the wave of heat. The plunge of ice around my head and neck immediately turned to a furious blazing fire. White flames heated my insides by the time they had barreled halfway up the plane. It was like being burned at the stake—only I hadn't committed this crime by choice. I'd never wanted this. I'd never wanted anybody to get hurt. And then I was dead.

23

I died. Every damn cell in my body died as my body ignited in flames. Obliterated. I got every ounce of what I deserved. It was my raw emotion that had brought that plane down, drawing it into the vortex of my fear. I sucked in a deep, shuddering breath before lurching forward. My eyes sprung open and I took in my afterlife. The odd thing was, it was identical to the life I'd had before. I was in bed at the cabin. Drenched in a cold sweat. My heart galloping as I struggled to slow my breathing.

My head pounded as if I really had crashed and burned. But hadn't I? I brought my hands to my face. My fingertips searched for marks. Evidence of the crash. But there was nothing. Nothing external anyway. My insides were clearly marked. Traumatized. I was still sick to my stomach, and my head . . . my head felt like it was torn in two and bleeding profusely. I reached up to my hairline, but there was no such sign. The whole thing had been a nightmare. A ruse. I couldn't wrap my head around it. I threw off the covers and jumped to my feet, my head pounding excruciatingly as I rose. I grabbed at my temples as the pain nearly took me to my knees. Tears pricked my eyes, and a low whimper shuddered from my throat. I closed my eyes, trying to breathe through the stabbing pain, and then slowly, ever so slowly, I stood upright.

If the plane crash had only been a nightmare, then the guilt could subside. I hadn't killed all those people, and I didn't deserve this pain. I told myself that over and over. *I didn't deserve this pain.* But there it was, persisting. Etched in stone, branded upon me for life.

I licked my lips and wondered what I would find downstairs. I couldn't be sure of anything. I lifted my hands before my eyes and scrutinized them. As far as I could tell, they were mine. The same old hands I'd always had. The weird-shaped fingers, the bulbous knuckles. My mom used to call them piano fingers. I just thought they were freakishly long. I went to the bathroom in search of a mirror. But as I stood in front of it, I couldn't bring my eyes to meet my reflection. I didn't know who would stare back at me.

I watched my hands trail around the rim of the porcelain sink, making slow circles, until I was ready to face myself. I lifted my gaze and stared deep into her eyes. She was a shell of the girl I once knew. Something was missing, too. Something I couldn't quite put my finger on. It was the thing that kept me from identifying with her. The reflection scowled back at me, and I cowered, pulling my gaze away from her intense stare. I grabbed my toothbrush and vigorously brushed my teeth, looking anywhere but directly at the girl in the mirror. I didn't know her, and I didn't want to. I remembered Walker. And I remembered my promise to help him.

I had to find him to tell him everything I knew. And together, we needed to find that damn girl. But I didn't know how to find him, and I was pretty sure that he'd never want to see me again. I recalled the look in his eyes as he'd stood over Trinity's dead body. I hadn't been able to read that look then, but now, I imagined his eyes had been filled with sorrow. I was the only person he felt like he could relate to, and in a world where he felt as alone as I did, I'd left him. Worse yet, I'd accused him of murder. He probably never wanted to see me again. But that wasn't going to stop me from trying. I had to finish what I'd started. Not because I was a badass, but because I had no other choice. I couldn't leave Baylor if I wanted to. The crash had proven that much.

I tiptoed downstairs, afraid of what I might find around the corner. Afraid of all the angry, judging eyes. I knew I'd left them to handle the investigation by themselves, and I'd have to beg for their forgiveness. I'd do it, though; I was prepared. I could live with that mistake. I could live with anything, as long as I hadn't killed off a plane full of people.

Scarlett May rambled, the sound of her light and airy voice meeting me on the stairs. I listened while making my slow descent. "I just don't know what I'm gonna wear. Because on one hand, I want to look cute, which would mean the heels, but on the other hand, it's like, how can I *not* wear the cowgirl boots?" It was a good sign that she had nothing more pressing to worry about than her clothing.

"Well, I think you have to wear the cowgirl boots. I mean, they're classics. And the Water's Edge Concert is country anyway. I was thinking of wearing a plaid flannel. Asher has this one that I like, blue and gray. It's oversized, so I can just wrap it around my waist. That'd be cute, right?" Kimber said.

I stared at them from the stairs. I wasn't sure how this conversation fit in the morning after finding Trinity's body, but I was about to find out. The next step I took, the stairs creaked, and both girls looked in my direction.

"What? What are you gonna wear?" Kimber asked. Their empty eyes waited for an answer. It was so simplistic that it hurt. I continued down the stairs, slowly trailing my hand down the wooden banister.

"Um, I'm not sure."

"You might want to figure it out soon. The concert's tonight. We're thinking of going country. We all should," Scarlett May said.

"Yeah, maybe," I said under my breath as I passed through the living room.

The girls continued to chatter as I walked into the kitchen. Everything was the same. Just as normal as could be. Nobody seemed shaken from seeing Trinity last night or being questioned by the cops. Nobody looked at me with judging eyes. It was as if it had never happened. Ethan looked at me and smiled, holding up a coffee cup. I looked at the blue ceramic mug and then back to him. It was as if he was almost . . . pleasant. Was that possible?

"Kinsley? Are you all right?" he asked when I failed to respond.

"Yes. Yes. I'm all right. Just a little tired. Coffee would be great, thank you."

He then poured me a cup of coffee, and I sipped it, assessing everybody one by one. There wasn't an ounce of guilt wafting through the air. No grief. No tension. It was almost as if I was living in a parallel universe. Was that possible? Had the plane really crashed? Could this truly be my afterlife? Somewhat the same but better in certain little ways? The caffeine did wonders to help me, and I almost felt myself succumbing to the positive vibe in the cabin. *Almost.* But no matter how much I wanted to stay and enjoy myself with my friends, I had a nagging voice in the back of my head telling me to get to that tower.

Mason sat in his boxers, debating with Kai who the opening artist would be at the concert. Noah sat alongside the other guys, but he paid them little attention. His eyes were trained on me. He, too, was in a good mood, a flirty one. He smiled out of the corner of his mouth and winked at me while I tried to put the pieces together. I couldn't get over how weird it was to see everybody happy.

It was as if it were the first day we arrived at the cabin with the best summer of our lives still ahead of us. I looked around the kitchen, scratching my head. Something else was off. There wasn't one single sign of the raging party we had thrown last night. No plastic cups. No hangovers. No muddy footprints tracked in from the storm. It was perfect. I almost expected Trinity to walk around the corner. Had she even died at all?

Kai turned up the volume on the TV. "One hundred forty-seven people died Thursday night on flight 351 to Decord City. Caught in the storm, the plane came crashing down in the middle of Grand and Fifth, demolishing the historical bank here in Charlee City."

My gut sank. The TV showed the wreckage of the plane crash. The crash I'd caused. The crash I'd *died* on.

"Wow, check it out. A plane crashed!" Mason said, pointing to the TV.

I nearly spilled my coffee and quickly put the mug down on the counter. I had to get out of here. Finding this girl couldn't wait one more second. I pulled the back door open and grabbed my shoes. I laced them up, ignoring the fact that, even though they'd been left out in the rain all night, they were bone dry.

At this point, nothing in my life made sense . . . but that could change. It could, if I found the girl. I was convinced of that. She could right this wrong. I'd do my part in finding her, and she'd do hers. She'd give me my life back. My sanity. I set out on the trail, and I didn't look back at the cabin as I disappeared into the woods. My sights were set on Walker and the tower.

Time flew by. The entire day passed as I searched for the tower. It wasn't where I'd left it—not at the clearing. But I'd stay out all night searching if I had to. And when I got cold, tired, and hungry, I'd just remember the faces illuminated by the explosion of the plane. I'd remember my gran sitting next to me when I'd visited her in the void. When I told her that I'd do everything in my power to find this girl for her. For me. And for my friend, Walker. Because he was a tortured soul, just like the one I'd become.

My legs were weak, and I was dehydrated, but I kept going. And when I felt the eyes of the forest watching me, I had enough grit to ignore it. *Let them watch me.* It wasn't going to consume me the way it had before. I was different now. I was on a mission. But the new me only lasted for so long. There were only so many twigs snapping that I could endure before my heart picked up speed, and I was utterly crushed to realize that I was the same old girl. A girl who was afraid of her own shadow. A girl who'd run away.

Whispers swirled in the wind, and a light mist rolled in from the west. A hand grabbed my shoulder, and I spun around to find Walker's golden eyes. I all but lunged into his arms. He laughed, happy to see me too.

"Walker! I'm so glad to see you! I'm so sorry I left. But I'm here now. I'm here now." I said. He pulled away and looked at me with an arched brow. The gash had healed into a bloodied scab. The scar would be worse than it had been before.

"I'm happy you came back. But I didn't know you left," he said with a shrug. The weight of a dozen bricks lifted from my shoulders. I never wanted him to feel abandoned by me, especially since that's what his ex had done to him.

"Yeah, I don't think anybody did. Hey, question—was there a storm last night?" I asked. Walker looked at me questioningly, and I hated the way it made me feel. Like I was crazy. Like he *knew* I was crazy.

"You're asking me if there was a storm last night? I mean, you were there, right? Do you not remember?" he asked.

"No, I know I was there. I just . . . can you just, answer the question?" My eyes dropped to the ground, unable to face him.

"Yes. There was a storm," he said.

"Okay. Did we happen to find anything down by the lake? Anything . . . abnormal?" I asked, my eyes still searching the ground.

"Well, if you consider Trinity's body abnormal, then yes. We found something," he said.

"Oh, thank god!" I blurted, giving him another hug. Relief washed over me, and I *knew* I wasn't crazy. Walker made me feel normal. It was always him. Only him.

"Don't sound too excited now," he said, his eyes wide.

"No! I didn't mean it like that! I just meant . . ."

"I'm just messing with you, Wilde. I know what you meant."

I reluctantly pulled my arms off his neck and took a step back. "You do?" I asked.

"Let me guess, nobody seems to care this morning?" he asked, his golden eyes boring into mine as he tilted his head.

"How? How did you know that?"

"Remember? It's that Baylor phenomenon. Everybody makes you feel crazy here. It's just the way it is." Walker shrugged and began to walk down the trail. I followed quickly behind him without a thought.

"I think I know where Layla Barns is." I had to say it. If I didn't say it then, I was afraid I never would. Walker wanted to know more about what happened to Layla. It was tangled in his family history, and he sought answers. I couldn't blame him. And for whatever reason, my gran had sent me to help him get those answers. Furthermore, I needed to help the girl. For all I knew, Walker had been summoned to help her too. She wasn't dead like everyone had thought; she was hiding. Hiding in the stone tower like in the fairy tale. I was convinced of that.

"Where she *is*?" he asked.

"She's alive . . ." I said, grabbing his shoulders.

"Really? What makes you think so?" he asked.

I tried not to let the excitement in his voice distract me from telling him all I knew. But there was that small nagging voice that said, *He's too excited. He'll leave you the second you tell him what he is looking for.* I ignored it. Walker and I were friends, he wouldn't leave me.

"Yes. It just clicked. All the signs. Layla isn't buried in the cemetery with her lover, she's hiding. And I think she needs our help getting home. Have you ever seen a tower out here in the woods?" I asked.

"No. What kind of tower?"

"It's this really beautiful old stone tower. There's no door at the base, but there is a window at the very top. I saw it one time when I was looking for the graveyard. I've been looking for it all day, but it seems to be moving on me. I can't find it." I lifted my hand in the air, then let it fall.

"Ah, that happens here, too. Things go missing. They get turned around and spit back out in a different location. But that's okay. We can still find it. Just takes a little work." Walker was optimistic, and it was infectious. I nodded.

"Okay. And how are we going to do that?"

"Stop right there. And close your eyes," he said, placing his hands upon my shoulders. I gazed into his eyes before I closed my own. Completely at his mercy, I breathed deeply, feeling his warm hands on me and wishing they would travel. "Remember the Baylor phenomenon?"

"Yes," I said, with my eyes closed.

"It doesn't just work against us. It runs both ways. We can make it work for us too."

"Like magic?" I asked, scowling.

"Shhh. Now just *be*. Listen to my breath, inhale and exhale." He took in a deep audible breath and let it out. "Match yours to mine."

I listened, tuning out all the sounds from the forest. The little branches cracking, the birds chirping, and the subtle wind rustling through the leaves. It was harder to tune out his touch, but eventually, I shut that down too. I focused all my energy on his breathing. Matching my breaths to his was easy; not completely falling for him was another story.

"Now imagine the tower," he said. I didn't want to. I wanted to imagine his hands slipping down to the small of my back. I wanted to imagine his breath on my neck. I frowned. Why did I do this to myself? Why did I like a guy who would never like me back? And why was I pretending to summon a stone tower? It would never work.

"You're not focusing. You need to focus for this to work," he said. I felt my cheeks warm, and I started over, drowning out the sounds of the forest and listening to his breathing. Then I imagined the tower as I had seen it before.

I could see the stone wall up to the window. I could see every single crack in the mortar, but more than seeing it, I could *feel* it. I could feel the cold, damp stone beneath my hands, and I could smell the moss on the stone.

"Now, imagine where it is," Walker said softly.

I didn't even have to think about it. I lifted my hand and pointed. It wasn't far. And it also wasn't where I had seen it last. My eyes shot open and narrowed on my pointed finger. There was no path before me, and I immediately doubted my telepathic skills. I cocked my head to the side and smiled at Walker, embarrassed for trying to be something I wasn't.

"Guess that didn't work," I said, wanting to shrink.

"What are you talking about? Of course it worked." Walker grabbed my hand and tugged me forward into the bushes where there had been no path before.

"Are you serious?" I asked, not paying attention to anything other than his hand holding mine. They fit together so perfectly. If I hadn't known any better, I would say we were meant for one another.

The bushes nipped at my legs as I tried to take large steps and tiny hops over them. "How far do you think it is?" he asked.

"Well, I mean, I don't think it was far, but that wasn't anything. I didn't *do* anything. We can't trust what just came up in my mind out of nowhere! This is ludicrous!" I said doubtfully. Somebody had to say it. Walker stopped and dropped my hand. Disappointed, I looked to the ground. My feet were hidden beneath the rapunzel bushes.

"Tell me this, Wilde . . . if I had closed my eyes and told you I had a gut feeling, would you think a thing of following it?" I imagined Walker telling me he had a gut feeling. Good lord, I'd follow his gut feeling anywhere. But I wasn't going to tell him that.

"But that's different—"

"How?"

It was a good question. I trusted him. I shrugged.

"Exactly. It's not different at all. You have to learn to trust yourself, Wilde. There are going to be times in your life when you can't trust anyone, and it's going to fall on you to take care of yourself. You need to show up for yourself." It was as if he was reading my thoughts. Could he do that? I looked up at him. And there was so much warmth behind his eyes in that moment, I almost *did* believe in myself. I nodded, and we trudged on through the thick bushes.

"Do you see all these purple flowers?" I asked, watching my feet disappear beneath the shrubs.

"The rampion? They're also known as rover bellflower."

"And rapunzel," I said before lifting my head to behold the stone tower. I stopped, and Walker looked back at me before lifting his gaze. He also seemed surprised to see it standing before us.

We both stood still, taking it in. It was a beautiful sight. Not the one I had seen before in the middle of the clearing. No, this time the tower was planted in the rocks at the water's edge. I had never seen it while out boating, but I wished I had. It was breathtaking. Walker looked back at me excitedly, and I felt like we had a small win. I smiled, the warmth of his eyes filling my chest. It was pride like I hadn't felt in a long time.

"Just like magic . . ." I whispered.

"See! I told you! You just have to believe in yourself!" he said, striding forward. I smiled to myself as I hopped over the bushes behind him. I guess I could do *something* right. This one small thing . . .

As we reached the tower, I was so overjoyed that I didn't realize at first that there was an actual door. But when Walker opened it and peeked his head inside, my brief pride was replaced with something pungent and cold. It was the familiar sorcery of insecurity. It felt like I was about to lose the only solid thing I had in my life. Because once we climbed those stairs, something bad was going to happen, and I was going to lose him.

Losing Walker wasn't the only thing I was afraid of. What happened when I found the girl? Layla. How was I supposed to help her? What was I to do? Was I really the chosen one for this particular mission? Or was I going to let my gran down? Somehow, I knew it was the latter. I couldn't do this. And if I could, it wouldn't be done right.

Walker urged me to hurry and join him. We climbed the steps, and I stayed close behind him. The tower was dark and cold. It must have dropped twenty degrees the moment we stepped inside. I reached out and touched Walker's back, and he grabbed my hand, holding it warmly and securely, giving me the strength to continue. We took the rest of the stairs together, and I never wanted it to end. Sure, my life had been hell since arriving at the cabin, but Walker made it right. Whatever was waiting for me at the top of the tower could wait a little longer because, in that moment, my hand in his, I finally felt whole, and I didn't want to let go of that.

24

The tower was cool and musty. We were losing daylight. It wasn't quite dark outside yet, but inside the stone walls, there was almost no light. With only one window at the very top, the spiral staircase was pitch black and ominous. I took the steps one at a time, slower than Walker would have liked. But, while he was eager to find answers, I didn't want this to end. Not just because I was afraid of failing, but because I was equally afraid of succeeding. Neither outcome worked in my favor.

Walker tightened his grip on my hand and gently urged me forward. I felt comfort knowing that he was right in front of me. I felt ahead with my foot, feeling for each step before I took it. My eyes were wide as I searched for light. The tension in the air loosened as we came up the last rung of the stairs and light from the sunset sky came through the single window. Pink and orange lit up the landing, and had the stakes not been so high, it would have been romantic.

Timidly, I walked to the middle of the open floor, slipping my hands into my back pockets and allowing my eyes to sweep the tower. There were no signs of the girl. Boards were piled up in the shadows, knickknacks stashed here and there. Trash and other belongings from transients that had sought shelter at one time or another. I wondered if we would run into the person who'd been sleeping here when my eyes landed on the burgundy leather jacket crumpled on the floor. *Trinity's jacket.*

"Whoa, what's that?" said Walker, grabbing my arm. I whipped my head around and followed his gaze up the tower wall. It was hard to see in the shadows, but I could make out numbers written in red paint across the rock. I took several steps forward, scrutinizing the sloppy numbers. It hit me like a ton of bricks. It was one through thirteen. The number one was crossed out in dripping red paint. At least, I hoped it was paint.

"What do you think it means?" he asked. He ran his fingers across the paint and then drew his hand back, examining the red chalky powder on his hand. I glanced back at Trinity's jacket.

"I've been seeing this in my dreams. I'm not sure what it means, but I have a theory."

"And what's that?"

"Well, it's always thirteen. And including myself and the dog, there's thirteen of us in the cabin. I never related it to people until one of the numbers was crossed off. It was only after Trinity went missing that a slash went through the number one. After that, I just had a feeling." More like a deep, sinking sense of doom in the pit of my stomach.

"I think it's kind of like a hit list of sorts. I think we all have a mark on our backs. It's stupid, and I have no proof. It's just a thought. A worry." I turned away from the red-painted numbers and looked out the window. In contrast, it was a beautiful view of the lake. I could see the crowd in the far distance waiting for the band to play at the Water's Edge Concert.

"You've seen this in your dreams?" Walker asked. Before I could answer him, a loud thump sounded from the base of the tower and echoed up the spiral stairwell, sending chills down my spine.

"What was that?" I whispered.

Walker made his way to me. At first, I assumed that it had been the wind slamming the door shut, or even an animal, but as the seconds ticked by, it became clear that what we heard were footsteps climbing the stairs. Not just any footsteps, but heavy, nefarious stomping that grew closer and closer. Much too heavy to be the Layla Barns I'd pictured in my head.

With each step, my heart pounded harder and my breath quickened. Walker slowly moved in front of me, spreading his arms in a protective stance. He had saved my life once before, and I didn't doubt he would try his best to do it again if necessary.

I craned my neck to look over his shoulder at the stairwell opening. A dark figure approached, and he was gigantic, both wide and tall. He grumbled to himself like a vicious animal—nothing intelligible. Just feral. There was a moment when he froze upon the landing and the three of us sized each other up. But this one man was bigger than the both of us combined. And once he realized it, he trudged forward. Walker took a step back, and I did too. And as he stepped into the sunset's rays, I recognized him from the grocery store. It was Big Jimmy.

He'd been unkempt the day I'd met him and looked even worse now. He didn't need to come any closer for me to know that he had gone off the rails.

And even through the dimming pink light, I could see the ill intent in his eyes. I didn't dare look away. He looked toward his stash of belongings. The empty liquor bottles, broken wood pallets, and Trinity's jacket. I remembered the stories around the campfire at Sampson's house. They'd said he was crazy. They'd said he'd hurt people. A liability, they'd called him. And now, we were in his hideout, and we had seen too much.

Jimmy pulled something from his belt buckle, and a switchblade flipped, catching the light from the window. I failed to swallow the lump rising in my throat. Jimmy held it out as if he were ready to strike, stab, and rip from top to bloody bottom.

"Jimmy! Jimmy, it's me. We met one time at the grocery store. Do you remember me?" I asked, trying to think of something to snap him from the trance he seemed to be in. Like a dog on point, he took another step forward, slow and stealthy. If he was the dog, we were the flock he was targeting.

"You gone and done it now, didn't you?" His voice was deep and gravelly.

"Did what?" I asked, taking another step back in unison with Walker.

"You went a-looking, didn't you?" He tossed the blade in the air and caught it again, his eyes never leaving us.

"Looking for what, Jimmy?" I asked, grabbing the backs of Walker's arms.

"You're looking for her. The girl!" he yelled, and a deep red flesh colored his neck and into his face.

"We're not looking for anybody! We just found this tower, and we were curious, but we'll be on our way now."

I took a step from behind Walker, but Jimmy called my bluff and lunged. I let out a yelp and jumped backward. But there was no more room, and my back slammed against the stone wall. Jimmy continued and Walker jumped in front of me, tackling him.

There was no fight—not even a chance. Jimmy threw Walker to the ground and continued coming for me. But Walker kicked out and snagged his leg, and Jimmy went down with a thud.

I tried to run, but Jimmy kicked his giant foot and caught me in the stomach. All the air went out of my lungs, and I dropped to my knees.

I was only vaguely aware of the scuffle that was taking place feet away from me; my focus was on taking my next breath. My arms were wrapped tightly around my stomach, my mouth open and hungry for air.

"I told you! I told you! The butcher will come back!" Jimmy yelled as Walker did everything in his power to keep him from me. "I told you! And now you're gonna pay!"

I had just gotten a foot underneath me to stand as Jimmy ran at me with the knife. And as I began to get up, Walker slammed into Jimmy's back. The three hundred-plus pounds of Big Jim tripped over me as I rose, and the force of his weight couldn't be stopped as he tumbled forward. He bashed into the wall and out the window of the tower. I was smashed to the floor, trampled by his momentum. What once was a tiny window that had barely let the light of the sunset slip into the shadows was now a gaping hole in the side of the tower.

Having been kicked again in the ribs, I lay across the floor of the tower gasping for air. The pain was muted by shock. I knew the threat was gone by the lifting of tension in the air, but I didn't quite realize what had happened until I looked at Walker. His hands were on top of his knees, and he was drawing in quick, shallow breaths. His forehead was creased, and his eyes were large with surprise. I looked out the window, the only viable exit, and I saw the multitude of missing stones. I scrambled to my feet, placing one hand around my waist and one on the cold rock wall, and peered out the gaping window.

Big Jimmy lay sprawled across the rocks below, the gentle water lapping at his limbs.

I sucked in a breath and whipped my head around toward Walker. "We killed him!"

I said it. I said it out loud. But just because it was true, didn't mean I was ready to accept it. Hearing myself say it was like an accusation. And even though it was self-defense, I knew my life would never be the same. Because I had killed a man.

"Wilde!" Walker whispered, his eyes not on the body below, but on the wall of the tower. I followed his gaze to the red-stained numbers upon the stone. Ever so slowly, a red slash etched its way through the number two, sending an electric tingle inching down my spine.

Neither one of us had any words. We stared in disbelief, panting. When the red paint had stopped dripping down the wall, the music began across the lake at the Water's Edge Concert.

"Thirteen people? Thirteen people have a mark on their back?" Walker asked.

I pressed my back against the stone wall and my knees trembled under the limp weight of my body. I slumped down to the floor, wrapping my arms around my knees and starting to tremble. At least . . . at least it wasn't only the people in my cabin that had the mark. Perhaps it was thirteen Baylor residents or visitors. Maybe it was at random.

"Wilde? Are you okay?" he asked. I nodded curtly. But I *wasn't* okay. Nothing was okay. I'd killed a man. I had crashed a plane. And now eleven more people were going to die—and for what? I raised my eyes to see Walker's concern in the fine lines around his eyes. He didn't seem to be rattled by what had happened here this evening, and that should've concerned me more . . . but I sought comfort in his warm eyes. His face softened with a smile and I sucked in a deep, refreshing breath.

"I'm sorry we didn't find what we were looking for here. I don't know what I was thinking. This girl, Layla. I kind of imagined her with the long locks of blonde hair flowing from this broken window down to the base of the tower, but it was nothing more than a fairy tale." I shook my head, my eyes wandering around the small landing.

"Don't apologize. It's not your fault we didn't find the girl. Maybe she doesn't exist anymore. Who knows? But if it's okay with you, I'd like to keep looking for her, with your help. I've gotten closer in the last few days with you than I ever have before. And I've been following this case for a long time." His eyes stared unfixed into the distance and his face fell with disappointment.

"Why is that? Why do you care so much? You have to give me some answers here." I said, looking up at him. He took a seat next to me and propped his forearms on top of his knees, interlacing his fingers.

"I . . ." Walker stammered, his gaze pensive and sad.

It felt like I'd asked the wrong questions. I knew there were secrets between us, but I never knew when something I said would draw out his pain. The tower was silent except for the country music echoing across the lake. I knew he didn't want to talk about it, but I needed to know who the butcher was, and why he was so invested. I'd promised my gran I would help him, and Layla, but I didn't even know what I was supposed to help them with. My eyes fell on the pile of stashed goods that were hidden within the shadows as I thought of how I'd failed to keep my promise to my gran.

"Long ago, I made a promise to help the girl, too. You're not the only one getting messages to bring her home," Walker said in a defeated tone.

"Really? Why didn't you say so?" I asked.

"I was afraid you wouldn't help if you knew the truth," he said.

"Why? What truth?" I couldn't imagine a reason to not help Walker look for Layla, especially after he had saved my life. I owed him so much.

Walker frowned. He tried to speak, but nothing came out.

"Who are you getting messages from?"

His brows creased and he dropped his head in his hands.

"Are they dreams, like mine?" I asked. But he didn't move, and he didn't speak. Why was he keeping secrets from me? Why wouldn't he just talk to me? I sighed. I couldn't go on like this. And I wouldn't leave this tower until my questions were answered.

Something stole my attention away from Walker's silence. I squinted into the darkness. "What's that?" I asked, nodding to the pile of Jimmy's stolen possessions. Something was lying in the shadows. Another personal item. But this one wasn't Trinity's. Walker jumped to his feet and picked it up. It was a purse. He turned it over in his hands, and I watched him intently.

"That's Trinity's jacket," I said. Walker looked back at me and swallowed, turning his gaze back to the bag. He didn't say anything. "But that's not her purse. I've never seen that before."

He stood there, rigid. After a long moment of silence, he came to sit by my side again. He handed me the purse and looked away, running a hand through his disheveled hair.

I pulled the zipper across the top of the bag and peered inside. I pulled out a small silver compact, tickets to the Summerfield State Fair, and a wallet. But something seemed off. The *tickets* were off. I scoured the fine print.

"These tickets are twenty years old! I can't believe this has been sitting up here for that long," I said, opening the wallet. Walker had no interest in looking at the compact or the ancient tickets. I didn't know if he was upset that we hadn't found Layla or that we had just murdered a guy, but either were feasible options. I continued to examine the wallet. I pulled out the ID of a beautiful girl. Luxurious long brunette hair and ruby red lips. But there was one thing even more striking than her looks, and that was her name. *Layla Barns.*

"Oh my god!" I said in a whisper. Walker turned even farther away.

It was all coming true. All my hard work, my premonitions, Gran's hints. I was meant to find this, and I'd been drawn straight to her belongings. I hadn't found the girl, but I had found a clue, and that was something. It was the first tangible clue. A step closer to understanding what all this was about.

"Oh my god! Walker! We found it. It's Layla's!" I said, holding out her ID. But for reasons I couldn't understand, he didn't want to look at it. I shook his arm, but he didn't budge. He hid his face in the depths of the shadows. I tried to read him, but I could only see the dim outline of his jaw. A tear caught the last of the light, sparkling at the top of his cheek, and ran down into the scruff where his dimples lay dormant. It wasn't the time for more of my questions, though I had them piling up by the dozens. It hurt me to see him like this, and it hurt to know that there was nothing I could do to help.

Slowly, I turned my attention back to the identification and flipped it back to reveal a personal photo of Layla and her boyfriend. Only this wasn't a boyfriend from twenty years ago, this was Walker St. James. *Now.*

My stomach dropped. Sucking in a sharp breath of air, I felt woozy and confused.

Walker wiped the tear from his cheek. "I wanted to tell you. I just . . . I didn't know how," he said. A million thoughts ran through my head, and I was unable to settle on any one in particular.

"I love her . . ." It was the only thing he could say, and it was full of nothing but honest pain.

I tried to pull the few things I understood together, but like a puzzle, pieces were missing. "I knew you had a girlfriend. Not right away, but eventually. And I knew you wanted to find Layla Barns. Probably as much as I did," I stated the facts, not for him, but for me to hear out loud. "But for the life of me, Walker, I just can't figure out how these two things go together." A tremble racked my body like an aftershock. I looked at him, but he was still shying away.

"Now, you just told me that you love her, and I'm trying to understand how you're in this twenty-year-old photo. Because when I look at you and I look at this photo, you're exactly the same."

"Isn't it obvious?" Walker asked, looking at me for the first time since we found the purse. The red in his eyes matched the dying sunset.

A nervous chuckle escaped me, "No! Not unless you're a ghost!" I blurted, half-joking half not. But when Walker's dimples failed to make an appearance and his gaze ran cold, an unsettled feeling seized my chest, holding it captive. Because I knew that this was no joking matter.

"You're . . . You're?" I clambered to my feet, the tiny hairs on the back of my neck rising. *Impossible . . .*

I stuck my head through the broken wall in search of fresh air to help clear my mind. A light breeze lifted a loose strand of hair and tickled my neck. My heart galloped in my chest as Walker slowly climbed to his feet, careful not to spook me any further. He rested his elbows on the edge of the stone and gazed out into the darkening sky.

I don't know how long we stayed like that, silently staring into the distance, but the shock wasn't wearing off. The sunlight had fully dissipated, and the artificial concert lights were glowing just beyond the lake. There were too many questions in my head. Was it possible that they canceled each other out? An odd calmness blanketed my mind. *He was a ghost . . .* There was a gnawing feeling inside me, and I was shocked that it wasn't dripping with fear, but curiosity. How? When?

This strange soul beside me—the one that had captured my heart—was not only taken but . . . but he wasn't even alive. He was a spirit. He was a phantom. I turned to him and let my eyes wander over his hair, his lips, his jawline that met the collar of his flannel. Unafraid, I reached out, grabbing his bicep, and when he looked at me with that longing, it hurt to know that he wasn't aching for me but for her. Maybe even his past life.

"How is this possible? You're real. You're solid. I can feel you. You saved me—" I could have gone on forever, but thankfully, he didn't let me.

"How did you not know, Wilde? There were so many signs. I kept waiting for you to notice, but you never did," he said, tears pricked his eyes.

"Signs? What signs?" I asked.

"You see your gran, and she's no longer here. That should have been your first sign." His voice was soft, sympathetic. This hurt him as much as it did me.

My eyes widened. I really *had* lost my wits. This was it. This was my new reality. I, Kinsley Wilde, was some sort of clairvoyant. I saw dead people, and I conjured fears.

"Yes. That probably should have been a clue. I . . . I guess I can see beyond the veil."

Walker ran his hand through his hair, shaking his head and sighing heavily. My eyes trailed back out to the concert, though I could barely hear the music over my shock.

I thought back to Layla's headstone resting in the forest. I guess she was dead after all. I felt the disappointment wash over me for failing my gran. How was I supposed to find her now? How could I help her if she had already crossed over? I thought back to Walker and how he'd plucked me from the lake the night we'd met. I supposed Layla would find me, now that I was a magnet for the paranormal.

I thought back to the day I'd looked beside Layla's grave and knew her lover was resting next to her. But how had I known that? An extension of the memory surfaced. One I'd forgotten, possibly on purpose. I wafted the heavy blanket of fog with my hands to uncover the name, Walker St. James, etched on the headstone next to hers. I felt sick to my stomach. Light in the head. Woozy. Like I was about to pass out. How had I forgotten that? It was so extremely important, how had I forgotten it? Or more importantly, why had I hid it from myself?

I rested my forearms on the window next to Walker's, trying to steady my breathing and strengthen my weak knees. "So, if you are Layla's love, then you *are* the butcher?" I asked.

"No. I told you, that's just an old wives' tale that followed a tragic love story. *My* love story," he said.

"If the butcher isn't real, then who killed Trinity?" I asked. Walker's eyes dipped down to the ground.

"Oh." I glanced down at Jimmy's remains and swallowed a lump in my throat and nodded. There was no real butcher of Baylor Lake, but there was a killer. It was justice. A life for a life. I hadn't done that to him; he'd done it to himself.

Shoulder to shoulder, we watched the concert from the best view in town. My thoughts were lost in space, beyond my grasp. I paid no attention to the body below, and I caught myself thinking that it was romantic. It felt that way. It felt like it could be. And it was far better than acknowledging the truth. The truth that I could somehow see beyond the veil. See the dead. And perhaps even fall for one of these special souls.

I had just tripped a man who had then fallen to his death. He lay dead on the rocks in the shallow water below. I had fallen for a guy who wasn't even alive. And I could tell that, somewhere inside of me, there was evil waiting to seep out. And with it came a great power, one I had yet to fully understand. I didn't know myself as well as I thought I did.

"Hey, Wilde?" Walker asked. I looked at him, and his eyes reached deep inside me, seeming to clench my heart. I wasn't afraid, only saddened that this extraordinary soul was no longer a part of my reality—and that one day, he would have to leave me behind. The day that I helped him find Layla would be the day he'd rest in peace. And the last day I'd have the honor of knowing him.

"Yes?" I asked, my tone breathy and laced with a desire that was impossible to fulfill. My heart was a bottomless well next to his.

"You know . . ." Walker winced as if it pained him to say.

"Just say it."

"You know you're dead too, right?"

Dark Reflections

Volume 2

DARK
REFLECTIONS

1

We stared out the broken wall of the tower, listening to the Water's Edge Concert, watching the spotlights rotate in the otherwise black sky, and trying to understand this world we found ourselves in. When the night chill rolled in, I didn't feel it.

"I'm . . . I've—" My mouth moved, but the thoughts were too tiny and scattered to come together and form a sentence. I rotated Layla's old silver compact in my hand.

"You're like me," Walker said. His golden gaze had dimmed to black under the night sky.

"Dead?" I asked.

Walker scanned my face and then nodded.

As I watched the searching spotlights of the concert, I recalled the plane crash. The light from the explosion of impact. The heat funneled up the cabin of the plane, disintegrating everyone on board. Including me. I never should have gotten on that plane . . .

"I remember. It was terrifying—" I stared unblinking at the pine trees, my eyes drying out and then overcompensating by watering. Walker listened to me patiently while I told him my story.

"I was upset with myself. I wanted to get off the plane. And the more I thought about being an awful friend . . . letting my gran down . . . Lainey and Emma . . . you . . ." I stole a glimpse of the compact, turning it over in my hands. Did I dare face my reflection? I wasn't sure what I looked like dead. "The more disappointed I got with myself, the more the turbulence shook the plane. And when I got angry, that's when the lightning struck." The country music faded away, and I blinked several times to keep the tears from pooling.

"I did this. I ran right into the hands of death. And I brought all those passengers down with me . . ." The tears streamed silently down my cheeks, and my heart constricted so tightly, I could no longer talk.

"Think . . . think back. To an earlier time," Walker said wearily. I looked at him, not understanding. His brows pulled together, pained, and his now black eyes shone with the moonlight.

"What?" I could barely hear him. The voice in my head was much too loud.

Walker sighed. "You didn't die in the plane crash."

I froze still. His quiet voice now piercing. My eyes darted around, searching for clues. "Well—then . . . when?" Was it when the thing chased me in the woods?

"The night we met," Walker said, his voice a whisper and his head tilted. He continued to speak, but this time, his voice faded just like the music in the distance had. A high-pitched tone rang in my ears, and I grew faint. Weak in the knees. I dared to open the compact but couldn't bring myself to look within.

I don't remember Walker taking me home that night, and I don't remember when the concert ended. I had been swallowed whole and caught in the throat of the night. I hadn't existed this entire summer . . .

I sat on the back patio as dawn broke. I had no answers, and I knew it would take a lot more than just one sleepless night to wrap my head around this reality. *My* reality. I watched as the sky lightened from deep hues of navy to lilac. My favorite was when the warmth of the orange broke through, illuminating the fog-covered lake below. I listened to the loons calling into the mist, and I wondered if they were haunting me or if it was the other way around.

My friends lay sleeping in the cabin behind me. Had I been haunting them all summer?

When my grandma had died, I had nothing but sadness for her. For me. I had worried about what my life would be like without her, but never once had I imagined what it would be like for her. To be a ghost.

And yet, here I was. Living the dead life. This wasn't how it was supposed to be. This was supposed to be the best summer ever. And now, I wasn't even alive for it.

I had just tagged alongside the living, unaware that I was in a separate realm. Thinking I'd been alive for the past several weeks. It was a strange deception. One I was sure that I'd never fully understand.

I felt many things about being dead, but being lonely wasn't one of them. I had Walker, and he understood far more than I ever did. Although, being trapped in the afterlife with the most beautiful guy I'd ever known and not being able to penetrate his heart seemed like some sort of personal hell. I was kind of okay with it. Maybe I wouldn't be in the future, but for right now, I was taking what I could get. And if that meant just friendship, I was all right with that. And oddly enough, I still had all my friends too. Apart from Trinity, that is. Did they know that I was different?

Even though loneliness wasn't an issue here, it didn't mean I wasn't disappointed. I had thought my afterlife would be filled with bright, shiny things. Glorious warmth, wings, and the potential to fly. Maybe I'd be able to eat as much chocolate and ice cream as I wanted and never gain a single ounce, or I could bounce from place to place at the snap of my fingers. At the very least, I expected there to be *available* guys. Needless to say, this wasn't how I imagined I'd spend eternity. Harboring a secret as outrageous as this one seemed impossible. I didn't know how Walker did it, but I would have to ask . . . Learn. I had a lot to learn.

The lake scintillated as the fog burned up and the sun rose into the sky. I was partially hypnotized by the sparkling water that held the secrets I desperately needed to uncover, but something was drawing my attention to my neighbor's yard. Mrs. Vandal had been gardening since it was dark out. And even though I had a lot more pressing issues hurtling through my mind, I couldn't help but wonder what was so pressing in her garden that she needed to tend to before daybreak. Every now and then, I'd watch and wait, but I'd always see the same old thing. A woman who couldn't sleep and spent her time gardening. Maybe she was running from something. A bad marriage, perhaps? I knew her husband could be a little weird. Even more so since I had died. Maybe he could tell. Maybe they all could, and nobody wanted to tell me. Walker certainly hadn't.

I'd been staring out at the horizon all night. I watched it even when I couldn't see through the black sky. Yet, I still knew it was there, just beyond the shadows. It reminded me of the ghost of my gran and all the times I'd known she was there, even though I couldn't see her. My eyes were dry and weary, my soul anything but content. I jumped when the door opened behind me and Gunner rushed to my side. I jumped forward, hands spread in the air.

"You're up early," Lainey said in a groggy morning voice, careful not to wake the others. She was already dressed, ready for a hike. The leash dangled from her hand, and Gunner knew. He pranced like he was on hot coals.

"Yeah, I couldn't sleep last night." I pulled my hoodie closed and mindlessly ran a hand through my hair. She was looking right at me. How could she not know?

"Have you been up all night?" she asked, coming to my side.

I shrugged apologetically.

"Oh wow! You look like death!"

A brick dropped in my stomach, landing with a thud. I winced. *Death? So, she knew?* "I do?" I asked, leaning forward, an arm wrapped around my waist.

"Yeah! You've got the worst bags under your eyes right now!" Lainey's eyes were bright, and she worked to hide the smile bunching in her cheeks.

Bags? I could deal with bags. As long as she couldn't see deeper. Past the sleepless skin that I wore so well. As long as she couldn't see that I was an outsider, that I was pretending to have a heartbeat, I could deal with that. I was used to looking like hell anyway—just not living in it.

"I'm sure I do," I said, rubbing at my eyes.

"Do you want to take Gunner on a hike with me?" she asked.

"Can I take a rain check? I'm really not feeling up to it."

"Sure, no problem. Is everything okay?" Lainey asked while leaning against the deck's banister.

How was I supposed to answer that? Lainey was one of my best friends, and I wasn't used to keeping secrets from her. But this was more than a secret. This was a way of life. Or more like . . . a way of death. I wasn't sure she would handle it well if I told her that I'd died nearly a month ago. Emma? Maybe. But Lainey? Lainey was of a holistic nature. Loved anything plants, animals, and nature. But I wasn't sure she could handle the supernatural. And that's what I was, right?

"I'm fine. Just have a lot on my mind, I guess." It wasn't a complete lie. I *did* have a lot on my mind. An unbearable amount.

"Is it your gran?" she asked. Lainey's head tilted to the side and her brows creased with empathy.

"Yeah . . ." I shrugged. My gran *was* part of it. She'd been visiting me in my afterlife. Maybe that's why I could see her and hear her. We were on the same plane.

"I know it's hard, but one day, you'll see her again. She's probably up there now, smiling down at you. She's probably so proud of you, going to college and everything."

I felt like a terrible person for drowning Lainey out. She meant well; she really did. But hearing about how my gran was *up there* . . . Up where? She was right here. And I was too. And nothing had changed. Except for the random glitches in reality. The stuff that didn't make sense but should have. No, my gran wasn't dressed in white, adorned with angel wings, and sipping champagne. She was reading fairy tales and murder mysteries. She was sitting by a fire that failed to heat the frigid air. And she was haunting my afterlife to no avail.

Mrs. Vandal had finished bagging her clippings and started the long haul to the trashcan in her front yard. Only her clippings looked abnormally heavy and oddly shaped. I strained my back, trying to get a better view.

"Do you see that?" I asked Lainey. Lainey whipped her head to the neighbor's house, and she straightened her back to get a better look. Her brows rose, and her face shifted from curiosity to bewilderment in the blink of an eye.

"If I didn't know any better, I'd say she was dragging a body to the trash," Lainey said from the side of her mouth. That's exactly what it looked like. It looked like a body in that bag. Long and slender, bulbous at one end, and sharp at the other.

"Right . . ." I watched Mrs. Vandal throw all of her weight into dragging the bag ever so slowly crossed her lawn.

"What are you guys staring at? Oh shit! Did they kill somebody?" Mason laughed.

"It sure looks like it," Lainey said. And then, as if it were nothing, Mason, Kai, and Levi, joined us on the back patio, making jokes about the neighbor.

"Guess her husband couldn't get it up last night," Levi said.

"It's all fun and games until you're taken out with the trash," Mason replied.

"Well, this has been fun, but Gunner has waited long enough. Are you sure you don't want to come?" Lainey asked, giving me a look that said, *anything is better than hanging out with these fools.* Gunner jumped to all fours, his tail slapping me in the shins.

"I'm going to skip this time, but thank you."

"I'll go with you?" Levi said.

"What! You can't go hiking! We have to sign up for the fishing tournament!" Mason said.

"Can't you just write my name down?" Levi asked. Lainey waited for the guys to decide while Gunner spun in circles.

"Whatever! It's going to be bad luck if you don't sign yourself up. You better bring your fishing game for that tournament!" Mason said.

"Don't worry about that! There's no way those three are going to beat us in the tournament. Asher has never even been fishing a day in his life," Levi said.

"So, you guys are entering the Baylor Bass Tournament?" I asked Mason.

"Oh yeah! Levi, Kai, and I are gonna whoop their asses. Asher, Noah, and Ethan don't stand a chance."

"Just so you know, I've fished with Noah before, and he's pretty good. Luck kind of just follows him on the water," I said, still wrapped tightly in my hoodie from my pensive night. *Do they think I'm alive?*

"Noah? What? He doesn't fish. You think we need to worry about him?" Kai said, laughing. The boys took it upon themselves to throw Noah under the bus. And if I hadn't been dead, maybe I would have been amused.

"Was Noah lucky when Sherry Miller spilled her hot chocolate on him right before senior pictures?" Kai asked.

"Or when he was the only one benched for ditching?" Mason said, backhanding Kai's chest.

"They just had to make an example out of somebody . . ." I said, but it fell on deaf ears as they dug into Noah's luck with the ladies. Things I didn't want to think about and certainly didn't want to picture in my mind. It was my cue to leave. I took a deep breath before prying my bones off the chair I'd been glued to for the whole mind-numbing night. My back ached, and I had to work hard to stand up straight as the pain crawled down my spine. *Why did I still feel pain?*

"What's wrong, Wilde? Too much for you?" Mason called out. I waved my hand over my shoulder, too tired to chime in. It didn't matter anyway. None of it did.

I passed the others making breakfast in the kitchen, but I didn't pay them any attention. They looked at me with alarmed eyes and I knew it was because I looked like . . . death. I could feel where my eyes had sunken in, and I didn't know if it was because I'd stayed up all night or if the worry had finally taken its toll on me, but I was pretty sure that I looked on the outside how I felt on the inside. Without bothering to brush my teeth, I crawled straight into bed. I pulled the blankets over my head, but my eyes refused to give up their fight.

I must have lain there in a catatonic state for several hours before Lainey and Emma came bounding into the bedroom, loud and boisterous.

"Hey, Kins! Oh—is she sleeping?"

I threw the blanket off my head, tearing out of the self-made cocoon. "No," I groaned.

"No, she's not," Emma echoed as she sat on the edge of the bed.

"Well, not anymore," Lainey said as she took a seat. They looked at me, and an uncomfortable silence spread throughout the room as their eyes scanned my face. "You really need some sleep. We can come back?" Lainey asked.

"You look like shit!" Emma said.

I threw my arms up in the air. "I can't sleep! I'm having an existential crisis, you guys!" My eyes burned as tears began to form. If my friends had looked uncomfortable at seeing the shadows under my eyes, they were even more uncomfortable now.

"It's okay. It's okay. What's the matter?" Emma asked, her mouth gaping open.

"I don't even know where to start . . ." How could I?

"Just start from the beginning," Lainey said.

So simple.

I looked at them in all seriousness, and I said it. "I think I'm dead." And then, I gazed into the two sets of empty eyes, waiting for their response. Maybe it was so far-fetched that they never comprehended it. Or perhaps they never heard me. But all they could do was look at me with giant black pupils that threatened to swallow me whole. "Did you hear me?" I asked, my voice rising.

"I feel that way too sometimes." Emma nodded.

"You're just in a funk. I've got an idea to snap you out of it, though," Lainey said.

Snap me out of it? Were they going to snap me back to life? This was unbelievable. Walker would never say that to me. He understood. He was of like mind, and it was clear that these two were not. My confession had traveled right over their heads. I sighed. It was probably best if they didn't know the truth. Not like I had a choice in the matter. They clearly didn't want to accept what I told them anyway. I played along. A slow, painful dance between the three of us.

"And what's that?" I asked through tight lips.

"Well, you know how every year I volunteer to work on the Fourth of July floats in Decord City?" Lainey asked. It was true; she volunteered every year. She'd been doing it since she was a little girl. Lainey loved everything botanical. She was a nature-loving creature, and she adored everything from plants to animals. If it was under Mother Nature's umbrella, Lainey was in love. Getting to glue live flowers to a float was like her dream come true. She was able to volunteer, but in all honesty, she would've paid to do it.

"Yeah, I remember."

"I just found out that I can volunteer here for the Fourth of July Baylor Parade!" Lainey said with a big, toothy grin.

"That's great, Lainey. I'm sure you were worried about missing that this summer." I could barely look at her. My mental state had been snuffed like a candle. And now we were talking about flowers . . .

"And that's not all! I signed you guys up to help too. We can get coffees, volunteer, and make a whole day out of it! There's no way it won't cure this little funk you're in. I promise," Lainey said.

I tried to smile, but I knew my eyes didn't twinkle the same as Lainey's had. I agreed, and Emma did too. But there was something in Emma's expression that also lacked luster. If I had to guess, I'd almost say she looked worried. Was she worried about spending her precious summer behind a glue gun? Or had she heard me when I said I died? *Really* heard me?

2

It was early the next morning when Gunner's barking had become so excessive that I could no longer lie in bed pretending to sleep. But no sooner than I was dressed and rushing down the stairs to find the spritely dog, there was a knock at the front door. I glanced around the cabin, wondering how I was the only person awakened by the non-stop barking. Not even Lainey had woken up to tend to her own dog.

I opened the door to find a man dressed in khakis and a polo shirt with a patch that resembled a police badge. "Hello, I'm looking for a Miss Kinsley Wilde," he said. I folded my arms across my chest. It was too early to be in trouble.

"Who's asking?"

"My name is Carl Stevens. I'm with Baylor Animal Control. I had a call about your dog this morning by an un-named neighbor of yours—" Carl stopped himself right there. His eyes rolled back in his head before shutting them all together. I only had one neighbor. The Vandals' cabin was the only cabin in Rock Creek Cove apart from ours. I couldn't understand why she wouldn't have just called me before calling Animal Control. It seemed uncharacteristic of her, but then again, they'd always been on the odd side.

"I'm Kinsley. What's the problem?" I asked.

"Well, it seems your dog has been barking non-stop since . . . since 5:23 a.m.," Carl said, flipping through his miniature notepad.

A creak on the stairs told me that Lainey had finally woken. "Lain—" I began. But it was only Emma. "Emma, can you get Lainey for me?" I asked.

"She's not upstairs. I figured she was with Gunner. Why is he barking so much?" Emma asked. I sighed. That was the question.

"Look, Carl, I'm sorry you got called out here. I'll talk to the *anonymous* neighbor and apologize. Honestly, I don't know what's gotten into the dog. He's not mine; he belongs to my friend. But the longer I stand here talking to you, the longer the dog will continue to bark. So, if you'll excuse me, I'm going to tend to the barking now," I said, passing by Carl and his notepad and shutting the door behind me.

I ignored the officer's grumbling disapproval as I ventured out the front and around the back of the cabin in search of Gunner. I found him easily by following the constant barking, which bounced throughout the clearing in the cove. He stood rigid, facing the dock, his bark as consistent as a leaky faucet. Drip by drip, he called out. It was so unlike him, and it was so unlike Lainey not to have shown up. The closer I got to the dog, the more I wondered where she was.

"Gunner? Gunner?" I patted my legs as I called his name. His ears perked but nothing more. He wouldn't pry his eyes off the dark water. I approached him slowly for fear of his uncharacteristic behavior.

Gunner wasn't just a good dog; he was an exceptional dog. Lainey had always had trouble with anxiety, and her mother had gotten Gunner for her as a kind of service dog. He served as her emotional support dog, and Lainey took him everywhere. But Lainey's mother was far more anxious than Lainey had ever been, and sometimes I wondered if the dog was really to help keep her anxiety at bay rather than Lainey's. Either way, when her mother said she could only come to the cabin for the summer if she brought the dog, we were more than thrilled to have the extra mouth to feed. We all loved Gunner, and I felt I knew him well, but at this moment, as we stood on the edge of the dock, I felt like I didn't know him at all.

The hair on his back stood rigid, and his bark had begun to turn hoarse. With every step I took closer to him, I found myself less afraid of him biting me and more fearful of what I might find in the water. What was he trying to tell me? For a moment, a reflection of a girl staring back at me with fearful eyes startled me. It was my face, of course, as I looked into the water. But my heart galloped in my chest at the thought of seeing one of the Baylor Butcher's victims seeking help from the depths below. I rested my heavy hand on Gunner's back and he snapped out of his methodical barking. He turned to me with a wagging tail and a whimper.

"What are you doing out here, boy?" I asked, scratching behind his ear. I turned to see Carl with his hand on his hip. He slowly picked up his notepad and jotted down something before turning away. My eyes wandered across the way to the Vandals' house, and I thought I saw a window shade ripple in one of the back bedrooms.

After securing Gunner inside the cabin, I conducted a thorough search for

Lainey. But she was nowhere inside. I called her cell phone, but she never picked up. "Did she answer you?" I asked Emma as she typed away on her own phone.

"No, nothing," she said.

"I bet she took Gunner for a hike this morning, and he got loose. She's probably out there now, looking for him." I shook my head as I turned away, searching for my shoes.

"Are you going to go look for her?" Emma asked.

"Yeah, do you want to come? She'll be out there all day if she can't find him." I stomped my heel into my shoe.

"Yeah, I'll come. Just give me one sec."

It didn't take long for me and Emma to hit the trail. The sun was still rising, and it was quite cold in the shadows. I didn't expect it when Emma brought up my comment from the other day. And my sudden burst of regret surprised me.

"So, you said something the other day that caught my attention. You said you had died . . . but . . . what did you mean by that?" she asked. I felt a sickening twist in my stomach. I never should've said anything. It was so ridiculous, the thought of talking about it made me even more unsure of myself. If I could just look for Lainey. If I could only have one focus, then maybe I could do this. But to look for Lainey and look for Layla Barns and not disappoint my grandmother and worry about my existence all at the same time was far too much.

"I didn't mean it. Not like that. I just meant, I *felt* dead inside." I felt the stress knit my brows together, and I looked away so Emma could no longer see my face as I lied to her.

"That's fine. You can blame it on depression or whatever you want. But just so you know . . . I know what you really meant." Emma's voice was small and quiet but was never mistaken for weakness.

My mouth ran dry, and I didn't know why, but I felt like crying. I wanted to ignore it. Suppress it until I forgot about it. Allow my mind to erase it from my memory. The plane crash. The ghosts. The haunting conversations with Walker. And the nebulous Ferris wheel and red door I'd seen right before I'd drowned. I'd thought if I could just focus on what was right in front of me, everything else that threatened my reality would slip away. But I couldn't control it the way I hoped. And a tiny piece of me was thankful to have a friend like Emma to open up to.

But opening up to anyone other than Walker was going to have its own bag of hardships. Walker was dead! His spirit caught in this realm and unable to move on. Nobody could understand it like he did. And Emma? Emma was very much alive. And the fact that I was walking alongside her was almost too much for me to comprehend. I couldn't bear to think how she would wrap her head around it.

I didn't want to see her eyes when she looked at me and realized that I was a figment of her imagination. That I was no more than a hoax or apparition. Because if I didn't exist for her this summer, then what about Lainey, who was wandering the woods in search of her pointer? What about Layla Barns? And the Baylor parade? Would it all go on without me? Probably.

"You know, I never told you this, but when I was thirteen, I was playing with my aunt's Ouija board . . . and it moved. All on its own. There was a woman there from the 1800s. I swear it. So, I believe you," Emma said confidently. It took everything I had not to burst into laughter. What I was dealing with wasn't in the realm of a preteen board game. People were dying. And worse was yet to come. Still, I was relieved that my sense of humor was still intact. "Emma, it's not the same thing," I began, but stopped when tears filled her eyes. This wasn't about me any longer. Something had been going on that I had missed. "What's wrong?" I asked.

"You don't believe me. Nobody believes me. But it happened. And I've been watching you this summer, and I can tell that something's up. I just wish you would talk to me the same way you talk to Lainey." Emma's face was pink. Her voice stern.

"I do! I do talk to you the same. And I believe you about the Ouija board or whatever. I didn't want to say anything because it makes me feel awkward, but it has nothing to do with you. I promise." I no longer knew what to say. Our steps were the only sounds that passed between us for some time. At some point, I gave in. "I haven't told anybody this, but I'm going to tell you now. But don't freak out, okay?" I asked. Emma's face lit up, and she nodded fiercely in agreement.

"Promise!"

"God, I don't even know where to start. Remember when I tried to go home?" I asked.

"When you tried to go home?" The crease in Emma's brows told me this was going to be a much more difficult conversation than I had originally expected. She didn't remember.

"Remember when I hitchhiked to the airport? We texted the whole night?" The frown on Emma's face grew deeper. "It was the night the cops came after we found Trinity," I said.

But Emma didn't know what I was talking about. She looked at me like I was sprouting a second head. "No . . ." She shook her head slowly from side to side. Her eyes slanting.

"You honestly don't remember? It was just the other day!" My voice raised as I felt the heat creep into my cheeks. I pulled my blatant stare from Emma, and I scanned the woods. Was this real? Any of it?

Ultimately, it was her lack of memory that would keep me from spilling the truth. Whatever I was going through, I had to do it alone. Well, not completely alone. I had Walker.

Emma was waiting for the secret. I had to tell her something. "I had a dream I died. There was a terrible plane crash." I picked up my pace on the trail, and Emma was quick to keep up.

"It was so real. I felt the terror, the heat from the explosion. And when I woke up from the nightmare, I was convinced that I no longer existed. It was slower than I'd like to admit, but I realized it was no more than a night terror. So, sorry for the fuss. I just wasn't acting like myself, I guess," I said. I let my eyes wander through the pines in search of Lainey, but there was no living soul in sight. The lie made me feel sad and lonely. Like I could no longer connect.

Emma nodded her head, accepting my story. Or so I thought. "But what if it wasn't a dream?" she asked.

"What do you mean?" slowing my pace once again.

"I mean, what if you did die, and this is your afterlife?" she asked. I let out a very-much-forced laugh.

"I'm serious!" said Emma, as she grabbed my arm, pulling me to a full stop. "What if this is your afterlife?" Her eyes were round and bright as suns.

"Okay. I'll play along. Say it is. Say I'm dead. Then, what does that make you? And why can you see me? Don't you think it's a little misleading that the entire cabin can still . . . I don't know, talk to me?" I laughed a harsh, gritty laugh.

"Well, they all think you've been a little . . ." Emma rolled her eyes.

"What?"

"A little . . . off," she said.

I frowned, letting her know I saw straight through her lie. But I didn't need to know what they really thought of me. I'd probably already thought much worse of myself.

"Look. I believe it. The weirder, the better," she said.

I thrust my hand on my hip, coming to a complete stop in the middle of the trail. This dreadful summer wasn't meant for Emma's entertainment.

"I'm sorry. Not like that. I'm just saying, I'm here for you." She reached out and placed her hand on my shoulder. A thoughtful gesture that I couldn't feel.

"Emma, this isn't one of your sci-fi, fantasy, paranormal . . . sex books!" I fumbled over my words. The truth was, I didn't know what she read, and I never really cared, but I recalled seeing oil-slick abs grace the covers of her books. And more often than not, they had some sort of glowing globe of universal power or a sharp crystal that always looked phallic to me. Either way, Emma was meant for a world much more interesting than ours. And given the chance, she was ready to make whatever it was that I was going through her personal dream come true.

"I know that!" she said, looking off to the side. Guilt washed over me. Who was I to crush a bookworm's dream?

"Look—" I started.

"But what if? What if!?" she pressed, palms up and eyes wide. She wasn't going to leave this alone, and part of me loved her for it.

It was the straw that broke the camel's back. The truth spilled from me like hot lava.

"I know! I swear, Emma, I died in that plane crash!" I ran my hands through my hair frantically and began pacing back and forth on the trail. I'd died in the lake, I'd died on the plane . . . how many more times would it happen? And how? I didn't want to know. "And you wouldn't believe it. You wouldn't believe it, Emma . . ."

"What?" she hissed.

"Walker! He said it!" I threw my hands up in the air.

"He said what?" Emma's voice grew.

"He said, 'You know you're dead, too, right?'" I crammed the heels of my hands into my eyes.

It took a moment for her to respond, but when she did, all she could say was, "Too?"

I stopped in my tracks and spun around to face her. It was the one thing I'd promised myself I wouldn't say. It just slipped out. "Emma, you can't tell anyone! It's a secret. I shouldn't have said anything!" I cupped my mouth and watched her, praying she'd abide.

"No. I won't say anything. I promise," she said. I held her gaze until I stopped, feeling like a terrible friend to Walker. I'd probably just spilled his deepest, darkest secret like it was gossip.

"Do you . . . Do you think I'm . . ." Emma whispered, her long fingers pointing to her chest, her face falling.

"No! No. *You* are happy. *You* are healthy. And you are going to live a long life. You hear me? Look, Emma, if anyone was in real danger here, it would be—"

Emma's eyes grew large, ticking up towards mine. "Lainey!" she gasped.

My stomach sank. I'd known something was off the entire morning. And there we were, talking about my problems instead of trying to find Lainey. I was a terrible friend. And I'd never forgive myself if we didn't find her.

We searched for hours. When lunch rolled around, we ventured back to the cabin to get Gunner. Emma thought he would be able to sniff her out, and I originally thought it was a good idea, too, until I remembered him barking at the edge of the dock. The pale face of the scared girl that reflected in the water passed through my memory, and acid rose in my throat. I said nothing.

I was pleased to see Walker gliding up to the dock when we got back to the cabin. I hadn't seen him since the night we killed Big Jimmy, and the secrets of our souls passed like whispers in the night. He flashed me a smile, and I could see his dimples all the way from shore.

"Emma, why don't you go see if anybody has heard anything yet. And I'll be right behind you," I said. Emma ran into the house, and I ventured down to the dock.

I couldn't help the smile that spread across my face, and there was no hiding it, either. We'd bonded in a way I'd never done with a guy before. I guess murder will do that to a couple. Well, self-defense, really. But it was less about the attack and more about the thing where he and I shared a special secret with one another. There was no other soul that I'd known that walked this earth like we did. We were living a lie. And nobody but us knew about it. And, I guess, Emma too. But something about the secret made me feel even more drawn to Walker.

"Hey, you look like you're in a good mood. What's going on?" Walker asked as I approached him.

"Oh, nothing. My friend Lainey is missing."

"And you're happy about that?" he asked.

"No!" My smile completely vanished. "No, I'm not. I just. It was you. Seeing you made me feel like I wasn't . . . I don't know. I was just happy to see you. I wasn't sure I would again." I tucked my hands into my back pockets and let my hair fall in front of my face.

"What? Are you serious? We've got big plans this summer, don't we?" Walker asked, wrapping his arms around me for a hug. I melted. I'd have him all summer.

"Yeah . . ."

"Of course we do! You and I are pals! We've got to stick together," he said, patting my back.

"Right. *Pals*," I repeated, taking in his scent as we parted. We were so much more than that, though. "Hey, do you mind if Emma comes to the library with us tomorrow?"

Walker's brow creased.

"It's just that she's really good at research, but if you don't want her to come . . ."

"No, it's all right. She can come. So, you have *another* friend missing?" Walker asked.

"It's my best friend." I looked back at the house. "It's one of them."

"Well, what happened? Do you think she was marked?"

"I don't know. We went to bed, and she was there. We woke up, and she wasn't. I think she took Gunner out for a run or something and he came back without her. Do you think you could help us look?" I asked, tucking the loose lock of hair behind my ear.

Walker rubbed the scruff on his chin, his gaze fixed on the lake. "I've got a better idea. You run back out with your friends. I'm going to head into town. There's something I need to pick up."

I nodded.

"Don't worry, Wilde. Everything is going to be all right," he said. But it didn't feel like that. It felt like everything was getting worse and there was no end in sight.

Late in the evening, when Lainey hadn't returned and Gunner sat staring out the window, Walker showed up at the cabin. With bags in his hands, he motioned for privacy. We went into the den, where nobody had gone since Mason had eaten the lightbulbs and the room remained dark.

"Did your friend show?" he asked.

"No. And nobody seems too worried either."

"That's the lake for you." Walker rifled through the bags in the dark.

"What did you get?" I asked, peeking inside.

Walker pulled out several surveillance cameras from an electronics store. "Trust me on this. I've got a theory." He took a wide stance, shifting his weight from side to side.

"Oh? And what's that?" I asked.

"Something's off. It always is. Kind of like we're missing bits and pieces, right? Like time is slipping away from us or something?" I knew what he meant. Since I'd drowned in the lake, so much time had vanished. And when I'd resurfaced, nobody knew I was ever gone. Could it have been a skip in time itself? I didn't know. I guess that's just what happens when you pass.

"So, what's with the cameras, then?" I asked, looking up at him.

"Well, we're going to set them up tonight when everyone goes to sleep. And after a few days, we're just going to see what we find. But I have a feeling . . . we're going to find some answers in these recordings," he said, finally stilling.

I wasn't as hopeful as Walker, but who could deny that smile? I knew I couldn't. And it's not like I had any other options. So, that's what we did. We hid in the den until everyone fell asleep. My head rested on his shoulder while we waited in the dark. We'd been kicked out of the game. We were outcasts. But we had found one another, and it was the glue that held us together. We spent the night wiring three cameras inconspicuously about the cabin. All I had to do now was wait for the answers to come to me. But waiting wouldn't be easy.

3

Emma, Walker, and I stood on the corner of Charleston and Grand, the heat beating down on our backs as we stared at what used to be the town library. Only, Baylor had swallowed it in the night. It wasn't there. Not now, not ever. Emma stole several quick glances at Walker, and I knew she was curious about him. About us. But she held it inside and I appreciated that. I looked down the empty streets for the tenth time.

"Are you sure it was on this street?" Emma asked.

"Absolutely positive. It's been on this corner ever since I've been coming to Baylor. It's the cutest vintage library I've ever seen. I can't believe they tore it down," I said, triple-checking the street signs.

"It doesn't look like anything was torn down. I'm pretty sure this liquor store has been here for as long as time," Emma said, her brows furrowed as she peeked into the window.

I scratched my head and craned my neck. Only Walker could understand an entire library going missing overnight, and he remained calm and patient while Emma and I struggled to understand. "I guess we need to ask somebody," I said with a shrug.

"Excuse me, sir?" Emma called out at the first sight of mankind. An older gentleman with kind eyes and a fragile body hunched over a cane continued to walk without so much as a glance in our direction. "Excuse me?" she called, louder this time. The man reluctantly hobbled to a stop and craned his neck toward us. "Do you know where the library is?"

"It's . . . It's . . . One block down," he said. Ever so slowly, he turned his focus to Walker and frowned before dismissing us altogether.

"Nice fella," Walker said.

There was nothing left to do but accept the impossible relocation of a historical library—there one trip and gone the next. We began walking.

I glanced at Walker, and he gave me a small nod, reminding me of the twisted way the Baylor phenomenon could make one feel as if they were losing their marbles. As we passed the old ornate pillars of Charleston, I began to pick up on missing person flyers taped to street posts and on storefront windows. At first, they were just text, and I figured that more people had gone missing than Trinity. But as soon as I saw Big Jimmy's mugshot plastered across a full page, sweat began to gather at the small of my back.

I hadn't realized that anybody would miss him. Not that it made it any more acceptable, but more like maybe it hadn't happened at all? If Emma couldn't remember the night I tried to fly home, then had Jim really died? I liked to think that he hadn't, even though the big guy had tried to kill us. Still, I hadn't wanted to see anybody get hurt.

When the body beside the tower had vanished the following day, it was easy to think of his death as make-believe. Stuff like this didn't happen in real life. Real life was cops, and real life was . . . missing person flyers.

I grabbed Walker's arm and dug my fingernails into his skin. His eyes flicked to mine, and I nodded toward the ornate pillars. I saw his face the moment he looked into Jimmy's pixilated eyes. It was enough to tell me he, too, had considered the entire event a figment of our imagination. His eyes only grew slightly wider, but I could see the panic. I lifted my finger and pointed. Flyers were on every corner, every window, and covering the bulletin board. I worked hard to swallow the lump rising in my throat. This wasn't something we could sweep under the rug. This was a man. And just because I didn't know where his body lay now, didn't mean I hadn't known where he had fallen. My chest tightened, the guilt like a tether wrapped tightly around me.

It was as simple as that. Responsibility. It didn't matter if things were unexplainable in Baylor; the responsibility I felt was still the same. It was within me to be a good person—whatever that meant these days. No matter my mental state, or my reflection in the mirror, I still strived to be the best that I could be—dead or alive. My mind tinkered with the possibilities of sitting through a trial and going to jail . . . or simply letting the guilt eat away at my conscious soul for all of eternity. There were no good options. That was, unless Walker had thought of something that I hadn't.

I peered up at him, and the crevice between his brows was so deep it reminded me of the great Baker Canyon. It also confirmed what I feared most—there was no way out. We were going to have to deal with this one way or another. And as far as I could see, it wasn't going to be a positive path for Walker and me.

We continued down Charleston, Walker and I both sweating buckets, partially due to the heat but mostly due to our impending doom. When we arrived at the library, it was the same old historical building that I had always remembered it to be. The only thing that had changed was the corner on which it sat. Emma walked in immediately, and I stood on the sidewalk, hesitating as I took in the street's location, the flyers catching my eye every now and again. Walker gave me the time I needed to wrap my head around the relocation of an entire historical building as he held the door open, eyebrows raised. I sighed, shaking my head before striding forward. As I walked past him, I took in his cologne and wished that I was back in the canoe wrapped in his flannel. And that there had never been anyone lying at the base of the transient tower.

I wished there wasn't a care in the world—only a boy and a girl and what could be. But that wasn't the case as things stood today. Today, there was one boy and two girls. There was one missing person and two dead people. Three —if I counted myself. It wasn't the summer I'd hoped it would be. And it certainly wasn't the running start into independence I had imagined. Somehow, somewhere along the way, my adulthood had ended before it even began.

I let my eyes wander across the books on the bookshelves. Not one new release. Everything was old and well-read. The books were dingy and outdated, and yet, the stories were still as rich as the day they had been written—the fantasies forever young and the infinite possibilities as fine as aged wine.

"I'm going to hop on one of these computers and see if I can locate any old newspapers relating to the accident," Emma said. Walker and I nodded. And as soon as she left, Walker grabbed my elbow and yanked me down an empty aisle. The books towered well over our heads.

"They're looking for him, but he's nowhere to be found," he whispered.

"I didn't realize that people were going to be looking for him. I thought he went missing because of the Baylor phenomenon. What are we going to do?" I broke down right there, nestled between the rows of books. My heart rate was picking up speed, and my eyes had gone shifty.

Walker ran his hands through his hair and paced the aisle. "We have to keep it quiet," he said, pinching his bottom lip in thought.

"What? We can't do that!" I hissed.

"The hell we can't!" Walker's eyes fixed on mine momentarily before he started pacing once again.

"I'm not going to spend eternity rotting in my own guilty conscience!" I said.

"I'm not going to spend eternity behind bars!" Walker said, his golden eyes ablaze.

For a moment, I was lost—not just in the amber flame behind his eyes but behind my moral compass. I was already dead. Hadn't I suffered enough? Was I supposed to spend an infinite lifetime behind bars as well? It probably wouldn't even work. I'd wake up the next morning in the master bedroom of the cabin on Rock Creek Cove. *Incarcerate me? Impossible . . .*

"You're right. That's not going to work for us." My gaze blurred before me. Walker was finally still, stance wide and hand on his hip. It was my turn to pace the aisle. Every time I passed him, I fought the urge to wrap my arms around him and beg for all of it to disappear. I wanted to be in this library with him, but I wanted my mind to be free. I wanted his heart to be available. And most importantly, I just wanted to be an eighteen-year-old worrying about which bikini I was going to wear that day. But because we can't always get what we want, I had to come up with a plan for Big Jim's disappearance.

While Emma searched records, Walker and I whispered between the old books of the historical library. "I think the best shot we have is to pretend it never happened," said Walker, shrugging as if it might be true. It had never happened. The body never flew out the window and crashed down upon the rocks. And we'd never listened to the concert from the tower, shoulder to shoulder, as he lay bloodied below.

"You're right. It probably never happened." I looked down to the ground, debating not only Jimmy's death but the existence in which Walker and I shared a bond unlike any other. If all of this never happened, then what we shared wasn't real either. He reached out and placed his hand beneath my chin. Electricity sparked where our flesh met, reminding me that some things are undeniable. Slowly, he lifted my head so that my gaze met his.

"It *did* happen. I know you feel like there's no reality because it's twisted and everything feels fake. But it happened. I'm here, and as painful as it may be—"

I sighed, the stress flaking off me and falling to the wayside. As long as I had him, I'd stay grounded.

"—it's important you realize that what happened in that tower was real. Now, I don't know where the evidence has gone. But just like this library, it's been relocated . . . somewhere. But it's not our job to find out. And we're simply going to step away from this case. We have no ties to Big Jimmy, and nobody will be looking for us . . ."

I nodded, taking his instructions in. He dropped his hand from beneath my chin, but I held his gaze.

"As far as anybody is concerned, he fell out a window. We were never there. Do you hear me? It happened . . . but we were never there," he said. Acknowledging that we were there was only for our sanity—not for the police to know.

It was a fine line to walk—insanity and reality. The lines were not made of rich, black charcoal, but that of a nebulous gray watercolor. The transition so vaguely defined that it might as well not even be there. And when the line was so arbitrary, I found myself lost between right and wrong. It was there, between the stacks of the well-read books, that I came to realize that, just like my reality, right and wrong had ceased to exist. And if that were the case, I might as well stop worrying about it. My shoulders relaxed when I realized my responsibility as a dead girl was next to nothing. I pinched my shirt and tried to air out the sweat that had been gathering on my chest and back. My head was full of tension and ached. I wasn't cut out for this. The fine lines across Walker's forehead told me that *nobody* was.

"Kinsley?" Emma whispered a couple of aisles down.

I looked at Walker, and it was clear that our decision had been made. We wouldn't be going to jail today. I gave him a quick nod, and he seemed to confirm that our case had been closed, never to be spoken of again.

"Kinsley, look what I found!" Emma said, coming down the aisle with a newspaper folded in her hand. "Read this!" she said, pointing to an article. I took the newspaper from her hand and read the title: "Midnight Collision." I scanned the article below, and much like my reality, the words blurred together in one jumbled mess. Letters rearranged themselves and continued without any semblance of a pattern. The white spaces between were just as prominent, if not more so, than the words themselves. I did, however, pick out a name. *My* name.

Another word that caught my attention was *accident*. I didn't know what Emma had found, but I knew it was important and pertained to me. Heat radiated down my back with embarrassment, as I knew the two of them were waiting for me to read it and come to a conclusion. A lump formed in my throat as I worried that I should have been done reading the entire article by now, but the truth was, I hadn't even started. I watched the words blur like a movie in motion, and there was no decoding this mess under all the pressure of my peers watching and waiting for me to finish. I passed the newspaper to Walker, peeking at him with questioning eyes and hoping to grasp the answers through him instead of reading the article myself.

He took it, never questioning my performance, and began reading out loud. And for that, I was forever thankful. "Accident involving Kinsley Wilde . . . On her eighteenth birthday . . ." He read, and my ears deafened as my mind raced to build a timeline before me. Eighteen? My birthday? I failed to recall the details but knew that something was terribly wrong. My birthday fell well before I came to the lake and before I'd drowned by the hands of darkness.

"—Car overturned from the bridge above. Paramedics estimate the accident happened some ninety minutes earlier, as there were no witnesses . . ." Walker continued, and I struggled to pick up bits and pieces of information.

"You were in an accident?" Emma asked, her face just as contorted as mine felt. Good question. I didn't know. I had no recollection of being in an accident, but it made sense. Perhaps that's where my life had actually ended. That's why I'd drowned and crashed in a plane and yet never really died—because I was already dead to begin with.

"I . . . I don't remember," I said, the ringing in my ears returning.

Walker reached out and squeezed my shoulder. His eyes filled with pain, and I wondered if he, too, had a moment in time that he couldn't remember. A moment when his life was stolen, and his mind worked ravenously hard to cover its tracks. I sought comfort in his eyes as I let the feelings of uncertainty settle deep into my stomach. I no longer felt the watching and waiting from Emma and Walker—only the cold, distant trepidation of not knowing my own past.

We left the library, having found more than what we'd come for. Emma knew about Walker and me being less than alive, and she did a pretty good job keeping that secret. As far as Walker knew, she was only with us to help with research about the Layla Barns accident. The article she uncovered about me came as a surprise to all of us. I was vaguely aware of the delicate dance the two of them did as they tried to figure out what each other knew. I had pressing concerns of my own. I couldn't recall much from my eighteenth birthday, let alone an accident. I heard trauma could do that. Make you forget.

As we walked down Chandler Street, there was a commotion outside the liquor store that stole my attention. It appeared that somebody was being arrested, and the three of us watched curiously. The closer we got, the clearer the picture became.

"Paul Cummings, you are being arrested for the murder of Jim Saunders," a cop announced.

Walker's eyes widened in disbelief as I felt my lungs expand in a quick, ragged breath. A part of me was relieved that it was all taking care of itself. But I knew I couldn't allow this man to take the blame for something he never did. I raised my hand to flag down the police and opened my mouth out of pure instinct, ready to confess. Walker grabbed my side, pushing me away from the cop's attention. Of course, Walker's hand on my waist was just about the only thing that could have stopped me in my tracks. And it did. My voice never came.

"Did he say *murder*?" Emma whispered.

"Some guy named Jim, I guess," Walker replied, his eyes trained on me. I remembered our agreement and closed my gaping mouth. I watched the cops slam the innocent man against the car as they read him his rights. I placed my hand over my stomach as it twisted in knots. Then, I looked away. I couldn't watch the man squint, writhing in pain as he was pushed against the police car when I knew it should have been me. I secretly vowed that I would make sure he got out of this unscathed. And as I did so, I couldn't help but wonder what evidence they had on the man they called Paul Cummings.

It was dark when we got back to the cabin. Saying goodbye to Walker was bittersweet. I didn't want him to go. But at the same time, I needed time alone to decompress. I needed to sit with myself, and I needed to shake this looming feeling of existential dread that hung over me like a dark cloud. And as I sat down on the edge of my bed, I realized that it was going to get worse before it got any better.

I'd had one accident I didn't remember and two I couldn't forget. A car accident on my eighteenth birthday, a plane crash that took 147 innocent lives, and a drowning. I was responsible for the death of one friend and the recent disappearance of another. Oh, and I'd killed a man. But if all of this had happened in my afterlife, then had it ever happened at all? I didn't know.

I didn't know who I was anymore. I brought a hand to my cheek and caressed it softly. My flesh was soft and plush beneath my fingertips, my jaw sharp and chiseled. I let my fingers fall just below my chin, and they settled on my carotid artery. If I had been dead, then why did my heart still beat? Why was there blood pumping through my veins? And why on earth was I surrounded by all my friends in this cabin?

I had never seriously questioned what happened after you died. But now that I knew, I suppose the answer was that our subconscious lived on. It lived on to imagine life as it had been. Perhaps as it *should* have been. Everything I saw as I looked around the room was make-believe. It was a memory that I had from previous trips to the cabin. My friends were a combination of memory and a projected outcome I had conjured in my head throughout my entire senior year of planning this trip. This was my best guess at what would have happened if I had lived past my eighteenth birthday.

And I was living it out. I was living it out just the same as if it were real life. The only difference? It wasn't real. And it was fragile, prone to breaking down in hellish fears. Maybe I was living out the nightmares I'd had when I was alive. Fascinated by this notion, my eyes lifted to the bathroom, where a large mirror covered the vanity wall. What would my reflection show? If it was all just a guess, how much did I get right? I imagined what I looked like when I was alive. Long dark-chestnut hair. Sun-kissed skin and red lips. Chocolate-brown eyes, with one small fleck of green. I stood up and slowly walked to the mirror, my heart pounding harder the closer I came. It was the only truth this world had, and it was just inside the bathroom. I kept my gaze low as I entered, and I grabbed the white countertop as I braced myself to see my true reflection.

Seconds turned to minutes before I found the courage to look deep inside my soul. The mirror would show a murderer. Someone unlovable. Someone . . . hideous. Only, when I stood square in front of the mirror, there wasn't a heinous spirit looking back at me. There was no reflection at all.

My deepest, darkest fear was then realized. I was *nobody*.

All my heart's desires, all my greatest wishes—they'd never come to fruition. The love I had for my family and friends would never be felt. They would never be warmed by my touch. And the only reason my friends at the cabin had acknowledged me at all was that I had wanted them to. I had imagined they had.

My existence now was as real as the reflection looking back at me. It simply ceased to exist.

4

As I stared into the mirror, my hollowness staring back with no eyes to question, I wondered if my lack of reflection meant that I had no soul. No heart. If I wasn't capable of true love. One thing I was sure of: I had a conscience. I had thoughts that kept me awake at night, and I had worries that drilled deep inside me, keeping this body running on anxiety and fear. If I had no soul, then how would I have feelings of guilt? And empathy? Why would I feel sick about Lainey's disappearance? Or how would I long for something more meaningful with Walker? And how would I wonder what could have been with Noah?

It must've been hours that I stared into that mirror, searching for my soul, but no passing time could bring me back.

Gone from this world yet somehow still present, I thought about my mom. I'd spoken to her since the accident, and there had been no mention of my passing. Should there have been? Or had my mind simply not wanted there to be? Whatever the case, with my newfound perspective, I picked up the phone and dialed.

I listened to the phone ring on the receiver and felt my hands grow clammy in anticipation. "Hello?" Mom answered in the vibrant tone of the living—a tone that reflected her daughter was alive and well. Had she not known? Or had I simply not wanted to live in a reality in which she was grieving?

"Mom?" I asked.

"Oh, hey honey. I was just thinking about you. Your ears must be ringing." I closed my eyes and imagined her on the sofa in front of a fire, her reading glasses sliding down the bridge of her nose and a mug of warm tea by her side.

"Were you?"

"Always, dear. How are you? How is everything going at the cabin?" she asked. I took in a deep breath, not knowing how to respond. Do I play the game? Or do I be myself? My authentic self . . .

"Mom?" I asked, looking for answers. The line was quiet on the other end, and I decided in that moment that I had nothing left to lose. "Mom, Lainey has been missing. We can't find her. And I know deep down that something is wrong. Gunner hasn't moved from the window, and he watches and waits for her return." My throat tightened as the words squeezed up and out.

"Well, that's a hard one, dear. Sometimes in life, people we love go missing. But there are lessons to be learned here—silver linings to look for. I know you'll find what you're looking for." Mom's voice was like a beautifully misplaced melody. It would have been comforting if it fit with the context of the situation.

It was almost as if I had made up different variations of answers a mother would give during a difficult conversation. But this particular conversation was one I'd never had with my mom—a missing person, the death of a friend. Since I had never had these conversations before, I assumed my consciousness had no way of projecting what she would have said.

There was an unsettled churning in my stomach as I realized the conversation I had with my mother was as fake as my new life.

"Silver lining? And what do you think that is, Mom?" I asked, simply needing to hear her voice.

"It could be anything, dear. When one door closes, another one opens. You just have to keep your eyes open. And you'll see the new opportunities that arise."

I imagined my mom on the other line, giving me her most heartfelt attention. And it warmed my almost-heart, as if it were there, beating within my chest. I knew now the conversation was fictitious, but that didn't stop me from needing my mother's love.

"Mom? I met a boy. And I know what you're thinking. It's not Noah." A small smile tugged at the corner of my lips.

"Oh? Go on," she said, changing her emotion to fit mine. A chameleon at its best.

"He's older than I am. And I never considered dating an older guy, but when I met him, I never gave it a second thought. It's like I saw him, and he could have said he was an alien from Mars and I would've happily nodded, accepting him. To be honest, he could be anything—a butcher, an alien . . . hell, he could even be a ghost—and I'd still want to crawl inside his flannel. I don't know, Mom, there's something about him. I can't quite put my finger on it, but it's this intangible light that surrounds him and invites me in. I feel this draw and I know he was made just for me."

"You know, when I met your father, it was like that. And your Grandma Green—she always said that Grandpa was her soulmate. She described it as much deeper than one life could possibly shed light on. That her love for him went back lifetimes. And you know what? I believe in fate."

I thought about that. Fate. I didn't know the meaning of my afterlife, but I had to believe that Walker coming into it was no mistake.

"I miss you, Mom . . ."

"I miss you too, dear."

"I better go. I know you need to get your sleep, and it's getting late." I fiddled with a tassel on the pillow, wishing my mother was there to give me a hug.

"I love you, dear. Good night." Her words lingered on the line long after I'd hung up. I wondered how the conversation would have gone if it had been real and she knew that I was dead. What would she say to me then?

And then something happened. An epiphany . . . like a lightning bolt, it hit me. The conversation I'd just had with my mother was conjured because she was alive, and I wasn't. But what would happen when I called my gran? What would happen when I called somebody who was in the same realm as me? I'd seen her in my dreams, and I'd seen her apparition in the woods and on the plane, but could I call her on the phone? Had there been a direct line of communication with her this whole time? One I had never taken advantage of it?

As quickly as I could, I picked up the phone and dialed her number. An ache spread across my chest as I realized I was calling a number I'd never thought I could again. The phone rang not once, not twice, but three long miserable rings before it happened. She answered.

"Hello?"

"Gran? Is that you?" I asked, flinching back.

"Kinsley? Kinsley, are you there, dear?" Gran asked.

"It's me! I'm here!" I said.

"I wasn't expecting your call. Is everything okay?" I sensed the trepidation on the other side of the line.

I sat quietly, unsure of what to say and how much. "I know . . ." I said.

"You know what, dear?" she asked.

"That I died—"

The silence stretched between us. And I played with the pillow's tassels as I waited for her response. Had I said too much?

"Is that really you, Kinsley?" her feeble old voice wavered.

"Gran, it's me. I'm here!" I said.

"Oh, honey, I've been trying to reach you."

"You have?" I asked. It was the first thing that had felt real in a long while.

"This is against the rules, so we'll have to be quick," Gran said.

"*Rules?* What rules?"

"I've been trying to reach you this whole time. But it's difficult. I've been having a hard time contacting you. And when I do, it comes out twisted and warped. I fear I'm doing more damage than good."

"What do you mean?" I asked.

"Every time I try, my words get twisted, and your visions become a blundered mess. I can't tell if I'm helping you or hurting you. But I keep trying, dear. I keep trying . . ." Gran said, her voice pained with sorrow so deep that I could feel it on the other side of the line.

"You're not hurting me. I'm just . . . I'm just confused. Are you trying to tell me it wasn't you I saw in the forest? Or on the plane? It wasn't you sitting by the fire reading books?" My head ached with all the questions I had no answers to. Yet, there was something more. Something real in how it hurt.

"Oh, honey, it's me. But only fragments. My intention isn't coming through the other side. And I try to help, but it doesn't seem to work. You're never there." Gran seemed frazzled.

"I'm here now. And I love you. I miss you so much." It was all I could say.

"Oh, Kinsley. I miss you too. I want you to know that I'm here for you and you don't have to do this alone. You're not alone. You're so strong, darling. You're so brave."

I began to cry as her comforting words wrapped around me like a warm hug. I could tell that this conversation was different from the rest. It touched me in a way that the others hadn't. And I wondered if I could reach her again when I needed to by simply dialing her phone number.

"Gran? Come back? Can you come back?" I asked—an impossible question. And if I only had one question to ask somebody on the other side, it was this. A request that I knew couldn't be fulfilled. The words simply tumbled out of my mouth and I couldn't take them back. I wanted my grandmother. I wanted everything to go back to the way it had been before.

I felt the disappointment in her ragged breath on the other side of the line. "Kinsley? Kinsley, are you there?" she asked, her voice dripping with worry.

"Gran? I'm here. Can you hear me?" Static filled the other side of the line, and I could hear her voice far away in the distance.

"Kinsley? Oh no . . . Not again . . ."

It broke me to hear her pain. I felt my heart break and shatter like an unreplaceable vase. I hunched over and sobbed. She knew I was hurting and scared, and she was doing everything she could to reach out to me in an impossible situation. We were both dead yet unable to find each other in the vast emptiness beyond the veil—just like Walker and Layla.

"Gran! I'm here. I'm here!" I said in no more than a whisper. The tears rolled off my cheeks and fell onto the pillow I grasped tightly in my lap. Nothing could bring her back. And I was to face this eternity on my own.

My insides felt paper-thin and delicate beyond belief. Like a house of cards that could topple over with the slightest breeze. Walker and I were two lost souls. Together, we were searching for answers. A way back to our loved ones. He to Layla and me to my gran. If I could find her, then maybe we could live our afterlives together the way they were meant to be. But what about everyone else in the cabin? The ones who were still alive but only brought together by my imagination?

It was hard to feel anything other than sorrow when you ceased to exist. But still—despite the fallen tears—I found something else to latch onto. Curiosity.

It peaked when I remembered the surveillance cameras I'd set up throughout the cabin. One pointing toward the lake dock, one in the kitchen, one in the master bedroom, one in the living room, and another in the den. If my friends were a figment of my imagination, then what did the cameras reveal? Did they have reflections?

Thankful for Walker's grand scheme, I jumped out of bed and wiped my cheeks dry of tears. I hurried to the camera set up in my bedroom, and I examined it front to back, watching as the green light blinked. Nerves of anticipation spread throughout my body as my gaze lifted to my laptop. Should I look now? Would I be disappointed? The answers would be undeniable. It didn't matter if I looked now or later. It didn't matter what the tapes were to reveal; it was the truth, and it was waiting for me.

I opened my laptop and logged onto the surveillance website. There were five cameras to scour footage from, but I chose the master bedroom first. I started from the beginning and I watched as I set the camera up and then crawled into bed. But soon after, the video feed glitched and then went black. I clicked here and there, but nothing brought the video back. I skipped forward, scanning for any sort of footage. However, there was nothing but darkness.

Four more to go. I looked back to the camera in the bedroom and the green blinking light. It seemed to be working, but I was no technician. I clicked on the footage from the kitchen, and to my dismay, it was the same deal. It had taped me as I set the camera up but froze as soon as I walked out of the room.

"What the hell?" I said aloud as I opened the footage of the living room with disappointment. It was the same thing as the kitchen. Frozen footage. It's like every single security camera I set up worked for thirty seconds and then gave out. I slammed my laptop closed.

I went around to every camera and checked the wiring. Everything seemed to be in working condition, but I unplugged them all and started them over just in case. It was the extent of my technical knowledge. And oddly enough, it fixed about seventy-five percent of my problems with electronics. I could only hope that it would do the same with these cameras. I made a mental note to ask Walker to look at them next time he stopped by the cabin, but for now, this would have to do.

When I got to the camera in the den, I never plugged it back in. With all the weird happenings at the Vandals' house, I took it to the patio and hooked it up so that it faced the neighbors' property instead. I'd probably get no footage again, but it didn't stop me from trying.

I'd known there was something fishy about my neighbors even before my eighteenth birthday. The odd happenings at their house weren't because of the Baylor phenomenon or tied to my afterlife. And I feared they had something to do with Lainey's disappearance.

5

I lay tossing and turning in bed at night, the thoughts of an innocent man being sentenced to life in prison racking my mind and torturing my conscience. If my mindset was all I had left, then why let it rot with guilt? I tossed and turned while forcing my eyelids to remain shut. When I heard the familiar sound of tiny stones clinking on my bedroom window, my spirits lifted. They were the pebbles thrown from Walker's hands late in the night when he couldn't sleep and knew that I couldn't either.

I popped my eyes open and hurried to my window, cranking it open and peering outside. The mist was thick with anticipation. I gave Walker a quick wave, held up a finger to signal that I'd only be a minute, then quickly slipped on pajama pants, grabbing a robe on the way out of my bedroom. I tip-toed down the stairs and passed the sleeping bags on the living room floor. Nobody was awake.

I smiled widely when I opened the door to the back patio and found Walker standing with his hands in his pockets and an apologetic look on his face. But he didn't need to apologize for waking me up, and he knew that. I guess the dead didn't sleep. Both he and I were tortured late at night as our minds struggled to grasp the boundaries of our lives.

"Hi . . ." I said softly.

"Hi. I hope I didn't wake you," Walker said, wincing.

"Not at all. Is everything okay?" I asked, pulling the robe across my chest.

"Yeah, yeah. I just . . . I couldn't sleep. I was hoping you . . . well, not hoping, but—"

"I know what you mean," I said.

"I just needed somebody to talk to, and these days, you're all I have. I hope you don't mind," Walker said as his eyes lowered to the ground. I wiggled my feet in my slippers. This revelation did weird things to my stomach, and it felt like I was in motion—namely, falling. I didn't know what to say to that. I wanted him to know how much it meant to me and how much I wanted to be that person for him. But by the time I thought of a response, the moment was gone.

"Your neighbors seem to have a habit of gardening at three o'clock in the morning." Walker scowled, looking over my shoulder. I peered over to the neighbor's yard, and sure enough, there was Mrs. Vandal digging in her planters.

"I wish I could say this was abnormal for her," I said with a sigh.

Walker raised his brows in question, and I answered with a smile and nod. It was true. I looked up to the wall where I had plugged in a surveillance camera, and I was pleased when I saw the green light blinking. It didn't mean I had captured anything, but I was still hopeful that there was a chance.

"You see that?" I asked, pointing to the camera.

"You aimed one at the neighbor's house? Good thinking," he said, and I felt proud of myself in the wake of his compliment. "Want to sit on the dock?"

"Sure," I said.

He led the way. "Do you remember what it was like to be in the car accident?" Walker asked as we headed down the grassy hill toward the lake. The cool mist planted kisses on my cheeks as I tucked my hands deep inside the pockets of my robe.

I shook my head. "I have no memory of it." My slippers were getting wet from the moisture in the grass, but I didn't care.

"Really? None at all? See, I'm envious of you. I wish I couldn't remember. But that's all I do. When I close my eyes, that's all I see. It haunts me like a nightmare, and I can never escape it." Walker hung his head and tugged at the bill of his hat. I felt the shift in his mood as it radiated off him and surrounded us. This man was hurt, and I'd like to be the one to help him. But I didn't know how. How do you erase the pain from a tragedy? It was impossible.

"Maybe . . . maybe if you talk about it? I don't know if you have anybody to talk to, but I'm here." I shrugged. "I'll listen," I said, peering up at him.

One of his dimples deepened, casting a shadow on his cheek. "I don't have anybody to listen. It would be an odd thing if I did. There aren't many like us wandering around Baylor Lake." I looked behind me on the dock as my slippers made wet footprints on top of the wooden planks. Walker's canoe was tied to the end of the dock. The corner of my mouth tugged into a small smile that I tried to hide behind a curtain of hair. I liked the way he traveled. It was romantic in its own right.

"Do you mean there are more people like us?" I asked, taking a seat. I tucked my hair behind my ear and peered up at him as he sat down next to me.

"I'm sure there are—amongst us. But it's not something you can see. It isn't detectable on their flesh. It's not a smell or sight."

"Well, what is it then? You knew that about me. How did you know?"

"It . . . It was in your eyes. Your eyes were scared and lonely. You didn't understand the world around you any longer, and that's because you were no longer in it. Not in the way you used to be," Walker said, peeking down at me. The thought of me not really being in this world was a scary one, and I imagined my eyes were doing whatever it was that had helped Walker identify the status of my soul in the first place. I looked into the black distance.

"You got all of that from my eyes?" I asked, drawing my attention back to him. And if I didn't know any better, I'd say that he blushed under the moonlight.

"Believe it or not, the eyes *are* the windows to the soul. And your eyes . . . they say a lot," he said, leaning back on the heels of his palms. His torso taut as he stretched out.

"I'm going to have to keep them in check. I wouldn't want them telling any of my secrets now," I said with a wink.

"Secrets? Secrets are for the living. What do you need to hide in your afterlife?" he asked.

It was a good question—and one I didn't have an answer to. I suppose my crush on him was the only one worth hiding away. I shrugged coyly and tucked a loose strand of hair behind my ear.

"I don't know. I was just messing around. Do you have any secrets?" I asked, wanting to know them all.

Walker stared out over the water at the moonlight glinting off the surface. The ripples danced like ballerinas, moving to a beautiful symphony.

"I do. And what a burden they are. You wouldn't believe what a guilty conscience can do to you over a couple of *decades*."

He steepled his four fingers beneath his chin, lost in thought. The night was beautiful, but nothing compared to Walker's profile. His nose turned up slightly at the tip, and it reminded me of the innocence of a young boy. His brows were dark and thick, and his cheeks were covered in week-old stubble. Yet, even beneath the five-o'clock shadow, his dimples were clearly marked. He didn't need to smile for me to see them. They were always there. Sometimes deep, sometimes shallow. They were my favorite of his features. I even liked the scar he had through his eyebrow.

"What would you have guilt about?" I asked.

"The accident I was in. I not only killed somebody, but it was my somebody. She was my person. The one I was supposed to be with. She was the one that made it"—he waved his hand through the air—"all worth it." Walker scowled, took off his hat, and ran his hand through his hair before securing it on top of his head again. "And I . . . I couldn't return the favor for her. I robbed her of everything she had and everything she was capable of."

My stomach churned, and I could finally see why he had problems falling asleep at night.

"She was the only person I ever really loved, and I threw it all away. I don't deserve to be happy. I don't deserve to let that go—that guilt." He buried his head in his hands.

"Of course you do. It was an accident. You're a great person. Don't say you don't deserve to be happy!"

"Tell me this, Wilde, do you deserve to be happy, after you killed Big Jim?" he asked, his words like a dagger in my back. I knew Big Jim had died because he tripped over me, and I had told myself a million times over that it wasn't my fault. That it was self-defense. That he'd brought it on to himself.

Still, the answer was no. I didn't believe that I deserved happiness after what I had done. I hung my head in admission, and Walker nodded. "I didn't think so."

"So, what?" My voice was a little louder now. "We're just going to live out eternity like this?" I asked, tightness coiling inside me. I hadn't chosen this life.

"Yeah. You and me. We're stuck trudging through this hell."

I frowned, angry at the cards I'd been dealt. "At least we have each other?" It was more a hopeful question than a statement, wondering if he felt the same way. But when he burst into laughter, I didn't know what to think. I felt as white as a ghost. I began to chuckle into my cupped hand as I tried to cover my mouth. I was only laughing because he was.

"At least I've got you," he said, as if it were a punch line. He laughed some more, and I cringed inside, wondering what I had said that was so funny. But when his laughter died, and he looked at me with all seriousness and a warmth behind the windows to his soul, I knew he was happy to have me around. "Yup. At least I have you," he repeated, nothing funny about it.

When the silence crept back, the tone turned serious once again. "What happened that day?" I asked. Walker swallowed a lump in his throat, and I could tell that he'd feared I would ask that very question. But he knew as well as I did that he needed to talk about it. It was crucial to him letting go of the guilt that haunted him.

"We were getting away for the weekend. It was a long weekend, a special one. We were just getting into Baylor late at night. I was drowsy from driving all day, and the roads were slick with fresh rainfall. It must've been the early hours of the morning. I remember my eyes burning as I tried to keep them open." Walker's fist tightened and released. The memory was consuming him, and I could almost see the stress coming off him in waves.

"We were so close to the cabin when it happened. It must've been a deer. It's the only thing I can think of. There was a reflex there that jerked the steering wheel. A hard right. The car flipped. The thought of me falling asleep and waking with the jerk haunts me to this day. It's not like a deer dashing in front of the car would have been any better. The outcome would remain the same. But there's something about me doing this all on my own, versus having outside influences that would change the way I feel about . . . who I am inside—what I've done."

I reached my hand out and grabbed Walker's forearm. I felt his muscles contracting underneath his jacket and I wished he could find peace within himself. I knew that time wouldn't be soon enough.

"The car rolled several times down the embankment and landed at the base of the lake. By the time I got out, she was already gone. She died before I could even say goodbye, or . . . I'm sorry."

Walker hid his face in the palms of his hands. I moved my hand from his arm to his back, rubbing up and down slowly. I wanted nothing more than to take his pain away. But he was back there at the site of the accident on that dreadful day, and there was nothing I could do to take him away.

"She didn't even know how much I loved her. She didn't know," he said, sniffling here and there.

"I'm sure she knew. I'm sure she did."

"I was going to tell her. I had plans that weekend. I was going to tell her how she'd changed my life and brought meaning to me when I had nothing. I was going to give her this . . ." Walker said, as he fished around in his pocket. It was a velvet box small enough to contain a ring. Possibly an engagement ring.

"Is that?" I asked in a whisper.

"Yes. I was going to propose."

I knew he'd had a girlfriend, and I knew it had been serious. Enough for him to have loved her. But I'd had no idea that he was going to propose. Or that he felt she was one in a million—made for him. They were soulmates. The same way my grandpa was with my gran.

I felt my heart sink lower inside my chest. Walker's heart couldn't be stolen, and worse, it would make me a bad person for even trying. At that moment, I knew what I had to do. I had to help him find his one true love and accept that it wasn't me. It never would be. And if I connected with him as much as I thought I did, then I needed to help him find peace.

"I'm so sorry," I said in a whisper. I knew it wasn't my fault. And for that, I had nothing to be sorry for. My apology wouldn't bring Layla back into his life. Yet, I said it simply because I had nothing else to say. Because there were no words to comfort the grieving. And I regretted it the moment it slipped from my lips.

"You have nothing to be sorry for," he said.

"I know! I'm sorry!" I said, wincing when it tumbled out again. I bit the inside of my cheek, hoping to silence myself. Walker took in a deep, staggered breath, and I watched from the corner of my eye as his back rose and fell again. I let my eyes wander over the dancing moonlight on the lake surface, and eventually, he did the same. *At least we have each other*, I thought.

"I need to find her, Wilde. The only thing I'm sure of these days. I have a loyalty to her, and if she's out there—stuck in this afterlife—then I need to find her. I found you, so I can't comprehend why I can't find Layla. It doesn't make any sense," he said.

"We'll find her," I said.

"I knew you were the one to help me. I just knew that you were the one who was going to find her. Call it a gut instinct."

"You're not the only one," I said with a chuckle. The amount of pressure these people were putting on me to find a phantom was astronomical.

"Oh?" he said.

"My gran keeps telling me the same thing," I said, shaking my head.

"That's what I'm talking about! You have connections that are going to help us find her. I feel it!"

"Connections?" I asked, tilting my head.

"Yeah, you have your gran. Didn't you say that she told you about the tower?" he asked. And while it was true, she had, I wasn't positive this was an ongoing thing—her helping and all.

"I mean, she did, but . . ."

"She's looking out for us. I don't know what's behind this for you, but I know it's going to change my entire existence. Once I find Layla, I'll finally have peace. I won't rest until it happens."

Walker was restless. He kept pulling on his sleeve and scratching at his chin. This was his life's mission, and without it, I wasn't sure what he had left. Besides me, that is. Another lost soul. "Why do you think she wants me to help you find her?" I asked.

"I don't know, Wilde. Trust me, I've racked my brain. I've stayed up countless nights trying to figure that out. The connection between us. As far as I see, other than us both being in this awful state of limbo—this afterlife amongst the living—I don't know why your gran would want to help me find her. But if she said that Layla needed you, it's worth a shot, right?" His brows raised underneath his hat, and his eyes were wide with hope.

"I would help you find her, regardless. I want that for you. I want you to be happy. And well, it's too late for me, but it's not for you. You have a purpose to find her, and I want to help." It was true. If Walker would be able to rest after making sure Layla was okay, then I would rest, too.

"What? You have a purpose too!" Walker said, surely out of instinct. But as soon as it left his lips, I could see it in his eyes that he regretted it. He had no idea what my purpose was, and he knew I was right. If I had to attach myself to his purpose to give myself a goal, that's just what I would have to do. It's not like I could go home and everything would be normal.

"Yeah, you're right. There's a purpose out there for me. Even if I haven't found it yet," I said, purely to make him feel better. I placed my hands against the damp wooden planks and leaned back. It was a beautiful night on the lake. Almost serene. It made me sad to think that all this beauty was lost in the mist. It touched my lips as I tilted my head back, and I wished it would always be like this. Calm and peaceful.

"Are you getting tired yet?" I asked.

"Who, me? Nah, I don't sleep. If I go home, I lie in bed and wonder till the sun comes up." Walker leaned back like I did, his head turned toward the cabin. "Hey, did you ever get any video feed from those cameras?" he asked, his tone lifting with curiosity.

"You wouldn't believe it. They all malfunctioned."

"Damn . . . I believe it," he said with a chuckle.

It was in this lighthearted teasing that we finished the night out on the dock. Walker was content until the sun began to rise. We talked a little more about the accident and Walker's life-long purpose. I imagined the times we spent together in the early morning hours by the lake had forged bonds that would one day become unbreakable. My hopes were that these early days were the pillars to our relationship, and that someday I'd look back on them with a warm heart—even if it failed to beat.

6

I went to bed early that morning after Walker and I had watched the sunrise together on the dock. I knew he said he didn't sleep, but I didn't have any trouble drifting off as soon as my head hit the pillow. But when I woke up, I wasn't cuddled safely between my bed sheets any longer. I wasn't in my bed at all.

As if transported in a state of sleep, I woke up wandering about the forest by my lonesome. Barefoot and still in my pajamas, I woke to the sound of a squirrel gnawing on a nut. My feet were cold and sensitive, treading the rough gravel and fallen pine needles. A fine mist surrounded me, making it difficult to see any distance. Goosebumps covered my arms, and I quickly tucked my hands into my armpits as I shivered, trying to understand not only where I was but how it came to be that I was out here in the middle of the night.

I was startled when an owl called out. My heart thumped as I recoiled. I took a step back and bumped into some bushes. It sent me lunging forward with a shriek. Eventually, I recognized that my attacker had been no more than a blackberry bush. I placed my hand across my heart and I took in several deep breaths. How it came to be night wasn't important now. I only needed to know how to get back to the cabin, and to do that, I needed to know where I was. But in the dead of the night, every tree looked identical to one another.

I heard a snap, and my deep breathing did nothing to calm me. I whipped my head back and forth, searching deep in the dark forest. Blackness to my left and blackness to my right. Little critters running over dried leaves and brushing up against the bushes grew louder as they ventured closer. That was until I heard a voice. A familiar voice. And all else dropped dead quiet.

"Kinsley? Can you hear me, dear?" It was no more than a whisper through the branches, but it was enough.

"Gran? Gran, is that you?" I asked, hoping that it was her come to save me. I searched all around, but the voice had come from every direction all at once.

"Kinsley?" she whispered again. It was no closer this time, and I looked up frantically to see a small clearing of a moonlit sky through the tall pine trees.

"Gran! Gran!" I took several steps forward and then retraced my steps. When the blackberry bush nipped at my bare calves, I lunged again, only to stop when I saw a small gray light in the distance. I stood still, my eyes laser-focused on the only light in the forest. I took one small step toward it, and it began to grow bigger and brighter.

"Gran?" I asked of the darkness. But there was no answer. The light flickered between the trees, and I could tell that there was movement there. It was coming closer to me. Winding in and out of the pines. I was both afraid and comforted by the unknown presence. I hoped it was my grandmother in rare form.

The light grew bright. The lumens were high as it became almost unbearable to look at. I squinted for as long as I could until I had to shield my eyes with the crook of my elbow. And as soon as I took my eyes off the mystical light in the forest, it went out again. Only this time, I could hear that it had closed the distance between us with a whisper-quiet breath. I pulled my arm down to the bridge of my nose and was surprised to see my gran standing before me. She wasn't of blood and flesh but of smoke or mist. Translucent. The bright light turned to a soft warm glow around her . . . and through her.

I said nothing. I let my eyes take in the beauty of my late grandmother. I'd never seen such a sight like this. She was a spirit, an apparition, but her eyes . . . her eyes were of incredible detail. Full of love and happiness, her eyes were as clear and vibrant as a warm summer's day. Almost clearer than my vision was capable of seeing. Though she stood several feet away, I could get lost in the crystals surrounding her pale green, emerald eyes.

"So beautiful . . ." I whispered. She floated through the mist like a slow waltz in the night.

"Kinsley?" she said with a shudder.

I smiled, and a single tear rolled down my cheek. For a moment, it looked like she was going to cry too, but instead, she reached her hand forward, cupping my cheek. She swiped her thumb over the tear, and her hand felt just like the cold mist—only more concentrated. It sent a shiver down my spine, and she smiled at my reaction.

"Oh, how I've missed you," she said.

"Was it you I spoke to on the phone?" I asked.

"Yes," she said, overjoyed that we had found grounds to communicate.

I couldn't take the excitement any longer. I lunged forward, putting my arms around her. I'd needed a hug more than I ever had in my entire life. And disappointment crashed down upon me when I fell forward and nobody was there to catch me.

I opened my eyes and my arms to find nothing but darkness before me. I spun around, my heart stopping. She was several feet away, her back to me. I circled back around her, and her head hung with disappointment.

"I'm so sorry, dear. We're not the same. I wish for nothing more than to give you a hug, but it's not in the cards today."

"It's okay, Gran. I'm just happy you're here." I rubbed my arms, chilly in the shadows of the night. I looked around and spotted an owl whose eyes were bright and yellow. "Did you summon me or something? The last thing I remember, I was lying in bed. I'm not sure how I got here. And as you can see, I'm not dressed for a midnight walk in the woods." I wiggled my toes across the gravel, and Gran peeked down.

"Honey, it's not nighttime," she said, looking around.

"What do you mean?" I asked, my eyes searching the depth of the dark and misty forest.

"I'm sorry, dear, did you say the woods?" Gran tilted her head.

"Yes . . ." I said in a leery tone. "What's going on, Gran?" I looked around sharply. Was I not seeing correctly?

"I'm so sorry, dear. I've been trying to make this visually appealing for you. I know the void can be quite a scary place if it's not decorated well. But I'm new at this, you see. I haven't lived here long. I didn't realize I had brought us to the woods, and to be honest with you, I'm seeing something entirely different," she said, looking around. She held her hand out with a small smile and I followed her eyes as they lowered to the tips of her fingers, as if a tiny bird or butterfly had just landed on one. But all I could see was the forest with its haunting shadows and secrets.

I'm not sure why, but I began to cry. There was only so much I could take. Only so many questions without answers. They bubbled up until the stress boiled over and poured out in streams of frustration. I didn't want to spend my time with Gran complaining. I knew my time with her was limited. But I couldn't help myself from the mental breakdown that had been threatening to burst forth for weeks on end.

"I can't do this anymore! I can't be blind to this! Nothing makes sense. Nothing! How are you there in my dreams and the next day we're out in the woods? How could I talk to you on the phone and now you're a spirit? How in the world do you not see the woods? They're surrounding us! They're everywhere!" I yelled with my arms outstretched. I spun around, pointing to all the trees. "You're telling me you don't see that one right there? Or that one next to it? What about this one over here? That blackberry bush . . . you don't see it?" My voice hitched.

"I'm sorry, dear. I'm trying to tell you what you need to know—"

"Then just tell me already! Tell me!" I yelled.

"I—" she began, but I couldn't take one more second without knowing.

"Just tell me!" I screamed with my eyes closed behind my balled fists.

Tears spilled from my eyes, and I grabbed my stomach in pain as I heaved forward. I let out loud, ugly sobs that echoed off the trees. I struggled to suck in jagged air, my diaphragm locking up. And when I thought to open my eyes, when I thought the worst was already there upon me, I found my gran far in the distance, her light dimming as she was on her way out.

"Don't go! Don't go!" I choked out, my hand reaching into the darkness. I dropped to my knees, and I felt the pine needles dig into my kneecaps.

I hunched over as my hands wrapped around my waist. My forehead dipped until it rested on top of the fallen pine needles. Tears rolled down my nose and fell into the dirt. I grabbed at my waist, the thin material of my nightshirt not enough to protect me from my fingernails as they dug into my sides. In a world that I was so unsure of, I welcomed the pain. There wasn't much that was real to me now, and if all I was sure of was this searing ache of my nails digging into my ribs, I'd take it. It was better than nothing. Better than the abyss.

I had never felt more alone than I did that night. I had thought that many times before, but each time I did, it was exceedingly worse. I had died before. And I didn't even remember it. And I didn't doubt that anybody else had remembered it either. I was nothing to anybody. And now, I was lost and lonely, half-dressed in the middle of the forest. Or what I assumed was the middle of the forest. And I could only hope that it was the woods near the cabin of Rock Creek Cove.

Even the ghost of my gran couldn't stand to be near me. I had shut her out by screaming. Demanding to know more. If I had only accepted what she'd given me. But I was too greedy with questions. I pried when I shouldn't have. And I hated myself for it. I hated myself for many things. I couldn't do anything right; I couldn't make anybody love me; I couldn't even make the conversation last. I was worthless. And why wouldn't I be? I wasn't even alive.

Truth be told, I had spent my afterlife at the cabin with all my friends and it was pathetic. I should have had somewhere to go—somewhere to be—but instead, I was following these people around like a lost puppy.

At some point, the tears ran dry. I lifted my head from the gravel and dusted off my face. And sometime later, the pity I had felt for myself went cold, allowing the fear to creep back in. That's when I knew. That's when I knew it was time to leave.

When the owl started calling out and sending chills down my spine. The point where I started to look into the forest and worry about predators. That was my cue to leave. I got to my bare feet, dusted off my knees, and began walking. I didn't know what direction I was heading in, but anything was better than being stagnant.

I had a long time to rethink how I was living my afterlife. There were a few things I was sure of that came to light after my gran left. One of them being I needed to help Walker find his soulmate. I needed to release his soul so that he could be free how he deserved. It was my priority—far more important than anything I had planned for myself. The second thing I knew for sure was that I was doing this all wrong.

If I was already dead, then what was I doing, spending my time worrying about any of this? I'd come here to have the best summer of my life before I went off to college. Many of us were moving away. And if I didn't take this summer to live out what should have been . . . then I don't think I'd ever forgive myself. Perhaps I wouldn't move on at all.

There was no point in worrying about the things I could not control—the things I couldn't even understand. And the things that made little, if any, sense. There was no point in worrying about things that may not even be real. And I had no way of telling what was. For this reason, as I walked through the forest, I realized I was letting this opportunity slip by me. To be dead and yet still alive, roaming this earth with my friends . . . It was a gift to have more time with them. There must've been something that I was robbed of. Unfinished business, placing me back at the cabin for the summer.

I had to make this the best summer ever, like I'd wanted when I was a senior in high school. I had to kiss boys. Fall in love. I had to go to concerts and fairs. I had to go to the farmer's market and sunbathe out by the lake. Soak up the sunlight before it penetrated right through me. I had to do it all because if I knew one thing, this was my last chance. And I was already on borrowed time.

It hit me like a ton of bricks. My stomach felt like I had fallen off a thirty-story building. I jolted and reached my arms out wide, surprised to discover bed sheets balled up in my fists. I shot up, my back straight as a board. I looked around the master bedroom of the cabin, and I was surprised to find myself in bed where I had thought I'd fallen asleep. The sun was bright through my window, and quite some time had passed. The room was hot, and the downstairs was loud with laughter. I must've been sleeping the entire time, but for the *life* of me, I couldn't believe it. My gran, her spirit, it had been so real. More real than anything . . . more real than life itself had ever been. I closed my eyes and shook my head, but all I could see were the crystals of her pale green, emerald eyes staring back at me.

If I ever saw her again, I made a promise to myself that I wouldn't attack her with questions. I wouldn't push her away, and above all else, I would never scream at her again. I wondered if she would ever come back to me after I'd treated her that way.

Gran had mentioned something about rules, and I imagined she had already been breaking a few by talking to me in the first place. I didn't know when or if I would see her next, but until then, I had defined some purposes, whereas before, I had none. I was going to help Walker find the girl, and I was going to have fun doing it. I was going to enjoy my friends because, like Lainey —whom I hadn't seen in days—I knew my time with them was limited. And I wanted to soak them up like the sun that was void in the dark forest.

7

It was the day before the fishing tournament, and I had convinced every girl in the cabin to secretly enter the tournament against the boys. Everybody thought it was a great idea, and we couldn't wait to see their faces when our boat pulled up next to theirs on the morning of the competition.

There was a different air to the cabin, and maybe it was because I had a shift in mindset, or maybe it was just going to be a good day, but either way, I was grateful that things had finally turned around. The summer of fun was just what I needed—it's what we all needed, and I was happy to be back on track. That didn't mean that I missed Lainey any less, and she still took up a lot of my mind. I still searched for her between the pines every morning when I took Gunner out for his daily walk. And though I had lost most of my hope of finding her, I knew firsthand that the alternative wasn't so bad. Secretly, I hoped she would come back to me.

I didn't know what death looked like for my gran. She seemed to be having a different experience than I. But for me, things were pretty much the same. It was a little weird here and there. I was by far the outcast of the group, but that was normal for me. I'd always been the outcast. My dyslexia had set me apart in second grade, and I had never come back from that. I'd always been pulled out for special classes, and I had always asked the other kids for help with directions. I had never been the leader, and I had never been independent, simply because I couldn't. Not at school. But maybe, just maybe, I'd find my place here in the afterlife. Maybe being the outcast wasn't so bad.

Scarlett May, Kimber, and Emma piled into the back of the cab, and I took the front seat. We told the guys that we were going out for breakfast, and when they wanted to join us, we insisted it was girl time. Kai didn't seem to care, but when Scarlett May complained about her period, he threw his hands up in the air and backed away slowly.

A sweet mountain of a woman named Henry—after her father—gave us a ride into town. She suggested Paula's Pancake House for breakfast. All the locals did. Not just because the pancakes were delicious, but because it was the only breakfast spot in town. If you wanted more options, you would have to go to the other side of the lake, which took forever to drive. It was worth it sometimes, but not today when our focus was signing up for the fishing tournament.

We had Henry drop us off at the local fishing store where we could fill out our entry forms and pay the fees for the Baylor Bass Tournament.

The door chimed, and two sportsmen stopped in their tracks when the four of us walked in.

"Hi, we'd like to enter the Bass Tournament," I said. The two men stifled laughter, and it irritated not only me but Scarlett May. I grabbed her arm when the men turned their focus and shook my head. They retrieved the forms we needed, and I scowled at Scarlett May, hoping she wouldn't say anything too snarky.

"How many of you?" one of the men asked.

"Five of us," I said, still accounting for Lainey.

"You're going to need two boats then," he said, pointing between us. "You won't all fit in the same boat."

"Sure. Two boat entries," I said, looking between the girls. Kimber nodded positively, and Emma was busy looking at a pink worm lure. Emma and I started to fill out the paperwork, and it looked like one of the boats was going to be short a member. When I counted out on my fingers, I realized I was accounting for Lainey. Emma's eyes fluttered down to the paperwork, and without much thought, I entered Walker's name on the line instead.

No harm, no foul. If he didn't want to join, he didn't need to. When all was said and done, when the fees had been paid and we were signed up, the girls and I decided to check out the pancake house. It was just what I needed—an actual girls' trip. Only a couple of blocks away, it was a short walk. The sun was still buried behind the morning fog but working diligently to burn it off. I noticed that the flyers for Big Jim had been taken down around town. The thought of it made my palms sweat.

We got settled in at Paula's Pancake House, and after looking over the menus, we were ready to order. All of us except for Kimber ordered the special. She got an egg white omelet.

"Have any of you heard about that guy that was murdered? I think he worked at the grocery store?" Kimber asked, eyeing my butter-soaked pancakes.

My stomach dropped, and I momentarily stopped chewing to survey the girls.

"Yeah, that was Big Jimmy. He's psychotic! He probably did it to himself! Everybody knows him, and he goes off his medication and gets super weird and violent. He's the guy that attacked Kinsley in the grocery store." Scarlett May gestured toward me with her fork. I felt my cheeks heat as all the girls looked at me for confirmation.

"Yeah, it's true he did," I muttered.

"Oh my god, do you think he's tied to what happened to Lainey?" Kimber asked. All the girls fell silent, as nobody wanted to think about it.

"I bet he is, that sick son of a bitch!" Scarlett May said, her fist coming down on the table.

"Do you think he did it? I mean, not just Lainey . . . but Trinity too?" Kimber asked, her voice quiet and solemn.

All of us looked at each other anxiously, and everybody was thinking about it, but nobody wanted to say it. I was the only one who had any insight on Jimmy. He had squirreled away Trinity's jacket in the tower. It was the jacket she'd worn the night she went missing. It was strong evidence that he was her killer. And I knew he had it in him from the attack on Walker and me. But he had nothing to do with Lainey's disappearance. Because he hadn't been alive when she disappeared. I feared something else was to blame for that.

There was something else. Something in the water. There was something bigger than all of us, including Big Jimmy, that threatened our lives here in Baylor. And if I had to guess, I would say their disappearance had something to do with the Baylor phenomenon.

"I don't know. I'm still hoping that Lainey turns up," I said quietly.

"You can't be serious?" Scarlett May said. Her brows furrowed, and I couldn't quite tell, but it almost looked like she was disgusted with me.

There were two groups of girls among our friends. Subdivided by popularity. Trinity, Scarlett May, and Kimber were the popular ones. Then, held together by the guys in the group, were us: Lainey, Emma, and me. There wasn't much overlap between us. We weren't friends on our own, and I imagined Noah was the one who brought our two groups together to build one. But Trinity's group wasn't just made up of the popular ones but the *mean* ones. They didn't have a problem saying what they meant or cutting you down to size. In fact, I think they liked it. I think they enjoyed making us feel small, and I imagined it made them feel more important.

Emma, Lainey, and I were the less liked and nerdier of the group. Lainey was always into plants and nature, while Emma was the bookworm. She'd read all day if she could. And I was just the introvert. I was the introspective, insecure one. I was always physically present, but my mind would be gallivanting somewhere else. Somewhere deep, full of self-doubt and observation. I looked for the reasons and the proof that I was a wallflower. And honestly, I think I liked it. I liked knowing that I was unseen. There's a lot less responsibility for an invisible person. And now that I thought of it, being dead kind of suited me. But for whatever reason, my voice was still heard . . . my face still seen. I had to deal with Lainey's disappearance, just like everybody else.

"She's dead, Kinsley. I don't know why you haven't accepted that yet." Scarlett May snapped. She brought her fork down, stabbing her pancake and scraping it against the plate. The sound of the metal scraping the porcelain was painful to my ears. I winced from both the sound and her comment.

I looked at Kimber. She had been so busy eyeing our pancakes that I didn't think she had heard a single word. She chewed mindlessly as her eyes darted from plate to plate. I felt the tension flowing off Emma, who sat next to me. Emma, Lainey, and I were always the best of friends, but it was Lainey and I who were the closest. Emma was always the third wheel.

"You don't know that," Emma said beneath her breath. It was unlike her to stand up to Scarlett May. But this time, it struck a chord. And I was proud of her.

"Oh, yes, I do. You'll see," Scarlett May said, staring deep into Emma's eyes. The rest of our breakfast was uncomfortable. It was hard to grieve for somebody you weren't sure had lost their life. It was almost as if I was teetering on the edge of hope and despair, and it changed from one moment to the next.

I hated how cold-hearted Scarlett May could be, and she had a way of making a bad situation worse. The only difference between Scarlett May and Trinity was that Scarlett May was all bark and no bite. Trinity, on the other hand—she'd let you pet her and then bite you when you turned your back.

I was thankful when Kimber finally joined the conversation and it turned from our deceased and missing friends to more lighthearted matters—like boys. I wasn't about to forget that my best friend was out there somewhere and needed me. But I was happy to engage in a conversation that pulled on the heartstrings a little less.

"Do you think that Noah and Trinity had a secret thing going between them?" Kimber asked me. It hurt to know that he was one of the last to see her, and probably he saw quite a bit of her.

Noah and I? There wasn't much to tell. He'd been my longtime crush, but something had changed when he'd gone into that bedroom with Trinity. Some sort of loyalty had been lost. He knew it. I knew it. But a part of me still had feelings for him. It was possible I might always be curious about him and what could have been.

"I can't tell you how Noah feels, but I wasn't convinced that he liked her," I said.

"That's because you thought he liked you?" Scarlett May asked, brows raised.

"No! That's not it," I said. My fork made that awful sound on my plate.

"He did, though, or *does*, right?" Emma asked.

I scowled, looking at her. It wasn't something I wanted the other side to know. What was going on between Noah and me was a secret. It was a secret because I wasn't convinced he really liked me. Or that he wanted to be seen with me. Sure, I was good enough to be his friend, but *girlfriend*? Probably not. But now that we were out of high school, things could be different. If I hadn't died, that may have . . . Well, it would never work now.

"I've been seeing you with some local. He always comes around the docks, even when you're not here at the cabin. Who is he? He's kinda cute," Kimber said. The thought of her calling Walker cute made my blood boil. I knew I couldn't have him either, but I still wanted to keep him for myself.

I found myself stuck between Noah and Walker. I couldn't have Noah because we were partially separated by a thin, translucent veil. One side living, and the other not knowing how to move on. On the other hand, I couldn't have Walker because his heart belonged to another. Yet, somehow, I still had feelings for both of them. It's true. My feelings for Noah had been seriously dampened since the thing with Trinity—and even more so since Walker came into the picture—but I couldn't deny that there was something still lingering every time I passed him in the kitchen or hallway. The tension of what-if?

"That's just . . . he's just a friend. He's staying at a cabin across the lake. He might do the tournament with us," I said with a shrug.

"Really?" Emma asked.

"Yeah. It's no big deal."

"Because I was thinking maybe you and I could be a team, and then Kimber and Scarlett May could be a team," Emma said. I looked at the other girls across the table, and one look was clear enough that they didn't want Emma in their boat.

"That sounds great. You don't mind if he joins us, though, right?" I asked.

"There's something in the water . . ." Emma said, though it didn't line up with the movement of her lips. And the voice a fraction lower than hers.

My eyes flicked from her lips to her eyes and then across the table to Scarlett May and Kimber. Nobody had a look on their face that told me something was out of the normal, and the more I looked at them in question, the more suspicious they became. I cleared my throat.

"I'm sorry. What did you say?" I asked.

"I said I don't mind. That's great," Emma said, shaking her head.

"Okay, great," I said, nodding. I let my eyes wander over the other customers in the pancake house. None of them were close enough to have spoken the secret message, but I'd heard it loud and clear.

"Excuse me, miss, we're ready for the check," Kimber said, waving down the waitress. A cute blonde nodded and ran off to get our check. But when she came back to the table to thank us for dining with her, there was only one thing I heard.

"There's something in the water . . ." she said. Her eyes fixed on mine when she said it. Although her lips said something much different. Like a bad voice-over on an old film.

I swallowed a lump that was rising in my throat and anxiously fiddled with my clothing. This had happened to me before when I was out in the forest. I didn't like where it was going, and I worried it would get worse before it got better. I reached down to my phone and called a cab immediately. I was thankful when Henry had still been in town and she arrived quickly to give us a ride back to the cabin.

I hadn't escaped the cab ride without hearing Henry advise me about the water in some secret message only I could hear. I wanted to scream. I knew there was something in the water! I had felt it firsthand. And it wasn't something I wanted to come into contact with again. I knew I would be out on that water the next day, and it was almost enough to make me cancel the tournament. But I knew I would have Walker by my side, and I felt safe when he was in my presence.

I decided right then and there, when Henry told me there was something in the water, that I wouldn't do the tournament unless Walker agreed to do it with me. Emma would be a nice addition to our team, of course, but it was Walker that I needed. When we got back to the cabin. I called Walker immediately. I was thankful he agreed to do the tournament with us. Moreover, he seemed excited.

Emma and I spent half the night hiding in my bedroom, trying to figure out how to spool the fishing poles. It was more complicated than it first seemed. And somehow, we continued to get knots in the line.

"So, breakfast was awkward. I wish Scarlett May wasn't such a bitch!" Emma said, her tone so out of character that it made me laugh.

"You know, don't let her get to you. She means well, but she says it in the worst possible way."

"The worst."

"Um . . ." Emma began. When she said nothing more, I glanced at her. Her lips were pressed into a thin line, and her cheeks were red.

"Yeah?"

"No. Never mind," she said quickly.

"What is it?" I asked.

"It's stupid. Never mind." She batted a hand through the air.

I put the fishing line down on the bed. "Just say it. What?"

"Well, I don't want to offend you . . ." she said.

Only slightly offended already, I pressed her to continue. "Just say it so we can both move on." I shrugged, picking up the line again, and examining a knot.

"I just want to know what it's like."

"What?"

"Um. What it's like to be a ghost?"

My stomach dropped. This life was so real, I had almost forgotten. The reminder came crashing down on me. What was it like? It was like nothing ever changed.

"I'm sorry. You're offended," Emma said, disappointed with herself.

"No. It's not that. It's hard to put into words. It's like the same life I had before, only my future's been stripped away. All the best parts of my life are now behind me. And sometimes I think I'm losing myself. Like my mind is deteriorating the further I sink into the afterlife. I'll never have anything real again, and I'll probably never find love."

Emma's brows knitted together. "Huh. I never want to die. Does it hurt?"

"I didn't either. Part of me is glad I don't remember it. I think it would be harder that way. Um, no it doesn't hurt. But I get these headaches quite often, and I'm starting to think they have something to do with the crash. They're only temporary," I said, biting on the fishing line, trying to free a knot.

"Are you going to tell your mom?"

I rolled my eyes, temporarily giving up on the knot. "I mean, I assume she knows. I did call her, but I only heard a one-sided conversation. I think I made up the whole thing," I said.

"She's probably heartbroken," Emma said.

I nodded slightly. She probably was. The thought of it made me unbelievably homesick. Emma must have realized she'd gone too far. She sucked in a quick breath and pressed on.

"Hey, did you notice Kimber was, like, oddly obsessed with our pancakes?" Emma asked, her eyes darting from side to side. I let out a chuckle because I actually had noticed.

"I totally saw that! I don't know why she didn't just order them, she clearly wanted them."

"Do you think that maybe she's not eating enough?" Emma looked at me, her eyes scrunched, as if she shouldn't be talking about it.

I sighed. "Sometimes I wonder the same thing. I catch her staring at the mirror quite often, and it's usually from her backside. She changes her clothes all the time . . . probably because she doesn't like the way she looks in them. I don't think she knows how pretty she is," I said.

"What a shame, to have it all, but not to see it," Emma said, baring her teeth.

"That egg white omelet? That looked gross." I shook my head, narrowing my gaze on the tiny translucent knot between my fingertips.

"I thought it looked good!" Emma laughed.

"You would," I said smiling, trying to bite the knot again. I rolled my eyes, giving up on untangling the line and dug through the lures we had bought. Of course, there was the pink one. Emma just had to get that one. I left the blue one for Walker and opened a small package of gold worms that felt like they had oil covering them. I smelled my fingers and made a face. Emma laughed.

"Do you think we should talk to her about it?" she asked, as I wiped my fingers on my jeans.

"I don't know. I wouldn't know what to say," I said, hating the way that I felt helpless.

Kimber and I weren't the closest of friends, but she was my favorite out of that side of the group. Scarlett May had her times when she seemed subdued, and Trinity had a few moments where she and I actually clicked. She could be a lot of fun when she wanted to be. But Kimber? She was the nicest. The only reason she hung out with the mean girls was that she was one of the most popular girls in school. If she hadn't been, I'm sure she would've come over to our side of the group long ago. But the poor girl had such low self-esteem. I'm sure the other two steamrolled her all the time. It was hard to watch.

"Maybe we can just tell her that she looks really skinny and that she should eat more," Emma said with a shrug as she tried to tie a hook to the end of the line.

"You know, I've thought about this a bunch. Sometimes when you say something to her about her looks, it's almost like she goes backward. It doesn't seem like a compliment to her. And I doubt telling her to eat more would feel like a positive thing, either."

"But why?" Emma asked.

"Because. I don't think she really wants to be skinny. I think it's like a skipping record that plays in her head. The problem is much deeper than that. Kimber doesn't see herself the way she really is when she looks in the mirror. It's all distorted by her insecurities." I held up the fishing rod, proud of my mangled mess. I was certain that when Walker saw it, he'd laugh.

I had never gone fishing before, although I had sat in the boat while Noah fished when we were kids. Sure, I held the pole every now and then, but I had no idea how to put bait on my hook or how to spool the reel. I had several knots here and there, and I was pretty sure I had done it completely wrong. But as long as the line was in the water and the worm was on the hook, I figured I would do all right.

Emma laughed, and when she showed me hers, it was even worse than mine. We both laughed together, and I buried my head in a pillow.

"We are *so* going to win this tournament!" Emma said.

8

It was early morning. Gray light, the cold mist upon my face, and the smell of the lake. Emma and I were the first to wake, and we snuck out of the house holding our fishing poles. I had a sack lunch. Emma had a huge cooler she struggled to carry but a big smile on her face, and I knew that we had done right by entering the tournament. This really could be a summer to remember. Maybe not the best—not what it should have been—but I was positive that we could find a few nuggets of joy along the way. And this tournament was going to be one of them.

We were making our way down to our boat, which was tied to the dock. A bunch of bananas was tucked under my arm. It was probably the only thing I knew about fishing. It was bad luck to have a banana on the boat. Strategically, Emma and I placed a banana in each of the guys' boats.

"Should I put one in Scarlett May's boat too? Or just the guys?" Emma asked. I looked up at her with a wicked air, and a slow smile spread across my face.

"Hell, throw *two* bananas in their boat!" I said. Emma smiled and tossed a couple in.

"Well, aren't you the devious ones!" Walker appeared out of nowhere. The fog was so thick I never saw his canoe coming. I stifled a laugh and ran to the dock's edge to help him tie up.

"Thank you so much for joining us," I said.

"Us?" Walker asked.

"I hope you don't mind. Emma's going to join us. Scarlett May and Kimber weren't exactly welcoming," I said in a whisper.

Walker looked at Emma with his head cocked to the side and a sympathetic stare. "I don't mind. The more, the merrier. Now, who are all the bananas for?" he asked.

"Boat one consists of Asher, Noah, and Ethan. Boat two is Levi, Mason, and Kai," Emma said, pointing. "Boat three is Scarlett May and Kimber. That boat there is ours." Emma dusted her hands.

"Waking up early to destroy the competition, I knew I was on the right team!" Walker said.

I held my hand out and Walker took it as he crawled out of his canoe. He didn't need my help, of course, but I was happy to give it. It was the small moments where our hands met that made me feel alive. I looked back to the house as I remembered that nobody had let Gunner out. Nobody took care of him the way I did.

"Hey, you guys, I'm just going to run up and let Gunner out real quick. He probably needs to go to the bathroom."

"We're really early, so take your time," Emma said. They situated the tackle as I jogged down the dock and back up the hill. When I got close to the cabin, I could hear him scratching on the door and knew I had made the right decision. But as I opened the door, he lurched out, blew past my legs, and took off running. Now I feared I had made a terrible mistake and that Gunner would run away. We didn't have time for this. Not this morning. I threw my hands up in the air as I watched him barrel down the hill, wondering where he was going and why he wasn't running toward the woods. It didn't take long for him to jump into the water. All he needed was a morning swim. I shrugged and held my hands out. I could hear Walker's laughter from where I stood on the back porch before I started down the hill again.

The sky was getting lighter now; everybody would be awake soon. I wanted to get on the water before they were up to find the bananas in the boats and give us all hell about it. But I knew I couldn't leave without having Gunner locked up safely in the cabin. "He really likes the water, huh?" Walker asked.

"I guess so," I said with a shrug.

"I don't think he's going to come out on his own, Kinsley. He looks like he won't go without a fight," Emma said.

I sighed, knowing that she was right.

"Let's bring him," Walker suggested.

"Bring him? That would be a disaster," I said, shaking my head.

"No, it'll be great. I used to fish with my dog all the time. Dogs like that love the water," Walker said as he tried to lure Gunner to the boat. With a little coaxing, Gunner was in the boat, getting all the seats wet. I turned to Emma, and we shared a look of trepidation.

"See? He loves it!" Walker said as Gunner shook off the excess water, completely drenching the inside of the boat. All I could think about was my jeans soaking through, making it look like I'd peed my pants. But if it was going to make Gunner happy, it was the least I could do. If Lainey had been here, she would probably want to bring him too.

We set off just as the sun made its debut. Walker did the rowing, and Emma and I sat huddled together for warmth. Gunner ran back and forth through the tiny boat, rocking it. We didn't need a banana on the boat when we had him. With all this running back and forth, I had no doubt that I would end up in the water by the end of the tournament. And the water was no place I wanted to be.

My eyes settled on Emma's pink fishing lure. There was no way we were going to win the Baylor Bass Tournament, and likely, we wouldn't even board a fish. But my goal here wasn't to beat the guys—as much as I'd like to. My goal in entering the tournament was to see the look on their faces when we pulled our boat up next to theirs. I knew it would be a moment to remember. And with any luck, Walker would have some skill with fishing and we could at least have one fish to dangle in front of their faces. It was about making memories, and we had already succeeded at that.

It was when the cabin was far behind us that I could hear the booming voice echoing across the lake. I didn't know for sure, but I figured it was Mason yelling over the bananas he found in the boat. It brought a warm smile to my face, and I couldn't be happier with how the morning started. Gunner hadn't settled down yet, but I was hopeful that he would.

"So, I think we're going to start off on the east side. There's a cove called Blackwell's over there, and I've been pretty lucky fishing in that spot before," Walker said, rowing in that direction.

"Yeah, yeah," Emma said.

"Whatever you think," I said and nodded.

It was a little quiet in the morning before our caffeine kicked in. I could tell that Emma was uncomfortable with Walker. Not uncomfortable because she didn't know him, or even that she knew too much about him, but more like she was uncomfortable because he was attractive. She avoided eye contact with him, and when he spoke to her, she often blushed and started to fidget. I couldn't blame her for that. If I hadn't gotten to know him, or if he hadn't saved my life, I doubt I would have felt comfortable enough around him to be myself. He was *that* attractive. Walker caught my eye and he smiled, his dimples piercing his cheeks. I looked at Emma and wrinkled my nose, laughing at how her cheeks were a rosy hue.

After catching a few bass—which apparently were small ones—we changed spots. It was beginning to get warm, and I knew that all three of the boats tied to our dock were now on the lake. I didn't need to see Scarlett May and Kimber flounder around on their boat, squealing over the bait, but I did want to see the guys. I wanted to tease them about the bad luck we gave them in the early morning. And I wanted to see their faces when we told them we already had a catch and release. But it was an enormous lake. Big enough that if we didn't know where they were going to be ahead of time, we might never meet up. Thankfully, I had listened in on Asher's conversation with Ethan last night, and they were going to fish fairly close to the cabin.

I wasn't too sure where Levi, Mason, and Kai were fishing, but if I had to guess, I'd say the two boats would stay close together. Heck, even the girls would probably stay close to the cabin. I'm sure that Kimber didn't have the strength to row the boat as far as we had. Walker's arms were broad and strong. But that's not all; he'd been commanding this canoe for some time. Twenty years maybe. He was conditioned for rowing. And I couldn't say that about anybody else in the cabin.

"Let's head back and see if anybody else caught anything," I said.

"Is anybody hungry? I made some breakfast burritos," Emma said. She took out a bag of three tinfoil-wrapped burritos from the cooler and closed the lid quickly. My mouth watered.

"That sounds fantastic. Thank you," I said, reaching out for the breakfast. Walker said the same.

"What else do you have in there?" he asked, trying to peek inside the cooler.

"You'll see. It's a secret," Emma said, bright red.

Before I knew it, we were drifting on the lake, no longer fishing or rowing, but it was the best part of the tournament. The pleasant conversation and tasty food. I'd had Emma's burritos before, and while they were always good, everything tasted better on the water. Gunner pressed his nose into my thigh, begging with a little whimper. Had he not been my best friend's companion, I wouldn't have sacrificed the butt of my breakfast burrito. But because he was, I shared, and he thanked me by nearly snapping my fingers off.

I found it funny that the best part of the fishing tournament was the part when we weren't fishing. Nothing but quality time with Walker and Emma. The more time Emma spent with Walker, the more she loosened up, and I could tell that her personality had started to come through. She was fond of Walker, but I didn't mind. I knew he was taken. And I couldn't blame her, because I thought he was adorable. Walker seemed to enjoy Emma's company as well, and I wondered if he'd had much interaction as a ghost for the past twenty years. And then I briefly wondered what would happen when everybody left the cabin and only I remained.

The day seemed to fly by. We caught two keepers, which Walker seemed disappointed by, and the three of us got ridiculous sunburns. It wasn't until afternoon that we headed back to the cabin and spotted the other three boats. It was as glorious as I had hoped. Mason stood up, throwing his arms into the air and yelling belligerently about the bananas. It was clear that he had been drinking, and none of us could understand what he was saying. We laughed so hard, Emma pointed at him, and I wrapped my arms around my stomach. Somewhere after the laughter lightened, I caught a glimpse of Noah's face. It was a look I didn't know well on him, and if I had to imagine, I'd say it was jealousy. I wasn't proud of it, but there was a part of me that enjoyed it just a little bit.

Noah had hurt me. He knew it, I knew it, Trinity knew it. The three of us knew I had feelings for him, and the funny part was, I believed Noah felt the same toward me. Why he'd done it? I'd never know. I had given up on trying to figure that out. Things never went back to normal for me and him, and . . . well, I liked to blame that on his actions with Trinity, but I knew there was a large part of it that had to do with my feelings for Walker. Still, to see him want me the way I had wanted him for the past year . . . it was satisfying in a deep and twisted way. I wasn't perfect; I knew that. Hell, I wasn't even human. I suppose I couldn't expect too much from myself. I looked from Noah to Walker and felt the uncomfortable pull of my heart in different directions . . . toward my old life and—with greater strength and possible pain—my new life with Walker.

"Hey, Wilde, catch anything yet?" Noah yelled. I held up the two fish we'd caught with pride. And Emma ripped open the cooler and stood tall and proud, holding a large salmon.

"Read 'em and weep, suckers!" Emma yelled, the salmon slipping out of her hands and hitting the bottom of the canoe.

"What!" I burst into laughter. Walker rolled onto his side, clutching his gut, laughing.

"Yeah, we're going to win the whole tournament! Caught this little guy over in Blackwell's Cove!" Emma yelled.

"Is that a store-bought salmon?" I choked out.

"Yeah, shhh. They don't need to know that," Emma shushed me.

Walker was dying of laughter.

"Is that a salmon?" Noah called out.

"Oh yeah. Just a little one," Emma gloated.

"Do they have salmon in this lake?" Mason asked Kai.

Emma's eyes grew large, and she whipped her head back to Walker. He couldn't speak, but he shook his head.

"Salmon don't live in Baylor Lake!" Kai shouted.

"You're a cheater!" Levi yelled out, laughing.

Emma sat back down and threw the slippery salmon back into the cooler. "Thirty bucks down the drain," she mumbled.

I grabbed her shoulder, laughing, and she cracked a smile. "Oh my god—"

"I thought I had this one in the bag," she said with a chuckle.

"It's okay. We got skunked too! I wonder why?" Noah said, holding up the banana. Gunner barked and rocked the boat.

"I got one!" Mason yelled, standing up as his pole darted around frantically. Kai and Levi jumped up in excitement for their first catch of the day, and their boat rocked back and forth. I imagined them falling into the water, and I watched with excitement as I tried to keep Gunner calm.

"They're going to beat us!" Scarlett May complained. The two of them looked like they had done little all day except float around Rock Creek Cove. Kimber pulled out her phone to take pictures and video of Mason pulling up his fish, and we all watched eagerly. Walker rowed the boat a little closer, but Emma's fishing pole suddenly bent. Our attention snapped from Mason to Emma, who started screaming with delight. It was her first bite of the day, and it wasn't even store-bought.

"You got this," I said, standing up in the boat, which continued to rock. Gunner ran back and forth in the tight space of the canoe, and I reached out, grabbing Walker's shoulder to stabilize myself.

"Oh, they've got one too! Why didn't we catch anything!?" Kimber asked.

"Come on, man! We can't let the girls beat us!" Levi said to Mason as he pulled up a small fish. The guys yelled at Mason for making a big deal out of an eight-inch perch, and I could hear their laughter booming in the background. I wanted to laugh with them, but I was so focused on Emma's fight that I couldn't pull my gaze from the water. Gunner barked, running in circles.

"Slowly pull the reel up, allowing the fish to fight. Then, you're going to start reeling as you lower the pole back down. Go slow, as we don't want the line to snap," Walker coached. He placed his hand on Emma's forearm and helped guide her pole up and down. I tried to grab Gunner's collar to make the rocking stop, but it was impossible through all the commotion. I was pretty sure that Emma would catch nothing more than seaweed and all four of us would end up in the water by the end of the tournament.

"It's really fighting hard, huh?" Emma asked.

"Yeah, I think you have a big one!" Walker said with confidence.

"It feels like a big one!" she said between breaths. I tried to get a look but didn't dare lean over the water too far.

The anticipation grew as Emma fought the giant bass. Walker was kind and patient as he taught Emma everything he could in such a short time. I held onto Gunner as tightly as I could so he wouldn't rock the boat. I let my eyes flicker to the other boats in the cove. Scarlett May and Kimber watched carefully. Meanwhile, Asher and Ethan ate slices of pizza while watching Emma.

I was surprised to find Noah's eyes on me instead of the water or Emma like everybody else. Our gazes locked for just a moment and somewhere in that space I thought jealousy had turned to pain. Regret. He hated himself for the decisions he'd made, and there was a part of me that wanted to make it all better for him. Tell him I didn't care and that I still had feelings for him. But that ship had sailed.

Emma screamed with excitement. I stood up, leaning over the boat to catch a glimpse of the Baylor Bass Tournament's winning fish. The boat tilted close to the water's edge.

"I've got it! I've got it!" Emma yelled.

"How big is it?" Mason yelled, hands cupped around his mouth.

"It's a big one!" Emma screamed as a figure slowly rose from the depths of the water. It was a big one. *Too big*. My stomach dropped as I realized this figure was no fish. It was huge. I wasn't sure what else would be in the water—something of this magnitude. Slowly, I leaned forward, trying to get a better look, but my eyes couldn't quite pierce the glare on the water's surface.

"What is that?" Walker mumbled to himself.

"I did it!" Emma squealed, looking around at everybody.

"It's really big . . ." I said in a warning tone. Fish shouldn't be that size.

As the prize-winning fish slowly rose. The glare from the water receded and medium-length brown hair surfaced. A body . . . *her* body.

A guttural scream ripped through Emma's throat as Lainey's freckled face breached the surface of the water. Emma dropped the fishing pole and flailed backward. I could hear shouts from every boat around us just as the cold water hit my back. I plunged deep into the lake, and I could see Gunner's paws hit the water just above me in the commotion.

His four legs thrashed about as my body sank deeper and deeper. I tried to swim back to the surface, but it was no good, because I wasn't in the lake alone.

Lainey's lifeless body was anything but dead—she came to life before my very eyes. Her flesh gray, and the whites of her eyes now yellow.

Her hands grabbed me as if her life depended on it. I let out a scream and wished I hadn't. It was the breath I needed to survive, and I'd just let it go. I clamped my mouth shut; the water escaping between my teeth. Fighting the urge to breathe as I wrestled my best friend under the water.

I kicked at her desperate eyes as she became more aggressive. She was oddly strong for how weak she looked, and I knew that there was no blood coursing through her veins. She opened her mouth, hissing, as I grabbed her arm and ripped her grip off my calf.

I delivered several kicks to her chest, finally freeing myself. I was swimming to the surface when I saw Walker dive into the water—he looked so far away. He swam down toward me, and I reached my hand out, but the distance between us was too far to grab hold.

Lainey's demon grabbed my foot and yanked me back down. I felt the fight leave my body, as I needed oxygen and had none.

I'd been here before, but the thing that had tried to kill me hadn't been my best friend. Neither was this, though. The thing that had me tight in her grasp, drowning me, wasn't the girl I had grown up with. She wasn't the girl I had shared all my secrets with. She was a monster. And that was no more than Lainey's skin that it wore, and I had no trouble kicking my feet into its face.

"Wake . . ." she hissed. I watched her mouth move, and somehow her voice was a whisper in my ear and not at all muffled by the water.

I stopped fighting for just a second as not only the fatigue set in but also the confusion. I felt Walker's powerful hands grab at my arm, and he yanked my body upward.

He was just in time because I had nothing else to give. And neither did Lainey's ghost. I watched her yellow, desperate eyes begin to disappear into the depths of the water. And one last time I heard her whisper as clear as day.

"Wake up . . ."

9

None of us won the tournament. Not even close. As if it mattered anyway. Finding Lainey was like a dark wet blanket that draped over us. We headed inside the cabin, leaving all our belongings in the boats. Walker joined us, and for the first time, he was one of us. I wished it was something else that had brought him close. Anything but the death of my best friend. It stripped away all the joy I would have had from him joining the team.

After the panic had subsided, silence followed. It was hard to understand how this could happen. Not once, but twice. To our friends, nonetheless. As a collective group, we didn't know what to do. Lainey was the one who had called the cops before, and as that turned out, it had never really helped anything. Not here. Not in Baylor. They showed up at our door asking questions, and they took a lot of notes, but beyond that, I don't think they did anything. And if the cops were so quick to arrest a stranger for the murder of Big Jimmy, I didn't know what they would do with this information. Perhaps the Baylor phenomenon had affected them as well.

It was a somber evening. Everyone sat in the living room. Seats were taken on the sofa, and when there was no more room, we sat on the floor. Everybody waited. Waited for somebody to speak up, for somebody to take the lead. I wasn't sure who was going to do it. By the looks of everybody else, nobody wanted the job.

"Are you sure it was her?" Mason asked, cutting through the silence.

"I'm sure," I said.

What I hadn't told him was just how sure. She was long gone, and whatever that thing was in the water, it wasn't her. I just kept thinking about those awful yellow eyes and how they had a message for me. I wondered if anybody else would've seen it or heard it. And how it was so clear even though we were submerged underwater.

"This can't be happening again . . . I can't . . ." Kimber stuttered and began to cry. Asher put his arm around her and pulled her in close. She whimpered into his chest.

"It's going to happen to all of us. One of us is going to be next. And it's not going to be me," Scarlett May said. I nodded in agreement.

"How can you be so sure?" Levi asked.

"I'm going to get out of here. I'm going home!" she replied.

That's good, I thought. *She should go home. They all should.* Why they hadn't already, I didn't know. Independence, I suppose. The fact that we were now adults. We can't run from this. We can't run from our lives the way we used to when we were kids. But they should now.

"You should go home. You should all go home. Now, right now!" I said, standing up in the middle of the group, urging them to save themselves from this evil.

"You should too. We all should," Noah said. His eyes flickered from mine to Walker's. I hung my head, remembering the time that I tried and failed.

It was then that Kimber pulled herself together. "I think I will," she said, reaching out to grab Scarlett May's hand.

"You guys go. I'll call the cops. I'm gonna stay back for just one extra day to contact the police. But I will be out on the very next flight. I promise," I said, my eyes fixed on Walker. He gave me a slight nod, and I knew we were both on the same page. He and I were tethered to this place. But there was no reason that the rest of my friends should endure the wrath of my personal hell. Walker and I could, and should, do this alone.

Scarlett May and Kimber jumped to their feet. They held hands as they left the room to go pack their belongings. Asher jumped online to buy plane tickets, and I went to call a cab.

"It's going to keep happening. And if it's not us, it's going to be them—somebody else. Somebody else's daughter . . . somebody else's girlfriend. I say we stay. We find this son of a bitch," Mason said, his voice booming with authority. It was leadership like I'd never seen from him.

"Yeah!" Levi said, jumping to his feet. The pit sank in my stomach. This was bad. They couldn't fight whatever this was. And if there was one thing I was sure of, they should've never come here. This was my mess. I don't know why or how they got dragged into it, but I was doing everything in my power to get them out. My eyes shifted to Walker, and I could see his worry. Being the older one in the room, he stepped forward.

"Look, the police are on this. They've already arrested a guy for Big

Jimmy's murder. They think it was the same guy who got Trinity. And if I had to guess, it was probably the same person who got to Lainey. For all we know, he's already taken care of. But that doesn't mean that you guys shouldn't go home. This lake's not safe—not now, not ever. Mysterious things have been happening here for the last twenty years. Go home. Get the summer you deserve. And then have a life to live afterward," Walker said, looking each of us in the eyes.

I watched Mason and Levi rethink their prior commitment to stay and fight. Levi's eye contact dropped off as he scoured the floor. He didn't want to admit it, but I could tell he wanted to go home too. It took little to sway him.

"I don't know about you guys, but I'm going home. I'm gonna take my girlfriend home," Asher said and followed Kimber out of the room to go pack.

"I'm sorry, Kinsley. I've got to go too," Ethan said, placing his hand on my shoulder. I forced a smile and nodded. I understood it. Heck, I even wanted them to go, but there was a small part of me that felt like they were leaving me behind. Because I was pretty sure it would be the last time I ever saw them again. And when all was said and done and Walker found Layla, I'd probably cease to exist.

What would happen when they went home? Would they find out about the accident I was in? Would they know they had spent the last few weeks at the lake with a ghost? Or would the phenomenon continue, and they would simply not remember, like Walker said happened to his friends. Time would leap, and they would look back on a hot and forgettable lakeside summer.

There were no flights that night, and everybody had to wait with their bags packed for an early morning flight. I tried to help Emma pack, but she insisted on staying with Walker and me. I couldn't tell if she was brave in the face of danger or so delusional that she believed this was one of her fantasy books. Maybe a murder mystery? I wasn't sure without the ending. But I insisted she leave with the others, and she came down on me very firmly, which was unlike her. I figured if Emma Olsen had raised her voice, it better be for a good reason, and I let her stay.

The night was long, but eventually the sun rose. We had big plans for the following day. It wasn't much, but it was the only thing I could think of. We were going to plant a tree in honor of Trinity and Lainey. Walker said he would go to town and get one at the nursery. As soon as he showed up, we were going to set out, find the perfect place in the forest, and give them the kind of memorial that they deserved. Of course, it wouldn't be in a church filled with friends and family, but it was the best we had in the reality we were suspended in.

"Kinsley, I wish I could say thank you for your hospitality, but this has been a total nightmare. If you were smart, you'd leave too." With that, Scarlett

May gave me a tight squeeze. She didn't know how to say goodbye or thank you without criticism, but I felt her twisted love in the hug she gave me. I glimpsed Asher's face just as he rolled his eyes. I didn't want everybody to leave, but I knew it was best, and beyond that, I may or may not have been excited to have some peace and quiet to wrap my brain around my new life.

"Just get home safe, okay?" I said to Scarlett May.

Levi came up behind her and grabbed her bags. As the night had worn on, he had become more and more eager to leave. He packed his belongings with increasing vigor.

Kimber came up to me next. She wrapped her arms around me, and though not as tight as Scarlett May, her hug was genuine. I felt her frail body shaking, and I felt terrible for putting her in any sort of distress beyond what she could handle. "I miss her so much," Kimber said.

"I know you miss Trinity. We all do," I said.

"Why don't you come with us? It's safer at home," Kimber asked. She pulled away to look into my eyes, but I avoided eye contact. The truth was, I wanted to go home. I wanted that more than anything. But from the conversations I've had with my mom, I knew that even if I could go home, it wouldn't be the same. My life was here. My purpose was here. And I needed to complete that so I could go to wherever it was that I belonged.

"I am coming home on the next flight out. I just have one little thing I need to do."

"What are you gonna do?" she asked, playing with my hair mindlessly.

"Well, for starters, we're planting a tree in Trinity and Lainey's honor in the forest this morning," I said.

"I think that's a beautiful idea. I wish I could be there to see it," Kimber said, her eyes dampening.

"I'll send pictures." I tucked her hair behind her ear and sent her on her way.

Asher was on her heels. He came up behind her, gave me a quick hug, and told me to be safe. I slipped my hands into my back pockets, and I watched as my friends left one by one.

"Thanks for having us at the cabin, Wilde. I'm sorry we're leaving you with such a mess. Are you sure that this Walker guy can protect you? Because I have my doubts," Ethan said, hooking a thumb over his shoulder. I remembered the time he'd kicked Walker out of my bathroom, his forehead bleeding. Ethan was the strength I needed.

"Yeah, yeah, he's a good friend," I said. And all the things I didn't say were lost behind my eyes. I forced a smile and gave him a hug goodbye.

Emma was hugging Kimber through the window while Mason started pounding the side of the cab. "Let's go!" he yelled.

Noah had been hanging back to say goodbye last. He came up to me, hands deep in his pockets and a sheepish look on his face.

"Your mom's gonna kill me for not bringing you home."

"No, it's okay," I said.

"I'm sure we can get you a seat on the flight. You can take my seat? Just come home." Noah's eyes were filled with worry. And I hated to see him like that. But he couldn't help me now. That's what he couldn't understand.

"I already have my flight booked with Emma. We're leaving tomorrow morning. It's just twenty-four hours. We're going to plant this tree in the forest. I have a meeting with the cops, and I've got some cleaning to do. Plus, I've got to tidy up the house . . . turn off the water—that kind of thing. It's easy work, but it has to be done," I said with a shrug. All of it was a lie, of course.

From years of coming up to the cabin. I had learned there was a checklist of things I needed to do before leaving the house vacant for months on end. Noah accepted my answer and gave me a hug. He pressed his lips onto my forehead. I could feel the hot air coming from his breath, and it spurred a weird tickle in my stomach—and made me curious—but I knew this was the last time I'd ever see him. I'd never know what would have happened between me and the next-door neighbor.

Kai picked me up and spun me around. He was more lighthearted than the rest. He said his goodbyes, but unlike everybody else, he wasn't worried about me staying in the house one more night. "Call us right when you get home, and we'll all go out. We'll celebrate for Trinity and Lainey," Kai said. And it sounded nice. I wanted to do that. And I hoped they would carry on without me.

"I will," I lied.

As the cab drove away, a sense of relief washed over me. A weight off my shoulders. I was happy they were driving away to safety. I wanted nothing more than to see them flourish. Have good lives. Long lives. But the selfish part of me didn't want to be left behind. A loneliness struck the bottom of my stomach. Emma slipped her arm over my shoulder, reminding me I wasn't completely abandoned. But there was safety in numbers, and those numbers were leaving us behind.

"Are you sure you don't want to go with them? I promise I won't hold it against you, and I can probably still call them to turn around. I have no doubt you can get a seat on that plane." Emma tilted her head to the side and frowned.

"Are you trying to get rid of me?" she asked. Her tone was somber.

"Are you serious? That's the last thing I'm trying to do. I just want you to be safe. That's all."

"I *am* safe. I'm with you. Nobody knows this town better than you do, and we have Walker. He's been here longer than your family has been, right? He's a local?" she asked, her brows rising.

"Well, technically, he just comes here on vacation. Kinda like us," I said, turning around and heading back inside.

"Whatever, I'm not worried."

"I wouldn't blame you if you were," I said honestly.

"I'm not scared! Do you know how many books I've read about murder mysteries? I know exactly what's happening here, and we will *not* be the next victims. Plus, for the first time, my life is more interesting than my books," she said.

This was her wheelhouse, and I wasn't going to argue with that. I'd never read a murder mystery in my life, but I didn't doubt that it had given her some ideas that she would find useful. Maybe we all would.

"Ready to go plant the tree?" I asked.

"Yeah, I guess we should go do that. I just don't want to say goodbye . . ." she said, her optimism fading.

"I know what you mean. But we don't have to say goodbye. We're just honoring them. There's a difference."

It wasn't long before Walker showed up at the cabin with an apple tree sapling in his hand. "It's all they had. I hope the fruit-bearing tree won't take away from the memorial. I wasn't really sure what I was looking for, but this was the only choice. You should see the size of that nursery—it was like a small hut," Walker said as he stepped inside. The branches were mere twigs, and they bent easily as he walked through the doorjamb. A few leaves fluttered to the ground, catching my eye.

"That's great. I had nothing particular in mind. Thank you for getting it," I said.

The three of us walked into the forest. Gunner ran off ahead of us as we walked down the trail in silence. I didn't have to ask where we should plant the tree; I knew the exact spot Walker was heading. It was off the beaten trail, where both the tower and cemetery lay. It was the landing that was different every time I had arrived. The part of the forest that changed daily. I wasn't sure we would ever find the tree again after planting it, but that wasn't the point. The point was to give back. Let roots grow where love was lost. Honor the life that they'd had, even though it was short. And we would do that by planting the apple sapling, even if we never saw it again.

Walker dug a decent-sized hole in the ground while Emma and I stood watching, our arms interlocked and her head resting on my shoulder. Once Walker had placed the sapling and covered it with the freshly turned soil, he stood by my side with dirt-stained knees and hands.

"Do you want to do the honors?" he asked me. But I didn't. How I felt couldn't be expressed in words. It was just a feeling in my chest. A feeling of hollowness without my best friend. I knew that, no matter what came out of my mouth, it would never be enough. I didn't say anything, though; I just acknowledged my pain.

"I'll say something?" Emma offered.

I nodded, encouraging her to do what I couldn't.

"Lainey, thank you for being the best of friends. Life's not going to be the same without you. I hope that wherever you are now, you're safe and your mind can rest. I love you and miss you already," Emma whispered. I squeezed her shoulder and fought the tears from forming in my eyes. I wanted to say so much . . . But I couldn't. And I knew I was going to regret it the moment we left, but the words just wouldn't come. The feeling of loss was just too massive. It reminded me of the time after my gran had passed and my mom asked if I wanted to talk about it. I hadn't been able to then either.

"And Trinity?" Walker asked.

Emma looked to me for an answer, and I knew we needed to say something in her honor too. Only she'd never really been nice to me. Therefore, I didn't feel qualified. But I found the words where they had been lost for Lainey.

"Trinity, I'm sorry we never had time to build the friendship I know we were capable of. May you finally find peace," I said. I didn't dare lift my gaze to Emma or Walker for fear of being judged.

Silence blanketed the forest as we took a moment to honor them. My throat tightened when I remembered Lainey on the days when the sun was hot and the wind picked up her hair. The days when she laughed out loud and her smile was infectious. I locked it up tight, for I had always wanted to remember her in the fresh, sunny air . . . and not in the depths of the cold, dark water.

10

The tree was planted and left in the forest to thrive on its own. I hoped it would. I hoped it would survive—grow strong and tall, and find sunshine so that its roots would grow deep and rich in soil. I hoped that one day, my friends would come back to the forest and see the tree and know that it had been planted just for Lainey. Trinity too. It was one small act, but at the moment, it felt like so much more.

"Do you want to watch a movie?" Emma asked.

The cabin was empty and quiet—if you could call it that. Almost static in its energy, the silence seemed louder than the voices ever had been. I never thought it would be as unsettling as it was. And I already missed the booming voice of Mason and the testosterone that flooded the kitchen. I even missed Scarlett May's obnoxious criticisms that filled the air with the constant flow of sarcasm. I missed it all more than I thought I would. But most of all, I missed Lainey. I missed how I felt like we were on the same page. Like whatever I was going through, I wasn't alone. She got me like nobody else did. And I always imagined that, whereas Lainey understood me, Emma thought too highly of me for that. I knew she looked up to me . . . but I didn't know why. It was a lot of pressure on me, and I felt like I needed to protect her from whatever evil was out there because she was too naïve—too whimsical. She wanted this to be her open door into a magical world because that's what she read in her books. But this wasn't Emma's calling. This was my life . . . or at least my *afterlife*. And somehow, for reasons I could never understand, she was trapped in it.

"Yeah, why don't you pick out a movie? I'm just going to get some pajamas on," I said.

The truth was, I needed a moment alone. I took my time on the stairs, my fingers trailing the banister. There was an idea on the tip of my tongue I couldn't quite extract. Something I needed to do—needed to check on. I couldn't remember though, as I looked around the cabin. But when I closed my bedroom door, I gave up on the missed thought and got ready for the movie. I wondered what she would pick and hoped that it didn't have an ounce of horror in it—my nerves couldn't take much more. That's when I saw the blinking light of the surveillance camera.

I remembered what it was I was supposed to do. I needed to check on the surveillance cameras. I glanced back at the door, afraid to look at the footage. Afraid of all the things I might find and the things I wouldn't. I opened up my laptop and logged into the security website. I didn't know what I feared most. Was it another malfunction? Or something that I had never even considered? Like seeing Lainey on these cameras or my gran. What if it picked them up? What if hauntings had been happening all throughout the cabin, day and night? What if there were messages carved into the walls? What if there was evil?

The page loaded, and all cameras had a tiny thumbnail—not a black square, but an actual feed. I clicked on the video from the kitchen and watched Emma grab a bowl of popcorn and sit down on the sofa. And then I took a deep breath and scrolled back for days. My neck flushed with heat as I found the video hadn't cut out like it had before. I watched myself set up the camera and back away like an idiot. Despite being alone, it embarrassed me, and I hoped that nobody would ever see it.

I watched Kimber sit down next to Asher when I went outside, as they thought they had a moment alone. He reached over and kissed her, and my envy surprised me. I wanted to be kissed like that. I wanted somebody to *want* me like that. Nobody ever did. Right then, the video feed froze. Serves me right for watching a private moment. I slapped the back of my laptop shut. "Come on!" I said under my breath, disappointed that the video feed still had problems.

I closed my eyes for a moment and opened my laptop again. I'd refresh the page, and when it wouldn't work, I'd check the other camera files. Just when I'd convinced myself that it was the terrible internet connection at the lake house, Asher and Kimber pulled apart. The footage came back on just in time to capture me coming through the back patio door.

I sped up the feed through all the inactivity. Surprisingly, there was a lot of it, and I stopped when I found a particular moment when the kitchen was full and everybody was making lunch. I stopped to watch for anything unusual. I checked the faces, looking for ghosts that had slipped back into the cabin when nobody was watching. Nothing out of the ordinary happened as I watched myself make a sandwich. Noah watched me intently as he loaded chips on his plate. I hadn't noticed that in person. Kimber checked herself out in the reflection of a mirror, which wasn't abnormal. Mason and Levi ate three times what any human should, but I knew they had ravenous appetites. These were football guys—big and muscular. The amount of groceries I had bought to sustain them was insurmountable.

I searched every inch of that screen for something abnormal. My gran wasn't there, and neither was Lainey or Trinity. No ghost hauntings, no flickers of screens. No spiritual beings crossing the video feed. There was absolutely nothing abnormal. And I should have felt comforted by that, but I was disappointed. I watched as I took my plate of food outside. And I remembered I'd gone and eaten alone on the dock that day.

I was just about to close my laptop when everybody seemed to slow down. Not quite like they had before, where the video seemed to stop completely, but actually slow down, as if in slow motion. I watched as my friends slowly froze until they were as still as could be. I brought the screen closer to my face, trying to see the detail. Trying to see if their eyes were still blinking. It was such a weird image that it almost looked like a setting from a wax museum. I assumed that maybe the camera had frozen again, but when I saw the seconds tick by at the bottom of the camera, my blood ran cold.

I skipped forward a minute, then two. They remained still—the time continued. I skipped forward a half an hour, and they had only moved a couple of feet. Mason's sandwich was finally to his mouth. Kimber's eyes had finally made it up the length of her body in the mirror. And I was still gone. I cocked my head to the side and placed the laptop down on my bed. I couldn't grasp what was happening. It was even weirder than the cameras failing to record.

"Kinsley? Are you coming?" Emma yelled from downstairs.

"One second!" I called back.

I almost looked away, but an image of my reflection coming onto the back porch caught my eye. And just before I opened the door, everyone sped up. Like life had been breathed back into them, they were no longer statues. Everyone carried on, just as they always had been. My stomach dropped, and I hit rewind to watch it all over again. I checked the time stamp and watched it tick at regular second intervals while my friends moved in painfully slow motion.

I raced forward to another time where we had all been together. It was last night—when I had convinced everybody that they should go home and it wasn't safe here. I watched myself talk in front of the group and convince them to go home. It was exactly how I remembered—how it should be. But when I left to help Emma pack, that was the exact moment that it happened again. Everybody slowed down. From the moment I left the room, their speed had slowly decreased until they were frozen still. A lump swelled in my throat as I watched them intermittently come back to life and then slow again.

They sat like statues in the living room until I came back downstairs. I couldn't make any sense of it, but when Emma called me down for the movie a second time, I knew I had to come back to this later. I slammed the laptop shut and shoved it under my pillow. I went downstairs and put on my best fake face. I decided it wasn't something I could tell her since she had been one of the frozen. It was then that I realized I was truly on my own. Whatever phenomenon had been happening to me, it wasn't happening to them. And I imagined all of them on the plane landing in Decord City and then heading home to Clover. I imagined them all with their families in the warm embraces they'd get from their parents. I imagined them safe in their beds and what it felt like to be alive.

And then—like an intrusive thought—I imagined none of that happening. I imagined their plane crashing like mine had. The fire they'd feel from the flames. I imagined them waking up in the cabin and cycling through the vortex that I had. I was thankful that it was only me that would suffer like that. No matter how lonely the path may be, I would never wish that upon my friends. I slipped on my pajamas and thought about what I'd tell Emma. I'd tell her my mom rang and I had to take her call—that I was sorry for taking so long. I would watch the movie and pretend to enjoy it, but really, I'd be thinking about the video feed and what it all meant. I wondered what Walker would say.

A commotion shattered the silence downstairs as I placed my hand on the door handle. My heart pounded one giant thunderous thud. Maybe the intruder had broken in again? As I heard the roaring voices and slamming of doors, I raced downstairs to Emma but was shocked to see Noah, Kai, Levi, and Mason. I stopped dead in my tracks, just like they had on the video feed.

"What happened?" Emma asked.

Noah looked at me, disappointed, and Kai shook his head, his jaw clenching shut. "You'd never believe it! We were just about to step on the plane when they said there were engine problems. They told us all to go home because the next flight out wouldn't leave until tomorrow. So we're here for another night," Mason said. He ran his hands through his hair and went to the kitchen. I listened to him bang around in the cabinets as I remained frozen on the stairs. Scarlett May and Kimber came in and they were even more disappointed—if it was possible.

"We better not get killed tonight!" Scarlett May grumbled. The blood drained from my face. *Don't say that . . .*

"That might be too much to ask," Kimber said.

My eyes grew wide. I couldn't believe what was happening.

I watched as they set their luggage in the entryway, and I was happy to have them back, but the fear was screaming in my head. There was never a chance for them to leave Baylor. They were stuck here just like I was.

Emma and I never watched the movie, but while I sat downstairs amongst all the conversation, I couldn't help but think of what I'd seen in the video feed. It was like all my friends had gone dormant. The second I left the room, they froze, and I couldn't figure out why. I excused myself early that night and went to watch the rest of the video feeds. It had been very clear that it was my absence that stopped the activity in the cabin. But it wasn't consistent. Sometimes, they would move when I was out on the docks or in the forest. I opened my phone and texted Walker. I sent him the login to check the footage online. Soon thereafter, he called me. Then, we went over the video feeds together and scoured them for answers.

"There you are," I said. I pointed at the screen when Walker walked into the cabin. Somehow, I was surprised to see him captured on the feed. But then again, I was on these tapes too. Whatever life force he and I shared, it was enough to be caught on tape. And certainly, enough to fool all my friends into believing that we were alive.

"It's so weird. It's as if they only exist in your presence. But why? Why would that happen?" Walker asked.

The phone was hot against my cheek, as we'd been talking a long time. "They only exist . . . when I am around . . ." I said, mostly thinking out loud.

"Maybe . . . maybe this *is* your reality. Maybe this is your afterlife, and it's what you make of it?" Walker said in an optimistic tone.

I liked the way it sounded. Of course, I'd like this to be my own personal world. Have everything and everyone revolve around me. I smiled. "That's ridiculous," I said with a laugh.

"No, no. Think about it. If you're in their presence, you're thinking about them, and that gives them life. But when you move on, and you venture off to the woods or wherever else you go, you stop thinking about them. And the only actual existence is whatever's happening around you—whatever or whoever you're interacting with. They move sometimes when you're not around, right?" he asked.

"Well, yeah, but . . ."

"Then that must mean you're thinking about them."

I lost my stomach, slightly embarrassed. They'd been moving a lot when I wasn't around. Had it all been because of Noah? Because I'd wondered what he was doing? Or how I had felt about him? But the thought of me being their only source of life was flat-out egocentric. I knew this world was a lot bigger than me and stretched far beyond my emotions. The thought of its boundaries depending solely on how I felt or what I thought was absolutely impossible.

"It can't be," I said with a shrug.

"Why not? We've seen a lot of weird things, haven't we?" Walker said. And while it was true, this was too weird.

"Because I'm not . . . I'm not that special," I said, wincing. I covered my eyes with the palm of my hand. I hated the way I sounded inferior. I wasn't a natural-born leader. A strong woman. And yet, I wasn't a child either.

"You know that's not true. You're the most special person I've ever met. I mean it, Wilde," Walker said. The back of my throat stung, and it brought tears to my eyes. I closed off my throat, not letting a single sound escape. I feared that he would hear me whimper. I clenched my jaw and held tight, but it was the sniffle that gave it away.

"Are you? Are you crying?" he asked.

I threw myself back into the pillows. "No . . ." I said, my voice quaking. Silence ensued, and I could feel his smile through the receiver.

"You're making me blush, Wilde," he said. I couldn't help it. I burst out into laughter. *Me? I am making him blush?*

"I'm sorry, I'm just . . . that was one of the nicest things anybody has ever said to me."

"It's true. I've met many people in my life, but none of them have perplexed me the way you have. You have no idea how special you are, and to be honest, I think the best is yet to come," he said.

I listened to his breathing. I didn't know what he meant by that. And it only made me sad that I had no more time left to blossom. How could I ever grow into the woman I was supposed to be when I was already dead? There was no *best to come*. I had no more days to make someone proud. And no more years to make someone love me.

11

I woke to the smell of bacon, doors closing, and heavy commotion throughout the cabin. I remembered their flight was early this morning, and I threw on a robe to wish them farewell. However, I didn't know if they'd be successful this time or if the Baylor phenomenon would suck them back to the cabin like a venomous vortex. I padded barefoot downstairs, tying the cotton string belt around my waist as Emma entered the house.

"Good morning," she said.

"Good morning." My eyes traveled down to the bag in her hands. It was evident that she had packed one last night without telling me. I was happy for her. I thought it was the right thing for her to do. She needed to go home—or at least try. And if it wasn't meant to be, she'd come back soon anyway.

"I'm sorry I didn't say anything earlier, Kins."

"No, no—don't do that. I want you to go. It's safer at home, and you should be with your family," I said, running my fingers through my morning hair.

"I just . . . When everybody came back last night because their flight got canceled, I thought it might be fate. Maybe it was the universe saying that I should have been on that flight with them too."

I gave her a tight hug, and after a moment, her shoulders dropped the tension they'd been carrying.

"Emma, seriously, I'm happy for you to go. I want you to go home. Can you do something for me?" I said, pulling away. Her eyes seemed to droop at the corners with the slant of her brows.

"Anything. What do you need?" she asked.

"Can you tell my parents I love them?" I asked. Her eyes fluttered softly down my face toward the floor, then she nodded. She said nothing, though, and I wondered if the message would get through to them. I guess I had no way of knowing. Emma took Gunner on a leash. She was taking him home to Lainey's parents. I patted his back as he passed by. I was going to miss him most of all.

"Levi, are you seriously making breakfast right now?" Scarlett May scoffed from the den.

"I'm hungry! We've got a long flight ahead of us. What am I supposed to do? Starve? Here, have some bacon. I know that's what you really want," he said. Scarlett May snatched a strip of bacon out of his hand.

"You're just making a bigger mess for Kinsley to clean up after we leave," Kimber said. She passed by, giving me an empathetic look. I shrugged it off. I was used to the mess, and I didn't mind having something to do. Something to occupy my mind.

Noah took my hand and pulled me aside. "Hey Kinsley, I know I didn't have time to say this when we left for our other flight, but I really regretted that, and I wanted to say it to you now."

I looked around nervously—nobody was listening. I pulled my hand away and tucked it into the pocket of my robe, giving him my full attention.

"I can't stop thinking about you. And I think you feel the same way. Now, I know I've messed up. The whole thing with Trinity . . . and I've apologized for that. I'm hoping that when you come home, I can take you out on a date. A proper date—without all these fools around. Maybe we can finally see if this thing between us has a chance. Would that be okay?" he asked, the lines creasing on his forehead and his denim-blue eyes burrowing into mine.

"That sounds . . . nice," I said, teeth clenched. I knew I wouldn't be coming home.

Noah smiled, but it didn't reach his eyes. He gave me a nod before continuing on his way. I crossed my arms and wondered if it would have ever worked had I still been alive.

We all stood in the driveway as several cabs arrived to drive them to the airport. Right before the last door shut, Walker showed up. I felt Noah's eyes like lasers on me. The sunlight lit one half of his face from the back seat of the cab—and the other side remained in the shadows. I knew what he was thinking. He was jealous of Walker. He had every right to be. Because I had feelings for him. And not just crush-type feelings. Deep-seated feelings, like maybe we were soul mates. Lovers in another life. None of that mattered though—because the truth was, in this life, he was already taken. And I was just some sad sapling, like the apple tree we had planted in the lush forest—it never stood a chance.

Walker and I waved goodbye as the cabs pulled out of the driveway. I watched until each of them disappeared down the road. Then, with nothing left to do, Walker and I went inside and sat on the sofa. It was truly quiet now. Only the dead remained. Was this my new life? My new existence? It seemed so empty. So still.

Without the distractions of my roommates, I noticed Walker's hint of cologne. The smell alone was alluring to me, but when I added everything else —his looks, his personality, the way he made me feel—I almost couldn't keep my hands to myself. Was I really supposed to spend eternity alone when I had this wonderful guy sitting just inches from me? My mouth salivated. I couldn't stop thinking about kissing him. What would happen if I tried? Would he reject me? My mind wandered blissfully.

"Quiet. So quiet. What should we do?" he asked, shattering my daydream. My cheeks turned hot. He knew I was fantasizing about him. It must've been written all over my face.

I jumped to my feet, guilty as could be, and stuttered. "We should. I don't know. Let's go . . . check on the tree," I said with a shrug. Check on the tree? Why not? It would be a nice goose chase for us. Sure, it wouldn't be where we left it, but checking on the sapling didn't seem like a half-bad idea. We walked out to the clearing just beyond the beaten path, and Walker told me about his family.

He'd been raised by his mother, and his father was never around. It made me sad to think about the things I'd always taken for granted. Having two parents—two loving parents—just seemed like a given. I'd never realized there were so many kids being raised so differently than I was. I wondered what kind of obstacles he'd faced without a father. I imagined it branched out further than not celebrating Father's Day. I listened intently as he talked about his family structure. How he was the man of the house, taking on a lot of responsibilities at a young age. How he tried to be a brother and a father to his younger sister, Wendy. I told him I, too, was the oldest. I thought of my little brother, Conrad, and an odd sense of tugging at my heart followed. I'd been gone for so long—I tried not to think of it. The walk was such a beautiful one that I tried not to think of my past life—it only made me homesick.

The sunlight filtered through the pine trees and danced slowly over the gravel path. Listening to Walker's voice was one of the best parts. If it was he and I for the rest of eternity, and it was like this day every day, I thought I could be happy. With all the others finally gone, the stress of trying to fit in left with them. I fit in with Walker perfectly. And I didn't even have to try. I looked up at Walker as he spoke of Wendy, and I realized he was my home now. He and I belonged together. And in this vast, vicious world of the living, it was only he and I that walked in the shadows.

The overgrown bushes scratched at my pants as I walked past the blackberry bushes. It was always cooler on this path. Like dark magic swirled around the corner. I only hoped that today wasn't a new nightmare. But as we rounded the corner and the temperature continued to drop, I was in for a big surprise. Today the cemetery rested in the clearing, and in the middle of it, amid the fog, was a fully grown, enormous apple tree. My jaw dropped. I was unable to speak, and so was Walker. I took one step at a time, unsure if we should get any closer. The tiny hairs on my arms stood up, and I knew that something was very wrong.

"It's magnificent!" Walker said, the corners of his lips tipping upward.

"Magnificent? This is some sort of witchcraft or . . . or . . . evil . . ." I didn't know what it was. I only knew that it was unnatural. And like everything else here at Baylor Lake, unnatural seemed to be a bad thing. A dangerous thing.

"It's a tree, Wilde. How can it be so terrible? You know, that's your problem," he began.

"My problem?" My eyes grew wide to match my open mouth.

"Yeah, you think that everything that's happening here is bad." Walker perched his hand on his hip.

"Well, isn't it?" I asked.

"No. It's not. I know you've seen a lot of bad things here . . ."

I sighed, rolling my eyes.

". . . But I think you need to open your eyes to all the beauty. Take, for instance, the pathetic sapling we planted for your friends . . . which grew into this substantial specimen overnight. Maybe it's Lainey's way of saying thank you. Maybe it's Trinity's life force that fed the tree so that it could grow so quickly. I mean, how can a tree be a bad thing? You've seen the most beautiful skies you'll ever see here, right?" he asked.

I remembered back to the night he'd paddled me to the secret cove—and the night he'd saved my life. There *was* something majestic about them. The stars were so bright and huge. They sparkled like none other. I put my hand on my hip, mimicking him and equally frustrated.

"I'm just saying, Wilde, not everything here is bad." With that, he moved toward the tree.

I knew he was right. I needed to start looking at the beauty. I needed to settle in and enjoy myself, and part of that was seeing the magic for what it was. I took another step toward the tree. The fog was rolling in thickly, coiling around my ankles. As I really looked at it, the fully grown tree was something to behold. It was manicured perfectly, just like in a painting.

"It's kind of . . . beautiful," I said, placing my hand on the trunk of the tree. It was warm to the touch, as if the energy within was enough to radiate outward. The sunlight hadn't penetrated this part of the forest, it was decently shady and cool. Yet the bark felt like it was alive. Like a warm life hid inside.

"Must be the magic . . ." I said, peeking over at Walker.

But Walker wasn't interested in the warm bark like I was. He was staring at a headstone underneath the tree. His face was white as a ghost. "What did you say Trinity's last name was?" he asked, his voice far away.

"I didn't. Why?" I asked.

"Trinity Myers, taken by sin," he said, sending chills down my spine. My gaze dropped to the headstone, and I came to stand by Walker. There it was, etched in the stone: "Trinity Myers. Taken by sin." My heart lurched. It was most unsettling. It didn't even look like the other headstones; it looked like her name had been scratched into the marker with claws.

"That seems awfully quick for a headstone. Don't you think?" I asked, peering up at Walker.

"Who do you think would have a headstone made and placed here in Baylor?" he asked, his brows furrowing. I'd never thought of it like that. Was this the job of her parents? And if it was, then why would they've put it here? It seems more fitting that they would put it in Clover.

It was then that another headstone caught my eye farther back in the shade of the apple tree. I sucked in a gasp when I saw Lainey's name. I slapped my hand over my mouth and turned to hide my face in Walker's chest. He wrapped his arms around me.

"Lainey Summers, taken by fear."

I knew the headstone wasn't made by Lainey's parents. The ground was dug up as if the headstones had been freshly placed in the night. The tree that we'd planted in their honor, just the day before, had moss growing over the roots as if it had been here for ages.

The tears started to fall, seeping through my fingers and landing on Walker's flannel, and he let me cry. He let me cry until the eerie forest would no longer allow it. The thick fog had almost swallowed us whole, encapsulating us in an opaque white cloud. Walker tapped me on the shoulder and gently pried me from his chest. When I looked up at his blurry face, I could see that his eyes weren't fixed on mine but on the rising mist around us. It was cold, and I could see that it was moving in fast.

"We should get out of here," he said, taking my hand and leading me away. I followed him, grateful that he was taking the lead because I was still thinking about Lainey, and I probably would have remained there until it was a total whiteout and there was no way back. When we'd gained some distance on the trail and the fog was a thing of the past, Walker held my hand for what felt like a little longer than necessary. We talked little on the way home. Both of us were deep in thought, but when he finally let go of my hand, it felt cold in its absence.

"Do you see that?" Walker asked, snapping me back to reality. I followed his gaze to the cabin nestled in Rock Creek Cove. It looked as if the door from the back patio had swung closed—or open, I couldn't tell. All I knew was there was movement there, and my heart skipped a beat because of it. Was somebody in the cabin? My thoughts fell back to the time I was alone, when Gunner had attacked the thing upstairs that never was.

"The cameras!" I said, grasping Walker's arm.

Whatever this ghost was, we were going to catch it on camera. I couldn't have been more excited to finally crack the case. Walker and I took off running toward the cabin, the curiosity driving us forward. But as we got closer, it was the rumbling sound of voices that perplexed me the most. Walker opened the back patio door and walked in first, holding his hand out for me to stay where it was safe. But as he slowly took a step inside, he dropped his hand of warning and I followed him inside to find the entire crew standing in the kitchen. My face paled as everybody started talking over one another.

"There you are! Where the hell have you been?" Mason said with a hand in the air.

"Oh my god, Wilde. You wouldn't believe it!" Kimber said, her hand on the side of her face rubbing her temple. My eyes flashed to Noah, who was quiet and stoic. He refused to look me in the eye, and I didn't know if it was because Walker was by my side or something else.

"It was like this flash . . . A flash and then we were here," Kai said, trying to make sense of it all, his hands out before him.

"No! No, it was like heat—heat spreading all over my body. I thought I was on fire. Until we were here," Levi said, looking around with eyes of wonder.

I took one look at Walker, and it was clear that the Baylor phenomenon had taken over the entire cabin, not just me. It may have spread out like fingers, touching those I cared about the most. Maybe it was a web, ensnaring those who came too close. Maybe *I'd* secretly been the one who'd spun it?

12

As the tension grew, so did my drink consumption. By early evening, everybody was plastered. Some celebrating, some in existential crisis, but we were all together, under the same roof, experiencing the same mind warp. As terrible as it all had been, I was thankful to have my friends finally get a glimpse of what I had been going through. I didn't feel as lonely as I had before.

Sure, I had Walker, but there was a safety in numbers that couldn't be denied. And I felt better knowing that my friends had experienced something otherworldly, too. It was selfish, I know, but I guess that's what it took to make me feel comfortable in my own skin. To make me feel like I was no longer an outsider looking in. And for the first time since the day we'd arrived at the cabin, we were a family of misfits again.

"It was like this glowing blue beam of light that sucked me in. I traveled through it at the speed of light. And before I knew it—before I could even think about what had happened—I was back here in this living room staring at all of you. Staring at this ugly mug," Mason said, pointing to Levi. Levi shook his head, unable to comprehend what had happened earlier. Even though many hours had gone by, everybody was still in shock.

"What if we're dead?" Levi asked, his eyes growing large.

My stomach dropped as I searched the faces of those around me, wondering if they believed that might be a very real possibility. Wondering if I had let my secret out. And wondering if maybe we had more in common than I ever realized.

"Whoa. I think I might be," Mason said, examining the back of his hand.

"We're not dead, you dumbass!" Scarlett May said, rolling her eyes.

"Oh yeah? Then how do you explain what happened?" Mason asked her.

"Maybe we are? Maybe, we're all in hell?" Asher said. I scoffed.

"Why does it have to be hell? How do you know it's not heaven?" Kimber asked. Asher looked from her to Mason to Levi.

"Because there's no way these two guys would be in *my* heaven," he said, pointing to his friends.

I smiled up at Walker. And I wondered if I was in some sort of heaven. I couldn't imagine Walker's dimples would be allowed in hell. Sure, he had some skeletons in his closet; he had a curse—and a girlfriend—and he was unattainable . . . Actually, the more I thought about it . . . Maybe this *was* my hell. To perpetually be enticed by something I couldn't have. It was pure evil. Maybe I was being punished for something. I took a swig from the bourbon and seven in my hand, and my cheeks puckered.

"What's that scowl for?" Walker asked. I stared at him. His beautiful face. His golden eyes. The scar on his brow. But I had no answer for him. He laughed and poked fun at me until there was nothing left for me to do but laugh with him. No, this wasn't hell—it couldn't be.

It didn't take long for Noah to see the connection between Walker and me, and he was quick to pull me away. "Can I talk to you about something in private?" Noah asked, his hand on the back of my arm. I glimpsed a hint of something in Walker's eyes. Jealousy? One could only hope.

"Sure," I said, following him out of the room. He pulled me into the den, where the lights had still been out. There was little light filtering in through the window. Night was upon us, and a shadow was cast across his face. My heart skipped a beat, thinking of the old me. The one who would have died for this private moment with Noah and that pensive look in his eyes. Now I was just dead.

"What's going on?" I asked him, swirling the ice around in my drink.

"I've been thinking it's so weird that we didn't get home again. I thought the first time was a sign that maybe I should be with you, but now I know. Now I know that this isn't my second chance but my third or fourth. I can't stand by any longer and watch you talk with that guy. I have feelings for you, Kinsley. I think I always have. Don't keep doing this to me. Don't keep me waiting," he said, his words slurring.

Had he been sober, this might have meant something different to me. Had I been sober . . . I might've felt something different.

"What is it?" he asked. He reached out and grabbed my hand, squeezing it tight. When I didn't answer, he took a step closer and leaned in for a kiss.

It was all I had wanted. I wished for it on my eighteenth birthday. It felt like a lifetime ago. I came to this cabin for the best summer of my life, and a big part of that was Noah. His lips grazed mine with a featherlight touch, and

I jerked back. The heat from his mouth left mine, and all I could think about was Walker. How something inside of me wanted him more. Maybe just a little bit, maybe a lot, but it was more complicated than my feelings for these two guys.

Noah symbolized everything I was—everything I used to be. He was the symbol of love, happiness, family, and warmth. He was sun shining down on me—the girl I used to be when I was alive. But if Noah was the sun, then Walker was the moon. Being with him was like living a life in the shadow of the night. An afterlife of darkness. With Walker, I was a ghost—scared, lonely, and cold.

Should I really leave the thing I had always wanted for the one thing I could never have? The one guy I could never get. Should I leave the daylight for a life in the shadows?

"I just . . . I just need a moment," I said, dropping his hand and running out of the dark den.

I went in search of Walker. I sifted through my dwindling group of friends as they came up with belligerent theories on what had happened to them. I heard everything from time travel to time warps to black holes and death. "Excuse me," I said, gently pushing on Kai's back.

I found Walker out on the back porch, all by his lonesome. I tripped over the doorjamb and stumbled out onto the porch, making my cheeks heat. He raised his brows, and I could see him silently judging me. "I swear . . . I swear, I didn't drink that much," I said.

He chuckled to himself, and I grabbed hold of the banister for support, my lips pursed in a thin straight line.

I needed to know right then and there if I was ever going to have a chance with him or if this was only a wild goose chase. Because I'd spend my eternity chasing Walker in the dark if I thought I had a chance at catching him. I needed a sign.

"Your friends are really creative in there. They're coming up with all sorts of theories. But none of them know about the Baylor phenomenon," Walker said.

"Yeah, they don't know what hit them." I looked out at the placid lake. The sky was a hazy dark lavender as dusk blanketed the water. And then I asked the question I wasn't sure I wanted the answer to. "You don't think they're like us, do you?" Walker came to my side, and I took my gaze from the calm waters to his rough hand, which rested beside mine on the banister. Our pinkies almost touching. Almost.

"Like us?" he asked.

"Passed. In their afterlife?" I asked, inching my hand closer to his until my skin rested against his.

"I don't think anybody's like us. I think we're two peas in a pod," he said with warm eyes and a kind smile trained on me. Goosebumps ran down my arms. *That.* That was my sign. I had a chance.

"Are you cold?" he asked.

I shook my head and then slipped my hand over his. Slowly, I lifted my gaze from our interlocking hands to find his face pensive and pained. In a gentlemanly fashion, he picked my hand up and placed it down on the banister. He tucked his hands into his pockets.

That . . . was my sign. Denied. He was absolutely, unequivocally, unattainable. And it didn't matter if we were the last two people on this earth—two peas in a pod—he would never have feelings for me. I would never measure up to his sweet Layla Barns. I nodded my head in understanding, the tears pricking my eyes, the sting in the back of my throat. I wasn't enough now, and I never would be.

"Wilde—" he began.

I turned back to the cabin. Back to my sure thing. My sunlight. At least Noah wanted me. "I'm sorry, I think . . . I think somebody's waiting on me," I said, fumbling to open the door. He let me go.

Walker didn't even try to stop me. I guess it was a good thing, because I couldn't take being denied twice. I opened the door and shut it on Walker, leaving him in the darkness.

"Because . . . What if we never go home? What if I never see my dog again? He probably thinks I abandoned him," Kimber cried, her face red on Asher's shoulder. It was the exact conversation I was avoiding. I didn't need to get sucked into the what-ifs and the whatnots. I had too many of them in my head as it was. What I needed was to find Noah. Find the person who saw my value. I licked my lips as I squeezed by Ethan and Kai. This kiss was going to be everything I'd always hoped it to be.

I peeked my head into the now dark den, and it was almost black inside, but I could see well enough to know that Noah wasn't there. I turned back to Kai and Ethan. "Have you seen Noah?" I asked.

"Yeah, he's right there," Ethan nodded his head, brow furrowed. I followed his gaze to find Noah passed out on the sofa. I sighed heavily. Denied not once but twice in one night. I walked over to him, his limp, lifeless body, and considered kicking his foot to make him wake and kiss me. But he was out. And I wasn't worth waiting for.

It was the following day, but Walker's rejection still stung. My head ached, and I had the sour taste of defeat (and bourbon) in my mouth, but everybody else seemed well. Slightly hungover, of course, but in good spirits. Kai was still trying to get home, and he'd taken a cab into town to rent a car and drive. Nobody had gone with him. Kai wasn't easily dissuaded. I couldn't tell if he really wanted to get home or if he was more interested in the phenomenon that brought him back. If I had to guess, I would've assumed it was the latter. Kai was a smart guy, into physics and science. He probably had all sorts of theories buzzing around in his head, and if I had to guess, he couldn't wait to teleport again.

The day was warmer than normal, even for summer. It was so hot that everybody wanted to go swimming. Probably to wash off the stench of the hangover. Scarlett May had spoken of the tree swing deep in the woods, and without question, everybody wanted to go. I'd never jumped off it before, but that wasn't because I didn't want to. I did. I was afraid, though. There were three giant boulders that you had to climb just to get to the swing, and they were tall. I didn't know how tall, but I knew it was enough to keep me from climbing. I knew my fear of heights would set in about halfway up the first boulder. And I would never get myself to climb all three, let alone jump off and swing from the rope. Had I made it that far, I doubted I'd ever let go.

But everybody else wanted to try, and I didn't blame them. We packed lunches. I scoured the kitchen and gathered all the scraps of food we had left. It was going to be a sparse lunch, half a bag of chips, three sandwiches, four yogurts, and a bunch of grapes. Nobody cared. They were just happy to be alive.

I was surprised to see Walker show up at the cabin as we were heading out to the swing. I thought it was clear now that I thought of him as more than a friend, and it put us in an awkward state. The pinkness in his cheeks and lack of eye contact were obvious to me.

Noah was no better. From the lackluster glaze in his eyes to the downward stares. He was embarrassed but didn't know what for. He probably didn't even remember talking to me or that he'd tried to kiss me. He did, however, know that something had happened, because he wouldn't address me in the slightest. He reminded me of a dog cowering in the corner, his tail tucked between his legs.

As for me, my mind was still a little cloudy, but I knew enough to know that heading back to Noah after my rejection with Walker had been a grave mistake. I shouldn't settle, even if it was for a guy I'd always dreamed of.

I walked with Emma in the back of our group. Walker talked to Mason in the middle of the pack, and Noah stayed as far away from me as possible. He was up front with Scarlett May. The tension bounced from person to person like a pinball, and being in the back of the pack made me the gutter. I let Emma speak of fate as I tried to sort through my feelings for the two guys I'd never have. And no matter how I looked at it, there was only one true answer —*This must be hell.*

I watched my feet fall on the path as I tried to stuff down the rising thought that something was wrong. It shouldn't be like this. This afterlife was my burden to carry and mine alone. I looked at the back of Kimber's head and then at Asher's. They shouldn't be here.

It wasn't until we had reached the rope swing and set out a large blanket and unpacked the lunch that Walker approached me. My palms grew sweaty, and I was hot. So unbearably hot.

I gave Walker an awkward smile, and he returned it just the same. "You're not going on the swing?" he asked.

"Me? Hell no."

He laughed, breaking the tension between us. Everybody lined up behind the boulder for the rope swing.

"Yeah, I'm not going either. The last time I was on that swing, I jumped tandem with Layla. And, I don't think I want to overwrite that memory," he said, picking up pebbles and flicking them away. I watched them land and tumble in the dirt. I wasn't sure if he'd brought her up to remind me the reason why he would never choose me or if he was simply stating the truth—but it felt like it was his explanation for the other night where he pulled his hand away from mine. It wasn't easy to accept, but I respected it. I respected his loyalty. He was such a good guy. It only made me want him more.

"I don't want to fall—jump. I mean, it's so high," I stammered.

"I didn't know you were afraid of heights." Walker blushed.

"So . . . so afraid," I said, shaking my head. It was true. I'd died, and yet falling for Walker was the scariest thing I'd ever experienced.

We watched as Ethan scaled the boulders. He was the first to jump, and everybody crowded around the base of the first rock to watch him drop into the water. It seemed so wrong—everybody having fun. They weren't even supposed to be here. This was my afterlife, and somehow, they were stuck inside of it. I held my breath as Ethan swung. He flew through the air, and he seemed to let go just a second too late. He fell rather ungracefully and belly-flopped into the lake. Everyone laughed, including Walker and me.

"That's gotta hurt!" he said, wincing.

I snickered, empathizing with the slap of the water against the softest part of the body. I remembered what it was like as a kid to hit the swimming pool like a solid surface before the water parted and took you under. I remembered that moment of pain spreading across your skin, but you couldn't yell because you were submerged under cold water. I saw myself as a kid screaming—the bubbles escaping my mouth and clinging to the corners of my eyes. And then it was Lainey's double as she pulled me down to the darkest part of the lake—the part where you can't come back from. I scowled and refocused my eyes.

Mason climbed the boulders like a monkey and it surprised me he wasn't the first to go in. Kimber tugged on her suit, readjusting the sides against her hipbone. As Mason took the rope swing in his hand, something pinged the depths of my stomach and I knew this wasn't right. This wasn't the way it was supposed to be.

Ethan hadn't surfaced yet. I arched my back, my eyes scouring the water. But there wasn't as much as a single bubble popping at the surface. "What's going on?" I said as I jumped to my feet. "Wait!" I yelled.

Mason looked back at me, and I ran to the water's edge. I searched the lake. Walker came up behind me, doing the same. "He hasn't come up yet!" I said, breathless.

"What the hell?" Noah said, running into the water. Seconds later, it was Walker, Asher, and Mason all diving in, one after the other.

I watched their heads pop up out of the water. I held my breath each time they plunged back under. I moved in close to Emma, and we held hands as we waited for one of them to rescue Ethan and carry his lifeless body ashore . . . but it never happened. Ten minutes had passed, maybe more, and there was nothing to show for it.

"How could he just disappear like that?" Kimber whispered. It was the question we had all been silently asking ourselves. I feared that whatever had taken the lives of Trinity and Lainey had now taken the life of Ethan Patrick—swallowed him whole in the black water.

It was ages before the guys gave up the search—but the water was murky, and their lips were blue. The rescue was a lost cause, and once they'd pushed their bodies to the point of exhaustion, it was time to call it.

I couldn't help but feel like it was my fault. I looked around at the dwindling numbers, our little family of misfits. Who was next? Who would be the next victim to get stuck in my web?

13

The tension rose on the way back to the lake house. It was a long walk, but that did nothing to calm everybody's emotions. We were one friend short, and the sense of defeat was insurmountable. We were fighting an invisible monster with our hands tied behind our backs—it was impossible. The fear grew as the heat beat down on our backs, and by the time we reached the cabin, we were nearly at each other's throats.

Walker headed home. He said he needed to find clues about Layla's whereabouts. He said he needed answers, and it wouldn't happen sitting around the cabin. I was thankful that he left to do the thing I couldn't, but as I looked back at the angry bunch before me, I didn't know how to deal with them alone.

Asher and Noah were particularly upset because Ethan was one of their best friends. Why they took their grief out on each other, I didn't know. But Asher shoved Noah as we were entering the back porch entryway. He stumbled forward, quickening his step to catch himself. I looked back to Walker climbing in his canoe and pushing off—I'd give anything to be in that canoe.

"Who was the first one in? Answer me that! I was the first one in!" Noah yelled, hammering his chest.

"Stop!" Kimber said in a helpless heap.

"Well, it didn't do you any good, did it? Did you find him? No! He's still at the bottom of the lake!" Asher yelled back, his outstretched hand nearly hitting Mason.

I took a deep breath, running my hands through my hair. I paced the length of the kitchen, searching for answers. How does this make sense? How does it fit together? I hated the fact that I hadn't figured it out yet. That my friends were dying on my watch. If I were smarter . . . if I hadn't been dyslexic . . . maybe I would have figured it out by now. My shortcomings affected not only me but everyone around me. I felt this huge amount of responsibility that I couldn't measure up to. I hadn't been able to save Ethan or Lainey; I hadn't been able to save Trinity. And I knew that for the rest of the people in this cabin, it was only a matter of time before I couldn't save them either.

I heard a gasp and spun around on my heels, just in time to see Asher's fist slam into the side of Noah's cheekbone.

"No!" I screamed. I rushed forward and then paused as the confrontation continued. Noah was hunched over, his hand to his face, when Asher jumped on his back, bringing him down to the floor. He brought fist upon fist down on his face. Blood splattered, marrying Asher's fist to Noah's nose. Noah never had a chance. From the moment he was hit, he never got a punch in, and Asher was relentless.

Scarlett May yelled belligerently. Kimber cried. Kai was still trying to get back home or break ground and discover time travel in his attempt. And Ethan was at the bottom of the lake. I flinched with every thud of Asher's wet fist meeting Noah's broken face.

Time slowed to a crawl. Mason jumped in and tackled Asher to the floor. At first, it seemed like the fight had grown. The three guys fumbled around on the ground, taking up the entire living room. Noah rolled onto his side and coughed up blood, clutching his nose. I ran over to him, swiping a dishtowel from the countertop as I passed by. Careful not to get hit, I pressed the towel up against his nose, trying to stop the bleeding—my hand trembling beneath the cloth. Mason wrestled Asher until he calmed down, but they shed no more blood.

"It's not fair! It's not fair!" Asher yelled, nearly incoherent. Streams of tears ran down Asher's red face. Noah's blood had smeared across his cheeks.

"I know, man. I know. We need to find this guy! We need to get him! But *that*," Mason said, pointing to Noah, "that's not your guy! You hear me?" Asher gave up his fight and Mason got off him, helping him up. But as soon as Asher got to his feet, his face came down on Mason's chest, and he wept.

Ethan always looked up to these guys. He'd followed them everywhere, and he was always so happy to be part of the group that he never cared about being on the bottom. He'd only wanted to be accepted, and they did that for him—they accepted him, and Ethan got to be part of the cool group. But what I hadn't realized was they actually loved him. They were actually best friends. True friends. They were friends like Lainey and I had been. My heart ached for them because I knew that pain. I would have taken it all if I could. I would have taken their grief into my eternity so that nobody else had to know it the way I did.

Noah groaned and pulled himself up to a seated position. I pressed the towel up against his nose, and he grabbed it with his bloodied hand.

"I think my nose is broken," he said beneath the towel. I didn't know a thing about broken noses. I'd never broken anything in my life, but I'd never seen a cast on a broken nose—I assumed it would heal itself. I looked over to Asher as he tried to pull himself together by wiping away his tears. In the process, he created stripes of blood across both cheeks and looked like a warrior, ready for battle. I'd heard that Asher had a temper, but I'd never seen it until now.

There was one time when Levi and Asher had come to school with bruises under their eyes. They'd both looked terrible. When we asked them what had happened, they both replied, "You should see the other guy." They'd never told us what happened, but it was clear that they had fought each other. The funny part was they were over it by the next day at school. Guys didn't hold grudges the way girls did. And I hoped that was the case for Asher and Noah now. There was enough tension in the cabin, and we didn't need to divide into sides.

"I'm going to get you some medicine," I said to Noah as I pushed to my feet. I rummaged through the cabinets looking for the ibuprofen, and when I finally found the bottle, it was empty. I slammed the bottle down on the counter. Of course, everybody had been taking it for their hangovers. I crossed my arms, leaned against the counter, and watched as the panic continued to progress uncontrolled. It was like a stream that was slowly fed as the snow-capped mountains melted—only, today was hot, and the stream of panic filled all at once. Kimber couldn't stop crying. She had been upset by Ethan's death but even more rattled by Asher's violence.

"You promised me you wouldn't do this again!" she cried out, beating on Asher's chest.

"And then he was gone—just gone. He never came back up . . ." Scarlett May said on the phone.

Levi came back in from the back patio. He must have been out with Gunner because when he let him in, Gunner ran through the house, excited to see everybody and wagging his tail. As if we needed more commotion. I groaned, wrapping my hands around my neck and tilting my head back. I closed my eyes and listened as everybody took their frustrations out on one another. I wanted to scream.

"If you don't like it, then just leave," Asher said to Kimber. I watched as she bashed her hands into his chest, crying maniacally. The tension was getting to us all. One by one, we were cracking. First, it was Asher and Noah, second, Asher and Kimber. I briefly thought about Kai and wondered how far he'd gotten today. And then I remembered—we needed to call him and tell him about Ethan.

"You don't want me. I'm never good enough. I'm never good enough," Kimber cried.

"I don't have time for your bullshit! I don't have time for this, Kimber! People are dying! Ethan died! And you're worried about how good you are? How pretty you are? How skinny you are? I don't have time for it! We're done!" Asher yelled before storming out of the cabin. Kimber wailed and took off running. I listened to her feet stomp all the way upstairs and heard the bathroom door in the hallway slam shut. Everybody else was quiet—even Scarlett May, as she held the phone away from her ear. Everybody was still except for Gunner, who was still looking for pets. I scratched behind his ears and he leaned into me.

Levi walked back out of the cabin, presumably after Asher. And slowly, Scarlett May continued her conversation on the phone about her horrific experience at the lake. She didn't care that Kimber was upstairs crying, and I felt bad for her because Trinity would have. I took one look at Emma, and we knew what we had to do. We headed upstairs to console Kimber.

With each stair we climbed, the sobs grew louder. Emma and I stood outside the bathroom door, my hand on the knob. I looked at Emma, concerned for what we might find. Her brows furrowed as she gave me a curt nod, signaling she was ready for battle. Slowly, I opened the bathroom door to find Kimber tucked in a ball against the bathtub. She lifted her head from her knees. Her face was beet red. She screamed through her tears, "Get out!" But it wasn't convincing.

"Get out," she whimpered, her hunched back quaking as she cried.

Emma and I slipped in, and I closed the door behind us. I looked at Emma and shrugged. I didn't know what to do. I bit the side of my lip and lowered myself to the floor. My back slid against the wall until my butt bumped against the tile floor. Emma joined me, leaning against the bathtub. I put my hand on Kimber's back and stroked it, but when it didn't seem to do anything except make her cry more, my eyes bulged, and I threw up a hand to Emma. "I don't know what to do . . ." I mouthed.

"Hey, it's okay. I'm sure he was just mad. He's just going through something. I mean, he and Ethan were really good friends. It has nothing to do with you," Emma tried. Kimber didn't respond.

After a moment, I tried my hand at it. "I know it's scary, Kimber. I'd be lying if I said I wasn't scared, too. We're all under a lot of stress right now, and

I think the best thing we can do is band together. We can't have a chink in the armor. Not now. So we need you to be strong. Can you do that?" I asked.

"Strong?" Kimber asked, her words muffled as her chin was tucked to her chest. "You want me to be strong?" she rasped, her tone growing sharper, and I knew I had said something wrong.

"Well . . ." I began.

"I've lost one of my best friends! And now, I lost Asher too. We can't come back from this. We're done," she said. They'd taken breaks before, but this seemed different. We were on the cusp of change. High school had ended; college was about to start. If Asher was on the fence about their relationship, this was as good a time as any to sever their bond.

"Asher was the best thing I ever had. I don't know why he loved me the way he did. But I'll never find somebody to put up with my shit like he did. I'm just this . . . *big*. . . nobody will ever love me," she wailed.

Big? Kimber was nothing but skin and bones. She was tiny. Borderline emaciated if I really thought about it. Emma and I shared a look of concern. I knew what she saw in the mirror wasn't grounded in reality. She was one of the most popular girls at our school, she was beautiful, and it wasn't until this moment that I realized just how disconnected her inner voice was from her outer appearance.

And then it struck me—maybe Kimber and I had that in common? Maybe my own mind had blocked me from seeing the truth within the mirror. Maybe I wasn't a nobody or invisible the same way that Kimber wasn't overweight.

I took my hand off Kimber's back and pushed off the wall. I stepped up to the vanity. I looked from Emma to the girl staring back at me in the mirror. I sucked in an uneven breath as I stared at my reflection, long dark hair, and ruby-red lips. My eyes were the dullest brown I'd ever seen. My skin was sallow. There wasn't one feature to adore. I was the plainest girl there ever was. But this time, I was visible.

Emma tried to console Kimber, but everything she said only made her cry more. I was stuck staring at my reflection in the mirror. I had always known this version of me. This girl. The one who was so plain that she might as well be invisible. I didn't know what was worse, seeing my true reflection or seeing none at all. I felt the burn in the back of my throat when Emma called my name for the second, third, or maybe even fourth time.

"Kinsley!"

I pulled myself from the dull brown eyes and looked down at Kimber. Things had escalated, and she was hyperventilating. The stress of it all made my head pound. I didn't know who to help first—her or myself. I grabbed my head as the migraine came crashing down on me and I bent at the waist.

There was nothing I could do for myself, so I tried to fight through the pain. I put my hands around Kimber's waist and pulled her to her feet.

"Breathe, Kimber. Just breathe," I said, leading her to the sink.

"Let's get some water on her face," I said to Emma.

With Emma and I on either side of Kimber, we helped her get to the vanity. I turned the faucet on, but as soon as she dropped her hands from her puffy eyes and saw her reflection, she screamed wildly.

She startled me, and I staggered backward. Her cries were like sharp daggers plunging into my head. I looked in the mirror to see Kimber had shrunken to seventy pounds, maybe less. Her skin stretched thin across her bones—so thin it was nearly translucent. With her mouth open and her cries screeching, a single tooth fell out of her mouth. It clinked several times as it fell into the porcelain sink. I watched with enormous eyes as it circled the drain.

I looked at Emma, who was as white as a ghost. And it shocked me to see Kimber as her old self, fully fleshed out as she stood beside me. I whipped my head back to the mirror to see her skeleton piercing through her taut skin.

It was like a fun-house mirror—the kind you'd find at a circus or a Halloween fright night. The reflections were hideous and grotesque—our deepest fears, our truest nightmares, all before our very eyes. It was so real, it was no wonder we couldn't tell fact from fiction—why our inner voices had fed us lies our whole lives. Because as I stood there beside my two friends staring into an alternate reality, I couldn't tell where my dimension had stopped and the truth began.

"Kimber's hyperventilating turned to wheezing as she stared at her reflection until she was no longer breathing. Her face turned blue and her knees grew weak. Her double in the mirror was a stark purple, and I saw every vein straight through her skin. Her eyes were bulbous as they rolled back in her head and several more teeth fell out, clamoring against the porcelain sink. Kimber passed out, hitting the ground with a thud. Emma and I kneeled at her side, torn between the tangible life before us and the dark portal of our own inner makings seen within the mirror.

I picked Kimber's head up and cradled it in my hand. "Go get help!" I said. Emma leaped over her limp body and ran into the hall, yelling for help. My head pounded with excruciating pain. It was one of the worst migraines I'd ever had, and my vision was starting to blur. I winced through the throbbing, agonizing pain. Lightheaded, I struggled to hold Kimber's heavy head in my hands.

Stop this!

Somehow, deep inside, I knew it was me who was orchestrating this. Like Walker had said, it was my manifestation. It was the things I didn't want to see that had a way of coming to life. I wanted to concentrate on helping Kimber, but my pain was blinding and all-consuming.

Asher burst through the door like a bolt of lightning. He took Kimber's limp body from my hands, and it was the last thing I saw before the darkness washed over me.

14

My head ached and my mouth ran dry. The bedsheets were bunched up in the palms of my hands. My eyes fluttered open to find a dark room. I had no memory after Kimber's meltdown in front of the funhouse mirror, but when I saw the blinking green light of the recorder, I figured I could at least piece it together. I sat up; my head pounded. I sucked in a sharp breath and clutched my temples just as Noah walked in. It shocked me to see him, and his ease of coming into the bedroom left me with questions.

"Oh, you're up. How are you feeling?" he asked, closing the door behind him.

"What happened?" I asked, relieved to see I was fully clothed.

"You passed out. Asher and I got you into bed. He's taking care of Kimber now and I just went downstairs to get you some ice water," he said, placing a glass on the nightstand. I turned on the bedside table lamp as Noah sat on the edge of the bed.

"Thank you. I'm sorry. I'm just a little groggy, I guess. I've never passed out before," I said, sitting up and bringing my knees to my chest.

"It's okay. I think you were just out for a little bit—maybe like five or ten minutes," he said.

"Jesus, you look like hell," I said, taking him in for the first time. His eye was swollen, a mix of yellow and blue; dried blood crusted around his nose. If he looked this bad now, I imagined in two days' time he would look like he'd been thrown in front of a bus.

Noah looked down at the ground and forced a smile. I could tell he was embarrassed about losing the fight. "Yeah, he got me good."

"I know you guys are upset about Ethan, but we shouldn't be taking it out on each other, you know?" I said.

"Trust me, I know." He inched his hand toward my feet and I wiggled my toes. It was weird having Noah in my bedroom with the door closed. I had run out of things to say to him, and the intimacy made me a little uneasy. If I was being honest with myself, I still felt the pull toward him from deep inside. But at this point, I couldn't tell if it was Noah that I wanted or if it was the girl I used to be before coming to Baylor. The girl I was when my gran was alive and school was in session. The girl who had only one problem in the world: getting noticed by Noah every day. I missed that life. That simple life.

"Do you remember that one time when I broke my arm and Joey had a birthday party? All the kids went swimming, and I couldn't get in the pool because of my cast, so you stayed back with me to watch a movie?" Noah shifted, inching closer.

"Yeah, I remember that," I said, smiling. The memory was so innocent.

"This kind of reminds me of that. Should we watch a movie?" he asked. It sounded nice. I wanted to escape this mess and leave it all behind. Get lost in a love story or comedy. Allow my mind to move past Ethan, if only for a little while. "I'd love that," I said. He leaped over me when I patted the open side of the bed. I laughed at his boyish ways as he got situated. I turned on the TV, excited to have my old friend back.

I flipped through the channels on the TV, and at first there was silence between us, maybe even a little awkwardness. But as Noah vetoed movie after movie, the tension eased. He'd come up with the most ridiculous reasons why the movies were no good.

"That one's too corny."

"That one's too romantic."

"That one's got a dog in it, and I think it gets hurt."

"I don't like that Scott Teek. He does the weird thing with his brows when he laughs."

I rolled my eyes and then realized he'd never really wanted to watch a movie. He'd just wanted to crawl into bed. I couldn't blame him for that. We all could use a friend right now, and we used to be the best of friends when we were kids.

"We used to be such good friends. What happened?" I asked in all seriousness.

"We're still good friends," he said, his tone climbing.

"I don't know. Somewhere along the way . . . maybe puberty—"

"Puberty?" he said, scrunching his face. "Ow!" Noah cupped his swollen eye.

"Oh, be careful." I paused, choosing my words wisely. "I thought you didn't want to be friends with me anymore because you thought everyone would think we were boyfriend and girlfriend or something," I said, a little embarrassed by my feelings back then. They had hurt a lot at the time, but I was used to it now.

"No . . . Maybe? I don't know. It was hard growing up, you know? I'm sorry I wasn't more mature about it, and middle school . . ."

I laughed. "More like high school," I said.

"What? Seriously? Oh my god, I've got to rethink my whole life now." Noah smiled and then winced from the pain.

"Well, you've got a plan at least, right? I heard you got into one of your top colleges?"

"Yeah, I got into HU, and I'm moving there at the end of the summer." Noah's eyes lowered slowly. It was just another reason why we wouldn't work out.

"That's great. What are you going to do when you're done with college? Come back home and find a job here? Or stay out east?"

"I'm not sure yet. If I had a reason to come back home, then maybe I would . . ." His eyes focused on mine. It was the first time in a long time that I'd lost my stomach with Noah. I squirmed under his gaze, cleared my throat, and sat up a little straighter. And when I dared to look back at him, there was a twinkle in his eyes. He knew he'd won some minor victory. But I wasn't giving up just yet.

"Well, I'm going away to college too, so . . ." I began.

Noah slowly leaned down. The seconds ticked by in slow motion. He was going to kiss me. The room was dark except for the movie trailers that played on an endless loop on the TV. This was everything I dreamed of—my one birthday wish. His battered face warmed my cheeks as he came closer. His lips touched mine gently for a kiss as I sucked in a quick breath. I stilled briefly, and he parted his mouth, kissing me deeper. My head swirled as I kissed him back.

It *was* everything I'd hoped for. I opened my mouth slightly, inviting him to get lost in the longing—but longing for what? I didn't know. I wanted so desperately to only care about this kiss. To be present in this moment. But the truth was, all I could hear were Kimber's teeth striking the porcelain sink. All I could see was Ethan's belly flop into the underworld. And it wasn't what I felt but what I hadn't. I didn't feel Walker's scruff scratching my face as we kissed, and I didn't have feelings for Noah.

I did, however, realize that I was no longer the same girl I was when I came to Baylor. And as much as I wanted to be that innocent, lighthearted girl with a crush, I had to let her go, because she wasn't coming back, and there was nothing I could do about it—not even kiss Noah Hampton. My life had changed significantly in the last handful of weeks. Nearly all of it was for the worse. All of it except Walker St. James. *My* Walker St. James. I jerked away, breaking off the kiss. This was all wrong. Noah stared at me, stunned. His breath quickened.

"I'm sorry, but I can't . . . I can't," I said, throwing my legs over the side of the bed and standing to my feet.

"Kinsley, wait," he said as I hurried out the door. Once in the hallway. I closed the bedroom door behind me and rested my back against the wall. I ran my hand down my face. It was clear as day. When I'd died, so had my feelings for Noah.

I hurried downstairs because, even though I knew I needed to tell Noah how I felt, it didn't need to be now. The cabin was pitch black and quiet. It must've been the middle of the night, and nobody was awake. Just as I got to the bottom stair, the front doorknob jiggled. I peered out the peephole and a sense of relief washed over me when I saw Kai under the glow of his cell phone light. I unlocked the door, and he rushed inside like a freight train. He scooped me up in his arms and gave me a big hug like it had been ages since we'd seen each other. Maybe it had. I didn't know why or what his reasoning was, but I hugged him back like it was the last time I'd ever see him—and it felt good. It felt good to be loved for just being me.

"You're back?" I said, trying to sound surprised. But I always knew he'd never escape this place.

"Wilde, you'll never believe it." Kai's voice was electric, and instantaneously my sorrows lifted. I closed the door behind us, and Kai spoke quickly, waving his hands in the air.

"I got the rental car, right? Then, I was driving down the highway—had been driving four hours . . . maybe three?" His eyes rolled up as he counted silently. "And then suddenly, the sky lightened! It continued to lighten until it looked like I was driving straight into a tunnel! And then, when all the windows were encapsulated in this beam of light . . . I felt like I was falling, and then guess what?" Kai's eyes were larger than I'd ever seen.

"What?" I asked.

"I was here. Not just in Baylor, but here on this doorstep. Right. Now." He pointed to his feet as if this was the very place where teleportation had been invented. Like we were upon something bigger than life itself. "Whatever it is, it's real, Kinsley. It's real. This is incredible. Do you even know what this means?" he asked.

"What does it mean, Kai?" I asked, loving how his spin on the phenomenon was incredible.

"It means we've stumbled on some sort of weird wormhole. It's like we're stuck in a time loop. Only it's not time that's passing by, it's space. It's direction. We have to test it. We have to test all the theories! Didn't you say this happened to you?" he asked.

"I was in the plane crash . . ." I said, the screams echoing in a far-off land.

"The one from the news?" he asked.

I dropped my head and he brought me in for a hug. "Yeah. That one."

"I'm so sorry. That must have been terrifying."

"It was." I tried not to think about it.

"And then what happened? You ended up here?" Kai asked, holding me at arm's length.

"Exactly. Walker says it's called the Baylor phenomenon. Maybe you can start researching it," I said, happy to have him on the team. Kai was a smart guy. If anybody was going to be on our research team, he would've been my first pick.

"The Baylor phenomenon . . ." Kai whispered as he walked past me into the kitchen. When I turned to follow, I saw Noah standing on the stairs. The heat crept across my cheeks. "Oh, um, Kai's back. He didn't get far," I said to Noah.

I was thankful that this news was big enough to take the attention off our failed kiss. Noah frowned and pointed in the kitchen's direction. He passed me as he searched for Kai. I trailed after Noah. I didn't want to, but I had to. I had to squash the awkwardness. We were living together for the summer, and I couldn't avoid him altogether. So hiding from him for one night wouldn't do me any favors.

"Wow, dude! What happened to you?" Kai asked. I sat down on the sofa, realizing how much Kai had missed in a single day. I pulled a lap blanket over my legs.

"Oh, this? That's compliments of Asher," Noah said, nodding to Asher in the sleeping bag on the floor. I hadn't realized he was sleeping downstairs, as I'd given him and Kimber a bedroom upstairs.

"Why is he sleeping down here?" Kai asked.

"After the fight, he and Kimber broke up. It was a big thing. I'm glad you weren't here for it," I said.

"Oh, shit. That's going to be weird tomorrow," Kai said.

"Yeah, awkward," Noah said. But the really awkward part wasn't the breakup or even our failed kiss—it was knowing that we had to tell Kai about Ethan drowning in the lake. My eyes flickered to Noah's, and his one good cheek turned to a pinkish hue.

"What was that?" Kai asked, smart as a whip. His eyes bounced from Noah to me.

I sighed. "It's Ethan, he—" I began, but I was thankful I didn't have to finish.

"—He jumped. He jumped into the water and never came back up. It was the last time any of us saw him." Noah looked like he had seen a ghost, and I could only imagine the movie that was playing in his head. It played in mine too, Ethan hitting the surface of the lake with a smack. Kai's expression had morphed from shock to grief to fear to empathy, all within seconds. I swallowed a lump in my throat and chewed on my lip while he gathered himself.

"Wow, I really missed a lot. How long was I gone?"

"Just today. You left this morning."

"You know, I was pretty excited about this . . . phenomenon, but now, I feel like maybe I'm just playing with fire. Maybe I shouldn't try to understand. Maybe we should run. We should all *run.* Because one of us is going to be next," Kai said in a low and eerie whisper.

He was absolutely right. We should run. But we'd tried that once, and we'd ended up right where we started. Only I knew that precisely thirteen people were going to die—that made for nine more.

"Man, I can't deal with this right now," Noah said, bringing his elbows to his knees and hunching over till his head met his hands. I knew he had the weight of the world on his shoulders, and our kiss was just another stone to carry.

"Tell us more about your experience. It's good for all of us to hear. Maybe we can piece everything together and find a way home," I said, knowing that I'd never get the chance to go home, but that maybe they could.

We stayed up for a while. The three of us huddled on the sofa, talking about our experiences. I told them how the plane went up in a blaze and how I woke up in my bed. They both agreed they probably would've thought I was crazy if I had said anything before. And they joked about me letting them get on a plane without warning of their impending doom.

By the time I went to bed, I felt hopeful for the first time in a while. Hopeful that Kai would figure something out that I had missed. Maybe he'd get everyone home where they belonged. I hoped things wouldn't be weird between Noah and I come morning. I still had to talk with him about my feelings, but talking with him and Kai had taken some of the awkwardness between us away.

I knew I also needed to have an open talk with the remaining group—a talk like I'd had with Noah and Kai. It was time that they were all on my team. Now that they were experiencing the strange flukes that I had been, it was time that I let them in on all the secrets and clues that had been happening around us. It was time for us to band together and fight whatever this thing was as a team. An army. Because I was done doing this on my own. I simply hadn't been strong enough. Or smart enough. But together, maybe we'd have what it took to finally find Layla.

15

The sunrise brought with it a friendly reunion. It was exciting for everybody to see Kai. And after losing Ethan, we were strengthened again by Kai's presence. His energy felt like renewed hope. Even Kimber was doing better. Though still thin, her teeth were intact. When she came to speak to me, I could tell that what we had seen in the mirror had weighed heavily on her insecurity by the way she rubbed her fingers across her jaw. Yet, for the first time, we were banding together. We felt like a team. That was, until Asher woke up.

He staggered to the fridge; his swollen hand covered in bruises grasped the refrigerator door. Asher wasn't the problem, though. It was his relationship. Asher and Kimber were the most popular couple in school. Kids had talked about them on the regular, and if they weren't gossiping about them, they wanted to *be* them. Everybody was in tune with the most apex relationship, and even though we were now out of school, our eyes and ears were still trained on them. And when their relationship crumbled overnight, leaving broken noses and fallen teeth in its wake, we all felt it.

As soon as Asher was up, the air in the room shifted. I looked at Emma and asked if she wanted to take Gunner for a walk. She nodded eagerly. Anything to get away from the brooding couple. I picked up Gunner's leash, and he jumped to all fours, bumping into chairs and slamming his tail into kneecaps. I grabbed a coffee on the way out and felt Noah's gaze on my back until the door closed behind me. As soon as we gained some distance from the cabin, Emma broke the silence, and I took a much-needed full breath.

"How are you feeling?" Emma asked.

With all the commotion, I almost forgot I'd passed out the night before. It was minor compared to everything else that had been happening. I shook my head. "Oh, I'm fine. But I have to tell you. Noah kissed me last night," I said, staring at her with bulbous eyes. She gasped.

"No freaking way!"

"I don't know, Emma, it was everything I had dreamed of for so long. And now? I don't know. I thought I liked it, but then I thought I would like it more if it was Walker, and then as soon as he popped into my head, I couldn't get him out. I pulled away from Noah, and I've hardly been able to look at him since," I said.

Emma looked back at the cabin as we entered the shady part of the forest. The wall of trees. "Wow, you really must like Walker. Didn't you say he has a girlfriend?" My stomach dropped because I knew I'd been lying to her. I'd been lying to everyone. But it had only isolated me. Alienated me from the group and made me feel like an outsider in my own cabin. And now . . . now that everybody was seeing things, I realized the secrets were just keeping us apart. Still, I didn't feel like Walker's past was mine to share.

"She's . . . unavailable," I said, dropping my head and feeling the defeat of just how true that overly broad statement was.

"You must really like Walker if you left Noah for him, even though he's unavailable."

"That's what I thought!" I said, and Emma giggled.

"So, I wanted to talk to you about something else that's been on my mind. You know how we talked about finding this girl? Layla?" I asked.

Emma nodded.

I hesitated. "Well, I think we should tell the group. I don't want to scare anybody—any more than they already are—but I think it's time. And I think they might be able to help us find her. Maybe we could get some answers about this place and how it all works? What do you think?" I asked.

"I don't know, Kinsley. I don't know if everyone can handle it. I mean, Kimber was nothing but a skeleton last night. You saw her. Do you really think they can deal with anything else? Especially after losing Ethan? And I read these stories all the time. I love this stuff. If it's paranormal, I'm in. Horror, I'm there. But Scarlett May? She's probably like a western romance kind of girl. And Kimber reads sci-fi—they can't handle real life ghost stories."

I reached down and let Gunner off the leash. He took off running as Emma babbled about how she judged people based on what book genres they read.

"—And you know Asher doesn't even read."

"I don't read either," I said.

"No, I know. But, I think you would, if you could—not like that. You know what I mean." I watched her fumble a little before lowering my gaze to the gravel path. I knew what she meant. It had just come out wrong. Anyway, I had bigger problems than being offended by Emma's analogy.

"Look, all I'm saying is I don't think that we should tell them about Layla Barns or the accident you were in." Emma scowled as she scratched the back of her head. "I don't even think the Baylor Butcher's connected to any of this. Maybe it's not even a *real* person—maybe it's a ghost . . . or some sort of entity, an evil one." I tried not to think about how she'd said *real* person. As if *I* were a fake. It felt that way sometimes. "And the Baylor phenomenon, isn't that just magic?"

I glowered down at the path and after a moment, nodded in agreement.

"Yeah. It's just magic that we don't know the rules to yet. I don't think any of our friends are going to believe this for one second. So, if you want to push them away, tell them. But I think this should stay between us. And Walker, of course," Emma said.

I let out a disappointed sigh. I couldn't help but feel she was wrong. I would think about what she said, but I wouldn't let it stop me from building the team I needed. Maybe I'd start to tell the group and then I would feel the room. Let it guide me. It was a slippery slope because I was harboring secrets from everyone. Once one stone came out, the whole tower would surely crumble.

We talked a little bit more about Kai coming home. I told her the things he had seen and experienced. And then I told her how Noah and I had broken the news about Ethan. I took the opportunity to persuade Emma to tell everybody the truth, because if Kai had set his mind to it, he could probably figure out the whole puzzle. And nobody could argue with that. We could've talked for days, but the words were stolen right from our mouths the moment we saw that an apple tree—*our* apple tree—had moved to the main path. It had grown even more, arching over the main pathway and now bearing fruit. An apple the size of a small melon hung right in front of my face. It wasn't just ripe; it was beautiful, red, and glossy. It could be award-winning. I reached out to touch it and the apple fell into my hand—perfectly ripened to the very second.

"I've never seen this apple tree before, have you?" Emma said, marveling under the branches filled with low-hanging fruit.

"I haven't seen it *here* before. But that's only because it was somewhere else yesterday. This was the sapling we planted." I spun the gigantic apple around in my hand. Not one imperfection was visible.

"Okay, maybe we should show the group *this*. They're never going to believe it. But this is . . . amazing." It *was* amazing. And it reminded me of something from my childhood. A book my gran used to read to me. A fairy tale filled with magic—both beautiful and poisonous.

It took me back to a time when my gran would tuck me into bed on the nights that she stayed for dinner. She'd never just kiss me on the forehead and turn out the lights; she'd sit and read me a story. My mom would always come looking for her, wondering where she'd disappeared to. She'd been right there by my side, reading bedtime stories until my eyes were heavy enough that I would drift off to sleep. Often, I'd dream of the magic. The fairy tales would whisk me off to a faraway land, and I'd fly with the monkeys, sing with the dwarfs, and ride in pumpkin carriages.

This particular apple was so perfect and lush, it reminded me of other things too—a story I couldn't quite place. My mouth watered. I brought the apple to my lips and opened wide. Emma slapped it out of my hand with surprising force. The apple flew from my hand, nearly taking my fingers with it.

"You can't eat that!" she yelled.

"What? Why not?"

"Do you know any of the classics? I mean, I know you don't read, but clearly, you've heard of the most classic fairy tales of all time, right?"

I shrugged. I had.

"Clearly, that's a poisonous apple, Kinsley!" Emma hissed with disapproval.

I scratched my head. That was it. I knew it had reminded me of something. She very well could be right. We were trapped in Baylor, after all. Surely there were poisonous apples and all sorts of things that could spin a spell so fast you could die . . . and never even know it. I shivered.

The apple had split against a rock, and a wisp of black vapor plumed from the crack. I smiled at Emma for possibly saving my life. *Afterlife?* I wasn't sure what she'd saved, but she's done well. She was a valuable member of our team.

On the way back, Emma and I discussed talking with the group. After seeing the apple tree grow without constraints and bloom in only forty-eight hours, she was convinced that we should tell the others. Show them, too. No more secrets, she said. And I agreed it was the right thing to do. But that didn't mean I wasn't scared. I felt like I was going through my own transformation. My own nightmare. And somehow, if I told everybody everything, it was like I'd be drowning them right along with me.

I nodded and agreed, but secretly I planned to hold some important details back. I thought about the first night when I'd drowned. How I'd come back into the cabin and nobody noticed I'd been gone. Nobody cared. The thought of telling them that was so mortifying, I didn't think I could. But it was the piece of the puzzle that told of the dark souls lost in the murky water. They needed to know.

As we neared the cabin, I realized there was something I needed to do. I had Layla Barns's purse tucked away in my closet. There were only a few items in there, but one of them was a mirror. And after seeing that juicy red apple—poisonous or not—I wanted to look in the mirror. I wanted to see if there was magic inside. Or, at the very least, the future. But even after the long talk Emma and I just had about not keeping secrets, that's precisely what I intended to do. Keep it secret.

Once we were back at the cabin, I headed for my room. I pulled the closet door open, halfway expecting to see the purse had been stolen, but it was there, tucked in the corner where I'd left it. My heartbeat quickened. This was a clue. I knew it. I could feel it. I was getting closer to saving my friends. The hems of my clothes touched the top of my head as I sat on the floor. I picked up Layla's purse and set it on my lap, admiring it like a wrapped gift on Christmas morning. I reached my hand inside, feeling for the compact, and I pulled it out. It was at least two decades old—probably more—and still, it was in great condition. It was gold with a round ruby button. I turned it over in my hand, examining it from top to bottom. There were only a few scratches on the side where it looked like maybe she had dropped it. I wondered if it had been scratched during the accident.

I opened the compact and was surprised when a small photograph, cut to size, fluttered into my lap. I shut the compact and placed it to my side. I picked up the picture and turned it over, instantly feeling sick to my stomach. Layla and Walker—*my* Walker. It was him in his other life. The one where he was happy and fulfilled. The one he preferred over his life with me. He was handsome, and I had never seen him smile like that before. It broke my heart thinking that I would never see him smile like that. He looked almost unchanged. As if the past twenty years hadn't aged him a day. I guess that's what happens when you die. You stop aging.

I looked at Layla in the photo. She was vibrant, full of life. Her eyes sparkled even in the old photograph, and I could only imagine how beautiful and warm she was in person. Her hair was lush and healthy, her cheekbones lifted so that her eyes had the most perfect shape. She was smiling here in the photograph, but I imagined even on her worst days, her eyes would glisten. She was that kind of girl—a happy one. And I knew that I could never achieve that level of beauty. Not just because of what was on the outside; beauty was from within, after all. And as sad as it was to say, my insides didn't match hers. The loss of my gran and the insecurities I'd grown up with surrounding my dyslexia had dampened my energy. And that's why Walker would never love me—not because I wasn't Layla on the outside but because I was broken on the inside.

The compact cracked open as I pushed my thumb into the ruby button. The mirror reflected my ugly insides as I peered into it. I hated it. I hated how

I was staring back at myself. This girl was dull, her skin lackluster and eyes two-dimensional. Her lips were dry and cracked; her hair brittle. And that was only on the surface. If this mirror was magic at all. It was showing me how transparent I was. I nodded, understanding it now.

Layla was never the one standing in my way of Walker. It was me. And who I was at the very core. I couldn't change that. And what I was coming to learn, I couldn't hide it, either. The mirror was proof of that. I snapped the mirror shut and tossed it back in Layla's bag, and a moment later, I threw the picture in there too. I rested my head on the back wall of the dark closet and stared up at the hanging clothes. I thought about the time I'd looked in the mirror and my reflection was vacant. Missing completely. The time I was a nobody. And then I thought about the time I saw Kimber, her skin stretched over her bones and her teeth falling into the porcelain sink. We had something in common.

Our reflections weren't that of our exterior—not our skin, eyes, and hair—but something much deeper. Kimber's eating disorder was reflected in the mirror the same way that my insecurities were reflected in mine. And at one point, I'd believed I was so insignificant that I didn't have a reflection at all. Now I knew better. I knew I had a purpose and that I held the power to get my remaining friends out of Baylor. And I supposed that was why I'd found my reflection again.

I thought about Walker's photo. He'd had the scar across his eyebrow. It was the same one he had on his eyebrow half the days I saw him. Some days it was magically gone; other days, it was a fresh wound—bleeding all over again. Could that be his reflection? Could he be so beautiful on the inside, except for that one little piece? A piece that refused to heal. I wondered what it could be. What marked his soul? What ran so deep that it showed on his surface?

If Walker had only one scar to bear on his face for all of us to see, then I had one hundred. I had a long way to go if I ever wanted to like what I saw in that funhouse mirror. It felt impossible, and at times it felt shallow. But I knew that this was much more than a beauty contest. There were answers hidden beneath our reflections. And if I could figure out what Kimber's truth was, then maybe, just maybe, I could figure out my own.

16

As I sat at the base of my closet, the darkness and clothing smothering me, I knew I had to tell the group what I'd learned about the Baylor phenomenon. It was snatching souls and destroying minds, and if they knew, they'd at least be better equipped to combat it. They'd have a better chance of fighting if they knew the manifestations began in their heads. I couldn't leave out a single detail. Because if I missed even one little thing, I knew it would inhibit us from solving this puzzle. One missing piece could bring us all down.

I didn't want to tell them about my gran, though. The nights that she had come for me, the twisted conversations I'd had with my mother over the telephone that were rehearsed and fake. It was too personal, and I didn't want them to see my weakness. But that's precisely why I *needed* to tell them. I needed to stand up for myself. Stand up to the fear that kept me caged inside. I scrambled to my feet, my face getting caught on hanging clothes. I batted them away and strode downstairs with newfound purpose. I tried not to let myself think of how terribly this could go, because then it surely would.

Kai and Noah sat making dinner plans in the living room. It sounded like an epic barbecue night, and they were making a list of items they needed at the grocery store. I didn't have to look for Kimber and Asher; I could hear them clearly from the other room. They were fighting like they had been ever since their breakup. They were tucked in the dark den; only it wasn't as private as they'd probably hoped. One look at Noah and Kai, and I could tell that everybody was annoyed with them. I sighed and headed into the kitchen to find Scarlett May and Emma washing dishes. It was nice to have the extra help.

"Do you know where Levi is?" I asked, trying to round up the troops.

"Levi and Mason are throwing a football outside," Scarlett May said, pointing a soapy finger out the window.

"What's up?" Emma asked.

"There's something important we need to talk about. I want to get the group together before dinner so we can all chat," I said, picking up a dish towel. As I started to dry the dishes, Kimber and Asher marched into the room, stealing the show.

"Don't make this about me! This is all about you and what you're going through. But you push it off on me like it's all my fault, and it's not! You make me sound so crazy!" Kimber yelled, stomping out to the back patio and slamming the door in her wake.

"What the hell?" Asher fisted a hand in his hair and then stormed off in the opposite direction.

"I swear, if those two don't get back together, I'm going to pull my hair out strand by strand," Scarlett May said. Emma took a deep breath, visibly stressed. We all were. The relationship fighting was just the icing on the cake.

We finished the dishes, and I had high hopes of gathering the group for the speech I never wanted to give. But now, Kimber was gone, taking Gunner for a walk, and a few of the boys were off to the grocery store in search of supplies. Emma retreated to her room to do some more research, and I grew more and more anxious about delivering my speech as the minutes ticked by. What if they didn't believe me? Or worse, what if they did? What if it elicited fear and everybody went crazy? What if it made *me* crazy?

I was worried that I was missing something. Something so simple that I hadn't seen. What if I told them everything, and they knew the answers almost immediately? Was I ready to face it? Was I ready to understand what was happening? I didn't know if I could handle all the responsibilities. I was most afraid that the terrible things that had happened to my friends were my fault—I couldn't live with that.

There were already monsters in the water, magical fruit trees in the forest, and the most handsome walking dead guy I'd ever seen. If there was even one more abnormal evolution, I might fall to my knees and crumble to ash. Yet, I knew if that were to happen here in Baylor, I'd be the phoenix and rise to do it all over again. There would be no break for me. Not until the hard work was done.

When the guys got back from the store, they fired up the grill. The smoky smell of barbecue permeated the air and rose to the second story of the cabin. I was riddled with anxiety about all the ways our conversation could go, and I was stuck trying to find the courage within myself to do it anyway. I was pacing back and forth in my bedroom when I heard one of the guys call out through the window. "Dinner is served!" It sounded like Mason.

I peeked out the window and saw the football rolling down the grassy hill toward the lake, left behind by the guys as they ran for dinner. Scarlett May grabbed a plate and got in line for dinner. Her jean shorts and cowgirl boots were the perfect attire for a lakeside barbecue. I looked down at my joggers and tennis shoes and briefly thought that I should try harder. Put on some real clothes. Especially if I was going to be speaking in front of everyone tonight. So, I did just that. I rummaged through my clothes and changed into jeans and a hoodie—only slightly better. I wasn't dressed up by any means, but at least I didn't feel like I had just rolled out of bed.

I loaded up a plate with a bread roll, barbecued corn, and steak. It smelled wonderful, and I had no doubt these guys had been perfecting their barbecue game over the course of the summer. When they went back to Clover, they were going to impress their parents and future girlfriends with their skills.

"There's something I wanted to talk to you guys about before dinner," I said in a meek tone. Only a few of them heard me.

"What's that, Kinsley?" Kai asked. He had compassion that reached out beyond his senses. He heard even the weakest of voices, and he worked hard to bring them to light so that everybody could hear. "Hey, dipshits, Kinsley's trying to tell us something," he said in a booming voice. Maybe he didn't do it with grace, but he got the job done. My face heated, as I had the stage. Everybody froze, holding their plates or tongs mid dish.

"Um, I just, I wanted to talk to you guys after dinner. It's about all the weird things that are going on, and I think I might have some insight that I haven't quite shared with you all yet. There are things I know. And, um, I think it's time that we all share the little bits of information that we've gathered. I'm probably not the only one who's had strange things happen to them or seen things that seem abnormal. I think if we piece them all together, as a group, we'll be stronger. And maybe we can go on the offensive for the first time if we're a team," I said.

"Sounds like a plan," Levi said, loading up his plate.

I nodded, my face hot. Kai patted me on the back. I looked around and couldn't find Emma. My stomach sank, hoping that she hadn't been the next victim.

"I think that's a great idea, Kinsley," Kai said. And I felt validated for the split second before I ran inside and searched for the only friend I had left.

"Emma?" I called out. But I heard no answer. I ran upstairs where I had known her to be last, and when I burst through her bedroom door, I saw her sitting at a small desk with earphones in. My heart pounded against my chest, and I felt dizzy in my relief. I backed up against the wall, hand across my heart.

"Hey!" Emma lurched, catching sight of me from the corner of her eye. Her expression remained unchanged with the passing seconds. Had I interrupted something? Perhaps Emma had secrets too.

"What's going on?" I asked, catching my breath and looking around the room for signs of secrecy. I found my sign the moment that Emma reached for a book and placed it over an article on her desk.

"Nothing. You just scared me, that's all," she said, her voice higher pitched than normal. I moved toward her desk, and slowly I reached out for the book. I didn't take my eyes off her. I watched as her face wrinkled with grief.

"What is it?" It must've been something terrible if my only friend was hiding it from me when we had just discussed secrets being off-limits. It had to be something absolutely atrocious. Something that made her think it would destroy me if I saw it.

She said nothing, but her eyes turned glassy as she looked down at the article. I, too, looked down at the article. The print was tiny, and the black spaces of the font merged with the white spaces in between the letters. They danced as I watched, knowing that if I could only focus hard enough, I'd know exactly what that article said. My name popped out, bigger and bolder than the rest. Words like accident were next.

"What is it?" I asked again.

"I found a new article. I swear it wasn't there the first time we looked. It must've just come online." Emma picked up the article and watched me intently. I took a moment to decide if I wanted to hear it, and my ultimate decision was that I had no choice. I was nothing more than a victim. Everything had been happening to me at lightning speed, and I had no control over stopping it. Or slowing it down. I nodded.

"It talks about the accident you were in. It talks about how you . . . *survived.*" Emma's eyes flickered up at me, checking for my reaction, but I had none. *Survived?* "It says you spent some time in the hospital recovering, but ultimately, you're a fighter." Emma paused, and my eyes turned glassy as the news soaked in.

She continued, "You were able to heal even when the doctors said you wouldn't. They're calling it a miracle." Emma's eyes drooped with sadness. My throat burned, and even though I was on the verge of crying, my mind was quiet. Thoughtless. It made little sense to me. And the fact that she was sad about it only confused me more.

"Do you believe it?" I asked. Emma's eyes floated back to the article.

"I don't know what to think," she shrugged.

"If I survived . . . Then why am I here?" The room silenced.

It was the million-dollar question. How could I be here, dead, amongst my dying friends at a cabin in the woods? How could the woods be filled with mysterious and surreal happenings? How could apples appear overnight? How could Lainey come to life under the water? How could she speak to me without ever saying a word? —If I were alive?

"Lainey . . ." I whispered, taking a seat on the edge of the bed.

"Lainey?" Emma asked.

I looked out the window. The wheels turning and grinding in my head. Gears I had never explored before. "When I saw Lainey under the water, she told me to wake up. She said *wake up*!"

My mouth parted, and time stopped altogether.

"Oh my god, Kinsley! *You're dreaming*. It's a dream! It's nothing but a damn dream!" Emma said, coming to her feet. Her eyes searched mine.

"I'm . . . I'm dreaming? That can't be . . ." I shook my head.

"Why not?" she asked.

"Because. I don't know, you're here. And Noah's here. And everybody is here!" I felt sick to my stomach. Like my world had come crashing down on me. "It makes no sense. How are you all in *my* dream? I mean, you're real, aren't you?" I asked, and a sense of dread poured over me the moment it slipped from my lips. I couldn't do this alone. I needed her to be real.

"Of course, I'm real!" Emma said, insulted. But after a moment of silence, I watched as a new thought creased her brows and her eyes lowered to her body. Slowly, she patted her arms and gripped her shoulders. "Yeah, I'm totally real," she said quietly. I wasn't so sure. I wanted to touch her too, but I couldn't insult her like that.

"Could we all be dreaming together?" I said.

Emma snorted. "More like you've summonsed us into your dream. I think you're pulling us into it."

I was like a dark vortex. I sucked in anybody who got close enough, and then swallowed them into the throat of the night.

Emma looked out the window, her eyes traveling the distance. When she turned back to me, she looked upset. "I don't want to be here, Kinsley. And if this is your dream, can't you send us home?" Emma nodded. "I want to go home. I don't want to die here." Tears spilled from her eyes, and I felt absolutely terrible. She cried on my shoulder when I pulled her in for a hug.

It didn't convince me I was alive yet, but somehow I had been hurting the people I loved most. Somehow, I knew this was my fault. I never put it past me to hurt the people I loved. But it was never my intention.

"Oh Emma, I would send you home if I could. But I don't think I can control this. I'm not convinced that I'm alive, let alone dreaming up this whole Baylor phenomenon. I'm just not . . . I don't know," I said, my thoughts a jumbled mess. I let go of Emma and pinched my arm. I shrugged. "I feel it. So, that means I'm real. I'm not dreaming, right?" I asked, unsure of anything at this point. I was worried that I was giving myself false hope, and I knew I couldn't survive another letdown.

"A pinch? That's all you've got? We need something bigger." Emma looked around the room, and I feared what she would do next. I watched as her eyes settled on a pencil, and I instinctively stepped backward, thinking that she'd bring it down on me, stabbing me in the back—just to test her theory.

"I feel . . . I feel! You don't need to stab me," I said, holding my hands out. Emma laughed. It had never been her intention. And I sure felt stupid for believing it.

"I thought I said *we*. I was thinking bigger. Much bigger."

"Bigger than stabbing me?"

"Hey, you know what would be really great?" Emma said, a smile broadening across her face. "If Asher and Kimber got back together and all the fighting stopped." I frowned. They were an unnecessary thorn in everybody's side, but I couldn't see how the two things were connected.

"I mean, yeah, that would be great. But—"

"—Make it happen," she said. Demanding the impossible of me.

"Make it happen?" Now it was my turn to laugh. It was so ridiculous. She acted as if I could dream up anything in the world and it would happen before our very eyes. Like a manifestation.

Manifestation . . .

Walker told me that my fears came to life here—and if that didn't sound like a dream, I didn't know what did. A weird feeling swirled in my chest, and I didn't know if I was about to like this theory or not.

"Just *try* to make it happen. Think about it. Think about what you would see if they got back together. Let's go downstairs for dinner, and I want you to feel as if they'd already gotten back together and the tension in the cabin was long gone. Go downstairs with the firm belief that everybody is getting along. Can you do that?" she asked. Who knew Emma could give motivational talks? If I had, I would've tapped into them more often.

"Okay, I think I can." And that's exactly what I did.

We went down for dinner. I'm sure my plate was already cold, as I had set it on the banister before running in to check on Emma. But as we walked down the stairs, I concentrated. I tried my hardest to feel what it would be like if everyone was happy, despite the fear, the anger, and the grief. Not just Kimber and Asher, but everybody. I imagined unity and laughter. And just the thought of it made me feel lighter, as if it had already happened. I smiled, feeling stupid, and embarrassed for believing it could work. It reminded me of the time Walker and I found the tower by way of sixth sense.

By the time we hit the bottom stair, I could see the change in Emma's face. Behind her smile and sparkling eyes, there was genuine happiness. Butterflies fluttered in my stomach as we opened the back patio door. The entire group was playing football out on the grass. Kimber ran and jumped on Asher's back as he tried to score a touchdown. She roared with laughter as the guys tried to rip the ball out of Asher's hands. A normally aggressive game of football was now child's play. And it was like walking into a scene from a movie. A scene of normalcy and happier times.

I couldn't pry my eyes off the faces out on the grass. They were happier than I had ever seen them . . . and all at the same time. The way I felt inside—I had seen it in their eyes. They felt it too. Emma grabbed my arm. And as we watched them with unhinged jaws and wide eyes, she laid her head down on my shoulder. The sun set, turning their figures into dark silhouettes in play. It was the summer I'd always wanted.

If this truly was a dream, then why had all the bad things happened? I was a good person. My soul was pure. If I was in control, then how were my best friends dead? It couldn't be. I couldn't be the only one flying this plane right now. There had to be outside factors contributing to the pain and misery we'd all experienced this summer. Because this wasn't my plan.

I rested my head on Emma's and we contentedly watched everybody play, if only for just tonight. When they caught sight of us, Kai waved us to join. Emma looked at me with a twinkle in her eye that reminded me of a child on Christmas morning. She slipped her hand out of my arm and took off running across the grass to join the team.

But if I was dreaming, then she wasn't real. And if she wasn't real, then what was she?

On her first step forward, I reached out behind her and touched her hair in curiosity. My hand touched nothing at all. It swiped through her brown locks as if they were nothing more than air—pushing little specks of particles around as they glimmered and disintegrated. Emma ran off to play football as I stood on the porch watching the pieces of her fall to the ground, sparkle, and fade into nothing.

17

After a long, sleepless night, I awoke to the sound of my alarm, though it was far too early to volunteer for the Baylor Fourth of July Parade. It was Lainey's commitment, but she'd enlisted our help before she had disappeared. Back home, she did it every year without fail, and she was more excited to glue live flowers on floats here in Baylor than to watch the parade itself. I'd done it once with her before when we were a little younger, but this time was different, and I wasn't looking forward to it.

Today was going to be full of Lainey memories, and it hurt just thinking about it. Walker decided last minute to join us, and I was thankful for his distraction. However, I knew I needed to tell him about what Emma had found online—the part where I'd survived the accident. *Survived*—it sent a shiver down my back. Maybe it was good news to tell, I didn't know. But I found myself worried about how he'd take it. Walker and I had always been two peas in a pod. The only ones of our kind. And today, I was going to tell him that it was simply him. Only him. That he walked alone in the shadows.

Theoretically, it should be good news. I wasn't dead after all—assuming the article was real. I wasn't totally convinced. But if it were, I'd have a life to live outside of Baylor. I'd go on to college—maybe even have a family of my own one day. But regardless, I couldn't help the terrible feeling that swirled in my chest telling me this was a bad thing. That I was leaving Walker behind. To a world of solitude. An eternity of it.

Solitude. It was man's worst punishment. Walker didn't deserve it. He deserved to find his real love, Layla Barns. And if she had died in that crash, there was no reason we couldn't find her and set him free. I knew he didn't look at me the way I did him, but I was still heartbroken to tell him that I would not be in his eternity. I'd always thought that he would find Layla and leave me behind, but if I was alive somewhere, then I'd be the one leaving him. We had become good friends over the summer. Better than friends. We had become afterlife mates. We shared a bond like nobody else. And today . . . today was going to be the day that I broke that bond.

Walker and I walked side by side as he handed me a hot coffee. I thanked him as we checked in for volunteering. There were several floats to be assigned to, and Emma was hoping to work on anything that originated from a book. If it had, she'd probably read and loved it at one time or another.

With that said, we were assigned to the furthest thing from a fairy tale. We were assigned to work on a beer float. An advertisement. But to me, sticking golden flowers on a cold brew was no different than placing the red flowers on a poisonous apple. It was, however, the ultimate blow to Emma. Her disappointment was obvious in her droopy gaze and pouty lips. I squeezed her shoulder.

"It's okay. I'm sure that an hour from now you can go stick flowers wherever you want." The corners of her eyes lifted, and she smiled mischievously.

The beer garden float was a long walk away. One of the farthest floats from the check-in stand. A kind old lady gave us volunteer badges and sent us on our way with a map. The place was a madhouse. It was crawling with volunteers, engineers, and even a news crew. There was a lot to see and a lot to take in. I knew as we passed each subsequent float that I wasn't enjoying the flowers to the fullest, how Lainey would have. I slowed, reaching my hand out, and my fingertips praising a freshly glued flower. I didn't even know the names of the flowers. If Lainey were here, she would have told me. She wouldn't have stopped telling me, and at some point, her words would have fallen on deaf ears. But I wanted to hear their names now.

"That white one right there—that's a carnation. The brightly colored ones in the front of the float are chrysanthemums. Mums for short. They symbolize death and grieving," I heard Lainey say in my ear. Her voice tickled, and I batted at my ear, checking behind me. I searched for Lainey and then realized it had only happened because I'd wanted it to. It brought a smile to my face, even if I'd made it up. Because it was her voice—her essence—and it lived on through my memory. And that much was real.

"You know, if Lainey were here, she would tell us all about these flowers. She wouldn't shut up about them," I said with a smile. Walker hadn't known her very well, only having had a few brief encounters with her, but I could tell that he enjoyed hearing about her.

Emma laughed. "Oh yeah. All day long. She'd tell us how they collected the flowers and have stories about each kind. She loved this stuff," Emma said.

"The bright-colored ones in the front of the float are chrysanthemums. Mums for short. They symbolize death and grieving," I said in my best impersonation of Lainey.

"Oh—how'd you know that?" Emma asked, taken aback by my comment.

I shrugged. "A little birdie told me," I said.

The smell of flowers was overwhelming, and it reminded me of walking into a flower shop to pick the perfect bouquet when my gran died. It wasn't a good memory, and the smell was intoxicating. My heart had broken while looking at the beautiful varieties of flowers and smelling the sweet petals. It was a terrible mix. The beauty, the nature, the colors, and the smell—all laced with grief. And what never seemed to make sense to me was that flowers were for every occasion. You get them when you're in love and when it's your birthday; you can get them with a new job or a raise. And how is it supposed to make you feel when all you can remember is the smell of heartbreak, and it takes you back to that space and time? It doesn't feel like a celebration of anything, but more like torture. Torture of the mind and soul.

But today was the day that I was going to overwrite that memory. I'd never inhaled so many flowers before, and I was pretty sure I'd smell like petals for the rest of my life. I didn't think a shower was powerful enough to rid me of the rose bath I was marinating in. I held my coffee close and took in a deep, cleansing breath, the roasted bitter beans under my nose. But there was only so much coffee I could drink, and at some point in the day, I'd have to get used to smelling flowers again.

They stationed me near the top of a giant beer stein. I had a million tiny white flowers to glue to the float, which would soon become the effervescent head of the beer. It all felt so elaborate for a small-town parade. Where in the world had all these flowers come from? Walker was below me with deep amber flowers at the base. Emma was on the other side of the float, gluing greenery to make grass for the beer garden. I watched as she pointed to a book in another girl's purse. They hadn't stopped talking since.

"How's it going down there?" I asked Walker.

"Slow. How long do we have to do this for?" he asked, stopping to peer up at me.

"We've only been working for eleven minutes. We have all day."

"I see. Can we take breaks?" he asked, hopeful.

"I don't see why not. We're just volunteering." I stuck another white flower on top of the beer stein.

"Now?" Walker asked. I laughed. He made his way up to me and started picking from my flowers. He wasn't supposed to be working on the same project as I was, and it made my heart smile that he wanted to be closer to me.

There were a million reasons why that could have been the case, but I settled on distance. He didn't like the distance.

"Any idea where our next clue is?" he asked, looking around. And then I realized he didn't like the distance between him and Layla.

"Actually, I think I might have a clue." I searched around for floats with seven dwarves, but I saw no such thing.

"Really? Did your grandma pay you another visit?"

"No. I haven't seen her in a little while. But, I've been thinking . . . and you know that apple tree we planted?" I asked.

"Yeah, the gigantic one. How could I forget?"

"Well, it bloomed. It's got the most beautiful, giant, red apples you've ever seen. They're perfect. Emma said they might be poisonous."

"Poisonous?" He glared at me with one eyebrow raised—the one with the gash running through it. It was healed today and looked as if it had happened a decade ago.

"I know it sounds weird, but didn't the tower sound weird? I'm telling you, I think these fairytale books my gran used to read to me are clues. And where there's an apple . . . there must be poison." I said, picking the sticky glue off my fingertips.

"Okay, so what fairytale are we in now?" he asked, leaning in.

"I'm thinking our next clue is going to lie on one of these floats. Look for anything with apples, seven doors, a witch, or . . . a magic mirror," I said.

We made it just shy of half an hour before Walker was so restless we ditched our stations and wandered around in search of fairytale floats. We came across superheroes, big-box labels, and mythological creatures but had no such luck when it came to fairy tales.

Since Emma had stayed back chatting with her new friend and working diligently to cover the float, I decided it was time to talk to Walker. I had to tell him about the article. But the more I tried to spit it out, the more it seemed to bury itself deep down inside of me. I considered keeping it a secret and never letting it see the light of day. I'd allow Walker to think that we were two of the same kind so that he'd never have to feel alone again. But I knew that was wrong, and it would never last. The truth needed to be told, no matter how painful it would be for him to hear.

"I found something. Or rather, Emma found something. She found an article on the accident that I was supposedly in . . ." I said, tiptoeing around the facts.

"She found another article? Did it say anything new?" he asked, his attention only partially on me as he continued searching floats.

"Yeah, I learned that I'm still alive—" I said, wanting him to stop looking for Layla and see what was right in front of him. It worked too well. Walker stopped dead in his tracks. He looked back at me with his brows stitched. I couldn't quite read his expression, but I knew enough that it wasn't a positive look. I grimaced.

"I hate to tell you this, but I don't think you have that right, Wilde. I mean, you're just like me, and nobody's ever been just like me."

My heart sank. "The article said that I survived the crash. It said that I spent a long time in recovery and it was thought to be a miracle. I think it's true. I think I might be alive. And this . . . this is all just a dream . . ." I said quietly.

Walker stepped close to me. Our faces were close enough that I could feel his breath upon my lips. "You think you're in a dream?" he asked.

I swallowed hard, questioning the real possibility. If I were in a dream, he'd kiss me—and that wasn't happening. "Well—" I began.

"—I'm not dreaming. This is my real life. My *afterlife*. This can't be your dream because I've been living it since long before you drowned in that lake. I'm sorry to be the one to tell you, but I don't think you're alive, Wilde. It just can't be. What about your gran?" he asked. His voice was harsh and filled with skepticism. But I knew that whatever the answers were, we were still in this together, and he would be by my side, no matter the state of my mind and soul.

"Well, I stayed up all night thinking about that," I said, leaning in closer, our heads nearly touching, my eyes searching his. "I think that maybe it's *because* I'm in a dream state that I can talk to you and Gran. I think I've passed the veil of the living and somehow gotten closer to wherever you and she live. I think my heart and soul are traveling at a different frequency somewhere closer to yours, on the other side. I think that's what makes us so similar," I said, nodding. He pondered my best guess as his face contorted.

I knew the moment he believed it to be a possibility. His forehead softened, and his eyes appeared deeper, more distant, like he'd already begun slipping away from me. I spotted a mum—the flower of death. I plucked it from the base of a float and held it between him and me. Then, with all my concentration, I imagined it evaporating like I'd seen Emma's hair the night before. I stroked the petals between my fingers and they turned to tiny sparkles and glimmered all the way down to the ground.

Walker's eyes lifted with wonder but quickly drooped with sadness. He nodded. If I was alive, he was alone. The special bond we shared was a double-edged sword.

"One living, one not," he whispered.

But Walker was living. He was—just not the way that I was, or like anybody else back home. He wasn't even living the same as my gran. She was in another realm altogether. And if I had to guess, I'd say that it was the torture he'd put himself through that isolated him in such a way. If he'd only believe that Layla didn't blame him for her death, then maybe he'd be free. Free to get out of Baylor and follow her to their happily ever after. But instead, he believed he was cursed. It sure felt that way now.

When Walker's expression darkened, I could see the hurt in his eyes. "What's wrong?" I asked.

"This is good news. I'm happy for you. I'm happy," he said.

I knew the possibility of it was good news, but it didn't feel that way, and I could tell he had mixed feelings about it too. With my old life still ahead of me, I knew that one day we would be broken apart, and I would no longer see him. It made all the time between us even more precious. We had grown to like our peculiar arrangement. We had learned to lean on one another in times of need. Our bond had been strong from the start, but it had only strengthened each and every day this summer. It felt like a lifetime ago. Like I'd known him my whole life—or at least my soul had.

18

After a long, failed attempt at locating anything remotely helpful to find Layla Barns in town, Emma, Walker, and I came home empty-handed. We had, however, honored Lainey and her love for Mother Nature by gluing countless flowers onto a giant stein of beer. She would have been proud.

But Walker wasn't ready to give up, so he headed home to do some research on the seven dwarfs. The fairytale lead was only a hunch at this point, but I recalled the bed of purple Rapunzel flowers blooming on the forest floor, long before the tower had appeared. And while we hadn't found Layla in that tower, we *had* found her purse—not to mention Trinity's killer. I'd also discovered some rather disturbing things about my existence . . . or lack thereof. But when Emma swiftly smacked the most perfect red apple away, mere inches from my mouth, I'd thought of another fairy tale. This one, in particular, would have a witch, seven dwarfs, and a mirror. I'd already found the mirror—I couldn't forget it.

Emma and I slumped down on the sofa and turned on a movie. It wasn't long before the entire cabin got sucked in and we were packed like sardines on the couch. We were sandwiched between the once-again-happy couple and Noah. Scarlett May was at our feet with Sampson. Mason and Levi were lying on the floor, and Kai was popping popcorn in the microwave. I couldn't help but look at the empty spots on the floor. There was a spot for Ethan, one for Lainey, and one for Trinity. Now and then, my eyes would wander to the empty spots and I'd imagine how they would have lain or laughed.

The movie was packed with action and kept everybody on their toes. But no matter how many explosions, fistfights, or car chases sprawled across the screen, Emma had something else working through her mind. She leaned over and whispered during a loud suspenseful crash. "I've been thinking about the dream theory," she said. I watched as two cars collided, one going up in a plume of smoke and fire. I knew nobody could hear us, so I leaned back and gave her my attention—I wasn't fully invested in the movie either.

"I want to test it again. I have an idea," she said.

"Shut up back there," said Scarlett May, swatting a hand at Emma.

I said nothing but gave her a curt nod. I was up for testing dream theory—it could be fun.

"You made it happen once. I think you could do it again," she whispered.

"Shut up!" Scarlett May hissed. Emma's face turned red, and we knew that this conversation would have to wait for another time. Emma said nothing for the next half hour, and my mind swirled with the possibilities of tests. Kimber and Asher could have been a fluke. They were bound to get back together at some point. Couples fight all the time, and they had a long-standing relationship, not to mention they were hidden away in a remote cabin for the summer. There was no way they *weren't* getting back together. The fact that I imagined it happening could very well have been a coincidence. The more I thought about it, the likelier this explanation seemed.

But the part that irked me most—the part that I couldn't get out of my head—was Emma's hair as she ran away to play ball. I questioned if she was real, and she just disintegrated. I didn't know what that told me, but when I tried it again to show Walker, there were particles of that flower that I saw disintegrate too. There wasn't much. But it was enough to get me thinking. Truth be told, I couldn't stop thinking.

The movie ended with Emma giving it one more shot. She leaned in and whispered in my ear, but this time, we'd caught Kimber's attention.

"What are you guys talking about? What could possibly be more interesting than Danny McCoy without a shirt on?" Kimber asked, her eyes glued to one of the most handsome actors ever known.

Emma shook her head, not wanting to divulge. But when the movie was over, and Emma and I snuck into the dark den to chat, little did we know that Kimber followed.

"It worked with Kimber and Asher, so I was thinking maybe you could try it again," Emma said in the shadows of the den.

I folded my arms and looked at her suspiciously. I wasn't okay toying with people's emotions, but that didn't mean I wasn't curious. "What did you have in mind?" I asked.

"Well, I was kind of thinking that maybe you could see if . . . possibly . . ." She twisted her fingers in ways they weren't meant to bend.

"Just spit it out," I said.

"Levi. I like Levi." Emma's face contorted, knowing that it was a paradoxical match. I stared at her, wondering if it could be true. Emma was smart. She was one of the smartest girls I knew, and she was sweet, too. Levi couldn't be more opposite than that.

Levi was cute—maybe that was the reason she liked him. I wasn't sure. He was built like a tree trunk, strong and stout. He had black, spiky shards of hair that were on the brink of flopping at all times. And he only smiled from one side of his mouth. There was a real bad boy air about him, and his reputation with the girls preceded him. If Emma truly did like him, she wouldn't be the first, and she wouldn't be the last.

If I could pair Emma with anybody, it would be Kai. Kai was smart, compassionate, and also attractive. But I knew that's exactly why she didn't like him. Because as much as it never made sense to me, opposites truly did attract. And Emma liking Levi was proof of that. "So, what then? You want me to make Levi like you?" Levi wasn't in it for the long game, and I didn't think he had the emotional depth to carry a relationship of any kind. He was easy to fall for, but nobody ever stayed, and nobody ever wanted him for more than a one-night stand. I knew this was a bad idea.

Emma fidgeted, tucking her hair behind her ear and looking down to her feet in the dark, even though they were buried in the shadows. "Come on . . . Just do this one thing for me. I'm asking for a favor. I've *never* . . ." My eyebrows shot up right before Kimber walked in.

"You've *never* what?" she asked. And even though the room had no light bulbs, I could see the horror written all over Emma's face.

"How long have you been there?" she asked.

"Long enough to know that you like Levi and you're asking for Wilde here to do something mysterious—maybe evil. I want in," Kimber said, folding her arms.

"No," Emma said dryly.

"I heard you did, whatever it was, to Asher and me. You did *something*. I need to know what you did." Kimber wasn't budging. And I shrugged. She had a right to know. Emma shook her head, mortified, but I saw it differently. If I was going to enlist everyone's help, it started with the truth. And I was going to tell them, eventually. Maybe not about this, but about other stuff. The dream theory included. It made sense to do some testing to make sure it had some merit before telling the others. I put my hand on Emma's shoulder and she tipped her head back, moaning exhaustively.

"It's nothing more than a little manifestation," I said, improvising.

"You . . . *manifested* Asher and I getting back together?"

I could see the hesitation in her eyes. She knew there was much more, and had it not been for Kimber's emaciated reflection in the mirror, we might have gotten away with simple manifestation. But just nights before, we'd watched her teeth fall out, one by one, and as she glared at me now, she was certain I was lying. There was something much bigger going on, and she wanted in on it. Kimber slowly tilted her head and stiffened her shoulders; she wasn't budging until I spoke the truth.

"Emma has a theory—a theory that this is just a dream. And if it's a dream, then we can basically . . . *will* what we want to happen." I strategically left out the part where this was *my* dream and mine alone. I didn't think it would go over well. I wasn't the star of the show here, and if I needed teamwork, there couldn't be a frontrunner; a single dreamer.

"And you tested this theory out on me?" Kimber asked, her head dipping and her eyes looking up at us through her lashes mischievously.

"Well, you and Asher fighting was hell for all of us. You two aren't the only people in the house, you know," Emma said, her tone higher than normal.

"Okay," Kimber said, taking the news with a grain of salt. She was used to hearing that she affected people in ways she never knew. It came along with being popular in school. She must have been sick of hearing about other people's feelings by now.

"So, we were going to try Levi and Emma next," I said, pointing a finger at Emma. I knew that this was wrong. I knew that playing matchmaker with my friends like they were marionettes was like playing with black magic. I was tapping into something mysterious and powerful, and I knew it wasn't for the right reasons. Unfortunately, my curiosity trumped my moral compass. If Emma wanted a little kiss from a guy who enjoyed kissing, then what harm was there in that?

"Did I hear that you've *never* . . ." Kimber said, her finger swirling towards Emma's pelvis in the dark.

"Stop," Emma said bluntly.

"And you want Levi to be your first?" Kimber asked. This was the other half of the bad idea that made this test one gigantic, terrible plan. It was bad enough to play with my friends' emotions, but Levi would end up hurting innocent Emma, and we all knew it. Even she did.

"I mean, he's really, really hot. You can't argue with that," Emma said, her voice jittery and her arms folded tight across her chest. I shrugged because I couldn't argue with that. Kimber took on the parental role that perhaps I should have.

"But you know he's kind of an asshole, right?" Kimber asked.

"Mmm . . ." I nodded and looked at Emma for her response.

"I know," she said, looking at the ground.

"Okay, are we going to do this? Or should we find a different test? A safer one?" I asked, wanting to test the theory any which way possible. Emma nodded her head vigorously, and Kimber rubbed her palms together like she was starting the kindling of a fire.

"Okay, that settles it. How do we do this?" Kimber asked, her eyes bouncing from one of us to the other. A swirl of excitement ambushed me, and for the first time since the naked cheetah races, I had something to look forward to.

"We . . . We just imagine it as if it were true. We imagine what it would feel like, look like, smell—"

"Eww—" Kimber grimaced.

"Not like that, no, we just kind of spread that feeling all throughout the cabin," I said. Emma nodded in agreement.

"But what feeling?" Kimber asked.

I sighed, trying to think of how best to describe it. "Think of it like this: Levi falls for Emma. Now imagine how that would change the dynamics of the group. Feel the charge of flirtation in the air like electricity—"

"—Just picture it," Emma said with wide eyes.

"Yeah. That." I shrugged.

We closed our eyes, and I imagined Levi taking notice of Emma for the first time. I imagined Levi flirting with her. Grazing his hand against hers. Smiling out of the side of his mouth. I pictured her swooning and him grabbing her for a deep and passionate kiss. I smiled when I thought of her reaction. She'd blush like she'd been swept off her feet. And then I imagined what she would do if he actually swept her off her feet. If he threw her over his shoulder and charged upstairs to the bedroom. She'd be giggling the whole way. She'd have the night of her life, and when all was said and done, she'd fall back on her pillow with flushed cheeks and fall asleep with the large goofy grin that spread from one ear to the next.

Emma squeezed my hand as she snickered. I opened my eyes to see both of them giggling at me.

"What's with that look on your face?" Kimber asked. I realized I'd been the one with a stupid grin on my face, and it faded as the embarrassment sank in. The feelings I'd felt were so real that I couldn't wait to see if it would come true.

"I was just imagining it all. You guys did it too, right?" I asked.

"Yeah, I imagined Levi ravaging Emma all right," Kimber said. Emma slapped her shoulder, and we all laughed.

"Okay, let's see if it works. Let's go," I said, heading out the door.

"Oh my god, I'm so nervous," Emma said, completely frazzled. She hung behind, and I grabbed her shoulders, shoving her out of the den. The three of us laughed as we entered the kitchen, and as soon as we did, Levi snapped to attention. He looked Emma up and down. Kimber and I stared at each other with wide eyes as Emma's gaze darted straight to the floor and her cheeks turned crimson.

"Hey Emma, catch," Levi said, holding a piece of popcorn high over his head. I'd never seen Emma so embarrassed. She opened her mouth and tilted her head back, her cheeks as red as port wine. Levi threw the piece of popcorn and it landed perfectly in her mouth, just like magic. Levi jumped and yelled, and without hesitation, he swept her off her feet. He spun her around in a circle and high-fived her.

"That was awesome!" he yelled.

Kimber and I backed up slowly and leaned against the back counter. We folded our arms and watched from the shadows. At first, they were just talking, but it didn't take long for his fingers to graze her hand. Emma wasn't as sly as she had hoped. She jerked her hands back and stuffed them into her back pockets. Her eyes continued to dart in our direction, and every time they did, we pretended not to be watching.

"Is this really working?" Kimber asked, huddled toward me.

"I think it might be . . ." I said, not believing my eyes.

"If we can make this happen, what else can we do?" Kimber asked. I glanced at her, and her blue eyes were dark as the depths of the ocean, but they sparkled with the light of intrigue.

Somehow, I knew this curiosity would get me in trouble, but it did nothing to stop me now. I waited for him to throw her over his shoulder. I bit my lip, willing it to happen, and we watched as he grabbed her waist to tickle her. He leaned in close and whispered something in her ear. Kimber and I were fascinated. The suspense was far greater than that of the movie we'd watched earlier. No gunfight, car crash, or explosion could match the intensity we felt from watching our own manifestation play out in front of us.

"*Holy shit.* It's really happening," Kimber muttered.

I couldn't believe my eyes. Whereas Kimber and Asher making amends very well could have been a fluke, this was like watching a pig sprout wings and fly over the cabin. Levi liked girls, but he only liked them for one night. I knew he'd never looked at Emma with anything other than a friendly eye. But this was different. He was looking at her like he was under a spell, and I knew I'd been the witch who'd cast it. But Emma was happy, and Levi certainly didn't mind, so that made me a good witch. At least, that's what I told myself in the moment.

"We need front-row seats for this. Come on." Kimber grabbed my arm, and I lunged forward. She ran upstairs, and I was quick to follow. Just as we reached the top, I heard Emma squealing, and I knew she'd been thrust up on Levi's shoulder.

"Come on," Kimber hissed, her hands tight around my wrist as she pulled me into Emma's room.

Levi's heavy steps were on our heels and we could hear Emma giggling the whole way up, getting closer and louder. The second that Kimber and I realized they were coming into the bedroom, she shoved me into the closet. Kimber jumped in and slammed the closet door shut. Levi barged through the bedroom door with Emma draped over his broad shoulders. I worked to slow my breathing as my eyes adjusted to the dark closet. Slowly, Kimber let go of my wrist and I could tell by her warm breath that she had moved her ear to the closet door. I stood frozen, not wanting to be discovered. I didn't have to place my ear on the door to hear everything that was going on. Neither Levi nor Emma was trying to be quiet.

"Damn, Emma, what's gotten into you?" Levi asked.

Emma giggled, unable to talk. It was quiet for a while. Nothing more than the sound of lips meeting and pulling apart.

When it was obvious Kimber and I were trapped in the closet and we would probably be in there for a while, I slowly made my way down to the floor and got comfortable. Kimber did, too, pushing some clothing on the floor that we couldn't see.

Levi moaned, and Kimber and I did our best to keep our snickering silent. "I'm glad you're hanging out with us. This wouldn't be the same without you," I whispered to Kimber in the dark. I listened for her response, as I couldn't see a single thing except for the illumination of the closet door, and it wasn't long before even that had darkened when one of them switched the lights off. I leaned my back against the closet wall and I felt Kimber do the same.

"Sampson is hanging out with Scarlett May. I didn't really have another choice, now that Trinity's gone," Kimber said. It should have burned that we weren't her first choice . . . not even her second, but her *only*. I didn't take it personally. I knew Kimber liked us well enough. And I could tell that she was having fun. I was too.

"Do you think this is what she really wants?" I whispered.

"I think it is. But I think she'll regret it one day," Kimber said. I nodded, even though she couldn't see it. I thought she was right. This is exactly what Emma wanted . . . in the moment. But I knew Levi would fall back on his ways, and soon enough, her heart would be crushed.

As the sounds continued from the bedroom, I wondered if I had accidentally imagined too much. Maybe I should've stopped with a simple kiss. I cursed myself for allowing my mind to wander. It seemed fun, but I'd probably taken it too far.

When Levi's moaning started, Kimber grasped my arm so tightly she nearly cut off my blood circulation. My hand was going numb as she tried not to snicker out loud. But as Levi's moaning began . . . and ended, shortly thereafter, the excitement in the closet had dwindled too, and I was now worried that maybe Kimber was right. That Emma would regret this one day, and it would be my fault.

I dropped my hand down, shaking out the pins and needles, and I felt a sweater that I knew to be Lainey's. It was one of her favorites. I wrapped the ribbed material between my fingers, knowing it was the blue sweater that she used to wear all the time. It was cinched around the waist, and I always admired the way it hugged her figure.

I wasn't sure why and how Lainey could've passed away, especially if this was my dream. Because never once would I have wanted that to happen. I never would have manifested that or conjured her ill departure in any way, shape, or form. And as we hid in the depths of Emma and Lainey's closet, buried in the clothes that she would never wear again, the thing I feared the most was the network of unexplored crevices in my dark mind . . . because perhaps there was no such thing as a *good* witch.

19

Even though the night had ended just as I imagined it would—with Emma's face buried deep in a pillow, hiding her blush, I had gone to bed with the swirling distaste of regret. I didn't know what kind of monster I had unleashed, but I feared the capability I now possessed. I wanted Emma to be happy. She was supposed to experience a night to remember with her crush. And even though that happened, it had still been with Levi, and he wasn't the right one for her. I battled between right and wrong into the wee hours of the night when sleep finally won over.

By the next day, Kai had come up with a new plan. He was going to hitchhike until one mile before the spot where he had evaporated. The spot where he had been sucked in and spat back out, landing him here, with us. He knew the exact spot, said it was burned into his memory, and he believed there was some sort of force field holding him in. Once he got to his spot, he was going to walk, step by step, looking for signs of change. He had all sorts of math equations tucked under his armpit as he shoved a banana and three granola bars into a backpack. He planned to document it all, take pictures, and report back.

"Are you sure this is going to be safe?" I asked.

"I'll be back before you know it. After I document everything, I'll turn on my recorder and step into oblivion, and I'll be back here, probably standing on the doorstep. I'll be back in time for the party tonight, and I'll tell you guys everything," Kai said. He gave me a wink before he left the cabin. And I sighed, knowing that it wasn't the best plan. But I couldn't stop him. He was a man on a mission.

Walker had plans to meet us at the party tonight—another bonfire at Sampson's house. It was good to keep the morale up. I spent the day watching Levi and Emma flirt. Emma had no regrets, and Levi seemed to enjoy himself as well. He had already enjoyed her company one day longer than I'd imagined, and I hoped I was wrong about him hurting her.

But as I got ready to go to Sampson's house and meet Walker, I had a knot in my stomach and an awful ache in my head. The headaches were coming more and more frequently, and even though I'd had them often as a child, this felt different to me. The pain, dull but widespread, was sometimes enough to blur my vision or make my stomach queasy. I went to the party anyway, as I was looking forward to seeing Walker. He always made everything better—no matter what reality I was living in. Dead or alive.

Once we got to the party, I grabbed a drink and headed out to the bonfire. Many of the girls stayed inside the cabin, grouped in cliques. I wore a beanie to keep my ears warm, and even though it was summer, the nights had dipped into cooler temperatures quite quickly. I wanted to be prepared for a night outside in the woods, and I was hoping for more campfire stories about Layla and the Baylor Butcher. The fire was warm enough for me to slip my jacket off, but as soon as I saw Walker striding toward me, my whole body heated from the inside out. I pulled my beanie off and ruffled my hair. I hated the way my body reacted to him, making it so obvious. There was no manifestation in the world that could knock down my feelings for him. And even if I could, I wouldn't want to. Because even though I hated the way my body melted around him, I loved the torture. The inner turmoil I felt when I saw him was addicting. I wanted Walker so badly that the torture of knowing he'd never love me was also welcome in my heart. Anything that came along with him as a package I had accepted long ago, when I thought we were the only souls of our kind. Even if I was just the girl to help him find his one true love, I would show up, every damn day.

Walker smiled at me by the fire, and my nauseated stomach swirled. I forced my gaze to the white-hot flames and made a deal with the Devil himself. I was going to make Walker fall for me. I was going to conjure up whatever I had for Levi and Emma, and I was going to see it to the end. I was going to dwarf his former epic love story with one of my own. And I'd do it, even if it made me the Wicked Witch of Baylor.

I knew it was wrong, but I wanted nothing more. And I was willing to take whatever consequences came along with it. Should I do it here? Should I do it now? What was the perfect way to make him fall for me? A slow burn? Or a tidal wave? Oh god, I wanted a tidal wave to crash down on me this very moment.

I smirked.

"If I could only read your mind," Walker said, peering over at me.

I snapped out of it, the blood draining from my face. Had he been watching me the whole time?

"Why would you say that?" I asked, my voice squeaky and wavering.

"You should see the look on your face. What were you thinking about?" he asked. Walker smirked, as if it embarrassed him to even ask.

"Is it hot? Super hot?" I asked, fanning my face. I tossed the beanie in my hands behind me with my jacket and tugged at my shirt for airflow.

Walker laughed and surveyed the crowd.

I looked at all the faces; many of them I'd seen at Sampson's house before, but there were a few new ones. I saw the girl who had been interested in Noah in the kitchen, and I picked out several of Jack Sampson's friends, whom I'd spoken to the last time I was here. But there was a tall guy with a freshly shaved mullet that I'd never seen before. And a girl with short, curly black hair and large hoop earrings who was quite flirty with Levi that I couldn't recall either. Many of the faces disappeared into the background like white noise.

Levi followed the girl around like a puppy dog, and it pissed me off. I knew Emma had been in the kitchen with some of the other girls, and I hoped she wouldn't see it. I leaned over to Walker. "So, last night was interesting," I said. He tucked his hands deep in his pockets and focused his attention on me.

"Oh yeah? Mine was uneventful. I should've stayed over. I found nothing useful about the fairy tale. Nothing relevant whatsoever."

"Emma and Levi hooked up," I said, trying to find Emma through the kitchen window. I couldn't see her.

"What? Isn't Levi kind of a . . . meathead?" Walker shrugged.

I laughed, nodding. Even Walker got it. Emma wasn't supposed to be with him. "Yeah, and now look at him," I said, pointing to a dark corner of the waterfront cabin. It was just Levi and that girl—the one with the hoop earrings. She was taking his baseball cap and trying it on. He was pretending to want it back. Walker rolled his eyes. I could tell he felt bad for Emma. I did, too.

"Does she know yet?" he asked.

I craned my head to see through the windows again; even so, I couldn't see her. "I don't think so."

Walker blew out a long and heavy sigh. "Hey, you want to get out of here? Let's take a little walk," he said.

Naturally, I'd follow him anywhere, so I nodded. I left my jacket and beanie behind, and I was quick on his heels. We walked in silence, not far into the woods. The heat from the fire left my skin and the night air cooled my cheeks. We were still close enough to see the bonfire and the cabin's front driveway where all the cars had been parked. But we were a few rows of trees deep in the forest. Hidden from everybody else. Hidden in the shadows. Walker leaned against a tree, and I thought this was my moment. I should ravish him. I imagined what it would be like to spread my hands over his chest and lift on to my tippy toes to kiss his lips. I'd be the wave crashing down on him.

"I've been thinking about you. Your dream state. Do you really think it's true?" he asked, running a hand over his chin.

I took a moment to shake my lustful visions free. This walk wasn't alone time for us, it was to get away from the listening ears at the campfire. "You saw what happened to the flower. It was like magic, right? Either I'm a ghost and I have the power to change my surrounding outcome, or I'm trapped . . . in some sort of reverie, and I'm lucid. I think those are the only options here. And to be honest, I don't like either of them," I said, running my hands through my hair, feeling stupid for even saying it.

"Or . . . It's the Baylor phenomenon. Just like I said before. It's the manifestation of our deepest desires." The way he said *desires* slipped me into a trance, and I felt the heat in my stomach dip even lower, spreading into my thighs.

"Deepest desires?" I said breathily.

"And fears. Lots of fears," he said, his eyes ablaze. Was he saying that he was afraid of falling for me? Or had I made that up?

I took a step closer, and he looked away. It was as if the word *fear* had soaked into my subconscious, making him turn from me. From then on out, all I could do was fear his rejection. So much so that I didn't even try to kiss him.

I took a step back and turned toward the cabin. My skin crawled with rejection. Like I had actually tried to kiss him, and he flat-out denied me. It hadn't happened, but it felt just the same in my head. All the heat that churned in my stomach dissipated, and the air turned icy.

"It can't just be deep desires. I never wanted Lainey to die," I said, crossing my arms.

"But it was your fear. Don't you see? Your fears are coming true too," he said.

"No. I never feared she would die. I never even thought about it. I never imagined her body floating in that water. So how did it happen?" I pointed to the shore and raised my voice.

"It's because of that damn calendar. That's how. You have it in your mind that thirteen of your friends are going to die. Thirteen deaths, all on your hands. Whether you thought it in the forefront of your mind or if it was a seed planted deep in your subconscious, you must've imagined that Lainey was on the chopping block. Just like with the rest of us." Walker pushed off the tree and took a wide stance.

"Are you saying that I killed my best friend?" I asked, turning to him and feeling sicker than I ever had.

"No! Yes. No."

"Spit it out, Walker!" I said in my full voice.

"I think there's a chance. I think there's a chance that you're manipulating this whole thing. This is your summer for the taking. Why don't you do something useful with it?" My chest burned like he'd sunk a knife into me. It was my deepest fear—that I'd hurt them, and that I had no control over it. He thrust his hands on his hips and leaned in.

"Your friends are all along for the ride. And I . . . by chance, I met you. I'm on my own mission here. I don't know what you're doing," he said, looking away from me as if he were disgusted. And that was a genuine fear of mine—anything to do with him not liking me or wanting me. Disgust was the very worst manifestation of rejection I could imagine.

I clamped my mouth shut and sank deep into my emotion, feeling the worry swirl around me and build like a tornado, until it just dropped, and it left me with nothing more than a thud in my chest. I looked up at Walker with teary eyes. "Are you mad at me?" I asked with nothing more than a whisper.

"Why don't you do something more? Something meaningful?" Walker's voice echoed in my mind, though I could see his mouth moving to a different tone. It was then that I knew our conversation was misleading. I wasn't hearing what Walker was truly saying. My mind was playing tricks on me again. And it was up to me to figure out what the truth was.

I could see in Walker's eyes a reflection of fear. I took a deep breath and fell back on my trust—something I wasn't very good at—that he wasn't telling me that I'd killed my best friend, that I was a bad person, or that I was doing evil things. There was no blame behind his eyes. And even though those were the words I heard in my head, I trusted the feeling I felt in my gut. He was scared—nothing more.

Walker's eyes turned glassy, and he looked like a trapped soul. He wasn't being portrayed the way he wanted, and it was my worry that was preventing the truth from coming out. He stared long and deep into my eyes, and I knew that he'd been subjected to my fear—that they all had been. I knew that nobody was safe when they were with me.

When it was obvious to both of us that our communication had failed, Walker slipped an arm around my shoulder and pulled me in for a hug. I held back my tears as I squeezed him tight. I pressed my cheek against his chest and breathed in his sultry, warm scent, which reminded me of the beach, knowing that this was the only communication we needed. In that moment, we weren't just friends; we were prospective lovers. We weren't the dead and the dreaming but two souls leaning upon one another.

I kept my head on Walker's chest, there in the woods, for some time. It took a while before his voice matched with his lips again—till my insecurities dropped back down to a manageable level—and we had come full circle. Yet, I didn't let go, and Walker didn't make me. We watched the party from afar, knowing that no matter what happened between us, we'd always be two of the same kind.

I didn't lift my head until I saw Levi follow the girl with the hoops into the cab of a truck. I scanned the crowd for Emma, but she was nowhere in sight. "Damn it," I muttered. Walker and I watched as the truck heated enough to fog the windows.

Anger boiled inside of me, and this time, I didn't try to stifle it. I hated what Levi was doing to Emma. I let go of Walker and crossed my arms over my chest.

"What an asshole. I can't believe him. He was just with Emma. It might have meant nothing to him, but it was her *first* time. It's always going to be important to her. She's always going to remember how he just ditched her the very next day. He's such an ass!" I went on and on, as the window completely fogged, and the truck began to rock like a wild animal had been caged inside.

I saw Emma walking around. She could have been in search of me or Levi, but I was afraid of what she might find. "No. No. No," I said, my heartbeat skipping.

"Maybe we should intervene? Maybe you should get Emma and go back to the cabin. Tell her you're not feeling well." Walker had a soft heart, and he cared about Emma because he knew she was my friend. I considered it. I could tell her that my stomach hurt, my head ached—all of which was true.

"Yeah, let's do that. Do you want to come with?" I asked. Walker nodded, and we hurried toward the cabin. When we approached the front row of trees, just on the outskirts of the clearing, something happened. The tall, muscular guy with the mullet approached the truck. He ripped the door open and started yelling. Walker and I froze as the girl scampered off with her shoes in her hand, and Levi stepped out, buckling his pants.

The arguing had caught the attention of everybody by the campfire. Heads started to perk, and it didn't take long for people to come out of the house and around the front yard to see what was happening.

"Oh no," I said, placing my hand on Walker's chest, keeping him back in the shadows. I wasn't upset that Levi was about to take a pounding; I was upset because I saw Emma come out of the cabin. "She knows . . ." I said beneath my breath. I backed up to a tree, and I was thankful that Walker and I had been hiding in the distance. I didn't want to get any closer.

Once the crowd formed, the tank with a mullet swung, his fist making contact with Levi's jaw. It only took one hit. The crowd stepped back, and Levi spun like a top. As he fell, the gasps echoed into the trees and beyond. I couldn't quite see what happened next, but I knew enough to know that Levi was still and he wasn't getting back up.

Screams ensued, and several of the guests immediately ran for their cars. Amid the commotion, a fine dark smoke rose into the air. Emma approached Levi, and I watched in horror as she slowly stood up, staring at her trembling hands.

Not like this! I didn't mean to do this!

Emma shrilled, and everybody at the party scattered like rats in an infested restaurant on fumigation night. I wanted to take it back. Take it all back. I wasn't mad at Levi any longer! I grabbed my stomach, feeling like I might throw up, but no matter how terrible I felt, I couldn't peel my eyes away from the brewing storm.

Walker and I watched in horror as every single soul departed that party and the smoke grew denser. Several bodies piled into single cab trucks and even more into the beds. Cars peeled out over the gravel, and trucks ran over planters and knocked over trashcans. Meanwhile, Levi lay on the ground as still as could be, black poison billowing above him.

I wasn't sure what happened because we had been some distance away, but I knew he was dead. Nobody wanted any part of it. Most of them had been at my cabin when Trinity's body had washed up on shore, and several of them had stayed back and been questioned by the cops. That couldn't happen again. Not without suspicion.

I had seen the inner workings of the fear. The memories of Trinity's death. I'd seen every one of my friends fight over involving the authorities. By the time Ethan drowned, nobody even mentioned the cops. And now, none of these people wanted to be tied to cold-blooded murder, either. I understood it. I wanted to run too. I would have, except my feet were planted like tree trunks, the roots deep within the soil. Neither Walker nor I could move a single inch.

Goosebumps covered my body from head to toe, and I was forced to stay and deal with the fears instead of running from them the way I always had. The smoke grew so dark and twisted, I couldn't see Levi's remains at all. Leaves and small bits of trash lifted into the air like a vortex, circling above where he lay. Black crows cawed into the night, taking turns diving into the mist. I knew it was my rage that had taken over and stolen his life. And I knew it was my regret that rumbled like a tornado before us now. If I hadn't loved Emma so much, would Levi still be alive tonight?

If hatred was the flip side to my love . . . then there was no telling what I was capable of. If my emotions were fickle and unpredictable, if they were deep and scarred with insecurities . . . Then I had just become the most dangerous thing in Baylor.

20

Walker and I stood side by side, unable to move as our feet were planted into the forest ground. Everybody was gone now except Levi, who lay in the middle of a black vortex in Sampson's driveway. My hair whipped wildly, and I squinted, turning away from the wind. It was my fault. No, I hadn't laid a hand on Levi, but I'd hated him for just a moment in time. I'd hated him for what he had done to Emma, and that's when it happened. I never thought that my anger could kill, but clearly, I knew very little about the power I possessed.

"I can't move!" I said, trying to lift a leg one at a time—they felt like they weighed a hundred pounds each. I looked over at Walker, and he was also trying and failing to move his feet.

"I can't either!" Walker yelled against the wind. He nearly lost his balance, trying to free himself.

The forest grew cold as the tornado raged. Deep in the distant woods, I heard a beeping sound. It was a long, drawn-out, high-pitched tone. At first, it was infrequent and random, but it was growing more repetitive now. Louder too.

Every now and then, I glimpsed Levi lying on the ground as the plume of smoke continued to rise above him, and I was consumed by the monster within me. I'd never thought very highly of myself, but in this moment, every worry that I'd ever had was solidified like my feet to the forest floor. I was no good. A rotten apple. Poison. I closed my eyes and let the guilt swallow me whole. Inch by inch, I sank into the ground.

"What is that!?" I asked, grabbing at my temples and whipping my head around when another beep sounded. It echoed off the forest trees and bounced back and forth until it hit us in waves. I couldn't tell how far it was, but I could tell that it was getting closer.

"What's what!?" Walker yelled, looking behind us.

"You don't hear that?" I asked.

The beep sounded loud and shrill. "That!" I said, looking all around me.

I tried to lift my feet, but the more I did, the deeper they sank. It was like quicksand, sucking me under. It was up to my ankles, but I deserved it. I deserved to be swallowed alive. Buried for the good of my friends. They were better off without me. Safer.

Soon, the cops would show up, and Walker and I would be the only ones tied to the murder of Levi. I was ready to accept my fate, rotting in the ground for the rest of eternity. If this was a dream, it was a nightmare.

The crows came in by the dozens and began diving into the pine trees. I ducked, covering my head with my hands. The birds cawed and swooped before me, causing me to reach out for Walker. I tightened my grasp around the sleeve of his flannel. The poisonous smoke had expanded, seeping into the forest and blooming high into the sky. The beep sounded sharply over the howl of the storm, as if it wasn't just behind us, but all around us. Inside us. I startled, opening my eyes against the wind and pulling Walker closer. But it shocked me to see that Walker was no longer there. I clutched his flannel in my hand as it draped to the ground.

In his place stood my gran. She was an ethereal light, drawing power from the dark of the storm. The storm I'd created. Tears pricked my eyes. She was always there when I needed her most. Even though I didn't deserve it. I whipped my head back to the deafening tornado, horrified that she would see what I had done, but Levi had vanished. The black mist had lifted to a light gray fog. And the sky was littered with hundreds of crow feathers that fluttered to the ground, but not a single bird was in sight.

In the distance, in Sampson's driveway, was a hospital bed. Doctors were running tests and checking fluids. The beeps came more frequently now as I was transported from the hell I'd created to a hell I'd never deserved. I was standing inside the hospital room. My feet were freed from the depths of the soil, my hair static from the storm as I stood at the foot of the bed, unseen.

It was so real; I could smell the antiseptic. The sterilization. It was more real than anything I'd ever felt. And in that moment of clarity, it made the rest of my life look like a dream. A memory, dancing in the wind.

The bright lights burned my eyes as I tried to refocus. I wasn't used to the sharp, defined lines or bright lights. I turned my head back to my gran, and I was somewhat surprised that she was still there by my side. I couldn't speak. I could only observe.

I looked back at the patient in the hospital bed, and I thought I saw a version of myself. The girl lying in bed was bloodied and swollen. Tubes in her nose and around her neck. She didn't look like me—especially not now—but somehow, I knew. Somehow, I felt it. That lifeless body lying in the hospital gurney—*it was me.*

There was a detachment there. Not because I couldn't recognize myself, but because I didn't remember, and I couldn't feel. After all, as far as I knew, I had been spending my summer in Baylor. I wondered if the detachment meant that there was no coming back. If I was so far removed from what lay in that hospital bed that I could never find my way home. I wasn't sure I wanted to. Could my life ever be normal with how battered I'd been?

Tears filled my eyes and pressure swelled in my throat. I wasn't exactly sure why, but it hurt to see myself like that. I ached for the girl I used to be. Not just the one that wasn't injured, but the one that hadn't hurt her friends by mistake. The one who was powerless, but safe. The wallflower. I missed her.

I watched as doctors ran various tests, and scribbled down various notes. I had no idea what they were doing, but I assumed the results were subpar. My head throbbed, and as I ran a hand over my temple, I could feel the wound that I saw on my body. It was all coming together. It was starting to make sense.

I didn't look in a mirror, and I was thankful there wasn't one around. I was afraid of what I might see. I knew my headaches were because of the accident that had brought me here to this hospital. An accident I remembered nothing about. I could not only feel the dried blood caked in my hair, but I could see it crusted on the body in the bed. It wasn't a pretty sight. And it felt even worse.

Slowly, my eyes dropped from the version of me in the bed, to my own body. The one I inhabited. I was wearing a hospital gown—a dingy white one with small blue flowers. My feet were bare and dirty as if they'd just been plucked from the forest floor. There was an IV taped to my wrist, and my hands were bruised and trembling. I turned my attention back to the girl lying in bed before us. It was easier to see her battered than me. There was no movement at all. She . . . *I* . . . was in a deep, deep coma. And I knew then that I had been dreaming of Baylor, my gran, and all my friends.

I'd been living a nightmare. A twisted lie. They were just stories I'd told myself while I tried to survive.

"Kinsley, dear, can you hear me?" Gran asked, tired, as if she'd asked the same question five times over. It took me a second, but I pried my eyes off the body and looked toward my gran. Unable to find the words, I nodded slowly.

"They're running tests on you. Looking for brain activity. Luckily, there is no shortage of that . . ." Gran looked at me with a wicked smile. She knew just how much brain activity there had been. *Way* too much.

"I'm alive. I . . . I didn't know it was a dream—"

"Yes. Very much alive, dear. I figure it's much like a normal dream. It happens every night, but people just forget about it when they wake up." Gran's eyes were glassy as she looked me over.

"Am I going to wake up?" My stomach turned with the question. It was the only question that really mattered. And yet, I didn't want to know the answer.

"Oh dear, of course you will. You're still at the beginning of your journey. I know it's hard, but the real work will begin when you wake up. There will be a lot for you to do to get back to your old self. This accident is going to change you forever. And it has the potential to change you in negative ways. But, it's ultimately up to you how you want to live your life. If you're strong enough—which I know you are—you'll fight this. You'll come back stronger. I know you will," Gran said, with encouraging eyes.

"You said I'm still at the beginning of my journey? What does that mean?" I asked.

I didn't know how that felt on my tongue. Was it the sweet taste of reality coming my way? Or was it sour? Sour because I'd be leaving Walker behind. *My* Walker. I couldn't leave him. I didn't want to. But if I felt this way now, it would be downright impossible to leave him by the end of summer. I was already on the trajectory of getting my heart broken into a million pieces. He'd told me once that he was cursed by love. I suppose the only difference now was that I knew *how* it would end. And *why* we couldn't be together.

"The accident was recent. Your body is healing. But your mind? That part's up to you. You're going to wake up whenever you decide to. You're stubborn like that. You always have been," Gran said.

I peered down at the IV connected to my wrist. "Can I wake up now?" I asked.

Gran chuckled. "Dear, you're not ready. And you know it."

"Well, why not?"

"Have you found the girl?" Gran asked, sending an icy chill straight through my veins. She stared at me blankly, and I couldn't tell if this was part of the dream or reality. Was it still her? My sweet grandmother comforting me? Or was this my mind, twisting and bending in dreamwork, fretting over a girl I'd never met?

"What's so important about this girl?" I asked.

"Some things need an end. They need closure. It's no fluke that you and Walker met. Just like it's no fluke that you and I are here, able to talk. He needs you, dear. And as fate would have it, you're able to see him. Help the boy out. You have a lot of growth to do. And when you're good and ready, you'll come home. Hopefully . . ."

"Hopefully?" I flinched back, and she was gone. Her word, *hopefully*, was floating in the air like a soft echo in her wake. Hopefully? When I was good and ready? Did she mean that there was a choice for me to stay? Why would I ever do that? Of course, I wanted to go home. Perhaps I'd just stay here. I thought back to the storm brewing in my dream. The crows swarming like bees, in and out of the poison I had created. *No, thank you.*

I watched as the doctors finished their tests, determined to live out my recovery as a ghost at the foot of the bed. But then, my mother came in. Her eyes were red and weary as if she'd been up for days. Weeks. Or maybe even longer. Her skin was sallow. I hated myself for what I had done to her, regardless of fault. She kissed me lightly on the knuckles as she cradled my hand in between hers. I lifted my own hand, taking inventory of the bruises, and wondered why I couldn't feel her kiss.

I moved in closer.

My mom sat on the edge of my bed, and I sat beside her. I tried not to look at my old self. She was a disaster. Barely hanging on by a thread. And it was hard to imagine that I could make a full recovery. It made me sick to look, so I kept my gaze on my mother, but her heartbreak didn't make it any easier. She started to break down, her back quaking as she sucked in uneven breaths.

I reached out for her, desperate to comfort her, but as I placed my arm over her shoulder, it sank completely through her back. And worse, she never noticed. It wasn't the first time I had felt invisible, but it was by far the worst.

Seeing my mom hurt so deeply and not being able to help. Being so close and yet so far away. It was soul-crushing. I was the very reason for everybody's pain and misery. And I knew that if I wasn't strong enough to turn this cyclone around, then I would rain nothing but terror and agony upon the ones I loved most.

I'd brought my deepest fears and subconscious insecurities to life. Everything I was ever afraid of wreaked havoc on me mentally, but now, it tortured my friends and family as well. It was happening in my dreams and in my reality. But what I hadn't realized until then was that I could bring positivity in the same creative way. I didn't know how I was going to pull it off. I only knew that it was possible for me to turn it around.

It was time that I learned to control and master my destiny. If not just for me, then for Emma and Walker. For all of them. And I was positive that as soon as I could, I would find Layla Barns. If I could master my destiny, then I was sure I could figure out where that girl was hiding. She was the secret to all of this, after all. She was the key out of here.

My mother was startled when a doctor walked in. I remained seated by her side as he told her the good news. There was lots of brain activity, as I had expected, and they thought I could make a full recovery. My mom nodded, listening intently for as long as she could hold herself together, then broke down in the middle of his explanation. She simply couldn't hold it back any longer, and I didn't blame her. I wanted to cry too. And I probably would have if I hadn't felt so detached from the other me lying in the bed asleep. In my world, it was summer at Baylor Lake. Things were a little bit foggy, and more than dangerous . . . there was a handsomely rugged stranger there who needed my help.

The doctor told my mom, now that the tests were done, they were going to push some meds to help keep me sedated. I still needed time to heal, as my brain was swollen. They injected a vial of something into my IV fluid, and I felt it instantly. A weird swirl of disorientation tore through my veins like a cyclone and whirled up toward my head. I grabbed hold of the bedsheets and scrunched them between my hands, gripping onto the reality that would be lost to me. The room spun, ticking like the hands on an analog clock. The edges of my vision became dark and clouded. The central tunnel of light was getting smaller and smaller. I was drifting away.

"No!" I called out, scraping at the bedsheets. Only my mom never heard me, and the doctor never saw.

"No! Mom! Mom!" I hollered as it swept me away to the land of broken dreams.

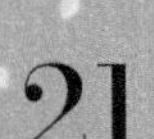

I came to, tangled in my bedsheets. When I opened my eyes, I realized I was back at the cabin. My prison. It was like a filter had been placed over my eyes. In comparison to the hospital, this was dingy and somewhat blurry. I saw now how I'd been living in a dream state. But just like stepping into the bright hospital lights, I knew my eyes would adjust quickly. And that soon I wouldn't be able to tell the difference between real life and the one I'd created for myself.

I let out a long breath of disappointment. Just once, I'd like to wake up back at home. I missed the smell, the way the light filtered in through my bedroom window, and I missed the quiet. I even missed my little brother, Conrad. It all seemed so far away now. Sanity was just out of my reach.

I could hear the rumbling downstairs of voices trying to trump one another. Mason. Scarlett May. They were the loudest. I grabbed my phone and checked the time. It surprised me to see that it was afternoon—though time mattered very little to me now. I drew the covers over my head. What's the point in any of this? The sheets fluttered down to my face, kissing my nose. Walker St. James. He was the reason this mattered.

If I didn't help him find Layla, he'd be lost in the afterlife for eternity. I would go back to my family, and I'd always wonder about him. I'd probably feel guilty, and I'd miss him far too much. Even though I wanted to be with him, I knew that him being with Layla was the next best thing. I'd worry about him less, knowing that he was happy.

Play the game. That's all this was. A mental game. I wasn't any good at those, but this time, I had an advantage. Nobody else knew what I did. I had the power to manipulate this realm any way I saw fit—if only I could figure out how. To build that control like a muscle would mean that I'd be the Sorcerer of Baylor. Then, I'd have Layla eating out of the palm of my hand. Hell, maybe Walker too?

I jumped to my feet, fully clothed, and walked downstairs, reminding myself this was only a game. I didn't want to know what they were fighting about this time. It all seemed so petty while I was out there fighting for my life. It was difficult wrapping my head around the idea that the body I possessed was an astral projection—an avatar in the silo of my mind. I had very little interest in parenting the rest of the group.

As my hand slid down the banister, I looked at the polished wood beneath my hands. *It wasn't real.* The voices I heard wafting through the air? *They weren't real.* And for the life of me, I couldn't figure out why I would imagine an argument at a time like this. It wasn't what I wanted. And if this was truly my dream, and that was really my body in the hospital, then why wasn't I dreaming of Walker alone? My literal dream man. Why wasn't I dreaming of the best summer ever? Was this the best I could do?

I came upon the group in the living room. They'd been in a circle, huddled over something, and their voices were sharp and cutting. "But there's five. Five! Not four but five!" Kimber exclaimed.

"Who is the fifth?" Noah demanded.

"There are seven of us here. Kinsley's missing," Asher said.

"She's just sleeping—as always," Emma said. And I felt the sting of the only friend I had left talking behind my back.

The temperature dropped as soon as they noticed I'd entered the room. Everybody froze, glancing at one another, but nobody wanted to speak. It was an uncomfortable moment of silence, which told me that they most certainly had been talking about me. And not just where I'd been or how much I slept these days—which, by now, I knew was erratic.

"What's going on?" I asked, genuinely curious, my eyes locking onto Kai's. He'd returned from his trip sometime in the night.

"Do you want to tell us what this is?" Scarlett May asked.

"What?" The group parted as I stepped closer, and I found a calendar in between them, sprawled on the coffee table. It was a thirteen-day calendar like the one I'd been seeing everywhere. In the tower. In the void. And by the looks on their faces, they knew I had something to do with it. I didn't want to be blamed for anybody's death. Or any negative notion that happened this summer. It was my biggest fear because deep down inside, I knew I was responsible. And I didn't know how to make it stop. They were all afraid. I was, most of all. The only difference was, I was afraid of myself. And all the dark places in my mind.

"I . . . I don't know . . ." I said, scratching my head. It wasn't a complete lie.

I didn't know where the thirteen-day calendar had originated. I only knew that I'd started seeing it early on this summer.

"Why are there only thirteen days, Kinsley?" Noah asked. It was clear this was bad when even Noah—who had feelings for me—had turned on me. *Really bad.*

"I . . . I," my eyes flicked from the calendar to Noah and then to everybody surrounding him.

They weren't real. But I couldn't help from getting sucked back in. They were all staring at me, demanding answers. And my eyes were quickly adjusting to the dark filter. I felt my reality slipping away.

"Why are there five crossed off?" he asked, his face deadpanned. I looked back down to the calendar and five days had been slashed through with the red marker.

Trinity. Big Jimmy. Lainey. Ethan. Levi. I couldn't say it. I didn't want to. How could I?

"You know why. It's us. It's the ones who have died," Emma said, her voice meek but still present. I felt the dagger slide into my back. I could understand why she was turning on me, but she was all I had left. She was someone I'd always imagined would be with me till the end.

"No! There's only four of us who have died. There are five on the calendar. Who is the fifth, then?" Scarlett May bickered with Emma.

"It's us! I told you. *She* told me," Emma said, lifting her eyes to meet mine. The room grew quiet and the shame heavy.

"There's Levi, Ethan, Lainey, and Trinity. That's four," Scarlett May said.

I choked back the tears and stuffed them down deep. I couldn't cry. Not while I was on trial.

"Who's the fifth, Kinsley? Who's the fifth!?" Noah demanded.

I took a deep breath, my foot starting to bounce. Part of me wanted to run out of the room. Out of the cabin and into the woods. But I knew I needed to face this. I knew there was no running from my mind. This was my guilt. It would follow me anywhere, and if I didn't learn to deal with it, it would eat me alive. Just like the crows did Levi.

"Big Jimmy," I said.

"Grocery store Jim? The crazy one?" Scarlett May asked. Her jaw hung as she looked around the group. I bit my lip and waited for their response to rain down on me.

"Why is he on this list with our friends?" Kai asked. It was a good question. But the answer was simple.

"Because he died," I said. My mouth ran dry.

"Is he the thirteenth person?" Asher asked.

I looked around the room and said what I knew to be true but never wanted to admit. "No. It's me. I'm the thirteenth person." I tried to swallow, but my tongue stuck to the roof of my mouth. Everybody looked at one another.

"So none of us will survive?" Scarlett May asked. Mason counted on his fingers over and over.

"But, if Big Jimmy was one, then maybe it doesn't have to be us," Kimber said, checking everyone's expression.

The chatter climbed until one question rose above the rest.

"Who's next?" Asher asked. It's what they all wanted to know. I took a step back, fighting my instinct to flee.

All I could do was stutter. "I don't . . . I don't know . . . I don't. I don't."

"Kimber told us. She told us this was a dream. She said you guys were somehow manipulating it. What else have you done? What are you doing now?" Noah asked.

"I'm not doing anything!" I said, taking another step backward.

"Did you or did you not get Kimber and Asher back together?" Noah asked. My eyes flicked to Emma's, and hers darted to the ground. Her face was red, and she almost looked sick to her stomach. I looked to Kimber, but she stared back at me with a deadpan expression, head cocked and waiting for the truth to spill.

I wanted to ask Noah why he was doing this. Why he was turning them against me. But I knew the answer—I'd hurt him. I'd rejected him. And somehow, hurting me back was making him feel better. Either that or I deserved it, and this was fate taking its revenge on me. I deserved more. I had killed a man. Come to think of it, I'd killed five people. Many more if I counted the plane crash. Tears streamed down my face, though I told myself I would not shatter. I held my breath as much as I could so that my back wouldn't quake. I locked my jaw so that the cries would not seep out.

These were my friends, and they were turning on me. It was time to face the facts. It was all there in the open, and there was no hiding it anymore. I was doing bad things to good people, whether I wanted to or not. And I had been the reason everybody was in danger. By the next time I looked at myself in the mirror, I'd be a monster.

"And you set Levi up because you were mad at him. Isn't that true?" Asher accused me. Kimber nodded. There had been a talk while I lay sleeping, and for the first time, I wished they had gone dormant.

If I could, I'd make it stop. All of it. Especially this interrogation. But, for whatever reason, I couldn't. I didn't know how. So, I stood there in the middle of the room, my head hanging and their accusations flying.

"Why is this only her dream?"

"Maybe it's all of ours?"

"It's not a dream. It's a nightmare!"

"Who else would have wanted Levi to die?"

"What about Lainey, though?"

It was that last question that lingered in my mind, lashing at me like a whip, slicing into my innermost memories. It stung. And it was lasting.

While it was true, I'd wished ill will upon Levi and possibly Trinity, I'd never wanted anything bad to happen to Ethan or Lainey. And Big Jim was just . . . it was self-defense, really.

While the comments flew like air darts, I thought about Lainey. I thought about why she'd gone missing. All I could think of was that I needed her. I needed her friendship when I was scared. And I was afraid to be alone in this. It must have been as simple as that. And Ethan? I didn't want him to drown. But I recalled the way I felt that day. It was an uncomfortable feeling. Something was off, and I knew it. I was looking for reasons, and as soon as Ethan jumped into that water—which I knew was haunted—the worry took over. I worried he would be the reason that the air was stiff and suffocating. And when he never resurfaced, my fears were solidified.

I didn't have to direct ill will at somebody for something bad to happen. That was the scariest part of all. All that was required to change the destiny of this summer was a simple thought. A simple worry. Insecurity. Something that would fester and grow, and as soon as the seed was planted, inevitably bloom into disaster.

I had never felt more exposed than I did standing in front of those seven friends. Seven parts of my brain telling me I was no good. It felt like elementary school all over again. Worksheet after worksheet, when everybody could read, and I harbored a secret—I wasn't good enough.

I knew I had to look everybody in the eyes and tell them the truth because they were already in my head, and there was no hiding now. There was no way for us to unite into one strong team if I ever wanted to wake up. And I wanted desperately to wake up. I needed all the help I could get.

I started with the death of my gran. That's when Noah's eyes dropped to the ground. I could see the guilt on his face for accusing me of all the harm I've done. Because he and his family knew just how much pain we had gone through recently. I told them how I started seeing her here at the lake. Even though she'd passed away. I told them how I thought I was crazy. That's when it turned around because several of them empathized with that.

A couple of them even had stories of their own. Stories I'd never heard before. Where *they'd* thought *they* were going crazy. Weird things were happening to all of us, not just me. But the one thing we shared in common was that none of us were comfortable enough to talk about it. It was the fear of judgment that had kept us silent and kept us tortured in solitude.

I was starting to feel like maybe we could be a team. I talked with them about the Baylor Butcher and my search for Layla Barns. The only thing I didn't tell them was that Walker St. James had been the phantom of the lake. I didn't tell them because he'd been isolated enough, and I didn't want them to pull out their pitchforks the way they had on me. And while he'd been the ghost in the story that haunted the lake for years and years, he wasn't a killer. That was merely a story changed by the hands of time. A scary campfire story is all. And if I knew Walker like I thought I did, he wouldn't harm a fly. He had a heart of gold, and he was just as broken as the rest of us.

I told them all how Layla Barns held the secrets to unlock the dreamwork that we had all been summoned into. I told them I knew because my gran had told me so. I told them how Big Jim had been determined to keep people like me from finding out. How he'd attacked us in the tower. Naturally, they wanted to see the tower, and I had to tell them I couldn't find it again. It lost me some credit, but I continued.

I told them all about my latest dream. Which hadn't been a dream at all. Quite the opposite. I told them about my glimpse of reality. How I was pulled back for a moment in time to a place unlike this one. To a place we all knew and feared—where death was final.

I told them how we were our own worst enemies in life and how we were out to get ourselves. That's when I saw the recognition in their eyes. Each one of them had a monster hidden within. They had tormented themselves in ways I couldn't possibly imagine. Kimber folded her arms across the tiny waist of her thin, frail body. Her demons were easy to see, but what about the rest of them? What torture had they put themselves through that was potentially going to come out at Baylor Lake? These were the questions that we all needed to ask ourselves. And as a group, we had a lot of work to do.

I wasn't out of the fire yet, but I tried my best to salvage the friendships I had left. I knew they needed to deliberate, so I stepped outside to the back patio for some fresh air and vitamin D. I watched the birds flock over the placid lake, and I let my memory lapse back to my mom's capsized frame as she cried on the edge of the hospital bed. As their voices grew louder and louder inside the cabin, I closed my eyes and tilted my head to soak up the sun.

They were fighting about whether or not to trust me. Whether I was their friend or foe. And the worst part was that Noah and Emma were inside, and I didn't know if they were fighting for or against me. The patio was my waiting chamber as the jury deliberated inside. I didn't know what the days and weeks ahead had in store for me, and I didn't know if I would ever return home, but I knew this: I knew we were stronger together. We were smarter together. And I knew I needed their help. In fact, I was desperate for it.

22

It was a long afternoon of deliberation inside the cabin. Voices rose and fell like the ebb and flow of the ocean washing over the sand. My emotions were no different. They changed like the tide, optimistic for change one second and riddled with angst the next. I contemplated leaving. Running away. Maybe I could seek a safe haven with Walker across the lake. After all, my friends would just go dormant, and as long as I didn't think about them, they'd be safe—as far as I knew.

But as the loons flew overhead and the sun set over the scintillating waters, I realized I couldn't run from this. I'd be running from . . . myself, and that was impossible. The only way out was the opposite of running. I had to dive in deeper, find the scariest place in my mind, and with the help of my friends, conquer it. I'd been so afraid this entire summer, but now I was just afraid of losing my friends. I needed to be the opposite of what I'd been. I needed to be a leader, the one they drew strength from. I just didn't know how to get there. I wasn't born a leader. I needed to find something inside of me that I never knew existed. And I had to be strong enough to pull it out to see the light of day. Then, I'd ride the power all the way home. Home to my mom, dad, and little brother.

I'd been hypnotized by the sunset—the bright oranges and neon yellows—but snapped back when the cabin door opened.

"Have you seen Gunner?" Scarlett May asked. I couldn't recall the last time I'd seen him. I glanced around to see if he was lying at my feet, but he had been nowhere on the porch.

"I haven't. Is he missing?" I asked. Scarlett May said nothing. Her brows furrowed, and she slammed the cabin door and disappeared inside. I listened to the voices rise again, but all I could think about was Lainey's dog. Where had he gone? And how long had he been missing? A few minutes later, Noah came outside, followed by Kai and Mason.

"You haven't seen Gunner?" Mason asked. His tone was accusatory, and I couldn't understand why this was now the primary focus.

"No, I haven't seen him. Is he missing?" I asked again.

"If you are the one making this all happen, then you are the one that caused the dog to go missing. Why did you cause your *best friend's* dog to go missing? Why would you do that?" Noah asked. His hands waving about in the air. I felt the dread drip down my neck and scatter across my back. I stretched my neck, uncomfortable in my own skin.

He was right. I'd been worried that something else would happen, something would tip the group over the edge and all hell would break loose. That I would get blamed for things beyond my control. And here it was: the dog. I shook my head. I should've known. But it was impossible for me to control all of my thoughts, feelings, and fears. They flowed freely, whizzing and whirling in circles all day long.

The accusations flew like darts, and I dodged them with agility, running into the cabin and up the stairs. The fighting stopped, and I felt their eyes heavy on my back. I wasn't hiding upstairs—though I wanted to—I was looking for evidence. Evidence to clear my name. I opened my laptop and went straight to the security website. I scanned all the video feeds until I landed on one with Gunner sauntering towards the neighbor's house.

It was late in the evening as he meandered into their backyard. It was hard to see. He was only a little black dot on the screen, but I zoomed in and watched him move around their yard until he ceased to exist. The dot disappeared before my very eyes. I watched it repeatedly until I was convinced that the Vandals had taken him. And then I marched downstairs with my laptop, eager to clear my name.

"Look at this. I set up surveillance cameras all around the cabin—"

"You what?" Scarlett May asked. I froze. Her mouth hung open like it offended her that her personal space had been invaded.

"I set up surveillance cameras."

"Why would you do that?" Asher asked.

"That's not the point, guys. Things are getting weird around here. I thought if I could catch something on video, then I would have a better understanding of what's going on. And it's helped; I know where the dog is," I said, pleading.

"She's right, guys. It's a good idea. We could use all the help we can get," Kai said. Finally, something had gone my way, and I appreciated Kai's kind words more than he knew.

"The dog went over to the neighbor's house last night. See the little dot?" I pointed to the screen. Everybody watched in silence as he disappeared into their backyard.

"What happened to him?" Emma asked.

"I don't know. I think they have him." To be honest, I wasn't sure if they did or not. But I was desperate to clear my name.

The tactic worked better than I had imagined. Within minutes, the guys were ready to break into the Vandals' cabin. They grabbed anything they could; a baseball bat, a meat cleaver, flashlights, and then they were ready to raid the place. This wasn't about the dog; this wasn't even about Lainey; this was about fighting back for the first time this summer. It was about taking what was ours and not living in fear anymore. This was about control. Every one of us had a reason to fight for that. And what better place to make a stand than at the Vandals'? They had been weird all summer long. And I knew they were hiding something.

Emma, Scarlett May, Kimber, and I crouched down inside the den, peering out the locked window. It faced the Vandals' house, and we had a good view of the guys as they crept across the yard. Mason, Asher, Noah, and Kai fell into step, making for a stealthy mission. They moved quickly across the lawn and only slowed once they reached the neighbor's house. We watched as two split off around the front, and the other two went around the back. I couldn't tell if I was watching a natural and incredibly talented sting operation or if it had simply been the inner child in these guys playing army. But either way, my eyes were fixated, and it was better than any action movie I'd ever seen.

"Where did they go? I can't see them," Kimber said, her nose on the windowsill.

"I can't see them either," Emma said, lifting her head.

"Open the window so we can hear them," Scarlett May said. I unlatched the window and slid it open. The four of us listened in silence. There wasn't much to hear, but we waited anyway.

"Is it supposed to be taking this long?" Kimber asked.

"No. We probably just lost all of our men." Scarlett May glared at me through the moonlit room.

"No. Don't say that!" I hissed.

The only thing we needed for that to come true was a seed planted in my mind, and her sarcasm was just that. I felt the panic rise inside me, as I couldn't stop my mind from exploring the option of the guys never returning and us four girls having to deal with this murderous summer all by ourselves. The thought of losing four in one night was too much to bear. And I wanted to rain down on her for even bringing the thought to light. If it came true, this was her fault. Not mine.

We watched, crouched on the floor, our fingertips gripping the windowsill as the Vandals' house lit up. A light in the front room illuminated the windows, and subsequently, it traveled back into what I had imagined was their kitchen.

"Why are they turning the lights on?" Emma asked.

"They're dead for sure," Scarlett May said.

All I could do was shove her. I did it with enough force for her to tip over on her knees and fall to her butt. "Shut up!" I said.

"Jesus! What's your problem? You're the one doing all of this!"

"That's not true. None of it's true. This is all happening because we're afraid of it happening. It's happening because people like you are planting the seed of them never coming home. And then we all think about it." I pointed to Kimber. "Haven't you thought about it?" I asked. Even in the dark. I could see her eyes lower to the ground.

"That's right. Now that she said it, we're all thinking about it. And our thoughts, here in Baylor . . . they come true. So, unless you never want to see them again, stop thinking that way!" I said in my full voice.

I stormed out of the room. Unable to stay for the aftermath. Afraid of what else Scarlett May might say and what might come to fruition. As I left the den, I heard whispers behind me. I went upstairs and crawled into bed with my laptop. I watched the surveillance camera, which had the same view as the window downstairs, but with night vision.

Although I was alone, I was in better company. I tried to make sure I did everything to bring those guys home safe. I took deep breaths and concentrated deeply. I imagined them coming back, that nobody got hurt, and that we were reunited as a team. I wanted so desperately for us to be the family of misfits that we were in the beginning of summer. I watched the video feed, as grainy as it was, and waited. I waited until I saw four tiny dots emerge from the neighbor's cabin.

Four dots became five, and the loud, boisterous voices of the guys echoed throughout the clearing. I slammed my laptop shut and ran downstairs with a smile on my face. Gunner was barking with excitement, and everybody was cheering. It had been a successful mission. The first of many. And we were a team celebrating our first victory.

"Hi, boy! Hi, boy! You're such a good boy! Yes, you are!" Emma chirped, scratching behind Gunner's ears. He barked and barked, his tail bashing the legs of everyone around him.

"So, they took him?" I asked, looking between the four boys.

"No. It looks like Gunner somehow got inside and was trapped. The neighbors weren't even home," Noah said, his head tilted apologetically.

"Those neighbors haven't been home for a long time," Kai said.

"What do you mean? I see them over there every day."

"Yeah, Kinsley and I see them do weird stuff in their garden," Emma said, agreeing with me. She'd been shy to speak up, but this was how she showed her support. She inched closer to my side. I gave her a small smile and nodded to Kai.

"I don't know what to tell you guys. That house was covered in boxes and dust. It looks like they started to pack and then just vanished. There are white sheets draped over the furniture. It looks like an abandoned house for sure," Asher said.

I scratched my head, wondering how that could be true. I glanced at Emma and my confusion reflected in her face. Her brows furrowed, and her mouth slightly parted. I suppose it wasn't the strangest thing that happened in Baylor, and it wouldn't be the last. For now, we were all just excited that Gunner had returned home. Our success at the Vandals' house had taken the spotlight that night, and it seemed that maybe I'd been let off the hook. After all, I couldn't be the only one responsible for all the terror brought to Baylor . . .

I didn't know when I started calling Gunner ours, but now that Lainey was gone, he felt like a team mascot. When he'd gone missing, like so many others had, it had felt like a turning point for us to get him back. Nobody had ever come back before. The hollow truth was finally fleshing out. This wasn't the afterlife—not yet anyway. And our thoughts had the power to produce magic and unleash terror. We were in control of our own destiny, and we had work to do to hone that power. Because right now, it was far too pliable.

One thought of negativity could bring the whole cabin down. And our insecurities had our teeth falling out. To be optimistic . . . That was going to take some training. And we were going to need to work together. As I watched everyone crowd around the dog, giving him love and affection, I wondered how I could bottle this moment and use it to spread light in all the dark places of the forest. I had some time left here in this realm, and I'd better make the best of it until I found a way out.

23

It was a crystal-clear day. The sun was high in the sky, and crowds came in from out of town to celebrate the Fourth of July at Baylor Lake. It was a special place to be on Independence Day. While the float parade wasn't anything like in the big city, it had a small-town feel that was even more festive. It was the busiest day of the year on the lake. Car doors slammed in the background, and boat motors idled on the once-placid lake. It was everybody's favorite time of year. Everybody's but mine.

The crowds made me anxious, and I was always worried something terrible would happen during the good times. Worse yet, today was the big day. I was ready to find Layla, and I now knew that I held the power to do so. I was nervous, though. I didn't know what finding her would mean, and I didn't have the time to figure it out. Walker and I had the clues that led us to this very parade on this particular day. The pressure of having only one chance to get this right had been weighing on me, and the crowds only amplified my stress. It was a mental space I needed to get out of if I wanted to pull this off.

Everybody in the cabin was getting ready to go enjoy the parade. Mason had been day-drinking, and Scarlett May was busy with her makeup and hair. Her sky-high shorts and cowgirl boots accentuated what great legs she had. Kimber chatted with her in the bathroom while Emma hid in her bedroom alone. Things between Emma and I had been awkward since she'd turned on me. But that was the least of my worries now. The entire house had been coming around since we saved the dog. We even ventured out one afternoon to show them how fast the apple tree had grown. The fact that it was right where we had left it was my saving grace. Had it not been there, I doubt they would've trusted me again, and I would've been fighting for my reputation instead of looking for Layla Barns.

As I waited for Walker to show, I checked the time repeatedly. I knew he had to be as nervous as I was, so I tried my best to relax. I knew he would feed off of my energy—the whole house would. I strived to be a beacon of confidence for them. But I had no idea what I was doing. I was just as unprepared as I could be, and I felt I was going into this mission blindly.

There was a knock on the back patio door, and by the time I turned, Walker had let himself in. He was wearing a blue and black flannel, and a dark baseball cap covered the scar on his brow, shadowing his eyes. It hadn't gone unnoticed that my stomach dropped the second my eyes landed on him. He was gorgeous. He was going to be the only reason I missed this place.

"It's a big day today," I said, wrapping my arms around him for a hug.

"It is. Are you ready?" Walker asked.

"As ready as I'll ever be," I said with a shrug.

"Shot?" Mason asked, holding up an amber-filled glass. Walker and I stared at him blankly.

"No, thanks."

Mason shrugged and knocked back the liquid, wincing as it went down. We all celebrated in our own ways. Scarlett May with her cowgirl boots. Mason with his alcohol. And me, with my suffocating anxiety. We were all a little crazy here.

Everyone was excited for the Fourth of July, and normally, I would have been too. But there was little chance of success today and a probability of failure. I'd already felt the disappointment of it before we even stepped out of the cabin. The sun beat down on my face as I placed my sunglasses on to shield the blaring sun. It was difficult to see, and I glared into the crowd.

There were people everywhere. Cars lined the windy road, driving five miles an hour trying to get good parking for the parade. Families sat in lawn chairs outside of our driveway. American flags swayed in the hands of little kids everywhere. Some people had music playing, and others had lunch spread out on their laps. Others had umbrellas, and I even saw somebody with a grill in the back of their truck. But everywhere I looked, there was a smile. And that should have made me feel good. Comforted. Reassured. Instead, it made me feel like an outsider.

It was in those smiles that I realized how different I truly was. While the thought excited them—a parade, a Fourth of July party all day and night—I was worried about survival. I was worried about my friends making it to live another day. And I was worried about my fears coming to life before me, torching the forest with flames of self-doubt. Nobody would escape that fire. Not even me.

I'd briefed the group on what to look for today. I'd shown them a picture of Layla Barns and told them she would be anywhere near a fairytale float. Anything that reminded them of their childhood. I told them we needed to capture her but not harm her. There were questions we needed her to answer. None of which I knew, of course. Other than why. Why couldn't I go home yet? Why was she so important to my survival? And I was curious about other things too—like why had she left Walker? I'd never leave him. In fact, I had conflicting feelings about that now, and he wasn't even my boyfriend, let alone my fiancé.

The parade stretched alongside the lake for a waterfront view. Rock Creek Cove, where our cabin was, was the tail-end of the festivities. The parade started in town, which was a little farther than a mile away and where most of the action was—where we were headed today. The town was lined with little mom-and-pop shops and the old historical library. We started out strong, walking into town, but it wasn't long before our team had parted.

Emma had Gunner on a leash, and his tail wagged constantly. She was stopped often by people asking to pet Gunner. She couldn't say no, and we couldn't wait for her. Walker and I continued through the crowds as Mason shouted loud and obnoxious sentiments behind us. Asher and Kimber kept to themselves, mostly. And Kai and Noah were focused on the hunt for Layla. Scarlett May had disappeared with Sampson's group the moment we'd stepped into the crowd, and I assumed she wouldn't be of help today.

I knew Kai's motive for finding Layla Barns was scientifically based. He had questions of his own; that I was sure of. But Noah? I wasn't sure why he was so interested in finding her. And I couldn't shake the feeling that maybe he was looking to get Walker out of the way. And what better way than to find his true love? It was the very reason I *didn't* want to find Layla Barns. But when it came down to it, my gran had told me that if I could only find her, then I would have a chance at coming home. And I wanted that more than anything. I wanted to go home to my mom and dad. I didn't want to live in a world where I had so much power. Because at the end of the day, I never truly trusted myself. There was more negativity in me than I cared to admit. And we were all the victims of it. I needed to get home. To a world where my insecurities affected only me and me alone. Where my dark side hid behind my smile.

It was about an hour later when the first float was underway. We made it into town, and there were more people than I ever remembered. Asher and Kimber left the group to buy corn dogs. Mason sipped from his tainted water bottle and weaved in and out of the crowds, looking for girls. We lost Emma somewhere with the dog. Kai and Noah, as far as I knew, were hunting for Layla Barns like trusty old bloodhounds.

Walker and I stayed close together. The group had come together for one mission and one mission alone. Find Layla and survive. And even though our goals had aligned, by the time the parade started, the team had fallen apart. Self-interest trumped any chance of finding Layla. We were a team, yet we weren't acting like one. And I should have known as much on our first try. It was hard to wrangle up a group of eighteen-year-olds with motivations that differed from my own.

They hadn't seen themselves lying on the hospital bed the way I had. And they never saw the hurt in Walker's eyes when he talked about his soon-to-be fiancée. A corndog or a pretty girl was far more interesting to them. I couldn't blame them, because I realized my friends were just pieces of my mind—fragmented. I couldn't pull them together. It was *my* interest, sprawling out like the tentacles of an octopus. *I* always enjoyed pretzels and hotdogs at places like these. The funnel cake and churros were a once-a-year delicacy. *I* was sidetracked by the cute dogs and the attractive guys in the crowds. And if I couldn't even focus myself, how could I expect them to?

The parade marched down the streets of Baylor whether we were ready or not. Our beer garden float had turned out quite nicely. Pretty girls in beer maiden dresses danced on top of the float with mugs of beer in their hands. Music blared up and down the street, and flags waved back and forth in the crowd. There was a lot of movement and loud sounds. The sun was blindingly bright. There was almost too much to take in, and it made it difficult to keep my eye out for fairytale clues.

Just when it started to seem that the venture was hopeless, I saw a dwarf. Then two . . . and three. Seven dwarfs turned the corner, marching in front of a float and singing. There was a giant apple tree on the float that looked just like the one in the forest. Snow White stood beautifully, waving to the crowd. As she turned the corner, my heart lurched, and I grabbed Walker's arm. I pointed toward the float. "That's it! That's it!"

"Shit! What do we do?"

I had no idea. The float was fast approaching, and I had absolutely no idea—no plan for what to do when it arrived. My eyes scanned the scene, now hyper-focused as I looked for ideas. It wasn't until I landed on Snow White's face that I realized she was more than just a character. She was Layla Barns, herself.

"Walker!"

I looked back just as he had made the realization himself. His face drained of blood, turning pale and peaked. He looked as though he might pass out. I reached for him right as he went down. He fell to his knees in the midst of the crowd. Tears streamed down his cheeks as he stared at Layla with wide, red eyes. My heart broke right alongside his.

I looked back as the float was directly in front of us. Time was closing in. I had to act quickly, and Walker was too riddled with grief to do anything at all. I searched the crowd. None of our group was around to help. I looked back at Walker one last time, and he was in so much pain he could hardly look away.

"I'm sorry. I'm so sorry," he uttered beneath his breath in a whisper that Layla couldn't hear.

I made the split-second decision to leave him behind and do what I needed for the both of us. I ran to the back of the float and lunged to the top. I heard the crowd gasp, and I knew I had made a mistake. Behind the trunk of the tree, I hid. The float stopped, and I knew it wasn't long before security would take me away. My heart pounded and sweat beaded on my forehead. But nobody was looking at me.

Everybody was looking at . . . I stretched my eyes far into the crowd and saw Mason on top of one of the dwarfs. They were wrestling, rolling around on the ground.

"Wilde! Wilde! I got one!" he screamed at the top of his lungs.

I felt my face flush, and I knew I needed to act quickly to use this distraction to my advantage. I crept up behind Layla. Her presence alone made me uneasy. I couldn't help feeling inferior as I stood next to her. Even in her costume, she was absolutely stunning. The perfect woman.

"Layla?" I asked. She whipped her head around and her eyes struck mine. I felt her look straight into my soul, and my blood ran cold. Her eyes dropped, examining me as a threat to her. Then she laughed. She threw her head back and cackled. It wasn't the sweet Layla I imagined her to be. She was a villainess. In a blink of an eye, she was off the float, running. She leaped and landed with grace, even in the giant dress and heels.

"No! Wait!"

As I tracked her into the crowd, I caught the seven dwarfs running after Mason down the street, in the opposite direction. I glanced back at Walker but couldn't find him in the crowd, so I charged after Layla myself. I jumped off the float with little grace and followed her. She was fast. Incredibly fast. But her dress made it easy for me to spot her.

"Wait, I just need to talk to you! Please!" I screamed out, running through the crowd.

Little kids stepped in my way and a grandmother in a wheelchair nearly ran over me. I tripped and fell as I tried to dodge a lady with a baby. Layla gained some distance as I picked myself up and continued. I vaguely felt the burn in my hands and realized I'd skinned my palms on the asphalt. But I kept after her.

She looked back at me now and then, laughing when she did. Whereas I was running full speed, heart pounding and lungs burning, she was frolicking.

Laughing. Playing. I'd never worked so hard in my life. I ran with every ounce of energy I could muster. My feet were heavy and it felt like I was running through a sand bank. Still, I managed to close the gap between us. I was winning. I was gaining on her.

Maybe I could do this?

I took my shot. I reached my arms out as I flew through the air. I grabbed hold of her shoulder, bringing her down to the ground with me. If she didn't want to talk to me, I was going to make her. This was *my* realm. *My* time. And I'd be damned if I let her slip through my fingers. But as we fell to the ground, it was only me who bashed into the asphalt.

The asphalt grated my elbows as I landed upon nothing. Layla had disappeared within my arms in the seconds it took for me to fall. I lay on my stomach on the boiling-hot asphalt as a crowd formed around me. My wrist was sprained, and road rash covered my forearms. I heard her cackle all around me, inside and out.

I rolled onto my back, staring up at the crowd. I knew at that moment that I hadn't caught her because I wasn't ready. I didn't know what that meant exactly—just that it wasn't my time. I wasn't worthy yet to go back to my body. And for that, I needed to stay here in Baylor for a little longer. It was a game I didn't want to play, but had to.

I'd come so far, yet I was still so far away. I'd gathered a team, but where were they now? Walker had been searching for her for twenty-plus years. And when he laid eyes on her for the first time, all he could do was crumble with guilt. It wasn't just me; it was all of us. None of us were ready.

"What are you doing?" Kimber asked through a mouthful of corndog. I focused my eyes and searched the faces above me to find Kimber and Asher watching me like a caged animal at the zoo. I extended a hand and Asher helped pick me up off the ground.

"Ouch," I said, looking at my wrists and forearms.

"Oh, that looks like it hurts," he said. I dusted the bits of gravel off my freshly grated skin, and the burn set in.

"While you guys were off snacking, Layla Barns was here, and she got away! And freaking Mason . . . charged after a dwarf! All seven of them ran after him! He's probably half-dead in some alley right now! Where were you guys?" My voice splintered. Kimber looked at me like I was stupid and then gave her corndog a shake.

I rolled my eyes, taking in a deep breath and pinching the bridge of my nose. I reminded myself it wasn't her fault but mine. "We need to find the others."

"Why? Don't we need to go after Layla?" Kimber asked.

I scanned the crowd even though I had known she'd disappeared into thin air. She was nowhere to be found.

"She's gone now. We need to find Mason," I said. We started down the street, but a little girl stopped me in my tracks when she pulled on my T-shirt.

"Excuse me. Excuse me. You dropped this," she said. I turned around to see a little redheaded girl with a fist full of my shirt. She had an envelope in her hand. I hadn't dropped an envelope, but as I started to deny ownership, I saw my name clearly written on the front.

"Thank you," I said, giving her a smile and taking the envelope from her.

Kimber and Asher thought little of it, and I slipped it into my backpack. We continued through the crowd, looking for a dwarf or two, and I kept my eye out for Walker and Emma. I didn't know what was in that envelope, but I assumed it was my next clue. A chance to go home. Another deadline.

24

The sun was high, making for a sweltering Fourth of July. The parade had ended, and the small town was crawling with families making their way back home. It took some time for the rest of our group to reconvene. We found Emma with another lady and her long-haired puppy. The leashes of the playing dogs had intertwined. She looked apologetic when she saw us, but I let her know there was nothing she could have done to change the outcome. I tried to hide the defeat on my face, but I just wanted out of here. I wanted to go home.

Home? I wasn't sure where that was anymore. A part of me wanted to go back to the cabin. It was only a mile or so down the road, and I could be there in fifteen minutes. I could kick off my shoes, get a drink, or take a cold shower. But the thought of going *home, home* . . . seemed so far away. It seemed like a lot of work—and I was tired. Too tired.

I guess I wasn't ready to get back to my reality and begin a new fight for recovery. And I could only hope when the time came, and I truly was ready, that I'd find a way to capture Layla. She'd be the one to send me back. I was sure of that now. And even though I considered this a failed mission, I was starting to understand what it would take to make a successful one.

Kai and Noah showed up with promising smiles on their faces, and hope rattled in my belly. At least the bloodhounds had done what they were supposed to. "We found the dwarfs. And guess what? They were chasing Mason!" Noah said, barely able to get the words out.

Kai stifled his laughter.

"They were what?" Emma asked.

I rolled my eyes. *What a shit show . . .*

"Apparently, he thought he was helping but must have misunderstood. He was supposed to look for anything resembling Snow White or a fairy tale. Instead, he made a mockery out of it," I said, bringing my hand to my forehead. "Does anybody know where Scarlett May is?"

"Yeah, I saw her earlier. She said Sampson's throwing a party tonight for the Fourth. He said he could see the fireworks really well from his cabin. She went with him to help set up. I think we're going to go tonight," Kimber said, looking to Asher.

"That sounds fun," Emma said, nodding.

I had other plans. Those plans were to be anywhere that Walker was. The first step was finding him. I'd left him back in the crowd, and he hadn't resurfaced since.

"I don't think I'm going to make it tonight. Look, we're missing Walker and Mason. Do you think you guys can track down Mason and get him back safely?" I asked.

I saw a subtle flash of aggravation in Noah's eyes. But ultimately, everyone agreed. Even though the parade had ended, the crowd was still going strong. Everyone had been on the move for some time, but the population hadn't thinned at all. I watched a mom scold her kid for touching something on the ground, then proceed to wipe his sticky fingers with a wet cloth. Gunner wrapped his leash around not one, not two, but three people, in one minute flat. I groaned, feeling the hopelessness wash through me. We couldn't do anything right. And I was the one in charge? *What a joke . . .*

I looked out, scanning the crowds. Hundreds of faces. All of them looking for something. I didn't see Walker, and I had no idea where he was. I tried to retrace my steps, but that didn't work. It wasn't until the group had made a collective plan and the crowds had thinned sometime later that I saw him sitting on a bench all alone—his head drooping down to his chest. Defeated. He looked like a kid who had dropped his ice cream one lick in and watched it melt on the hot sizzling cement. Or better yet, he looked like a man who had lost his only love.

I wished I could do more. But for whatever reason, when I'd locked my arms around Layla, it hadn't been enough. And if only I knew why my grasp wasn't strong enough, I would at least have some way to fix it. A direction to run toward—something to work on. But I had nothing, not even an idea. All I knew was that I had failed because I wasn't ready. I felt as terrible as Walker looked.

I took a deep breath and then made my way to him. He didn't lift his head when I sat down on the bench, but I felt his pain ease with my presence. We sat in silence for what seemed like forever, and then at some point, I reached over and grabbed his hand. I pulled it onto my lap and encased it in both of my hands. Gently, I rubbed the back of his knuckles with my thumb. He not only let me keep his hand in mine, but I think he felt comforted by it, too. There wasn't much else I could do, but I could be there for him, and I knew how to show that.

I laid my head down on his shoulder, and a moment later, I felt the weight of his head on mine. We stayed like that for quite some time, watching the people dissipate until it was a ghost town, and we were the only souls in sight.

I was wrapped up in a dream world. My mind, body, and spirit separated into three silos. Yet somehow, with Walker's hand in mine, I felt whole. I didn't understand, and I didn't try to. I just enjoyed the moment. I took full deep breaths, and for the first time in a long time, I felt optimistic that everything was going to be all right. Despite the rocky road we had been on and the long treacherous path ahead, as long as I had him by my side, I felt . . . almost . . . good?

"Will you watch the fireworks with me tonight?" I asked. My eyes fixed on the littered road before us. The remains of the parade painted the street, and bits of trash fluttered by the curbs.

"Yeah. We can do that. But I don't really want to go to Sampson's house," he said.

"I don't either. Not really in the mood for a party. Let's watch them from the canoe. I'm sure there's a secret spot you haven't shown me yet?"

"Yeah, actually, there is." His voice perked up for the first time since seeing Snow White.

We took our time on the bench, enjoying each other's company, and then we went our separate ways. By the time I showed up at the cabin, it was alive with festive sarcasm. Everybody was there joking about Mason's extravaganza with the seven dwarfs—everybody except Mason.

"Where's Mason?" I asked, my stomach dropping in fear. If I lost another one on my watch, I'd give up right here, right now.

"We found him. He's in the drunk tank," Noah said.

I took a sigh of relief. "Figures," I said, shaking my head.

"Yeah, he has to stay there for twenty-four hours. We're allowed to pick him up tomorrow," Noah said.

"It's probably best." I thought of all the things Mason would do on a night like tonight to draw attention to himself.

"Are you sure you don't want to go to Sampson's tonight?" Emma asked. She was trying to make things as normal between us as possible. It was her way of saying, "I'm sorry for turning my back on you." But I wasn't about to hold grudges—not at a time like this. Noah's eyes and ears were open to my response, so I locked arms with Emma and led her away.

"Walker was pretty upset today. I didn't tell anybody else, but I found

Layla Barns. I actually caught her. I wrapped my arms around her and then . . . then she . . . she just disintegrated like she was nothing. She left this world for another . . . I don't know," I said in a low voice. Asher mimicked Mason's wrestling match, and Kimber laughed as he jumped on the floor. We ducked into the den.

"You did?" she asked, eyebrows raised.

"Yeah. She was beautiful. She was dressed as Snow White," I began.

"Oh! Because of the apples," Emma said, piecing it together.

"She kept laughing. It was like this sinister laugh. And even when she disappeared, I could hear it echoing in the air. It was almost like she was here, even when she wasn't. I don't know. It was unsettling, really." I sighed.

"And Walker?"

"Oh, boy. He didn't do too well. One look at her and he crumbled. Fell to his knees and started crying." I winced at his pain fresh in my memory.

"He cried?" Emma's brows arched.

"Well, his eyes were glassy and red. He kept saying he was sorry. The whole thing really damaged him. I feel terrible for him." I crossed my arms over my chest and leaned against the wall.

"Are you sure you guys don't want to go to Sampson's?" she asked. "It could be fun."

"Yeah. I don't want to see the whole scene again. You know, with Levi and all. I don't want to remember that night any more than I have to. Plus, I think Walker needs me. We're just going to have a quiet night on the lake."

"Okay." Emma leaned against the wall, deep in thought.

"Are you okay?"

"Yeah. Yeah. Just thinking about Levi," she said.

"I'm sorry. I shouldn't ha—"

"No. It's okay. Call me if you need me," she said, placing a hand on my shoulder. It felt good to have her back. She was the only friend I had in my corner.

As everyone left the cabin to go across the lake to Sampson's house, I watched the group and remembered when there were twice as many of us. An eerie feeling trickled down my spine, knowing that so many of us had disappeared and we were only halfway through summer. I watched each one of them leave, and I prayed it wouldn't be the last time I saw them. But I tried not to dwell on it, because the more I thought about it, the more it had a chance of coming true.

I turned my focus on the night I had ahead of me. I showered and changed into some warm clothes in case the night brought a cool breeze. And after the sweltering day that we'd had, I hoped it would. I didn't know what hoops I'd have to jump through to get out of here alive, and I didn't want to think about it. All I really wanted to do in the moment was make Walker feel better. The hurt I saw in his eyes made me feel hollow inside. Like a hole had been punched through my heart. Like there was nothing I could do to ever feel better.

I imagined that was how he felt. I didn't know what it was like for him to be constantly chasing his soulmate in a realm that she couldn't be reached, but I had to guess it was miserable. Devastating, each and every day. And to spend eternity like that? What I'd seen in his eyes when his knees hit the pavement was probably a small fraction of what he felt on the inside. It was then that I realized, his guilt was the scar that sliced through his brow. It was his wound on the inside that showed in his reflection. Sometimes it was fresh; sometimes it would bleed; and other times, it looked almost healed.

When Walker paddled the canoe into the cove, I grabbed his flannel in the crook of my arm and locked Gunner inside the cabin. I stilled on the back porch when I saw him standing at the end of the dock with his hands tucked deep into his pockets. He was too far to see the details of his face, but I knew that he wore a somber expression under the bill of his hat. As if his feelings reached out in the space between us for me to sense. I crossed the grassy hill down to the dock, and stopped to pick up a daisy. I plucked it from the grass and twirled it between my finger and thumb until I reached him.

"Here, it's for you," I said, holding the daisy out to him. It was simple enough, but it worked. A small smile spread across his lips. Instantaneously, my lungs expanded, and I could breathe again.

"Are you ready?" he asked, admiring the flower.

"Yeah. I hope you don't mind. I brought your flannel."

"I told you, it looks better on you, anyway."

My stomach dropped, and I vaguely wondered how long I would torture myself with the impossibility of him being mine.

My mind said I shouldn't have come. I shouldn't be spending my time with this lost soul. I shouldn't be wearing his flannel and picking him flowers. But I was. I wanted to. And it was going to be the death of me. Yet, I threw caution to the wind, because that's where my heart wanted to be. If it was my dream, I would live it the way I wanted to. And right now, it was the Fourth of July, and I was going to spend that night floating on the lake with this ruggedly handsome guy. And I wouldn't convince myself otherwise.

Walker pushed the canoe off the dock after I got situated. His strong hands gripped the paddle, and his muscles bulged as he rowed us into the middle of the lake. I tried not to stare. I only stole glances when it seemed I wouldn't get caught.

"So, today was a bust," he said.

"Was it, though? We saw her. Have you seen her before? I mean, after the . . ."

"No. I haven't. It's the first time in twenty years that I've seen her. It makes me wonder, has she been here the whole time? Maybe she's been avoiding me? I don't know. I . . . I just froze up. I'm sorry I didn't help you." Walker turned his head to the side and looked out to the dense forest. His profile was my favorite because I could gaze all I wanted without ever getting caught.

"Don't apologize. I was pretty close to catching her, but she was too fast," I said.

Walker chuckled as if remembering a time when he'd chased her. I didn't want to think about it. I also didn't want to tell him that I'd caught her. And that she'd laughed at my attempt. That she'd mocked me for even trying. I thought it might hurt his feelings to know that she chose not to give herself up.

"Yeah, she is fast," he said, looking behind himself at the lake. I forced a smile and looked out at the channel we were entering. Another finger of the lake I had never seen before.

"I think we're getting close, though. I mean, she didn't know who I was, and I was chasing her. Of course she ran from me. But we're going to find her again. And when she sees you, she won't be running anymore."

"Yeah, you're probably right. But we don't know where we're going to find her next. She's gone, and she didn't leave a single trace. Unless your gran has something to say? Another hint? Another book?" Walker asked with brows raised, with an inkling of hope. It reminded me of the envelope the young girl gave me after I collapsed on top of Layla's ghost.

"Actually, I have a little something. . ." I dug around in my bag, and once I found the envelope, I pulled it out.

"What's that?" Walker asked.

"I don't know. A little girl gave it to me. It had my name on it. I think it might be another clue. Do you want to open it?" I asked, holding out the envelope. Walker's eyes flickered from mine to the envelope, and then he slowly withdrew his hand from the paddle to take the envelope. The canoe drifted as he ripped the seal open. I watched his face contort with pain as I saw the back of another photograph in his hands. It took a little time for him to soak up the memory, and then, when he was ready, he handed it to me. The photograph was of him and Layla in a hot-air balloon. It was a great photo. The sun was setting behind them, and they looked perfect together. I could see that they were true soulmates, and they were meant to be together. It hurt to look at the picture, but not for the same reasons it hurt Walker.

"You guys rode in a hot-air balloon?" I asked, trying to hide my heartache.

"Yeah. That was the Baylor Balloon Festival. The summer before the accident was when we did it. We were planning to do it again. We had big plans that summer."

"Sounds like me and my friends. We had big plans this summer, too." My gaze dropped to the dirt clinging to the belly of the canoe.

"At least you're doing them," he said.

"Yeah, kind of."

"Do you think that's her clue?" Walker asked. For the first time that night, his eyes had a sparkle. Aliveness behind them I hadn't seen since before the parade.

"The balloon festival? Maybe she's going to be there . . ." I said. It was only a couple of weeks away. And if we had her next known location, there was a lot I needed to do to ensure that she remained in my arms if I caught her again.

"Yeah. Maybe," Walker said, beginning to paddle again.

We rode in silence, the balloon festival on our minds and looming in our near future. It was another chance for me to escape. And a chance for Walker to live out his life the way it should have been all along. The last thing I wanted to do was screw it up again. Because who knew if I would have another chance. I felt the stress of the balloon festival thick in the air. The stress to be successful was suffocating.

A loud blast exploded. I startled, falling off the bench and landing on my back with my feet in the air. I gripped the wet rim of the canoe as Walker let out a loud and boisterous laugh. The first of the fireworks danced across the sky in a brilliant aqua blue. I laughed, awkwardly sprawled across the bottom of the canoe, and then I lowered my eyes to Walker laughing—because he was more beautiful than a sky full of fire.

25

By the time the fireworks fluttered down and fizzled out on the water's surface, I realized just how deep my feelings for Walker had grown. I started to have thoughts of abandoning my mission to survive and living out my eternity with him by my side. It was a dangerous mindset to be in. Far more worrisome than the fears that took root and grew into monsters of the deep, turbulent lake. Because the love that was spawning inside me would surely seize my heart, and I wouldn't be leaving Baylor alive.

This had all been a game. A game of the mind. A game I had no choice but to conquer. Win the game and I'd go home. But that was never certain. My gran's words played back in my head, *"And when you're good and ready, you'll come home. Hopefully . . ."*

Hopefully was the key word. And for the first time, I realized what she had meant. If I fell in love with Walker, I may choose to never go home, and that was absolutely horrifying.

Another thunderous crack above startled me as I climbed back to the bench. Walker clutched his stomach, and his head tilted back with a rolling laugh. Then another and another. The sky lit up in yellows, greens, aqua blues, and pinks. Walker's laughter was contagious, and for no reason at all, I laughed too. We both looked up at the sky to see the embers fluttering down all around us. It was gorgeous. The sound echoed off every corner of the lake like surround sound. The sizzle of the fireworks going out as they touched down on the water was electric. It was the most beautiful thing I had ever seen, and my heart swelled. I never wanted it to end.

It encapsulated us in falling fireworks and the soft glow of the night sky. I didn't see the fireworks slowing at first, but as my laughter died down, I noticed they hung in the sky a little longer than usual. And the more peculiar it seemed, the more I realized something surreal was happening. They slowed to a complete stop. They still glimmered all around us like streamers in the night sky, but they were no longer falling. Overhead, fireworks were no longer bursting.

"What's happening?" Walker asked, looking all around him.

"I don't know!" I said, my back arched with alarm.

It was as if time had stood still for everything except us. I reached my hand out to a bright, luminescent, blue ember and cupped my hand around it. It shimmered like magic in the palm of my hand. It was warm against my hand with buzzing energy. Fascinated, I closed my hand around the ember, and when I opened it again, the ember was gone. Smothered in my tight grasp.

"Did you do this?" Walker asked.

"Did I do this?" I asked, slightly offended, as I looked for signs of the snuffed ember in my hands. But when I turned to Walker, I could see he meant no harm. His eyes were like a child filled with wonder. In fact, he meant it as a compliment. I blushed with an inkling of pride.

"It's like you stopped time . . ." he said, marveling at me instead of the sky.

And then it hit me. That's exactly what I wanted to happen. It was the moment I knew I was falling in love with him, and I never wanted it to end.

My jaw dropped, and I looked out at the millions of embers floating in the sky. I had stopped time here in Baylor. Did the clocks still tick back in reality? Did I even care?

"I did it," I said in a whisper.

Walker laughed, his dimples deeper than I'd ever seen. "Yeah, you did," he said.

"I was just thinking about how special this was. How beautiful the night sky was with the fireworks. And you laughing. I didn't want it to end," I said, feeling the warmth hit my cheeks.

Walker's gaze was intense. His eyes were smoldering, and my cheeks were burning hotter than the surrounding fire. I couldn't hold his gaze any longer, and even though I wanted to be brave and forthcoming, I looked away, embarrassed for what my heart had done without my permission.

"It's magnificent. I've never seen anything like it. You are so . . . wow," he said. My heart sang with joy but was quickly snuffed like the ember I held.

"I feel bad for you. I feel bad that you're stuck here, in my world. It's not where you belong."

"Your world?" Walker chuckled, somewhat surprised.

"Yeah, you're stuck in my dream," I said, pointing to all the glimmering streamers suspended in the air. It was a vulnerable thing, falling for someone when your feelings painted the world around you. Like I was made from glass, and everybody could see inside. No secret safe.

"That's funny because I always thought *you* were stuck in *my* world. I felt bad for *you*," he said with a smirk.

"And how do you figure I'm in your world?"

"Because, Wilde, you can see me. Nobody can see me. Or at least, they hadn't until you came around. I'm dead without you. I've been gone a long, long time. And the fact that you're here with me proves that you're in my world. You may not be a ghost, but you're in my realm," he said. Walker let go of the paddle and rubbed his hands together.

"I don't think so." I shook my head. "I think I am in my dream realm. And you . . . you're over there, in the afterlife. Maybe we're in two separate worlds," I said, regretting the sound of it. I didn't want to be in separate worlds.

"Side by side?" he asked.

I nodded. And it hurt too much to think of the day that I might wake up without him.

"I don't know what I'm going to do without you, Wilde," he said, reaching up for a fallen ember.

"Don't say that." My throat seized like I wanted to cry.

"I remember the first time I woke up without Layla. The first time I realized I was invisible. That I had died." He snuffed the ember in his fist. "I was living out my punishment alone, and it was torture. It's been torture." He took his hat off and threw it into the boat. He ran a hand through his hair and let out the breath he'd been holding. "But pulling you out of this lake was the best night I've had in forever," he said.

"I almost drowned that night," I said with a sarcastic tone.

He chuckled. "You know what I mean. It felt like a gift had fallen from the skies. Just for me."

I found myself lost in his words. Had he really felt that way? Like I was a gift from the heavens? Like I was just for him?

"I know what you mean," I said. Thinking about how I'd never felt so comfortable with somebody before. How he completed my other half even though we were realms apart.

"God, it was so hard seeing her today. I can't tell you how much I miss her," Walker said, batting at a stream of simmering fireworks. They crumbled like dust, and my stomach turned over. He didn't feel like I came from the heavens because I was his soulmate. He just thought I was going to help him find Layla.

"Hey, Wilde? Do you think . . . do you think you could wish me away? Wish all this pain away?" he asked. His brows stitched together, both in pain and grievance.

"What do you mean? Like make you forget her?" I asked. Thinking back to the time I made Kimber and Asher get back together—or Levi and Emma. I cringed, thinking of the mistakes I'd made.

"Maybe? Do you think it would work?" He was desperate.

I felt the sickening spread of greed cross my stomach because I wanted to do it. I wanted to erase her from his heart and soul. I wanted to become his everything. And I knew I would absolutely hate myself if I did.

"I can't." I swallowed back my tears. I was standing in the way of the only love I'd ever known, but I couldn't do it. I couldn't live with a black heart.

"I didn't think so," he said, hanging his head.

"But, Walker, don't forget all of this." I motioned to the sky full of twinkling lights. It was gorgeous. They were dazzling as far as the eye could see. "Don't forget the beauty that's here, too. I might not be able to make you forget her, but there are things I *can* do," I said, not fully understanding the full depth of my talents. My power. My magic.

"Like what?" he asked. His tone was rough like gravel. Almost like he was taunting me. Pushing me. Like he wanted to play with fire. Like he had nothing left to lose. It made me nervous, like I might take his heart and relish his love, even though I knew . . . I knew it didn't belong to me.

"Well, for starters, I can make the backdrop absolutely stunning. I waved my hand, and the fireworks twinkled from reds to blues to greens. My eyes widened with surprise, as I hadn't known I could do that, but there it was right before us. I cracked a smile and looked back at Walker, but he was no longer happy. He was no longer interested in the fireworks. What he needed now was so much more. He needed to fix the hole in his heart.

"But if this is a dream and you can make things happen by just imagining them, then can you make this better? Can you make her come back to me?"

"You know, I saw my real self, lying in the hospital. When the doctor came to talk to my mom, she was crying. I held her hand. This is a dream and I know it. I know it. Here." I placed my hand over my heart. "But for whatever reason, I just lack the control to make it my own. I don't know how to do the things you ask. And all of this . . ." I waved my hand at the fireworks, "I don't know how it happened. It was just a feeling deep inside. A want. A hunger."

"You wanted to stop time that bad? Why?" he asked, considering the possibilities as he looked into my eyes.

I glanced down at my shoes and clicked my heels together nervously. He knew the reason. We both did. It didn't take a rocket scientist to see that I was falling for him. My love was gleaming all around us, and it was breathtaking.

"Because there was a feeling. Something I'd never felt before. A warmth deep in my chest. Your laugh made me happy, and I felt content." I didn't dare look at him.

"I feel that way too," he said, crossing the canoe and sitting next to me. The boat dipped, and the water rippled out. His warmth heated the side of my body, and he wrapped his arm around my shoulders. "I've never met anybody like you before, Wilde. I'm really glad we found each other," he said.

I sighed heavily. "Do you really think I could just wake up?" I asked.

"Look at what you've done here. It's nothing short of magnificent. You might not believe in yourself, but I believe in you."

"You do?" I asked, peeking up at him. He gazed into my eyes and nodded. He was saying one thing, but I was feeling another. My heart fluttered, and I wanted to close the distance between us and kiss him.

"I think you can do anything. You just have to really want it. I don't know why, but I think you just need somebody in your corner. I know you want to get out of here, so that's not the issue. I think the problem is that you don't believe in yourself. But I believe in you." He leaned over and planted a warm kiss on my forehead. I all but melted. "And I'm going to teach you what it means to have confidence in yourself. And before you know it, this is going to be your lucid dream." He waved a hand through the air, making Baylor seem so big.

"My lucid dream?" I asked.

"Yeah. It's a dream that you control. It's a dream with awareness. You're already aware; now we just need to work on the control. You have that power. And whether or not you like it, you've got the time to build upon that strength. And I'm here to help you. Hell, if I'm stuck here for the rest of eternity, the least I can do is set you free," he said with determination.

I pondered over that. How *I* had wanted to set *him* free, just like he wanted for me. We cared about one another, that much was clear. But did I want to leave? Right when things were getting good?

"You believe in me that much?" I asked, needing to hear it just one more time.

"I do," he said. I felt his face inch lower towards mine.

A firecracker burst.

"Whoa!" he gasped, grabbing my arm.

It surprised me to see the entire lake illuminated. It was like a giant flashlight had sunk to the sandy bottom, lighting the depths from within. What once was a lake of secrets now appeared a lake of hope.

The fireworks burst overhead, and the streamers waltzed down to the glowing lake. Swans glided in and out of the sizzling firework streamers that trickled down to the water. There must've been hundreds of them. Beautiful, elegant, white swans. Their necks were sleek and their feathers pure. They glowed like floating candles in a bathtub. It stole my breath. The beauty was almost too much to take, yet I couldn't steal my eyes away.

Walker stood up, rocking the boat. "I told you! I told you, Wilde. You can do anything you set your mind to!" he said, wide-eyed and giddy.

I turned away from him, amazed to see all the swans swimming in the sacred lake. I had made all of this? It was hard to imagine that this serenity poured out of me the moment I realized I was falling in love. The moment I thought he might feel something for me in return. I wondered what else I could bring to life. What my world might be like if I had everything I ever wanted.

"Woohoo!" Walker yelled, arms outstretched and head tilted toward the fiery sky.

If Walker was right about one thing, it was that I had time to develop my strength. I watched him hoot and holler, and my dark little secret rose from the bottom of the lake to the surface. And just as the water had illuminated with my hope, it shed light on the only real problem I had here in Baylor: I might not *want* to wake up.

Haunted Waters

Volume 3

HAUNTED
WATERS

1

The path through the woods was narrow and twisted. The sun had set long ago, and the chill was starting to settle in. So was the mist. It hovered in the treetops like a blanket over the forest, shielding the outside world from what lay within. I'd once thought of this realm as a prison, but I no longer felt that way. If this was a prison, and Walker was here, then I would voluntarily offer my wrists and stay shackled for eternity.

The gravel settled beneath my feet as my pace quickened. I needed to tell my gran about my revelation. I wouldn't be returning home. I knew I could find her ghost in the depths of the haunted forest. It was where the mist collected and stirred in the air, bringing her world and mine together. Unfortunately, it also brought other things, like malevolent, skinless creatures; hauntings of the unseen; and lush, beautiful poison. The unseen was the worst.

I'd thought about it long and hard, ever since the Fourth of July fireworks show. Walker and I had been encapsulated by the glowing embers of falling fireworks. The lake had been illuminated by an aqua light and was no longer a scary place. I didn't have control over this realm yet, but I thought maybe one day I could. I had every intention of learning how to hone my skill and make Baylor the place of my dreams.

Beautiful poison would just be beautiful. Skinless creatures would only be forest critters. And the unseen . . . That would be a feeling of wonder, and nothing else. I'd swim in Baylor Lake again, and instead of manifesting nightmares of people who'd passed, I'd visit with their spirits. It would be a magical place where I could have cupcakes with my gran, and she'd read me her latest novel. I'd swim with the fish all afternoon. And when it was time for dinner, Walker would be waiting for me at the dock with a towel. It wasn't a place that existed yet, but it was a world that I belonged to. All that was left to do was create it.

If I created this magnificent world here in Baylor, under the blanket of mist, then why would I ever want to go back? Sure, I'd miss my parents and my brother, but who's to say I couldn't visit? After all, I could see my gran, and we weren't in the same realm. Perhaps I could go to my family in a dream. And as for my friends, they were here with me; well, most of them. And then there was Walker—the love I'd never known existed. Now that I'd found him, I didn't think I could let him go. What kind of life would that be?

I searched the treetops when I heard crows calling above. They dove, piercing through the mist and swooping back up again, disappearing into the gray blanket of fog. I hurried along the trail, walking even faster than before. The forest at night was not the place for me to be alone. I needed to find my gran, tell her the news, and then get back to bed. I pushed my hands deep into my pockets and pulled my coat across my chest. The temperature continued to drop as the fog slithered closer to the ground. I wondered how much longer it would be before my gran appeared, and I could only hope that it was before the mist settled at my feet—that's when the bad things happened. I checked over my shoulder for the umpteenth time. She was nowhere to be found.

I wasn't sure how to tell her I wouldn't be going home. She'd known it was a possibility when we'd spoken at the hospital. I hadn't known what she'd meant at the time, when she'd said that I would *hopefully* return home, but I did now. This was a tempting world to live in. I wondered if Gran would be happy that I'd decided to stay. After all, I'd get to stay in touch with her. Going home would mean that I'd have to say goodbye to her, and I wasn't ready for that. I doubted I ever would be.

A crow called a long and gravelly warning that sent my eyes searching once again. There was a flash of movement in the distance, but it was only a dense shadow. I fixed my eyes on the path and scurried through the pines. Even though this world was still new to me, and much of it spawned from a nightmare, I felt the power deep in my belly that could grow into something magical. I wanted to see it come to fruition, and I couldn't bear the thought of leaving without having my wildest dreams come true. What lay before me was an opportunity.

Walker and I were going to train every day. Train like we were headed for combat. Like a war was on the horizon. He was working on developing training sessions for me to build what he called muscle memory, but for my brain. I'd learn how to control the dream using a multitude of techniques, and eventually it would become natural to me. I'd train myself regardless, because this was a war I couldn't afford to lose, but if practicing meant I'd be spending countless hours under Walker's instruction, I'd willingly be there all summer. And maybe I'd even fake it a little, so that I could get extra help . . .

A twig snapped behind me. I whipped my head around to see who was there, fully expecting it to be my gran, but it wasn't. A figure stood in the distance, draped in a red cloak. I froze, then took a few steps backward, watching intently and looking for signs that I should run. The crows swooped down again, and my eyes jumped toward one of the massive black birds. In that brief moment of inattention, the stranger had disappeared. I looked all around me but saw nothing. The crows called out in warning, and goosebumps prickled my arms. I started walking as fast as I could, eager to see my gran.

"Going to grandmother's house . . ." the wind whispered.

I wanted to share my news, tell her I was in love, and that my love was a double-edged sword because I would not be returning home. The heavy fog settled into the trees, and with it came a cool breeze that ruffled a loose strand of my hair. The mist curled around my ankles, and I knew that if I didn't see my gran soon, this could very quickly turn into a nightmare.

"Gran?" I called out.

No answer.

I scanned the trees, checking for her one last time before closing my eyes and wishing that I was back in the cabin. I didn't think it would work, but I was getting desperate. As soon as my eyes closed, I again heard the whisper in the wind, "Going to grandmother's house . . ."

My eyes sprang open, and I started to take off toward the cabin. Checking over my shoulder one more time, I saw the cloaked figure hiding behind a thin tree trunk. I stopped, trying to get a better look. A dark crimson cloak poked out from both sides of the tree, and the large hood bowed in my direction. Two piercing eyes glinting in the moonlight were all that could be seen in the blackness beneath the hood. The figure ran from tree to tree, pausing momentarily behind each one and checking to see if it had been noticed. I glanced down the path. Maybe I should investigate. It couldn't have been *that* dangerous if it was hiding from *me*. I'd come into the forest intending to find someone, and someone had appeared. I suppose it was my job to find out who. And why.

I took a slow, measured step off the path, followed by another, venturing into the thick forest. The further I got from the path, the colder it grew, and the fog became denser. The red-cloaked figure took notice of me and scampered more quickly, stopping to peek at me frequently. I hurried after it.

"Wait!"

Laughter wafted through the air and swirled all around me. It reminded me of a time before. A time when I'd almost caught Layla Barns. *Layla*. It was just like a witch's cackle. Was I chasing Layla? I slowed my pace, uncertain. The trail was so far away. My stomach twisted uncomfortably. I shouldn't be this far off the path. Could it be a trap? I could hear her laughter growing. It was all around me. The fog pooled at my feet and began climbing up my shins. I *really* shouldn't be out this far alone. The red cloak appeared behind me, only two trees back, and I saw Layla's face peeking out beneath the crimson velvet.

"Layla?" I asked.

A slow, sly smile appeared on her face. And with a twinkle in her eye, she turned and ran. I darted after her.

"Layla! I just want to talk. I'm not trying to hurt you!" But no matter how fast I ran, she was faster.

I jumped over fallen trees and weaved through the pines. "Wait!"

The crows screamed overhead, and twigs snapped under my weight. My lungs burned. I couldn't keep up. She led me deeper and deeper into the forest—to the deepest parts of my mind. This wasn't a place I wanted to be, a place I ever wanted to know.

"Layla?"

As the woods closed in around me, I realized I was not getting closer to finding my answers, but in fact getting further from them. She was leading me into a trap. I slowed to a steady walk, pinching a cramp in my side, and finally stopped completely. I panted as I looked around, uncertain of where I stood. All the trees looked similar in the darkness. I'd run far enough that I couldn't see what direction the trail was, and I had no way of getting back. My chest rose and fell quickly, as I looked up toward the stars. But there was no midnight map sparkling above; there was only fog.

"Don't stray from the path . . ." the wind whispered.

I swallowed hard, knowing I'd made a deadly mistake. There was something about this girl that seemed familiar. Not just that she was the mysterious Layla Barns, or even the cackle that filled the air around me. It was something that I couldn't quite put my finger on. It was almost as if it was a story I'd heard once before . . .

A massive crow dove at me, swooping in front of my face and missing my cheek by mere inches. I stumbled backward, half stunned, then changed directions. The crow screeched, and I had an odd feeling that it was trying to tell me something. Something I should have known. Something that should have been obvious. In the blinding fog bank, I took a few steps, but halted when the crow swooped again.

I flinched and spun in an entirely new direction. Had it been telling me which way the path was? A single black feather cut a path through the mist as it fell from the sky. Before it hit the ground, I thought of Levi. I wasn't sure how he passed; all I knew was that the crows had taken him away. In the storm's wake that night, millions of pitch-black feathers had fluttered to the ground. *Levi.* I tilted my head toward the treetops, and several shadows flew overhead. There was one shadow unlike the rest. It was magnificent, really. Its wingspan was twice that of the others, and its eyes were so yellow they pierced through the fog. It was the one who had moved into my path when I had lost my sense of direction.

"Thank you, Levi," I whispered into the sky.

I hurried through the pines toward safety. The sinister cackle came at me from all directions. A flash of red here, a flash of red there. She was all around me. And yet, never really there at all.

I didn't know why she hid from me. And truth be told, I wasn't sure I wanted to find her anymore. If I wanted to stay under the Baylor phenomenon spell, then why should I pursue her? I felt obligated to do right by Walker, and help him find his happily ever after, but maybe the best thing for him was not a girl who had run away, but rather a girl who was willing to give up everything just to be with him.

I had been looking for Layla all summer, but aside from the sighting at the Fourth of July parade, she'd kept herself hidden well. And tonight, she had steered me in the wrong direction. If I didn't know any better, I'd say she was dangerous. Perhaps I should be the one running from her.

All I'd wanted to do tonight was tell my gran I'd fallen in love and that I was here to stay. Instead, I was led deep into the woods, chasing a red cloak of ill will and mystery. And then it hit me all at once. The red figure was a symbol, and I was in another fairy tale. That was the *something* I'd remembered about her. Something that was familiar. It wasn't déjà vu. It was a story my gran had read to me, time and time again, when I was a child.

The fairy tales my gran had read to me had always been the key to finding Layla. But maybe I didn't want to find her anymore—in fact, maybe I wanted to hide from her. She was out here in the woods with me, and I wanted nothing to do with her. The fairy tale wasn't a key to finding answers; it was a warning sign. Gran was reading the stories so I would know how to prepare myself for what lurked around the corner. Poisonous apples, witches, and warlocks hidden in stone towers. I looked over my shoulder, because the only thing missing now was a wolf.

As soon as the thought entered my head, I felt the presence. It had been stalking my every step. Watching and waiting for the moment I grew weak and frightened. Because the moment I let my guard down was the moment it would pounce on me. My heart galloped in my chest. My skin broke out in tiny goosebumps. I trembled, because that moment was right *now*.

A deep, wet growl ripped through the fog, piercing my ears as I gasped and spun around. I shut my eyes tight and held my breath—one that would surely be my last. But the attack never came. Instead, I found myself tangled in my gran's crocheted blanket. My heart was nearly leaping out of my chest, and my skin was covered in a thin sheen of sweat. My wide eyes searched my surroundings. The dark bedroom. The cabin. Again. *Always.*

I closed my eyes, rolled onto my belly, pressed my face deep into my pillow, and I screamed.

2

I was standing on the back deck waiting for Walker. The morning dew had evaporated, and the air was warm and dry. The daisies were sunbathing and the bees were buzzing. Gunner played on the shore with a stick, and the guys were down by the dock practicing their golf swing using my dad's old clubs. Most of them had probably never played, but that hadn't stopped them from entering the Baylor Celebrity Golf Tournament.

Baylor was a small, hokey town around the base of a Great Lake. Needless to say, we didn't have celebrities. The golf tournament celebrities were usually B-list TV anchors or a basketball player who nobody had ever heard of, and of course there was always a lot of alcohol. The alcohol was for two reasons: to keep the cash flowing freely, and so nobody called attention to the missing celebrities. I could never understand why they hadn't just changed the name of the tournament. The Water's Edge Golf Tournament sounded just as good to me.

"Hey, Kins, why don't you give it a shot?" Noah called out. I'd been in the tournament several summers ago, but I wouldn't be attending this year.

"Maybe later," I yelled back.

"There's not going to be a later. We're leaving soon." Noah rested the golf club across the back of his neck and lazily draped his wrist over the other end of it. It sent my eyes traveling down the length of his body.

"Sorry!" I held up my coffee mug as if I were too busy. The truth was, that ship had sailed long ago.

"Well, you're at least going to come watch us, right?"

I opened my mouth to reply, and then clamped it shut when Emma stepped out onto the deck. "Are you ready for the library?" she asked.

"Yeah, I'm just waiting for Walker." I checked the time. "He should be here any minute."

Noah jogged up the hill, and I hid my face behind my mug. I didn't want to do this song and dance with him any longer. But having *the talk* with him was even more daunting. I had been trying to convey my feelings toward him through bodily cues, and I'd thought it was working—but it apparently wasn't enough. I could tell from the look in his eyes that he knew our time had come and gone, but it didn't stop him from trying, and I respected that, though I didn't have to like it.

"Hey, Kins, you're coming to the tournament, right?" he asked, a little winded.

Emma scoffed. "Golf? We have research to do."

Noah looked at me, and I sighed. "Sorry, we have plans for the library today." I spotted Walker out on the lake. He was only a tiny dot on the water. Noah must have noticed my change of expression, and he looked over his shoulder. He stared at Walker for a moment, and then glanced down to the ground, defeated.

"What's more important than the golf tournament? They have alcohol . . . and Sampson says he knows a girl who works the cart. We can buy beer from her. And Mason is going to bring some mixed drinks in his thermos."

"I'm sure you guys will have a blast, but—"

"There are celebrities there!" Noah continued, as he checked over his shoulder again.

"Oh my god, do you mean Parker Shallon?" Emma asked.

"Who's Parker Shallon?" I should have known by her expression that it didn't matter who Parker Shallon was. I'd probably never heard of the guy.

"He's the childhood actor from that show with the fence. You know, they were always meeting in the backyard? And the fence covered that guy's face?" Emma covered her face with her coffee mug, and I laughed.

"Oh yeah, that guy. He's the celebrity this year?" I asked.

Noah clenched his jaw. He'd lost the argument, and he appeared ready to concede defeat. He looked over his shoulder again, and I followed his gaze. Walker was paddling into the cove. A swarm of butterflies erupted in my stomach, but I tried not to let it show on my face.

"They have golf carts. You can be our caddie, and I'll let you drive," Noah said.

Emma looked between us and tapped her foot. "You realize she has a golf cart in the garage, right?" Noah glanced behind him again, and I widened my eyes at Emma.

He was trying awfully hard to get me to join him today, and I was starting to feel bad. "Look, we need to figure out this whole dream thing. If we can understand it, we can control it. And then we can do whatever we want." I shrugged, making it sound simpler than it was.

Noah took some practice swings as Walker climbed the hill to the cabin. "Like what?" he asked.

"I don't know, Noah, like win a golf tournament. Wouldn't you like that?" He glared at me, silently reminding me that there was something else he wanted. If only he had a choice. My eyes flickered to Walker, and I smiled.

"Morning," Walker said. Noah took a swing—a warning shot. "Nice swing you've got there. Try twisting at the hips, you'll get a better follow through." Walker swiveled his hips in demonstration, and my brows shot sky high. Noah's face turned red with fury. Emma's was red for an entirely different reason.

"D-did you used to play?" Emma stuttered.

"A little when I was a kid. My uncle used to take me to lessons." Walker smiled up at me, and his dimples cast shadows on his cheeks. A small hum escaped my throat, and Noah shot me a deadly glare.

The air thickened with enough tension to attract a curious bee. It buzzed by, taking multiple passes. Noah swatted at it mindlessly as he tried to talk up Parker Shallon. The rest of the guys climbed the hill to join us. My back stiffened when I saw the bee fly toward Walker, but before I could say anything at all, it flew straight through him. My breath hitched in my chest. The bee had flown *through* him, as if he was made of air . . . Maybe he was?

I watched Walker's expression closely. He hadn't noticed the bee penetrate his chest and pierce through the other side, and neither had anyone else. It reminded me just how different Walker was than the rest of us, and I wondered if he was invincible here in Baylor.

"Kins?" Kai asked.

"Huh?" Everybody was looking at me. Waiting for something.

"She was the weather girl on channel five. She was the celebrity in the tournament a few years back . . ." I looked at Kai blankly as his words trailed off. "Her name. Do you remember her name?" Kai laughed, shaking his head.

"Oh! Um, Shelly Trot," I said. Kai snapped his fingers, and everybody agreed.

"I wish Trot was going to be there instead of Parker Shallon." Mason suddenly recoiled, swatting at the bee.

"Oh, shit!" Asher jumped sideways. We laughed at him as he ran, belly first, across the lawn. He waved his hands aimlessly through the air, making us laugh even harder.

The kitchen window slid open, and Kimber yelled out, "Run!" without an ounce of humor in her tone.

"Oh, yeah, isn't he allergic?" Mason asked.

Asher tripped and rolled down the hill, causing the laughter to stop. "Like how allergic?" Noah asked.

"*Deathly* allergic!" Kimber yelled from the window. I froze in place, unable to think of a way to help. Asher scrambled to his feet, kicking up tufts of grass in his wake, and charged for the cabin.

"Hurry!" Emma waved him on.

Asher took the steps three at a time; the bee was mere inches from his back. I swatted at the air, trying to fight the beast off, but it was no good. At the exact moment that Asher reached for the door, Kimber barged through from the other side brandishing an EpiPen. The door slammed into Asher, pushing him backward into the bee.

We held our breaths and watched helplessly as Asher gathered his wits. At first, we didn't know if he'd been stung or if he was simply stunned from the blow to his head. He stood, eyes wide and blinking rapidly. I couldn't see or hear the bee any longer.

Everyone looked at one another uncertainly until Asher made a small, scratchy sound in his throat. Kimber pulled the cap off the EpiPen and dropped to her knees. She raised her arm and thrust the needle into Asher's thigh. I gasped. Emma dropped her coffee, splashing it on everybody near her and shattering one of my homemade ceramic mugs. Gunner barked with excitement.

Mason and Kai grabbed Asher and carried him inside. Kimber dropped the pen, fell to her butt, and started to cry. I kneeled down next to her and stroked her shoulder. "You were so brave, Kimber. How did you know how to do that?"

"His mom taught me. She tells me all the time where he keeps the pen. We practiced together one night when she was drunk. She accidentally injected her sofa," she sobbed.

Walker squeezed my shoulder as he passed by. He went into the cabin to check on Asher, and Emma busied herself picking up broken pieces of ceramic from the deck. "I don't want him to die. Kinsley, I don't want him to die!"

"Nobody is going to die." It wasn't until the words left my mouth that I realized just how foolish a statement that was. Somewhere inside, there was a calendar that showed precisely how many more of us would die this summer. Eight. Eight of us would. And the probability that one of those eight was Asher was pretty high.

"That's not true. You know that's not true," she said.

I ran my hands through my hair, trying to think of something else I could say to help calm her, but there was nothing.

"Look, maybe we can learn how to bring him back?" Emma said, hopefully.

"What?" I shot Emma a look. Not only was that doubtful, but it wasn't something I wanted to try. I'd seen movies before about raising the dead—it never ended well.

"Can you do that, Kinsley? Can you bring him back? Because I can't live without him." Kimber's eyes glistened a pale, sky-blue.

I opened my mouth, but nothing came out.

"Can you?" she asked again, dipping her chin and giving me doe eyes.

I was about to lie when Walker opened the patio door, bumping into my back. "Sorry," he said, looking down at me. My stomach dropped in preparation for the news.

Walker lifted his gaze to Kimber. "He's okay. We couldn't find the stinger, and no sign of swelling—" Kimber scrambled to her feet and blew past Walker mid-sentence.

"He wasn't even stung?" Emma asked.

"Looks like it was a false alarm," Walker said, shrugging. Emma looked at me in surprise, my labor of love broken in her hand. She went inside to see for herself, and I sat on the floor, deep in thought.

Had *I* saved him? Just by thinking about it? There was no way of telling if it was luck or magic, but if I had a choice, I'd say magic.

"What are you thinking?" Walker asked, no longer hiding his concern. His face reflected the same confusion and worry I felt.

"I don't know. I think, I think maybe I reversed it."

"Do you think he was stung?" Walker asked.

"Yes, and then because I was worried for him, I changed the outcome so that he wasn't allergic?" It was a stretch. Walker's lips twitched. I could tell he didn't think I was ready to pull off that kind of magic. And truthfully, he was probably right.

"Well, whatever it was, we need to work on it. If you had full capability and total control of your dreamwork, you could have extinguished that bee the second it came around. Hell, you could make bees extinct, if you wanted." Walker scratched the back of his head, and I could tell he was imagining the possibilities.

"Do you really think so?" I asked. A world without stingers sounded like a nice touch.

"I really do, Wilde. I really do." Walker's eyes burrowed into mine, and I could feel that he was being honest with me. He believed in me.

I smiled, feeling the heat across my cheeks. "Then let's get to it," I said, reaching my hands out. Walker grabbed my hands and pulled me to my feet. While standing, our bodies touched, and we were closer than *just* friends should be, but he didn't seem to mind. It felt natural. We were more than friends, after all. No, we weren't boyfriend and girlfriend, but we weren't just simple friends either. There was something between us. Something bigger than life, and even he couldn't deny it. I planned to whittle it away until there was nothing left except the bare truth.

Walker pushed open the door to the cabin, and I followed him inside. Asher looked perfectly fine. His face was red, but I imagined that was because of embarrassment more than anything else. "Are you feeling okay?" I asked.

"Yeah, I'm fine. Everything except my thigh," Asher said, glaring at Kimber and rubbing his leg.

"What? I was trying to save your life!" Kimber argued.

"You stabbed me! I wasn't even stung!" he said in a high-pitched voice.

"How was I supposed to know that?" Kimber raised her hands and turned away, shoulders hunched.

"Listen, we'd better get going or we're going to be late for the tournament. Kins, you're coming with us, right?" Noah asked, nodding as if it was a done deal.

I jutted my head back; did he really think I was going with them? I had already told him I wasn't. Walker looked at me questioningly, and I frowned. "No. I said we were going to the library. We're doing research." My tone was quick and cutting, and Noah's cheeks flushed under my scorn.

"Okay, okay. Sorry. I thought you told me you were going to go." He shook his head and looked at the floor. I knew what he was trying to do, but I wasn't giving in. It aggravated me that he was being so pushy. He didn't like Walker one bit. And that was going to be a problem.

Kimber and Asher stayed back in the cabin. As much as Asher would deny it, I think he was more rattled than he let on. His hands were shaky, and he looked sick to his stomach. The others headed off to the golf tournament, and I knew they would have fun. A piece of me was jealous. I wanted to go, but I knew my work at the library was far more important. When all this was over, and I was the master of my destiny, I could make everyday Celebrity Golf Tournament day if I wanted. For today, Emma, Walker, and I headed out to the library. It was a nice day, so we walked the mile and a half into town.

3

While our walk had started out pleasant enough, it had warmed significantly by the time we were halfway to the library. The nape of my neck was hot and sticky, so I pulled my hair back into a bun with the elastic I carried on my wrist. We talked about how bizarre it was that Asher hadn't been stung and all the ways it could have ended, but hadn't. Emma was convinced that he was going into shock from the trauma, and I thought I'd seen signs of that too. But Walker said that it was just the Baylor phenomenon. That I wouldn't have been able to reverse a moment in time without proper training.

"Do you think she will be able to time travel?" Emma asked, using one hand to shade her eyes from the sun.

"I think that's just the tip of the iceberg. I think this thing is massive. We have no idea what she is capable of, or how quickly she'll learn. From blowing out candles with her mind, to bringing back the dead . . ." Walker's words sent a chill down my hot spine. Goosebumps prickled my arms despite the heat of the day.

He looked up at the sky and frowned. I followed his gaze to see an enormous black crow circling above. *Levi.* By the look on Walker's face, he'd known there was something peculiar about the bird, but he didn't say anything. It made me wonder about all the times we had shared before. How much had I missed? And how much had he hidden from me?

"Bring back . . . the dead? As in, Lainey?" Emma asked. It was a nice idea, of course, but it only reminded us she wasn't here to begin with, and the sadness seemed to hit both of us again.

"Maybe," Walker said.

Emma glanced at the bird and her breathing deepened. "And Levi?" she asked, in a small, faraway voice.

"Maybe."

The crow cawed above, and I wondered how long he'd been following us. I wondered if was possible for me to bring Lainey back? And Levi? But what kind of person would that make me? Would I be dark? Would I be evil? Or would that make me a goddess?

"And what about *you*? Could she bring *you* back?" Emma asked.

My heart froze in my chest. It stopped beating completely and then sputtered, kicking back into rhythm. I bent at the waist, coughing, and Walker patted my back.

What about him? I wondered. Could I bring him back? Was it possible? He'd been a ghost for so long. Was there an expiration on this type of magic? I cocked my head to see Walker's expression, and it alarmed me. He wasn't in shock like I was—he'd thought about this before. His jaw was set firm and square, and his eyes narrowed into tiny slants. Had this been his plan all along?

"Are you okay?"

"Yeah," I said, slapping my chest. But Emma's question went unanswered as we reached the library.

"After you," Walker said, holding the door open.

Emma smiled and dipped under his arm, seeming to forget all about her question. But my thoughts were a jumbled mess. I couldn't stop thinking about that bird stalking us and the idea of raising the dead. I paused, passing Walker, staring him in the eyes. It seemed he'd had big plans all along. Ideas that he'd never shared. He'd said he wanted to train me, but what for? I wasn't sure. His golden eyes told no secrets. I bit my bottom lip and entered the library. Walker's gaze was hotter than the sun could ever be, and passing him in the doorway was like jumping through a ring of fire. I was thankful for the cool air conditioning.

The library was small but rich in literature. What it lacked in size was made up for by the cozy ambiance. It was an old historical library, and it had been here for as long as I could remember—apart from the fact that it had recently moved itself down the street. Regardless, it had all the classics. But perhaps the best part was the smell. The smell of the books, worn thin and well loved. I'd never been a reader, but that didn't stop me from wishing I were. I'd always wanted to lose myself in a good story, the way my gran did—the way Emma does. Instead, I lost myself in the depths of my twisted subconscious. Oh how I wished I could dog-ear the page and close the book on my mind when I grew weary and tired.

Emma's eyes beamed, all but forgetting the crow in the sky and how somber she'd felt just moments ago. "Do you mind if I—"

"No. Go for it." It's not like Emma would be able to concentrate until she checked out whatever book was on her mind, anyway. She'd been trying to get through the library's fantasy section over the summer, and she had made a sizable dent already. Emma scampered off to the back of the library, disappearing into the aisles of books. Walker took my hand and led me to the small section of personal development books. I picked through them, frowning at the titles and feeling like I was broken and in need of self-help. I turned to glare at Walker, but he was oblivious to my concerns.

"I've heard of this book; it teaches you how to become lucid in your dreams. There's technique involved, stuff I don't know yet. Probably stuff I can't find online. These books are ancient, and there is information here that you can't find anywhere else. Trust me, I've tried." Walker glanced at me and flinched. "What's wrong?"

"The self-help section. Really?"

"No, it's not like that . . ."

"Oh, yeah?" I held up a book titled *How to Be Everything You're Not*.

Walker rolled his eyes and turned his attention back to the shelf, running his fingers down the spines of the books. "It's not here. That can't be right."

"Are you sure they had it?" I asked, stuffing the book I probably should have checked out back on the shelf.

"Positive. I called before we came." Walker looked frantically through the bookshelf.

"Well, maybe we can just start with another one?"

"We can't start with another one. That is the *only* one. It's called *Waking Dreams*, and it is the only book here about dreams and the first one ever written on the topic." Walker crouched down, checking the books at knee level.

"I'll go check with the librarian. Maybe she pulled it, expecting you to come?" I asked.

"Okay. Good thinking. I'm just going to poke around here. In case it was put back out of place."

I turned around slowly and went in search of the librarian. But when I got to the checkout counter, she wasn't there. As I waited, idly drumming my fingers on the counter, I let my eyes wander around the little library until they landed on a girl drawn into a book at a small desk against the back wall. I hadn't seen her when we'd come in. She had lush dark hair that draped in front of her face as she read. Nobody has hair that pretty . . . except . . .

"Can I help you, dear?" a rickety old voice asked.

I spun around to find the librarian standing behind the counter as if she'd appeared out of thin air. She was an elderly lady, probably not more than four feet tall. Her nose was bulbous and red, and she had short, gray scraggly hair. Her eyes were beady behind her thin-rimmed glasses, and for reasons I couldn't understand, it felt like her eyes could see right through me.

"Hi. My friend called earlier this morning about a book. I think he said it was called *Waking Dreams*. We're having trouble finding it. Do you know where it is?" I asked, averting my eyes.

"Oh . . ." The librarian patted her pockets and then reached up to the top of her head, searching for something. She only stopped looking once she pinched the silver metal rim of the glasses that were resting on her nose.

"I thought maybe you pulled it earlier. Could it be up here with you?"

"I remember a young man calling about that book, but I didn't take it off the shelf. A young lady came in asking for it just moments ago. It must be a popular book today."

"Really?" My stomach tumbled. I knew there was something going on with that girl in the back.

"Sorry dear." The librarian gave me a smile. "Is there anything else I can help you find?"

"No, thank you."

I peeked again at the girl in the back, and I found Emma nose deep in fantasy, one aisle away. She was so entranced in what she was reading, she didn't see me coming, and I spooked her. She let out a squeak, drawing attention to herself. The librarian scowled, and I smirked.

"Dear god, never do that again," she hissed.

"Sorry. Hey, did you grab the *Waking Dreams* book already?" I asked. I pointed to the book she was reading.

"No. Sorry. This is all dragons and castles."

"Do you mean dragons and castles with big barbarian shirtless men with oil-slicked, tan bodies?" I asked, with a tilt of my head. It was like confronting an addict.

Emma's face turned a swarthy red as she lifted the book to hide her face. The cover was exactly what I'd imagined it would be. Bronzed pecs and an eight-pack of abs. I shoved Emma, and she stifled a giggle.

"I think you'll find that in the philosophy section, right? Or maybe personal development?" She pointed in Walker's general direction, dismissing me to anywhere in the library but here. I grabbed hold of her book and lowered it from her face. Her pupils were dilated, and I briefly wondered what exactly she was reading.

"Look, you have all night to read this book, but right now, we're in search of the dream book. The librarian said that a girl already checked it out, and I hoped it was you."

"Yeah, no. I'll help you look. Just let me finish this page real quick."

"Okay. Come find us when you're done."

I headed back to Walker but stopped when I saw the girl in the back corner. She was the only other girl in the library, and she had to be the one reading that book. I peered at her through the bookshelves, trying to get a clear view of her face. She absently brushed her hair back, revealing her profile. "Well, I'll be damned," I whispered. It was Layla after all. I knew I'd recognized her hair.

From the moment I'd decided I didn't want to find her, she'd started finding me.

I strolled down the aisle, peering over the tops of the books, trying to get a better glimpse of the mysterious Layla Barns. My heart pounded in my chest like I was about to enter a battle. With Layla being here, so close, this could all end for me in a matter of minutes. I could go back to my real life—wake up in the hospital bed in Decord City, just outside of Clover. I could deal with my wounds and properly mourn my grandmother. Or should I pretend I'd never seen her? I could stay here in Baylor for the rest of my life, learning magic and figuring out how to get Walker to fall in love with me.

Layla tucked her hair behind her ear, exposing the bridge of her nose, the curves of her lips, and the line of her chin. It was the first time I had taken in her beauty, and in that moment she reminded me of the beautifully poisonous red apple in the haunted forest. She seemed perfect on the outside, but what lay within?

Layla had what I wanted. She had Walker's heart. But now that I wanted a life here, she had so much more than that. Layla symbolized a great threat to me. That girl had the power to take my love, take my manifestations, and take my dreams straight out from under me. And I didn't like it one bit. I felt utterly powerless compared to her, and that made my skin crawl.

And now, of all things, Layla wanted to learn about lucid dreaming. Why? Somehow, she knew I needed that book. Somehow, she'd known that Walker and I would look for it today. There was something in *Waking Dreams* that she needed to get to before I did. I had to get that book.

Without realizing it, I had taken several tiny steps, inching myself toward Layla. I found myself standing directly behind her, so close I could reach out and run my hands through her silky brown locks. I froze in place and tried to swallow through my suddenly dry throat. All I wanted to do was run away, but instead, I found myself drawn to her like a magnet.

I worried Walker would find her sitting in the back of the library and realize she had no desire to close the distance between them. She must not love Walker the way I did, and it broke my heart. She didn't deserve him.

"Hey, I'm done reading. I made myself close the book for you. Do you even know how hard it is to close a book once you've read the first line of the next chapter?" Emma whispered from behind me, startling me from my trance.

I wanted nothing more than to hide Layla's presence from Emma and Walker, but she was right here, inches away, and hiding in plain sight. In slow motion, I saw Walker heading in our direction.

"*No. No. No. No.*" I whispered maniacally.

"What? What's wrong?" Emma asked. I whipped my head back toward Layla, and she was looking directly at me. Our eyes locked, and her lips curved in a small, impish smile.

"Can I help you?" Layla asked, her tone like a full-bodied dark chocolate —rich and savory.

Only it wasn't Layla by the time she was done speaking. The curves of her lips had spread wider and flatter. Her long brown hair turned ashy before my very eyes. And by the time Emma laid eyes on her, the girl looked three years younger, and her cheeks were dusted in freckles.

"Oh my god, I'm so sorry. We'll be quiet." Emma placed her finger in front of her lips and motioned for us to find a new place to talk.

The young girl's eyes bounced from Emma to me to Walker. Her chair screeched on the floor as she jolted backward, apparently stunned to see him. She slammed all her books shut and scrambled to collect her papers into a messy heap in her arms. She jumped to her feet, causing her chair to tip over behind her and land on the floor with a thud. She took off running, nearly bumping into Walker on her way out of the little library.

"Miss! You need to check those out! You can't take those books without checking them out!" the librarian called out after her. She waved her fist in the air, but by the time she had gotten out from behind the desk, the girl was gone. And so was the book.

"Doggone it. Kids these days. No respect. No respect at all," the librarian grumbled beneath her breath.

"What was all that about?" Walker asked, approaching us.

"Shhhh!" the librarian hissed. Emma stifled a giggle with her hand.

"She had our book," I said.

"*Waking Dreams*?"

"Yup."

"Dammit. And she just stole it, too." Walker said.

"I doubt she's going to come back here and return it after that debacle," Emma said.

"Well, Wilde, I guess it's just you and me. I've got some things that we can start working on. It won't be as advanced as I'd hoped, but in the meantime, I'll try to keep looking for that book." Walker forced an apologetic smile.

"Don't worry about it, we've got this," I said, nudging his shoulder.

"Hey, maybe we can find that girl?" Emma asked.

"No, I don't think that's necessary—"

"That's a great idea!" Walker said.

"Yeah, she's probably just sitting at the coffee shop two doors down. It's not like this is a big town. We'll just ask her to borrow the book," Emma said.

"Yeah."

"Nooo, I don't think we really need it . . ."

"Come on Kinsley, find the girl, find the book, master your dreams. It will be fun. Plus, what else do we have to do today? Go to the golf tournament?" Emma said with a laugh.

"Shhhh!" the librarian spat at us, still fuming from the stolen books. Emma rolled her eyes and linked her arm with mine. With a slight tug, we were moving through the library and toward the exit.

The last thing I wanted to do was go on another hunt for Layla Barns. It didn't matter if it really was Layla or just a young girl with ashy hair and sweet freckles; whoever she was, she had something we desperately needed. I tried to convince myself that I could do this on my own. And with just a little bit of luck, or perhaps a manifestation, we would find the book and not the girl.

We did, however, see a middle-aged man holding a heap of papers and a stack of books in the coffee shop's window as we passed by. He glared at me through the glass with distrustful eyes. Nobody recognized her but me, and I kept my mouth shut.

4

Walker stayed over for dinner that night, and we talked about all the different ways we could start my training. He thought that channeling my energy seemed like a good place to start, and it would give us something to build on. We were going to start after dinner, and I was eager to see how creative I could get under his direction. I remembered the time he'd coached me to find the lost tower, and how it had felt like make-believe. This time, I would know it was real, and the possibilities were endless. With Layla and I having somewhat of an understanding that she would not interfere and I would keep my distance, I could very well have this whole thing in the bag.

Kimber, Emma, and I made spaghetti while the rest of the group was still at the tournament with their one B-list celebrity. Asher and Walker were talking at the table, and it was nice to see him integrate into the group.

"My leg is a little sore, but it could be worse," Asher said.

"Oh my god, he is such a baby," Kimber muttered.

We dished everything up and brought our dinners to the living room. I sat cross-legged on the carpet, and the TV played faintly in the background. We talked about the fun things we could do if we gained control over the Baylor phenomenon. Mostly funny things, sometimes outrageous—we laughed all the same.

"I don't know about you guys, but I'd start my own football team. I'd be the starting quarterback, and I'd win every single game I ever played. I'd be famous and make loads of money. I'd even be on commercials, and I'd sponsor sports drinks and protein powders," Asher said with stars in his eyes.

Kimber slapped his arm. "Are you serious? That's what you're going to wish for?"

"Yeah, why?"

"You wouldn't take away your bee allergy? Or do something good with your power? You'd just play football?" her voice hitched.

"Well, I mean, it's my dream, right? Why wouldn't I be rich and famous?" Asher scoffed.

"God, you're so pig-headed sometimes, I swear." Kimber shook her head. We all laughed. They sounded like an old married couple.

"Why? What would you do with all the power in the world?" he asked Kimber.

"Well, for starters, I'd pray for you!"

We laughed even harder.

"I think I might open up a library," Emma said. "Maybe I could be a book critic? I don't know, something where I had to read all day, and I would get paid for it."

"Why don't you write a book?" Walker asked.

"Write a book? I don't want to *write* a book. I want to live in one. I want to step into a different world and marvel at every twist and turn. Make one up myself? What's the fun in that? There wouldn't be any surprises . . . That's actually so sad. *Write* a book . . ." Emma had a horrified look on her face. I nodded, thinking she'd already gotten some part of her wish. She was living in a fantasy that she had no control over, and there were certainly twists at every turn. If only I could find a way to get her a paycheck.

I took a bite of spaghetti and then wiped my chin with the back of my hand, wondering what I would do when my powers rolled in. Perhaps I would start to read books. Maybe I'd enjoy them? I could take away my dyslexia, and then I could transport Emma and me into different worlds for the day. We could call them "book trips." Hell, I could even take away Asher's bee allergy. I'd leave the bees but take away their stingers. There would be no venom left in my world. And certainly no poisonous apples.

"What would you do Walker?" Asher asked.

The air shifted, and the room turned quiet. Walker licked his lips and then brushed off the question with some generic lie, but I could tell that whatever he would choose for the world of his making, it absolutely wasn't possible.

We spent some time cleaning the kitchen, and when the dishes were done, Asher and Kimber put on a movie. Emma popped popcorn and joined them on the couch. Walker motioned for the porch, and I nodded, following him outside.

"Aren't you guys going to watch the movie?" Emma asked.

"You start without us. Maybe we'll join later," I said.

Night had fallen and blanketed the cove. The waves lapped gently on the shore below. I stared into the night, knowing the mysterious lake was just beyond the grassy knoll.

"So, I think we need to start out small. Here, take my hands," Walker said, holding out his hands. He didn't need to ask me twice. I slipped my hands into his, eager for his touch.

"Now, see if you can feel the energy." It was hard to concentrate with his golden eyes staring into mine. I felt the energy all right, but it wasn't in my hands.

"What *kind* of energy?"

"The kind that passes through you. Your whole body is made of energy. Try to channel it and draw it into your hands. Once you do that, try to send it through mine."

My hands grew clammy in his, but I blamed it on the energy. I chewed on my lip as I stared up at him, and I began to breathe in quick, shallow breaths. It was late and dark, so I couldn't quite tell, but I thought I caught a blush on Walker's cheeks. If I was right, he was good at hiding his feelings. He kept his stare locked on mine, and I blew out a long heavy breath through puckered lips.

"Here, try to breathe with me. Sync your breath to mine." Walker drew in a deep breath, and I did too. "Wilde?" he asked, tilting his head.

"Yeah?"

"Close your eyes."

Heat spread across my cheeks. "Oh. Yeah, right."

I squeezed my eyes shut and found it much easier to focus without Walker's dimples to distract me. I concentrated on all the energy I had swirling inside of me, and I channeled it into my hands. It must've been working, because my hands grew hot and slick with sweat. A few moments later I felt a tingling in my fingertips. I tried to merge my energy with his, sending little waves of electricity through our touch.

"I think I feel it. It's like tingling all over my hands," he said. I smiled, feeling prouder of myself than I had in a long time. If this was working, and he could feel the tingling of my excitement, I wondered how he would react if I sent my feelings for him through. I dug deep, drumming up all the emotion I had in my heart for him, and I started to push it down my arms, past my elbows, and into the palms of my hands.

"Do you feel that?" he asked with a shiver.

My smile grew, but I kept my eyes shut, and I continued to push and push until he felt the full force of my feelings for him. But just when things started getting interesting, the door behind us was flung open, and a very drunk

Mason and Noah stumbled outside onto the deck with us. I pulled my hands out of Walker's, dropping all the energy I'd collected.

I couldn't read the expression on Walker's face. It had almost looked like he knew what I was trying to do. As if it had actually worked, or was about to. Either way, he looked like he knew a secret but didn't know what to do with it. I could feel the heat rising in my cheeks, and I was so afraid of being rejected, again, that I darted to the bathroom to hide.

"I'll be right back," I said, as I pushed between Noah and Mason. I felt Noah's eyes heavy on my back, but I couldn't think about him right now. I wished I could send my feelings for Noah through a glare; then I'd never have to say it aloud. Regardless, he was drunk now, and anything I said or did wouldn't be remembered come morning.

"Whoa, easy there," Scarlett May said, as I burst through the bathroom door.

"Sorry."

"What's got your panties in a bunch?" She puckered her lips in the mirror as she retouched her lipstick.

"I-I'm falling for a guy who doesn't feel the same about me," I said, shutting the door behind me, trapping Scarlett May inside. She patted her lips with her middle finger and glanced at me through the reflection.

"Oh, you mean Noah?" she asked with a nonchalant tone. I scoffed. Apparently, falling for the wrong person was a thing I did. It was on par for me, and everybody knew it. I sighed, pressing the back of my head against the door.

"That was so last month," I said with a small laugh. Scarlett May smiled and turned to me in a moment of understanding that I hardly recognized in her.

"Oh, is it that new guy? That ruggedly handsome one that you've been hanging out with? Walter or whatever? Yeah, he is kind of out of your league." She winced, as if it brought her discomfort. That was the Scarlett May I knew. I could always count on her for the painful truth.

"Walker. And you have no idea . . ."

"Why don't you just tell him how you feel about him and get it out of the way? Sometimes, confidence is the sexiest thing about a person. And the best part about that is, you can fake it." Something shifted in Scarlett May's face, and I could tell that this was a candid moment for her. A moment where she was letting her guard down and showing her true self. She was never like that with me, although I imagined she had been with Trinity.

"I've done it before, and it works like a charm. Almost every time. And if he doesn't like you, then you just keep on acting. Act like you couldn't care less and it's his loss. Usually, if it doesn't work the first time, it'll work the second time." Scarlett May placed a hand on my shoulder with a tender touch. Maybe there was a caring side to her after all. I smiled at her in a split second of gratitude before her tender touch turned icy and she pushed me out of the way. She was just trying to leave the bathroom. I sidestepped, feeling slightly stupid.

"Thank you," I said. She winked at me before disappearing.

Scarlett May was right. I had nothing to lose. I was on my deathbed somewhere out there, and either I fell in love with this world that I'd created, or I'd go back home, to all the problems I never wanted to see again. I'd never told Walker that he should be with me instead of Layla. I'd never told him I was falling for him. But that was going to change. I was going to march right out there, and I was going to tell him. Tonight. Right now. I might not look him in the eye while doing it, but the words were going to come out. And when he turned me down, like he always did, I was going to pretend that it was his loss.

I opened the door and strode down the hall, through the kitchen, and out to the back patio. But when all I saw was Mason and Noah, my plan came crumbling down in a heap of failure. "Where's Walker?" I asked.

"You didn't even ask how our game was," Noah said, slurring his words. I looked around, aggravated.

"Where is Walker?" I crossed my arms.

Mason laughed. "I told him that Noah was basically your boyfriend, and that he was breaking code by hanging around. I told him he better leave you alone, or else . . ."

"You what!"

I turned to scan the lake for Walker, but the night was too dark, and I couldn't see past the halo of the patio lights. I pushed past Noah and Mason as they continued to make fun of Walker. I ran down the hill, nearly slipping on the dew-slick grass on my way down. I ran to the end of the dock, and I could just see the tail end of a canoe disappearing into the night. I threw my head back, panting, as I looked up toward the stars. Would I ever catch a break? I listened to the quiet trickle of his paddle long after the canoe was out of sight. I stood staring at the twinkling stars until I couldn't hear him any longer. He was gone, and so were my hopes of faking confidence.

Noah had been a problem for me since the incident with Trinity, but I didn't know where Mason had gotten the idea to ruin things for me too. I intended to find out. I marched up the hill with the same determination I'd originally had for faking my confidence. I marched right up to Mason, chest to chest, and I put my finger in his face. "What the hell did you do that for?" I said, seething.

"Whoa. Calm down, Kinsley. It was just a joke." Mason held his hands up in the air.

"Does it look like I'm laughing Mason? Why did you do that to him?" I asked, pointing toward the lake.

"Honestly? Because Noah can't get you on his own. He needs help from his wing man—"

"Nooo . . ." Noah said.

"That's me. I'm the wingman. I told him I could do it. And I did. Right?" Mason held his knuckles out to Noah and they fist bumped.

"Walker was my guest. And I don't appreciate you telling him to leave my cabin. How would you like it if I told *you* to leave?"

"Whoa, whoa, whoa. You can't tell me to leave! We're trapped here, remember? We're trapped here because you and your twisted little mind got us caught here. You're like a black widow and we're just stuck in your web." Mason flailed around, pretending to be caught in a web. He barely managed to lift one leg without falling to the ground.

"Yeah, Kinsley. You don't need that guy. You should be with me."

It was Noah's turn to feel my wrath. "Look. I didn't want to do this right now, when you only have half a mind, but you leave me no choice. *I. Don't. Like. You.*" I said, poking his chest with every word.

"Whoa there, you don't need to be such a b—"

"Hey! Hey, don't talk to her like that!" Noah said, shoving Mason. I took a cautious step backward.

"I'm just saying . . . "

"Well don't say!" Noah snapped.

Noah got in Mason's face, and I pushed them apart, squeezing myself in the middle. Out came my finger one more time. "Mason. If you don't go to bed right now and leave me be, you will see the full wrath of my *twisted little mind.*"

I was acting, of course—something I'd just learned from Scarlett May—but it worked. Mason clamped his mouth shut and turned around. He stumbled into the cabin, never turning back. I had fire in my eyes by the time the door slammed shut.

"Noah, I don't know how much of this you are going to remember in the morning, but I want you to understand right now that I don't have feelings for you. And if you continue to get in the way of Walker and me, we're going to lose our friendship as well."

Noah's face took on a swarthy hue, and he looked like he had sobered up considerably.

"But you used to have feelings for me, right? Or did I make that up?"

"Yes, Noah. I liked you. I liked you a lot. But the moment you chose Trinity over me, that changed. You're a great guy, and we've been friends for a long time. There *was* a chance for something more. But what we had, all the flirting, it's over now. It's nothing. And you have to let me go." It was difficult being angry with someone who looked so sad.

Noah's blue eyes were flanked red with broken blood vessels. I could tell that his last shred of hope had finally died. He opened his mouth to say something and then ultimately shut it again and nodded. He turned to walk away but stopped when his hand reached the doorknob. "Just tell me one thing. Why him?" he asked.

"I don't know, Noah. I guess I'm a sucker." It was the only thing the two guys had in common. They both had eyes for another girl. And I deserved more than that.

"I'm sorry about Trinity. Nothing happened. *Not really*. I mean, a little bit . . . but—"

"I know!" I pinched the bridge of my nose. "It's okay. It's over."

Noah's head dropped, and he opened the door. It slammed shut behind him with a bang, causing me to jump. I took a long, cleansing breath and ran my hands through my hair. It was over. The long-awaited talk was over. I only hoped I wouldn't have to repeat myself in the morning.

If I'd learned one thing tonight, it was how to fake my own competence. I looked toward the invisible horizon, and I wondered if that was the key to manifestation, too. If I pretended I believed in myself, would it be enough? I wrinkled my nose, a bit giddy with the thought, and turned when I heard the sound of a shovel digging into dirt.

It was dark enough that I could only make out the shadow of a man digging a hole, but I knew who it was. And I also knew that he and his wife had moved, or were attempting to. That house wasn't being lived in, yet Mr. Vandal was gardening late in the night? Why?

I rested my chin in the palm of my hand as I watched him dig the hole, wondering how deep it had to be to hide a body. What the hell was going on over there? The boys had broken in before to rescue Gunner, but I wanted to see it for myself. Something weird was going on with the neighbors, and I wouldn't be able to rest until I knew what. I had a weird feeling in my chest, a whispering in my ear, that he might just be the wolf.

5

I was still exhausted when I woke the next morning. We had to do something different today. I was starting to resent this cabin, this bed, and these sheets. The only thing that changed here was the dwindling number of roommates I had. I didn't want to go downstairs and face Noah and Mason. The thought of having to tell Noah I no longer had feelings for him all over again was excruciating. I squeezed my eyes shut, hoping that when I opened them again I'd be somewhere else. Anywhere else. I lay in bed like that for an hour, maybe more. And I didn't get up until I'd convinced myself that I could at least change something today. Something small. Today, I'd leave Baylor.

I got out of bed, and shouted down the hall, "Emma, Scarlett May, Kimber, get ready! We're going out!" I yelled.

I went back to my bedroom, excited for something new. On the opposite side of the lake, there was a train station. We were going to ride it as far as it would take us. We wouldn't get far, of course, and at the end of the day, we'd be back here eating leftover pizza. But at least I would feel free momentarily, like a dog with its head out the window of a car and its jowls flapping in the wind. I needed this for me. And the girls? They probably needed it just as much.

"Where are we going, Kins?" Emma asked.

"We're getting train tickets. We can eat lunch on the train. It will be fun."

"But, I mean . . . where are we going?"

"Well, I figured we'll get tickets to San Pearson, and we'll see how far we can get," I said.

Emma shrugged. "I don't mean to be rude, but what's the point of that?"

"Emma, it's not the destination, it's the journey. You know that." I smirked.

"Okay. You're right. Let's go explore."

Scarlett May never asked where we were going. She was just happy to get out of the cabin. She'd been spending a lot of time with Sampson and his friends, but he was busy today. And after spending the previous day with Asher berating her about the EpiPen stabbing, Kimber was also eager to get out. I wanted to talk to Walker about what Mason had told him last night, but he wasn't answering my texts, and I figured it would be best to give him a little space as well. If he didn't answer me by tomorrow, I'd march over there myself and bang on his door.

The taxi dropped us at the train station. It was busy for a Wednesday, but most days were buzzing like this during summer. It was always easy to tell who was coming, who was going, and who the locals were. Some families were sunburned; the ones who were heading back home from a stay at the lake. The newly arriving families had a polished look, like they'd just stepped out of air conditioning. The humidity hadn't frizzed their hair yet, and their skin wasn't yet scorched by long hours in the sun. The ones in flip-flops with brightly colored bathing suit straps peeking out from under their tank tops were the ones who lived here or had been here for at least a couple of days.

The four of us sat down on a bench and waited for the train while I profiled every person who walked through the station. I liked to imagine who they were and who they strove to be. Sometimes I wondered what their love life was like. Were they lonely? Were they happy? Creative? Disciplined? A secret genius? Were they even human . . . ?

I watched a girl dig through her backpack looking for something. She was most likely a student. Studious and high-strung. I wondered what she was trying to find. A snack? ChapStick? Or perhaps she had lost her cell phone? She pulled out a book, and the title stunned me. *Waking Dreams*. I sucked in a quick breath as the stranger's hair grew long and lustrous, bounding over her shoulders and stretching to her waist. Her button nose morphed in her sunlit profile, and the shadows shifted on her cheeks, making her jawline sharp and angular. Before I knew it, I was sitting one row over from Layla Barns. I couldn't help but stare, wondering if she knew I sat before her. Or had she bought a ticket for the train today because she knew I'd be here?

I glanced over at Emma, trying not to cause alarm, but it was clear she hadn't seen Layla yet. Kimber and Scarlett May had no idea who she was because they'd never seen her before, but if Emma spotted her, all of this would be over. If I could somehow hide her, there was a possibility that Layla wouldn't show herself to them. Just like she'd hidden in plain sight at the coffee shop as we'd passed by searching for her. She opened the book to a dog-eared page and began reading.

"Kinsley? Are you listening?" Kimber asked. I tried my best to engage, but all I could do was worry that my name had been called out loud.

"What? What? What did you say?" I peeked back at Layla, who was still reading her book.

"Are you feeling okay? You look a little pale." Emma said.

"Yeah, I'm fine." I swallowed a lump in my throat.

"So? When do you think we'll get back home?" Kimber asked.

"Oh, Kai said that he made it as far as Pacer Bay, and I figured we would probably do the same. I'm not really sure, but there's no harm in trying, right? Plus, it's probably best to know our boundaries."

"I can make a map," Emma said in a rush. She seemed really excited about the geography project, and I didn't see anyone else fighting for the job.

"Yeah, that's a great idea. You should do that," I said, peeking back at Layla, who was now staring directly at me. I froze. My breath stalled and my chest tightened. I couldn't pry my eyes away. Staring into Layla's eyes did weird, unexplainable things to my insides. The seconds stretched by until somebody walked between us, breaking the eye contact. I looked down at my hands in my lap and fidgeted with my fingers. Had my nails always been this shape? They seemed more square than normal.

"All boarding, San Pearson, Monroe, and Yearsgold. You may now take your seats," a voice called out over the speaker.

"Is that us?" Kimber asked.

"Yes!" Emma said, jumping to her feet. She scooped up her backpack and tucked her book under her arm. "Pacer Bay is about halfway to San Pearson, but we'll just ride it as far as we can."

I fell into step behind the girls, and I didn't dare lift my head. I didn't want to meet Layla's brown, piercing eyes again. It felt like she was looking into my soul, like she could see things in there that nobody else could. Things I didn't want to look at myself. Things . . . I didn't even know existed. I guess being dead did that to you. It was like that with Walker, too. He saw me like nobody else did. And I liked the way he looked at me—really looked at me. But when Layla did it, it was intrusive. *Rude*.

"Where should we sit?" Kimber asked Scarlett May.

"Try to get one of those little cubbies where the two benches face each other. That way we can all fit together. I think they're in the back," Scarlett May said, pointing to the rear of the train.

I shuffled my feet behind Emma, and once we stepped into the train, I lifted my gaze. The carriage was long, and the aisle seemed to go on forever. Some sort of optical illusion. I squinted to see if it would help and then recoiled when I saw Layla. She was sitting in the first row, and she was staring up at me.

I let out a shutter and jolted back, stepping on the stranger's toes behind me. I whirled around to apologize, but stopped cold as I met her soul-piercing eyes. Standing behind me with a scowl was another Layla. I looked down at my feet and muttered something like an apology.

When I turned around again, the line had moved forward, and Layla was back in the first row. Still staring. My head pounded. I couldn't take the tricks she was playing on me. I felt weak, incapable of defending myself against her power. As I scurried to catch up to my friends, I passed a third Layla sitting on the opposite side of the train.

I winced at the throbbing in my head. I searched row after row. More Laylas. There must have been dozens. And each of them was staring at me with those god-awful eyes. I hooked my gaze over my shoulder, and all the Layla's had turned around, watching my every move. I was the entertainment, center stage in a sea of brown eyes.

Emma, Kimber, and Scarlett May hadn't noticed that all the passengers had looked like a clone of one another. They chatted easily among themselves.

"There! There's one in the back. Hurry, grab it!" Scarlett May said. Emma slid into the seat, tossing her backpack to the ground.

"This is perfect," Kimber said.

Had the illusion been curated for my eyes only? Could they not see her? *Them*?

"They have food on these things, right?" Emma asked.

"You've never been on a train?" Scarlett May asked.

I sat down slowly on the open bench, my gaze fixed on the Layla to my left and the book at which she held. She must be the real one, if she has the book . . .

"When would I have gone on a train? We live in Clover," Emma said.

I leaned into Emma, nudging her with my elbow. When I had her full attention, I discreetly tilted my head toward the Layla on my left. Emma pretended to need something in her backpack. She kicked it to her feet and leaned forward, looking discreetly. Layla's eyes never left mine in a menacing glare. Emma grabbed a ChapStick and put it up to her lips, smearing on a sweet summer watermelon scent, as she whispered in my ear. "What about him?"

Him? I looked back at Layla, and a slow, lazy smile crossed her eyes.

"Well, don't look at him!" Emma hissed in my ear.

"Yeah. You're right. I thought I knew her. *Him.* But I was mistaken." I glanced over one more time, unable to stop. I was drawn to her, like an endangered specimen that might only be seen once in a lifetime. She was rare, and as equally ethereal as she was terrifying. She scribbled something frantically inside the book.

"Seriously, you gotta stop staring at him. You're going to make him anxious," Emma said. "Either that, or he's going to think you like him."

"Oh my god, Kinsley, do you have the hots for that old man?" Scarlett May asked. They were all looking at Layla now. My cheeks flushed and I felt faint.

"No. I thought I knew him from somewhere. That's all."

"Did you ever tell Walter that you liked him?" Scarlett May asked, absentmindedly.

"Who's Walter?" asked Kimber.

"*Walker* . . . And no," I said.

"Did you chicken out? You're such a chicken-shit!" Scarlett May threw her hands in the air.

"No, I was going to, honestly. But when I got outside to tell him, he was gone. Mason told him not to come around anymore. They told him that Noah was my boyfriend," I said.

"Nooo!" Emma gasped.

"Boys will be boys," Kimber said with a shrug.

"More like assholes will be assholes," Scarlett May said.

"Whatever. I just needed a day away from it all. I didn't want to see them after last night. I was glad they were still sleeping off their hangovers this morning when we left. Um, thanks for coming out with me today. I'm glad we're doing this." I kept my voice quiet, conscious of listening ears. I knew Layla would have my head if she knew I was after her man—but what sat next to me wasn't Layla, it was just my fear. An apparition of self-judgment, tucked in the deepest parts of my mind. I tried to ignore it.

"Oh yeah, anytime. We should do it more often. I mean, we are stuck here after all, right? Better make the best of it," Emma said.

"Hey, I've got an idea. How about you figure out how we can win the lottery, and then every day we'll win," Scarlett May said. I raised my brows, pretending to entertain the thought, but I couldn't help myself from glancing over at Layla. I watched as she tore a page out of *Waking Dreams*.

"No, how about you figure out how to reverse time? And then we can reset the day every twenty-four hours like a loop," Kimber said.

"Why? Why would we want to do that?" Emma asked.

The sound of the page being folded in half and creased between running fingertips was louder than the train barreling down the tracks.

"Well, because then we could rob the bank every day, or do whatever the hell we wanted, and there would be no consequences. They'd simply never catch up to us," Kimber said.

I liked the idea of no consequences, but if I were ever to reverse time, it wouldn't be to rob a bank. It would be to get Lainey back.

Layla placed the folded note on her table and stood. When she walked away, it fluttered down to the aisle. She didn't look back as she disappeared down the seemingly infinitely long carriage. My eyes fixed on the piece of paper she'd left behind.

"I'm headed to the restroom," I said, pushing to my feet. I swiped the note from the ground and hurried down the aisle. I could hardly wait to open it. It felt like the note was burning a hole in my hand as I passed row after row of Laylas. When I reached the narrow bathroom door, I hurried inside and slid the lock into place. I took my first full breath since first seeing Layla at the train station. The cabin was tiny, but within these four tight walls, I was free from judgment. I opened the note with trembling hands.

Layla's handwriting was a scribble between paragraphs: *you don't belong here*. I closed my eyes to the throbbing pain at the top of my head.

I know. That was the first thought that came into my head. I knew this wasn't my world, just a temporary holding cell. I couldn't stay here long. But Walker's world was the afterlife, and that belonged to everybody at some point or another. That would be my new home once my transition had completed.

I opened my eyes and faced myself in the mirror. I didn't like the girl staring back at me. *You don't belong here.* I belonged with Walker, though. Our souls were intertwined. How else could he have saved me? How could he have come from an entirely different realm and met me between the living and the dead if we weren't meant to be?

Layla just felt threatened. That's all. She was jealous of me, in the same way I was jealous of her. We were both fighting for Walker's attention. The only difference between us, was that she'd had the chance to be with him all this time, and she'd never taken it. I would not let that happen to me. I would not let her scare me away from Baylor with her stolen books and her red cloaks. I looked away from my reflection. I wouldn't let her deter me either.

I flipped the ripped page over and skimmed through the labyrinth of words. It spoke of dreamwork and how our minds use symbols. This was the exact kind of thing that Walker wanted to read up on. The thing he couldn't find on the internet. I wondered if she'd ripped out this particular page for a reason. I folded it back up and stuffed it in my back pocket. I'd show Walker the next time I saw him. Right after I apologized for Mason and Noah's prank.

When I left the bathroom, I was relieved to see that all the Laylas had reverted to the unique individuals they once were. I smiled at the old man sitting next to us. He looked nothing like Layla, and I was embarrassed to think he may have heard me and the girls talking about him.

"Where did Scarlett May go?" I asked.

"She's getting a snack from the bar. I told her to grab something for you, too," Emma said.

"Thanks."

"Honestly, though, what are we going to do all summer? Are our lives going to be one long endless summer in Baylor Lake? Will I have a perpetual tan, year-round?" Kimber rambled.

"Yeah, Kinsley, we gotta find a way out of here. I mean, I need to go home at some point. My mom's going to start to worry. And I have college in the fall," Emma said.

"I know. I know. I'm working on it," I said, feeling the full weight of the message burning a hole in my back pocket. *You don't belong here.*

I'd made my choice. I wanted to stay. But it was they who didn't belong here. Emma shouldn't have to miss college, and Kimber could have a year-round tan anywhere she lived—even if she had to pay for it. But she didn't have to be trapped in Baylor for that. And Asher, he may never become a famous athlete, but he was going to play football in college. And he had many years ahead of him to do whatever he pleased. It was my responsibility to get my friends home. The ones who survived, anyway.

The train jerked violently, and the passenger car seemed to jump beneath us. Scarlett May came crashing into our cubby, and a variety of snacks flew to the floor as she fell on her hands and knees.

"Whoa, what was that?" Kimber asked, hands pressed against the walls.

The train continued to jerk and jump, as we slid helplessly on the benches, unable to catch ourselves. The horizon jumped by in a zig-zagged motion. A sapling tree slapped the window and scraped alongside the car making a screeching sound like nails on a chalkboard.

"We're off the tracks!" Emma yelled.

I leaned over, trying to get a good look out the window, but everything was moving too fast for me to focus. It was a blur of bushes and trees, and it was clear we were off the rails and still traveling at alarming speeds. The train's whistle sounded, two long cries for help.

Scarlett May climbed onto the seat, and we tried to hold on to anything we could. My hands were spread wide across the bench, and I had one foot pressed against the adjacent seat, pinning me in place. Emma tried to hold on to the walls, but her hands continued to slip.

"No, no, no. Not again," Kimber cried.

"Holy shit! We're going to go off the cliff if we don't stop!" Scarlett May yelled, her face as white as a ghost.

"We have to jump. We have to jump!" Emma screamed, scrambling to her feet, and looking for an exit.

Panic ensued. Screams sounded throughout the passenger car, and the man sitting beside me was frazzled and pale. He looked like he may be having a heart attack. His lips were gray, and the collar of his shirt was ripped open. I wished they were all Laylas now, but they weren't. They were families. *Children.*

"We can't jump; it will kill us!" Kimber screamed.

"What do you think is going to happen when we plunge off that cliff?" Emma yelled back, trying to open the emergency door.

Scarlett May slipped and was knocked down to her knees again. She scraped my legs trying to pull herself up.

I leaned back in my seat and let it all happen the way it wanted to. I knew we'd be home soon, and this was just the way to get there. It wasn't nice. It wasn't neat. Or pretty. It certainly wasn't fair. But the sooner everybody accepted it, the sooner we could move on.

I'd be lying if I said I wasn't scared to plunge off the side of the cliff. I was terrified. And I had an incredible fear of heights. But just like watching a scary movie, I told myself it wasn't real. If I could just close my eyes, it would all be over soon.

I knew how to fake confidence now, and it was a trick I tried while everyone else panicked. My jaw was clenched tight, and my back went rigid, but I would not run this time.

Emma got the door open, and a small handful of passengers jumped. Their screams lingered briefly in the air like tiny wisps in the wind. Emma leapt, and her scream snuffed like a candle as the train barreled forward. She didn't even look back.

Kimber wanted to jump, but she stalled for one second too long, and then it was too late.

The bumpy ride stopped as quickly as it started. We glided through the air. The ground beneath us was just a cloud now, and we soared like Levi had. My stomach leapt into my throat.

The ground was getting closer and closer. Bile filled my mouth. I closed my eyes to the chaos. I tried to ignore the screams as I waited for the crash.

But that wasn't the worst part. The worst part was when I woke up, tangled in my bed sheets, feeling like a prisoner of my own making.

6

The night was long. The girls kept me awake, too frazzled to sleep after crashing to the bottom of the canyon. Emma was the only one who'd made it out in time, and even she was struggling. I couldn't help but feel like they were blaming me for their terror. I knew their fate rested in the palms of my hands, and it wasn't something I was happy about.

I assured them I was heading to Walker's house first thing in the morning, and we were going to get to work on my training. I told them things would be different in no time. And I may have even bribed them a little. It was all I could do when I grew tired and they were still angry with me. Nothing like year-round tans for everyone.

Walker hadn't been answering my texts, but I knew he was staying at the Williams' cabin across the lake. The drive would have taken too long in the golf cart, so I took a cab. By the time I got there, I had checked Layla's note about three times. Each time I expected her handwriting to have disappeared, but it was still there, and it was bolder than ever. As if somehow the indentation from the pen had deepened and the ink spread. I grew anxious about Walker's reaction to her message. Would he take her side? Would he agree with her? Would he forgo my training?

I'd never been to the Williams' cabin before, but I admired the unique cove. The dock was wide and adorned with a fire pit and outdoor lounge chairs. It was a far cry from the rest of the rickety old docks that barely stood on their pilings. Most of the cabins were half dilapidated, and the docks were worse. The Williams' cabin was one of the nicer ones on our end of the lake.

The north side of the lake was something entirely different. It was covered in tiny townhomes, hotels, and summer camps. The coves on the south side of

Baylor Lake were privately owned lots and were usually passed down from generation to generation. That's how we'd gotten our cabin. It had belonged to my uncle Tanner, who got it when his parents passed.

I knocked on the door, surprised by my own strength. I was excited to see him, and it showed in the way my knuckles met the wooden door. I shifted my weight from foot to foot as I waited eagerly. When Walker opened the door, shirtless, I lost the words I'd prepared during the cab ride.

"Kinsley?" he said, looking me up and down. The scar on his brow wasn't bleeding, but it was bruised badly.

"Are you okay?" I reached out to touch his brow, and he pulled back. My hand lingered by his cheek before dropping to my waist. "I'm really sorry about Noah and Mason. They were just being idiots."

"Yeah, I'm not worried about it. You don't have to apologize for them," he said, beckoning me inside. This cabin was more spacious than ours and had an expansive open floor plan. I could see the kitchen, dining room, den, and living room, all at the same time. The view of the lake was breathtakingly beautiful through every window.

"So, this is where you've been hiding out all summer?" I asked, admiring the art on the wall. A buffalo painting hung at eye level. The artist had used thick and textured strokes. I wanted to run my hand over the canvas, but that's not what art was made for. *Look with your eyes, not with your hands,* Mom's voice chimed in my memory.

"More like for a couple decades, but yeah." I pulled my eyes from the painting and watched as Walker's expression turned heavy and solemn.

"It must be lonely," I said, thinking of Mason's threat. "The last thing you probably want to hear is somebody telling you to stay away . . . god, they're such assholes."

Walker scoffed, "Nah, don't worry about it. Walker grabbed the shirt draped over the back of the sofa and slipped it on. I soaked up the sight of his obliques before his white shirt draped lazily over his torso. He was better than the art on the wall. *Look with your eyes, not with your hands . . .*

"What are you doing over here Kinsley? You've never come here."

Kinsley? It felt like a demotion. I liked it better when he called me by my last name. "You weren't answering my texts, and I thought maybe you were going to listen to Mason and stay away."

"No. I wouldn't do that."

"Are you sure?" I asked. I could see that he was mulling something over in his head, and since he'd just called me by my first name, it seemed like there was a lot more going on than he wanted to admit.

"Yeah, I'm sure."

I didn't believe him. I trailed my finger across the back of the sofa, taking slow steps in his direction. "You know Noah isn't really my boyfriend, right?" I asked.

"I mean, whatever. Right?" Walker frowned and turned his back to me.

"Well, no. Not whatever. He's not my boyfriend." I needed him to understand.

"Okay?" Walker said with an aloof shrug.

"Okay. He's *not*. And I'm one hundred percent single." *Did I just say that?* I was so taken aback with my ability to humiliate myself, I forgot to close my mouth, blink, and whatever else it was humans did.

Walker turned around slowly, and I was both mortified to find that he was holding back laughter and relieved to see that he was his old warm self again. I'd somehow managed to single-handedly take all the awkwardness between us and wrap it into one sentence I could never take back. Still, I needed him to know. I couldn't have him walking around thinking I belonged to somebody else. I knew from experience that was a painful burden to carry.

"I . . . I . . . Um, I bet you wish all these things were yours. But this stuff belongs to the Williamses, huh?" I asked looking around, hiding the heat in my cheeks by pretending to look at more artwork.

"Yeah, I don't have that much."

"What do you do when the Williamses come into town?" I asked.

"I mean, I'm not really here, right? I'm only here because you're here, and we want to see each other. I don't exist for the Williams family." Walker sat on the sofa facing the picturesque lake-view window. I sat next to him, my foot tucked beneath me.

"But what about my friends? And everybody in town? They see you?" I studied his bruised brow. It was mostly yellow, with bits of green and blue blooming from the center.

"Does everybody see your grandmother?"

"No, but that's different," I said.

"How so?"

I thought about it long and hard, but in the end, I didn't know the difference. I'd always thought my gran lived in a different realm than Walker, but maybe she didn't. Maybe, just maybe, Walker wanted to be a part of my world in a way my gran didn't. Or perhaps she was just busy looking after my grandpa.

"We're all just ghosts. Most of us don't live in the physical form like I have with you. You're my friend Wilde, and I wouldn't be like this if you weren't here."

"Where would you be then?"

"Oh, I don't know. I'd probably be eating grapes and drinking champagne from one of those white puffy clouds up there," Walker said with a wink. His swollen brow stiffened the wink, but he got the job done. I smiled.

"Hey, I have something I wanted to show you," I said reaching for my back pocket. I felt the corner of the note through the denim of my pocket, but hesitated to pull it out. Something inside me seized up. Would he still want to spend his time with me if he knew Layla disapproved of me being here? Would Walker go back to wherever he'd come from, the realm my gran lived in, and the place where Layla lived when she wasn't haunting me?

I fumbled around my back pocket, sliding my hand inside my jeans and pretending I came up empty. The thought of living under the Baylor phenomenon without Walker was not a pleasant one. And if that were the case, I'd happily return home to the beaten and battered body that lay in the hospital bed. Who knew what awaited me there? Struggle . . . lots and lots of struggle.

"I must have forgotten it," I lied.

"Forgot what?"

"Oh, I heard this thing, it was called a dreamwork. I was going to ask you what you knew about it. I wrote it down . . . just a couple of notes, but I thought you might be interested. It was something about symbols, I can't really remember now," I said, rolling around in the lie I'd just spun.

"That's right. Your mind is a complicated place. A dreamwork is exactly the thing that we need to learn about. That's where your latent mind stores information, and your conscious mind manifests it into a dream like this." Walker waved his hand about. "But your subconscious self doesn't want these dormant thoughts to be out in the open, so it uses dreamwork to manipulate them into signs and symbols to keep them hidden from yourself."

"Dormant thoughts?"

"Yeah. Everything you've ever thought or felt has a home. A place to live, in a dark forgotten corner of your mind."

"That's a scary thought. Are you saying that Baylor Lake might not even be a lake? That it could be a symbol for something that I'm feeling or thinking?" Lainey's ghost pleading to be heard flashed through my head and her voice rang in my ears. *Wake up.*

I jerked my head and shook the thought loose. Walker paused for a moment, studying me. He must think I'm crazy.

"Well, I guess it's possible. Sure, the lake could be a symbol for something you fear. Water can have a lot of meanings. It could mean the thirst for knowledge—"

I laughed. The thought of me dying to learn more was a joke. School had always been slow torture for me.

"—it could mean fear of something you don't have control over. Or new beginnings."

Something I didn't have control over . . . That was more like it.

"Of course, it could be none of those, or several. A body of water in your dream could mean something entirely different from a body of water in mine. That's what's so complicated about dreamwork. Every symbol is unique to its dreamer."

"And just so I'm clear, we can, or we cannot, interpret this dream?" I asked, feeling more exposed than ever. My eyes turned to the expansive window. If that lake were my emotions, we'd have a vat of worries to sort through.

"No, we can't interpret your dream. I mean, we could try?"

"No!" I shook my head, disinterested.

"But it would just be an interpretation. There's no actual way of knowing what your mind is really trying to tell you or hide from you."

"You think my mind's trying to hide stuff from me?"

"Well, yeah. Everybody's mind does that. I think it tries to protect you from the truth. Sometimes, the truth is what we fear most."

I wondered what my mind was hiding from me. If all the terrible things I'd seen here in Baylor were easier to swallow than the truth, I never wanted to wake up. The real world was a scary place. At least in my dreams I could tell myself it was make-believe.

"What do you think your mind is hiding from you?" I asked, tilting my head to the side, enjoying the tables being turned. Walker laughed and an uncomfortable smile crossed his face.

"Let's just focus on you. Are you ready for training?" he asked.

"Okay. I'll get it out of you someday," I said with a smile.

"We'll see about that. Let's start with the basics. Lucid dreaming. Lucid dreaming is when you are aware and conscious that you are dreaming." Walker jumped to his feet and started pacing back and forth in front of the window. The bright morning rays made his form look like a black silhouette of thought, bouncing from one side of the room to the next. "You're conscious you are dreaming right now, right?"

"Yes." Obviously, this was a dream. Look at how handsome he was . . .

"Most of the time, when somebody is aware that they are currently in a dream, it unlocks a sense of control. But this is where we're running into a problem. You don't have that sense of control."

"No. Not all the time."

"Would it be safe to say that *most* of the time you lack the control?" he asked.

"Yeah. Everything seems to happen to me, or around me. Sometimes I feel like I'm on the outside looking in, and very, very seldom I will feel like I can manipulate what's happening. And even then, when I do, it usually turns out badly. Like I shouldn't have meddled with it in the first place." I hooked my arm over the back of the sofa and watched Walker rummage through notes on the kitchen counter.

"I think the very first thing you need to do is remind yourself that you are in control and that you have the power to change what you see. So, remind yourself of that as often as you can. Sometimes a token can help. Um—" Walker patted his pockets and then looked down at a ring on his finger, twisting it for a split second before pulling it off.

"Here, keep this on you at all times. Every time you reach for it, or notice that it's there, remind yourself that you're dreaming, and you hold the control. Nobody else," Walker said, holding out a gold band.

"Are you sure? I don't want to take this from you," I said, simultaneously reaching out for the ring.

"I want you to have it. It was my dad's. I never really knew him, so it can't mean that much, right? My mom gave it to me when I was a teenager."

"I'm sure it means something to you." I slipped the ring on my finger, but it fell right off. I tried it on my thumb, and it was a perfect fit. I liked the way it looked, and I liked the way it felt even more. Like I had a piece of Walker with me wherever I went. I wanted to give him something of mine as well, but I had nothing to give. "I'll take good care of it," I said, admiring it.

"Just remember to be lucid."

"Every time I look at it, I swear, I'll remember this moment." My heart warmed with his generosity. Walker smiled at me, and I knew the ring meant much more to him than he let on.

When he turned back to his book, his face glowed in a way I had never seen. If I didn't know any better, I'd think he felt honored that I was wearing his ring. Could he possibly have feelings for me? Did he like me back?

"I would say don't get excited, but we don't need to worry about that," Walker mumbled as he ran his finger back and forth across a page of the book.

"What do you mean we don't have to worry about that?" I asked.

"It means, when most people are in a dream state and they realize that they're lucid dreaming, they tend to get excited, and then they wake up. You, you're different. You're stuck here. Unable to wake up because of medications from the hospital. So, you can get excited all you want, but you're stuck here at their mercy." Walker gave me a sympathetic shrug.

I didn't like the thought of getting overly excited and jolting awake in a different realm. What would become of my life here? "What do you think will happen when they try to wake me up?" I asked, feeling vulnerable in an entirely different way.

Walker closed the book and pulled it close to his chest. "I'm not sure. I guess you go home," he said somberly. I chewed on the inside of my lip, wishing and hoping there was another way. Gran said it was my choice, and I only hoped that, when I found my self-control, I could will myself to stay. But fighting against real medications sounded challenging, if not impossible.

"What's next?" I asked, eager to start training.

"I say we kick this into high gear. Let's take it from the top. We'll go hard in your training, and you'll get this in no time, Wilde." Walker placed the book on the kitchen island and came to the back of the sofa.

I nodded my head in agreement; I was ready. I needed to cram like I was studying for finals. Because I never knew when it was going to be my last day here, and I would need every trick up my sleeve if I wanted to stay and fight.

"I'm ready."

"Then all there is left to do is leap . . . literally," he said, with a wicked gleam in his eyes.

I recoiled. "You know I'm afraid of heights, right?"

7

"You won't be afraid of heights when you learn to fly," Walker said.

"Fly! I can't *fly!*" I glared at him, hands on my hips. *Was he crazy?*

"Look, flying is the ultimate dream training. Everybody knows that if they have control over their dreams, they can fly. It's the first thing people do when they turn lucid."

"I don't think that's necessarily true, Walker. Plus, do you really expect me to fly with no training whatsoever?" My voice was a sheer squeal.

"You said you wanted to jump into the deep end. We've got to try this. You can do it. I believe in you," he said, placing his hands on my shoulders and giving me a small shake. I stared into his golden eyes, and I trusted he had my best interests at heart.

"If you say so . . ."

"I know just the place," Walker said with a clap.

The next thing I knew, we were on the forest trails weaving in and out of something that looked to have been a path decades prior. I fell into step behind him and tried not to think of how humiliating this was about to be. "So, what exactly did you have in mind?"

"Do you remember that boulder with the rope swing?" Walker asked, swatting at a bug.

"You mean, the one . . ."

"Yeah. That one."

Silence stretched between us. It was the rope swing that Ethan had jumped from, and he'd never resurfaced. How could I forget? The training had already taken an ominous turn, and we hadn't even started yet.

"I don't know about this," I said, thankful he couldn't see my face. His pace slowed on the trail, but we never stopped walking.

"You have nothing to worry about. I'll be right here the whole time. I won't let you fall," he said. Well, if that were the case, I'd have to make sure I failed. The thought of falling into his arms all day long didn't seem so bad. I even caught a pep in my step.

When we arrived at the boulders, it brought back memories of that dreadful day. I remembered I'd felt disconnected from Walker, and the rejection had been a fresh pinch on my bleeding heart. Ethan's jump played in my head on repeat, and the panic returned to my chest where it had once squeezed like a corset.

"I don't want to jump in the water," I said.

"You don't have to do anything you don't want to. If it makes you uncomfortable, we'll skip it."

The tightness grew as the rope swing came into full sight. The rope hung like a bad omen that only I could see.

"Why don't you crawl up there, and then you can get a feel for how comfortable you are. And if you're up for it, you can jump—"

I stood at the base of the first boulder and took a deep breath, shielding my eyes from the mid-morning sun. I looked warily at Walker. "Noooo . . ."

"Could you jump onto the ground?" He searched my eyes, trying to gage how stubborn I'd be before we came to an agreement. "It's not that far. And if you fall, I'll be here, with my arms out to catch you."

I knew jumping didn't pose any actual risks, other than humiliation. I agreed, begrudgingly, but only because I didn't want to disappoint him.

Walker interlaced his fingers, giving me a step up on the rock. I dug my hands into the crevices of the boulder and pulled myself onto the first landing. Then I made the mistake of looking behind me. I knew it was the worst thing you could do when you're afraid of heights—look back to see how far you've come. It must've been five feet from the ground, but it felt like three times that. I wasn't meant to be this tall.

Walker gave me an encouraging nod and smile, accompanied with a nerdy thumbs-up. I swallowed hard and climbed up the second rock. By the time I was at the top, all I had left to do was stand, but it felt impossible. It must've taken a full minute for me to rise from a crouch to my full height. This was *so* stupid. I had a better chance of passing out and falling off the rock than flying.

"I don't think I can do this!"

"You can do it!"

"No. You're going to have to climb up here and get me down!" I yelled.

"Wilde . . . would you do me a favor?"

I said nothing in return. I just stared down at him through angry eyes.

"Would you look down at your thumb please? What do you see?"

I didn't have to look. I closed my hand over my thumb, and I twisted the ring back and forth. The metal warmed with my touch. He was right. I was in control. I could do this. But I couldn't do it if I thought about it any longer. Without warning, I took one long stride and jumped off the boulder.

"Wait!" Walker yelled.

I didn't think about flying; I didn't even try. I dropped like a brick through thin air. Walker lunged to make good on his promise, but I had given him no warning, and he was only able to barely brush my arm before my feet hit the ground. The shock splintered through my shins, causing me to drop and roll. Walker's hand barely grazed my back.

"Oww . . ." I moaned.

"Are you okay?" Walker dropped to his knees.

I took a moment to count my blessings. Thank god I was back on the ground, and nothing had broken.

"Did I fly?" I asked in a sarcastic tone. Walker laughed.

"Um . . . Almost?" he lied. I slapped his shoulder, and he fell to his butt beside me, pretending it hurt.

"You didn't catch me. What the hell?" I sat up slowly, feeling the sudden onset of a headache.

"You've got to give me a little notice next time, tiger," he said, pulling a twig from the long strands of my hair. There was something about it that seemed intimate. His hand in my hair. *I could get used to this.*

There was a heat in his eyes that was both warm and sultry. I wanted to lean in and kiss him, but that had never turned out well. Instead, I let myself get lost looking into the gold flecks of his eyes. He smudged his thumb over my cheek, and I melted under his touch. My stomach dropped, and if there had been any pain from the fall, I wasn't feeling it now.

"You've got some dirt," he said under his breath.

All of a sudden the heat in his eyes went out, and exchanged for something I didn't recognize. Hurt? Guilt? It didn't last long; he jumped to his feet. Dusted himself off and held out a hand to help me up. Even his grasp was cold. I picked through the various bits mother nature had deposited in my hair as I tried to make sense of the array of emotions that had flashed through his eyes.

"So . . . what's next?" I was afraid to ask, but I didn't want to think about the pained look I had seen any longer. I'd rather jump from another boulder.

"Maybe we came out too hot. Let's rein it back in. You can jump off something small."

"There's a creek not too far from here that feeds into the lake. It's tiny and has a cute wooden bridge over it. We could start there?" I asked.

"That's perfect."

A short, quiet walk later, I found myself standing on a two-foot-tall bridge. The creek was pretty much nonexistent in the heat of summer. It was only a dry bed of rocks nestled within the trees. I worried about twisting my ankle; if there was a way this could go wrong, I'd find it.

Instead of jumping off the middle of the bridge into the dry bed, I planned to run over the bridge and leap on the descent. It was no more than a jump and skip I might have done on flat ground, but I was trying to appease Walker and his attempt at training me.

I felt stupid even trying, but Walker made it better. After failing to keep his promise earlier, he decided that if either of us were going to do something stupid, it was going to be him first. He ran over the bridge—passing me in the middle with subpar speed—and leapt into the air like a wannabe ballerina. He made a mockery of himself and came tumbling down on the other side. I laughed so hard my knees weakened, and I couldn't hold myself upright.

"I'm going to miss this," he said as he sat up, dried leaves caked to his back.

Something pulled at my heartstrings. "What did you say?"

"I'm going to miss this," he said again, his laughter turning to loneliness.

All I wanted was to watch him laugh. I didn't like it when he was sad. These days, he appeared sad way too often, and it crushed me. "What? This?" I asked, running and jumping off the miniature bridge.

I didn't fly. He was so delusional. We did the only thing we could do now; we joked about it. Walker laughed at my pathetic attempt, and I came to his side with my hands on my hips. Slightly winded and in a more serious tone, I said, "You don't have to."

He took a deep, solemn breath, and reached out to push my hair behind my shoulder. "Let's not talk about that right now." He turned away and started to walk down the path unnaturally fast. I had to jog just to keep up. It was almost like he was running from something, but I imagined, being trapped in this realm, he couldn't get very far. Maybe the lake symbolized the depth of his sorrows.

Was he sad to think that one day I'd leave him? Or was he sad because he wanted me to stay? It felt like our relationship was growing into something more than two peas in a—one-of-a-kind—pod. It was branching out into new avenues, stretching and strengthening. It was hard to trump the way we'd begun, him saving my life and all, but we had never crossed the romantic bridge before, and I had a feeling we were getting close. Walker's eyes had twinkled a little differently in recent weeks, and there was a strong sense of sadness that emanated from him when we talked about me leaving Baylor.

There was a part of me that was riddled with insecurities. That feared he only wanted me to help him find Layla. That he would be sad when I left, because his chances of eternal love would dwindle significantly. That I was his only shard of hope for a life with her, a life of happiness. But there was another part of me, the more rational part, that told me he wouldn't look at me the way he did if he didn't have feelings for me. His eyes wouldn't gleam when they fell upon me. His dimples wouldn't flex. And I wouldn't get that pull in my heart, like two magnets being drawn to each other.

I've been wrong about a lot of things in my life; I'll admit that. I've been incompetent, and I've been blindsided. But I couldn't shake my instincts on this one. I wasn't the only one with feelings here. However deep or shallow? That I didn't know. The reason he'd been denying them? That could be just about anything. There were a hundred reasons why we shouldn't be together, starting with the day he'd died and ending with a curse. None of which I wanted to think about now.

I'd been so entangled in my own web of thoughts, I hadn't realized we'd arrived at our next destination. We were on a small bluff, the lake below us. It was a beautiful lookout point, with a wooden bench in the clearing. Tufts of overgrown grass clumped around the legs of the bench. Walker stood at the edge of the cliff peering over, and I didn't like the feeling that dropped from my chest into my belly. He turned, beckoning to me, and I instinctively took a step backward. There was *no way* I was jumping off that cliff, and there was *no way* I was going to *fly* off it.

"I think this is the perfect blend of height and safety for you to grow your wings."

"No. I'm not doing that. Are you crazy?" I shook my head, taking several more steps backward.

"If all else fails—"

"And it will!" my voice trembled.

"—you'll jump into the water and swim to shore," Walker cautiously approached me, like I was a rabid dog baring its teeth. I took another step back.

"Walker, I can't. I can't." I shook my head maniacally. He managed to grab my wrist in one quick motion and pull me close to him. Tears pricked the corners of my eyes, and he lowered his forehead to mine. He took a deep breath, and I did the same. We were breathing the same air, and it was filled with the forbidden fear of falling. Not falling off the cliff, but falling in love. Falling . . . and not being caught.

When my breath steadied, Walker's grip lightened to a whisper touch across my back, and I blinked my eyes open with conviction. I was going to do it. I wasn't just going to jump off that cliff; I was going to fly. And I prayed he would be the one to catch me. Because that's what happens when you fall in love; you fall without ever hitting the ground. You trust that your person will be there to catch you when the ground approaches. I was ready to take that leap, and the better half of me thought Walker was too.

"Are you ready?" he asked, his voice was like a low vibration I could get lost in. I pulled away from the small bubble we'd made for ourselves and gulped at the ever-thinning air.

"I'll go first. I'll wait for you in the water. That way, if you fall, I'll be right there with you."

"And if I don't?" It had seemed funny before, when we were jumping off the bridge. But there was nothing funny about it now. It felt like life or death. Which was ironic, because that's what we were. I was life, he was death.

"Then I'll swim to the shore, and I'll meet you wherever you land." I nodded, and he wrapped his hand around the base of my head and pulled me in, kissing my forehead.

The tender moment ended before my eyes could open. He dove off the cliff with all the ease of a first-class diver. I heard the splash and started to count. By the time I hit three, it would be my turn. Not another thought about it.

One . . . My heart was pounding with the excitement of new beginnings.

Two . . . My palms were sweating with the fear of failure.

Three . . . I did it anyway.

I ran toward the cliff. No turning back now. I pushed off the edge of the cliff and clumps of dirt gave way under my feet and crumbled into the water below. I clapped my hands together into the fine point of an arrowhead. I felt the air wrap around my body, supporting me as I flew.

But my heart was heavy, and the magnetic pull I had for Walker was fierce. The force was otherworldly, sinking its talons into me like I was its prey and pulling me down into the water to meet him. It was more than gravity; it was something else entirely, something I had no words for. Had I not wanted to fly? Had I not believed in myself? Or was my soul simply diving down because that's where he was?

The needlepoint of my fingertips split the water in two. The lake cracked open and swallowed me whole. The force was so strong, it didn't stop when I broke the surface—I plunged down with all the weight of the universe, cutting through the water like a missile aiming toward the deepest channel of the lake.

I opened my eyes, anticipating the evil darkness I'd grown to expect from Baylor Lake, but instead, I could see everything. It was like another world under the water. Perhaps another realm altogether. The sunlight dappled the water and filtered into a glow of dancing searchlights. It was a fortress of underwater plants and tiny bubbles floating like champagne streamers. The deeper I sank, the darker everything became. The green plants turned a murky dark gray, and the sun-dappled aqua was transformed into a dingy darkness.

When I finally stopped, it was only because I hit the bottom. My feet sank into the mud as I looked up toward the surface. The sunlight was but a tiny dot, so very far away. Walker was nowhere to be seen.

There was no way I could make it back on a single breath. But then I remembered, I didn't technically need to breathe. I closed my hand over my thumb, and Walker's ring. *I'm in control . . .*

I knew I should swim up, because that's where I belonged, but the urgency was lost somewhere in the wonder of the vast lake. Did I belong on the surface? Layla seemed to think I didn't belong in Baylor at all. All I knew was that I didn't belong here at the bottom of the lake, with Lainey and god knows what else.

I saw her then. Like she had come when I called. Lainey wasn't the double I had first encountered in the lake after she'd disappeared; she was sweet. Angelic. Like a mermaid or some underwater goddess. Her medium-length hair formed sweeping curls around her face. Her freckles glowed like twinkling stars in the night sky. And she was happy.

"Wake up," she said. Her voice cut through the water and surrounded me with its persuasive influence.

I was tempted to stay with her. I wanted to be happy and angelic like my best friend. I wanted to float like an underwater angel and swim forever by her side. But then she said it again. "Wake up."

The water seemed to close in around me, and I stiffened a little. The temptation to stay faded.

"Wake up!" Lainey's words grew louder and more demanding. I took a step backward and stumbled in a bed of rocks.

"Wake up!" The sound waves of her message rippled out and knocked me to the ground. I scrambled to get up, pushing my hands through a sea of silky plants and sharp shells. Something slimy wiggled across my wrist, and I panicked. A strong sense of danger raced through my body, telling me I wasn't where I belonged. That Layla had been right all along.

The lake turned icy as my fear grew. I wasn't alone down here. There were things in this water; secrets of the deep. Secrets I didn't want to know, and probably couldn't handle if I did. Symbols I wanted to keep hidden. Whatever my subconscious was telling me, I wanted to run from it. Because the thought of living two lives at once was a scary thought, and I knew it was unsustainable. I kicked out of the dark silt and started to swim to the surface. I needed to get out of here.

A whisper-like touch tickled my toes and wrapped around my heel, then slinked up my ankle. Lainey had my foot in her grasp. Her hold was soft but strong—gone were the claws of the dead I had known before. She drew my eye to something I hadn't noticed before. She pointed to a door at the bottom of the lake.

It was a red door, bright against the mud and algae. The gold knob gleamed with a warmth that both intrigued and invited me. I stopped fighting for the surface and floated neutrally in the cold water. My arms rose from my sides as I relaxed, staring at the red door. I felt at peace.

Where did it lead? Was it a door to the afterlife? Was it a door to the living? Or maybe it was the door to Walker's heart? It didn't really matter what the answer was, because I was drawn to open it either way. There was something luring me toward it, at the same time that I was pulled to Walker on the surface. Suspended between him above and the door below, I didn't know what to do.

In that moment, I wanted Walker more. But it scared me that it wasn't by much. A decision that important should never be that nebulous. Especially one involving the heart.

Lainey's eyes turned from an ethereal glow to dull and dimensionless. Her starlit freckles turned to craters that ate through her flesh like acid in a rolling boil over her face. Her dancing hair turned to pond scum and drifted to the bottom of the lake in clumps. She deteriorated before my very eyes.

The door was abruptly hidden between rows and rows of headstones that hadn't been there before. Guarded by lurking shadows and leopard-spotted eels. Whatever admission I'd had through that red door was now gone, and so were the warm and fuzzy feelings.

I could suddenly see Walker trying to swim down to get me, but he could only make it so far before having to turn around and go back for air. I kicked my feet and propelled my arms through the heavy water, fighting with all my might. His faint cries pierced through the water, and I knew I had to hurry. I kicked frantically. As soon as I'd made the decision to return to the surface, the need for air had ripped through my chest, and my lungs had tried to expand but couldn't.

My limbs were growing weak with exhaustion when the sun-dappled light finally reappeared. I was getting close. I kicked through the nightmares until Walker met me fifteen feet from the surface. He pulled me to the top where I took a huge, labored gulp of air. He spun me onto my back as I tried to stay conscious, wrapping his arm around my chest and swimming me to shore.

The sky spun, and my head was woozy. There was a piece of me still sunk at the bottom of the lake, lost and scared. I felt like I'd never take a full breath again. I was splintered in two. A chunk of my heart was somewhere beyond that red door, and it left me homesick.

"Are you okay? Wilde, are you okay?" Walker asked, slapping my cheeks as I lay on the sandy shore.

"I'm okay. I'm okay," I said, glaring at the scintillating water.

"I'm so sorry. I'm *so* sorry. We never have to do that again. I never should have pushed you to do that. I'm sorry." Walker held me tight to his chest and rocked me back and forth.

"It's okay. . . I think I was close to flying," I said absentmindedly.

8

From head to toe, we were all dressed in black to hide within the shadows and camouflage into the darkness. I'd never broken into a house before, but it wasn't the Vandals I was afraid of. It was the wolf.

I pulled on the drawstrings of Emma's hoodie, tightening the hood around her face. Only her petite features poked out through the center. But I didn't need her wrinkled forehead to tell me she was frowning; I could see it in her worried eyes. I loosened the strings, allowing her cheeks to breathe. "What? You can do this," I said.

"I just don't understand. If you think the Vandals are the bad guys, then why are we going over there?" Emma said, as I tugged on her sweatshirt.

"Because we're going to kick some wolf ass!" Scarlett May said.

"But it's not like we can fight. Do you even have pepper spray? Or something? A prime rib to throw? A net? Do we have a net?" Emma rambled, her eyes fluttering with questions.

"No, but do you think we should grab a hot dog or something?" Kimber asked. I guess it made sense. What dog didn't like meat? It was the perfect distraction.

"Yeah. Grab the whole package."

"Or whatever's left; Mason eats those things like Tic Tacs," Scarlett May said. Kimber ducked into the kitchen.

"So, what do we do when we get inside?" Emma asked.

"Look for anything suspicious. We're just going over there to figure out what's going on. And we don't want to get caught, so don't touch anything. Don't move anything. And don't make any noise," I said.

When Kimber returned with two hot dogs slumped in a dripping wrapper, we were ready to cross the yard. We hadn't told the boys what we were up to, because there was no way they would've let us go alone. We weren't on a mission to trap the wolf and feed it to the fish; we only wanted to know the truth. We wanted to know what we were up against so that we could be better prepared to fight the evil that lurked in the woods. Since it looked like the neighbors were half packed and between moves, we were confident we could get in and out without ever being seen. They probably weren't even in town.

"Ready?" I asked.

"Let's do this," Scarlett May said, slapping a flashlight against her palm. Emma met my gaze with wary eyes, and I gave her a nod of encouragement.

"Just imagine it's one of your stories. You're the main character, and you're investigating a crime scene," I said. Emma's brows rose into her hoodie and her eyes softened. I could see that she liked the idea.

We set out, huddling together like sheep. Only we didn't know where the herding dog was. We crouched, crossing into the middle of the clearing that stretched between the two cabins. The lawn was wet with dew in the night. The excitement coursed through my veins. It was the liberty to be free and to do what we wanted. We were no longer sitting ducks. We weren't the victims. And we would not sit and wait until the wolf came to us. We were going to find it, and it felt good. Empowering.

Emma let out a shriek when the floodlights turned on. It was the motion-sensor light on the Vandals' house. Perhaps I was the only one who felt empowered. Scarlett May shoved Emma, as she cupped her hands over her mouth. The four of us crouched, frozen in the clearing with the spotlight on us.

"What do we do?"

"Just don't move."

"No. That doesn't make sense. The lights are going to remain on as long as there's motion. We need to get out of the clearing. We need to hurry and cross to the Vandals' house," I whispered.

"Okay. Let's go," Scarlett May said.

We moved forward with the spotlights cascading down on us. Only this time, the air felt cooler and crisper on my side. Our pack felt smaller. Like one had already been plucked off by the unseen dangers of the yard. It was Emma. She was crouching in the middle of the yard all by her lonesome. Frozen in fear.

"Emma what are you doing?" I hissed, beckoning to her.

"I can't do it. I can't do it." She shook her head frantically.

"Yes, you can. Come on."

Scarlett May and Kimber had reached the shadow of the Vandals' cabin.

Emma and I were separated in the yard. But I didn't want to go backward, and she didn't want to go forward. She stood to her full height, abruptly abandoning the mission, turned and ran back to the cabin. A small whine escaped her, the sound waning with the growing distance. I threw my hands in the air and watched as she climbed onto the back deck and crouched behind one of the lounge chairs. I sighed heavily and then turned back to the others. They waved me forward and, reluctantly, I left Emma behind.

"We're better off without her," Scarlett May hissed.

"Yeah. She probably would have screamed or something. Don't worry about it," Kimber said.

We made our way to the back door and found that, just as we'd expected, it was locked. Scarlett May checked the windows as we made our way around the cabin. The front door was also locked, as well as the garage. But Scarlett May found a small window in the bathroom that had been left cracked open. She signaled us with a flicker of her flashlight.

Kimber and I boosted her up, and she crawled through the window. There was nothing graceful about it. She floundered, halfway in and halfway out. Kicking her legs, she landed on top of the toilet. The three of us froze, two on the outside, one on the inside. But nothing else sounded throughout the cabin. No voices. No alarms. And no lights.

I helped Kimber next. I lifted her light frame with ease, and she crawled through the tiny window without so much as a sound. I was next. But there was nobody to help me scale the wall. The window was just tall enough to where I couldn't pull myself up. I tried twice, my feet kicking against the wood shingles. I was determined to get in. Kimber and Scarlett May spat suggestions at me until somebody had the bright idea to open the front door.

I found myself lurking around the side of the cabin by my lonesome. And it was then that something rumbled in the bushes. I was several strides from safety when I saw the bush sway from side to side. I took off running, and a darkness lifted from the bush into the air. A cloud of my own personal fear came from the woodwork to greet me. As I lunged forward, the front door opened, and I tumbled inside just in time to escape my dreaded imagination.

My breaths came in short, shallow pants as the cabin door closed behind me. I didn't have long to catch my breath as the girls wandered throughout the cabin, arms linked and whispering. It smelled like the cuddy cabin of a small boat, or the abandoned grandparents' basement with periodic water leaks. It was dank and musty. Whatever it was, it didn't smell like a home two people were living in.

Their sofa was draped in a white sheet, and most of their furniture was clumped together in the middle of the room. A painting tarp crinkled beneath my shoes. I found it odd that the cabin was not freshly painted nor stained. It would have smelled better if it was. Boxes lined the kitchen counters with various appliances stuffed inside neatly. A bread machine. Wrapped coffee mugs. A blender.

"Do you see anything?" Kimber asked. The truth was, I saw nothing incriminating. This didn't look like the den of a wolf. This looked like the cabin of two people in the middle of a move, selling their vacation home for something more manageable in their later years. But I didn't want to admit it. Because admitting that there was nothing wrong with the Vandals meant there was everything wrong with me. And I didn't want to take that blame. Not today. Not ever.

Perhaps, I didn't know what I was looking for. Had I expected to find a pile of carcasses? Bunny rabbit tails, a bobcat's hide, putrid fish skins with flaking scales that glimmered like glitter across the cabin floor? Had I expected to find a warm spot in the living room where the wolf curled up to sleep? Had I thought the walls would be covered in claw marks and the cabin would reek of wet dog? No . . . I hadn't expected any of those things. But I simply hadn't expected this either. I didn't expect the Vandals to be *so* boring.

And then it hit me like a lightning bolt. This wasn't the den at all. "The garden!" I hissed.

"What?"

"That's where it all happens. Mrs. Vandal's pottery shed out back. It's got to be where all the evidence is."

Kimber shook her head slowly.

"Go outside? Are you stupid?" Scarlett May asked.

I thought for a moment—maybe I was. But I knew trekking out to the shed could clear my name. We would find the Baylor Butcher. The wolf. Whatever the threat was that still haunted me and my friends long after Big Jimmy had died. I was sure of it.

"Come on you guys. We've already come this far . . ."

"You mean across the lawn?" Scarlett May scoffed.

"No!" Kimber said in a voice that was anything but a whisper.

As if waking a giant, the floorboards creaked above our heads. The three of us froze, heads tilted toward the ceiling. My eyes followed along the ceiling as the steps crossed from one side of the cabin to the other. Scarlett May clicked her flashlight off, and we waited in the dark listening until the footsteps approached the staircase. Then all hell broke loose.

The three of us scampered like mice on a kitchen counter after the lights flickered on. No longer were we careful or quiet. We bolted for the back door, the three of us fighting over the doorknob. Yelling and pushing, we bolted outside, off the back deck, and into the grass. That's where we divided.

Kimber and Scarlett May headed for the safety of our cabin. I was the only one who ran toward the potting shed.

"Wait!" I hissed. The whisper was lost in the heat of the moment. They didn't hear me, or maybe they didn't care. "Wait!" I yelled.

The girls stopped in the middle of the clearing as the floodlights illuminated them. Scarlett May waved me on and Kimber clung to her arm. "Come on Kinsley!"

My body locked up. I wanted to join them. I wanted to run far away from here. I wanted to run straight out of Baylor. But I was frozen. Frozen in fear. Frozen in time. I just stood there unable to move. The girls fled the scene as the Vandals' porch light came on and a figure peered out the window. The girls ran full speed back to safety as I dropped to my stomach and lay in the shadows.

I watched as Emma's figure appeared on the back patio underneath the porch light. She waved the girls forward then peered out into the blackness, looking for me. My heart pounded, and I felt like I was sinking into the wet grass. The Vandals' patio door swung open, and I sucked in a gasp of the chilly night air and a mission gone wrong.

With no thought at all, I army crawled to the potting shed. Once I hit the soil surrounding the shed, I popped to my feet and patted the door down in search of a way in. My hand wrapped around the cold metal handles, and I pulled the door open and shut myself inside. Once inside, I slowed my breathing and tried to think.

I tried to steady my trembling body, but I felt the unknown closing in on me. It was pitch black inside the shed, and Scarlett May had the only flashlight. I had no way of knowing if I'd found the wolf's den or not. Unlike the vast dark cove, this confined space was small and suffocating. I didn't know how long I would have to wait inside the shed, but I already itched to leave.

Slowly, I checked over my shoulder, but I couldn't see a single thing. I told myself there should be nothing there except rakes, shovels, potting soil, and seeds, but I didn't believe it. There *should* be shelves of tools, like bush-trimming clippers and rooting powders and plant growth nutrients. In a normal shed, there wouldn't be anything mysterious. Nothing paranormal. And definitely not malevolent. And under no circumstances would there ever be a large, hairy, grizzly wolf . . . standing behind me.

I scrunched my eyes shut and pressed the palms of my hands against my sockets. But *should be* and *probably* were two very different things, and I knew that, with my luck, I'd just run straight into the wolf's mouth and asked him to swallow me whole.

Stop! Stop thinking of that . . .

I knew by now that I would conjure my fears if I fed my mind nothing but worry. But wasn't that what I was doing now? Wasn't that why my heart was racing? Wasn't it why the potting shed felt like it was closing in on me? Because the fear was growing? It was changing and morphing to life before me?

I felt it come together, pull itself from thin air behind my back. The tiny hairs on my neck prickled. My pupils dilated and my hearing piqued. Had I ever really been in control? Or was this all happening *to* me? Was I the victim? Because I certainly wasn't the hero. I felt like a victim now, in the dank, dark shed that felt more like a coffin with every passing minute. I was going to die in here. *Die again.*

Footsteps slinked through the wet grass, the sound growing further away. I tried to push it all out of my mind and stay focused on the facts. Listen to the footfalls. Mr. Vandal had chased the girls away. He was probably at my cabin now, pounding on the back door. The girls were probably hiding behind the pool table or upstairs in the master bedroom. It was the perfect time to escape. If there was evidence in the shed, I couldn't see it anyway. I took a deep breath and gripped the handle. I turned the lever just as I heard a twig snap outside the door.

I stilled, pushing my ear to the door. It was quiet. Too quiet. The door ripped open. I screamed. I pulled the door shut as I jumped backward. Once a coffin closing in on me, the shed was now my sanctuary.

I gripped the doorknob with two hands leveraging my weight to keep the door shut. My body jerked violently back and forth as the thing shook the door on its hinges. I held on for dear life. It took everything I had, and more.

As quickly as it started, it stopped. Everything stilled in the dark. But my dread only grew. I remained rigid, holding the door shut with all my might. I counted the seconds—the calm before the storm.

One. My breaths were quick and shallow.

Two. My joints were locked, my body braced.

Three. "Kinsley?" A deep voice called from the other side of the door.

It wasn't the wolf. It was Mason. *Mason?* Slowly, I straightened. I kept my hands on the doorknob but loosened my grip. Blood rushed back into my fingers like tiny pins sticking me.

"Mason? Is that you?" I asked.

"Yeah. It's me."

My shoulders dropped, and my body slackened. He was here to rescue me.

"Open the door!" he said eagerly.

I began to do as he said, but then I questioned—was he *too* eager?

Why would Mason come to save me, and not Noah?

"Why?" I said, wincing as it left my mouth.

"Why do you think? Don't you want to get out of there? Or are you going to hide in the neighbor's shed all night?"

I didn't answer.

"Come on, hurry up. He's almost back," Mason said.

My heart walloped in my chest. I knew Mr. Vandal would be back soon. A matter of seconds was all I had to escape unseen. But there was something holding me back.

How much did I really trust Mason?

Could he be the wolf?

He was the one who had told Walker I was taken. He was the one who had spread the lies and sent him home. He was the one who had threatened my relationship. I felt the weight of my scowl before I even realized I was upset. I wasn't suspicious of Mason; I was downright angry.

I'd done nothing to Mason. Why would he treat me that way? Is this how he repaid me for inviting him to my cabin for the summer? By eating my light bulbs? By getting in the way of Walker and me? He wasn't just a wolf in sheep's clothing; he was an *asshole!*

"No!" I yelled.

"Seriously, Kins? Come on!"

"No! I'm not opening the door. I'll stay here all night if I must!"

The doorknob jiggled lightly, and I tightened my grip. And then the storm hit.

A snarl ripped through the night, and the commotion rattled the shed. The whole door shook with such force it could topple the entire shack over. *I was right.* Mason *was* the wolf! And that made me his prey.

The door was pulled halfway open and then slammed shut, forcing in a brief gust of cool air. I threw my weight backward and felt a sticky web kiss my cheek. I yelped and flinched, letting my guard down for a split second.

Screams echoed in the distance. Three girls. I couldn't make out what they were saying, but I knew that Emma, Scarlett May, and Kimber were watching the whole thing from next door.

The wolf grumbled ferociously. Its snarls cascaded down from ten feet, maybe more. The slick drool gurgled in its growl. I could hear something rip, the tare of something salacious. I imagined Mason breaking out of his skin and growing to twice his height, into a beast this world had never known.

Eight tiny legs tiptoed down my neck and across my clavicle, forcing me to let go of the handle and flail about.

I screamed, scraping at my neck and clawing at my hair. My body danced beyond my control. The door sprang open when I let go, and I toppled out of the shed, rolling on the ground like I was on fire. Wet smudged across my chest and balled under my hand. The miniature threat gave way to the enormous one standing in front of me.

A large, grotesque wolf stood on its hind legs. Upright, like a human. The edge of its fur was lit by the moonlight and glinted a silvery white. Its eyes glowed fluorescent yellow flanked by fire orange. And its drool shimmered like a prism of promised pain.

It took a large breath, expanding its beastly chest and growing impossibly taller. I scooted back on my butt. My hands dug into the soil beneath me as I tried to push away. I gained inches, nothing more.

I scampered backward whimpering until I ran into something. A body. Still warm, but eerily still. And wet.

The girls continued to scream in the background as I pried my eyes away from the wolf to the warm body. I expected to see Mr. Vandal beside me, but it was Mason. *Mason!*

My heart stopped. He wasn't the wolf—he was a victim.

I coughed as my heart kicked back to life. The wolf pounced down upon me—its paws on either side of my shoulders—and it let out a growl so deafening that my ears rang and my blood turned to ice.

Its jaws seemed to unhinge, and its mouth gaped wide open. It could easily fit my entire head inside of its mouth. I winced from its hot breath, like I'd stuck my face inside an oven. I closed my eyes and tensed for my last moments. I'd died once or twice before; I thought I could do it again.

In that moment, when the sharp teeth grazed my chin, all I could think about was how wrong I'd been about Mason. That maybe he'd be alive if I'd trusted him more. And that guilt was the last thing I would ever know . . .

The wolf's jaws snapped shut, engulfing me in the pits of guilt. I startled. My eyes flew open to a calm, starry night. Crisp, cold air rest upon my cheeks and swirled in my lungs. A shooting star blazed across the sky and covered me in shame.

In that moment, I realized one thing. I'd rather die of fear than guilt. Because if the guilt didn't kill you—the regret would eat you alive.

The wolf was gone now, but the threat was far from over. I was shoulder to shoulder with Mason, and only one of us was breathing.

9

As I lay next to Mason under the dazzling starlit sky, I didn't think of Mr. Vandal or the repercussions of our break-in. I didn't think much at all. I'd just been swallowed whole by the tallest, meanest wolf I'd ever seen, and all that was left was the intrusive self-doubt. I should have believed in Mason. I should have opened the door. I should have escaped when I had the chance. But instead, I ran right into this mess. It was a habit of mine. *So predictably me.*

One by one, my friends were being picked off. They were disappearing. They were turning into crows, sinking to the bottom of the lake, and being mauled by ten-foot-tall wolves. And, somehow, *I* was supposed to have the power to combat it. *I* was supposed to control the Baylor phenomenon and turn it into something pleasurable. *I* was single-handedly supposed to turn this world upside down. If that seemed like an impossible feat, it's because it was. I wasn't as optimistic as Walker was. And I was pretty sure that I'd burn the forest down if *I* was left in charge. It was a frightening thought.

I wasn't the right fit for the job. But what if I didn't have to be? What if I gave that title to someone else? Walker would be excellent. But he was dead, of course, and I was pretty sure a living mind was a prerequisite.

Emma would be perfect. She'd be the main character in whatever book she wanted. But, unquestionably, she'd turn everybody in this town into oil slicked cover models. Shirts would be a thing of the past. I could live with that. It'd be far better than whatever I'd done here tonight.

The warmth from Mason's body was fading fast. Several footsteps swished through the wet grass and whispers floated in the air. They were coming for me. And I was ashamed of what they'd find when they did.

Gunner got to Mason first. He sniffed all around. His tail tucked between his legs. "It's okay, boy." *It wasn't okay.*

"Is that?"

"Is he?"

Kimber whimpered, stifling a cry in the palm of her hand. I lay helpless right where the wolf had left me. I couldn't cry for Mason. I'd gone numb. Something Kimber could never do.

Scarlett May picked up Mason's arms. She threw all her weight backward, and he moved a mere inch. "Are you just going to stargaze? Or are you going to help me?"

"What are you doing?" Emma asked.

Scarlett May said nothing, but her cold stare and clenched jaw said enough. The worry trickled back in, and I became very aware that Mr. Vandal was somewhere in the clearing, and we had to get this body out of his yard before bad things got worse.

I took one of Mason's wrists and Scarlett May took the other. Gunner wagged his tail as if things had just become exciting. We started to drag Mason, but in opposite directions.

"Where are you going?" I hissed. Mason's arms were spread wide.

"We can't go that way! The floodlights will turn on!" Scarlett May said.

"We can't just drag him a mile out of our way. We *have to* go this way. The cabin is right there. If we all help, we can have him across this lawn in a couple of minutes," I said.

Gunner barked.

"Shhhh!"

"No!"

Gunner sat, cocking his head to the side.

"But what about Mr. Vandal?" Emma asked.

"What about him?"

"He was banging on all the doors; he's probably still over there. We can't come back like this," Emma said, waving her hand at Mason.

"What else are we going to do? We have to act now." The seconds were ticking by at an alarming rate. We didn't have time to fight about it.

"Kimber, Emma, grab his ankles. Let's just get him across the clearing to the cabin. We can fight about what to do later," Scarlett May said.

They did as they were told, and we were moving Mason a little quicker than before, though his butt still grazed the grass, slowing us down. The four of us wobbled back and forth for what seemed like an eternity until the floodlights kicked on and revealed Mr. Vandal standing before us. That's when the slow crawl of time stopped altogether.

"What the hell have you girls been doing? Did you break into my home?" Mr. Vandal demanded answers.

His balled fists were clenched by his sides. Half his scowl was lit from motion-sensor light. The other half was hidden in the shadows, like Mason's body behind us. We bumped up next to each other, the four of us forming a wall in an attempt to hide the truth.

"Mr. Vandal, I am . . . I am so sorry about earlier," I stuttered, my eyes shifting, looking for lies to pluck from thin air. We'd broken into the man's home. There was no real excuse to give.

"You're sorry?" he yelled, with his hands in the air. "Do you have any idea what time it is?"

"We're sorry. We thought maybe . . . that maybe something was wrong. Like the house was abandoned, or you guys were out on vacation . . ."

"And what if we were? You have no right to break into my home! Did you steal something? Were you stealing from us?" Mr. Vandal's swarthy face grew closer with each accusation. But the girls and I couldn't take a single step backward. Our heels were already pressed against Mason's body.

"What's going on over there?" Noah yelled across the yard. All of us looked to find the guys standing half-asleep on the back patio of the cabin. All the yelling and pounding on the doors must have woken them. It was over now. We were caught. How could I explain this to any of them? Their best friend had been killed by a creature that didn't exist.

I felt the hollowness in my chest. Mr. Vandal yelled some more, but I could no longer hear the words coming out of his mouth. The idea of Kai, Noah, and Asher trying to get a better look at us and seeing the situation for what it was . . . was terrifying. The more they looked, the more they'd see, and it was an awful sight. One I couldn't shield them from but wished I could.

I tuned back in to hear Mr. Vandal threatening to call the cops. He stared at the four of us with a threatening glare. There was nothing we could say, so we just stood there silently eyeing one another. When he made his first move back toward his cabin, we flinched. He froze once more and glared at us one last time. Scarlett May tried to cover the corner of our man-made wall as he walked away. Fortunately, Mason was well hidden in the shadows, and out of sight. We didn't move an inch until Mr. Vandal's back door slammed shut, and then we each took a breath of relief.

Gunner whimpered, not understanding the rules of the game we were playing.

"Seriously, what the hell you guys?" Asher grumbled throwing his hands in the air and making a big show of his frustration. Noah shook his head and went back inside. Kai followed.

"Wait, we need you," Kimber said. Asher was the only one to hear her. He paused with his hand on the open door and then came back to the edge of the porch, lifting to his toes and craning his neck. He couldn't see what we were hiding, but he would soon find out. He jogged down the stairs, made his way across the clearing, and joined us in the bright floodlights.

"It's okay, guys. He can help us," Kimber's voice trembled.

I sighed heavily in anticipation of Asher's devastation. I glanced back at Mason, but he wasn't there. I squinted, searching the damp grass around us. *Impossible . . .*

"What's going on you guys?" Asher asked. Kimber immediately wailed and ran into his arms.

I looked all around us, but I could only see as far as the floodlights' illumination. Beyond that was a mystery of darkness.

Had Mason gotten better? Had he crawled off on his own?

Asher pushed Kimber aside and came at us. We parted, unable to speak. It was show and tell, only there was nothing left to show.

The girls gasped upon seeing the bare grass, and Asher grew frustrated.

"What?" he demanded.

"Where is he?" Emma asked me.

"You guys? Seriously, this isn't funny," Scarlett May said. But none of us were laughing.

I was chewing a hole in my cheek the size of a green pea. We scattered in the yard searching near and far. Gunner pranced about looking for a ball. None of us wanted to explain to Asher what had happened.

"Can we go home?" Kimber whimpered, pulling on Asher's arm.

We followed behind them in the wake of her tears. They reminded me of flower petals dropped down the aisle of a chapel. Our footsteps passed over the salty tears and blood-stained grass. It certainly wasn't the happiest night of our lives, but it was one we'd never forget. Or at least I wouldn't forget it, the others might.

When we were under the bright lights of the kitchen, Kimber really let loose. Asher wrapped his brawny arms around her tiny waist, and she snuffed her nose into his neck. I stood awkwardly staring at them as Kimber seemed to sink into herself. And I knew she was simply too weak to endure this kind of torture. Maybe she could draw strength from Asher. She would have to if she wanted to survive.

"Mason is gone, you guys. *Gone,* gone," Scarlett May said.

"What are you even talking about? What happened out there?" Asher asked, pulling Kimber off his neck. She quivered by his side, rubbing her arms.

"We broke into the neighbors'—"

"You what!" Asher's voice deepened.

"They have been doing all sorts of weird stuff. This entire summer, they've been gardening at midnight. Dragging bags back and forth through their garden. They've been watching us through the windows at night," Scarlett May said, pointing toward their cabin.

"So what?" he replied.

"We thought maybe there was a threat. You guys said it looked like nobody was living there. But clearly, they are. We wanted to see for ourselves," I said.

"Are you guys stupid?" he asked.

"I am sick of waiting around for something bad to happen!" I said, my tone sharp as a knife.

"So, you went to go find it? Is that what you're telling me?" Asher scoffed. He was right. We'd done a stupid thing tonight, and worse yet, I'd been the one to convince the girls to do it with me. I wasn't a leader and never should be.

"At least we're trying," Emma said, her eyes trained on the floor.

"Trying? You didn't even make it over there! You left us high and dry!" Kimber said, wiping her nose on the back of her hand.

"Okay, stop! Everybody stop! Just tell me what happened." Asher held his hand in the middle of the group like a traffic cop. Nobody spoke. We just looked at one another, not wanting to say it out loud. The things we'd seen. The things we'd endured. The things we'd let happen.

"You're up, Kinsley," he said, waiting. Everyone looked at me.

I took a deep breath and searched the floor for words. My voice was meek as I tried to recap all I'd done, and all I hadn't.

"We broke in—" Emma sucked in a sharp breath.

"All of us except Emma." I corrected.

"We'd looked around the cabin for only a few minutes when we heard something and ran outside. I ran into the shed where Mason found me. He wanted to help me, but I wouldn't open the door."

"Why?" he asked.

"Because. I don't know. I was scared . . . I didn't trust him." The truth was a tiny whisper from my lips. I didn't want to give it any more merit than that.

"A wolf attacked him," I said.

"A wolf?" Asher frowned.

"It's true! We saw it!" Scarlett May said.

My back straightened with surprise. They'd seen it? For the first time, my friends had seen the monster. It wasn't all in my head. That thing was really out there, lurking in the woods.

"It looked like a werewolf!" Kimber added, her hand pressed against her temple as if the very memory was making her suffer all over again.

"Well, technically, if it were a werewolf, it would have to transition in and out of being human, and we have no evidence of that," Emma said.

Scarlett May shot her an exasperated look. "The beast was on two legs! And it was gigantic!"

"Okay, okay. Everybody settle down. Kinsley, what happened next?" Asher asked.

"What's going on?" Kai asked, rubbing his eyes as he walked into the kitchen wearing only his boxers.

Nobody wanted to say it. Everyone's eyes turned away, pushing the responsibility off to someone else.

"The girls broke into the neighbors' cabin, and supposedly got Mason killed. Yet there is absolutely no evidence—"

"We didn't do it! We didn't kill him! The wolf did it—" I slapped my hand down on the kitchen counter, and it sent a zing of pain through each finger. Everybody stopped to look at me. I couldn't think with my heart pounding so wildly in my chest.

"I didn't mean *you* killed him," Asher said, just as Noah walked in. *Great. Now everybody's here.*

"I didn't open the door. I should have, but I didn't trust him. He lied to Walker. He spread rumors that Noah and I were together, and we're not! We're not!" My voice cracked into something inaudible as the tears flowed down my cheeks.

For a moment, I felt everyone's gaze leave me for Noah, but it didn't last long. There was something in the way they were all staring that felt like I was being interrogated in front of a jury. Only I knew how guilty I really was, and they were just on the cusp of realizing it.

Emma wrapped her arms around me and patted my shoulder. Everybody else mumbled in the background. Accusations. Assumptions. But mostly questions. What happened to Mason? Where was he now? What did we do?

The guilt boiled up inside. At first it was a simmer, like a stew on the stove being prepared for dinner. The questions filled the open space around me. Their voices became louder and louder until I couldn't take one more second.

"Stop it!" I yelled.

They continued despite my plea.

"A wolf?"

"What kind of wolf?"

"Is he out there now? Does he have Mason?"

"Stop it! Stop it, stop it, stop it!" I couldn't believe the shrill voice was my own. I was screaming. My fists were balled tightly next to my temples, and my eyes squeezed shut. The stew was a rolling boil, the pot forgotten, and dinner ruined.

The lights flickered and clapped overhead. The light bulbs exploded, and glass rained down on us in the now dark kitchen. I covered my head with my hands.

In the blackness, everyone's breath became audible. My stomach churned as the shock settled. *I did that*. I was capable of terrible things. Somewhere, hidden deep within me, were pockets of darkness, places I'd yet to see or know.

I closed my eyes and clenched my jaw. I drowned out the whispers that something was wrong with me and the sounds of broken glass under moving feet. I hadn't wanted this to happen. I wanted us to be a team. I wanted us to work together. To be there for one another. I wanted this to feel like a family away from home. I wanted Walker.

"Hello?" Walker's voice penetrated my thoughts.

I opened my eyes to see the lights back on and everyone looking around the room in awe. Walker was in the doorway, just as confused as the rest of them.

There was no glass shattered on the kitchen counters, no glass shards on the floor beneath my shoes. I squinted up at the bright light to see everything was perfectly intact, as if the explosion had never happened.

I did that, too.

I'd broken the lights, but more importantly, I'd put them back together. But before I let my mind run away with possibilities, I saw I hadn't changed everything. The scowls remained on the faces of my friends. The one thing I couldn't do was change the minds and hearts of everyone around me. And they were more suspicious now than ever before.

10

My hands trembled and my fingers jammed in the wrong holes on the dial of the old rotary phone. I choked back tears as I frantically tried to call my gran. This needed to stop. It needed to stop *now*. I was *done* with it. I was done with feeling out of control. I was hurting the people I loved most, and if there was a power deep inside me, now was the time it needed to come out. My gran was the only one who could help me. I knew she had the answers. A simple call was all it would take—if I could ever get this old telephone to work.

"Wilde?" Walker asked softly as he pushed the bedroom door open.

My chin wobbled as I messed with the phone. Was it six nine? Or nine six?

"Wilde, what are you doing?" he asked.

I sniffled, shoving my fat fingers into the tiny holes and trying desperately to circle the dial around the face of the phone. Each number took an eternity to wind back, and I kept forgetting Gran's phone number and how far into the sequence I had dialed. I slammed the receiver down not once, but twice, and then I closed my eyes tightly, letting the tears fall to my lap. I didn't want Walker to see me break down, but more importantly, I didn't want him to see the guilt I harbored for what I'd done to Mason. He crossed the room and sat next to me with his hand on my back, soothing me with slow, methodical strokes. I fought the urge to break down completely. I opened my eyes to face him and bare my heartache. I felt so small for all that I was. In the face of great expectations, I was falling short.

"What is it?" Walker asked.

I took a deep breath and glared at him through burning eyes. "I can't do this."

My eyes flickered to the phone and picked up the receiver again. Walker stopped me with his hand on mine. Slowly, we put the receiver down. I didn't have it in me to fight for a phone call I knew I wouldn't go through. She probably wouldn't have answered anyway. Walker held my hand until I gave him my full attention.

"You can't do what?" he asked calmly.

"Everything. Anything. All of it," I stared him dead in the eyes. If eyes were the windows to the soul, I was exposing just how weak I really was. And I hated to face my vulnerability.

I was afraid I was going to let all my friends die, right here in Baylor. I was afraid they were going to get picked off, one by one. Not only would I be unable to help them, but I'd be the one who set them up. The one who served them a cold plate of my poisonous mind. I didn't have the power Walker saw in me, and I never would. I was scared he would figure out that he was wasting his time with me. I was sure of these fears and so much more.

I didn't tell him I was afraid he would never love me, or that I was afraid he was using me to help him find Layla. The entire world was crashing down on my shoulders, and I wasn't strong enough to keep standing.

"We can do this, Wilde. I can help you." He rubbed his thumb methodically across my knuckles.

I shook my head, protesting.

"I need to talk to my gran."

"Here. What's her number?" Walker picked up the phone to dial for me. I rattled off her number effortlessly. It seemed so easy when he did it. He handed me the receiver, and I waited miserably through the never-ending rings.

"Try again," I said, when she didn't answer.

I waited as the phone rang, the tone growing louder, mocking me and my failure.

"Try it again," I said.

With each ring, I felt more and more alone. I was lost between the realms of the dead and living, and I wasn't sure I'd ever find my way. My answers were on the other end of this old Victorian phone—if she'd only pick up.

She didn't.

"Try it again!" I snapped. My hands shook when he took the receiver from me, and I wanted to pry it out of his hands and hold it to my chest. Why wouldn't she answer my call? Why wasn't she there when I needed her? Didn't she know she was being summoned? Was she gone forever? What if I never got to speak to her again?

Walker pulled me into a tight embrace. It was the straw that broke the camel's back. "I need to talk to her . . . I need to . . ."

"Shhh." He ran his hands up the nape of my neck and scratched the back of my head, tangling my hair into a mess.

"I know you think you need your gran to get you out of this mess. But I'm here. I might be all you have, but I promise you, it's enough. I can help . . . you just have to let me."

"Did you hear what I did to Mason?" I asked. He'd probably leave me when he heard, just like my gran had. If he knew what a monster I was, he wouldn't want to help me. And I didn't deserve it anyway. "Did you hear that I locked him out of the shed and let a wolf attack him?"

Walker's head tilted to the side as he looked at me empathetically. "Kinsley, you didn't *do* anything. You didn't do it," he repeated firmly, with his hands pressed against my cheeks as he held my head to stare into my eyes. "*You* didn't do it," he said again. Clear as day.

"It was gigantic. It ripped him apart, and I did nothing to help him . . ."

"Shhh."

I quivered, opening and closing my mouth like a fish out of water.

"Shhh."

I let him hold me for a long while as my emotions ran the gamut. We didn't speak for some time. I let the silence wash over me until every single emotion battling inside me solidified into one sole winner: defeat.

"Look, if you want to turn this thing around, you have to start slow. You're going to have to work at it. There's no other way around it," he said.

"I'm going to," I promised. "I'll work all night if I have to." If there was a way to right my wrongs, I'd do it.

Walker smirked. "It's going to take longer than that. You'll have to be patient."

"Well, I'm free now. Should we get started? I'm not going to sleep tonight anyway. I have nothing but suspicious friends downstairs—and not that many of them left. For all I know, they could barge through that door at any moment brandishing sage and pitchforks. If they don't go hunting for a wolf tonight, they're likely going to come for me. I saw the way they were looking at me . . . like I did it. Like I was doing it on purpose. But I'm not. I swear." I begged him to believe me.

"I know you're not."

"I have to harness this power. It must be now." I was determined to strong-arm the magic. Walker smiled from one side of his mouth, and a dimple appeared. He was somewhere between pitying me and being sincere. But I didn't care. I needed this. I needed to show my friends that I could turn it around. Otherwise, each one of them would fear me until the day they died.

Walker looked around the room and stepped away, snatching something from the dresser. He sat on the floor and placed a small peach-scented candle in front of him. He took a lighter from his pocket and lit it. Eagerly, I took a seat across from him on the carpet.

"To control this power, you need to harness your focus. There is a small stream of smoke rising from this flame. I want you to bend it."

It seemed kind of boring. I'd rather work on changing its color or scent. And to be honest, it took me longer than I'd like to be able to find the stream of smoke in the first place. But there it was, a small shadow that rose from the white-tipped flame. It was small and steady, so it should be easily pliable. *This was a joke.*

I took my time staring at the smoke without results. And then I imagined that I had cupped it with my hand. Immediately, the smoke flickered.

"Hey, I think it's working," Walker said eagerly.

I frowned. It wasn't quite what I was imagining. I tried again. The flame flickered slightly to the side. The scent of peaches danced in the space between us, reminding me that this should be fun.

"Good job, keep going," he whispered, careful not to distract me.

But the only thing distracting was how pathetic this was. It was only smoke; it should be easy.

I could extinguish the flame with my breath if I wanted to. I tried again. This time, I imagined my hand was made of steel, and I was forcing the smoke to contour to the curves of my palm. But clearly, by the lack of transformation, strong-arming this manifestation wasn't the way to succeed. I sighed and peeked up at Walker. He hadn't lost a single ounce of patience. His eyes beamed with excitement. He looked as if he could do this *all* night long. He believed in me, far more than I ever had.

I tried again. I imagined a pencil in my hand, and the flame was my drawing. I pictured drawing it in a different angle and smudging the smoke off to the side with my thumb. If anything, I was getting worse at this. Nothing happened at all.

"I just don't understand. I've done more than bend smoke before. Why can't I do this?" I leaned back on my hands.

"It's complicated. You must be in the right mindset. You've got to believe in yourself. If you can't do that, then nothing will ever change. You've got to find that something inside of you that won't take no for an answer. You've got to change your entire identity if you want to believe in yourself. Are you the kind of person who can bend smoke? Or not?"

That was the problem. I'd never believed in myself. From the day I began school, I learned I couldn't keep up with the masses. There was something fundamentally wrong with me. The funny part was, in the eye of that disappointment, I never totally gave up. I kept trucking along, meeting failure at every step. It was the only path I'd ever known. Regardless of whether I believed I could do it or not, I knew I would never give up.

I tried to think about that feeling now. What was it that had made the magic work before? How had I stopped time to enjoy a moment I never wanted to forget? Slowly, I looked up from the candle to marvel at Walker. His encouragement was palpable. His patience was everlasting. *It was him.* It was the way he made me feel. It was the way he made me feel . . . about myself.

I'd told him many terrible things about myself. I'd told him I'd killed a man. He'd said it wasn't my fault. I'd told him I was a monster. He'd said I had to believe in myself. Walker had always made me feel like I was more worthy than I gave myself credit for. He was my biggest fan. And I wanted to live up to the image he had of me. The girl he thought I was. I wanted to be better. I could identify with that, right? I could be all powerful? Magical?

I turned to the candle again, imagining the smoke sprawling off to the side. I squinted my eyes, focusing all my energy toward the tiny flame. And when the stream of smoke didn't so much as flicker, I blew it out, just like I had the candles on my eighteenth birthday cake.

The room went dark. I could hear Walker's lips part in a smile.

My cheeks warmed with embarrassment. I couldn't do it. It was such a stupid small thing, and I couldn't do it. If I failed at the start, the lowest point of entry, then where could I go from here? Flying was clearly far too advanced, but so was smoke bending. I didn't understand myself, and I never would. My mind was a labyrinth of locked boxes.

"What?" Walker chuckled.

I rubbed my eyes, and a small smile formed.

"What was that?" He laughed openly.

"What? I couldn't do it." I said, thankful the room was dark, and he couldn't see my face very well.

"Oh, but you did! You certainly found a way." He said laughing even harder now.

That I had. I'd found a way. He always saw the good in me. I wasn't dumb in his eyes. I wasn't powerless. I was the girl who found a way.

His laughter was like music to my ears, and I wished I could see his dimples, because I knew they would be glorious. A treat sweeter than any summer peach.

The room illuminated in a soft orange glow. *There they are.* Those dimples, his smile. It warmed my heart, and I got lost in his presence.

His laughter dwindled, and his dazzling smile faded. His eyes dropped to the floor between us, and I grew alarmed.

"Did you do that?" he asked looking at the candle.

"Do what—"

The candle was lit. I froze. When did that happen? More importantly, *how* had it happened?

"Wow . . ."

"You didn't bend the smoke; you lit the flame. You're amazing!" Walker bounded to his feet, arms spread wide. I leapt up and hugged him, drawing in his coastal scent, and filling my lungs with pride.

I didn't know how I'd done it, but that correlated with all the times before. I never knew how. It sort of just happened all on its own. When my mind turned off and my heart swelled . . . that's when the magic happened.

I began to pull away so that I could tell Walker what I had just realized when his arms tightened around me. I froze momentarily and then sank back into his hold. He didn't want to let go. He wanted to hold on to me a little while longer. Did he have feelings for me? It felt less of a celebratory hug and more like the hug you'd give somebody that you missed. Like he was soaking up all of me. Like he'd missed me, even though I'd been right here all along.

I laid my head down on his chest, and he rested his chin on top of my head. His hands slowly rubbed the middle of my back, diving a little deeper with each stroke. *What was happening?*

My heart beat against him. The low thuds were audible, and I knew he could hear it hammering between us. Hell, he could probably feel it. But it wasn't just my heart; it was his too. Whatever I was feeling, I wasn't alone. I dared to raise my head, afraid to snap us out of whatever this was, but longing for a kiss. Slowly, I lifted my eyes, trailing up his neck to his stubbled chin and resting my gaze on the bow of his lips. I swallowed the lump in my throat and then took the leap, looking deep into his golden eyes.

His gaze was intense. Like he was at war with himself. I swore he was trying to tell me something, but what? Did he want to kiss me?

He winced as if he was in physical pain and then pulled away abruptly. Just as quickly as it came, the moment was gone. He ran his hands through his hair, turning away from me. Had I done something wrong?

"Is everything okay?" I asked softly. I slid my hands into my back pockets and gnawed on my lip.

"Yeah. Yeah. No, it's great. We're getting somewhere. Pretty soon . . . we'll be able to find Layla again." My stomach sank with the sound of her name on his lips. The room turned icy and hollow. It was stupid for me to think there was room in his heart for anything other than her.

"That's right. I'm sure we'll find her soon." I did what I could to reassure him and not look like a fool.

I thought back to the last time I'd seen her. She hadn't even been interested in Walker. I didn't know what was worse, knowing that he didn't want me, or knowing that he'd chosen her. All I wanted was for him to be happy. And sure, in a perfect world, I'd get what I wanted too. *But why her?*

"So, what do you think is going to happen when you find her?" I pried.

"Well, shit . . . . I guess I'll apologize," he said, like it had knocked the breath out of him.

"For what!?" I snapped. Didn't he know he'd done nothing wrong? That it was an *accident*?

"If it hadn't been for me, she would have lived a long, full life. She's out there, lost and probably scared, because of what I did. It doesn't matter if it was an accident, it was my fault. I did it. I stole her life." His voice sank into a pit so deep I wasn't sure he could crawl out. Maybe he never had.

I didn't like the way this sounded. Somehow, it felt personal. "Wait a minute, if you think you killed her . . . Then you think I killed Mason." I cocked my head to one side.

Walker spun around in shock. "Whoa. No, no, no. I didn't say that . . ."

"Yes, you did. That's exactly what you're saying. Oh my god, you think I killed them? All of them? Trinity? Big Jimmy? Lainey? Ethan and Mason? Oh my god . . ." I pressed my fingers to my temples as I took it all in. He thought I was a mass murderer. Was I?

"No!" he snapped.

"You've just been pretending that you think I'm amazing so that I don't lose my magic. You've been trying to keep me on track so I would find Layla for you!" I took a step back.

The flame flickered madly, and Walker held his hands out in front of him. "Wilde . . . That's not what I said, and that's certainly not what I think. Don't put words into my mouth."

"It was an accident. They all were," I said.

"I know . . ."

"Are you using me?" My heart stilled in anticipation of his answer. I didn't know what I would do if the answer was yes. I certainly hadn't been prepared to ask.

"Wilde, listen to me . . ." he began, as several other candles in the bedroom lit, casting dancing shadows on the walls surrounding us. "While it's true I'm trying to keep you on track, and that I'm trying to teach you to find yourself and your power, it's for you. I care about you. I . . . I *love* you, Wilde!"

The flames froze, and the shadows fixed in place.

"You're the only family I've got left. You're my only friend here. And it just so happens, you're the only hope I have to find Layla."

My heart thumped with disappointment. The flames grew tall, thrashing frantically about. Of course, he didn't love me romantically. But was I so wrong to latch onto those three little words?

"Do you think I killed those people? Do you think I'm capable of bad things?" I asked.

"I think we're all capable of making mistakes. Grave mistakes that have outcomes far beyond any premeditated measures. I know what happened was an accident. It's just hard for me to admit that to myself." Walker shook his head and swiped a finger at the corner of his eye. He wasn't using me. He was just a guy riddled with guilt, in the same way that I'd been. We really were two of a kind, and I couldn't believe I'd thought otherwise.

"You can't call it an accident when I did it then take the blame when you do it. Either we're *both* killers, or we're *both* total screw-ups. You choose," I said.

Walker closed the distance between us and wrapped his arms around me. We'd been doing a lot of touching tonight, but I wasn't complaining. Maybe it was the new normal? This one was different yet again. It wasn't passionate like the last one, and it wasn't celebratory like the first. This hug was . . . *brotherly*. It was the kind of hug you give to somebody that you both love and love to hate. It was firm and a little aggressive.

"Come here, you screw-up," he said. I laughed and slapped his back with my own frustration.

"I love you too, *buddy*," I said with a laugh. Walker flinched. It was barely noticeable, but it was there. That jab stung. He didn't want me to love him like a buddy any more than I wanted the same from him. And I couldn't help but wonder, what would our relationship be like if Layla ceased to exist?

"You think you can turn down your flames of rage now?" Walker joked as he eyed the candles. The room shook with the furious silhouettes of my heightened emotions. The light of a half-dozen candles burning like tiny torches.

"Oh my god! That's what I wanted to tell you. I think I figured it out. The magic isn't made from thought. The magic is made from feeling."

"What does that mean?"

"Well, all this time I've been trying to make things happen by imagining them, but it always seemed like it was when I stopped trying that the magic happened. I realized it was a feeling—an emotion—that turned the magic on."

"Do you think you can control your feelings?"

"I don't know?"

"Try it! You have about one, two, six candles lit in this room. Try to blow them out."

I considered the half dozen candles spread throughout the master bedroom. Walker placed a finger over my lips. "No cheating," he said.

I smirked and closed my eyes. It was hard to think of anything other than his skin upon my lips. I promised myself I could relive all the moments another time—if I got this right.

This time I didn't think about the candles at all. I knew I wanted to blow them out; I didn't have to imagine it. Instead, I chose to feel the subtle warmth leach from the room, envision the dim glow fade to black behind my eyelids as the flames extinguished, and feel the pride swell in my lungs like fresh air. And just like magic, the room went dark with victory.

11

The next morning, I woke to a low hum outside my window. I thought little of it as I got ready to meet Walker. But just as I was about to leave the bedroom, the buzzing noise nagged at me. What was it? It was too quiet for a lawnmower, too constant for a plane. I crossed the room and slid the window open, sticking my head outside to look around. The hum turned to a buzz, and I noticed tons of tiny dots flying frantically about. Several of them took notice of me and swarmed, trying to scare me off.

I pulled back, slamming the window shut and windmilling my arms through the air. There was a massive beehive tucked into the eaves of the cabin just outside my window. And now there were several bees inside, buzzing around me as I darted in wild bursts around the bedroom. I swatted and twirled, but it only made them angrier. I let out a yelp and ran into the hallway, slamming the door shut behind me. I came face to face with Emma.

"What's all that about?" she asked, eyeing me suspiciously.

"So many bees. There are *so* many bees outside my window right now," I said breathlessly. I thought I felt something on the back of my arm, and I swiped at it violently and craned my head to see if it was a bee.

"Really? Oh my god," Emma said, flinching from my wild theatrics. She'd tied her hair back in a ponytail. Her black leggings and hot pink sports bra under a loose muscle tank told me she was on her way out. Her sneakers were caked with dried mud from all the hiking she'd gotten in while being in Baylor.

"Are you taking Gunner out?" I asked.

"Yeah, do you want to come?"

"I would love to, but I have plans to meet Walker this morning. We're starting my training. There's a theory I want to test today, and I'm hoping for a breakthrough." I rolled my eyes, knowing my breakthrough wasn't coming anytime soon.

"Oh yeah?" she joked, as we walked downstairs. Kai and Asher were in the middle of an intense video game in the living room. Kai was still half tucked in his sleeping bag, like a butterfly only half emerged, stopping his metamorphosis to play Night of Emerald's Kingdom.

The coffee pot was only halfway filled, and Emma didn't bother waiting for it to finish before she got on with her hike. Gunner did pirouettes out the back door as I waved goodbye to them. I wished I could get that excited about exercise. But right now, caffeine was the only thing I was enthusiastic about.

"Oh! You can't do that!" Asher yelled, and a sleeping Noah stirred.

"Shut up, dude. You can't wake up the entire house just because you're losing," Kai said.

I curled up on the sofa and watched the guys battle it out in the Castle of Greenland. I knew the game all too well. My little brother used to make me play with him. I used to pretend it was such a bother, but I secretly enjoyed it. But the one who'd liked the video games the most was Mason. It seemed odd that he wasn't sprawled out on the sofa, controller in hand.

The cabin seemed a little quieter in his absence. Smaller, in a sense. The guys were so captivated by their game. Had they forgotten what had happened to Mason? And why wasn't anybody blaming me? Surely, with my breaking all the lights in the cabin last night, somebody would have recognized me as a monster. I wanted to ask why they weren't sad, but I knew I'd be getting myself into trouble if I did. Forgetting about Mason was better for everybody. And honestly, I was jealous. I wished I could unpack the guilt and grief, the worry and shame, and spend my day in the Castle of Greenland. I supposed I would have to mourn alone. That's how it always felt, anyway.

The coffee maker beeped, and I leapt from the sofa. "Coffee?" I asked. I poured four mugs—two of them to go. As the coffee swirled at the top of the mug, I had a bad feeling about Asher. I mixed in creamer and sugar while I contemplated saying anything. I didn't want to give any credence to the thought, as that's when the bad things would happen. I handed the guys their coffee and said, "Hey, be really careful today. There's a beehive outside," as if it were nothing.

"Wait, what?" Asher asked. I rolled my eyes. It wasn't nothing when he was deathly allergic. I knew that. He knew that.

"There is a huge beehive in the eaves of the cabin. Right outside. We need to call a fumigator or something."

"Shit," Asher said, raking a hand through his hair.

"Looks like you're staying inside today," Kai laughed.

"I'll call somebody. I just don't know who takes care of these kinds of things. But I'll figure it out," I said, taking the to-go coffees and backing out the patio door.

"Be careful!" Kai yelled.

"Dude, shut up!" Noah grumbled from within his sleeping bag. The door slammed shut and I flinched, hearing the muffled groaning inside. I turned away and ducked my head while I hurried off the patio. The coffee spilled down my knuckles as I reached the lawn.

It was going to be a warm day. There wasn't a cloud in the sky, and the waters were calm. I sat on the end of the dock, sipping my coffee and searching my phone for bee removal in the Baylor Lake area. There were a few chat threads, but nothing official to be found in the small town. What did these people do when a swarm of bees moved in? I scrolled, searching for answers, and ended up calling the only option I found. Bobby Keller, a retired fumigator who still did side jobs for neighbors. I shrugged; it would have to do. I couldn't have hundreds of bees swarming the cabin, especially when Asher was allergic—and I had a propensity to make bad things happen.

I scheduled Bobby for that evening.

When I heard the gentle lapping of lake water against a canoe, I knew that Walker was paddling into the cove. I could only make out a baseball cap and an amber-colored T-shirt, but I felt his smile.

That guy right there, he loves me.

Maybe like a sister, but still. I'd been holding onto the thought that maybe he'd been lying to himself. I bit my lip in anticipation and watched him slowly glide toward the dock. Today was going to be a good day.

"Are you ready for this?" I asked, clapping my hands together.

"Am *I* ready? Are *you* ready?" he smirked.

"What have we got planned today, boss?" I was eager to test my theory.

"I don't know, how do explosions sound?" He took the coffee from my hand and helped me into the canoe.

"Explosions?" Now that was exciting. Way better than the elementary task of smoke-bending.

"Have you ever gone trapshooting?" he asked, pushing away from the dock.

"No, what's that?"

"It's when a machine throws clay pigeons and you try to shoot them while they're in the air."

"Oh, no. I've never shot a gun before." I searched the canoe for a shotgun.

"Who needs a gun when you have magic?" he said, a twinkle in his eye.

What? Was I the smoking gun? Did he expect me to shatter a clay pigeon with my mind? And then I remembered, that's exactly what I'd done to the light bulbs in the cabin last night. I shrugged, unsure of myself. "I guess we could try it." I eyed a small fishing boat near shore.

It took twice as long to get to our destination as I had expected. Maybe it was the performance anxiety, or maybe it was because I had drunk a large coffee on the way over, but either way, I had to pee. *Bad*. When the canoe bumped against the shore, I leapt out and ran into the forest to find a spot completely hidden from Walker.

I sighed in relief, zipped my shorts, and peered around. I'd been so focused on hiding from Walker, I hadn't realized what a great job I'd done. I must have gone farther than I thought, because I couldn't even tell which direction the lake was. The forest was dense with trees and seemed to go on forever. I listened for the water and the distant sound of motors on the lake, but all I heard were the bird songs emanating from the treetops.

"Walker!?" I yelled. My voice echoed in a way it shouldn't. Like my call had bounced off an invisible bubble and ricocheted back to me. Tiny goosebumps prickled my arms. Something was off.

Was I in the void? I spun around, trying to read between the lines. What was I not seeing here? What was right in front of my face?

I heard her before I saw her. A giggle that sounded pure as the songbirds and as joyous as a child playing in sprinkler water on a hot summer day. But Layla's echo was cut short. The sound was not traveling the distance as it should. Whatever was happening, we were trapped in it together.

It wasn't until I saw the red cloak from the corner of my eye that I realized she *wanted* it to be like this. She took pleasure in it. She wasn't trapped like I was; she reveled in the twisted shapes of the Baylor phenomenon.

Layla darted behind trees and dropped behind large rocks. She hid behind things that were a quarter of her size, and yet, no red peeked out for me to see. She slipped behind a sapling no wider than my wrist and disappeared completely. I sucked in a sharp breath. It was impossibly frustrating and magnificent all at the same time. What *was* she? And why wasn't Walker like that? Maybe he didn't want to spook me like she did.

"You're really good at hide and seek. You must have been playing for a long time," I said, stepping cautiously through the forest.

Layla giggled behind me, and just as I spun around, the red fabric passed in front of my eyes with lightning speed.

I groaned deep in my throat, feeling trapped and disadvantaged. I followed her deeper into the forest, not because I wanted to, but because I *had* to. She'd been so elusive that I couldn't ignore her, even if I tried.

But with every flash of red, and every turn, I might as well have been walking in circles. There was no way of telling which way I had come or how to get back. And there was no way I'd ever win this game if she was the one I was playing against.

I became more and more tense with every sighting of the red cloak. When she stilled long enough to deliver a genuine, mischievous smile, her eyes pierced mine, grabbing hold and refusing to let go.

Her long hair danced behind her as if she were floating in water. She was like a majestic animal, beautiful, but dangerous. We both stood still, sizing each other up. My heart hammered in my chest. She was a good several strides away, but I knew that even if I caught her, I'd be unable to hold her for long.

What did she want? Why did she provoke me like this?

"I don't want to play anymore, Layla," I said through gritted teeth. "I'm done!" I turned away, severing the intense eye contact, and stomped off. I became hyperaware that I'd just turned my back on her, and I feared what she might do to me because of it.

I wasn't sure where I was headed, but I knew it was away from her. Until, of course, it wasn't.

She materialized in front of me, blocking the path. I startled but tried not to show it. I put my hands on my hips, more frustrated than intrigued for the first time. I hated what she did to me. The way I felt around her. I didn't need her like I used to. I didn't want to find my way out of this mess. If anything, I was looking for a way to secure a life here amidst the weirdness. And I had a special day planned with *her* boyfriend that I didn't want to miss. My decision was made; I wanted to stay in Baylor. And she could go away now.

Layla's stare was playful at first, but quickly turned menacing, as if she'd read my thoughts. Her pupils dilated, darkening her eyes to coal. She pulled the *Waking Dreams* book out of her cloak, and I instinctively lunged for it.

But Layla wasn't an apparition of my mind like most of them. She was a true ghost, and my hands swiped right through her. She threw her head back and laughed, loud and boisterous. I hoped Walker wouldn't hear. This was the only time I wished he wouldn't come save me.

"That's mine!" I snarled.

She tilted her head to the side, and her lips curled upward.

All my gran wanted from me was to find this girl. And now that I had, I couldn't help but wonder *why*? I was expecting a wise old mage. One who knew the secrets of the world and would bestow a single answer to the one burning question inside my heart. But what I got instead was a twisted joker, a funhouse of disappearing acts, and more questions than I knew what to do with.

Did I have the wrong girl?

Gran said she needed my help. But this girl didn't need help, and if she did, she certainly didn't want it from *me*. She loathed me. She was like the

Cheshire Cat, and I was her mouse. Little more than entertainment to bat around in the afterlife.

A branch snapped, stealing my attention. Walker spun around on a ridge, far in the distance. He was looking for me. I saw him cup his hands to the corners of his mouth and call out. I couldn't hear a single word.

"What have you done!?" I demanded, taking another swipe at the book. We squared off. She held the book out of reach, and I was ready to pounce on it.

This time, Layla didn't look as amused. I could tell that she didn't like Walker here. It was her intention to bait me, and *only* me. Walker's eyes scanned right past where Layla and I stood without ever stopping. Couldn't he see us?

"Walker!" I yelled, stepping out and waving my hands overhead. He ran both his hands through his hair and then called out in silence once again.

"Walker . . ." I whispered. A loneliness coiled in the pit of my stomach, and for some reason, it made me miss home.

He wandered aimlessly, weaving in and out of the trees and yelling my name silently. He came so close I could reach out and touch him, but I didn't dare. The way his frightened eyes passed right through me sent a never-ending chill down my spine. Was this what it was like to be a ghost? I hated it. I hated everything about it.

Baylor had become my dreams, and my nightmares . . . and everything in between. But if there was a chance that I'd live here like Layla, unseen and unloved, this truly would be hell. I winced at the very thought. The *torture* she must bear . . .

My eyes watered as I pulled my gaze from Walker back to Layla. She looked just as frightened as he was. I no longer saw the twisted dark joker, but a lonesome girl who had lost her way. *No, no, no.* I couldn't feel bad for her. She was the enemy.

My heart sank even deeper as Walker passed by me, searching for something right in front of him. I lifted my hand, ever so slightly, and felt the wake of cold air pass by. Sure, being unseen hurt, but it was downright agonizing to think of Walker losing both Layla and me.

If he had to roam Baylor for another twenty years looking for me, my heart would crack in half. I'd go absolutely crazy. I'd be just like Layla—playing adult hide-and-seek with the only person who wanted to find her.

Had she been right in front of Walker this entire time? Unseen? That would drive anybody mad.

It was so sad to think he'd been tortured with the guilt of the accident for all this time when she was right here with him. Layla had probably tried to get messages through but couldn't.

I now knew why Layla needed my help.

My chest squeezed, causing me to bring a hand to my heart. Walker spun around, eyes wide and mouth agape. Something had happened in his world that hadn't happened in the bubble with Layla. He frantically ran back the way he had come, leaving Layla and me alone.

I whipped my head around to see that Layla had vanished. In her wake were a dozen pages from the book fluttering to the ground. I lunged for them, falling to my knees and grabbing them, pulling them close.

Walker was out of sight, and Layla was gone. It was just me and the pages. I flipped them over, looking for titles, but they were all bodies of text. Tiny print from top to bottom. An anxiousness passed through me. How was I supposed to read all these pages and get back to Walker in time?

And then something changed. The print was getting lighter. I frantically looked through all the pages, and they too were changing. The words were fading, the ink leaching from the pages. I started scanning as fast as I could before there was nothing left for me to consume. But they were just words. Random words. And I wasn't fast enough to read them. All faded but a single line.

You don't belong here.

I sat back on my heels. The phrase stung the back of my throat. I knew she thought I didn't belong here, but that wasn't the complete story. I looked back, afraid that Walker would find me, and I would have to explain that his beloved had been sending me letters. Little notes telling me to leave him behind, the same way that she had. Were there more girls like me? Had Walker met other girls in this realm who Layla had scared away?

Fearing Walker's family curse—that love would never find him—I dug a hole in the dry soil. Staring at the page with a single line left, full of insult and judgment, I ripped it into tiny pieces, letting them fall into the hole. Layla didn't know me. She had no right to tell me where I belonged or who I belonged with. I pushed the dirt on top of the ripped pages and covered the evidence from Layla's visit.

I walked back in the direction I had last seen Walker heading, wiping the dirt from my hands onto my shorts. It wasn't long before I found the clearing and our canoe.

"Kinsley! Are you all right?" Walker came running up to me.

I should have felt relieved that he could see me and I could hear him, but all I really felt was sadness for both Walker and Layla. Coming so close and failing to unite all these years. Tortured side by side and not even knowing it. At least *he* hadn't. She, on the other hand, she knew it, and that had been enough to make her crazy. I rubbed at the ache in my chest. Layla wasn't the threat I'd always imagined her to be. She was the girl who needed my help.

"What happened?" Walker asked, flipping my hand over and examining the dirt underneath my fingernails.

I pulled my hand back. "Sorry. I just hid behind a tree and kind of stumbled down a slope. I'm okay." I said hiding my hands in my back pockets.

"God, I've been looking everywhere for you. Didn't you hear me?" he asked.

"No." It wasn't a lie. But it wasn't the complete truth either. It was better he didn't know. It would only hurt him more. At least, that's what I told myself.

"Didn't you hear the explosion?" Walker scratched at his head, confused.

"Explosion?" I suddenly noticed the pieces of clay pigeons scattered around the canoe. "No. What happened?"

"I don't know. I was out there looking for you, and I heard an explosion. They all spontaneously burst. Now I have nothing for you to practice on." I thought back to when Walker had looked surprised and taken off running. The box of clay discs had burst, but why? How?

"Is something wrong with your chest?" he asked, eyeing me.

"Oh, it's nothing." I dropped my dirty hand. But the truth was, there was an ache in my chest. Call it guilt, call it sorrow, but I'd had it when the explosion happened. Maybe I had already completed today's mission, and I didn't even know it. I picked up a tiny piece of clay that fit in the palm of my hand and flipped it over. "We could still use these, right?"

Walker shrugged, taking the piece from my hand. He looked at it for a moment and then chucked it as hard as he could out over the water. Without hesitation, I let the excitement spark something inside of me, and the piece of clay shattered over the water.

"Whoa, did you see that!" he exclaimed.

Somehow, his excitement was contagious. I stifled a giggle behind my hand as Walker picked up another piece. Before I could let the fear of disappointment if I failed enter my mind, Walker had thrown the piece of clay and it was breaking into dozens of pieces.

With each piece we broke together, the ache in my chest became lighter. But I knew it would never fully fade. There would always be a doubt that refused to disappear as the single passage had. And the worry that I wasn't where I belonged would fester until it became infected. But for right now, while Walker had a huge smile on his face and I was getting the hang of this thing we called magic, I would let that piece of me rest.

12

Walker and I cleared the shore of broken clay pigeons that had been created in the explosion. I'd shattered every single one. Even the sneaky one he threw while trying to tickle me. I hadn't missed a beat. And with every little win, my confidence grew stronger. That seemed to be the key to it all. Locking in on a feeling and working it like a muscle. Once I trusted that I could break the next piece of clay, the explosions were bigger and louder, like thunder cracking overhead.

I got so good that, about halfway through, one clay chip exploded after it had barely left Walker's hand, and I had to pull back a bit. I learned to wait for the piece to be far away from Walker's hand, and at the highest point above the water, before shattering it into thousands of pieces. I couldn't have our fun end short with a burned hand. Though, knowing Walker, it probably wouldn't have affected him anyway.

It was the most successful day I'd had yet. I'd learned not only how to work the magic, but I'd also learned how to hold back, even if it was just for a few seconds. I had tapped into the spot inside me that made everything possible. It was the trickiest spot of all—my confidence—but at least I knew it was there, fickle as it may be. I didn't want to leave when we ran out of clay pigeons, but I had to get back before the fumigator came.

The ride back was quick and left me longing for more time with Walker. I hardly thought about the eerie sighting of Layla in the forest; I wanted to forget about it all together. Feeling sorry for her would not help me win her boyfriend. And I couldn't possibly survive being torn in another direction.

When we paddled into the cove and found Noah and Kai running around the clearing like little boys playing tag, I knew our magical day was over.

There was always tomorrow, I supposed. And as long as I played my cards right, my tomorrows would be endless. We would build a life here, so full of magic that *nobody* would want to leave. And nobody would have to.

"What are they doing?" Walker asked, stifling a laugh. I frowned as I watched Kai take his shirt off and swing it around his head. Gunner ran around barking at all the commotion. Were they drunk? What on earth was happening? I started to laugh, but the feeling faded fast.

"Oh my god, oh my god! It's the bees!" All I could see from the water were the two guys. Asher was nowhere to be found, and I prayed he was safe inside. I watched Noah pick up a rock and chuck it into the eaves near my window. "No! Don't do that!" I yelled, standing and making the canoe rock. Walker grabbed the sides and held on tight.

As soon as we could tie up, I hopped out onto the dock, but the boys had disappeared into the cabin. "Sometimes I think they left their brains back in Clover," I said with a sigh.

"Now the bees are going to be angry when you walk up the hill. How are you going to get into the cabin without getting stung?" Walker asked. It was a fair question; one I didn't have an answer to.

"You mean I can't just explode my way out of this?" I asked.

"Please don't," he said, laughing. I smiled, taking in his dimples.

"I had a lot of fun today," I said.

"I did too."

"What are we going to work on tomorrow?" I asked, lingering on the dock as Walker remained in the canoe. He was heading back home, and I wanted him to stay.

"Well, now that you're a professional—"

"Hey, I wouldn't go *that* far." I could feel the heat creeping into my cheeks.

"Seriously, you did really well today. I'm proud of you."

"Thank you," I said, softly enough to be a whisper. I wrapped a lock of hair around my finger and let his words soak in so deep, I'd never forget them.

"I'll come up with a plan tonight, but I think it's fair to say we get to move on to something more advanced tomorrow. You've earned it." He winked.

I smiled, but the hoots and hollers coming from the cabin interrupted the moment. The back door slammed shut. Kai and Noah came outside looking oddly thicker than before. "What are they doing now?" I mumbled under my breath. Gunner was chasing them, barking with excitement. We had to be careful, otherwise the neighbors would call Animal Control again. I swiped my brow and gritted my teeth.

Emma stormed outside, shielding her head with her hand as she ran down to the dock. "Kinsley, you have to make them stop. They're trying to knock the beehive down to get the honey! They're wearing like five pairs of pants just so they don't get stung!"

"They don't need to do that; I've got it covered. There's a fumigator coming this evening," I said, looking at my watch.

"What! You can't do that!" She marched down the dock waving her hands in the air.

"Why not?"

"Because that's inhumane!"

"But it's Bobby Keller, and the neighbors love him . . ." I said, reciting one review. Now that she was right in front of me, I could see her eyes were narrowed and her cheeks flushed.

"But what about Lainey?"

I felt a tinge of pain in my chest and sucked in a breath, looking back at Walker. "What about Lainey?"

"Lainey loved all things nature. How do you think she would've felt if she knew you hired a fumigator to *kill* the bees?"

"But Bobby—"

"*Bobby . . . Freaking . . . Keller . . .* How do you think she would feel?" she repeated.

I sighed. She was right. Lainey would've hated this idea. With her love for flowers, I could only imagine how crazy she was about the bees. I thought back to the time she'd rescued a bee from our swimming pool.

"Okay," I said with a shrug.

"Okay?" she asked.

"Okay. I'm canceling the fumigator." I pulled out my phone and sent him a text.

"What are we going to do about these fools?" Emma asked, still fired up. That was a whole other problem.

I looked back to Walker for answers, but he shrugged. "Don't look at me." He held his hands up. He reached over and released the rope from the dock, and I knew he was leaving me to deal with this disaster alone.

Just then, Kai yelped, and his gleeful dance turned into one of panic. One cry became two, as he ran around hysterically, waving his arms all about like a sky-dancer at a used car lot.

Noah was quick on his heels as they chased each other onto the lawn. "This is like watching a train crash in slow motion," Walker said.

Emma shot me a look, and my blood ran cold. We'd never told the guys about our incident on the train, and the complete scene unwillingly played through my head despite my best efforts to stop it.

"Can't you do something?" Emma asked. But this didn't feel like shooting clay pigeons over the lake for fun. This felt like they were depending on me to save them, and there were a million ways it could go wrong.

"What do you expect *me* to do?" I asked.

"Yeah, Wilde, can you make the bees stop like you did with the fireworks?" Walker asked. This wasn't like the times before; it was intense. So much pressure came down on me that I nearly seized up. Instead, I forced myself not to think about it at all. Because if I'd learned one thing, it was that my thinking got me in trouble.

I acted quick like I had earlier when Walker was tickling me, and things were fun and flirty. I threw my hand out like a gun and pretended I was shooting the clay pigeons, just like before. Only this time, it wasn't a clay pigeon that exploded; it was the beehive. Pieces of the hive blew apart and thousands upon thousands of angry bees flew out.

A dark swarm gathered in the air as I took off running straight for Noah and Kai. Walker was quick on my heels, but Emma plunged into the lake. The buzzing of forty thousand bees vibrated in my very skull. The sound alone should have sent me running.

"Run! Run!" I screamed. I didn't know much about bees, but I knew they wouldn't chase you for very long. Less than a mile, my dad would say, and they'd be back with their swarm. "Run!"

Kai took off running straight into the forest. The dark cloud split in two, and half followed Kai into the woods. Gunner ran after him, barking hoarsely.

Noah fell to the ground and started rolling like he was on fire. I flung my hands wildly as I entered the killer swarm. I dropped to my knees by his side and tried to shield him, but it was too late. The bees were so tiny and fast. There was nothing I could do. He kicked and flailed as I tried to calm him.

The fear inside me rose, reminding me of when the lights had shattered in the cabin. The feeling grew as hundreds of bees pelted Noah. I didn't know if the bees *couldn't* sting me, or if I was so numb with adrenaline that I couldn't feel it, but there was no pain on my part. I sat by Noah's side unable to do anything to protect him.

"Kinsley, do something!" Walker yelled. I looked back, afraid to take my eyes off Noah. Walker was barely visible as the swarm dove straight through him. He was untouchable. Invincible. "Kinsley! Do. Something!" Walker's voice rang through my ears louder than the drone of the bees.

I don't know what to do!

I scrunched my eyes shut, the bees crawling over my face, and found a feeling. Not the feeling that I wasn't good enough, or that I might be a disappointment, but a feeling of protection. I tried to zero in on it, but the bees entangled in my hair kept me from concentrating. I tried to stay still. I tried to focus.

"Kinsley!" Walker yelled.

"I'm trying! I'm trying!"

Noah's writhing slowed beneath my hands. Tears streamed down my cheeks as he grew tired. He stilled, and I feared his time was over. "I'm trying . . ." I cried.

Nobody here could help me. And no matter how much Walker had tried to teach me, *I* was the only one holding my power back. I was holding them *all* back.

Everything grew louder. I heard Emma's screams from the lake, and I noticed banging on the windows for the first time. The drone of the bees waned, the crawling on my skin lessened, and the vibrating in my hair stilled. Everything calmed down. Except Walker. His voice was something I was tuned into, and I could hear him now.

"You're doing it! You're doing it!" he yelled. I used it like fuel to grow the magic.

Moments later, I dared to open my eyes, just as the last bee crawled across my lips and fluttered away. The large swarm lifted into the sky and left just as quickly as it had come. I looked down at Noah in utter shock. His arm was draped over his face, shielding him as best as he could. His lips were twice their normal size. Walker got behind his head and cradled it in his hands. Carefully, I lifted Noah's arm.

"Noah?" My voice strained.

Noah's face was red and swollen. His eyes were glued shut, but he was still breathing. A shallow breath, but there was hope. "What do we do?" I asked Walker. I heard Emma come up behind me, dripping. She was sopping wet with lake water. "What do we do?" I looked to her, pleading. But nobody had an answer.

"What do we do?" I whispered to myself. But even I didn't know. The back door slammed as Kimber barreled down the steps. I watched her fierce stride cross the yard. She dropped to her knees and stabbed Noah in the thigh with an EpiPen.

"Wow!" Walker gasped.

"Where'd you get that?" Emma asked.

"I picked it up today because I used Asher's other one. Thank god he stayed inside the cabin all day!" She pointed to the master bedroom, where Asher was watching from the window. His hand was pressed against the windowpane as he watched his best friend lying unconscious on the lawn. I couldn't be more relieved that he was okay. He never would have made it if he had been out here. I wasn't sure Noah would, and he wasn't allergic to anything.

"Thank you. Oh my god, thank you." I prayed that the medicine would work on him and that it wasn't too late.

"Yeah."

"We should do another. Is that the only one you have?" I asked.

"Yes, it's all that was prescribed. It *should* help. Where's Kai?" Kimber asked, worried.

We looked toward the wall of trees. Kai was a powerful athlete, and I was certain he could run until he was no longer being chased by death. "He'll be back. I know it," I said.

"Let's get him inside," Walker said, lifting Noah's shoulders.

We positioned ourselves to help move Noah when we heard a pounding on the window. All of us paused to look up. Asher cupped his hand over his neck as his face grew ashen. He stiffened as we all watched helplessly from the ground.

"What is he trying to—"

"The bees!" I jumped to my feet. Kimber popped up next to me.

"But he's inside. He's safe!"

"No!" I said running to the cabin. "There were several in my room this morning!"

"What are you talking about?" Kimber yelled frantically as we reached the deck and passed through the kitchen.

"This morning. A few bees had gotten inside, and I ran out of my bedroom. They were locked in all day." I gripped the banister and lunged up the stairs.

"But I used the last EpiPen!"

We pushed through the bedroom door just as Asher fell backward. There was a loud thud when he hit the floor, followed by Kimber's cry. My stomach sank. How could I be that stupid? How could I have forgotten there were bees inside the cabin too?

"Do something, Kinsley! Do something!" Kimber demanded.

I ran my hands through my hair and paced the length of the room. What could I do? I could barely get the bees to leave us alone; there was no way I could siphon the poison. The EpiPen was gone, and there was nothing left to help Asher . . . but me. It was too much. And I was drained from fighting off the swarm.

Asher began convulsing, and Kimber pounded on his chest, tears running down her cheeks. "You can't leave me here! You can't!"

I crumbled under the pressure and ran out of the bedroom, shutting the door behind me. I pressed my back against the wall and cradled my head in my hands.

"This isn't real. This isn't real. This isn't real."

"No! No! No! Asher, no!" Kimber sobbed. I knew he was gone by the tone of her voice. I felt sick enough to vomit.

What was this world? What had I created here? And why? I grabbed at my stomach, clenching my T-shirt in my fists as I broke out into a cold sweat.

The door swung open and banged against the wall. Kimber stormed out. "What are you doing?" I asked, pushing off the wall and following her.

I expected her to be weaker than this. Smaller. So small that she would disappear in the wake of Asher's passing. But she was a lot stronger than she looked. She strode downstairs, her feet stomping with every step.

"Kimber what are you doing?" I asked again, trying to grab for her hand, but she yanked it away. I jogged to keep up with her stride as we went out the back door to where Noah lay.

"Is he okay?" Emma asked about Asher.

"I think he . . . I don't think he made it."

"This is bullshit!" Kimber said in a tone much deeper than I had known to be her own.

She strode right up to Noah lying on the ground. His skin was pale and, surprisingly, he didn't look any better. In fact, he looked . . . *Had he died too?*

His skin was purple and blue—bruised from the stings. His lips were large and his eyes swollen shut. I looked toward Walker, and my heart stuck in my throat. I knew Noah hadn't survived when Walker gave a small shake of his head. I cupped my mouth in shock. Then my knees hit the ground.

I'd grown up with Noah. I knew his mother like a relative. We weren't just friends; we were so much more than that. I'd thought about him all the time. This summer was supposed to be about us. I had wished for his kiss . . .

"I'm not staying here for one more second without Asher!" Kimber announced. Her tone was sharp as knives and her face determined.

Everybody froze, watching and waiting. If there was anybody who could find their way out of this realm, it would be that of a person with a broken heart. For they would forge a path where there was none before, just to find their other half.

13

"I'm *not* staying here without him," Kimber said maniacally. She turned in front of Noah's body so that they were heels to heels and lifted her arms out from her sides.

I couldn't pry my eyes off her. My focus narrowed and my mouth fell open. *What was she doing?*

Kimber closed her eyes and tipped back onto her heels. Only she never quite stopped herself. With arms spread wide, she did a trust fall back on top of Noah's lifeless body.

Nobody was there to catch her. Nobody alive anyhow.

"Wait!" I yelled, reaching my hand out.

As Kimber landed, she appeared to sink through Noah, hitting the ground with a muffled thump. At that exact moment . . . Noah sat up, gasping for air.

He grabbed his chest and patted his legs—which were oddly both hers and his at the same time. He shuddered and scrambled to his feet, sidestepping away from Kimber's body, which now lay motionless in his place.

Her skin bubbled and bruised with the wounds of a thousand bee stings. Her lips swelled, and the color of her skin darkened to a swarthy mix of purple and blue.

Noah ran his hands through his hair and patted his face, chest, and thighs, checking that his body was in fact his own.

My eyes bulged. I couldn't believe what I was seeing. *A life for a life.*

"How did she—" spilled from my lips.

Kimber had given Noah his life back. I hadn't even known that was possible. My question echoed on the lips around me as everyone muttered the same thing: *how did she do that?*

Even Walker was taken aback, as he now cradled Kimber's head and shoulders, instead of Noah's.

"Is she . . . ?" Emma asked. My eyes flickered, meeting everybody else's disbelieving gaze. Nobody could believe what had just happened, and Noah looked like he was going to be sick.

"I don't know. I think . . . I think she sacrificed herself," I said, my eyes meeting Noah's for the first time.

"She can't do that. Oh god, she can't do that." Noah grabbed his stomach and staggered forward. He made it to some nearby bushes and dry heaved over weak knees.

"But she did," I said, my eyes meeting Walker's. His eyes were a burning blaze of amber gold, and his eyebrow dripped with fresh blood.

Kimber didn't give her life so that Noah could live instead of her. She'd given her life so that she could be with Asher—wherever that may be. Regardless of why she'd done it, Noah was alive. And I knew, by Walker's fresh wound, that if he had known this was possible, he would have sacrificed himself for Layla.

He would've taken her place in a heartbeat. He would have lived his life in the shadows, and he would have done it happily, knowing that she was alive and well. If Layla could feel the sun on her face and her heart beat in her chest, it would have been enough for him. I could see the wheels turning in his pained eyes, and I knew he was wondering the same thing I was: was it too late now?

I looked over as I heard Gunner's bark from the woods. Kai came running through the dense forest and into the clearing. He was still thick with several layers of clothing and visibly exhausted. Seconds after breaking through the woods, a thick shadow ballooned out behind him.

There had been three casualties and one revival in the brief span since he had taken off, but I wasn't worried about that now. There were thousands of bees flying after Kai and Gunner, and they were headed straight for us. In the real world, they never would've followed him for that long. At least that's what my dad had always told me. But we weren't anywhere near the real world, and these weren't regular bees.

"Run! Everybody, get inside the house!" Walker yelled, as he lowered Kimber's head to the ground.

Emma took off running, and Noah staggered from the bushes up the stairs slower than I would have liked. But I was the slowest of all—I was frozen. All the power I had to blast the clay discs was not enough here. There was no amount of training that I could ever achieve to prepare for each unique situation that arose in Baylor. And yet, somehow, some way, Kimber had known. She'd known exactly how to get what she wanted, and she hadn't had to read a single book to get it.

Layla's words echoed in my mind: *You don't belong here.*

Walker grabbed my arm, snapping me from my trance and pulling me inside the cabin. Once inside, I collapsed like Noah had on the floor. Walker held the door open for Kai and Gunner as they barreled across the threshold, and he slammed the door shut behind them. An army of bees pelted into the door, sounding like hail in a torrential storm.

Kai fell forward onto the floor, barely able to hold himself up on hands and knees and panting in pure exhaustion. His face was red, and he had purple welts where the bees had stung him. There were two on his forehead, one on his cheek, and, as far as I could see, one on the nape of his neck. I peeled myself off the floor and placed my hand on his back. I could feel the sweat that had soaked through his many layers.

"He's overheating! Help me get him out of these clothes!" I said. Walker pulled at one of his many shirts. Noah—still layered himself—helped peel layers off Kai. I crawled to Kai's feet and unlaced his shoes. I'd heard once that heat escapes from the head and feet.

"Is he going to be okay?" Emma asked, cowering in the corner.

"Emma, help us out. Grab his pants," Walker ordered.

I yanked off Kai's other shoe, and Emma came to my side to help me peel off his sweatpants. There must've been five layers of pajamas and sweats over a pair of jeans. All damp. He needed water, and maybe a cool wet washcloth on the base of his neck.

We worked together to strip Kai down to a single layer. Kai wasn't saying anything at all, and his breathing had yet to calm down. The entire cabin buzzed with the army of bees outside, making it sound like we were inside the hive ourselves. They bashed themselves against the windows, making small knocking noises. My mind splintered thinking of all the ways they could get inside. I paused to look around the room on high alert, and a chill ran down my spine.

The knocking bounced from one window to the next as the swarm of bees tried desperately to get in. They moved around the cabin, and I watched the darkness leave the living room and eclipse the front entry windows. My mind raced. Something was there . . . something important that I couldn't quite remember. Every second mattered as I tried my best to pin down the thought pestering my brain. It hit me like a ton of bricks. The bathroom window near the front of the cabin. It was completely open, and there was no screen.

"The window!" I yelled, as I leapt over Kai. Running full speed through the kitchen, I grabbed the banister and swung around the stairs. It was a race against the bees, and as far as I could tell, I was coming in last.

I barged into the small bathroom. The bees had just found the opening. I froze for a second, and without thinking, I slammed the door shut—trapping myself inside.

I let out a yelp as the bees swarmed around me. I flung my hands around and spun in tiny circles. The bees surrounded me. I squinted to keep them out of my eyes and tried to shield my face. I wanted to run, but opening the door wasn't an option.

There was nothing I could do. Spinning in circles wasn't getting me anywhere, and I refused to unleash them onto my friends. I couldn't see. I couldn't run. I couldn't yell. They covered my face, looking for ways in. Yet, never once was I stung. Which only worried me more.

They wanted something else from me. It didn't matter what it was, because I wasn't giving up without a fight. I was done with this. I was so angry with myself for not being enough to fight this world. I was so, so angry. I opened my mouth to scream a deep guttural shriek, but the bees filled my mouth before I could make a sound.

Angst tightened in my chest as I held my breath—the scream trapped somewhere inside.

Wings thrashed against the roof of my mouth. I hunched over as they packed in tight, pressing alongside my cheeks and pushing against tongue. My mouth had become their hive, and I had become their creator. Were they searching for a new queen bee? I didn't have time to think about it. All I knew was I was in danger, and my power to explode things would not help me here.

Walker barged into the bathroom, and the second he did, the second I saw him, the bees vaporized into a fine black-and-yellow mist. I sucked in several shallow breaths.

The mist was oddly beautiful. It swirled, catching bits of light. The yellows turned golden, and the blacks were just a shadow. The vapor danced like a slow whirlwind as it lifted out the window. Walker and I watched in silence. The cabin was no longer buzzing, and the knocking on the windows had finally stopped.

"*You* did that. How did you do that?" I asked Walker, as I tried to catch my breath. I grabbed his shoulder for support, and he embraced me.

"I didn't do that. You did." He stabilized me as I leaned over the sink and spat several times. I wiped my mouth still feeling the tiny legs crawling across my lips, but there was nothing there. "Are you okay?" he asked.

My insides were shaking, and I was fighting back tears. I had become a human hive—I wasn't okay. None of it was okay. In that moment, there was a part of me that envied Kimber. I didn't know where she'd gone when she'd taken Noah's place, but it had to be better than this.

I wiped my lips with shaky hands, and Walker wrapped his arm around my waist, ushering me to join the others. But as soon as I stepped into the entryway, I heard them talking about the calendar. I stopped immediately. "I can't do this. Don't make me do this." It was too much.

"What's wrong?"

"They're talking about the calendar again. They know that I'm doing this to them. They're judging me for it. I'm a damn *monster*, and they know it," I hissed, tears stinging the back of my throat.

"Wilde, you're not a monster. Nobody is judging you . . . We're in this mess together." His arm tightened in a comforting hug.

"I am," I said. I was. All this time, I was. Every second of the day. I was my own worst enemy. And in some ways, my judgment of myself was worse than theirs. Simply because it was the loudest. A constant echo in my head.

"We're going to get through this. You did so amazing today with the clay pigeons. And you did it again with the bees. Under pressure, too." I could hear the hope in his voice.

"I exploded the hive and released thousands of angry killer bees upon my friends."

"You *stopped* the bees. That's what I saw. You made them disappear. You turned them to a fine mist. I know it's hard, but you're doing it. And with more practice, there won't be a limit for you. Don't give up now. We're so close . . ."

I took in a deep breath and nodded, even though I swore he was the one who had vaporized the bees. I stole one more moment of quiet before joining the others. A moment to stare into Walker's eyes just a little longer. My friends were still arguing over the numbers on the calendar, and it was time to face them. Those that were left.

"The bees are gone," Emma said with a nod of hope. I gave her a small smile.

"Yeah, I noticed that," I said, scratching the back of my head. I didn't know how it had happened, and I was uncomfortable taking the credit.

Kai was sitting up against the base of the couch taking small sips of water. His black hair was plastered to his forehead, and his skin was covered in a thin sheen of sweat. He looked ill—but he would survive. "How are you feeling?" I asked.

Kai tried to clear his throat but struggled to get any words out. He patted his chest a few times and winced.

"It's okay. Just rest," I said. Noah took off one of his many shirts and tossed it to the ground. It landed near my feet, and a weird feeling swirled in my belly. I was both happy he was alive and conflicted by the turmoil I'd felt when I'd thought he had passed. He still meant more to me than a friend. Part of me wanted to run straight into his arms and give him the biggest hug ever.

But I knew my loyalty lay with Walker, which made it all feel so wrong. Either way, I was grateful for what Kimber had done.

"Hey, Kins, did you see the calendar?" Noah asked with a pained expression. He suffered no bee stings, causing me to think his pain was purely guilt. He was probably happy to be alive but feeling guilty that Kimber had sacrificed herself. He pulled his shirt off, revealing a thin white ribbed tank underneath. I caught my eyes skimming over his torso the way they used to when I'd liked him, and I frowned.

"How are you feeling, Noah?" I asked. I averted my eyes from both the calendar and his physique.

"I'm fine. I'm better than fine. I'm just hot. But did you see the calendar?" His denim-blue eyes bore into mine as he peeled off his tank. I felt my skin flush and immediately peeked at Walker. How uncomfortable would it be if they all died except the three of us? Leaving me with Walker and Noah to roam the realms of eternity together. I really had to find a way to keep everybody safe.

"I haven't," I said. Noah nodded his head toward the wall. The calendar had eight slashes through it. Only five were left unmarked. I looked around the room and counted on my fingers to be certain. There were more than five of us left.

"Where's Scarlett May?" I asked.

"I don't know. She's probably with Sampson," Noah said.

"There's thirteen days, and eight of them have been crossed off. But only seven of us are gone. Who is the eighth?" Noah asked, scowling at the calendar.

"I thought we went through this? It was that store clerk who went missing. Right?" Emma asked, looking to me for clarity.

"So, there are five of us left? Kinsley, Emma, Scarlett May, Kai, and me?" Noah pointed to each of us, his brows stitched. "Why isn't *he* on the list?" He stared at Walker enviously.

"How do you know I'm not?" Walker asked.

"I just don't understand how the store clerk is on there. Does that mean that it doesn't have to be us on that list? It could be anybody?" Emma asked.

I knew that was wrong. Something about it was very wrong. I had already crashed a plane with over a hundred people on it. They weren't on the list. So why was Big Jimmy? And was I on the list? Or Walker? It was either both of us, or we were going to be separated, and I would not let that happen. I wouldn't leave Walker to this realm all alone. No, there was something off about this calendar, but I couldn't put my finger on it. I didn't want to tell anybody about the plane crash, but there was another accident that I could talk about. Make an example out of.

"Hey Emma, remember when we were on the train? What about all those people? Why aren't they on the calendar?" I asked. It was enough to shatter the whole theory. We were missing something here. But more importantly, maybe we weren't all doomed to be picked off, one by one.

"What train? What people?" Noah asked.

Emma's eyes searched the calendar. "You're right. If this isn't the calendar for how many people are going to die, then what's the calendar of?" she asked, a horrified look in her eyes. Somehow, that question seemed scarier than a calendar hit list. It was the unknown that we feared most of all.

"I'm not sure, but we need to find out," I said.

"What train? What people?" Noah repeated.

Emma told the story of our trip to the depths of the canyon, only to reappear here as if it had never happened. But it had. And my physiology could attest to that. My heart rate picked up speed. I couldn't bear to listen to it again. I left the kitchen and joined Kai on the floor. Walker came and sat by my side.

"I'm just so sick of it all. When is it going to click?" I asked.

"We're going to get it. This is a unique mess that we're in. It's twisted. If normal life was a linear line, this mess is a tangled knot. It's going to take time," Walker said, with all the patience in the world. I guess that's what happens when you have all of eternity.

"You've got that right," I said, slouching.

Kai made a sound in his throat, and I thought that he was trying to smile. Although his cheeks were so puffy, I couldn't be sure.

"We've got to stop thinking normally. This isn't a rational thought process here. There is no logic behind this mess. Or at least none that we can see. What we really need to do is start reading between the lines . . ." Walker shook his head, deep in thought. His dimples disappeared, and the sharp lines of his jaw popped.

Read between the lines? Why did that remind me of seeing Layla in the woods? Her notes telling me that I didn't belong. I already knew that my being here had caused this whole mess, but if I wanted to stop the chaos, maybe I needed somebody as crazy as her to help me figure it all out. Maybe that's why my gran had told me I needed to find her. She was like the Cheshire Cat; the loony one that actually isn't so crazy. She's a little different, but maybe that's because she sees what we don't. Maybe she's been trying to guide me all along. My throat ran dry at the thought of needing the one person I wanted most to stay away from. The one person who could take everything from me.

"We need a twisted mind," I said, thinking of Layla.

"Not a twisted mind, just a nonconforming one. We just need to look at the world a little differently than we're used to. Flip it on its side, or look at it upside down, or backward."

"You need one of those atypicals," Noah said from the kitchen.

"What's that?" I asked, taking in his bare chest and sorrow-filled eyes.

"Yeah. That's exactly what we need," Walker agreed. I whipped my head around. *Atypical?*

Emma joined us in the living room. She crawled onto the sofa and pulled a pillow onto her lap. "Well, Kinsley's dyslexic," she said.

"Hey! What does that have to do with anything?"

"Oh my god. You're right. Maybe that's why all of this is happening in the first place. You're atypical," Walker said, staring at me with wide golden eyes.

"What the hell, you guys? What does that even mean?" I already had one title. I didn't need two.

"It's just like being left-handed in a world full of rights. You get the job done, but you come at it from a different angle. It's nothing bad, really," Noah said.

"Well, it's not nothing," Walker disagreed.

"What he means is that you have a distinct, creative pattern for processing information," Emma said. But what did that mean? I didn't want to be different.

"Um . . . If by creative you mean broken, then yeah, it's creative all right," I said. I couldn't process a three-letter word without switching the letters around like a magic trick; there was nothing creative about that, just sinister.

"No, seriously. I did a bunch of research on it the last time you wouldn't read one of the articles I showed you."

I frowned at Emma, like she had gone behind my back. She shrugged.

"Your dyslexia isn't *just* a learning disability. It's two-sided. It's a distinct pattern in the way your brain functions, so you learn and organize information differently than most people do."

I crossed my arms and rolled my eyes. I wasn't about to let somebody tell me I was gifted.

"Seriously! Dyslexic people are really advanced at three-dimensional spatial reasoning, and they can recognize complex and ever-shifting patterns." Emma made cubes out of her hands and rotated them.

I sighed, embarrassed by the entire conversation. If it was true, I would have figured this calendar out long ago.

"It's true, Wilde. That divergence might just be the ticket to unlocking your ability," Walker said.

Kai still wasn't talking, but he made it a point to look me in the eye and nod. Even Kai was jumping on this wagon?

"I don't know, you guys. It's been nothing but a hindrance for me. Maybe it is a special power for some, but it's only held me back. Sorry to disappoint." I grabbed Kai's water glass and headed to the kitchen to refill it.

"No, I think we might be onto something here. The stupid calendar makes little sense to any of us, but maybe you could figure it out. You know, because your brain is working off the beaten path and stuff," Noah said with a shrug. I scowled at him over my shoulder. Emma slapped his arm, and his eyes grew wide as he looked at her in confusion.

Good lord, was that how they thought of me?

We were interrupted by the sounds of boots stomping up the stairs on the back porch. "Oh shit, Scarlett May's home," Noah said.

The air in the cabin shifted as we waited for her to come inside. My stomach flipped in dread as the doorknob twisted. She came in like a breath of fresh air, but that all changed the moment she slid her sunglasses onto the top of her head.

"Um, hi guys?" she said, surveying the room.

She slid her phone into her back pocket and cautiously walked into the kitchen. I tracked her eyes as they landed on the calendar, and I gnawed on my lip as she stared at each one of us, slowly counting down. When she took in the sight of Kai on the floor, she knew.

I came to her side and put my hand on her shoulder, but she shoved it off and stormed out of the room. Kimber had been one of her closest friends, and now she had nobody. It wasn't the kind of thing I wanted to connect with somebody over, but I understood how she felt. And it seemed like, for the first time, Scarlett May and I had something in common.

14

Kai slumped over, his eyes shut, and his chest moving slowly. It could have been the stress from the chase, or the handful of antihistamines I had given him, but either way, he should sleep through the night. Hopefully, he'd feel better in the morning. What wouldn't heal come morning was Scarlett May. And I worried that she might try something like Kimber had.

Emma took a pillow from the sofa and placed it next to Kai. I helped her tip him over until his head rested gently on the pillow. His body was radiating heat. It must have been from the venom. Emma grabbed a throw blanket from the couch, and I shook my head. He'd been through enough; we didn't need to cook him too.

Once we got Kai situated, Emma left to get ready for bed and Noah turned on the TV, leaving Walker and me on our own. I didn't want him to leave, and by the way he was lingering, I could see that he didn't particularly want to go either. He clapped a fist into an open hand and nodded toward the back patio. I stole a glance at Noah as we slipped out into the night. I was on high alert for the bees. Not only the killer ones buzzing around, but the dead ones that lay on the floor, dusted the seats, and sprinkled the railings with their little bee bodies and their sharp stingers. In the glow of the porch light, I scoured every inch of that patio. There wasn't a single bee to be found, though the hive still lay cracked open on the ground. It looked petrified as if it had fallen months ago and dried out in the day's light.

"There are no bees," I said, still looking.

"No. I think you took care of that," Walker said with a chuckle.

"What do you mean?" I asked.

"Wilde, you turned them to smoke. You vaporized them into a fine mist. They disintegrated—all of them. You know, I don't think you realize how badass you are." He rubbed my tense shoulders.

Badass? That would be the very last way I would describe myself. "I'm not all that you think I am," I said, careful not to disrupt the massage with too much movement.

It didn't matter, his hands left my neck as he craned to get a better look at me. "Are we going to do this again? Are you serious?" He breathed a deep sigh and wiped his lips with his hand. "What's it going to take for you to realize just how special you are?"

A laugh escaped me. This was ridiculous. "You guys literally just told me that my biggest weakness in life was actually a superpower. Who's trying to pull the wool over whose eyes here? Me? Or you?" I asked, cocking my head to the side.

"Don't you realize? It's true. Whereas most people have a processing pattern that goes one way through the woods, yours takes another path and—"

"—Yeah, yeah, yeah. I heard you guys. But what you failed to mention is, it's the wrong way."

"It's not the wrong way! It might be . . . longer, sure."

I laughed and rolled my eyes. I didn't need him to sugarcoat this. I'd had plenty of years to get used to it. I knew what dyslexia was and what it wasn't.

"Listen to me. It may take you a little longer, but that's only for the reading and writing. You're missing the whole other half here. Your kind of processing allows you to see things that most people don't and never will. It's backward, it's upside down, and it's exactly what we need in a situation like this."

It never felt good to be called backward, no matter how much of a light was cast upon it.

"Like this?" I asked.

"We're fighting your subconscious demons, Wilde. Whether you like it or not, this is a world of your making. If only you could realize that, while it is your weakness, it's also your strength, then we might have more dreams than nightmares. That's all I'm saying." Walker stared out at the full moon in a pensive gaze. I could tell he was getting tired of trying to convince me.

I looked at the moon too. We sat in silence for a little while, watching the night pass by. Noah's TV show flickered a neon blue that reflected on the cabin windows, and I let myself breathe deeply in the silence. I doubted I would get much sleep tonight, and I didn't want to be alone to try. But I didn't think Walker would spend the night if I asked. It might be crossing the line that he'd drawn for our friendship. So, this is what I had instead: moon gazing until our eyes burned and we parted ways. I'd go off to bed and stare at my ceiling while he did whatever he did at night. I just wanted him to stay. I wanted to stretch this part of the night out. If only till the sun came up and there were no more shadows to steal my mind away—telling me lies about my worth.

"I wish . . . I wish you believed in yourself how I did," Walker said, in a whisper. It floated like a failed spell that just wouldn't stick—in one ear, out the other.

"If my dyslexia were a strength of any kind, then I'd be powerful. I'd be this almighty witch who could freeze time. Just like this. Right now. I'd freeze it. I'd keep this moment in a bottle locked up tight, so I'd be able to have you by my side whenever I wanted. Whenever I needed. Then I wouldn't be left alone with my thoughts at night. It can be so haunting." I smiled shyly at him and then looked back to the low-hanging moon.

"The bees would never have snuck inside the cabin. They certainly wouldn't have crawled inside my mouth. They wouldn't have stung Asher. And if I was a witch, I wouldn't be afraid of Baylor Lake. I'd swim right down to the bottom, and I'd throw a party there with Lainey."

I dropped my head as the heartache gripped my chest. "I'd go back home and tell my mom and dad I was all right. I'd tell them not to worry about me, because I had something I was doing here on the other side. Something important that I couldn't walk away from. I would tell them I was with my gran."

Walker was silent, taking it all in, and it felt good to speak freely. No judgment.

I examined my fingers, picking at my nails. "You know, Walker, I know I can't go home right now, but if I could, I don't know that I would want to. If it was a chance I had, I'm not sure I'd take it. There's just so much here that I feel is within my grasp. And I don't think I could ever leave you. The thought of leaving you behind, leaving my gran behind . . . It makes me sick. Physically sick. I can't imagine my life without you." My eyes burned. I was afraid if I blinked, a tear might roll down my cheek.

Still, Walker said nothing. I could see from my peripheral vision he was still staring at the moon. It was a beautiful moon; a gigantic one. I could see the craters from here, and it almost looked like a face. Even so, I had expected a response of some type. He seemed to be deep in thought. His brows were knitted and his eyes glossy. The gash in his eyebrow glistened just a little, and I could tell that his wound was opening again from our conversation. I didn't want that. I didn't want to open his wounds. I'd done it again. I hurt the people I cared about most.

But when I looked more closely, Walker was eerily still, and I realized he hadn't even blinked, let alone responded. I flinched. "Walker?" I asked.

He said nothing. Did nothing.

I spun around to see the TV's glow hadn't flickered in some time. The cabin windows were lit by a constant blue haze. I turned back to Walker and reached my hand out, shaking his shoulder. He was still and stiff. Stiff, like he'd been turned to stone. I grabbed at his face to pull him close, but I couldn't get him to move.

"What the hell . . ." I whispered. Looking out at the night sky, not even the stars were twinkling. And that's when I realized what I'd said. That if I were a witch, I would freeze time.

If I were a witch . . . If my weakness was my strength . . . *Was my weakness my strength?*

Oh my god, my weakness *was* my strength! I'd been so conditioned to think I was broken because I couldn't perform like the other kids in school. But I had never been in a situation like this before. I was only eighteen. And this was no longer the classroom. I looked toward the woods and the world seemed so vast. Here, I could be my own wizard. I could control the dimensional space around me to my liking. Maybe I wasn't lost like I had always thought? Maybe I was simply on the scenic route.

I laughed out loud in embarrassment. It was absurd.

But was it? Could I really be in control of all this?

I scampered down the grassy knoll to the sandy shore, checking over my shoulder often to see Walker's silhouette. It surprised me how the lake ceased to lap against the sand. I kicked off my shoes and peeled off my socks. I touched a single toe to the water, and it was a hard, glass-like surface. I pushed my weight down on top of the frozen lake water, and it felt sturdy. I stole a glance back at Walker. He was like a statue leaning against the deck railing. I smiled before stepping out onto the water. It wasn't slippery like I'd imagined it would be, but chalky and dry. It was still cold, though, and incredibly strong. I eased into my first few steps and then took off.

I ran. My heart beat thunderously in my chest. The cool night air kissed my face as I ran on top of the lake. Time was frozen, and I had no fear of being chased by a predator of the night. For I had cast them all to stone in my spell and they lay motionless in the shadows. I was a free spirit. I must've run a half mile before I stopped to lie on my back. Breathless, I stared up at the frozen stars. And after a while, I found the tail end of a falling star. A constant shimmer of gold etched in the sky.

I made a wish. But not like the wish I'd made when I blew out my eighteenth birthday candles. No, this wish wasn't for a kiss from Noah. And I'd be lying if I said I hadn't considered wishing for a kiss from Walker. But if I'd learned one thing here in Baylor, it was that a wish was not to be wasted on a fleeting moment such as a kiss. Don't get me wrong, I wanted it. I dreamed of the day where my lips would touch Walker's. But it was far more important to me now that he find happiness. I took my time crafting the perfect wish. Because who knows, if I was a witch after all, it might come true. Maybe . . .

I wished that Walker's curse would be lifted and that he would find love to carry him through the rest of his life. *Afterlife?* Whatever path he was on, it made little sense for him to walk it alone. And if he truly believed that I wasn't the person for him, then I would help him and Layla reconnect. But, luckily for me, I *knew* I was the one. And I was pretty sure he did too.

I walked back to the cabin deep in thought, remembering the time that fireworks had glimmered around Walker and me like streamers in a magical lagoon. I guessed this time I just needed to be alone. Time to think. To explore. I promised myself I'd try this freezing spell again, but during the daylight, so I could explore further into the forest and deeper into the lake.

With each step, I watched my feet meet the hard, glass-like surface of the lake, and I wondered what it was like below. I thought of the red door glued to the bottom of the lake, and I felt a subtle pull drawing me downward. Like the door was made for me and only me. Like my hand turning the doorknob was its life purpose. Sure, I was curious, but I think more than anything I was afraid.

What was the door? My door. The question created a feeling in my belly that I didn't particularly like. I didn't let myself think about it any longer because, somewhere inside me, I think I knew the answer. And it scared the living hell out of me.

Living hell . . .

If I had to guess, this was the very definition: a place you lived in that was evil in nature. In the real world, there might not be wolves that stand on their hind legs or killer bees looking to inhabit your body. There might not be bodies in the lake that whisper secrets. But hell was hell, and I supposed it was different for everybody.

I wasn't sure what hell was like for adults . . . Taxes or something. I guessed I would never find out. I'd just go on living here, in my own personal hell, trying my damnedest to make it my heaven. And if what I had always considered to be my biggest weakness was indeed a strength, then that should be an easy feat. In no time, the nightmares would dissipate, and the accidents would wane.

I looked near and far, searching the trees in the distance. The glow of the cabin was nothing but a small dot in front of me. But with my yearning to see Walker so far away, my sight strengthened. Magnified. Walker was leaning against the back railing deep in thought. I saw it before I could even think it. A simple feeling. A dyslexic thought . . .

If I could see clearly, then what if I didn't have to walk all the way to the cabin? What if I was already there?

Startled, as if I was teetering on the edge of a cliff, I windmilled my arms and slowly lifted my gaze from my bare feet to the stairs of the patio. Behind me, the lake was calm and placid. A smiled creeped up on me, and for the first time I started to believe. To believe that maybe I *was* the person for the job. Maybe I *did* have the power to unlock the Baylor phenomenon.

If I were a witch . . . Maybe I didn't have to be a witch at all? Witches were inherently evil, weren't they? That's what I'd always thought I was in Baylor: evil. That part of my soul was steeped in the black malignant water. Why else would everybody die on my watch? Go missing in the woods or sink to the bottom of the lake? Why would birds flock from the sky and steal my friends from below? Because I was bad. I was wrong. I was the dreamer.

But what if I could control it? Then I no longer had to be bad. And I could stop thinking of myself as an ugly girl, with a long, pointy, and crooked nose. Green-hued skin covered in warts the size of grapes. A girl with a cackle so unnerving it sent chills up your spine. I didn't have to be that girl at all.

Standing there with a goofy smile on my face and nobody to see it, I thought of all the mischievous, glorious things I could do right now at the whim of a thought. A feeling. I could spy on everybody. Even the neighbors. I could hunt for the ever-fleeting tower. I could get free ice cream from the store. I could go to the mall . . . *The mall?* How far was the mall? Could I leave Baylor? If time was frozen, and I could do anything, then could I leave Baylor? Could I go home? Could I check on my parents? My body?

I felt the sudden pull. The wanting. The ties I had to my family beckoning me to come back. I looked at my hands as the odd feeling crept through my body, and they began to disappear. I felt the sucking of my soul drawing me.

No, no, no! I didn't want this! I didn't want to leave. I'd only thought about it.

But just as I had crossed the lake with a simple thought, I was abruptly standing in the corner of the hospital room.

I sucked in a ragged breath as I surveyed the room, afraid. It was dim and quiet. The monitors beeped rhythmically. My mom slept against my bed. Her chair was pulled close and her head on the edge of my thin mattress. Her arms stretched over my legs.

My dad was there too. He was semiconscious, dozing off in a chair in the corner. His head was slipping from his balled fist. He looked broken in a way I'd never seen before. Weaker by unseen measures.

And then there was me. A version of me; one I couldn't identify with any longer. There was so much pain in the room that I could hardly stand it. I didn't want to see it. I didn't want to smell the antiseptic. I didn't want to know anything about it. I just wanted to go back to the world where I was in love, where I was learning to conquer myself.

The now familiar feeling of transporting my soul into another realm began. It started with the sinking in my stomach and moved to a crawling under my skin. Then it felt like my insides were lifting away from my shell. Like I was no longer standing there with my body. I felt like there were two of me, and one was invisible, separating to a new and distant land.

As my soul left, the outer parts of me crumbled in its wake, unable to live without the support. My hands wavered like a mirage until they were no longer there, and neither was I.

My eyes pressed shut as I took in a deep breath. I breathed in the smell of pine trees from the forest and the wood from the deck. It was a breath of fresh air after the antiseptic smell of the hospital. I took comfort in Walker's faint cologne that reminded me of the beach, and I knew I was home.

I opened my eyes slowly to see the guy of my dreams still frozen in place, and I was home. The life I'd left at the hospital didn't seem like my life at all. If anything, it was more like a past life. One I had begun to separate myself from as I dove deep into this one.

As much as I was afraid here in Baylor, it really wasn't very different from my real life. My past life. I'd been afraid there too, just for different reasons. Like not being noticed or getting a poor grade. The stress of an exam or what college to go to. It was nothing like this, of course, but the stress felt all the same. I might as well have been chased by a phantom wolf.

At least here in Baylor, under Walker's wing, I was learning the skills to combat these inherently evil threats. I only wished I'd been able to get training like this in my real life. I wished I'd believed in myself when I was back in school. Maybe then I'd have realized that classwork wasn't a one size fits all, and I was smarter than they led me to believe. How would that have changed my struggles? My dreams? My ambitions? I guess I'd never know.

15

I stood on the deck staring at Walker. For the first time, I could gaze as long as I wanted without being noticed. Without being shy and having to avert my eyes. Without the embarrassment creeping into my cheeks and turning them warm. I looked at his broad shoulders stretching beneath his flannel. I took in his trim waist and strong stance. I walked around him, admiring his jawline, but when I came to his side, it wasn't how beautiful he was that stopped me in my tracks. It was the sadness that emanated from his eyes.

The tense way he balled one fist and hid it within the palm of his resting hand. It was the ache that poured from him, even though he was frozen, encapsulated in time. It was all the things I hadn't seen when I was so worried about what would come out of my mouth. I'd been so worried about how I came across to him, and the stress I carried, that I hadn't taken the time to notice how heartbroken he was.

I wanted to put my hand on his back and rub away all the stress. My hand lingered in the air, inches from his shoulder, and then dropped. I slipped it into my back pocket and leaned against the railing next to him. My eyes fell to my feet. If I stayed here in Baylor, would I be enough for him? Or would he always be looking for Layla? Would she always haunt us? There was a part of me that wanted to help Layla too, now that I knew her struggles. I couldn't help but wonder where my place was in this Baylor web. Where did I fit in? *How* did I fit in?

I sighed heavily and pushed off the railing. Inside the cabin, I found Noah fast asleep in front of the TV. I didn't linger long before heading upstairs. It was Scarlett May who I needed to check on. She'd been so hurt over Kimber leaving that I was afraid she might do something just like Kimber had. And if anybody was strong enough to do it, it would be her. I climbed the stairs, still in awe of how strong-willed Kimber had been. It made me wonder if I had imagined her all wrong. Maybe she wasn't the girl I'd always thought she was. And I wished she was here now for me to take a second look. A deeper look. One that I could only get by freezing time.

I grasped the bathroom doorknob with a light touch and turned it slowly. The door was unlocked, so I pushed it open just enough to peek my head inside. Nobody was in there. It only left one more spot for Scarlett May to hide—Kimber's room. I found her there on the floor, hunched against the wall. She cradled Kimber's jacket in her arms. Her chin was wrinkled, her face pink. A tear was glued to her cheek, frozen mid fall.

It was a private moment of grief. One that I had walked in on, unbeknownst to her. I took a single step backward with the notion that I should leave. Give her the privacy she deserved. But something stopped me from leaving. She needed me. I crossed the room in a few long strides and enveloped her in a hug.

It was difficult hugging her stiff body. But I let myself mold into her hard crevices and sharp edges. I hugged her tight, as if she were awake, so she'd know she wasn't alone.

"I'm sorry . . ." I whispered. I pressed the back of my head against the wall, both of us mourning, but for different reasons. Sure, I was gonna miss Kimber and Asher. The loss of Lainey still weighed heavily on my heart. But most of all, I was mourning the person I used to be. The girl that I had always known no longer existed. And in her place was somebody I had yet to know. Trust. Love. I didn't know who I was in this dimension, and that scared me most of all. I could be magical and powerful. I could be in love and happy. Or I could be dangerous and misunderstood.

I patted Scarlett May's knee and went to check on Emma. It was no surprise that she was sitting at her computer. Dressed in flannel pajamas, she hunched over the desk, a pen tucked between her fingers. Her cheek rest in the palm of her hand as she read an article, probably something about the inner workings of the dyslexic mind. I chewed my lip thinking the only thing worse than the pressure to succeed and the fear of failure was knowing you didn't try at all.

I stormed out of the room, across the hall, and into the master bedroom. I paced the length of the bedroom trying to think of ways to test the theory. Had being atypical always been a power? My eyes landed on the open window and then flickered to a framed picture of my brother when he was still in diapers. I didn't *want* to break it, and that wasn't the plan, but I had to test the theory, and it was the quickest way. I threw the framed memory hastily out the window, squeezing the windowsill as I leaned out into the open air to watch it fall.

When it stopped right before shattering against the patio, a wide smile crept across my face. I turned around and ran down the stairs, through the kitchen, and out the back door. Walker was still hunched over the railing, but this time, the picture was there too. It was suspended in air a mere inch above the patio. I marveled at it, touching the corner softly and watching it spin as if held by an invisible string. I chuckled and looked toward Walker, but my smile faded when I realized he hadn't seen it. The wonder still clung to me, despite not being able to share the magical moment. I grabbed the picture and ran back upstairs to do it again.

This time, it was going to be something bigger. I scoured the room. A million thoughts flooded my head. I grabbed my feather pillow. Twirling it around in my hands, I mused over the possibilities. Suddenly, I ripped off the pillowcase, grabbed a pair of scissors, and mindlessly cut a large slash through the center of the pillow. I tried not to think too much. I wanted it to be a feeling. And right now, I was excited, and hopeful. Maybe even a little playful. I hurled it out the window, and the feathers plumed into the air and fluttered both inside and outside the bedroom. I leaned out the window, full of hope, and I smiled with anticipation for a show unlike any other.

The white feathers stilled and separated. A glow deep within the veins of the feathers spread out to the soft edges. Each one lit in the dark. Like a million tiny lanterns, the feathers gleamed a warm golden radiance, lighting up the night. Unlike the picture of my little brother, I didn't want the feathers back. I wanted to send them out into the world. I wanted to free them—unleash them to spread the magic.

Go. Go now. A light wind ruffled my hair as I leaned out the window. The feathers stirred.

I watched as hundreds of golden feathers invaded the sky and sailed off into distant lands. Why would I want to give this up? How could I to go back to a life where magic didn't exist? A place where I was a nobody? I watched the feathers until I could no longer see a single glowing ember, and I wondered where they would end up. Who would find them? And who needed them most?

When the night sky was rid of magic, I thought I'd better wake up the rest of the world. To be honest, I was missing Walker. The magic was glorious, but it would have been better if he'd been awake to see it. I made my way through the cabin and resumed my position. I leaned my forearms on the railing and relaxed by his side. I was home. This was my *home*. I belonged here.

I wasn't sure if it was the magic of Baylor or the fact that my greatest weakness was a strength in this realm. It could have been that my gran lived here, and I had family on this side. And it very well could have been that I was falling in love with Walker. But I felt like I was in my forever home. And the longer I stayed here, the more my other life felt like a distant memory.

When I was good and ready, I willed my life to resume. Walker's still figure lifted ever so slightly with his first breath taken in hours. And I felt warmth touch my heart and a smile lift the corners of my eyes. He was back.

Walker dropped his head and looked at me with sad eyes, continuing the conversation we had been having before my adventure. "If you just believed, I know you could do great things, Wilde. You are the only one standing in your way."

I finally understood. I did believe. He'd been right the whole time, and I just hadn't been able to see it. I chewed on my nail nervously, afraid of how our relationship would change if he learned what I was capable of. I decided not to say anything about the mischief I had gotten into while time stood still. At least for now. He gazed back out at the moon.

"I know. I know. I hear that all the time . . . I'm trying," I said. I wasn't completely ready to take on this world, but I *was* trying. Just because I now believed that I *could* hone my manifestations didn't mean that I had mastered the process.

"I know you're trying. We'll get there. We just need more practice." Walker squeezed my shoulder and then turned to go home. He never gave up on me. It only made me feel guilty for keeping the secret from him.

I saw the remains of my pillow by the stairs. Walker bent down and picked it up, examining it. I swiped it from his hands and hid it behind my back. Obviously, it was too late. His brows rose and his mouth opened like he wanted to say something, but ultimately, he didn't. An embarrassed smile crossed his face and he turned away. I could only imagine what he was thinking. My face heated with humiliation.

"You're up to something . . ." His voice rang like a melody—taunting me.

"No! I'm not." But he knew better.

I heard him chuckle as he disappeared into the darkness. I pulled the pillow remnant from behind my back and examined it. A lone feather escaped through the tear. The golden glow rose before me and trailed off after Walker, following him home like a lost puppy.

I went inside and climbed the stairs to Kimber and Asher's bedroom. I knocked softly on the door, knowing that Scarlett May wouldn't answer. I knew she was huddled against the wall crying, and I could imagine her fretting over pretending that she wasn't. I imagined her wiping her tears and trying to catch her breath. I gave her a moment, not that she needed it. I wasn't judging her. I understood what she was going through. More than I would've liked to.

I opened the door slowly and walked inside. She didn't raise her head to look at me. I closed the door behind me and sat on the floor, just like when she'd been frozen. But this time, I didn't give her a hug. I didn't think she would be open to it. Scarlett May liked to appear tough. And I didn't want to do anything to threaten that. Out of the corner of my eye, I saw her swipe a tear quickly, but I pretended not to notice.

"Kimber and Trinity were my best friends," Scarlett May said in a shaky voice.

"I know."

"And they are just . . . gone." She waved a hand through the air.

"I know."

"I don't get it," she said, looking at me for the first time. Her eyes were flanked red with pain.

I wanted to help her, but the truth was, I didn't know how. When my gran had died, I'd shoved the pain deep down inside. I'd forced my mind to think of something else. Anything else. I'd refused to acknowledge any of it. It had simply hurt too badly. And I hadn't known where to start. How do you process death? How does it make any sense, that somebody could be there one second and gone the next? Where did they go? And what did that mean for the rest of us?

I chewed on my lip as the uncomfortable thoughts swirled in my head. I only wanted to be there for Scarlett May. I didn't want to confront my own grief. And a small part of me wished I hadn't come into the room. I hadn't thought that she would actually talk to me. And now that she had, the tightness in my throat was almost too much to bear.

"I don't either," I said, my voice wavering as I tried to keep from crying.

My vision turned blurry with tears, and I did everything in my power to stop the feeling. Stop thinking. Stop the hurt. The truth was, the more I thought about it, the more questions arose. The more I started to look at life like a cruel game. One where players were plucked away at any given time. Regardless of whether they were playing by the rules or not. I wanted to scream.

"What do we do now?" Scarlett May's forehead was creased with worry and confusion.

The only thing I knew how to do was to ignore it. And I knew that wasn't what I wanted to pass on to her. It wasn't helping me in the long run. I wanted better for Scarlett May. And the only thing that I could think of was the small power I had inside me. The power to make things happen before our very eyes. It paled in comparison to what she actually needed, but it was all I had. It wasn't going to bring Kimber back. And it wasn't going to send Scarlett May home. But maybe, at the very least, it could be a distraction. A bridge to get from one impossible moment to a time where it was more bearable.

I grabbed Scarlett May's hand and squeezed. She glanced over at me and then startled when the room turned pitch black. I heard her gasp when the ceiling lit with a billion sparkling stars. Hues of orange lit the galaxy where the ceiling fan would have been. The Milky Way streamed in aqua across the back wall. And the temperature dropped to match the outside air. I heard Scarlett May sniffle. But the best part was that she squeezed my hand tighter. This meant something to her. And even though it didn't take the pain away, I knew that we were getting through it. Together.

Scarlett May and I lay down on the bedroom floor head-to-head. We took turns pointing out shooting stars for hours. We talked very little about the pain that we were living through. Mostly, she spoke about Sampson. She told me how she had always liked him far too much to date him. Because, in her words, he wasn't the dating type. He was the marrying type. She told me how she kept him close because she was waiting for the time when she was ready to settle down. That's when she would make her move. And I learned I had pegged Scarlett May all wrong. It was turning out to be a bad habit of mine. And it was only when the world had stopped that I was able to see Walker's pain, Scarlett May's heart, and my strength. And I wished the world could stop a little more often, giving me a chance to see all that I hadn't before.

16

Several days passed, and with them my confidence grew. An instant pot of coffee brewed, a slide of a hairbrush in the bathroom, and clean socks when I'd had none before. It was the simple things that I put my mind to—the things I didn't care if I failed at—that I practiced with. And I was getting good at it.

When Sampson showed up at our door with several of his friends, I was excited to try my new tricks in a crowd. With the passing hours, the cabin grew thick with partygoers. More than I would have expected for the middle of the week. But it was summer, and ambitions were low. There weren't many job opportunities in Baylor, and I figured most of these people were here for summer vacations like we were.

I was pretty sure that every college-aged kid in Baylor had come to my cabin, apart from Walker. I figured I would glimpse his flannel through the crowd later in the night. But I still didn't want to tell him about the night a golden feather had followed him home. So, it was good that he wasn't here to witness what I had planned. The cabin was crawling with distraction, and it was the perfect place for me to train. If I could master the magic in this environment, I would be a full believer in the power of my twisted mind.

And if I couldn't, I suppose I'd be disappointed. But with that disappointment would come the security of keeping Walker by my side. The responsibility I'd carry to save all my friends would be next to none. How could I save everybody if I was powerless after all? Although failure seemed like a terrible thing, I wasn't convinced it was all bad. Nonetheless, I was going to put it to the test. And all these people were test subjects tonight.

I found Emma fighting for space on the couch. She squeezed in, barely getting the back half of her butt on the sofa. She tried to take a drink but nearly spilled it after being bumped by the rowdy group next to her.

"Some party, huh?" I asked, leaning up against the arm of the couch.

"Yeah, it's something all right. Who invited all these people anyway?" she asked with a scowl.

I looked out into the crowd and found Scarlett May playing pool with Sampson and Skid. I smiled, remembering her feelings for him. "I have an idea," I said, nodding toward Scarlett May.

"It's always her," Emma said, finally managing to take a sip of her drink.

A boundless energy grew within me. It was time to play. "What's wrong Emma? Is this party not entertaining enough?" I said with a mischievous wink.

Emma's eyes sparkled with curiosity as she waited to see what I was going to do. I quickly scoured the living room and picked the closest guy to us. It wasn't much of a manifestation. Just a quick little yank in my mind, and his pants dropped to his ankles. Instant reward.

I peeked at Emma, and her eyes bulged as she cupped her hand over her mouth to stifle her laughter. Red boxers with little yellow bananas were thrust into Emma's face as he bent over to pull up his pants. All the girls nearby laughed, causing a bit of a commotion. Quick were the phones that drew to take pictures. Emma threw herself backward on the sofa, laughing and spilling her drink onto her chest.

I shouldn't have felt a surge of pride with my pantsing of an unsuspecting guest, but I did. And it was better than I'd imagined. It felt so good, I couldn't wait to do it again. I took Emma's cup from her as she stood and tried to swipe away an ice cube that had fallen down her shirt. I briefly wondered, if Walker were here, would he have known that *I* was behind the spontaneous pantsing episode?

"Cold. Cold. Cold," Emma said, pulling her bra away from her chest. The ice cube dropped to the floor and spun out. I couldn't help but laugh. Emma's shoulder slackened, and she looked at me helplessly. I grabbed her arm, beckoning her to follow me. As soon as we stepped away, a girl walking behind us slipped on the ice cube. I heard her scream just before she hit the floor with a thud. I flinched backward, tightening my grip on Emma as the girl startled me. A tall blonde girl knelt to help her up, and Emma looked at me with questioning eyes.

"Did you do that?" she asked.

"No," I said, though I was unsure. *Did I do that?* I didn't think so.

Emma aired out her shirt by pinching the fabric between her fingers and fanning it back and forth. I set my eyes on the pool table.

"So, it must be true then?" she prompted.

"What?" I asked, still staring at the green felt table.

"Your twisted little mind is actually a great power." Emma looked at me smugly.

"Well, I don't know about that . . ."

"Kins, you just dropped that guy's pants with the flicker of a thought," she deadpanned.

"Well!" I laughed, shrugging.

"Welllll?"

"I guess. Maybe. A little bit." I looked innocently at the ceiling. Emma squealed batting her hands on my shoulder.

"I knew it!" She hid her grin behind a balled fist. Even with the loud sounds of the party, I could still hear her excited whimper.

"Okay. But seriously, don't say anything." It was all so new that I didn't want it getting out.

"No, I wouldn't say anything." Emma stared at me, waiting.

"I'm just not ready to have everybody's eyes on me. All their expectations to send them home. It's too much, you know? I'm not ready."

I watched the dynamics at the pool table; Scarlett May looked upset. Angry even. I wasn't sure where Skid's girlfriend was, but there were two girls vying for his attention. One of them had a special interest in Sampson, too. I watched as she whispered something in her friend's ear and then made her way to him. Seductively, she trailed her finger down his cue stick. Scarlett May barked at him.

"Sampson! You're up!" she said, tongue-in-cheek.

He leaned over, positioning his cue stick. The girl stopped him, taking the cue stick from him.

"What's going on here?" I mumbled. Emma looked but was unamused. She didn't know how Scarlett May felt, so it didn't seem very significant to her. Still, it wasn't my place to say anything. Especially not after the night Scarlett May had spilled her secret to me under the make-believe starry night sky.

I had only turned to look at Emma for a split second, but when my eyes returned to the pool table, Sampson had his arms around the girl, and he was attempting to teach her how to play. He drew the cue stick back and forth between the girl's knuckles, and I couldn't bear to look at Scarlett May.

"Who else should you pants?" Emma asked, trying to get my attention by patting me on the shoulder. I shook her hand off.

I didn't know how to remedy this. All I really wanted was for the girl to go away so that Scarlett May could play pool with Sampson. And I doubted very much that pantsing him was going to achieve that. Pantsing *her* would be even worse.

They drew the stick back one last time and drove it into the ball. To my surprise, the ball shot back and forth like a ping-pong ball. It hit the side wall and flew off the table, heading directly for Scarlett May's stomach. I gasped as she absorbed the blow to her gut. She wrapped her hands around her waist and dropped to her knees, breathless. Sampson rushed to her side.

"Oh no!" Emma said.

The flirty girl ran her hands through her hair, shrugging, as her friend laughed out loud. The two of them scampered off with Skid.

"Oh my God. That looked like it hurt," Emma said. She started for them, looking to help, but I caught her wrist as she passed by.

"I think Sampson has this," I said, watching him on his knees next to her. Emma looked at me and then back at Scarlett May huddled on the ground. She nodded, not thinking much of it, but I saw how he rubbed her back.

I was a little leery of getting involved when Scarlett May got hurt. And even though I'd achieved my primary goal of uniting her with Sampson, I hadn't intended to cause her any harm. It was a setback in my mind. Maybe I didn't possess the control that I thought I had. And just maybe I was playing with fire.

"Hey, Kins, you know what would be really cool? If you pantsed another guy." Emma said, scanning the crowd for another victim. I briefly joined her and then scrunched my eyes shut. *No.* Pointing this magic at somebody was like playing Russian roulette. You never knew if there was a bullet in the chamber.

"Yeah, until something bad happens," I said.

"Like what? You accidentally pull down his boxers too?" Emma giggled. Her amusement faded as an attractive guy walked by. Her eyebrows rose as she looked over his arms in a muscle tee. She gestured toward the guy. "Oh, come on! Just one more!" she whined.

It didn't take much for me to cave. After all, I didn't like ending on a grim note. You always hear you should quit while you're ahead, but how many times does it take to get ahead? How many times should you risk the failure?

"One more. Then were done," I said in my most serious tone.

Emma smiled and pointed to the guy with the shoulders. "That one!" she said.

"That cute boy? The one with the perfect smile and muscles sculpted from god?" I asked.

Emma nodded. Her eyes fixed on her target.

I licked my lips, getting ready. But Emma didn't really want me to pants the guy. She didn't want to embarrass him. She was attracted to him. She just didn't know it yet.

"Okay. Get ready. Here we go . . ." Like clockwork, the apple of her eye turned to face her. Emma's eyes darted to the floor, and then she spun to hide her red face in my shoulder, but I was already gone. I smiled, watching from a few people away as the guy strode right toward her. Emma spun in circles looking for me, and I hid behind a mountain of a man.

A group of guys made their way out of the living room, pushing me backward into the hall. By the time the sixth or seventh guy squeezed by, I made my way back inside to find Emma deep in conversation. I smiled, standing alone in the hallway, watching. Emma wasn't naturally comfortable with the opposite sex. She was a little clunky and a lot nervous, but right now she was killing it. And I wasn't going to interrupt her.

I was looking over the crowd for somebody to talk with when I noticed the garage door open and close out of the corner of my eye. I knew if any of these partygoers found the golf cart, there would be hell to pay. It wasn't going to happen on my watch.

I hurried down the hall, ready to do whatever it took to keep the golf cart parked but stopped five feet shy of the door. Something registered in my mind; a flash of red. I looked over my shoulder, shocked to see a red door in the middle of the hallway. I was pretty sure that on the other side of that wall was the office. And I knew, beyond a shadow of a doubt, that door was for my eyes only. Slowly, I turned. I approached the door, touching the doorknob. Its gold hardware matched nothing in the cabin. And there was something in the way the metal was lukewarm that made me hesitate.

Was it a trap? It reminded me of the door I had seen at the bottom of Baylor Lake, and it beckoned me to enter just the same. If I had felt any control over my power tonight, it was gone now. I was helpless when it came to the door. My curiosity was like the pull of a six-horse carriage—powerful and very much unstoppable. I never even looked back.

I opened the door and was immediately sucked in with a gravitational pull. My feet slid over the floor as if it was ice. The door slammed shut behind me. I spun to open it, but it had vanished. My heart pounded, and I immediately felt hot. I was now trapped within the walls of the cabin, and nobody knew it but me.

"Help! Let me out!" I yelled. The lights flickered and buzzed in the overhead two-by-fours. The sounds from the party faded on the other side of the wall into a muffled, distant murmur.

"Hello?" I called out, meekly. There was nothing but exposed beams and the backside of the drywall. I patted the wall in the dim flickering light, looking for a way out.

The door had vanished as quickly as it had appeared, and there was no way out. A short hallway led to something bigger, brighter. I had no choice but to walk it alone. I stretched my eyes as far as they could go. Where was the light coming from? What would I find when I rounded the corner? I could only hope my gran was there, waiting.

I took one step, and then another, leaning into my footsteps cautiously. As I walked down the narrow hall, unfamiliar voices arose.

These were not the voices of college-aged kids partying at a lakeside cabin for the summer. These were the voices of professionals. They belonged to another time, another place. Anywhere but here.

"Dan isn't going to make it here if he keeps running his mouth like that," a man's voice said, calm and collected.

"I'm so sick of these arrogant residents coming in here thinking they're god's gift. Every single one of them," a woman replied quietly.

"It gets worse every year. Maybe it's my age—"

"No. It really does get worse. This year is especially bad," she agreed, her voice a monotone, like the conversation was overly mundane.

I took another step. I didn't know who Dan was, but by the sound of it, I didn't want to. It seemed that my head ached more the closer I stepped toward the light. But by the time I rounded the corner and saw the doctors, it was my knees that threatened me the most. Quaking and weak, I almost collapsed.

Several doctors crowded around an operating table. Machines glowed, bags of blood and fluids hung on metal poles, and a continuous beeping chimed sharply. I sucked in a breath, but the air seemed so thin. There was so many of them, and only one of me. It reminded me of the night that Levi had been swept up in a tornado of crows, and I found myself at the foot of a hospital bed. *My* hospital bed.

Was that me? Was this happening in real life? Now?

The doctors talked like they were having coffee or lunch with a colleague, but the truth was, they were working on somebody's head. *In* somebody's head. My stomach turned sour when I saw the male doctor lift a portion of skull from the patient. He placed it on a metal tray draped in a blue napkin.

As if connected to the skull myself, my head screamed with pain. I reached up into my hair, grabbing my head, whimpering. I was only semi-aware that my head felt whole, and I continued to search for a missing piece—the cause of my pain.

It was one of the quiet men who noticed me first. As if he could hear my pain. He lifted his head and stared at me.

"Hello?" My voice cracked wearily through the pain.

He stared cautiously, unblinking. Sitting in a chair by the patient's head, he appeared to have little to do.

My face winced as the sharp pain grew unbearable. With nowhere else to go, I took a step toward him, looking for help. I was desperate and on the verge of passing out.

His eyes rounded and his face paled. He was the only one present who could see me. "Oww!" I groaned. My voice like that of a frightened little girl. A little girl calling out into the night when she was afraid a monster might reply but prayed it would be her mother instead.

The pain stabbed, and I sucked in a seething breath through my teeth.

"Patient is starting to wake. Pushing anesthesia," the man said, taking his eyes off me and focusing on his equipment.

But as soon as he said it, everybody in the room stopped. They all turned to look directly at me with wide eyes. My mouth dropped open as I stared back, just as surprised as they were. What was this place? Where was I?

I felt incredibly exposed, like I was being seen for the very first time, and I wasn't ready. The monitor's beeping slowed as the wooziness took over. The pain in my head subsided, and the bright lights dimmed. When the worst was over, the doctors went back to work, and I went back to being invisible. Invisible to all but the man in the chair, who watched me carefully.

Released from their snare, I turned and ran down the hall, away from the pain and exposure. The red door appeared between the exposed beams, summoning me. The golden handle called my name.

I barged through the door and shoved my way through the crowd, grabbing Emma by the shoulders and pulling her away from her beautiful stranger.

"Emma!"

"What! What is it?" she asked in annoyance. Her eyes flickered back to the brawny muscle tee as I pulled her away. "Kinsley, what?"

I dragged her all the way upstairs. Away from the crowd and into the bedroom. When I flipped on the lights, a couple lay tangled in each other on my bed. They made a show of protesting.

"Get out!" I yelled.

The couple scampered off the bed and out of the bedroom, mumbling choice words beneath their breath.

"What is going on?" Emma's voice rose as she demanded answers. The room was still, and the music was muffled through the walls.

"I went back!" I said, breathless.

17

I ran my hands through my hair, pacing the length of the small bedroom. Emma stood still, trying to grasp it all.

"I went back. I saw it all as it was happening."

"You went back where? You saw what?" she asked.

"I went back to the hospital. They were performing surgery . . . Oh god . . . Was that me? Was that my head?" I patted my hair where the pain had pierced through.

Emma frantically examined my head. "What are you talking about? There's nothing here!" There was no dried blood, and most importantly, no missing skull. I turned around slowly as she sat on the foot of the bed, patiently waiting.

"Tell me what happened," she said softly.

"They pulled out this piece of bone and put it on a tray. They were talking like it was nothing. Like it was nothing to remove somebody's skull. Like they did it every day." I grabbed my stomach, afraid I was going to be sick, but the nausea passed by.

"Whose they?" Emma asked.

I pulled the computer chair out from the desk and wheeled it over to the edge of the bed. "The doctors. Me. My *other* me. The one that's real, back home. I saw them. For a moment, I was there. It was like I was spying on them." I sat in the chair and looked Emma in the eyes.

"How did you do that?"

"That's the thing. I didn't. It was like it summoned me. This door showed up out of nowhere and when I opened it, it pulled me through and then vanished, trapping me inside the walls." Oh god, I sounded like a lunatic.

"The walls?" Emma tried to keep up, but I could tell I wasn't making much sense.

"Yeah. The hallway downstairs by the garage. A mysterious red door appeared."

"The tapes! We have to watch the surveillance!" Emma said, popping to her feet and rushing to the computer. Relief washed over me when I realized she was on my side and not silently judging me like I did myself. It was nice to have a friend to count on.

"At first, they didn't see me, but then they all looked at me . . ." I was lost in the memory, my unfocused eyes staring at the corner of the room where the carpet met the baseboards.

Emma typed away on the computer.

"You said by the garage door? I wonder if the kitchen surveillance would have captured it." Emma was quickly sifting through video.

"The worst part was the way they looked at me. Like they were disgusted. Like there was something wrong with me. Like I shouldn't be there," I said in a whisper. But if I wasn't supposed to be there, then where the hell did I belong? Did they even want me back? Or had I been banished to the realm of dreams and nightmares, the realm of Baylor Lake—my phantom reality.

"Here! I found it!" Emma said, pointing to a tiny figure on the video feed. She zoomed in. The video showed me standing by a bare wall in the hallway. There was no red door.

"No. That can't be it. Rewind it. Start from the beginning when I came into the shot."

"That is the beginning," Emma said, scowling.

"Just do it!" I snapped. I wasn't crazy. I knew what I'd seen.

Emma rewound the video. I watched myself in reverse. There were only a few steps taken backward before I was out of the shot. She hit play, and I walked into the hallway and stopped. I froze, bawling my fists at my sides. I appeared to be in some sort of trance. I glanced at Emma nervously as I struggled to make sense of it. It wasn't her mind lost in translation. It wasn't her up on that screen proving that she was crazy.

The video showed me turning around and placing my hand against the wall, like I was trying to listen in on a conversation happening in the other room. I stayed there like that for long enough to feel the shame and embarrassment spread across my skin in waves of heat.

"That's not what happened! It's a lie!"

Emma gazed at the screen, her brows knitting together as she looked for clues.

"It's not real! There was a door, I went through it," I said, on the verge of hysterics. My voice didn't sound like my own as it was much higher than normal. Quicker, too.

Emma held her finger up, motioning for me to wait. Something seemed to snap inside me on the video, and I appeared to wake from my trance. I spun around and took off running through the crowd. That's probably when I'd gone looking for Emma.

Emma hit pause and turned to me with an open mouth, but she couldn't seem to find the words to say.

"I swear, Emma, it didn't happen like that."

"It's okay." Emma nodded. She didn't believe me, but she loved me all the same. She accepted me, even through my psychotic flaws. But I didn't.

"They looked at me! They looked at me like I wasn't supposed to be there!" I said fanning my face. It was so hot. My throat tightened, and my eyes watered. Where did all the time go? I had been trapped inside the walls for ten to fifteen minutes, but the video showed no more than sixty seconds pass before I fled in search of Emma.

A guy and a girl barged in, laughing. "Get out!" Emma and I yelled in unison.

I took a deep breath and sank to the floor, dropping my head to my bent knees.

"Hey. It's okay. Remember, if that video feed wasn't real—"

"It was real."

"*If* it wasn't real, then who's to say any of it is? Who's to say *this* is real right now?" she asked.

I looked up at Emma as she tried to give me her best *it's okay* speech, and I pinched her before she had a chance to finish. Just like a viper, I struck without warning.

"Ouch!" She rubbed her arm. If she hadn't thought I was nuts before, she did now. Her scowl said it all, and her mouth hung open in shock.

I rolled my eyes.

"Point taken. You didn't have to pinch me." She slumped on the floor next to me.

"I don't know where I belong anymore, Emma."

"I think we need to get you home," she said.

"I don't think they want me there. You should have seen how they looked at me." A tear dribbled down my cheek as I thought of how unwelcome my presence had been in the operating room. I didn't want to go back anyway, but regardless of choice, it still hurt to know I didn't belong. And I didn't want that choice made by anyone but me. Was it too much to ask to be the only one in control of my fate?

"Of course they want you. Your mom wants you there. Your dad does. Even your brother. Don't think for one second that you've been banished to Baylor because they looked at you weird."

"But I have been banished here, haven't I?"

"I think you're just here to heal. And when you get your strength back, you're going to set us free, and we're all going home. That's what I believe."

"And if I can't?" It was a tall order. What if I couldn't save everybody? What if I couldn't save Emma?

"I can't let myself think about that. You know, I'm trying to be strong here, but I really, really want to go home. You can't lose hope, Kinsley, because if you do, we all will. And I don't want to see Baylor with lost hope. It's already haunting enough."

I felt the weight of responsibility crash down on me. I needed to thrive, because there was no other way out for them. When the time came, I could send them home, and then I would stay here with Walker.

"Too haunted for *you*?" I asked, trying to lighten the mood.

"You know, it's one thing to read it, and it's an entirely different thing to live it. I can't close the book on this. I can't turn out the lights and go to sleep knowing that tomorrow will be a sunny day and breakfast will be waiting for me downstairs on the kitchen table come morning. I don't even know if there will be a morning here. I don't know if we will survive the night."

"I'm so sorry, Emma. I'm so sorry I'm putting you through this." What kind of friend was I?

Emma rested her head on my shoulder, and I heard her stifle a sniffle. The girl was homesick, and I knew the feeling.

"Can you just make it better? If only for tonight?" she asked. I sighed, knowing that it would only be a bandage. That I would be fixing the symptom and not the cause. That the fear would still be there tomorrow . . . *if she were to wake*.

"I think I can." It was one small thing I could do for her now.

I closed my eyes, and I imagined Emma curled up on her window seat with her favorite book in her bedroom at home. There was a candle lit on her nightstand, and her cat curled up by her side. It was her happy place, and right now, it was her safe haven. She didn't have that here, but she needed it.

"Ceecee," Emma exclaimed.

I opened my eyes to see that we were no longer in the guest bedroom of the cabin, but in Emma's bedroom sitting on the floor. Her cat, Ceecee, purred rhythmically. Emma scratched behind her ears and under her chin. Emma's eyes lit with wonder, and she stood up, spreading her arms wide. "It's been so long!" she exclaimed.

"Is it how you remembered?" I asked, paging through the book on the window seat.

"It's exactly how I remember it. How did you do it?"

"Don't worry about that. Just enjoy it." I made my way to her door.

"Hey Kins . . ." I had almost made it out of her room, escaping the question that I knew would come next. "Can I stay?" Emma's eyes were pleading when I glanced over my shoulder. I wanted so badly to tell her yes, that she was home now, and the nightmare was over. The truth was, I couldn't lie.

"Only for tonight," I sighed.

I watched a flicker of sadness cross Emma's face as I turned to leave. As soon as I closed the door to her bedroom, I was in the hallway of the cabin. I'd given her a dream to live in, but it was only temporary. The dream would turn back into a nightmare soon enough. There was only so much I could do, and I rode that guilt like a wave across the hall to my bedroom.

I vaguely remember a wandering girl stumbling through the hall looking for an extra bathroom. I pointed her in the right direction as I crossed into the master bedroom. A faint smell of raspberry and vodka wafted behind the girl. I locked the door behind me. If Emma could escape for a single night, could I escape too?

I dressed for bed and turned out the lights. I closed my eyes and thought about what I really wanted. If it was just for one night, which dream could I live in? I wanted to go home just like Emma had. I was homesick too. I wanted to see my mom, but there was a part of me that was afraid of knowing it was fake. Worrying that her love was disingenuous. A figment of my imagination. I presumed that would hurt more than not seeing her at all. For that reason, I chose to stick with my bedroom. I could pretend I was home for one night, just like Emma, and we could commiserate together come morning when we woke in the cabin.

I opened my eyes, and I was in my bedroom, just the way I'd left it. My bed was unmade, and my graduation gown hung from my windowsill. I smiled and touched the fabric of the navy-blue robe. My shoes were on the floor, still toe to heel, as if I had just stepped out of them yesterday. Several clean outfits lay scattered on the floor outside my closet.

It triggered a memory of me getting dressed on the night of my birthday. I was going to celebrate, and I remembered I was running late to pick up Lainey. My eyes drifted over my desk where my journals had been bookmarked. My backpack sat in my computer chair. It was just the way I remembered it, and it almost made me feel like I was home. It didn't take away the nagging homesick feeling completely, and I knew that had something to do with my family not being here. But even though the familiarity of my belongings eased the pain in my heart, in no way had it healed it.

Now that I was here, I felt the emptiness that lived inside me. It was never my home that made my heart full, but the people that lived within it. I paged through my journal, opening to the bookmarked entry. I read a passage full of my hope to steal the heart of Noah Hampton. I blushed thinking of the time when that was my biggest dream. I'd had big plans the night of my birthday, and I had hoped that he would kiss me. I had been so naïve. It seemed like years ago, but I had no way of telling just how long it had really been. I sighed, feeling almost lonelier here at home than I ever had in Baylor. Which was saying a lot, because nobody understood me there. Nobody but Walker.

I turned back to my bed and my heart seized. Walker St. James lay on my unmade bed. His fingers interlaced behind his head and his ankles crossed lazily over one another. He smiled a wicked smile, and his dimples burrowed into his cheeks. I swallowed the lump in my throat as my mind raced in a hundred different directions at once. How long had he been here? Had I summoned him? Was he real? I had so many questions, but the one overpowering thought was how he could single-handedly close the gap in my heart. My world wasn't complete if he wasn't in it, and that scared me more than the devil of Baylor himself.

"Walker," I said breathlessly.

"Wilde," he replied.

"What are you doing here?" I took in how glorious he looked sprawled across my bed. And I was suddenly utterly horrified at my dirty bedroom. I stepped on a pair of shorts on the floor and kicked them underneath the bed, thankful that they slid across the hardwood floor effortlessly.

"What are you talking about? You wanted me here. Right? Isn't that how this all works?" he asked. Did he know I was just thinking about him? Did he know how I felt right now? I was uncomfortably exposed.

"No! And yes. I mean . . . maybe?" My voice hitched as I dropped to the floor, crawling on hands and knees after the laundry strewn everywhere. I slid half of it underneath my bed, and after popping to my feet, I kicked the rest of it into my closet and shut the door with a huff. My eyes widened as Walker left my bed for my desk and picked up my journal.

"No!" I lunged for him, but he was much taller than me, and he held the journal high over my head.

I jumped like a child, trying to swipe it from his grasp. His proximity made my cheeks flush, and I took a step back. He already knew I wanted him here, and now here we stood, alone in my bedroom.

He held the journal in which I had described my feelings for Noah in depth high above his frame. If this wasn't vulnerability, I didn't know what was. I felt exposed, like I was naked in front of him. I was afraid of how he would respond, and if getting a deeper glimpse of who I was would change his mind about me. Sometimes, being naked could be a funny thing—sometimes it was anything but a joke. I didn't know how Walker really felt toward me, and that scared me to the very core. I knew he cared, but I was pretty sure I was the only one with romantic feelings.

"What? I can't read it?" he asked. I couldn't tell if he was being sarcastic or not.

"Are you *insane?*" I didn't like how frantic I had become. Walker saw it too. The only difference between him and me, was that he liked it.

"Maybe?" he said seductively, with one brow arched. My heart hammered in my chest.

I stood staring at him like he was a feral beast until he slowly lowered the journal. As soon as it was in reach, I snatched it protectively. Walker held his hands up and backed away slowly. I shoved the journal inside a desk drawer and slammed it shut, barricading it with my body. He'd have to go through me if he wanted it now.

Walker let his hands fall and turned his attention to a painting hanging on my wall. I had painted it when I was eleven years old.

"No!" I stopped him again.

Walker laughed and held his hands up again. I stood between him and the painting, a small space for my exploding heart. I felt like the fireworks from the Fourth of July were bursting in my chest. I was nervous, excited, and petrified all at once. I couldn't tell if it was beautiful or horrific. I couldn't tell if having Walker in my home made me complete, or completely insane.

Walker smiled down at me as if feeling for himself what I had felt all along, and he backed up slowly, giving me space to breathe. He was amused, and I was about to have a breakdown. He turned around, spotting the collage of photos behind my nightstand.

A small whimper escaped my throat as I buried my head in my hands. *Please make it stop.*

"Is this you?" he asked, pointing to a photo of Lainey and me in sixth grade.

"Yep," I said, shoving my hands in my back pockets and chewing nervously on my lip. There was a photo of Noah and me when we were younger pinned right next to it. I hoped he hadn't seen that one, or at least didn't recognize him.

"So, this is your room?" he asked, turning around and taking it all in. I cringed seeing the strap of a pink bra underneath his shoe. I really should have kept my room clean like my mom always told me.

"This is my room," I squeaked out.

"I like it." I sucked in a breath, not realizing I'd been holding my breath until now. Why did this make me so nervous? Walker was my friend. We hung out almost every day in Baylor. But there was something about having him in my bedroom that made it all so real. Like he'd come to visit me in my realm and was really seeing me for the first time.

"So, Wilde, why did you bring me here?" he asked, the same smug look on his face as when he'd held my journal.

18

My bedroom was dim. I almost never turned the lights on. The summer before I'd started high school, my mom had gotten me a light shaped like a giant branch that sprawled across my wall, and with each stem, there were dozens of twinkling lights intertwined in the twigs. If I was home, it was plugged in. It may be a little childish now, but I'd always adored the soft glow of light scattered throughout the corner of my room. It was on now, and it only made Walker's chiseled jaw more alluring . . . and more out of place.

Why had I brought him here? I guess because I couldn't live without him, or I didn't know how to anymore. He was still a ghost, and I was still a dreamer, regardless of which realm we drifted through. But if that wasn't hard enough to wrap my mind around, the truth was, this wasn't my bedroom at all. This wasn't my reality, but a phantom of one I used to know.

I couldn't walk out that door and converse with my mom and dad. My brother wouldn't barge in at any moment trying to find my candy stash. And if I walked out that door, I wouldn't see the spindled stair rail of my house or the family photos my mom made us take every year at Christmas. I'd see wandering strangers looking for a private bathroom in the cabin at Baylor Lake. If I jumped out my window, I'd land on the grassy knoll of Rock Creek Cove. It would probably be the party trick of the night, and I would be thrust up on the shoulders of two or three muscular guys and paraded around like I was a demigod. Maybe that wasn't a half-bad idea . . .

But the part that *was* real was the connection I had to Walker. My feelings for him, regardless of backdrop, were unmatchable. I'd never felt this way about anybody before. My feelings for Noah stemmed from attraction, friendship, and maybe even the need to fit in. Noah had always been so comfortable in his own skin and so popular that I felt like maybe, if he liked me back, I would finally have a chance to relax and be accepted. I wouldn't have to try so hard to fit in.

But all of that was different with Walker. Walker never tried to fit in. He couldn't. He wasn't even alive. Actually, he stuck out like a sore thumb, and he owned every bit of it. I think it was one of the things I'd fallen in love with first.

High school is hard. It has its own little ecosystem. It's delicate, and difficult to find your place. But from the moment you graduate, that little world opens up—growing on a scale that is impossible to imagine at the time. The ecosystem you live in becomes the one you create. But I was neither in high school nor out in the real world. I was somewhere else entirely. I had my own realm laid out in front of me with infinite possibilities to create . . . *and destroy*. If I'd thought the real world was a big place, it paled in comparison to the silo of my imagination.

Living in a realm where anything is possible, and the path you choose could go on indefinitely, is a scary thing. Worse when you must do it alone. I didn't just want somebody like Noah, where I could fit in by his side. I needed somebody like Walker, who knew himself and was confident enough to allow me to find myself. I didn't have to change for Walker; I only had to grow into my potential . . . I had to find *myself*. And he would be there to walk the winding paths with me while I grew.

"Wilde?" Walker asked, head cocked to the side with a patient gaze.

"Huh?"

"Why did you bring me here?"

"Oh." My throat ran dry as my eyes scanned the bedroom I'd grown up in. "I wanted you to see this," I said simply.

"Really?" He laughed, running his hand over the stubble on his cheek.

I raised my eyebrows and nodded. Was it so hard to believe?

"Then why won't you let me see any of it?" he asked.

"You mean my journal? You can't read that."

Walker turned back to the collage of photos and my heart thumped in my chest. He un-pinned a picture of Noah and me at one of our mothers' get-togethers. We were wearing aprons and serving hors d'oeuvres; we couldn't have been older than eight.

"No, no, no," I said, plucking the photo from his hand.

He didn't say I told you so, but he might as well have by the way he was looking at me. I plopped down on my bed with a heavy sigh.

"Look, I just wanted to try it. I wanted to try to see my old bedroom. I thought it might ease some of the homesick feeling I get in my chest. And once it worked, I didn't really want to be alone. I didn't want to see my parents, because I thought it would be heartbreaking to know that it was only my imagination."

"Did it work?"

"Well, you're here, aren't you?"

Walker smiled and sat down next to me. "No, I meant, do you feel less homesick?"

"It didn't work as well as I thought it would. It's nice to be here, and it's comforting in its own right. But there was something missing."

"The home part?"

I nodded, feeling the burn in the back of my throat. "I can look out my window and see the row of houses . . . But I know nobody is home. It's as if, everywhere I go, I'm alone. Isolated. The cabin is filled with my friends, yet I'm the only one dreaming." I threw myself back onto the bed and stared up at my ceiling. Walker lay down next to me on his side, his elbow propping him up.

"I'm glad you brought me here. I don't want you to feel alone. You know, Wilde, we might be in different spaces, but we're connected here. I think our souls found each other for a reason."

My stomach dipped. I loved the way he was looking down at me. "And why is that?" I prompted him.

"I haven't figured that out yet. But if we're talking about home, you're the closest thing that I have felt to home in a very long time. I can't thank you enough."

I wanted him to lean down and kiss me so badly. I pled through my eyes. We were soul mates. He'd just said it. Yet he still didn't want to kiss me. I saw the sadness that I had grown accustomed to pass through his eyes. It was the same sadness I had seen when I'd frozen time and he was gazing up at the luminous moon. He was a hurting soul, and he didn't need kisses. He needed a friend.

He fell back on the bed, and for a moment we both lay on our backs staring at the ceiling through the dim light of my twinkling branch. But then Walker pushed his arm under my shoulders and pulled me to his chest. I looked up to see his glassy eyes before my head landed on his shoulder. I wasn't sure if he needed a hug or if he didn't want me to see him cry, but I wrapped my arm around his chest and melted into him. I wasn't the only one missing home.

I breathed in his beachy, coastal cologne and closed my eyes. It brought me back to the night we'd met. I was just a scared, drowned girl he'd plucked from the lake. I had sat in the canoe in my underwear, my hair dripping down my back and chest as I checked for claw marks on my thigh. But in the time it took to see the sky had illuminated with stars, I'd inhaled his smell, and his warm presence had me forever snared in his trap.

We drifted off, each drowning in our own despair, and clinging to one another like life rafts in a turbulent ocean. We held each other, trying to stave off the homesickness. Our heartache was a shared well of pain. We were two lost souls seeking refuge in each other, and I never wanted to let go again. I fought sleep, but it was inevitable. Walker's chin fell heavily on the top of my head as my mind quieted and we fell asleep.

In what seemed like no time, the combination of heat and light coming through the window lifted me from slumber. But it was the heavy arm around my waist and the heat against my back that fully awakened me. My eyes flung open as I stared out the window at the magnificent view of Baylor Lake. Just like a pumpkin carriage created for a magical night, my bedroom back home had disintegrated with the stroke of dawn. But it wasn't the pumpkin that had made the night magical. It was the prince. And my prince, Walker, was holding onto me tighter than ever. He'd never left, and he never let go.

His breath was hot against the nape of my neck. His hand rested at my navel, and his thumb was tucked into the waist of my jeans. My eyes widened, and I sucked in an alarmed breath, causing Walker to stir behind me. It was the last thing I wanted. I wished I could stay like this forever. I would have pretended to sleep for the rest of eternity if he'd keep holding me. But as my luck would have it, I ruined it the second I realized it was even happening. Walker stretched behind me, pushing into me as he did. His thumb caressed the skin just below my belly button as he slowly withdrew his hand from my waist.

I dared to be brave. I turned around to face him, but he was just getting up. He leaned over and kissed the top of my head, causing my stomach to churn with excitement. But then he did something unexpected. He ran his hand back and forth over my head, messing up my hair. He leapt out of bed, stretching once more and taking in the view from the window.

I lay in bed utterly confused. The kiss on the top of my head was something lovers did. But the ruffling of my hair was something that big brothers did to their annoying siblings. It said a lot of things, but it didn't say I think I'm falling in love with you. Why did he have to be so confusing? It was almost if he was fighting a battle within himself, and I wished he would just surrender already.

The way he'd held me while we'd slept would say something different entirely. I wasn't sure if it was a reflection of his true feelings unmasked as he'd slept, or if he was simply dreaming of somebody else. Somebody I had been avoiding. Somebody who had his heart but didn't want it. Part of me felt like Walker had been lying to himself. That he'd loved me all along but just wouldn't let himself admit it. But there was an even bigger part of me, a part driven by fear, that wondered if Walker really did have the curse of broken love. That he would always love somebody who didn't love him back, and furthermore, would be incapable of reciprocating the true love that I gave him.

When I found myself checking my morning breath in a stealthily cupped palm of my hand, I assumed I had been complicating things far too much—the guy just didn't like *me.* I rubbed my eyes and ran my hands through my hair, fixing the mess my dreams had left me with.

"So, Wilde, when did you master teleportation?" Walker asked, turning from the window to look at me. His mussed hair and wrinkled shirt were a good look on him. I liked the way he looked right after waking up, and I knew my nights would never be the same if he weren't in them.

"I guess, last night?"

"Really?"

"Yeah," I said with a shrug. He wasn't buying it. He knew I was omitting the truth, but he wasn't sure why. He didn't know I was afraid he'd ask me to use my magic to find Layla, and that if I did, he might finally move on, and I would be left to this web of dreams all alone.

"Okay." He didn't argue. I wished he would have. I wished I could scream *you don't want me* at the top of my lungs and burst into tears. But he was more the type to watch and wait. I would go on allowing the guilt to cannibalize me as he quietly collected evidence of my dishonesty. It would come out eventually, we *both* knew it. I sat in awkward silence as he waited calmly for me to change my mind. But my lips were sealed.

"I think we need to up your training." I didn't enjoy lying to him, but I simply couldn't tell him the truth. There was too much on the line for me to lose. He was the one thing that kept me sane, and I surely couldn't live without him. Or perhaps I would go crazy like Layla had. And I had already been banished from my real life back home.

"What did you have in mind?" I wasn't sure there was much else he could teach me now that I'd unlocked what had been holding me back.

"It's a good question. I guess I need to evaluate you first."

I swallowed, trying to moisten my dry throat. If I wasn't willing to tell him, he was going to make me show him.

Walker disappeared downstairs to brew a pot of coffee, and I ran to the bathroom to brush my teeth. I splashed cold water on my face and slapped some pinkness into my cheeks. I ran back out and jumped into the bed, pretending I'd never left, and waited for his return.

Emma screamed a long, drawn-out cry across the hall. It ended in a muffled gurgle. I knew that cry. I knew she'd fallen asleep at home and rudely awakened here. I also knew that she was screaming into her pillow, because that's exactly what I had done the first month I'd been trapped in Baylor. I worried she would come in and curse my very existence, but she didn't.

By the time Walker came back with two steaming mugs of coffee, I had a plan. I was going to hold my magic back. Dampen the manifestations. I wasn't going to show him what I was truly capable of. That, I would explore my own. And he would be none the wiser.

He handed me a cup of coffee, and I thanked him, taking a sip before resting it in my lap. He sat opposite me on the bed. "I want you to go back," he said in a serious tone.

"Go back where?"

"If you are truly lucid dreaming, you should be able to travel wherever you want. I want you to go back to your home, your body, to the life you used to have before you came here, no matter how hard it is."

"What are you even talking about? Why would I do that?" I asked in a flustered tone.

"Why?"

"I mean, how? *How* do you expect me to just go back? And what would I even do there?" I asked.

"Take me with you. We can try to figure it out together. Maybe you could just lie down on top of your body and your soul would reconnect?"

It hurt knowing he was trying to send me home. And it only confirmed my biggest fear, that he could never love me back. If that was the case, maybe I shouldn't stay. My heart ached at the thought of leaving.

"But then, I would never see you again." I scoured his golden eyes for answers. Was that what he wanted?

"No, perhaps you wouldn't. But Wilde, this isn't where you belong." Walker's face contorted the same way it had when he'd told me I had died. I was beginning to know it as his uncomfortable truth face.

"Honestly, I don't think I belong there either."

"What? Why would you ever say that? Of course you belong there. That's your body, your family, your home." It made sense to Walker, and I could see why, but he hadn't seen the looks the doctors had given me in the operating room.

"Maybe . . ." I lied.

"Let's go back. Together. Just to look around."

I couldn't let him down, not without at least trying. I nodded and closed my eyes. Walker reached forward and took my open hand in his. He waited for the magic to pull us through a wormhole, sending us to my battered body in the hospital bed. But me, I let the minutes tick by as I enjoyed holding his hand instead. I didn't let myself think of the hospital or the home I'd left behind. I stayed fully immersed in that moment, concentrating all my focus on his skin touching mine.

After quite some time, he squeezed my hand. "It's okay. We can try again another time." He'd been so patient and so supportive that it only made me feel worse for deceiving him.

"Sorry . . ."

"Don't be sorry. It's not your fault. You're just not ready," he said. He was taking half the blame for my failure, but he'd done nothing wrong. An uneasy knot formed in my stomach, and I was hating myself more and more with every chance I had to tell him the truth but didn't.

"Well, let's get this straight. You can't fly."

I broke into laughter. "Nope."

"You can't make yourself teleport."

I shrugged apologetically.

"But you *can* shoot down a clay pigeon telepathically," he said with pride.

"And apparently, beehives too," I added.

Walker laughed. "Yep. You have a real machine gun on that hand of yours."

His laughter died down to a small upturn of his lips as he gazed into his mug. His voice softened. "But you can't find Layla. And you can't find your way back home."

It felt like a punch to the gut. I averted my eyes, also looking into my coffee mug. I *could* find Layla. She'd been coming up to me, and it was I who had been avoiding her. Of course, he didn't know that because I'd been lying about it.

I could find my way home, too, although it wasn't a place I liked to be. The hospital scared me, and the doctors intimidated me. The bloated and bloodied patient I saw was not a girl I knew, or wanted to. My mom's tears made me feel sick to my stomach, and the bright lights hurt my eyes. I felt incredibly exposed and more invisible than ever all at once.

I never wanted to go back again. In fact, I would gladly stay here with the werewolves and wormholes, the haunted waters and the nightmares. I would stay here chasing after Walker for eternity if he'd let me.

19

Several days had passed and not much happened. One evening, when I was sitting on the back deck with Kai and Gunner, we'd spotted a glimpse of red between the trees. I played it off as nothing, but I knew it was Layla in her red cloak checking up on me. I'd told Kai I was tired and went to bed. I forced myself not to look out the window at night for fear she'd be watching. Like a rabid animal, she was gaining confidence and getting closer. It was inevitable that she would strike, and it was better to keep my distance for as long as I could.

I stayed up half the night tossing and turning. The curiosity pushing me to jump to my feet and open the window, searching for the girl in red, was almost unbearable. I had made up my mind to stay, and I didn't need her or the *Waking Dreams* book any longer. I was getting good in my abilities and growing confident in myself. I hid most of it from Walker by avoiding him. I knew I couldn't hide forever, and I would have to come out to him eventually, but I was waiting for the right time. The right place. A feeling of certainty. I was so afraid that he would send me home, tell me I couldn't stay, that I just avoided him.

There was one thing nagging in the back of my mind that had been there for a while now, that had contributed to my hesitation. The red door at the bottom of Baylor Lake. Somehow, I got it in my head that if I knew where the door led, or what its purpose was, then I could tell Walker everything. How else was I supposed to tell him that I had found my strength and still wanted to stay when there were so many questions left unanswered? It didn't seem very responsible of me. I wanted to be prepared in case I had to argue my reasoning with him. I couldn't fight for my right to stay if I couldn't answer any of the questions he might ask.

Of course, Walker wouldn't be asking about the door in particular—I'd never told him about it. That was a question I had pondered all on my own. It had been smoldering in the back of my mind since the day I'd found it, since the day it had beckoned me to open it, but the idea had grown into a raging fire of curiosity after I'd found a similar red door in my hallway. If the cabin could open a portal to an operating room, a realm where half of me lived, I had to imagine that the red door at the bottom of the lake was the exact same thing. A gateway between worlds.

Training with Walker was like baring my soul to him. I'd been avoiding it since the night he'd slept over. Call me superstitious, but I've been waiting for a sign. A moment in time where I knew I could tell him everything and he would not turn me away. Today was the day I was going to investigate the red door. Because the more answers I got on my own, the more confident I would be to tell him I belonged here—and believe it myself.

I laced my shoes for a hike and pulled my ponytail through the back of a baseball cap. I was slightly afraid I would never come back, so I lingered in the kitchen when I saw Emma. She was feeding Gunner scraps from breakfast.

"Good morning," I said.

"Hey. Going for a hike?" she asked, taking me in.

"Yeah. I should be back this afternoon. I'm heading out to the cliffs," I said, pointing, and then standing awkwardly. I wasn't ready to leave, even though the door had been calling. Emma turned around and shot me a weird look. I chewed on my lip, but my feet didn't move an inch.

"Uh, did you want company?"

"Oh no, you don't have to do that," I said, waving a hand. Emma nodded and went back to cleaning up her mess on the countertop.

I stood quietly at her back as the seconds ticked by.

"That's it. I'm coming." Emma slammed the oven mitt down. "Let me get my shoes."

I shrugged as she left the room. I couldn't argue with that. When she came back, she walked right past me, grabbing the leash on the way out to the back patio.

"Looks like you get to go, buddy," I said to Gunner. He wagged his tail and barreled out the door, running like he was slipping on ice. His legs went twice the speed that his body carried him, and he whacked the door frame on his way out. "Ouch!"

Emma wrapped the leash around the back of her neck and Gunner ran out before us.

"Did you have a fight with Walker or something? I haven't seen him around lately."

"No. Everything's going good," I said defensively. She knew I was covering something up.

"Did you have a fight with Noah then?" she prodded.

"No, why?"

"You're acting weird. Don't think I don't notice."

I frowned. Of course she'd noticed. I'd practically begged her to come without ever saying a word. She must have known there was a reason.

Gunner locked up on a bush, his front leg bent in a pointing position. He was frozen still, his tail unwavering as an arrow. Emma and I giggled, breaking the tension. We stopped to watch for a bit. He dropped his foot slowly and inched forward, ever so slyly. He was a predator hunting his prey. Eventually, his creep turned into a lurch as he ran into the bush and a covey of birds fluttered out.

We laughed, clapping, and cheering him on. "Good boy!"

"Do you think he senses that something is off here?" Emma asked.

I watched Gunner look into the sky at his missed prey. "I don't think so. I think he's more of a hunt, eat, sleep, and dig kind of guy," I said.

"Yeah, you're probably right. I found some more holes in the front yard the other day."

"I'll have to fill them this weekend."

We got to the part of the hike where we ascended a steep dirt path. Both of us were breathing hard, and Gunner was nowhere to be found. Emma didn't seem like her regular self. She hadn't been since I'd sent her home for a night. I should have gifted her a starry night sky like I had Scarlett May, because allowing her to go home without any of the things that made it real, like a family, was probably more torture than it was worth. It was a shell of the life she used to have, and I think it made her withdraw from this one even more.

I had to reengage her, but how? "Hey Emma, I have a secret . . ." I said, dangling it in front of her like a carrot before a mule.

Emma stopped dead in her tracks and turned around to wait for me. There was nothing quite like the power of a secret.

"I figured out how to stop time." I wasn't sure how she would take it, but I hoped it would give her something to look forward to.

"You did? How? When?" She cocked her head to the side and tucked some loose strands of hair behind her ear. She seemed more perplexed than anything else.

"I guess I did it when time ceased to exist for you. Remember that time?" I said, laughing.

"Wait, are you serious? You can stop time?" Her eyes grew wide with excitement.

"Yeah. You want to see?"

"Yes, please!"

It happened quickly. More quickly than ever before. I didn't have to concentrate this time or work with my breathing. I just leaned into that feeling of wanting to please Emma. I wanted to make her happy and proud of me. Everything froze except us.

"No way!" Emma said, turning to look at her surroundings. The leaves on the trees no longer swayed. The blades of grass were crisp and unwavering. Gunner's tail peeked through a bush in the distance. And the air was stagnant upon our skin. Emma ran her hands through the air feeling the drag for the first time.

"It's weird how the air stops too. It kind of becomes heavy in a way," I said, playing with it between my fingers.

"It's so weird. The entire world is like this? Frozen? It's just you and me?"

"I guess?" I said, shrugging. I didn't really know.

"Wow . . ." Emma mumbled under her breath as she walked off to investigate.

I smiled watching her like a child on Christmas morning as she walked through the clearing, full of wonder. But then I caught sight of the cliff where Walker and I had jumped. Where I had seen the red door for the first time. I was so scared to meet my fate that I froze Emma too. She didn't need to see this, and I didn't want her to worry. I'd be back by the time she even turned around. As far as she had to know, this wasn't anything more than a hike where I'd told her one of my secrets.

I left her in the clearing and made my way to the edge of the bluff. As I peered down to the lake below, I realized that it too was frozen. I looked back at Emma, wondering if I had enough time to unfreeze, jump in, and then freeze again before she turned around. I needed time to stand still, but I also needed the lake to be placid. Otherwise, I'd never get in. Could I stop time *above* the lake, but continue it *below*?

It was getting too complicated, and I could sense myself making up excuses. I couldn't talk myself out of this, and that's exactly what I had begun to do. I had to believe that everything would work out just the way I wanted, the way I needed.

I jumped before I had time to talk myself out of it.

Even though time was standing still, free falling felt like a rush. The stagnant air didn't riffle through my hair the way it would have if it was free flowing; it wrapped around me, as if I were a knife slicing through warmed butter. I windmilled my arms and held my breath as I prayed that the glassy lake would break, and I would fall into the water. But it remained solid, and it was fast approaching, and I feared I would splatter like a bug on a windshield.

I closed my eyes inches before the sheet of water, and felt the slap of the lake as I broke through and plunged beneath the surface.

Success.

As soon as I felt the cold water on my face, I knew Emma would be looking for me and my cover would be blown. I needed to freeze time again before she turned around to see that I had vanished.

My arms and legs were suddenly pinned between the layers of rock-hard water, and I wasn't able to move an inch. I'd stopped time, and the lake had frozen with it.

Like being stuck in dried cement, I couldn't move so much as a fingertip. My hair stretched out in front of me, and a million tiny bubbles had frozen mid-burst. My eyes were the only thing that could move, but I couldn't see much through the effervescent stir of the water. My chest had no room to rise, there was no air for me to breathe, and I couldn't expand my lungs, anyway.

Fear snatched me much like the water had, and I knew I was in over my head. What if this was it? What if this was the rest of my life? I knew I hadn't died yet, and I knew I couldn't, just as long as my body was appropriately taken care of in the hospital. I wanted to take a breath because it was my instinct to do so, but I didn't need it to survive.

My mind screamed for Emma to notice me trapped here, but I had frozen her too. How could I be so mindless? I was the only one who even knew I needed help, and the only one with the power to fix it.

My heart hammered in my chest; it was just about the only thing that could move. I remained still as stone as the adrenaline coursed through my veins telling me to run, to fight, to do anything but freeze. I was utterly powerless against the full weight of the lake. And I was in no mindset to manifest. My emotions had to rise and fall before I'd have the clarity to help myself.

It felt like an eternity all on its own. I felt like a fossil etched in stone and buried for a lifetime. My fear ran so hot I swore the water was starting to melt around me. But after a long and dreadful stint of terror, I started to calm.

I moved my fingers at first, and then a slight bend of my knee. I arched my back, and the water became like sludge. I dropped further into the wet-cement-like water, still falling from my jump. When my mind fully cleared, I was able to release my spell and resume time.

My hair covered my face, then lifted for me to see the lake and the trail of bubbles above me. I knew Emma would be looking for me, but I couldn't think of that now. I had one mission for the day, and I wasn't going to turn back after the hell I'd gone through to get here.

I desperately wanted a breath of air, but I didn't want to risk never coming back down, so I dipped my head down to my toes and started swimming to the bottom of the lake.

I swam hard and fast. Everything inside me told me it was wrong to swim downward with no air, but about halfway down something took over. Something began to pull on me, and the weight of the water itself pushed me down quicker than I could've swum. I sank like a ton of bricks.

I searched through the water, looking for the door, but everything was too murky to see. It felt like I'd been under the water for a solid year, and still, there was no end in sight.

I startled when I saw a hand breaking through the poor visibility, and I realized I wasn't alone in the haunted lake. I paddled fiercely as somebody neared, swimming next to me. A wave of emotion washed over me as I saw Lainey's freckled face paddling by my side.

I couldn't tell if she was real or a memory. She simply swam alongside me during the long and brutal trek through the water, like a good friend would. And it was at that moment I knew I was on the right track. I knew this door was something more than a figment of my imagination, and I was right to explore it.

A golden glimmer pierced the dark water, and like a string anchored directly to the door, I descended right on top of it. The red door grew more vibrant with the closing distance, and the pull grew stronger.

There, at the bottom of the lake, was a single red door set into the sand. The hinges latched to a pile of rocks. My feet planted heavily on the bottom of the lake next to Lainey's. The familiarity drew me in, and without thinking, I reached out and grabbed the doorknob. Lainey encouraged me excitedly. I twisted the knob and pulled the door open just a crack before stopping myself.

What was I doing? I didn't want to open the door, I only wanted answers. What if the draw was so strong, there was no escaping it? A bright light shone through the crack, but there were no answers to be had. I couldn't tell what was beyond, other than light. Lainey grabbed a hold of my hand over the doorknob and pulled with all her force.

No!

The door swung open all too fast, and Lainey's eyes lit up like fireworks on the Fourth of July. I too was dazzled by what was inside.

Through the door, white, fluffy clouds drifted by, and the sound of an airplane hummed somewhere in the distance. The water warmed around me from the sunny day. I sucked in a deep luxurious breath of the fresh air that flowed through the door.

Cautiously, I kneeled on my hands and knees and peered over the edge of the door frame. Lainey did the same next to me, and we marveled at the sky. It was definitely another world, another realm. Without a shadow of doubt, I knew it was the world I had grown up in. The world I now called "The Real One."

But as I sat back on my heels, I wasn't quite as sure it was the one I belonged to. There was something in Baylor that called to me, something other than Walker. I was getting to know myself here, better than I ever had at home. I was starting to believe in myself, and I wasn't ready to give that up. I felt the pull in both directions equally. My soul yearned for its body, but my heart refused to follow.

Lainey nodded encouragingly. Slowly, I shook my head to communicate that I wasn't ready. That I didn't think I ever would be. I watched as Lainey's face fell into deep disappointment and then verge on the edge of something else entirely.

I reached forward to close the door, and I felt Lainey's knobby hands on my back as she pushed me through.

I screamed, falling through the open door and into the thin air, grasping the edge for dear life. My body dangled above the clouds as my arms grappled in the sand and water. Lainey stood above me as I screamed and fought to get back. I tried to hitch a leg onto the doorjamb but failed miserably.

She bent down and grabbed my hand, but not to help. She lifted my fingers off the sandy floor and bent them backward until I lost my grip.

"No! Lainey! Help!" I screamed out, hanging on by a single outstretched hand.

The weight of my drenched clothes made my body feel even heavier, and my wet skin erupted in goosebumps. I was helpless, and so very foolish.

I looked down between my dangling feet as the clouds parted, and I could see the tiny neighborhoods below. Immediately, I knew I was over my hometown of Clover.

My gut wrenched, and the air became difficult to breathe. She was supposed to be my friend. She was supposed to support me. But this wasn't the Lainey I knew and loved; this was the ghost of her. The thing that had grabbed me in the lake before, trying to drown me.

It reached down lifting my pinky finger, and I screamed. "Stop it!!"

My voice rumbled like thunder, and all the fear and anger of betrayal flew out of me like a storm, knocking Lainey backward into the deep water. I slung my free arm into the lake and reached for a rock to grab hold of. I thrust one leg over the doorjamb and wedged it into the corner of the frame. I struggled, kicking buckets of sand through the open door, stopping briefly to watch it fall into the sky. I mustered all the effort I had left, heaved my body through the open door, and rolled onto my back at the bottom of the lake.

Holding my breath, I rolled onto my side, looking for Lainey. I saw her in the distance, swimming toward me like a shark in the deep sea; unnaturally fast and alarmingly compelled. I scurried to my feet and trudged through the thick water to the door. I lifted the door from the rocks. It was as heavy as an iron boulder, and pushing it through the water made it even more difficult.

Lainey was closing in on me, and it took everything I had to get the door up and over the midpoint. Once it stood upright, it was easier to close, as gravity helped pull it shut. I pushed all my weight on top of the door and rode it to the ground as it fell.

Lainey was five feet from me as the door made its descent. And by the time it clicked shut, I could feel her hands upon my cheeks, reaching to ensnare. But instead of the hard nails and the deadly grasp that I had anticipated, her fingers turned to a whisper-light touch as she, and the door, faded into oblivion.

The door disintegrated into the sand. I whipped my head around and saw nothing but the strands of my dark hair floating around my face and tiny bubbles that escaped my nose pirouetting in the water.

There was no ghost of Lainey left, and there was no more portal to the life I'd once had. If I was unsure whether I belonged in this world, none of it mattered anymore, because my decision had been made for me in a heap of betrayal and rage.

I was here to stay . . .

20

I broke through the surface of the lake, flailing my arms and gasping for air.

"Kinsley! Kinsley!" Emma screamed from the top of the bluff.

I hammered the water, fearful that Lainey's ghost would materialize once more beneath my feet.

"Kinsley are you okay?!" Emma yelled frantically.

"Yeah." But my small broken voice was much too quiet for her to hear. I tried to gather myself, brush the hair out of my face, and focus on her pacing back and forth at the top of the cliff. She was worried, and who knew how long I had been down there.

"I'm okay!" I yelled the best I could.

With all the strength I had left, I swam toward shore. Emma took off running, and it wasn't long before she and Gunner met me in the shallow water.

"Oh my god, Kinsley, you scared me! You were down there forever!" she said, tromping into the lake. Gunner barked excitedly and swam in circles, biting at the ripples in the water. Emma hugged me tight as I stood weakly in a foot of water.

"I'm sorry. I didn't mean to scare you. I tried not to, but it almost took my life." I sloshed my way to shore.

"What!?"

"I tried to freeze time so you wouldn't know how long I was gone and you wouldn't worry. But I froze the lake with me in it. It was like being stuck in cement."

Emma gasped.

"That wasn't even the worst part. The worst part was . . ." I pictured Lainey and how desperate she'd been to betray me. It wasn't how I wanted Emma to remember her, so I kept it to myself. "I think I died."

"I've heard that before. How many times do you think it's happened now? Two? Three?" Emma plopped down in the sand and unlaced her shoes.

"It's not something a person gets used to Emma," I snapped. I plopped down next to her, but I was too tired to take my socks and shoes off. I fell onto my back, closing my eyes to the sun and welcoming the warmth on my cheeks. "Not here . . . *there.* I think maybe my body died in the *real* world."

Emma looked me over and then poked my arm. "You don't seem any different?"

She couldn't possibly understand what I'd been through. "Okay. Promise not to say anything to anybody?" I asked rolling onto my side. The dry sand caked to my wet skin like a blanket of warmth.

"Yeah. Even Walker?" she asked.

"Especially Walker."

"Yeah, okay," Emma said, shielding her face from the sun with her hand.

"I think I found a way back home—"

"What! No way!" Emma's face lit up, and in that split second I realized I had made a devastating mistake by telling her. She would either want me to go through the door like Lainey had pushed me to do, or she would want to find it herself, and it no longer existed.

"No, it's not like that. I mean, it was. It was a portal of sorts, but it closed."

"Where is it? We can open it again." Emma stood, dusting the sand off her butt. She was ready to go home.

"No, it's not like that! You can't just open it," I argued.

"Noah is really strong, and Kai is super smart. We can do this as a team. We have to tell them! We have to go!" Gunner came tromping out of the water and shook off all the excess water, splattering us.

"The door isn't locked Emma. It's destroyed."

"We can put it back together!"

"It vanished. Disintegrated into nothing. It disappeared, Emma. It is no longer at the bottom of the lake. It's gone."

"Well . . ." Emma began but couldn't finish. She placed her hands on her hips and bounced her foot up and down. She was trying not to cry, and I hated myself for not having the foresight to have seen this coming. I unlaced my shoes and peeled off my socks. I gathered them up in a heavy, sandy mess, and Emma and I started the long walk home—barefoot and drenched in defeat. She sniffled the entire way home as Gunner pranced happily before us, finding twigs to take as souvenirs.

I couldn't help but think that I had been the one to cause her so much pain. And maybe, if I had just dropped through the open door, I would have landed in my bed at home, recuperating from the accident. And then Emma would have gone home too. Maybe they all would have.

But what about Walker? He would stay here all by his lonesome. He'd wander around Baylor looking for Layla. And Layla would follow him around driving herself crazy because he couldn't see her. It was an impossible feat. On the one hand, I was torturing my friends, keeping them from their homes and their lives ahead. But on the other, I would be forcing Walker to be tortured with a life of solitude. He didn't deserve that. None of them did.

When we got back to the cabin, Emma gave me a half smile, dumped her shoes by the deck, and disappeared into the cabin. Gunner drank a gallon of water, and Kai made fun of me for going hiking and coming home in wet clothes.

"Kai, can I ask you a hypothetical question?" I tossed my shoes into a pile with Emma's. It wouldn't take long for them to dry in the summer heat.

"What's up? Did Emma push you into the lake or something?" he said, chuckling.

"Do you remember when you drove to the edge of the Baylor phenomenon?" I leaned against the patio railing next to him.

"Yeah. Did you find a new edge?" he asked, suddenly serious.

"Kind of. But it didn't send me back to the cabin. I think it was more like a portal. The gateway back home." I hated seeing the excitement light Kai's face. I was doing it again—giving false hope. "But it's gone now . . ."

"What happened, Kinsley?" He leaned in.

"There was a door. It was at the bottom of the lake—"

"How did you get there?" he asked, brows furrowed. Nothing got past Kai.

"I didn't really need to breathe. I guess I can hold my breath for quite some time here if I put my mind to it. But that's not the point."

"Right. Go on," he said eagerly.

"I opened the door, and on the other side was Clover. Well, I'm pretty sure it was Clover. I was high above the clouds, looking down on the neighborhood. Time seemed slower there, and the air was . . . different, familiar. I don't know how to explain it."

"No way . . ." His back stiffened, and I could tell he was ready to go on a hunt for the door, just like Emma had.

"But when I closed the door, it disappeared. It completely disintegrated into nothing."

"Maybe we can find it?" Kai asked hopefully.

I shook my head. "I think it's really gone."

Kai straightened, suddenly eager to end the conversation. He turned to head inside the cabin, and I realized I'd never asked my question.

"Hey, Kai?"

"Yeah?" He looked over his shoulder.

"If the gateway closed . . . hypothetically . . . does that mean there's no way back?" I was unable to say the word *died*.

"There's always a way back, Kinsley." He turned and headed inside, leaving me by myself.

I rested my forearms on the railing and gazed out at the lake. I wish I knew for certain. I had planned to stay here in Baylor either way, but if there truly was no way home, I think it would end the plague of uncertainty. I could tell Walker, and there would be no convincing me otherwise. It would be beyond my control. Noah, Kai, Emma, and Scarlett May could lay down roots here, and we could stop fighting. Maybe we could even have some fun. But I had to know. There was nothing worse than the uncertainty.

My clothes were nearly dry by the time I finally came up with a plan. I would need to find the hidden cemetery. When Trinity died, her headstone had appeared immediately. And I assumed it would be the same for me. I would have a headstone next to hers and Lainey's. The only problem was, I didn't want to go alone. The woods were a place of nightmares for me, and if I found my headstone, I didn't want to know what would happen when I felt my world closing in on me.

I couldn't bring Walker, not without telling him the truth first. Emma and Kai were freshly scarred, and I didn't want to put them through seeing headstones. What if they had headstones of their own? What I really needed was Scarlett May to come with me. She was strong, and I knew she could handle anything she saw in those woods.

By the time I had changed my clothes and started searching for Scarlett May, I couldn't find her anywhere. In fact, I couldn't find anybody. I was so desperate, I was willing to take Noah, but I couldn't find him either.

"Emma?" I yelled down the hall.

"Kai?" I called, jogging down the stairs.

"Gunner?" I peeked my head out the back door.

I paced the living room, wondering where they had gone in such a short time. "Noah?" I called, softer yet.

I would have taken him had he answered. I just didn't want to field questions about my feelings for him the entire time. Not that he would ask. I was sure he didn't even like me anymore. It had been weeks since we'd talked last. Still, I often felt his eyes on me. Especially when Walker was around. He didn't like him.

But he also didn't want to end up like Mason—missing after a wolf attack. A sickening feeling twisted my gut. Was that why Noah hadn't talked to me? Because he thought the incident with Mason was my fault? That I did it on purpose because I was angry they'd turned Walker away with a threat? Well, I guess I *was* still angry about that . . .

I was doing it again. I was stalling. Only this time, I didn't have Emma to fall back on. If I wanted to check out the graveyard, I was going to have to go alone. Asking Walker was not an option for me. Not now. I could do this. I could be brave and courageous. I could face the forest and its mysterious ways.

I scribbled down a message on a pad of paper. *On a walk*. And I left it on the kitchen counter where I thought it would be most visible. I caught a glimpse of Gunner's water bowl on the way out and wished I had him to come with me. But none of that mattered now. I was going to do this. I was going to see if I was dead or alive. If I had a chance of going home or if I was already there. I was going to march into those woods, and I was going to discover my fate. I just had to put one foot in front of the other.

As it turns out, fate is a hard thing to find. I must have walked for hours. Dusk had settled in, and my stomach growled from hunger. I'd stomped through so many rapunzel plants that my jeans had a hazy, light-purple dusting below the knee. I glanced up into the trees now and then to see the same crow watching me. It didn't matter how far I walked, it was always there, perched in a new tree high above me. It seemed a little wider than most crows and reminded me of the crow we'd seen flying overhead on our way to the library. It reminded me of Levi.

It was probably just my imagination. A way to protect myself from the evils that lurked deep within this forest. But I didn't care what it was, I only cared how it made me feel, and I no longer felt alone. I was still angry with Levi for how he had treated Emma, but I was more upset with myself. I'd caused the storm that night, and if it wasn't for me, Levi would still be here. And he deserved a chance to live. They all did. No one deserved my wrath.

The crow called out as it swooped down between the trees in my path. The bird was gigantic. Twice the size of any regular crow. It flew in front of me, so close that I could reach out and almost touch it. But it was faster than my walking gait, and I ended up jogging after it.

"Levi?" I called out. It was stupid. Of course, it wouldn't answer me. But could I at least get it to slow down?

"You're going too fast," I said, through burning lungs. I liked talking out loud. Like somehow I was less crazy because a bird might be listening, instead of nobody.

The bird took a sharp right, and I stopped briefly to analyze the change in path. But there wasn't much for me to figure out. The crow perched on a headstone. My fate had found me.

I walked slowly, catching my breath. My eyes flickered from the bird's black, beady eyes to the multitude of new headstones scattered throughout the trees. With every step I took, the temperature dropped, and I became more leery.

Another crow called out above us, and I saw a single black bird circling the cemetery. "Your friends are calling you," I said.

The bird didn't move. Its eyes were trained on me as I slowly dropped my gaze to the stone it was perched on. Its sharp claws dug into the stone. My heart sank when I read *Levi, taken unfaithfully*.

Oh no . . .

It was more than just a hunch now. I was convinced the crow was the embodiment of Levi. Why else had it taken me directly to his grave? I clenched my jaw, suddenly feeling awkward in front of the bird. Had it known what the headstone said?

"You shouldn't have hurt Emma like that. You messed up." I scowled at the bird, and it did nothing to show its remorse.

"You did this to yourself," I said, getting more upset with its silence than anything else.

I looked up at all the other headstones, crooked and worn, and Levi turned to assess them with me. His claws made an unsettling scraping sound against the stone, and I cringed. I wanted to tell him to stop, but I seriously doubted he had the capacity to understand me.

The next stone I came to was blank. I was thankful for that. But I couldn't help wonder why it was here in the first place. Somebody or something had planted it here in anticipation, and that should have worried me. I think I was just so relieved that whoever it belonged to wasn't marked yet. So much so, that I didn't care about the expectation of another death on the horizon.

The next two stones I saw were for Kimber and Asher. It didn't seem like that long ago that the bees had invaded the cabin, but these headstones were decades upon decades old. Moss had grown up the sides, and the sun had stained patterns into the rock. *Asher was taken by weakness*, which wasn't his fault at all. He was genetically weaker than the rest of us when it came to the bee's venom. But what really surprised me was that Kimber's headstone said she was *taken a coward*. And Kimber had been anything but cowardly.

The way I saw it, Kimber was the bravest one yet. She was the only one who had known how to escape this place. And instinctively, she was the only one who had known how to bring Noah back. She'd sacrificed herself. She was courageous. I couldn't for the life of me understand why the legacy etched in her headstone would read that she was a coward. What was it that I hadn't seen before? I placed my hand on top of the headstone waiting for the answers to come, but they never did. When Levi flew to Kimber's marker, I scowled at the awful scraping noise and moved on to the next.

Ethan had a headstone now too, and apparently he was *taken by worry*.

That I understood. I remembered how worried I had been on that walk. I remember looking for something to explain it all away. That unsettled feeling I had cinched my chest. When Ethan had jumped into the water, I had just assumed it was him. That he wasn't safe. That he wouldn't come back to the surface. And because I was worried—so dreadfully worried—he never had. My heart sat heavy in my chest, and there were so many things I wished I could take back. But I couldn't.

"I'm sorry, Ethan. You didn't deserve that," I said in a whisper.

I passed two more headstones with fresh clean slates. No lives claimed. Not yet. Levi flew overhead and perched on the next marker. Mason's marker. I rubbed my arms as the temperature continued to drop. New birds called above, and I could see that there were three or four of them now. Circling.

It didn't surprise me that *Mason was taken a liar*. He never should have told Walker that I belonged to Noah. It simply wasn't true, and he had no right to meddle in my affairs. But he wasn't just taken because he'd lied, he was taken because of my anger toward the lie. I shook my head, upset with the mass destruction I had caused.

"I'm sorry, Mason. I'm sorry," I said, patting the headstone. Suddenly, I was glad I'd come to the cemetery alone. This wasn't something I wanted my friends to see.

I looked into the distance to see another clean slate, and one with just the beginnings of a name. My stomach dropped, wondering if it was my name slowly being etched into the stone. I kneeled and examined the chiseled mark in the stone. One long line, the beginning of the name. The first of the letter was covered with a string of ivy. I reached out with a shaky hand and lifted the vine. My mouth ran dry as I lifted the strand of ivy, and a *K* was revealed.

I swiped my hands over the stone, desperately searching for more clues, lighter scrapes, anything that would tell me how I had died or why I was taken, but there was nothing left for me to see. Which could only mean one thing. It wasn't set in stone yet.

I sat back on my heels as Levi jumped to the ground next to me. *It wasn't set in stone.* Nothing was finalized. And if I wanted to go home, I would still have a body to return to. I hated the way relief washed over me. I hated it. It only confused me more. What did I want? What the *hell* did I want!?

Tears pricked the corners of my eyes as I realized that I would not get any answers today and the weight of the decision would come back to the cabin with me, resting heavily on my shoulders. The secrets I needed to keep from Walker were draining, and I was getting tired of keeping them. I was tired in general. I wanted it to be over, only I didn't know which life needed to end. I only knew that I couldn't keep living two lives at the same time. It wasn't fair to me, it wasn't fair to my family, and it was incredibly exhausting.

A name had clearly been started on this headstone, and if I had to guess, I'd say that the *K* was made when I'd shut the door in Lainey's face. When it disintegrated beneath me, and the gateway closed. But if that hadn't ended me right then and there, that could only mean one of two things.

Either there were more doors out there, more than one way to get back home, or I hadn't fully made up my mind up yet. I had thought I was stuck in Baylor, but the sense of relief that had washed over me when I saw the incomplete headstone had me second-guessing. I was torn. I needed to talk to my gran. She was the only one I trusted to have my best interests in mind while guiding me toward a decision.

The scraping grew louder, casting a shadow on my thoughts until it was all I could hear. I turned to yell at Levi, but he was perched quietly in the dirt. A dozen or more crows cawed above, creating the beginnings of a vortex. I had seen this before, and I didn't want to get caught in it. It was time to leave, but the scraping held me in place.

What was it? Where was it coming from? It was close, I knew that much. I got to my feet and dusted my hands on my jeans. The ivy twitched, drawing my attention back to the headstone. I reached out and gently lifted the vine one more time. The letter A was freshly carved into the stone, causing me to gasp and flinch backward.

I wrapped my hands around the ivy and tore it off the headstone. The grinding of the stone grew louder as Kai's name slowly etched its way into the rock.

"*No* . . ." I cried, wrapping my arms around myself.

Levi lifted into the air and joined the murder. I took off running.

21

The crows circled above, calling out to one another and funneling in the sky, high above the cemetery. I ran through the rapunzel, weaving in and out of the pines as I tried not to look back. Whatever was happening in the sky was a bad omen, and I didn't want to stick around to find out what might happen on the ground.

It was dark enough that the colors had faded from the forest and the trees were just a blur of dark, muddy shadows. I couldn't tell if I was running deeper into the forest or if I was heading toward the cabin, but I knew the storm was brewing behind me in the graveyard, and I was doing everything I could to get far away. I was alone and afraid in the forest, and that was a terrible combination for me.

My lungs burned, but I refused to slow down. I was going to run until I couldn't hear a single crow screeching in the distance. I hopped over fallen trees and small bushes. I checked behind me, my hair eclipsing my sight. But when I turned back around, I ran straight through a spider web. I opened my mouth to scream and flailed my hands about as the sticky string pulled across my lips and clung to my cheeks. I tried not to cry as I grasped the invisible threat, trying to free myself and run away at the same time. I felt the tears on my cheeks, anyway.

I swore to myself that I would never come into these woods again. Especially not alone. The forest had become the accumulation of my worry, and on the darkest of nights, my fear. It was no place for exploration, and I promised myself to stay far, far away. Some things were best left unknown. The etchings on the headstones were none of my business. There was probably nothing I could do to save Kai anyhow. He was probably already gone.

This couldn't have been my fault. I didn't even know where Kai was. Everybody had been gone when I'd left for the woods, and I certainly didn't have any ill will toward Kai. He was one of my favorite people. He was kind, intelligent, and he was a safe place for me in my rowdy group of friends. It *couldn't* have been my fault. Unless I had seen his name being etched into the stone for a reason. Maybe it wasn't over until the inscription was complete. Until the words *taken by* were followed by something obscure. Something speculative. A single word like kindness or courage. Could he be taken by kindness? I didn't doubt it.

My ankle rolled, and I lurched forward. My foot caught on a pile of rocks, and I tripped, driving my hands into the dirt. I let out a small grunt when I hit the ground. Sprawled in the dirt where no path had been, I listened for the birds. Their calls were growing louder and louder, drowning out the sound of my hammering heart.

I could see them in the distance. Small black dots against the darkening sky. Somehow, I was getting closer to them . . . or they were getting closer to me. I scrambled to my feet and took off in a hobble. I couldn't sustain a run any longer. My body was drained, and my mind was giving up. I couldn't run fast enough to save Kai. And if I could, I wouldn't even know where to look.

Running water babbled over rocks. A small stream appeared by my side, and I suddenly recognized where I was. The lake wasn't far, and down by the water was a small path that would eventually lead to the cabin. I picked up speed, being careful not to stumble again, and I ran alongside the stream. I gained distance on the crows, and the suffocating air began to lift as the dense trees opened to the clearing of the lake. I weaved through the last of the trees, relieved when my feet hit the sandy shore. I hunched over to catch my breath.

"Quick, get in!"

I barely had the energy to lift my eyes, but when I saw my gran sitting in a canoe perched in the rocks, my back straightened with renewed hope. "Gran! Gran you're here!" I called out in a sob.

"Get in, child!" she said, holding her hand out for me to take. I mustered a fresh burst of energy and plunged into the water, soaking my shoes. I clambered into the canoe ungracefully and then lunged for my gran. I enveloped her in a tight hug, and I couldn't have been more thankful when she hugged me back. I didn't know what I would've done had she disintegrated or disappeared like times before. I needed her now, more than ever.

"Gran, I love you! I've missed you so much. You have no idea."

"Ohhh, I've got some idea. I love you too, dear. More than you'll ever know." Her voice was music to my ears.

Her eyes shifted from me to the sky, and it was then that I noticed the crows had grown louder again. They were catching up to us, but I didn't dare look back.

"It's time we get out of here," Gran said, taking the paddle. The canoe began to move swiftly through the water. Surprisingly, Gran was quite strong for her age. Strong like Walker. I wondered if strength prospered after death.

"I've been trying to get a hold of you. The phone didn't work, and you haven't been visiting. I was worried," I said, my grip tight on the sides of the canoe.

"I'm here now. It's difficult to reach you. Our planes are more different than you can imagine." The canoe glided through the water faster than I thought possible.

"How? How are they different?" I asked hungrily. I wanted to ask everything in the world. I wanted *all* the information from her. I didn't know when I would see her next, or if I ever would again.

"Where I live, I can go anywhere and be everywhere, all at once. There are no rules or restrictions. But finding you has proven to be difficult. It must be the drugs. They keep your mind shut down and locked away. It's hard for me to break through. The dream state that you're in is like a prison. It's governed only by your emotions. Unfortunately, your fear seems to be the driving factor. It must be so scary for you." Gran tilted her head with empathy. "It's a dreary place, and I'm *so* sorry you must be here. But it shouldn't be much longer now."

A prison? Was Baylor my prison? If it was, then why was Walker here?

"What do you mean, it shouldn't be much longer?" I asked, suddenly worried my time was coming to an end.

"You'll wake soon. I promise it won't be much longer. You're healing quite nicely. There have been some . . . *hiccups* . . . along the way. It's been rough on your parents, your brother, and aunt. It's been rough on your grandpa. But when you wake up, everybody is going to be so happy. It won't be easy dear; I'm not saying that. But it will be better than this cold, dreary place." Her chin wrinkled and her brows creased with distaste. A visible shiver ran down her back, causing me to look away.

It wasn't *that* bad.

The guilt hit me like a tidal wave. I had no idea how to tell her that I planned to stay here forever. I was going to make a life for myself here. I didn't want to devastate her and my grandpa. I didn't want to hurt my family at all. But Baylor had become my home. Walker was my home. I couldn't leave him.

"But Gran, remember when you said *if* I come back." I chewed on my cheek nervously as I waited for her reply.

"Oh dear, you *will* make it. You were *always* going to survive this. I'm sorry if I made that unclear." Her forehead creased with pain.

"Then why did you say it? Was there ever a chance I wasn't going home?" I leaned in. The answers couldn't come fast enough.

"I said *if* because there was a small, very small, chance that you *theoretically* could *choose* to stay here. But that's not in the cards for you, dear," she said, searching my eyes.

"About that . . ." I hesitated. I was glad she'd brought it up, but I was still so scared to tell her how I felt.

"Oh dear, are you thinking about staying?" she asked. I thought I saw a flash of disgust pass through her green eyes.

"Gran . . . there's this guy." I said with tears in my eyes.

"I know. I know there is." She dropped the paddle to the bottom of the canoe and held her arms out for a hug. I crossed to her and fell into her open arms. The canoe dipped but didn't slow. We propelled forward by an otherworldly force, as if Gran was still paddling.

"I can't tell you what to do, honey. You're going to have to make that decision on your own." She held me tight.

I cried on her shoulder. I cried for Walker, I cried for my family back home and all the pain I'd put them through, and I cried for my gran and how deeply I'd missed her. Nothing was ever going to be fair or easy. Whether I was living or not, I was imprisoned. I only wished the answers were clear, because it was the ambiguity that rattled my mind the most. I wished my path was laid out before me and I'd never come to a fork in the road. I feared I would choose wrong.

"I don't know what to do, Gran. *I love him.*" I looked deep into her eyes.

Her cataracts had cleared, revealing a brilliant emerald green with tiny glimmering flecks of gold. That was how I knew she was real. That this conversation I was having with my dead grandmother was real, and not one I had conjured from grief. I soaked it all up. I cherished every moment.

"I know you do. I can see that. Just like I know you love your family. But hearts are made to break, honey. And with each break they become stronger, and you love deeper. Sometimes, if you love something, the best thing you can do is let it go."

The air left my lungs in a whoosh. *Let him go?*

"You need to take care of yourself, first and foremost. I wouldn't ask yourself who you love more, your family or a boy, I would ask yourself where you belong. Where do you belong, honey?"

My stomach churned. It was the question that haunted me most. I didn't know. "What if I belong in both places? . . . Or neither of them?" Was that possible?

Gran ran her gentle hands over mine. "You belong."

I closed my eyes, letting the two simple words wash over me. It hurt to hear them, and for the life of me, I couldn't understand why. If she was speaking the truth, then I had been lying to myself. Not just this whole summer, but my entire life.

"I want to stay . . ." I said in a whisper. "This world is different to me. I feel like I get to be somebody here that I never was back home."

Gran patted my hand, and I pulled away. She began to paddle again while she chose her next words carefully.

"There is no right or wrong here. But I will leave you with this: you will find your greatest happiness not from luck nor fate, but through hard work, grit, trials, and tribulations. Your fullest heart will come from breaking, time and time again, and loving despite the vulnerability."

I took a deep breath. Nobody wants to hear how hard it will be. I had come so far here in Baylor, but she was talking like the journey had just begun, and it put the fear in me.

"When the time comes, go down the steepest, most treacherous path. Don't shy from the dark nights—lean into them. I know you will find your way. Whichever you choose, know you belong, wholeheartedly. I will be with you every step of the way, even if you can't see me." The canoe nudged the shore.

I arched my back, wondering where we had beached. I recognized the cove by the unique formation of boulders nearby. It was close to where I had dove early that morning.

"Don't leave, Gran. Stay," I pled. I wasn't ready to say goodbye.

"I'll be here," she said, smiling.

"Did you find him?!" Scarlett May's frantic voice traveled across the lake.

I looked from Gran to the lake, searching the open waters. Through the darkness I could see what I thought were two heads bobbing in the water. My heart sank. *Kai.*

"No!" Noah yelled.

I leapt off the canoe. My feet plunged into the water as I ran ashore. My instincts stopped me, held me still, as I remembered my gran sitting in the canoe. I was torn between helping Kai and knowing I may very well never see my gran again. I looked from her to my friends and back again. She encouraged me with a nod.

"Go . . ." she said, and then she was gone. Just like she'd never been. The canoe, everything had disappeared, and I was standing alone on the shore in the shadows.

"Kai?!" Noah screamed. The hoarseness of his voice told me they'd been searching for far too long.

I ran into the lake, dragging my legs through the resisting water until I was deep enough to dive in. I swam as hard and fast as I could, taking in my surroundings as I came up for air. Emma was on shore pacing back and forth, crying. Scarlett May and Noah were some distance apart, yelling to each other between diving for Kai.

"How long has he been missing?" I asked, breathlessly.

"He's gone! He's gone!" Scarlett May yelled, splashing around in hysterics.

"He's been under for ten, fifteen minutes now," Noah said.

It was bad news. I'd seen Kai's name etched into the gravestone, but I'd hoped it wasn't final yet. The inscription hadn't been complete when I took off, and a small part of me clung to the idea that maybe it never would be. That maybe Kai wouldn't be taken by the lake of dark secrets, and that he would come home with us tonight.

I gulped a giant breath and dove under the water. It was pitch black. Even if I could stay under all night searching, I couldn't see a damn thing. I swam straight down toward the bed of the lake, where the portal to my distant reality had once lived. Something brushed against my arm, and I startled, stalling momentarily before continuing. It happened several times on my way down, but I continued anyway. I couldn't be afraid of the dark any longer—I wouldn't be.

Lean into the darkness...

Suddenly, I feared the others would think that I'd drowned too, and it would send them searching deeper into the water. I worried that my prolonged absence would cause yet another death. I pushed it out of my mind, and I used the worry as fuel to swim deeper.

By the time I hit the bottom, it was obvious that I would never find Kai. I patted my hands against the soft, silty lake bottom, feeling around in the rocks and unseen plants. Something prickly, something muddy, something slimy. An open sandy floor, and gobs of seaweed. I couldn't see any of it, and feeling around in the dark brought on new challenges.

I was helpless under the weight of the lake. Hindered by the darkness. If Baylor was a phantom world where magic was real, then the forest was where the evil mist lived, and the lake was where the poisons drained and gathered.

I couldn't do it. I couldn't find Kai. There was something about being under the water that kept me from crying, and for that, I was thankful. I pushed off the bottom of the lake and started my ascent empty-handed. There were only three of them left. Only three. No matter how much training I received, I couldn't save them.

In the dead of the night, the four of us huddled on shore, shaking, soaking wet, and drenched with grief. Noah wrapped his arms around me and Emma, and I stroked Scarlett May's head on my lap. Now and then, a shiver would rack through one of us and extrapolate through the group as if it was contagious.

"We were trying to find the door . . ." I wasn't sure when Emma had said it, but her words played over and over in my head, haunting me for hours on end. The red door to Clover had claimed its first victim, sight unseen.

22

It was early morning by the time we got back to the cabin. We were like a mob of zombies, cold and wet, beyond exhausted, and half asleep. We walked through the cabin door, and everybody scattered. Scarlett May had been sleeping in Kimber's room ever since she and Asher had left, and Emma was across the hall in her and Lainey's room. Noah took the couch, since it was now open. Every time somebody didn't come home, one of us got a better bed. Even though I was sure it didn't translate to a better night's sleep.

I lingered, watching Noah crawl into the sleeping bag and punch his pillow aggressively. It was almost like we didn't have tears left to cry. Like we had been through so much trauma in Baylor that it couldn't affect us any longer. Instead of breaking down, we hardened. We shut down, and we isolated ourselves. Maybe it was the path of least resistance. I felt the effects of it too.

When Trinity had died, I'd wanted to run far, far away. I'd felt a very deep sense of danger, and all I'd wanted to do was flee. But so many times later, all I wanted now was to crawl into bed. By the looks of it, everybody else felt the same way. We didn't love Kai any less; we just didn't have the strength to feel the pain, and we didn't have the energy to run. There was nowhere left for us to go.

I waited till Noah settled before turning out the lights. And with my hand on the light switch, my eyes wandered helplessly to the calendar on the wall. Out of thirteen days, there were only four left. I didn't know who the fourth was going to be. My jaw hardened when I remembered my gran saying I was always going to survive this. I was starting to gather that, when she said survival, it actually meant death in Baylor. The last thing I wanted was to be another X on that calendar.

She'd said I would be waking soon, and it was hard for me to comprehend what that meant for this realm. What would happen to Emma and Noah if I woke up? What would happen to Scarlett May and Sampson? Would they disappear? Would they die? Would they disintegrate like the door on the bottom of the lake? Or get swept up in some extravagant vortex like Levi? There was no way to know. I had to come up with a plan to set them free before anything else bad happened. I needed them to go home alive. I flipped the switch, and the lights went out. My feet were heavy on the stairs as I dragged myself to bed.

From the moment my head hit the pillow, I was asleep, and I didn't wake until late the next morning. But I remembered dreaming of a war.

There was a battlefield under ominous gray clouds filled with thunder and lightning. There were hundreds of doctors dressed in light blue scrubs holding their scalpels and syringes as weapons. Their first line of defense was . . . my family. My little brother and his buddies were covered in war paint, striped across their cheeks and the bridges of their noses. My parents, my aunt, and my grandpa stood front and center. Even in the distance, I could see the anger on their faces. They were ready to fight, and they would show no mercy.

On the opposing side, my side, stood Noah, Sampson, Scarlett May, Emma, Walker, Layla, and me. It was a far cry from the hundreds they had on their side. But we had heart, and I knew I had a secret weapon that would put their needles to shame. I could manifest anything I wanted, and I could end the battle with the drop of a hat, if that's what my heart really desired.

We were getting ready to fight. The seconds were ticking down when something terrible happened; Layla crossed over.

I wasn't entirely surprised; I knew she didn't want me in Baylor. I was falling for her soulmate after all. But when she joined the opposing side, Emma, Scarlett May, and Sampson did too. It broke my heart that Emma wouldn't stand behind me, but I understood why she wanted me to go home. Because she was stuck here until I did. They were only a quarter of the way across the clearing when Noah turned to me and shrugged. He didn't walk; he ran.

By that time, only Walker and I stood against what felt like the rest of the world. I remembered the worry I'd seen when I looked to him with questioning eyes. Whose side was he really on? Because it was now or never.

That's when I woke up. I never got to see what Walker chose, and I never got to see the war between my past life and my phantom reality. But I had to imagine it was a dirty fight.

I rolled over in bed and stared at the white wall, playing the dream over and over in my head. Any way I reworked it, the battle ended when Walker chose the other side. Because when he left, there was nothing left worth fighting for. I let the doctors uproot me from this realm and take me back to Clover.

Several days passed in a blur. Even though the sun and moon danced across the sky, time never really existed here. No parties raged at the house, no video games played on the TV, no cues hit winning balls into the pockets of the pool table. Walker's dimples never came, and my heart began to freeze over. I was so devastated by the idea of leaving that I pulled back from everything. It was clear my mood affected the others too. The once lively cabin was quiet and still.

The Baylor Balloon Festival was the following day. It was the day we were to capture Layla. I recalled the picture of her and Walker in a hot air balloon. She had been gorgeous and very much in love. They both were. We were supposed to go to the festival, find Layla, and then what? They would go off happily ever after, and I would have no choice but to return home? Suddenly, I wished it was Layla who had disappeared in the lake instead of Kai.

I'd been avoiding Walker because I knew he wanted to send me home too. I knew which side of the war he was on. And the rejection I'd feel from him would be far worse than anything I had experienced so far this summer. But something changed on the morning before the festival. The fight inside of me smoldered with the simple question—*what if?*

If my days were limited here, I wanted to spend them with the person I loved most. I was done hiding from all of it. I laced my shoes and grabbed Walker's flannel, tying it around my waist. I planned to take the golf cart straight to his cabin and demand answers. I was going to tell him that I wanted to stay. I was going to bare my soul to him, and if he didn't want me . . . I guess I wouldn't fight the war.

As soon as I made my decision to see Walker, I heard a commotion outside at the dock and peered out the window. Walker was tying up. I immediately took off running down the stairs. I hadn't realized how much I'd missed him until this very moment. I swung the door open and ran halfway down the grassy hill before calling out, "Walker!"

He threw the rope down and froze when he heard my voice. "Wilde?" His voice rang with something I'd never heard before. Anger?

He marched down the dock and I slowed, cautiously. "Where the hell have you been?" He waved his hands in the air.

"I've been here. What do you mean?" I flinched.

"I haven't been able to get over here. I haven't been able to get close to Rock Creek Cove at all!"

It could have been a week since I had seen him last. Maybe longer. I searched his eyes, trying to understand why he was so angry with me.

"You used to summon me. You used to want me with you so badly that I had no choice but to come. And now? Now I can't even get across the lake? It's like you put up an invisible shield. What the hell is going on Kinsley?" he asked, hands on his hips.

I hated when he used my first name.

"I . . . I . . . I didn't know it worked like that. I'm sorry." I had no idea that being afraid to see Walker would keep him from me.

"You didn't know it worked like that? Why don't you want me around? I thought we were *friends*.."

An ache settled in my chest.

"If we are *just friends*, then why are you so mad?" I took a step forward, the smoldering in my belly igniting to a small flame.

"Because we're a team. You don't shut out your team."

"But what does that even mean?" I asked, needing more.

Walker ran his hands through his hair and spun around. He dropped his hands to his hips as I stared at his rigid back. I wanted to reach out and touch him. I wanted to run my fingertips down his back and rest my forehead between his shoulders . . . I didn't dare. I waited patiently for him to turn around while the flame in my belly flickered with insecurity.

"It means, we do this together." Walker turned around, his face softer now. Saddened almost. "In a world of smoke and mirrors, you are the only thing that's real to me. Don't shut me out." Walker's eyes fixed on mine.

"I'm *not* shutting you out, I promise."

"But you're hiding stuff from me. There are things that you don't share with me. Why?" he asked, his face contorted in a mix of emotions that I couldn't read.

"I'm not hiding anything from you," I lied. So much for being brave.

The pain on Walker's face melted to disappointment. That look I knew. I didn't know which hurt worse. He reached behind him, pulling something from his back pocket. A glow radiated from his hand as he held the golden feather between us. My eyes flickered back and forth, from the feather to his face. And as my thoughts raced over the secrets I hid from Walker, his jaw hardened.

"You've been hiding *this* from me."

The fire in my belly snuffed immediately. I was marked a coward. I certainly couldn't tell him that I was going to spend the rest of my life with him now. "That's nothing." One more lie toppled out.

His eyebrows arched. "Nothing? You think I don't know what this is? This is a Wish of Warmth. The floating element, the warm golden glow."

Walker let go of the feather and it gently floated between us.

"This wish followed me home one night. When I took my clothes off, the feather slipped out from behind my jeans and hovered in the corner of my room. The damn thing has been following me ever since. I've only seen you once since that night. It was the time you summoned me to your childhood bedroom. And you were hiding stuff from me then, too." He reached out, his hands hovering over my shoulders, before he gave up, dropping them to his sides.

"I've done a lot of research on this wish. The Wish of Warmth. It's typically given as a parting gift. A wish for good fortune and happiness. Did you give it to me? Or does somebody else in Baylor possess the same power as you?"

I remembered sending the feathers out by the hundreds. Those wishes were for anybody who needed them. I shouldn't have been surprised that Walker needed it. "I sent it with you," I admitted.

He snatched the feather and stepped closer to me. I could feel the intensity of his gaze and the heat of his breath on my face. "Is this, or is this not, a parting gift?" he asked sternly.

The proximity between us heated the nape of my neck, and I fought the urge to fan my face and step away. Was this the time to tell him? I didn't know. I was afraid. I dropped my gaze to the round marbled button of his flannel. "It's not a parting gift." I would stay forever . . . If he let me.

He took a deep breath. While he was relieved, I was bound by my lies tighter than ever. I was surprised by the bear hug he gave me. Startled with shock, and suffocated by his shoulder, I adjusted my head for air and then wrapped my arms around him. He held me like he was never going to let go. I held him like I was halfway gone.

"Just promise me one thing?" he asked.

I said nothing.

"Don't leave without saying goodbye first."

"Um, Walker?" I asked. *Now or never . . .*

Before I could get the words out, he continued, "We're still going to the Baylor Balloon Festival tomorrow, right? You'll let me come over?" I felt his chin rest on the top of my head, and a part of me melted into him.

"Yeah. Of course. We've got to catch Layla, right?" I pulled my armor back on, shielding my heart from the unknown. I knew it was what he needed to hear.

"Yeah." His tone was slightly higher than normal. Excitement to find her? Or was I reading too much into it? Was there something else he wasn't saying? I bit my tongue.

"We have less than twenty-four hours before the festival." Walker pulled away and checked his watch. "To be honest, I'm afraid to go home. I'm afraid you won't let me back over." He shot me a half-joking smile, but it didn't reach his eyes.

"Of course, I'll let you back. I just . . ."

"What is it?"

"I was afraid to see you, because I didn't want you to know about the magic."

Walker's brows rose, and he took a step back, forcing me to explain.

"Do you remember when you said this was a puzzle for somebody with a twisted mind?"

Walker nodded.

"Do you remember when Emma said that I was atypical, and that my mind worked in mysterious ways?"

Walker nodded again.

"I thought, if it was true, then the magic would come, and I could control it. The Baylor phenomenon would be what I made of it. And so it was. That very night, when we gazed at the full moon from the porch, I froze time. I walked across the lake. Not around it, but on top of it. I sent hundreds of Warm Wishes out into the world. I didn't know what I was doing, it was just a feeling of hope. The feathers traveled on their own, seeking a destination. And when you left that night, I was just as surprised as you were when one of them followed you home. I've been testing the atypical theory ever since, and most of the time it works."

"Why would you hide that from me? Isn't that what we were trying to achieve together through your training?" Walker shook his head, completely confused.

"Well, yeah, but what would happen if I didn't need training anymore?" I asked.

"What do you mean?"

"What would happen to us if you no longer needed to teach me?"

"I don't know. I guess I would come up with more difficult challenges for you. And at some point, I assume you would pretend that you still needed me as a teacher. And we would go on doing lessons that both of us secretly knew you didn't need. Maybe one day, *you* would teach *me*. And we would do that forever, because there's no way I'd be as quick of a learner as you—"

"You mean, you would still stick around if I mastered the magic?"

"Of course I would," he said, slightly offended.

I was too afraid to ask how this would change our hunt for Layla. I decided to quit while I was ahead. That would unfold tomorrow anyway.

"Come on. Did you think we would stop seeing each other or something?"

I shrugged.

"Don't do that. We're so much more than that. You mean the world to me.

I'd never cast you away." He swiped his thumb across my cheek. "I mean, if you're here . . . I'm here, right?"

"Yeah, okay . . ."

When push comes to shove and we meet Layla face to face tomorrow night, I'd find out just how true that statement was.

"You said it only works *most* of the time. What about the other times? What happens then?"

"Oh, yeah. It seems that my fear blocks the magic. And when that fear comes, when it rises inside of me, there's nothing I can do. Kai—" His name stuck in my throat. It was too soon, too raw. "Kai drowned. And all the magic in the world couldn't bring him back."

"Kai?" Walker folded an arm around his waist and cupped his mouth.

"We can't even cry anymore. We're so numb to the pain . . . we can't even cry."

"I'm so sorry," he whispered.

"I have to send them home. I must get them out of here. I just don't know how," I said shaking my head.

"We're going to find a way."

"Will you help me?" I asked.

"Of course, I'll help. We can do this, especially now that you can freeze time. It can't be much more advanced than that. I keep checking on the *Waking Dreams* book, but it's never been returned to the library. I'll check again tomorrow. I know there is something in there that would help us figure this thing out."

I cringed thinking about the book but nodded regardless. I was hopeful we'd find a way, but something inside of me wondered at what cost? What sacrifices needed to be made to send the three of them home? The cabin door opened and closed with a slam, and it wasn't long before Gunner's wet nose pushed against my leg.

"Hey, we have a big day tomorrow. Let's take your mind off everything for a while. Do you want to take a break? I know of a great drive-in movie theater . . . We could take the golf cart?" Walker forced a smile as he absentmindedly petted Gunner.

"Actually, that sounds perfect." My heart pitter-pattered in my chest when I considered that maybe the movie was a date. But of course, it wasn't a date; it was only the two of us killing time before trying to find his ex-girlfriend. Twenty-four hours until I'd knew which side of the war he would fight on.

23

We parked the golf cart in the open field. About a half dozen vehicles were parked in a line, and several groups of moviegoers sat on blankets before them. The movie screen was gigantic, even from a distance. It didn't matter which movie played, only who you came with. And tonight, I'd come with the one person I wanted to spend my time with.

I grabbed the blanket from the back seat of the golf cart and left the keys in the ignition. Nobody came to the drive-in to steal. Especially not the people rocking the single cab truck with foggy windows. I smirked as I looked at the heated truck and then quickly averted my eyes. Walker and I found a spot halfway to the screen and placed our blanket in the dirt and sparse patches of grass among the others. Most of them looked to be on dates.

"Do you know what movie is playing tonight?" I asked, settling down on the blanket.

"*Between You and Me.*"

I forced a smile. *Between You and Me* wasn't just any movie. It was a popular movie about love and sacrifice. About a boy and his family who live in another world. He leaves everything behind to chase the girl of his dreams, even though she lives on a different planet. One day he realizes that being with that girl is costing him his life. He can't live outside of his world for any sustained time, and he has no other choice but to return home without her. He was willing to lay down everything he had, just to be with her. But in the end, he'd never really had a choice. He'd chosen to sacrifice, but fate chose otherwise.

I didn't want that to happen to me. I wanted to be the one in charge of my destiny. And I'd already chosen to sacrifice. The only thing that would send me packing would be Walker's rejection, and even then, it would be a tough choice.

"Have you seen this movie?" I asked.

"Yeah. It's a great one. Have you?"

"Yeah, but don't you think it's kind of sad?"

"Sad? Maybe. I kind of look at it as a journey, though. Samuel Chesson gets to experience another world, and he gets to fall in love, what could be better than that?" Walker settled on the blanket, perched on his elbows behind him. I leaned forward, grabbing my knees in a bear hug.

"Oh, I don't know, staying with the love of his life, and *not* having to leave her?" *Just a thought . . .*

Walker tilted his head, weighing the options. "When you're cursed in love, you take what you can get. The time he spent with her was way better than sitting in his world all alone," he said, staring at the blank screen.

It hurt thinking that Walker was so starved for affection that he would choose the broken heart over the lonely one. I was pretty sure that avoiding heartbreak was not only the safest bet, but the smartest one too. I would have done it, if I'd had a choice.

"So, you're saying you would rather fall in love and have your heart shatter a *million times over*, just for the experience?" I asked.

"I think so. Yeah. Isn't that what life is all about?"

"Heartbreak?" My voice squeaked.

"The ups and downs. The journey." Walker stole a glance in my direction then quickly looked away.

"Call me crazy, but my life's a little different. A little safer. My journey is all about avoiding land mines. I would like to be whole by the time it's complete." I rested my chin on my knees.

I wasn't really whole as it was. Half of my heart was in another realm; half was wrapped up in a ghost of a guy. I'd been in some sort of accident I couldn't even remember, and I'd fallen deeply for someone I could never keep.

"You can't go through life being so scared, Wilde. If you're afraid a bomb is going to blow, then you stop seeing what's right in front of you." I thought I saw his pinky finger stretch toward me on the blanket.

"Is that how you felt with Layla?" I regretted the words the moment they slipped from my lips.

Walker's fingers withdrew as his hand clenched into a ball, and his face contorted.

"I mean, even though it hurt, you were thankful for the time you spent with her? Would you do it all over again?" I asked, reading him carefully.

"I . . . I *would* do it again." He reached up to touch his brow, and when he pulled his hand away, there was fresh blood on his fingertips.

"Oh!" I scrambled around the blanket looking for something to hand him to stop the bleeding.

"It's okay. I'm fine." He smeared the blood across his temple in an attempt to remove it, then rubbed his hands together.

I hated how the very mention of her name caused his wound to reopen. It wasn't something he would ever heal from; I knew that now. I had so many more questions to ask, but I didn't want to cause him more pain than I already had.

"You said that maybe I could teach you the magic one day. What would you do with it?" I asked, trying my hardest to take his mind off Layla.

It had the opposite effect. He took a moment to think about it, and then he dabbed at his brow again.

"Honestly? I would change the day it happened. I'd go back in time and stop the accident. I would do whatever it took to keep her safe."

I sighed heavily. I'd asked the wrong question again. "But what if it took not being with her anymore?"

"You mean like the movie?"

I looked up at the screen as it darkened. "Yeah, I guess."

"Absolutely. Whatever it took."

The movie screen flickered to life, and the sound was adjusted from too loud, to too quiet, to just right. Trailers for old movies I'd seen several times played in the background, and my mind wandered.

He certainly loved Layla, and I had to imagine she'd been a different person back when he knew her, because the Layla I knew was a little bit crazy. I lay back beside him as we watched the trailers in silence. I pretended not to notice when he swiped the blood from his eyebrow, but I internally cursed myself for making it happen. With less than twenty-four hours left before we met Layla, the last thing I wanted was to focus on her all night. From here on out, there was only room for two on this blanket.

The movie started with a scene from the boy's world. It was an inhospitable place, lacking color, joy, and safety. But the boy didn't notice, because it was all he knew. I chewed on my lip, thinking about the Baylor phenomenon. I couldn't compare myself to the boy in the movie because I *had* known better. And surely, my life before this wasn't so far away that I had forgotten what a predictable environment felt like. I wasn't choosing to stay in Baylor because I couldn't remember life was better somewhere else. I was choosing to stay here because I was in love. Because this was where my heart had found its home. Still, I couldn't help relating the entire movie to my situation, comparing my realm to his planet and my relationship to his.

The movie did very little to quiet my mind. If anything, it made me think about my situation even more. I couldn't help but feel like time was of the essence. Gran had said that I would be going home soon. I didn't know how long *soon* would be, but I felt the need to prepare for the war. I knew an army would try to take me home, and more than ever, I needed to know if it was worth fighting for. I needed to know where Walker stood. Would he stand faithfully by my side? Or would he stand across the battlefield?

I couldn't just ask him. If I did, I knew he would tell me to go home. He would be chivalrous. His way of showing me he cared. He would sacrifice my company and live a lonely life because of his love for me. Whether it was a friendship kind of love or something more, it didn't really matter. But if I just stayed quiet, I might be able to stay as long as . . . forever. He'd said so himself. He'd said he would train me *forever*. Whether he admitted it or not, I knew he didn't want me to leave. And I wasn't sure he could survive another heartbreak.

But he'd also said he would stop the accident from ever happening if he had the gift of magic. Even if that meant leaving Layla. Maybe it meant that all he wanted was her safety, not her heart. Maybe he would pick Layla's safety and *my* heart? And that would be our forever. Forever with Walker in Baylor would truly be an infinity of time and space. I would have endless days by his side, and one of those days, he would have to admit that he'd fallen in love with me somewhere along the way. The excitement swirled in my stomach like the wings of butterflies lightly stirring.

On the big screen, the boy reached out and touched the girl's cheek. Without moving my head, I tried to peek at Walker. My hand twitched slightly in his direction, and I tried my hardest to not make it obvious. But as I tried to steal tiny glances at him, I caught sight of something else. Something red. A girl in a red cloak standing near the steamy truck.

Disappointment washed over me. *Not now . . .*

"I forgot something in the golf cart. I'll be right back," I said, eyes trained on the red target. She wasn't supposed to come so early. I had until tomorrow before she ended this for me.

"I can get it. What do you need?" Walker asked.

"It's okay. I'm just going to grab a water," I said, patting his shoulder as I left.

I walked straight back to the row of parked vehicles. I weaved in and out of the cars before approaching the truck, staying in the shadows. I didn't have a plan and was suddenly afraid that Walker would see us together. What would he think then?

The edge of the cloak peeked out from the bed of the truck, and I stilled when I saw it. Did I really want to talk to her? Make a scene? What would I say? Something flipped inside of me, and I no longer wanted to confront her.

This was a terrible idea. I looked down at her black boots and saw a flash of her face peeking around the truck bed. But by the time my eyes flicked up, she was gone. Slowly, her shoes took a step back.

I made the decision to let it be. She didn't want to talk to me. She was here to spy and nothing else. I turned around and headed for the golf cart. I didn't even know if I had a water bottle to retrieve, but I had to look. I couldn't come back empty-handed—that would be weird. I glanced at the blanket and was pleased to see that Walker was still there, watching the movie. I rummaged through the golf cart and managed to find little more than an empty crumpled soda can. I supposed I would have to tell him I couldn't find my water. I was just about to head back to the blanket when I heard a swipe of gravel behind me. A flash of red disappeared one car over. *Dammit.*

Layla made it difficult to know if I was being spied on or chased down. Was she trying to get closer or keep her distance? I felt foolish for fearing her, but I couldn't help how my heart rate doubled with her proximity.

I saw her shadow clear as day when the big screen lit up. She was crouched behind the car like a child playing hide and seek. I felt bad for her, but also incredibly threatened. It was an odd mix. My body told me I was in danger, but my mind said she was harmless and needed help. And it was my gran who had conveyed she was a job. A task I must complete. *Find the girl . . . Help the girl . . .*

Maybe she was lost and couldn't find her way to a more restful afterlife? Could I really send her on her way when I knew that Walker had been looking for her? Would it make me a terrible person if I did? I bit my lip and made the split-second decision to try to talk to her. What's the worst that could happen? I was growing sick and tired of wondering where I belonged. I crouched, like her shadow, and snuck around the back of the car.

"Wilde?"

I jumped. My heart hammered in my chest, and I let out a shudder. "Walker?" I asked, extending to my full height.

"What are you doing? You're missing the movie."

"Oh, I can't find my water." I raised my empty hands.

The movie screen lit up, revealing three shadows instead of two. I swallowed a lump in my throat waiting for him to notice, but he never did.

"Do we need to make a run to the store?"

"No, no. That's all right. I can wait." I closed the distance between us, and we turned and headed back for the blanket. Walker slipped his arm around my shoulder as we made our way to our spot in the clearing, and I peeked over his arm to see if Layla was watching. She was no longer hiding in the shadows. She stood, openly visible, in front of the golf cart, arms crossed. Black boots and a red cloak. Long tresses of dark hair cascaded over her shoulders. Her brows were furrowed, and her lips were pursed. Her head tilted ever so slightly to the side, as if she didn't know what to make of us. I felt sick to my stomach.

We sat down on the blanket. Walker lay back, immediately comfortable, while I sat up nervously shredding a single blade of grass into thin strips.

"Are you okay?" Walker asked.

"Yeah. I'm all right." I lifted my gaze from him to Layla.

It was my job to reunite them. But was that my only purpose here? To help them find each other through the veil? Layla had told me I didn't belong here, and that echoed everything my gran had said in her cryptic visits. But I didn't believe it.

But at the same time, I couldn't bear the thought of letting my gran down. I had to find a way to stay with Walker and help Layla. *Separately*. It was an impossible feat, especially since I couldn't even help my friends escape. I didn't know what to do. My friends needed me, Walker needed me, Layla needed me, everybody needed something from me! But what did I need?

I stole a glance back, and Layla was no longer there. Frantically, I searched the darkness between the cars and across the blankets. Nowhere could I find a red cloak and a lonely girl.

An epic space battle began on the big screen. The boy's family was trying to get him back to the safety of his planet, but the government had intercepted them. I couldn't focus on the movie because I refused to believe that Layla was gone. And an invisible threat was far worse than one I could track with my eyes, no matter how uncomfortable her glare. I looked back, searching once more, and this time Walker took notice.

A stream of light blazed past us at lightning speed, knocking Walker onto his back.

"Whoa!" I said, breathlessly.

"What the hell!?" Walker exclaimed, looking for answers.

Another laser shot through the crowd. And then another. A high-pitched squeal whizzed by with each streak of light. The small crowd screamed and ran for cover, leaving their blankets and belongings behind. Car doors slammed shut. Somebody's alarm went off.

"They're missiles!" I yelled.

The missiles being fired in the movie were coming straight through the screen, unleashing their firepower into the crowd.

Another one shot overhead, and I ducked, wrapping my arms around my head. The cars peeled out and sped off, kicking up a cloud of dirt and dust. Even the couple in the truck with steamed-up windows took notice, starting their ignition, and speeding away.

Five more shots fired off. One landed in the forest behind us with an explosion. The ground rumbled as orange flames ignited into the sky.

The last of the cars disappeared from sight, leaving only a cloud of dust in their wake. Walker and I were alone as the fire grew in the distance.

If Layla was hanging around the cars before, she certainly wasn't there now. Breathlessly, I searched the movie screen and tried to recall when the battle scene ended. Walker was the only one who was unafraid—probably because he was already in his afterlife—but it surprised me when I thought I saw a pass of amusement cross his face. He wasn't just entertained, he was . . . *proud?*

He was actually proud of all the hard work I had put into manifestation, and he couldn't care less that it came out in twisted ways. What could have been an embarrassing, tragic night was nothing but excitement for him. He had been trapped in what probably felt like Groundhog Day for the past twenty-some years, and what I suddenly understood was that unpredictability was his friend. Which made it a friend of mine.

A missile shot by, missing us by several feet. The heat blew past us, nearly singeing my brows. The gust kicked up my hair, leaving half of it toppled over my face. Walker broke out in laughter as I swiped my hair back. I couldn't believe he was laughing at a time like this. He reached over me, and my eyes grew wide as he grabbed the edge of the blanket. *What was he doing?*

He pulled the excess blanket over us, and we hid there listening to missiles fire off. I couldn't see the golden amber of his eyes or the dimples in his cheeks, but I could hear his smile through the darkness, and I could feel his energy through waves of heat. He covered me with his body, a human shield, protecting me from my own imagination. His forearms pressed into the ground on either side of my head as the blanket pitched over his shoulders. Missiles whizzed by, and the light from the lasers flashed underneath the blanket, momentarily lighting his face.

I couldn't leave this realm even if I wanted to. I was *incapable* of leaving Walker. He had become my existence. He was my only reality.

Every time I thought he might see the desire written across my face, another life-threatening missile would graze by. Another explosion would sound in the distance, causing Walker's body to tense on top of me. I licked my lips and waited. I fought every desire to turn my gifts on him. *Make* him want me. *Make* him kiss me. But it wasn't right. And I knew that it would never taste as sweet if I did.

I was so into him, I didn't even notice when the battle scene stopped. I only noticed when Walker relaxed, and his energy turned from heated to curious. That's when I heard the roaring fire gaining momentum in the distance and the soft sounds of a piano playing a sad melody.

Walker threw the blanket off, and we took in the surrounding destruction.

We got to our feet, amazed by all the smoke and embers glimmering in the sparse tufts of grass. The blankets and trash had blown all about the field in a whirlwind. It was nothing short of mass destruction, and I had caused it with my typical indecisiveness.

But that's not what stuck with me long after the night ended. The thing that really stopped my heart was the main character, brought to her knees in the middle of the field. The girl was tucked into a ball amid the smoke, crying quietly. The movie continued to play in the background, but she had come to life before our very eyes. Her heartbreak was palpable, and the music leaked from the movie screen and floated all around us in a heart-wrenching melody of a love that could never be.

24

The Baylor Balloon Festival was alive with sightseers, townspeople, and travelers alike. Everyone within a sixty-mile radius of Baylor Lake had come to see the balloon festival, including Walker and me. My thoughts lingered on Emma, Scarlett May, and Noah back at the cabin. None of them had wanted to see the balloon festival. They really hadn't been the same since Kai left.

I thought it had more to do with failing to find the red door than Kai's absence. We'd lost many of our friends along the way, and everybody had seemed to bounce back—quite unnaturally. This was different. This had affected them in a way I hadn't yet seen this summer. Their hopes of going home were waning.

I scanned the crowd, looking for Layla. I had been on pins and needles the entire afternoon. Just because I didn't see her didn't mean she wasn't there, watching and waiting. I knew she was around us. She was *always* around us. I couldn't understand why she would make herself visible to me when she hadn't done it for Walker all these years. Perhaps it was her way of intimidating me. I imagined she had a laundry list of reasons why she thought I was unworthy to be by Walker's side. I glanced up at him and saw his eyes flickering through the crowd. If I was feeling nervous, I couldn't imagine what he was feeling.

My uncertainty had shot missiles through the woods last night. I'd caused a forest fire just by weighing my options. And I was incredibly thankful that Walker didn't possess the same power. Because I couldn't fathom the trepidation racking through his mind as he looked for Layla, his long-lost love, in the crowd.

"I still can't get over last night. I mean, did you think about the movie coming to life? Did you have to physically pull the light show out of the screen? How did it happen?" Walker's face was alive with possibilities as we swerved around a family with lingering small children.

"Light show? That's a little generous don't you think?" I looked up at him. His eyes were sunken, and light purple shadows lurked below his lashes. Neither of us had slept much last night.

Walker chuckled and shot me a sleepy smile. "I know you were scared, but I quite liked it."

"I wasn't scared!"

He laughed louder, bringing an unwilling smile to my face. "I wasn't!" *Maybe I was, a little.*

"You were so scared, you know it."

"I think you were scared when the movie ended and you realized the entire forest was going up in flames," I exaggerated.

"Well, how was I supposed to know that you could turn it off just as easily as you started it?"

I smiled crookedly, shaking my head. I hadn't known I could do it either. But after last night, after seeing the actress in a heap of tears and her heart broken into a million pieces, I'd just wanted the night to end. I'd wanted the whole thing to shut down. I got lucky is all.

"It was just a flick of your wrist. You clenched your fist, and the entire fire went out." Walker reached his hand out in front of us, snatching at thin air. I felt my cheeks warm.

"Stop it . . ."

"It was nothing short of amazing," Walker said. I rolled my eyes, completely embarrassed, but the truth was, my heart was singing. He was proud of me, and I was too.

"What do you think happened to the actress?" I asked, my heart still hurting for her.

"What do you mean? She got sucked back into the movie."

"You think she was just part of the movie?"

"Well yeah. Why? What did you think?"

"She just seemed so real." I said in little more than a whisper.

Walker chuckled like I was a total sap. But I couldn't tell the difference between the actress from the movie who had come to life in the clearing and the girl in my mirror. She was just as real as any of us, and that frightened me.

Walker tugged my arm and steered me to a small cotton candy booth. His face lit up like a little boy, and it quickly pulled my mind away from last night's movie. "Good call. Cotton candy is always a good call." My mouth watered at the thought of spun sugar.

I pinched the pink cotton candy and pulled a clump off. The web of candy melted instantly into tiny granules of sugar in my mouth, and I wanted more. Walker pulled off a piece far too big for his mouth, and I laughed at him as he tried to fit it in one bite. We walked aimlessly around the festival eating candy and people watching. I knew we were supposed to be looking for Layla, but it didn't feel that urgent. Neither one of us was on the hunt for a change. We were simply enjoying each other's time in a slow and lazy manner. When we became too relaxed, Walker would pull out the photo from his back pocket. It was his way of reminding us to stay focused on the mission. Still, his actions seemed forced, like he was driven by guilt.

The photograph was of a yellow balloon with green stripes and the most beautiful couple there ever was. A tinge of jealousy crept through me every time I saw the picture, but as soon as it was folded away in his back pocket, I did my best to enjoy myself. I didn't need to actively look for yellow hot air balloons with green stripes; I was pretty sure it would be obvious when we saw it. That meant we just had to cover as much ground as possible, and our job would be complete.

But our steps were slow and our eyes nearsighted. It wasn't a stretch to say we were having fun. In fact, it was the first time I felt Walker ease into contentment. And I felt like I might be enough for him to be happy. If this had anything to do with last night, I would have fired off missiles a long time ago.

We strolled through the crowd, passing families with little kids, seniors who still held hands—my favorite—and a wide variety of couples. I spotted a young boy, maybe three years old, peeing behind his parents' backs as they purchased food from a vendor. The little boy's pants were around his ankles, and he leaned back in a practiced and proud stance.

I grabbed the crook of Walker's arm and pointed as the crowd parted around the child, looking at his parents with furrowed brows. We laughed, collapsing into each other. When a random little white dog came up beside the boy and peed with him, my knees grew weak, and I grabbed hold of Walker's shoulder for support.

The hours passed seamlessly. We tried ridiculous treats that you could only buy at a festival, and we laughed . . . *a lot*. It was far different from the last hunt we'd gone on. The stakes were high at the Fourth of July Baylor Parade, and Walker's heart had been crushed.

We rested on a bench under a sparse sapling of a tree, picking apart funnel cake and cracking jokes. Nearly the whole day had passed, and dusk was fast upon us. Walker had finally stopped pulling out the photo of Layla, which told me his guilt was waning. I kept a careful eye on his brow, which remained a healed scar the entire day. I didn't know why I'd been so worried about coming to the festival.

"Look, aren't they so cute?" I said pointing to an elderly couple sitting at a nearby table. They wore matching purple shirts, and they were incredibly into each other.

"What makes them so cute?" Walker asked, eyeing the couple. I frowned at him, and he laughed at me. "What?"

I swiped powdered sugar from his cheek. "What makes them so darn cute is the fact that they've probably been together for sixty years and they are *still* very much into each other. Probably as much as they ever have been. Most people get sick of one another. They get complacent and grumpy. But they're the opposite. They even dress alike. They love each other so much. You know, I bet they still hold hands." I smiled up at Walker. *Maybe I was a sap.*

He dipped a strip of funnel cake into caramel sauce and handed it to me. I cupped my hand underneath the hot caramel, catching a single drip of sauce.

"I guess that *is* kind of cute, but don't tell anybody I said so," he said with a boyish smile. I laughed, bumping my shoulder into his.

"Do you think that will be us one day?" I asked. It tumbled out of my mouth before I could even think about it. The look on Walker's face made me wish I hadn't grown so comfortable after all.

Had I ruined it? Had I just ruined the entire day? Was this the part where he told me we were nothing more than friends, and this wasn't going to last forever? Was this the part where he chose which side of the war he was on? My throat tightened as I waited for him to say something. Anything.

"Us?" he asked. I stared at him, unblinking.

There was no way to remedy it. I'd said it because I looked at him as the love of my short life. It was very clear that he didn't see me that way.

"Wilde . . ." he drew out my name.

"I know. I'm sorry." I scrunched my eyes closed and hid behind my hand.

"I'm *never* going to grow old," he said, breaking the silence.

He's never going to grow old? That's what he was worried about? Not whether we'd be together, or if we loved each other, just that he wasn't going to grow old like the couple at the table? Maybe I hadn't spoiled the day. Maybe the idea of him and me wasn't so far-fetched.

"I know. I'm sorry," I said, still hiding my eyes. Now, I was afraid he might see my confusion.

He pulled my hand from my face and peered into my eyes. "*I'm* never going to grow old, but you will. I'm going to find a way to get you out of here. I promise."

It was the saddest thing I'd ever heard. Walker never growing old, me leaving him behind, and the sight of two elderly people in love—something neither one of us would ever have. Especially not together.

"But I don't want to leave you behind," I said, dipping my toe in to the conversation I really wanted to have.

"I know you don't. It's okay. I'll be okay."

My eyes burned as tears threatened to spill. Walker seemed to grow more nervous as he looked into my worried eyes, and he turned away as if searching the crowd for answers. "Hey, have you ever gone up in a hot air balloon?"

That caught me off guard. "Me? No."

"Let's go."

"I can't do that. You know I'm afraid of heights, right?"

"You'll be fine."

"I can't even jump off the rocks at the lake, and that's with a rope swing and forgiving water below. What makes you think I'm going to be *fine* in a hot air balloon?"

"Wilde, trust me, I'll be there the whole time. It's about the experience, right? Let's do this together. We might not have another chance."

My jaw hardened as I thought about all the ways it could go so terribly wrong. The second I began to think was the second the balloon ride would turn into a tragic event. "You understand that when I become afraid terrible things happen, right?" I asked, slowly, putting emphasis on each word. "Walker, I'm already afraid just looking at the thing!"

A flush crept into his cheeks, and his dimples flashed beneath his unshaven face. I couldn't quite read the look, but I thought it might be embarrassment. "Yes. I understand. And I will have to try *very* hard to keep your mind occupied."

My eyes widened. I didn't know what that meant, but it sounded like an invitation that I couldn't turn down. I jumped to my feet, suddenly eager for the hot air balloon ride. Walker's lips pursed together, creating a thin straight line. He held my hand as we walked to the nearest unoccupied balloon. It was then, at the worst imaginable time, that I spotted the yellow and green stripes we were looking for. My heart skipped a beat as I considered not telling him. Or maybe I could tell him afterward? But when I looked up to his bright eyes, I knew I couldn't deceive him, even for an hour.

I squeezed Walker's hand, and he turned around to look at me. "Um, I think I found it," I said meekly.

"Found what?"

"The balloon. It's over there." I pointed with a shaky finger. It was a sacrifice I wasn't ready for, but I made the choice, regardless. I would rather Walker's happiness before my own, and I suppose I would rather his heart be full for an hour longer than for me to get my balloon ride. It had *nothing* to do with the fact that I was petrified of heights . . .

Walker froze, staring at the yellow hot air balloon. I turned my body slightly in its direction, anticipating the change of course, but Walker's hand tightened around mine. "It's okay. We'll head over afterward?" His eyes were fixed in the distance.

"Are you sure? I know you've been waiting . . ."

"I'm sure." He turned away determinedly, and I jumped to keep up with him. I couldn't believe he was choosing a hot air balloon ride with me over his chance at finding Layla. Who's to say she would wait? He didn't say much else about her or the balloon waiting for us across the field, but he was quietly ruminating to himself. My eyes flickered to the scar running through his eyebrow, and I noticed it had turned pink but wasn't bleeding.

We stepped into the basket, and I quickly became anxious. The wicker was sharp against my palms as I grabbed at the edge, looking for anything I could use to secure myself. Why was the basket so old and rickety? The other balloons had leather-wrapped baskets that were newer and stronger looking. Our balloon was a sun-bleached navy blue. The skirt blended into a merlot red and then bloomed into a bright orange on the top pole. The basket was smaller than I would have liked, only large enough for three people: the pilot and one lucky couple.

Our pilot was a tall, thin man with scrawny arms and a long handlebar mustache. His eyes were droopy and glassed over. I was pretty sure he was stoned. I wasn't comfortable in a hot air balloon as it was, but having our pilot be under the influence made me even more nervous.

"My name is Chad, and I will be your aeronaut today. Please keep all hands and feet inside the basket. Do not lean over the edge. Do not crawl over the edge. And if you must use the restroom, please go now. There will be no opportunity to relieve yourself in the sky."

I peeked at Walker, slightly concerned, but his thoughts were elsewhere. I took a deep breath. "What's that thing?" I asked, stalling.

"That's the burner. This is the vent line. That is the envelope. The hot air is released into the envelope, trapping it inside and lifting the balloon into the air. I'll pull this line when we ascend too quickly. Ready for takeoff?" Chad's voice was monotone. I looked at Walker with gigantic eyes.

Were we ready for takeoff? Should we maybe rethink this? Maybe chasing after Layla wasn't such a bad idea after all?

"Great. Ready for takeoff," Chad said when nobody answered.

I squeezed Walker's arm as the burner started and I heard a loud rumble as flames ignited. The basket tilted sideways, and I let out a yelp. It skipped and jumped before lifting smoothly into the air, and I felt immediately sick to my stomach. Walker seemed to be in a trance, and I couldn't snap him out of it. It was a recipe for disaster.

"Walker?" I asked. But he didn't hear me. His wound had turned from pink to purple, and I could tell that his heart was hurting.

"Walker!" I yelled. He snapped out of it. His eyes tried desperately to focus on mine, but he seemed to be having trouble. "I'm scared."

The purple bruise immediately receded, and his golden eyes turned warm and compassionate. "I'm here. I'm here."

I steadied my breathing and found comfort in his eyes. We lifted into the air far quicker than I would have liked. The crowd below shrank the higher we lifted. I watched everybody pointing at our balloon as the orange flame glowed into the nylon, and the colors lit like a stained-glass window from within. Walker turned me around facing outward and wrapped his arms around my waist. I felt secure in his hold, but the height did weird things to my stomach, and I felt slightly dizzy, like I could collapse at any moment.

"See? It's not that bad, right?" he asked, his mouth pressed behind my ear.

"How high are we going?" I asked.

"We're on a tether. We're not going very high at all. These balloons are meant for the crowds. They go up and down all day but stay right here in the fields." The other balloons were all tethered by thick ropes attached to the bottom of the baskets. I immediately felt better, and the adventurous part of me wondered if I could enjoy it with time.

"Is it okay that I'm holding you like this?" It felt more right than anything had all summer long. And it reminded me of the night I'd slept in his arms.

"Yeah. It's okay. It actually helps. Don't let go, okay?"

"I won't." His voice was riddled with trepidation. I was glad I couldn't see his scar, because I didn't want to know how badly it hurt him to have his arms around me. Especially knowing that Layla was so close.

The basket hitched as the rope caught and the ascent had reached its limit. "This is as high as we're going today folks. Enjoy the view," Chad said.

Walker and I inched forward, his arm still wrapped tightly around me. I grabbed hold of the basket and dared to peer down at the ground. We could see everything from up here. *Everything* . . .

The yellow balloon with green stripes sat anchored on the festival grounds. A splash of red painted the bench by its side, sticking out like a sore thumb. I knew it was Layla, and I knew she was waiting for him.

All this time I had been told to find the girl. Now that I'd found her, I wanted to keep her hidden. I wanted nothing more than to stay in Walker's arms for the rest of eternity, but seeing the girl in the red cloak waiting for her soulmate to appear pulled at my heartstrings. I really did want to help her, but I didn't want it to be at my own expense.

If Walker told me today that all he really wanted was her, I'd turn away. I'd dust my hands and walk straight through that red door. The problem was—I didn't really believe that's what he wanted. And I was too afraid to ask.

"Time's running out . . ." Chad said.

What?

Walker rubbed my arms in the cool air.

"Time's running out," Chad said again. I stretched my neck to look at the pilot.

"What did you say?" I asked.

He looked perplexed. "Excuse me?"

"Did you say something?" I asked.

"Me?" he said pointing to his chest.

"Never mind," I said, looking back at the remarkable view. I was hearing things again. I let my eyes fall over the horizon. The dense topography met the sky in an artistic smudge of color.

"Time's running out, Kinsley!" Chad exclaimed. I spun around, causing Walker to let go of me. Chad pulled the vent line with a crooked smile. His handlebar mustache turned lopsided. Was time running out? Was I being a coward?

Layla was on the bench waiting for Walker, and as soon as this balloon landed, we were going to meet her face to face. The only thing stopping Walker from leaving with her and not me might be my confession. Maybe I *was* running out of time. Maybe Chad was right. I took in a rattled breath and peered at him one last time for confirmation, but I was shocked to find he wasn't there at all.

I went rigid, afraid Walker might see that our pilot had vanished. On the one hand, it was more private, more romantic this way. But on the other hand, if my feelings were to get hurt, there was nobody to land this thing.

Regardless of risk, the flame in my belly was back. Only this time, I wasn't going to let it fizzle out. I was going to speak my piece, and if this balloon crashed down to the ground, then so be it. At least I would have my answer.

I watched Layla on the bench checking her watch and growing impatient. Time was of the essence. I'd found the girl, but I had something to say first. I turned to face Walker and he kept his arms wrapped around the small of my back. His eyes were a warm mix of spun honey and compassion. I placed my open hands on his chest.

My time was running out . . .

"Walker, I want to stay . . ."

25

His eyes squinted ever so slightly, and his mouth twitched nervously. The basket began to rumble, but my eyes were glued to his.

"I want to stay here, in Baylor, with you. *Forever*." I grabbed hold of his arms as the basket lurched forward. My worry escalated. The tether suddenly snapped, sending the balloon racing into the sky.

Walker was immediately alarmed, but he tried to hide it. We braced each other through locked arms as he whipped his head around looking for the pilot.

It was happening . . .

My fear was getting the best of me. He either had to accept it as part of who I was, or he didn't truly love me. His face paled as he realized we were climbing out of control with no pilot. Despite the burner not turning on, the balloon continued to rise. But that was the least of my worries.

"What about your family, Wilde? You can't do that to them!" His voice was rushed as his eyes flickered to the disappearing festival grounds. And perhaps to Layla below.

"My gran is here. Either way, I'm losing family."

"I don't think you belong here. I think you are meant to go home and live a long, happy life." His eyes deepened with sadness as he seemed to finally admit the truth to himself. But I wouldn't accept it.

"I belong wherever I choose!" I was so tired of people telling me where I did and didn't belong. It wasn't anybody's choice but my own. And I had the right to be whoever. Wherever. Always.

"I don't think you understand the gravity of the decision."

"I understand plenty!" I snapped. The basket whipped back and forth as the winds became violent. My hair lashed at my face, and the air became thinner and more difficult to breathe.

"You would be choosing death! If you stay here, you will *die* back home. I don't want that for you." His voice broke up as he yelled into the brewing storm.

"I am more me here than I ever was back home! The Baylor phenomenon has shown me my deepest fears, but it has also shown me my strengths and desires. I may not always know how to control it, but I know what I want. I want *you,* Walker. I want *us*."

"I want you too. Just . . . Just not like this," he said, his eyes searching mine. It was everything I was afraid to hear, and it struck me like a knife.

I reached for the vent line, wrapping my hand around the cord. I pulled down as hard as I could, letting the heat vent from the balloon. It was supposed to let the hot air escape from the envelope so the ascent would slow, but that's not what happened. I didn't have control of my emotions after being rejected by the only person I'd truly fallen for.

All the hot air escaped in one heaping whoosh. The balloon turned flaccid, whipping back and forth as it dropped through the sky. The basket turned sideways, rocking like a pendulum. Walker and I held on for dear life. I grabbed hold of the supporting ties as we flipped entirely upside down.

A scream pierced my ears. As my throat grew sore, I realized it was my own. I wasn't even sure if it was fear, shock, or the pure frustration I'd felt. Dangling upside down from a falling hot air balloon, when I was terribly afraid of heights, could do that to a girl.

The fear of heights seemed so insignificant now that I faced a life without Walker. I had convinced myself that going home was the worst thing imaginable. I couldn't just lie in a hospital bed, beaten and battered, heartbroken and alone. No magic to perfect and no missions to complete. What would be the point? This was my home. *He* was my home.

I clung to the outside of the basket, my hand wrapped fiercely around a dangling line. The basket finally flipped right side up, and Walker crawled inside. He grabbed my arms and pulled me in. The old, rickety basket scraped my forearms and legs as I clambered in. We collapsed together at the bottom of the basket sprawled out and panting. I jammed my feet into one corner and wedged my hands into another.

"Wilde, you have to control this! We can talk when we're on the ground, just bring us down safely!"

"What if I do it, anyway? What if I stay? Would there ever be a chance for us?" I yelled through the wind tunnel.

It was an impossible question for him to answer. And I could see the torture it put him through. A single drop of blood ran down the side of his face.

"I don't know what to tell you! My heart . . . It's broken!" he yelled, slamming his hand into his chest.

"You're not broken! You're perfect to me. I love you just the way you are. You're not cursed. You're *not* cursed!"

"I am!" His voice strained.

"Do you love me?" My voice splintered as I wrestled to my feet. The ground was coming up fast, and we were going to crash. But I wasn't afraid of crashing. I was afraid of the next words to come out of his mouth.

"I do! I do! But . . . You're not the only one," he said, right before he looked over the edge of the basket.

Screams split through the turbulent air as the families below turned to run. I was running out of time. My world was ending.

The basket spun and crashed down into picnic tables and several retail booths with a loud racket.

I landed square on my feet. Like a meteor strike, I shook the ground, completely unfazed. The basket broke into pieces beneath my feet, and the balloon fluttered down, eclipsing our sight. Sun-bleached navy and merlot enveloped the broken tables like a sea of nylon.

I had no idea where Walker was. I pushed at the balloon until I found a way out. Panicked, I slid it off my shoulders and began to rifle through the heavy fabric.

"Walker!?" I yelled.

No answer.

I searched the grounds. Almost everybody had fled, except for a few stragglers who had stayed to watch. They stared in disbelief.

"Walker!?"

"You don't belong here, Kinsley!" Layla called out from the distance. Her red cloak fluttered behind her as my worry for Walker caused the brewing storm to worsen. What was she still doing here?

"You can't tell me where I belong! You don't even know me!" I yelled, lifting the navy scraps of the hot air balloon.

"Stop fighting it!" she demanded.

"Walker!?" I called out. He was the only thing that mattered now. I needed to know he was safe.

"Go home, Kinsley!" she said forcefully. The threat blew across my face in a fierce wind, and it was clear I wasn't the only one with a mind for magic.

"He loves me! He said he loves *me*!" *I wasn't afraid of her.*

"He loves me more!" Layla said in an all-powerful voice that enveloped me from all directions.

"No!" I yelled. Electricity lit the gray clouds a neon blue. A crack of thunder growled overhead.

"Don't do this!" Walker pled. He stood unscathed. His arms were spread wide as he crouched down ever so slightly.

The three of us were at a standoff, three points of a triangle. The remains of the hot air balloon lay splattered like navy and merlot paint between us.

I watched as Walker's eyes flickered between her and me. He loved me, *but I wasn't the only one.*

It was the first time he had seen Layla since the parade. But he was no longer the guilt-stricken boyfriend. Now, he was neutral. Caught between two, as if his heart had been torn down the middle and each of us had been given half to keep. Neither Layla nor I would ever have his full heart. And Walker would never experience the marvel of true love. He was right after all; he really was cursed.

I took a step toward Walker, and he inched toward Layla. She took a small, calculated step away from him and closer to me, as we circled around the fallen balloon. Two of us were incredibly dangerous, and Walker was caught in the middle. It was probably a good thing he couldn't die twice.

"Who do you love more Walker?!" I yelled, my eyes fixed on the threat. I had everything to lose, but I was going to lose either way. If he chose me, I'd die. I'd lose my life at only eighteen years old. That was the cost of being with him. But if he chose her, I'd lose my heart, my strength, and my opportunity to live a life I'd only dreamed of.

I inched closer to him, and he took a step further away. *Was he afraid of me?*

"Both! My heart is split down the middle. I love you both," he yelled, no longer amused by my wicked sense of manifestation.

"Don't tell her that!" Layla hissed, and the air grew thicker with humidity. Dark clouds full of angry rain cast a haunting shadow upon us.

"Don't listen to her! She's crazy!" I said, trying to make him understand. He hadn't been there all the times she'd approached me. He simply hadn't been able to see her, and the one time he could, she'd wanted nothing to do with him.

"Be careful what you say, Wilde. We're not in training anymore!"

He knew something. Something he'd never told me. How else would he know that I should be careful? I took another step toward him, and he sidestepped toward Layla, not letting me get close to him. Why didn't he want to be close to me? I was clearly upset, but I would never hurt him.

Layla moved toward me again, arms spread wide. I couldn't quite tell if she was keeping her distance from Walker or trying to keep close to me. What was she going to do? Would she hurt me? Would *I* hurt *her*?

"Walker! Listen to me. Do. You. Love. Me?" I demanded. My sight narrowed in on him, willing him to answer.

"Yes!" he exclaimed sharply.

"Nooo!" A guttural cry came from Layla, and lightning split the sky in half. Thunder broke above, and the clouds unleashed heavy, pelting rain.

I'd had enough of her. I took a step toward her, and she moved away. The three of us turned counterclockwise for the first time, still skirting the remains of the broken balloon.

I didn't know why she was standing in our way when she didn't want Walker for herself. When she had been hiding from him for two decades. I was done with her and her games. But whichever direction I turned, the two of them kept an equal distance, like we repelled each other.

The anger inside of me boiled as the rain pelted my head and streamed down my face, narrowly missing my eyes, and sputtering across my lips.

I felt protective of Walker, and Layla's storm was a threat to him. The fire in my belly had grown to new levels. Total mayhem was on the rise. I seethed with power and anger. My heart drummed in my chest like a hungry predator.

My vision stretched and distorted, turning everything a shade of red. From bright and alarming to deep and alluring and everything in between. There was something so freeing about giving in to my power, and I let myself surrender to it fully.

At first, I thought Layla was shrinking into a powerless form, but I soon realized that I was growing taller. My skin was uncomfortably tight. It felt like it was tearing. A shiver trailed down my back and ripped through my spine. My head pulsed with pain as my jaw extended. Something sharp grazed the skin of my lips and chin.

Walker was terrified. He stumbled backward with enormous eyes.

"Stop it!" Layla screamed.

The few remaining onlookers fled the field, screaming in terror.

I stepped toward Walker and the ground shook beneath my feet. I caught glimpses of myself in the shards of the smashed glass from the tiny broken boutiques. I must've been ten feet tall, covered in dark brown, shaggy hair. It was jarring to see myself as a grotesque monster, but it matched the greed and jealousy I felt on the inside.

"Kinsley, stop it! Stop it! Don't do this! You're going to ruin everything!" Layla's voice came from every direction. It penetrated my head and drove deep into my mind. She had no right to be there.

I shot her a silencing glare. Her mouth sealed shut as she tried to scrape the spell off her lips with her fingernails. She writhed back and forth, moaning within, but she couldn't get a single word out.

With Layla finally silenced, I turned my sights on Walker and stalked toward him. I cut through the center of the balloon wreckage, no longer edging around it. The nylon caught on my foot, and I knocked several benches over trying to free myself. With a single swipe of my paw, the remaining pieces of the basket flew through the air. Layla ducked as the debris narrowly missed her.

Walker startled and tripped, falling backward. He never took his eyes off me. They were the size of saucers and gleamed with adrenaline and terror. He hadn't blinked once since I'd given in to my power. I was only vaguely aware that I had morphed into some ungodly figure, because I could only focus on one thing at a time. And right now, it was him.

He crab-walked backward as I inched toward him. I was done being weak. I was done hiding my true self. My *twisted* mind. My feelings for him. I knew what I wanted, and I wasn't afraid to take it. I was a predator with a one-track mind. I licked my lips in anticipation of my marked prey. All I felt were teeth, long and serrated, as my tongue slinked over the wet bone.

Layla let out a muffled scream, breaking my focus. A clap of thunder rumbled in the remote forest, and with a silencing glare, I drew a lightning bolt down upon her. I used the storm we had both created to end her. She lit up in a magnificent blue light. Her eyes filled with fright as she turned to a fine black smoke. A patch of singed grass smoldered where she'd once stood, and tiny golden embers fought for survival against the rain.

As the thunder waned, so did my blood lust. I stared at the patch of wet, black grass as I slowly came back to myself. Layers of greed sloughed off me, and color seeped back into my vision. I sucked in a sharp breath. My power was greater than I'd realized.

Walker was on the ground, confused and afraid. I'd never intended to harm him. Either of them. What had I done? This wasn't who I wanted to be. I scanned the deserted grounds. If Layla wore the mysterious red cloak, then she couldn't be the wolf. And possibly, wasn't my enemy either. My creepy neighbor certainly hadn't been the wolf. Neither was Mason . . .

I caught the reflection of a hairy monstrosity in what was left of a mirror hanging from a collapsed jewelry booth. Two yellow eyes peered back at me. Scrutinizing me. *I was the malicious wolf.*

I was the killer we'd been hunting for the past month. I had embodied the very fear I'd felt all summer long. I was angry, jealous, greedy, and so very powerful. I was dangerous. And the only thing I wanted was for Walker to want me as badly as I did him. I wanted to be loved.

I couldn't stop what I'd set in motion, because only half of me wanted to. The better half of me wanted to save Walker from myself. But the darker half wanted to devour him. My claws sharpened and my fangs grew like blades against what little will I had to control myself.

"You should leave!" I somehow managed to heed a warning. There were two sides of me now, and I didn't know which was more powerful.

He scampered backward. The terrified look in his eyes made me sad.

"You should run!" I hissed, still stalking toward him.

He uttered something inaudible, and I kneeled down, grabbing his shirt at the collar. My eyes glowered into his like I was hypnotized. I lifted him with ease, my strength immense. His feet dangled six feet from the ground. He squirmed, fighting me every step of the way as I pulled him in for a deep, ferocious kiss.

My mouth claimed his as my heart hammered in my chest. My fangs were deadly, and my strength was unmatchable. I gave in to the pure instinct to take what I wanted, and I had all the power in the world to do it. I kissed him ravenously. My tongue exploring every inch of his mouth as I tasted him for the first time.

I pulled away, breathless. A small voice screamed inside my head, just like Layla had. *You're going to ruin everything!*

I felt my sight narrow, and I was shocked to see my wolf's paw was made of human flesh. We were both on the ground. At some point during our kiss, I had reverted to my natural size and form. Though I didn't think I'd ever be completely normal again. I knew the wolf's blood still coursed through my veins, because the anger and strength remained.

Walker's eyes were terrified, and the wound across his eyebrow was gaping. The blood was diluted from the rain, and a sea of red ran down half his face. His dark, wet hair was plastered to his forehead and cheeks, and his golden eyes popped like the fierce summer sun.

Kissing me had hurt him, and I knew why. It wasn't because of my ferocious fangs, but because he loved both of us at the same time. He knew being with me hurt Layla and vice versa.

"Go! Run!" I blurted out. Fighting my own drive and now-twisted genetics.

Walker turned, and I let go of his collar. He got several strides away but then stopped unexpectedly. Thunder cracked ahead and rumbled the ground. It felt like the world might split in two, and I was standing on the fault line.

I closed my eyes and tilted my head up to the heavens and the angry storm. I begged for forgiveness. Though I wasn't sure who from. The rain washed over my face, and I felt the wolf's anger disperse through my fingertips. I opened my eyes to see black smoke emanating from my hands and pluming up around me in a massive dark cloud.

I was relieved to see it go. No matter how badly I wanted Walker, I never wanted to be filled with that poison again. And it scared me that, deep in my bones, a part of me liked it. I didn't know who that girl was. But I'd been fighting her all summer long. The strength of the wolf drained out of me, and the fire in my belly dissipated. Watching Walker leave was heartbreaking, but knowing I'd hurt him was even worse.

He turned to face me, as if reconsidering, and then slowly he took a step closer.

"Walker, don't come any closer!" I held my hand out in warning.

He took another step. His face half bloodied and etched with sorrow. Still, there was something else. Curiosity? Trust?

"I can't control myself! I'm a beast! A monster!" I spat into the rain.

He suddenly closed the distance between us and crashed into me. His hands tangled in the back of my wet hair as his lips met mine. He kissed me so deeply and passionately my heart melted into a puddle at his feet, and I could have sworn it sent us floating into the air.

The kiss was everything I'd wanted our first to be and more. It felt like the death of me and the birth of something stronger. Something better. Something addicting.

His mouth was warm on mine, erasing the chill from the rain. His eyes were a blaze of golden amber and danced like flames of a fire. They were set deep with desire and framed with crimson blood. He smiled mischievously, a look I'd never seen on him before. He wiped the blood from his mouth with the backside of his hand.

"We're more alike than you realize."

"What?" *I didn't understand.* I'd been through a lot in the last hour, and the pieces weren't adding up.

"You didn't think you were the only one fighting our draw, did you?" he asked.

"What do you mean?" I touched my mouth and stared at the diluted red rain on my fingers.

"Wilde, I've wanted you from the moment I first saw you. But it wasn't right. *This* isn't right."

"You have?" All this time, I'd tortured myself? And for what? *What was I missing?*

"You! Don't! Belong! Here!" His shout was as clear as day in the cascading thunderstorm.

"Then why did you kiss me like that?" I snapped back. The taste of copper spread across my tongue.

"You started it!" He flailed his arms in the air.

"I was taken over by a wild beast! I grew ten feet tall! I couldn't stop that thing, even if I wanted to!" My voice was shrill.

"Did you want to?" he asked.

I opened my mouth but couldn't make the words come out.

"You didn't want to stop the animal inside. And *I* didn't want to stop *this* . . . Wilde. I've been fighting my feelings for you for a long time. I've tried to do what's best for you. But when you kissed me like that, I couldn't see straight! And I lost the strength to fight it. I want what's best for you, but it's *so* hard when you're standing right in front of me looking like that."

He motioned to my body, and I glanced down. I was drenched in rain and covered in blood. Long scrapes covered my legs, and my shorts were ripped, leaving the front pocket dangling by threads. I didn't understand.

"I haven't felt this alive in a very long time. You do something to me, and I think I need you—more than you need me." His eyes lowered to my lips, and he sucked in a shuddering breath.

"Then let's stop fighting each other. Let's stop pretending. We can have it all. We have the power to create it and forever to build it."

"But it's so wrong . . ."

"I'm okay with that . . . if you are?" I could hear the thread of hope in my voice.

He stared into my eyes, weighing his thoughts for what seemed like an eternity. My heart fluttered in my chest as he finally leaned down and kissed me with all the urgency in the world. As if time was slipping by and this was all we had left. Our worlds couldn't be further apart, and yet, somehow, our souls fought to be next to one another. I was going to stay here forever. And I knew now, undeniably, I belonged here.

But as I held Walker tight, kissing him like my life depended on it, I couldn't help but see the bright lights of the Ferris wheel spinning in my mind's eye. Images of the red door screamed for my attention. They were the visions I had when I'd drowned the first night in Baylor, and they were still haunting me.

I'd had the power to silence Layla, but I knew she wasn't gone forever. If I wanted to finally be rid of her in my new life, I'd have to listen to the wise words of my gran. Find the girl, and help her. I needed to help her cross over, and I needed to sever my ties to the realm I once knew and loved. And, somehow, I had to save my friends from the darkness that sometimes crept into my mind and distorted my reality, placing them in unspeakable danger. I had only weeks left to do it. Maybe less.

Now that I knew which side Walker was on, I was ready to fight for my place at his side. The haunting Ferris wheel in my visions told me the battle would find me at the Summerfield State Fair. It was going to be a knockdown, drag-out fight, and I was nearly ready. Now that I wasn't afraid of losing Walker, I had no reason to shy away, shrink, or cower.

I was ready to get what I wanted, and there was a monster inside me that knew just how to get it. All I had to do . . . was give in to the poison.

Beautiful Poison

Volume 4

BEAUTIFUL
POISON

1

Change was on the horizon. It wasn't something I saw, like a storm front blowing in from the south, but more something I felt from within. The summer was coming to an end. Most of my friends had died in one horrific nightmare or another, and the ones who remained were trying everything to get back home. It was only a matter of time before they found a way. Or died trying.

When the calendar had one unmarked day left, that's when it would happen. I had to imagine that my body was healing somewhere in the Decord City hospital. The swelling in my brain must have decreased by now, and they wouldn't keep me on the meds forever. Nor would this limbo I'd been in last forever. If that wasn't a clear enough message that my time in Baylor was ending, I had Layla sneaking me reminders. *You don't belong here . . .*

I've often heard that when one door closes, another opens. I suppose that means I should be looking at the end of summer like an opportunity. But it didn't really matter if I died at home or in Baylor, because either way, I'd suffer. There would be no happy ending for me. I couldn't live two lives forever. I put off the decision any way I could.

Thankfully, I now had some control over my unconscious thoughts, and had I could secretly reset the days as often as I needed. Today was one of those days. It never gave me an extra day on the calendar, but it pushed the Summerfield State Fair back, and that's all I really needed. Now that I had a little taste of wolf's blood, and the power that came with it, I knew the next time I saw Layla would be the final showdown. That girl was crossing over, one way or another. And when she did, I'd agree to meet my destiny.

Since the car accident, I'd been dreaming of the crash. I'd see it on the news or browse past it in the newspaper. Though at the time, I hadn't known it was *my* accident. That *I* was in the car. I didn't even recognize the car, let alone remember the night it happened. But when I discovered I was still alive somewhere in this world, I stopped having those dreams. Maybe the idea became too painful to relive. Or maybe I would be too inquisitive and search for answers beyond the bounds of my dream state. Either way, the rules of this consciousness were breaking down, and things were getting weird, even for Baylor. When I had that dream again, I knew it wasn't like any time before.

I stood under the overpass. Gran was by my side. The night was misty, and the fog was dense. Seemingly in slow motion, we watched as the blue sedan with tinted windows flew overhead. Gran's hand tightened around mine, and I took notice of how cold her skin was. Even in the afterlife, she was frigid. Though I doubted she could feel it. Her skin was paper-thin, and even though I could feel her veins across the top of her hand, I knew there was no blood pumping through them. Maybe that's why she was so cold? It was the little things like the temperature difference between her and me that stood out in my mind. I always thought of us as being similar here in Baylor, but actually, that couldn't be further from the truth.

She had definitely passed on, and I was the opposite of that. I assumed I was in transition, but the way my gran looked at me said I was only here temporarily. I couldn't imagine my life resuming back home after a full summer in Baylor. What used to be surreal was now quite natural. I imagined that going back to my previous life would be dull and somewhat depressing. It didn't mean that I enjoyed everything that happened to me here—quite the contrary. But at least it had always been engaging. I couldn't fathom working at the art gallery for peanuts per hour, plugging numbers into a spreadsheet and talking to the random customer about paint strokes. What was the point?

I had fought off skinless monsters of the mist, conjured a tornado of crows, and swam with familiar but vile shapeshifters. I had become a human beehive and grown ten feet tall. It wasn't glorious work, but it was exciting. And I held on to the hope that I could make more beautiful things here, given the time. Now that the fear of Walker's rejection wasn't in the forefront of my mind, maybe I could have that dream. Or a proper date. Was that too much to ask of a girl in a coma? I didn't think so.

I contemplated my existence as it was, and as it could be, while I watched the undercarriage of the four-door sedan plummet to its demise. Glass shards exploded into the sky like confetti as the car smashed into the street. The front of the car compressed like an accordion, and the remaining intact windows burst like fireworks. The car stood on end, perpendicular to the road, before teetering over. It landed flat on its roof, the metal frame bent like a tin can.

The fog lights flickered in the nearby condensation, illuminating the moist air and the particles of glass and debris.

Before, I'd only been vaguely aware of the yellow fabric pressed against what remained of the driver's side window. Now that I knew it was me pressed against the window, I recognized the blouse as one of my favorites. I obviously chose that top for my eighteenth birthday celebration. I used to love how it contrasted with my dark chestnut hair and thought it made me stand out in the usual sea of black tops. I winced, wondering what my funeral would be like.

The sympathy in Gran's eyes met mine. I'd had this dream so often that I now recognized the sadness that flashed across her face as different from before. Because all the times before, my gran had shown no emotion. Her green eyes had been no more than the distant fog of cataracts, her voice as cold as her skin. But as we stood under the overpass now, her eyes were a brilliant green, just like they had been when she was alive. Yes, change was on the horizon.

"We should go," she said, just like she always had. She coaxed me to leave the scene with a tug on the arm. But this time, I didn't move. I was lucid, and I finally knew what that meant.

"Not yet." I shook my head and watched as Gran's face creased with worry. She didn't want me to see this. Nobody should have to see their own death. But I had seen it many times before, though this was the first time I'd seen it with open eyes. *I* was in that car. And I wanted to know why. I wanted to see myself. Talk to myself. Could I do that?

I slipped my hand out of Gran's weak grasp and walked toward the car. A small protest choked in her throat as I stepped out of the shadows. The night was silent but for the settling of the car that groaned in the distance. I cracked my knuckles as I approached the car. I didn't want to see myself beaten and battered, but I was still curious. I'd already seen a version of myself in the hospital that I hadn't recognized, and I knew this would be far worse. Dark hair covered my face, and for that, I was thankful.

I kneeled next to the upside-down door, trying to look inside. An unsettled feeling washed over me. This was harder than I imagined it would be. The unexpected urge to protect the girl dressed in yellow came over me, and I reached out instinctively. I tried to grab hold of her shoulders—my shoulders—and shake the girl awake. I tried to swipe her hair out of her face. I called out to her.

"Wake up!"

My hands were useless as they passed through her.

"Wake up!" I yelled. She couldn't hear me.

I searched frantically for ways to get her out of the car, but I couldn't even grasp the door handle. My help was of no use to the girl now, for she was in reality, and I was anything but. I was a phantom. An apparition. Just a projection inside her delicate mind. I withdrew my hands, staring at them. My breath billowed out in front of me. How could I be so alone? How could *she* be so alone?

"Gran! You've got to do something!"

Gran stood several strides away, averting her gaze from the accident. Her eyes drooped with sadness and the admission of helplessness. But I was not as easily persuaded.

"You *have* to help her!"

"I am, dear."

But she was just standing there. "Then do it! Help her!" I thrust my hand toward the motionless body. Why was she so calm at a time like this?

"It's not as straightforward as it looks."

"You're not doing anything! I can't grab hold of her. Help me pull her out!" I turned my attention back to the car, trying again to scrape my way in.

Gran placed a feeble hand on my shoulder. "That's not how you help her now."

I knew it was true, but I wasn't ready to accept it yet. What was done, was done. There was nothing that Gran or I could do now. I sat down with my head in my hands, watching my breath cloud between my bent knees. I half-heartedly listened to my gran's words while I tried to come up with ways I could stop the accident from happening in the first place.

"Listen, this accident already happened, and we can't fix that now. But if you wish to help her . . ."

"We need to! We need to help her . . ." I cried. That was me in there. A version of me I couldn't quite recognize, but it was still me, nonetheless. That was *my* beating heart strapped inside. I didn't always like the girl, but I loved her.

"Oh dear. You're not going to like what I have to say . . ."

"Just say it!"

"The only way to help her now . . . is to *go home*."

I flinched back. That was the last thing I expected her to say. I looked up and met Gran's gaze. She knew how I felt about it.

So it was my life, or hers . . .

The girl in yellow lay still, but not peaceful. There was something behind her closed eyelids that wreaked havoc on my soul. I knew the things she'd have to endure, and I didn't want that for her. Yet, I wanted to continue this life I had found in Baylor. It was different for me than it was for her. I loved her, but how much? Would I give my life for her? The girl I used to be?

"We should go." Gran held out her bony hand. She helped me rise, and together we walked away from the wreck. How could I feel like two people at once?

As I looked back over my shoulder, I felt the familiar tug in my heart. I was walking away from something I shouldn't. I knew that. Yet, I did it every time. Steam climbed into the black night and the sedan's fog lights illuminated the desolate distance. It was eerily quiet; no sirens on the horizon. I wondered how long it would be before somebody would find me.

"What happens if I don't go home?"

"You mean, if you stay here?" She wouldn't meet my eyes.

"Yeah, if I stay."

"She can't live without you. She would die. And everybody you love would have a piece of them die too."

I sighed heavily. I could have done without the last part. Clearly, it's not what I wanted. I never wanted to break my mom's heart. It seemed like there was no good option for me. It was the first time I wished the void would take me away.

As we returned to the overpass, my eyes trailed upward, taking in the surroundings I'd never paid attention to before. The bumper of a car jutted slightly over the broken guardrail. I wasn't entirely alone. That must have been the car that hit me. I never noticed it before, probably because I had never ventured out from the shadow of the overpass. I'd never even considered the fact that I wasn't in the accident alone. Had I hit them? Had I hurt a family? A sick feeling twisted in my gut. I couldn't live with myself if I had.

"Do you see that?"

Gran looked around aimlessly.

"Up there," I said, pointing to the car. "Did I hit them? Or did they hit me?"

Gran's brows furrowed and her lips pinched. Her hand dropped from mine, and she faded into the darkness. Her green eyes held mine until there was nothing left of her.

"Gran?"

I spun around, surprised I was still in the dream without her. I looked into the darkness, knowing that's where the dream usually ended. A black space that led into the void. A portal from one dream to the next.

"Gran?" I called out one last time.

Seemingly impossible, it was even quieter now that she was gone. Darker too. This was definitely a world I didn't want to live in without her. Where did she go when she left me? My heart rate sped up. I wanted to run straight into the void, but my feet wouldn't move.

A shadow of a man appeared out of nowhere and stood on the overpass. I hadn't wanted to be alone, but the presence of this stranger scared me even more than my solitude. I feared for my safety, even though I knew he couldn't hurt me. Perhaps what I feared most was that he would hurt the *other* me. The vulnerable one.

I shot a quick glance toward the girl in yellow and was alarmed to see another shadow emerge. A tall, lanky figure stood just outside the shattered window. It was as if an invisible human being was standing there, and their shadow had distorted behind them. My heart raced, and I had the undeniable feeling that I was seeing something I shouldn't be. Something no eyes should ever see. Who was it? *What* was it?

Was it the Grim Reaper? Was he coming to extract me? Had I solidified my choice, and my life was now coming to an end? Was I going to have to watch?

It was difficult to pry my eyes away from the figure by my car, but I had to see what the other shadow was doing. Conflicted, I forced a quick glance to the overpass and sucked in a quick shallow breath as the figure disappeared. Where had it gone? I spun around, fearful it was coming for me, but I couldn't find it. A black shadow lost in the darkness.

Slowly, I stepped backward, inching my way toward the void. I would have to turn and run. If only I could build up the courage. I wasn't sure what was happening here, but I wasn't safe without my gran. I was ready to wake up in the cabin. And this time, I wouldn't scream. I wouldn't shove my head into my pillow, feeling like I was trapped in a web. A nightmare. No, this time I'd welcome it.

When the second shadow figure reappeared, it was by my car. The two figures stood side by side. A meeting of sorts. One was slightly bigger, taller, and lankier than the other. But they were equal in darkness and depth. I didn't know what exactly they were, but they were two of a kind. I watched in terror, waiting for something to happen.

Side by side, the figures walked away from the car. The shadows grew smaller the farther away they got, and my heartbeat gradually slowed as the threat moved on. It surprised me to see the yellow fabric still pressed against the window of the car, and I was unsure if the Grim Reapers had taken me with them. Much like the time I had found myself both between the walls of the cabin and inside the real-life operating room, I felt the distinct feeling that I should not have been allowed to witness what I had. Somebody or something was breaking a lot of rules with me.

I needed to get out of here before the feeling swallowed me whole. I turned away from the shrinking shadows and the birthday girl who lay tangled in her seatbelt, and I ran straight into the black void. The temperature dropped into an icy bath of nothingness, and I knew I would soon sink into my days spent at Baylor Lake.

2

The sun had settled behind the treetops long ago, and the sky was quickly losing the last of its color, giving way to nightfall. I readjusted my seat on the stiff bench of the canoe, stretching my back for just a moment. Walker paddled mindlessly. Spending time with him was my favorite pastime, but it hurt me tonight, knowing he was in pain. His scar had been an open wound since the day he'd admitted to having feelings for me, and he tried to hide it—rather conspicuously—behind a baseball cap. I didn't pry. I knew what it meant.

He wasn't completely over Layla, and being with me was somewhat of a painful choice for him to make. It hurt me too. It hurt to know that he'd given me part of his heart, but not all of it. How much had he given me, though? And how much was reserved for Layla? That part I didn't know. I didn't think I wanted to. I wished I could be content knowing that my feelings for Walker were reciprocated, but from the moment he told me, I only wanted more. I feared my longing was a bottomless pit that would never be satisfied. It felt that way tonight as I watched Walker's pensive gaze. I wondered which of us he was thinking of.

He'd said it was wrong for us to be together. There were a hundred reasons that might be true, but I didn't know which one he was thinking of when he said it. I contemplated asking him, but I wasn't ready to hear the truth.

"It's a nice night," I said, breaking the ice. Walker blinked rapidly, as if waking from a stupor. He examined the night sky.

"Sure is," he agreed.

It wasn't really, though. Actually, it was quite average. The stars weren't even out yet. Walker's fresh wound was bothering him, and he was preoccupied with thoughts from beyond the canoe. And if I had to be honest, I was too. There were several trees on fire on the north side of the lake. At least, I thought it was the north side. I sometimes got turned around and only had the glow of the flames to orient myself with.

The fires had started the night of the balloon crash. The night I'd turned into my enemy—the wolf. A ten-foot tall, hairy, bloodthirsty beast. The night that greed coursed through my veins and all that mattered was that I got what I wanted, when I wanted it. Despite the rain, the patch of smoldering wet grass never died. I didn't think much of it at the time, but ever since, I'd been seeing fires come to life in the most uncanny of places. Trees were on fire, pinecones were glowing with embers, and sometimes even patches of the sky were catching fire. As if the blue sky had a piece, invisible to the human eye, cut out and soaked in something flammable, then hung back up for everyone to see. It had been odd to see flames licking up the backside of a low-hanging cloud. But that wasn't the most disturbing part. The part that bothered me most was that nobody else had noticed. Nobody mentioned that the world around them was burning down. Nobody saw it but me.

I glanced at the small grouping of trees from what I still thought was the north side of the lake and wondered why Walker hadn't seen it. He was a ghost, after all. Couldn't he see the things nobody else could? Maybe it was just me making it all up in my head. Maybe it was the idea my gran had put in my head; that I'd be going home soon. I certainly could see how that fear would make the world crumble around me. But it wasn't just the fires; it was little things too. Like Walker wearing the flannel that he'd given me. The same flannel I *knew* was strewn across the foot of my bed at this very moment. I wore it often, and I'd intentionally never given it back to him. Yet he wore it now, as he stared absentminded into the abyss. Why?

Had the world I created for myself become too much for me to hold without dropping pieces here or there? Was I losing little bits of dream-mapping that should be obvious? Like the sky isn't flammable. Like Walker's flannel was now mine, a gift I held dear to my heart. Would I forget about gravity, because I was more focused on the script that Layla had snuck me on the train? Or because I had added too many manifestations to remember them all clearly? Would I begin to drop parts of my dream like marbles falling out of a brown bag with a soggy bottom? And would the whole collection of marbles fall at once, bouncing out of my grasp, causing total mayhem? Or would it be a slow unnerving process that unraveled before me?

"What did you mean when you said that we were more alike than I realized?" I asked, trying to distract myself from my bag of marbles.

Walker straightened his back and paddled the canoe with longer and stronger strokes. But no answer came.

"It seems like things are changing. Little things. Do you think I'm transitioning into your world? Do you think it's a slow change over time? Or does it happen all at once?" I waited for an answer, but grew impatient while he chose his words. "Is it like a whoosh of freedom that captures your soul and sets you free?" I squinted into the night, trying to imagine it.

"No. Not quite."

"What was it like for you? Could you feel it?"

"Not really."

"Can you explain it? I want to know when it happens to me." I ruffled my hair as I peeked at the glow of burning trees.

"Wilde . . . I don't think we should let that happen." His voice was small and pained, like he had changed his mind but didn't know how to say it.

"What do you mean?"

"I—"

"I thought we agreed I was going to stay here!" Immediately I heard the betrayal in my tone. He didn't want me. He never had.

"I want you to stay!" he exclaimed. "But it's selfish. I think we both know the best thing for you would be to go home. You have a chance to live your life. Why wouldn't you take it?"

"But I *am* living my life. I'm living it right now. Here, with you."

"You know what I mean. It's not the same thing, Wilde. You have so many people counting on you to make a recovery. I would never forgive myself if I let you stay with me."

His words sank in, leaving a chill on my arms and shoulders. I rubbed the goosebumps away, but the rejection remained, not so easily removed. "With all due respect, Walker, it's not your choice. I don't need your permission to stay here."

"No, you don't. You're right. Can I ask you something?" He rested his arms across the paddle as he took a break.

"Okay."

"What is it you like about this place? Hasn't it been somewhat awful?"

That was a fair question. I could see why he and Gran hadn't seen the appeal. "I feel like I'm getting to know myself here. I'm growing into something I could never be back home. You don't know what it was like for me to be—"

"Ordinary?" he interrupted.

I thought about his assumption. No, it wasn't ordinary that I detested. It was far worse than that.

"Behind." I let the word float between us. Was that the right description? Had I been left behind in life? "I felt like I was always in a race that I could never win. I always felt one step behind everyone else. It was a constant feeling of not being good enough. It weighs on you, you know?" I shrugged, hoping he understood.

"Yeah, I get that."

"But here, I . . . I'm—"

"Powerful?" Walker guessed.

While that was true—I had been powerful in the wolf's guise—that wasn't what drew me to Walker's world.

"No. It's not the magic, though that is a nice perk. It's more about having the option to choose who I want to be. I don't have to be behind here. I don't have to be dyslexic. It's as if I can choose which life I want, and it's always within my grasp if only I work hard enough. It's not like that in the real world."

I thought silently about what his world meant to me, and my heart swelled with the opportunities I saw in my future. I stood up, suddenly full of excitement. "I can swim to the bottom of the lake if I want. I can freeze the water and walk on top of it. And I bet I could climb the night using a ladder of stars, given the time and practice."

"You probably could," Walker laughed.

"I can't do that at home."

"You certainly couldn't." His smile faded, and I thought maybe he understood.

"I can't shed who I was and start anew." I shook my head, looking for a way to explain myself. "If earth was a cage with intricate brass bars holding us within, then the afterlife would be . . . limitless, I suppose."

A splash sounded not too far away, pulling my attention in the direction of the burning trees. It was too dark to see what had caused it.

"But you're not in the afterlife. What if it's different from what you expect? Are you really willing to give up everything for a place you've never seen?"

I sat down like a deflating balloon as the excitement withdrew. "What do you mean? This *is* it, isn't it?"

Walker looked away, and even in the dark, I could tell he was hiding something from me. "You are in a dream state. Not the afterlife. They are completely different dimensions."

"I know that." I knew they were different, but how different could they be if we could see each other?

A loon sang its long, mournful call into the night and sent a chill down my spine.

"Your gran is in the afterlife, and she is barely around. She can hardly communicate with you. Where do you think she goes when she's not with you?"

I'd thought of this before, but couldn't come to a plausible conclusion. "I don't know. But you're here with me. So it has to be similar, right?" Walker sighed heavily, keeping his secrets locked behind pursed lips.

A splash came from the middle of the lake, drawing our attention away from the debate. We craned our necks, trying to get a better look at the dancing fish, but it was far too dark to see where the lake's surface kissed the night air.

"All I'm saying is, everybody's reality is unique to themselves. Don't believe all that you see." Walker refocused on me.

"Ahhhh!" A guttural scream ripped through the night, and water hammered frantically.

"What the hell?" Walker said beneath his breath. I couldn't see anything, but it sounded awful.

"What is that?" I asked.

"I don't know." Walker picked up the paddle and started moving us toward the screams.

"What are you doing!?" I asked, alarmed.

Another gurgling scream echoed off the bordering forest. This time I could make out a girl's voice, afraid, and clearly in danger. What was she doing all the way out here, in the middle of the lake?

"Are you all right?" Walker called out.

I searched desperately in the dark water, looking for anything that resembled a girl in danger. I hated the part of me that wondered if it was a trap. If my mind was playing tricks on me. Or if we shouldn't save her life, in hopes of protecting our own. A loon called out again, reminding me just how haunted the lake could be when the sky was this dark and the nightmares came out to play.

We bumped against searching hands, and I could hear the girl panting from pure exhaustion. Walker leaned over and instinctively pulled the helpless girl into the canoe, splashing water across my face. The girl trembled in fear and what looked to be confusion. I watched her shoulders rise and fall and her hands quake with adrenaline.

I looked at Walker with the same confusion that the girl wore. His dimples were piercing, even through the tight clench of his jaw. The stubble from his unshaven face caught the glimmer from the peeking starlight. When had the stars had come out? It was really quite something, just how many there were. It didn't seem at all something that would accompany such a frantic event.

"Hello?" Walker asked.

The girl trembled as she tried to regain some sort of control. I wiped the water from my face and noted the swirling unease in my stomach. Something wasn't right. It was wrong. Very wrong.

"Hello?" Walker repeated himself.

"Ya-yeah. Yes," the girl stammered.

I recognized her voice and leaned over to get a better look at her face. She brushed the wet hair from her eyes, and I almost fell off my bench.

It was me. I sucked in a sharp breath and grabbed the edge of the canoe to brace myself while my world spun out of control.

"What the hell were you doing all the way out here? We must be miles from the nearest shore." Walker was seemingly unaware of the misprint.

The girl before me perched on her elbows, and I flinched back. I didn't want *it* touching me. I had no clue how there were two of me sitting in the canoe. I had to get Walker's attention, but I didn't want the girl to look behind her and see me. I felt something terrible would happen if her eyes met mine.

I waved my hand overhead, and Walker's eyes ticked up. "That's me!" I mouthed, pointing in an exaggeration.

Walker's back slowly straightened. His eyes flickered between me and the girl. A terrified look stretched across his face, and the girl tensed. She crab-walked an inch backward, bumping into my shins.

She was as real as I was. The past me and the present me had just collided with the slightest touch. I sucked in a sharp breath, and she spun her head to see me.

For just a moment, our eyes met. It was like looking into a mirror and seeing your past self come to life. It was like knowing yourself, but not being able to trust it. Like wanting to protect the vulnerable, but equally craving to heave it off the life raft and let it sink to the bottom of the lake. It was love and hate, all wrapped up in one.

Her eyes were my eyes, and we were both horrified to be looking at one another. I knew the look she gave me. I could read her face well, but I couldn't feel her emotions. Perhaps mine were too loud to feel someone else's.

Something in my brain told me this wasn't right, that there shouldn't be duplicates of me wandering around Baylor Lake.

The girl faded.

I watched her fear-filled eyes disappear into the night. She left nothing but a puddle of water behind. And even that shrank as it evaporated. The puddle dried, and I reached down to touch the once-soaked wooden planks. *I couldn't trust my mind any longer.*

"What was that!?" Walker asked, more afraid than I'd ever seen him.

I looked at him in shock. "It was me!"

"But why? Why were you just in the middle of the lake?"

"I don't know. It's like it was some sort of weird replay from the first night we met!" I glanced into the water, looking for myself out there, but only saw the reflection of the brilliant stars twinkling above. I remembered that. That the stars had come from nowhere that night, and it had been the most beautiful night I'd ever seen. It was like that now. I eyed Walker's flannel and wondered if he would have given it to my wet, distraught self if I hadn't interrupted.

"Were you thinking of the night we met or something? Did you manifest her?"

"No! I don't know why that happened. It shouldn't have happened!" I said, thinking of the trees on fire. The sky shouldn't have been burning the other day either, yet it was. I knew Baylor had been a breeding ground for mischievous phenomena, but this was different. This was almost like the system was breaking down. Like the very connections that allowed this world to come together had begun to falter.

So, it was true. My time here was ending. I wasn't meant to dream forever. I looked up at the tranquil sky and felt the pending doom wrap around me like a weighted blanket. The Milky Way was tinged pink and teal, and golden embers twinkled from bright to dim in a never-ending waltz.

"You might just get your wish," I muttered.

"Which one?" he huffed.

"I don't think I'm allowed to stay here much longer." I tried to swallow through the tightness that clenched my throat.

"Oh."

My chin began to tremble, and Walker crossed the canoe and wrapped his arms around me. I rested my head on his shoulder and hid my tears beneath a curtain of my hair. "I just don't have the strength to go home."

"I know it will be hard. But I promise you, it will be worth it."

"How? I don't want to leave you . . ."

"I know. I know."

The weight of Walker's body felt ten times heavier as the thought sank in. I brushed my foot over the dried puddle. It was hard to think that I was in two places at once. Three, if you counted the version of me that was in the hospital. It took tremendous effort on my part to conjure three from one. Separated were the body and the mind, and the mind into halves. I felt the exhaustion of it all. I was tired.

As my body grew stronger back home, my mind grew weaker here. Wires were getting crossed, and the past was commingling with the present. I would never get my underwater tea party and endless celebrity golf tournaments. My summer at Baylor Lake was ending just as my relationship was beginning.

"Just promise me one thing?" Walker asked.

"What's that?"

"You won't leave without saying goodbye."

"I'm *not* leaving. Not without a fight, anyway."

"Just promise."

I clenched my teeth. It felt like I was conceding defeat if I agreed. But I knew he needed to hear it, so I said it for him. "I won't leave you without saying goodbye."

3

When I came back to the cabin that night, the lights were out and everybody was asleep. I desperately needed to talk to Emma about seeing my double nearly drown. I had to sort out my feelings, because I both wanted to harm the girl and simultaneously save her. I didn't exactly understand it, but I had a theory; the dream was crumbling, and what little understanding I had before was now gone.

I hesitated in front of Emma's door, contemplating waking her, before I hung my head and strode across the hall. I crawled into bed and lay awake for what seemed like an eternity. Maybe it was. I found an edge of the blanket and fiddled with the fabric while staring at the shadows in the corner of my room. When I got restless, I headed to the bathroom to splash cold water on my face.

I closed my eyes and dipped my face into a small puddle of cool tap water in my cupped hands. The chill did wonders to orient me. I blotted my cheeks with a towel and stared up at myself in the mirror. I was nothing more than the dark shadows I had seen in my bedroom. I could make out the outline of my jaw and, most of all, my dark hair. I searched for discerning features but found none. No features to say that I was, in fact, Kinsley Wilde. For all I knew, I could be looking into the eyes of my double.

I flipped on the light switch and took a long, hard look at myself. My hair was tousled and chestnut brown, my lips pouty, and my eyes dark. Soulless though? I looked deeper. I searched for the green fleck in the bottom right corner of my eye. For a moment I panicked, leaning closer to the mirror until I was nearly pressed against it. That's when I saw it. The small memento from my gran. I leaned back, my heels touching the floor once again, and I sighed a breath of relief.

I was still myself. At least for now. My whole world might come crumbling down, but in this moment in time, I knew who I was. That should be enough to let me sleep. I flipped the lights off and staggered back to my bed, unbearably weary. I tucked myself in for the tenth time that night and closed my eyes, hoping there would be no more interruptions in the world of my making . . . at least, until I woke.

I wasn't so lucky. In the faraway distance, I heard a sound. Music? A quiet melody that I couldn't quite put my finger on. I recognized it from somewhere, but the more I focused on the notes, the quieter it became, fading out until almost disappearing. As I began to drift off to sleep, it would grow louder again. I played the guessing game for quite some time before one of the quiet lulls finally put me to sleep.

When I went down for breakfast after a restless sleep, replaying the melody in my head like an addiction, it was already evening. Late evening. Noah was outside stacking wood for a bonfire, while Gunner dug a hole nearby. Scarlett May was draining a pot of noodles for what I assumed was spaghetti, and Emma was finishing a book on the couch. I felt a little insecure joining them this late in the day, but nobody seemed to notice my absence. Sometimes their oblivion could work in my favor, and this was one of those times. I slipped into the conversation as if I hadn't just woken up, and my worries about missing out dissipated quickly.

"Is Sampson coming over tonight?" I asked Scarlett May, as I checked on the breadsticks I'd seen her slip into the oven.

"No. I don't think so. I couldn't get a hold of him."

"Is Walker coming over tonight?"

"Nope. Not tonight. We have plans tomorrow night, though. I'm going to take him on our first date."

Scarlett May threw the potholder down and stared at me in surprise. I laughed and covered my face with my hands. "What?"

"What!? You didn't tell me you guys were dating!" Honestly, I didn't think she'd care. But now that Kimber and Trinity were gone, I supposed I should include her more often. I shrugged apologetically. Emma jumped from the sofa and joined us in the kitchen.

"Well, it's still really new. We kind of admitted to having feelings for each other at the Baylor Balloon Festival. We've talked little about it since, so I wanted to take him out for an official date. I thought it might help solidify things."

The truth was, we had talked little about it, but I didn't like where we'd left things. I felt nervous about Walker changing his mind on me, and I wanted reassurance. I wanted to show him what we *could* have if I stayed. I wasn't sure how to plan the date, but I knew I had to blow his mind. He seemed to have liked the missiles flying from the movie screen at the drive-in, so I wanted to make some grand gesture again.

"What are you going to do on your date?" Emma asked.

"I'm open for suggestions. I've never planned a date before. The only thing I can think of is a picnic, but it seems kind of silly." I turned off the oven and took the breadsticks out. They were perfectly browned and smelled of butter and garlic. My mouth watered.

"You guys could go swimming in one of the remote coves around here. Take the golf cart?" Emma suggested.

Scarlett May moaned. "Come on. That's *so* boring!"

"What? She could wear a cute little bikini and bring strawberries and wine coolers. It could be great!" Emma chirped. I briefly wondered if that's what she had planned to do with Levi before he broke her heart.

"No, no, no. What you need to do is get a bunch of candles from the store. Light them in a trail from the dock all the way to your bedroom—"

Noah walked in dusting his hands and scowled. I shrank in his presence. "Candles? For what?" he asked, swiping a breadstick from the hot pan.

"Uhh—" I muttered.

"Kinsley is taking Walker on a date! I'm teaching her how to do it right, so she'll get lucky," Scarlett May said, with a smug look on her face. I smacked the oven mitt across her arm and she flinched. Then I scrunched my eyes shut, not wanting to see the disappointed look in Noah's eyes. When I opened them, the look was even worse than I had imagined. It only lasted a moment before his mood shifted into something icy.

"You should take him swimming," he said.

"See! That's what I said!" Emma exclaimed.

"Take him to the three boulders and practice jumping off the rope swing," he continued, his denim blue eyes turning to glaciers. Both Scarlett May and Emma turned away, lips pursed. My stomach sank as I thought of Ethan dropping from the rope swing and never surfacing.

Was that what he wanted? Did Noah want Walker to jump off the rope swing and drown, like so many others had? I knew Noah wasn't a fan of Walker, but did he really want him dead? My mood lightened when I realized Walker already was dead. There was nothing Noah could ever do to hurt him. The joke was on Noah, and he didn't even know it.

"Or you could take him to the Summerfield State Fair. Maybe you guys could have your first kiss on the Ferris wheel! That would be . . ." Emma piped in, trying to temper the room. It worked, somewhat, to dispel thoughts of Ethan, but Noah was still gritting his teeth. He grabbed the lighter fluid from the kitchen counter and went outside. As soon as the door slammed shut, the three of us let out the breaths we'd unconsciously been holding.

"On second thought, Emma is right. The Ferris wheel *is* really romantic. You should do that. And then the second date could be the candle thing." Scarlett May mixed the spaghetti sauce with the noodles and threw a pair of metal tongs into the bowl.

I had thought a lot about that Ferris wheel. I'd seen it the first night I drowned. Maybe my destiny was waiting for me at the top of that large sparkling wheel, and all I had to do was ride it with Walker. Perhaps it would be a kiss at the stroke of midnight. Maybe a lightning bolt from a summer storm. The electricity would strike the metal of the wheel, and I would transition into eternity. A butterfly emerging from its chrysalis. I yearned for the possibilities of something great but feared the more likely outcome. Our first date would be our last.

I dished up a plate of spaghetti, covered it in Parmesan cheese, and threw a garlic breadstick on top while mulling over the possibilities of my soon-to-be future. The state fair was only two days away—assuming I didn't get cold feet and add more rising suns to the summer. As it was now, I had forty-eight hours to figure it all out. It hardly seemed like enough time. Emma dished up plates for herself and Noah. Balancing the two as she opened the door to the patio. Scarlett May followed, talking about how wonderful it would be to fall in love at the fair, and I knew she was thinking about Sampson.

"Do you think he's going to win you one of those big stuffed animals? The ones that are so gigantic you have to carry them on your back?" she swooned.

"Or maybe he'll say something like you owe him a kiss if you can't pop a balloon with a dart," Emma said, before abruptly clearing her throat at the sight of Noah. The three of us stiffened as he shook his head. Emma handed him a plate of spaghetti, and we took our seats around the campfire. It must be lonely to be the only guy left. It was too bad he and Walker couldn't be friends. Though that would be incredibly awkward for me.

"Actually, I wanted to talk to you guys about the state fair." I redirected the subject away from Walker. "I have a theory. Hear me out, okay?" I asked, before shoving noodles in my mouth.

Nobody said a word; instead, they eyed each other nervously. Theories in Baylor have proven to be useless, and they usually ended in crippling disappointment. I could see it on their faces now. They didn't want to get their hopes up.

I covered my mouth as I spoke. "I think that I've been getting these signs, or premonitions, about the state fair. Little signs here and there. And I think it means there will be another red door present."

This had everybody's attention. "You mean, like the one we tried to find at the bottom of the lake?" Emma asked warily.

"The portal?" Noah demanded, his fork frozen just in front of his mouth.

Of course, I already knew there was going to be a red door at the state fair. Summer was ending. The calendar was nearly filled with X's. And the dream was crumbling like a house of cards in the wind. The three of them would go home to their families if it was the last thing I did. But I hoped I'd have time to ride the Ferris wheel with Walker and live in eternal happiness. It seemed like a tall order. Gunner placed his paw on my knee and licked his lips. We would have to get him home, too. I ripped off the corner of my breadstick and tossed it for him.

"Yes, the portal. I've seen more than one before, and I think there are even more out there. We just have to find them."

"We just find it, and then we can go home?" Scarlett May looked at Emma with a wrinkle in her brow. She appeared to be questioning the ease of it all. "What about Layla? I thought we had to find her?"

"The only reason I'm stuck here is to find her and get her through that door. Just like you guys. I mean *us*. My, um, my gran told me she's having trouble getting to where she needs to be, just like we are. And that red door isn't just a portal home. It can take us anywhere. Anywhere we really belong, that is." I wondered what would happen if I fell through the portal. I wasn't sure what side I would end up on. Would the portal spit me out with the living, or recast me to the afterlife?

"Your gran?" Noah asked. I swallowed a lump lodged in my throat. *He caught that.*

"I've sort of been in contact with her." I shrugged, eyeing the dirt beneath my feet. Noah sighed, frustrated with the amount of information I'd been withholding. He ran his hands through his shaggy, sandy hair and tipped back in his chair, causing the front two legs to lift from the ground.

"Why is Layla stuck here?" Emma wondered.

"Who cares? We just need to find the door and shove her through it," Noah said sharply. He was done with me and this entire summer. And I didn't blame him.

"I'm not really sure why she's trapped here. I think she's relying on all of us to help get her home. Wherever that may be."

"Is Walker going to come with us?" Scarlett May asked through a mouthful of spaghetti.

I'd never thought about him coming home with me. I'd only imagined me staying here with him. Was it possible? Could he come home to Clover and exist among the living? Could I date a ghost? I guess I already knew the answer. I had been dating him all summer long, or at least trying to.

Nobody would see him back in the real world, though. And I imagined that would weigh heavily on our relationship. It would probably put me in a mental hospital. It would only be a matter of time before my mom caught me talking to myself, or worse. I shuddered.

I frowned, and Emma looked at me sympathetically. She was the only one who knew that Walker and Layla were ghosts. I never dared to tell Scarlett May or the others that Walker had been the Butcher of Baylor Lake. I imagined if I had, this summer would have gone differently. For starters, I wouldn't be getting dating advice.

"Yeah. Walker and I are going through the portal, too. He's dying to get back home," I said, lying through my teeth. I saw Emma's brows furrow, but she said nothing. The other two bought it easily enough, and we dropped the subject as Gunner came back begging for food.

My gaze rested on the orange flames flickering between the logs in the campfire. I couldn't tell the truth because they would surely lose hope. And right now, hope was all they had. And they weren't the only ones. I had hope for them getting home, too. I really wanted to find the door and get them through it. But when it came time, I planned to skip away, holding Walker's hand.

I wondered if Layla would go willingly or not. I imagined it both ways. She'd either give me a hug and tell me thank you, and the feud would finally be over, or the war I saw in my dreams would begin. Either way, I had to be prepared for the worst. I had to assume that she would stab me in the back, given the chance. And by the look Noah had on his face as he stared absentmindedly into the fire pit, I might have to watch my back around him, too.

My eyes met Emma's which seemed to convey a sadness. She knew I wasn't telling the whole truth. I bit my lip and felt the guilt wash over me. I knew she would miss me when I didn't return home. I thought about my family and then quickly pushed the thought away, burying it in butter and garlic.

"We'll have to bring this guy, too," Emma mumbled.

Everyone watched Emma feed Gunner. She held a single, long noodle above his nose. As the noodle swayed, my focus was drawn to the forest. Layla crept between the trees. I felt my heart rate rise but remained still and kept my composure. It was the first time I had seen her since the lightning strike, but I'd known she'd be back. A girl like her wasn't so easily dissuaded by a little magic. The first thing I noticed was she no longer wore the crimson cloak. That fairy tale had ended. Had a new story begun? I wondered if she'd heard us talking about her. Did she want to pass on? Was she happy to have us looking out for her, or did she only care about ruining me?

"Ouch!" Scarlett May yelped and shot out of her chair. A burning hot ember flew out of the fire pit and slammed into her bare shoulder. She batted at the sparkling coal, swiping it off her arm.

"Whoa! It burned a hole right through your chair!" Noah said. A red glowing circle ate through the fabric and began to spread outward.

I checked back with Layla, but she had made herself scarce during the commotion. Emma was assessing the burn on Scarlett May's shoulder, while Noah just stared at the chair. The taut nylon continued to burn, though there were no flames. The tiny embers fed until they consumed the entire thing. When Scarlett May was ready to sit back down, her chair was nothing more than metal legs and two long posts where the back had once stretched between. The trees weren't on fire tonight, but that didn't mean the flames had been extinguished.

We spent the evening talking around the campfire, and I was well aware it was one of our last nights together. It made me miss my family of misfits to think of them gone. Scarlett May sat in my lap, and we wrapped a blanket around both of us. Inevitably, the blanket caught fire from another rogue ember, and Noah put the campfire out with a bucket of lake water. We all went to bed early, but I couldn't turn in before taking one last glance out my window. Layla was sitting at the edge of the dock. What was she doing so close to the cabin?

It hurt my heart to see her hunched back and dangling legs. The girl was a broken soul. It was hard for me to understand how someone so powerful needed help from someone so wounded. I was a nobody in this world. I didn't even belong. And she made sure I knew that.

But still, I couldn't stand to see her in pain when it was just the two of us. I knew she lived an invisible life alongside Walker, which seemed to be a torture of the worst kind. I couldn't imagine looking into his golden eyes and having him see straight through me.

I decided right then to go to her. I slipped a hoodie over my head and stepped into my slippers. But when I opened the patio door, the ghost was gone. There was nothing but thick fog wafting over the dock and the smell of campfire lingering in the air.

4

I was anxiously awaiting Walker's arrival for our first official date. I sat on the dock, my legs hanging over the edge and my bare feet barely skimming the top of a wet paddleboard. I'd rented two of them in a watersports rental shop in town earlier this morning. While I was worried about falling into the haunted water, I wanted to recreate the night of the Fourth of July. It was the first time I had experienced the magic that Baylor had to offer, and I longed for that curiosity and excitement again.

Then, it had been nothing more than a simple thought of wanting the night to last forever. And it was that one fleeting thought that had brought on the serene glowing lake, the elegant white swans, and the fireworks that fell like blazing streamers from the sky. I could only imagine what my feelings for Walker would do on a day like this. I secretly hoped that we would swing from the stars and bask in the clouds. Nothing was too far from reach in a place like this, with a guy like that.

I rummaged through my old backpack as I waited impatiently. Stuffed at the bottom were two thin towels I grabbed off the back railing on my way out. On top, I'd gently laid our lunches in a clear Ziploc bag. I had prepared two sandwiches and added a couple bags of chips, sodas, and a bag of fresh strawberries to share. It wasn't the most romantic lunch, but I was hoping to make up for that with the water show.

How I was going to manifest it, I wasn't sure. But I had seen various water shows on TV. Massive fountains with shooting water in intricately timed spurts, streaming over and under each other in a beautiful design, and lit by colored lights that cut through the night. I hoped all I had to do was tap into my emotions for Walker and think about the fountains I'd seen on TV, and then they would appear just as beautiful as, if not better than, I had imagined. I zipped up the backpack and double-checked the smaller pouch on the front of the bag. It contained a tube of sunscreen and a very old lip balm. Could that expire?

The door slammed behind me, and I turned to see Gunner running out of the cabin. Nose to the ground, he followed an invisible trail that led him to the dock. Once he spotted me, he came running.

"Hey, boy!" He pushed his nose forcefully under my arm, begging me to scratch behind his ears. I did as he asked, and he bowed his head, leaning into me for more loving. I giggled just as Walker glided around the cove. With my thoughts trained on Walker, my hand slowed. I watched my future come toward me, brighter with each stroke. Gunner wouldn't have it, though. He pushed into me with all his might, his tail painfully flogging me in the back. "Okay! Okay! I love you too," I said, giving him my attention once more.

"Hey, Wilde. You look nice."

I smiled, more embarrassed than I should have been. It certainly wasn't the first time I'd tried to impress Walker, but I had taken more care than usual with my appearance today. Which is precisely what he noticed first. I had put on a lip stain that usually dried my lips out, but I found it to be pretty and well worth the sacrifice on a day like today. Scarlett May had put some eye shadow on me that I wasn't quite used to, but it looked good enough to get my approval.

I wore a more feminine tank than I was used to wearing at the lake. I hadn't packed nice things for our summer trip. There wasn't usually an opportunity to wear them. The silky tops stained with sunscreen, and the beautiful whites that I'd worn in years past always came home with a barbecue stain of some type. But when Scarlett May had insisted I wear her white tank top, I readily agreed. I loved the petite buttons that ran from top to bottom. She insisted I unbutton the first couple to show off a V neckline, rather than the boring straight cut. It didn't really matter to me, but I liked the way her hot pink bikini peeked out from underneath the thin straps.

"Thank you," I mumbled.

"Wow, what have you got there?"

"Paddleboards. Have you ever tried it before?" I asked, kicking them off to the side so I could help tie the canoe to the dock cleat.

"I have not," he said, somewhat unsure of himself. I laughed, but I was worried that I had set us up for disaster.

"We don't need to take them," I shrugged, suddenly deciding against the entire plan. Had I really thought a picnic on paddleboards was a good idea?

"No. It will be fun. I'm looking forward to it." He smiled encouragingly. "Honestly."

The canoe scraped against the dock as it came to a full stop. I held it as Walker hopped out, and we tied it up together. He gave me a brief side hug before awkwardly looking away. Was it awkward for him, too? Or was I the only one who felt the pressure of a day like today?

I didn't doubt my insecurities would play tricks on me, in Baylor of all places. Still, it seemed odd that he hadn't kissed me. Wasn't that something couples did after admitting their feelings for one another? When was that going to start? I hung my head slightly, thinking that sometimes, our relationship felt like the beginning of an endless road, while other times, like now, it felt like it was the end. A dead end.

"Shall we then?" I asked, motioning to the paddleboards.

"After you . . ." Walker eyed me warily.

I smirked as I tossed my backpack over my shoulder. I sat down on the dock and pulled the boards over, one by one, using my tiptoes. After trying rather unsuccessfully to get on the boards from the dock, we finally pushed them to shore in hopes that getting on in shallow water would be easier. It was.

I kneeled on the board carefully and dug my paddle into the silt to push off. Walker followed my lead. "See? That wasn't so bad," I said, feeling quite proud of myself. I'd been worried over nothing.

"Oh yeah? That's the easy part. Why don't you actually stand up, and then tell me how easy it is." Walker glided next to me, his legs dragging in the water and brushed against pads of water lilies. He looked like a natural. I bet he was good at everything he tried. I felt the heat creep into my cheeks. He stared at me with one brow raised, daring me to stand on the board.

"Okay." Of course, I was going to stand up. That's what you did on a paddleboard. I took the backpack off and placed it on the back of the long board, then carefully got a foot beneath me. I crouched, the board wobbling beneath my feet as Walker laughed. "Stop it! I'm . . . I'm focusing." And I needed it. I needed all the focus in the world to keep me upright.

"Oh! Oh! Oh!" He willed me to fall, but I did no such thing.

"See? It's really not that bad!" I said, nearly erect and trembling like the last leaf on a tree at the end of fall.

Walker wouldn't stop laughing, but I didn't dare take my eyes off my feet. Somehow, staring at my ten little toes gave me the confidence to push through and stand upright. I took one tiny step forward, positioning my foot in a more comfortable spot as I windmilled my arms, the paddle waving in the air. Walker's laugh grew into hysterics. "What? Let's see you do it." I finally looked at him, surprised to see that he wasn't laughing at me. He wasn't even looking at me.

I followed his gaze behind me until I couldn't turn my head any further. I whipped my head in the opposite direction, nearly losing my balance. Gunner was paddling as fast as he could to keep up. He was headed directly for my board. "No. No. No! Gunner, no!" I shouted, crouching down.

Gunner slapped one heavy paw onto the back of my board, and then two. "No!" I screamed as the board slipped from beneath my feet. The paddleboard went one way, and I went the other. I splashed into the lake, cursing myself for such a stupid idea for a first date. The water was cool, but not refreshing. It could never be refreshing after the things I'd seen in its depths. I wanted out as soon as my skin touched the mirrored lake.

I took in a gulp of air as my head breached the surface. Gunner had just tipped my paddleboard, and the backpack slid into the water. Walker tried to grab it, but it was too far.

"No!" I yelled before diving under the water. I opened my eyes, searching for the backpack before it disappeared. I kicked down, barely able to reach it, but managed to grab hold of a single sinking strap.

"Here, boy. Here." Walker patted his board, and Gunner's head bobbed just above the water as he made his way around the mess he'd created. Walker grabbed hold of Gunner's collar and pulled him onto his board, somehow managing to stay upright. I frowned.

I side-stroked to my board and struggled to tip it over. Once it was upright, I threw the wet backpack on top and began the long process of heaving myself up. I was only slightly relieved that I managed it in one try, because just about the only thing I could feel now was sheer embarrassment. I must have looked like a seal trying to board a channel marker. As ungraceful as it felt, it must have appeared ten times worse to my date. By the time I was upright, soaking wet and most likely with makeup marred cheeks, Walker was no longer laughing.

"Did you like that?" I asked, eyeing a very dry Walker and a soaked but happy Gunner. "You know he's going to do that to you too, right?" I willed it to happen. Magic don't fail me now!

"He won't do that to me. He loves me."

"Uh-huh." Walker passed me the paddle that he rescued, and I took it from him with a sharp jerk. "So much for our towels," I grumbled.

"Is this what you imagined when you rented the paddleboards?" Walker asked with a hint of sarcasm.

"Yup," I lied, trying not to let the rocky start ruin the rest of the date, but I worried it was the first domino to fall. It took a little effort, but finally I was able to look past the humiliation. I had a water show to perform, and I would need all my focus.

We paddled around Rock Creek Cove into a smaller deserted area. Boats almost never came here because the fishing was bad and the strip was too short for any water sports. It was the perfect spot for our first official date. We pulled our boards close together and held onto one another's paddles while we ate lunch. Thankfully, I'd shoved the sandwiches inside of a large Ziploc bag, and most of our lunch remained dry.

"Tell me more about Layla," I said, surprising myself. The question passed through my lips before I registered it as a thought in my mind. I'd always wanted to know more about the girl, but I'd intentionally avoided asking Walker. I knew it hurt him too much. But the words were out there now, and it was too late to take them back. He seemed to ponder the question, his hand twirling in the water lazily. I zipped up my backpack, heaved it behind me, and then, ever so carefully, I used the wet bag as a pillow.

"What do you want to know?"

"Honestly? Everything." I knew so little about the girl, other than she was important and beautiful. But at large, she was a mystery to me.

"She was everything to me. I was ready to build my life around her. I wanted to . . ." Walker followed my lead and lay down on his paddleboard, placing his hands behind his head, and his feet before Gunner. I remained quiet, giving him ample time to remember his past love.

"She wasn't perfect by a long shot. She was stubborn and insecure, and sometimes I feared I loved her far more than she did me. Who knows, maybe I was the insecure one?"

"Maybe," I echoed his thoughts, as I twirled my fingers in the cool water like he did.

"She was a lot of fun to be around. She was really creative and always coming up with these crazy ideas. Often, we would talk about the most hypothetical situation she could imagine, and we would laugh about how ridiculous it all was."

I wanted to know everything about Layla, yet I didn't want to listen. It was difficult to hear Walker gush over somebody else. I let my mind drift to the water show I'd wanted to give him. Anything to take my mind off how much he loved her and the brewing fear that I'd always be second best.

"She had the biggest heart. And I had no doubt that one day we would find ourselves old and gray, side by side."

I squinted into the sunlight, trying to get a glimpse of Walker's eyebrow. I couldn't see it very clearly, but I knew that at least the pain wasn't too bad. His cheek was clear of blood, and I'd seen worse before.

Quickly, I lifted my fingers from the lake. A stream of water shot into the air and curled around Walker and me. Walker flinched as the water came pouring down on the other side of him. He looked at me in surprise and then slowly relaxed.

The water had moved somewhat like I had imagined, but smaller. I pushed it higher into the sky and added a second stream, and then a third. We watched the water move across the sky like a running rainbow in a moment of silence. Soon, Walker continued speaking, and I wondered if it felt therapeutic to him. He'd probably never talked about her before. All these years . . .

"She was the best person I'd ever known, and I dedicated my life to her when I made the decision to propose. And just because I never got the chance to ask doesn't mean I feel any different."

I squinted at Walker, afraid of what I was hearing, but the sun reflecting off the water was too bright, and I could barely see him. I needed to see his eyes and, most important, the depths of his wound. I needed to see what this meant for me and my future. The sun grew dark with my needs, and the cloudless sky cast a mysterious shade upon us. That's when I saw it. His gash was opening, and the skin surrounding it was turning purple like a fresh bruise.

"Do you feel guilty for having feelings for me?" I asked, no longer squinting under the sun. It was another question that flew from my lips before I had time to really consider it. Walker didn't immediately answer, so I rotated the streams of water to keep my mind busy. The lake water encapsulated us in a perfect cave, reminding me of a private grotto. Private enough for this conversation.

"No," he said eventually. "That's not where the guilt comes from."

The shock of his answer rippled through me. I thought I knew. If he didn't feel guilty about loving two girls at once, then what was it? I'd always imagined that he felt like his love for me took away from Layla, as if there was some finite amount to be given away.

I waited for him to continue, but he didn't volunteer. "Then where does it stem from?" I prodded.

"I feel remarkably terrible for bringing you here." It was difficult to hear inside the cave of rippling water.

"Bringing me here?"

"Allowing you to stay!" Walker shook his head, riddled with pain and what looked to be distress. I sighed heavily and rolled my head across the makeshift pillow to look away. I'd heard this before. "No. Listen to me. You shouldn't be here."

"I know that! Everybody keeps telling me!"

"Because it's true, Wilde! Your fate is written, just like all of ours. And you're meddling with it!" I sat up, my jaw dropping. Who was he to tell me what I was meddling with?

"How do you know what my fate is?" I accused. The sky darkened outside our fortress of water.

"I mean, isn't it obvious? You're healed. You should go home now. I can't keep you here for myself. What do you think that would make me?" Walker held his arms wide in question, and Gunner inched toward him offering comfort.

"What do you mean? It wouldn't make you anything, because it's not your choice. I *want* to stay here with you. Are you saying that you've tried to hide your feelings toward me because you're afraid they would persuade me to stay in the afterlife?" Wouldn't that be a shame? If he'd had feelings for me all along, but hid them, making me feel like I wasn't worthy enough to penetrate his heart?

"I'm incapable of love, Wilde. What's the point of all this? As far as I can remember, my family has never had a love that lasted. I don't want to be the reason your heart breaks. We're not even the same kind of entity. It could never work beyond this *twisted* dream of yours."

"I don't believe that," I mumbled, taken aback by his confession. The vulnerability that washed over me was suffocating. We'd been living inside my dreams and haunted by my fears all summer long. I hoped he could feel the depth of my love for him, but all he saw was a twisted dream. That my love was wrong. I didn't know how to make it right.

He gave a resigned sigh. "My father disappeared when I was little," he began. I twisted his father's ring on my thumb, remembering when he'd given it to me.

"I know."

"I wasn't honest with you. While it's true he disappeared, it wasn't in the sense that I led you to believe. He was in an accident." He paused, pinching his bottom lip between his finger and thumb. "He was drunk and got behind the wheel. Nobody in the accident went home that night, or ever again."

"Oh. I see." It was starting to make sense. It must have made him wonder if his father had the chance to return to his family and decided not to. I could see why he encouraged me to go home.

"My mother, sister, and I had to survive without him. I was much too young to remember the immediate fallout, but I grew up in my father's shadow. I grew up watching my mother, a widow, and my little sister, fatherless. I could only imagine what happened to the other family who lost their other half. They didn't deserve it. *We* didn't deserve it."

"I'm so sorry. I didn't know." The walls of our water cave thickened, pumping copious amounts of fluid above our heads. What had started as streams of shooting water was now like being under a raging waterfall. It was thunderous and difficult to hear Walker's words of sorrow. Gunner tucked his tail, and I pulled the paddleboard closer to mine.

"I never drank much because of it, and when I bartended, I often hated the customers that frequented. I wondered how they were affecting their families and if they would ever leave them like my father had us. Of course, the apple never falls far from the tree. I thought by not drinking I could spare the life I was destined to repeat, but I didn't have to drink to destroy the lives around me. Falling asleep was just as dangerous."

"Is that what happened, you fell asleep?"

"Yes. I think so."

"It was an accident. You can't blame yourself for that." I was adamant that he understood that.

"I killed her. And I won't rest until I make it right."

I sucked in a sharp, painful breath. I now understood the depths of Walker's wounds. I knew why his brow would reopen and heal, only to split again. It was because his heart was broken, and it couldn't even begin to heal until Layla safely crossed over into the afterlife. It would never right his wrong, but it was a step in the right direction. Both of them remained in purgatory, waiting on the other's safe return.

I didn't suppose he had much room in his broken heart for me, I thought selfishly. But I couldn't think of myself right now. "How can I help?" I asked, fearful of what he would say next.

Walker sat up, suddenly alive with determination. "We have to get her through that door. It's the only way!"

I nodded eagerly. I was on board with this. I wanted to get her moving along just as much as he did, if not more. "We can do that. I'll get Emma, Scarlett May, and Noah to help us too. We already have a plan in the making."

"That's good. That's a start." Walker ran his hands through his hair, and I could tell he felt slightly better. I did too.

"Hey, Walker?" I asked after a moment of silence. "What would happen if I stayed? Would you feel the guilt like you felt for Layla all these years? I mean, could you ever be happy?" The mist peppered my face, and even though Walker had never fallen in the water, he was beginning to look damp, like he had taken a dip too. The water rumbled, and the cave-like structure continued to close in on us. I was eager to paddle out of my failed attempt at impressing Walker.

"I wasn't lying when I said I came from a long line of cursed love. If you stay, I will love you . . ." I tried to hide the smile budding on my face. "But I'll hate myself for what I've done to you."

I lurched forward. It was no way to live. The water turned dark and the tiny bits of sky that peeked through the fortress of water were nothing but shadows. "And if I go home?" I held my breath, awaiting his answer. The cave began to break apart and rain down on us.

"If you go, I will love you just the same. But every day will be gray, as I wander through eternity."

The water cave collapsed, as I could no longer think of anything other than my two dismal options. Like a tidal wave, the water crashed down upon us, tossing us from our boards and leaving us bobbing in its wake. In the haunted lake, as turbulent as the deep blue sea, we were no more than two lost souls.

5

"Are you sure this is going to work?" I asked, setting a candle down on the first step.

"Trust me," Scarlett May said confidently. Too confidently, if you ask me.

After my disastrous date last night, I'd spent a good hour crying on Emma's bed. Scarlett May had comforted me in a way she'd never done before. It reminded me of the time we had spent in the guest bathroom downstairs. The night Walker told me about Layla. She was comforting then, sympathetic even, but she still had her edge. I recalled her shoving me away from the door so she could escape when she so pleased. It was a brutal end to the endearing moment we had shared just moments before. But last night was different. She'd genuinely cared that my date had gone sideways, and she wanted desperately to help make it better.

If I was going to take advice from anybody on dating, it might as well be Scarlett May. With her short, wavy blonde hair, her killer legs, and her wicked sense of confidence in a pair of cowgirl boots, she was the queen of attraction. I had always thought that Trinity was more alluring, but that was in a mysterious, almost dangerous way. Scarlett May was the girl all the guys wanted to be with, and all the girls wished they had on speed dial. But her shell was too hard to crack for most. It had taken me months, and even then, I think the only real reason she opened up to me was because she had nobody else. Because Trinity and Kimber had found a way out of Baylor, leaving the rest of us behind.

Scarlett May had a reputation for being fun, and at times crazy. She was a lot closer to Trinity than Kimber. I think that may have been because they used to egg each other on. It was a sort of competition between the two that they liked to feed on. But even though Scarlett May had countless boyfriends before, she was far pickier than anybody realized. Even me.

I hadn't known the depths of Scarlett May's desire until we'd spent a night under the make-believe galaxy in Kimber and Asher's room. She had told me about Sampson, and I never would have guessed. She held him up on a pedestal, and even though she could have him as her boyfriend right now, she was waiting until she knew she could treat him the way he deserved. How a long-term relationship, or perhaps even marriage, deserved. I never expected that from her. She knew I thought the same of Walker, and that's why I put my trust in her tonight.

"But what about Noah? He can't be here. He'll ruin everything," I said, pulling another tea light from a cardboard box and placing it on the top step.

"Emma has Noah covered. She cut a wire in the golf cart and told him it wasn't running any longer."

"What!" I gasped.

"Yeah. They're off to the auto shop. It will take them forever to get there and back. Apparently, that kind of thing is an emergency," Scarlett May said, a proud smile stretching across her face.

"Well, yeah! What did she cut?" For a split second, I feared my parents would kill me. But then I realized they weren't a part of this world, and perhaps I would be dead in twenty-four hours anyway. I took a breath. Why was it Emma couldn't lie dormant when I wanted? How were any of them walking around when I wasn't dreaming them up? I winced. I didn't like the way it made me feel to think of such things. Like simply thinking about the dream state might pull me out of it. Take me somewhere closer to home, to the living. It made my head feel fuzzy and my fingers less dexterous. Maybe I was going dormant myself. *What a terrible thought . . .*

"How am I supposed to know? She just snipped something and then scratched the hell out of it to make it look like a rat gnawed it."

I rolled my eyes, thinking of the dozens of things she could have done to steal Noah away that had nothing to do with the golf cart. "Does Noah even know how to fix it? I thought he flunked auto shop?"

"Who cares? Get the rose petals."

I groaned but did as she said. Seeing the dozens of candles we had placed from the end of the dock to my bedroom, I suddenly grew nervous. Scarlett May began tossing flower petals on her way out of the cabin and onto the back patio. I went to the window and watched her lightly dust the dock in a covering of romantic red petals. Is this too much? It almost looked like a proposal of sorts. *Oh god, I hope I don't scare him off.* A wave of heat crept down my neck and spread across my back. I clasped the neck of the brown bag while I paced back and forth, fanning myself.

Several minutes later, Scarlett May walked in. "What are you doing? You haven't even done the stairs yet. I'm all out of petals." She raised her hands in frustration when she saw me just standing there.

"Is this a little overboard?" I asked warily.

"What? No!"

"I think I'm going to scare him off." In fact, I knew I would.

"Absolutely not. Don't be ridiculous. Give me your bag." She held her hand out.

Reluctantly, I passed her the bag of petals and followed her up the stairs. "He gave me this weird side hug yesterday. It was really awkward. And I think he hinted that expressing his emotions to me was a mistake. This whole thing might be a mistake. He's not going to like it. And if anything, it might push him away. It's all too much . . ."

"Hey. Stop that. That's just your insecurity talking. Remember what I said before? Just fake the confidence?"

I sat on the bed and nodded, trying desperately not to hyperventilate. The last thing I needed was a new nightmare to take hold.

"Most likely, if you're confident, he will follow your lead. So just fake it. Can you do that?"

I nodded once more, and Scarlett May continued to toss flower petals on the bed. *Oh god, not the bed.* What was he going to think?

She put a firm hand on my shoulder and looked me in the eye. "You've got this. You're going to snag his heart. And then tomorrow, he's going to follow you through that red door like a lost puppy." She smiled and then trailed off to dust the stairs with the last of the petals.

I slumped over, resting my chin on the palm of my hand. I had been manipulating the time in Baylor. Pushing the final showdown out by one day at a time. I needed more days. I wasn't nearly ready to face whatever waited for me at the state fair. If anybody found out that I was intentionally prolonging their time here, they would kill me themselves.

Walker wasn't going to follow me through the red door. But what if he did? Had it really been Walker's cursed heart that kept us apart? Because I was starting to believe it was *me* who was cursed. I had spent the last couple years pining after Noah, and he'd gone after a girl he could never truly have instead of me. Then, I fell for a ghost. What could be more unforgiving than that?

My life hung in the balance between life and death, and the only thing holding me on that balance beam was a phantom. Walker was more real to me than anyone else had ever been, and I was willing to put my life on the line for him, but he was still a ghost. He wasn't real in the world I came from. And most likely, he couldn't survive there. The only way to keep him alive was to join him.

I anxiously played with my fingers as I stared out the window, watching the bend around the cove. I watched as the sun glowed a bright fiery orange and then disappeared behind the forest. Walker would be here soon, and either the awkwardness we shared on our first date would grow into something insurmountable, or it would be squashed and . . .

I peeked at the bed covered in rose petals. My stomach turned at the very thought of us spending the night in that bed together. I knew I loved him, but I wasn't sure we were ready for this. For all of this, I thought, looking at the trail of petals and tea lights. This wasn't me.

Something was off between Walker and me. It had been that way since the night of the balloon festival when he saw me cloaked in the wolf's guise. I imagined it was quite the turnoff to see me as an ugly beast, but I feared it was much deeper than that. The thing that stood between us was a matter of fate. Something he saw and I didn't.

Something he told me I was meddling with. Surely, if I believed in fate, I wouldn't run up against it. But it was not something tangible to me. If it had been, I would bow at its feet and surrender. But fate was something that Walker had only spoken of in riddles, like a secret he kept locked in a box. Was there something he had been hiding from me? Did he know more than he let on? I would ask him tonight. If I was going to make a decision that affected the rest of my life, and possibly beyond, I needed to know what was in that box of his. I needed him to be as transparent as possible, even if it hurt.

My ears perked. I homed in on a melody far, far away, stealing my focus from the window. The sound wasn't just in my head, it was everywhere. It surrounded me from all directions. And it was just faint enough to take all my attention to listen. I turned my head slowly, trying to hear the melody better, but every direction was the same. It was on the tip of my tongue, a melody I recognized from my former life. But just as before, I couldn't pinpoint the origin. I closed my eyes and gently lifted my hand in the air, tracing the rhythm with my fingertips.

"We're all set. He should be here any minute!" I startled as Scarlett May clapped her hands behind me. I spun around to a room full of romantic ambiance and dancing shadows cast on the walls. I turned to peer out the window. She had lit the dock candles, too. A trail of warm glowing lights led down the grassy knoll toward the dock. I must admit, it was beautiful. Breathtaking even. I bit my lip, wondering what Walker would think. How he would feel.

"Thank you."

"I'm just going to wrap a few things up, and then I'll get out of here. I promise he won't even see me. I'll keep an eye out for him, and if I see him coming, I'll sneak out the front." Scarlett May waved her lighter at me and then disappeared. It was time. Ready or not, Walker would soon be paddling around the cove. I wondered if I would see his reaction from this distance. Would I be able to tell if he hesitated? Hesitating would be bad, I decided.

I pumped my hands open and closed, narrowing my eyes toward the bend of Rock Creek Cove. I could hear Scarlett May banging around in the kitchen as the haunting melody grew louder.

I tried not to get drawn in like before, but the more I pushed it away, the louder it sounded. My mind scraped at the edge of my callused memory. My past life seemed so far away, making it difficult to recall the nuances of my earlier years. But the memory was there, hidden in a dark forgotten corner, just waiting to be uncovered. As I tried to recall the distinct song and its origin, the words slowly came to me.

"My heart blooms. Blooms for you. Wildflowers because of you," I muttered with my eyes closed. The song grew louder, enveloping me in its lullaby.

It was a song my mother used to sing to me as a young child. It was a song she favored and played in the car during times when she felt melancholy. No matter how sad the song, singing it always seemed to make her feel better.

I breathed it in, each piano stroke moving me in a way that felt almost euphoric. The song surged as if I were standing in the middle of a symphony being performed in a grand opera house. The music echoing off the tall arching ceiling that I knew was not actually over my head as I stood in the cabin. Then, as clear as day, as clear as an unveiled realm, I heard my mom's voice. She serenaded me with the sweet chords of her favorite song. "My heart blooms. Blooms for you. Wildflowers because of you."

I brought my hand to my heart.

"Come back to me, baby," she whispered. My eyes flew open as my spirit dropped. I grabbed at my ear, still feeling the tickle in my hair where her whisper lingered. My heart pounded in my chest. I heard my mother's voice. Somehow, I knew it was happening at that exact moment, worlds apart.

"Mom?" I looked around the room frantically. Smoke billowed from under the bedroom door. "Mom!?" I called out, my voice now trembling with fear. *What was happening?*

I had not wanted to go home. Not until the connection with my mother was made. Now, I was torn. I wanted nothing more than to run into her arms. She called me to come home, and I wanted to answer that call.

"Mom, I'm here! I'm here!" I called out.

I closed my eyes and dug my fingernails into the meat of my palms. I tried desperately to connect with her again. But I could no longer hear her singing. And I could no longer feel her whisper upon my ear. "Mom . . . Don't go . . ." I murmured.

My panic grew as I smelled the smoke. This couldn't be happening. Everything I touched turned to dust. And everything I dreamed turned to nightmares.

I sprang into action, alarm growing as I grabbed the doorknob and felt the heat transmit through the metal. I opened the door to find flames blazing throughout the hall. Smoke filled my lungs, and I immediately started coughing. No. This couldn't be happening.

I covered my mouth with my hand and took one step into the hall before realizing I couldn't bear it. I jumped back, coughing and shielding my face. My eyes burned. I ran back to the window, hoping that Scarlett May had made her way out. I needed to get out too. I would have to jump. I grabbed the windowsill and tried to slide the window open, but it was locked. My fingers fumbled over the latch, but it wouldn't budge. How dare it slide open effortlessly when killer bees swarmed the eaves, yet stuck when I would surely burn alive.

"No!" I yelled.

The fire roared, and my heart drummed. I had to make it stop. But how? I ran my hands through my hair, grabbing my head and squeezing my eyes shut, and wished it all away. I wished everything to go back to normal. But this time, when I opened my eyes, nothing had changed. Despite the emergency, I couldn't push the connection I'd made with my mother away.

I hadn't felt her that close for so long. I had talked to her on the phone. I had even seen her in the hospital. I sat next to her as she wept for the health of her child. But I'd never *felt* her love. Not until now. I knew she was sitting there holding my hand as I lay unconscious in that hospital bed. I searched my hands, looking for hers in mine, but I couldn't see them.

"You should get some rest," I heard my dad say in that faraway land.

"Dad!" I called out, hysterical now. They were here. They were here with me, and I was closer to them than I had been this entire summer. I wanted to scrape through the veil that kept us apart and hug them. But . . . I remembered my promise to Walker—I wouldn't leave without saying goodbye.

My mouth grew dry, and the room grew dark with smoke. I coughed, lurching forward and grabbing at the window again. For a moment, time stood still. Walker paddled the canoe around the cove. And just as I imagined, he hesitated. But I couldn't think of that now. I pounded on the glass. "Walker! Walker! Help! Help!" I cried.

Slowly, he evaluated the glowing path of candles and flower petals, contemplating something that no longer mattered. Then he heard me.

"Help!" I yelled, pounding on the window, begging it to break and let fresh air in. Walker spotted me and immediately raced the rest of the way to the dock. He jumped out of the canoe and took off running toward the cabin. I spun around, hoping for help but expecting the worst.

Flames lurched from the walls and crept up to the ceiling. The heat was unbearable, but the smoke was the worst. I dropped to my knees, unable to breathe. I took quick but shallow breaths filled with soot. I felt it coat my lungs in black, suffocating death. My head grew light and my body weak.

"Mom . . ." I called out with what I was sure was my last breath.

"Wilde!" Walker yelled, running into the room. I whipped my head up to find the fire dissipating from raging flames to a soft yellow hue with the magic I knew Walker had secretly possessed.

My next breath was clean and oxygen rich. I sucked it in, panting frantically. The temperature dropped with every step Walker took toward me. He helped me to my feet, and I collapsed in his arms, crying.

"Shh. It's okay. I'm here."

"I miss my family," I cried. He squeezed me tighter, and I held on for dear life. Feeling torn in two. Is this what he felt like? Did he feel like his heart was torn between Layla and me? Just like mine had been torn between two worlds? It wasn't fair to either of us. Neither one of us could win.

"I know you do. I'm just glad you can see it now."

I buried my face in his shoulder until the tears ran dry and the depression sank in. When I finally opened my eyes, it was clear that even though the fire had cleared, the destruction remained. The walls were stained black, and I could see into the hall where everything appeared decimated. The more I tried in this world, the worse things became. And for the first time, I thought maybe I wasn't meant for this life after all. Maybe Walker was right. Maybe they all were.

Still weak in the legs, I let go of Walker and moved to assess the damage. With every step I took, I kicked ash into the air. Everything was crusted in black and burned to char. The staircase railing was gone, cannibalized by the hungry flames. I stepped slowly down the staircase, unsure if they could support my weight. They creaked and groaned, bowing under my feet. My foot broke through one step, but I managed to stay upright. I stepped gingerly down the last of the stairs.

Thick ash fluttered all around us like a snow globe, lightly dusting Walker's hair and smudging across his chin. I surveyed the den, which looked like the remains of the fireplace after a cold front. This was my home. Where was I supposed to live now?

My heart stopped as I spotted the toes of a beautiful pair of cowgirl boots peeking through the sea of ash.

I paused, feeling for Walker's hand. I grabbed hold of him and held him close as I kicked through the remains of the cabin to get to her. Scarlett May's body lay perfectly covered in soot and ash. Black from head to toe, still as a statue. I leaned closer, supporting myself with Walker's strength. I reached out with trembling hands to feel for a pulse on her neck. Just as my fingertips grazed her burnt skin, her eyes sprung wide open, stark white and beaming with fear. My heart seized.

"Ahh!" I screamed, springing backward and falling onto my butt.

"What? What is it?" Walker asked, kicking up a fine dusting of ash.

"Sss—shh—" I stammered, looking at Walker briefly, and then back to Scarlett May. My lips parted, but no words came out. Walker looked behind him to where Scarlett May's body had lain just seconds before. Of course, she was gone now. Nothing but a memory to haunt me. The ash lay flat; not even her boots remained.

"What is it, Wilde? What did you see?" Walker looked back and forth between me and the spot on the floor.

My mother sang. Her beautiful soft tone floated in the air, swirling, and mixing with the hideous, black death all around us. Creating something of a paradox, both hopeful and heartbreakingly tragic. The end, and yet still, a new beginning. "My heart blooms. Blooms for you. Wildflowers because of you."

Walker looked all around him now, even more confused than before. Could he hear it too? His lackluster golden eyes settled on me.

"Do you hear it?" I asked.

"She's calling you..." he said, as he lifted a soot-stained hand and cupped my cheek. "She's calling you home." His brows furrowed, creating a deep line of pain. I rested my heavy head in the palm of his hand and found my tears once more.

6

A new day is a symbol of new beginnings. With the rising sun comes hope, change, and opportunity. But there was something off about the sun in Baylor. As if it were hidden behind a silkscreen, the sun's optimism never struck Rock Creek Cove. It never bestowed its magical powers of renewal upon me and my friends. And with each rising sun came not only a new day, but a new challenge. A new struggle. A new nightmare.

As I walked through the cabin, the morning light filtering through broken glass windows and I saw not an opportunity to seize the day, but the ruin that I had caused from my own self-interest.

I eased my way down the stairs, testing my weight on each decrepit board. The ash still floated in tiny particles, like a snow globe of horror, and there was a chill in the cabin that seeped deep into my bones. I had the distinct feeling that I would not be warm in Baylor again. The state fair was tomorrow, yet again. And for the first time, I wanted no more delay. I wasn't ready for what was to come, but I could no longer stay here. I finally saw what everybody else had been telling me; Baylor was a dreadful place.

The cabin walls looked as if they were painted black, and the ceilings were peppered with swatches—lashings from the flames. The air was desperate and cold, even in the peak of summer. I felt an ache in my heart that I could only describe as being lonely. Not the typical loneliness one would reflect upon in a time of solitude, but the god-awful kind that is sometimes felt in a room full of people.

For the first time this summer, I realized that I wasn't here with my group of friends—my family of misfits. I was here by myself. There was truly nobody here except me and my own rambling thoughts.

And what a scary thought, to be in a remote cabin for an entire summer with nothing but ghost stories to fill your mind. Haunting you with illusions from your subconscious, twisting and contorting in ways they were never meant to be. What had I done to myself? Why did I have to dream at all? And how could I make it stop?

I snuck behind Emma as she kneeled over a small black puddle in the kitchen. She knelt in a mound of ash that covered the balls of her bare feet. The back of her head bobbed up and down mechanically. There was a wash bucket to her side and a stained rag in her hands. She scrubbed the floor in tiny circles as she wept.

The cabin was charred black, and piles of ash littered the floor. The sofa was mostly disintegrated, with a small piece of armrest sitting on the ruined floor. The pool table was gone, the windows were broken, and the doorframe to the back patio was hanging at a slant with no door to help support it. The fog wafted in the house having no protection from the outside elements.

I didn't know how long I watched Emma scrub the floor, wring the rag out in the bucket, and begin again. There was something about the sight of a broken soul, endlessly working toward something that could never be fixed that captured me. Hadn't she seen the destruction? Couldn't she tell it wasn't worth the effort? That it was impossible to do so? Or was she simply the small part of me that wanted to salvage this place? A tiny piece of me that clung to the idea of living in a fantasy.

I approached her slowly as she hunched over the never-ending task. By the time I was in front of her, my shoes nearly in her path, it was clear that she was refusing to acknowledge me. She sobbed gently as she scrubbed the same square foot back and forth.

I opened my mouth to say her name, but my breath hitched in my throat. What could I say? Nothing could fix this. Maybe that was the reason she wouldn't look at me. Because she knew I'd gotten her into this mess, and I was more caught up in my love affair than getting her out of this place.

After a long moment, I left for the fair. I had to do everything in my power to get Emma and Noah out of here. Even if they were just pieces of me, just figments of my imagination, I still owed it to them. To me. I deserved better than this. And they certainly did. I couldn't stand around and watch them deconstruct into apathetic robots. I had to help them, and Gunner too.

There was just one thing I had to do first. I had to find my gran. Maybe there was a deal I could strike with her. Maybe she would help release Noah and Emma and open the door for Walker and Layla in exchange for my coming home. Could she do that? It was my selfishness that continued to make a bad place worse. I'd been so caught up in where I belonged, I'd lost sight of everybody else. I made my decision; I would get everybody home, regardless of which realm I ended up in.

I stepped to the doorway and stood within the collapsing frame, surveying the view. The deck was gone, and the drop was some five to six feet to the ground. Noah threw a handful of two-by-fours onto the grass and sighed heavily. He scratched his head, staring at the empty space where the deck had once been. Defeat was etched in the lines of his forehead as he dragged his hand down the side of his face. He wasn't handling this well.

Noah was great at football, even better at swimming. He was a decent fisherman, I thought. But he was *not* capable with mechanics and construction. Yet there he stood, just like Emma, trying to fix what I had broken. I cleared my throat, but he didn't look up. A recurring theme this morning.

Rose petals were scattered across the yard, pinched between wet blades of grass. Metal tins from the tea lights were scattered in a trail that led to the dock. And a blanket of fog covered the lake as a pair of loons swam near shore. I had an odd sense that somebody was watching me. And since Noah and Emma had yet to acknowledge me, I searched the surrounding area.

I wasn't surprised to find Layla standing just at the edge of the forest. Without thought, I jumped, landing next to a pile of charred patio furniture. Though I was right in front of Noah now, he seemingly never saw me. I plodded past him, watching for signs of life, but his eyes never lifted, and his demeanor never changed. I didn't think it was possible to feel lonelier than I did last night, but I was wrong.

As I crossed the yard to Layla, I passed Gunner ferociously digging a hole, pausing only to shove his nose deep inside. I patted my leg inconspicuously, fearing he would reject me, too. For a second I thought his ears perked when I beckoned him, but it was something in the hole that piqued his attention. Was I the ghost now? Was that my punishment for not returning home when I was called to do so?

Layla turned and disappeared into the gloom of the forest. There was no reason for me to stay here any longer. Nobody even knew I was there. I took off at a jog to catch her. Somehow, she had always been the answer to all of this. Yet for most of the summer I avoided her. I saw her, and I ran the other way. I had even admonished her with lightning.

And now, just like in the beginning of summer, I chased her. I needed her more now than ever before. *I* needed *her*. Not because my gran told me so, but because Walker needed it as a condition to move on. She was the key to unlocking him from his prison. Plus, if I was honest with myself, the girl didn't deserve to live in a realm where nobody acknowledged her. I'd just had a small taste of that myself, and it was far more miserable than any wolf or ghoul of the lake. Being invisible was the worst kind of torment.

I ran straight into the disorienting fog, chasing hints of long brown locks as they whisked through the trees. I couldn't tell which direction I had been running, but it felt like I was going in circles. I was briefly aware of the apple tree that we'd planted for Lainey. Its red, luscious apples were more than alluring in the sea of gray fog. But I knew one bite would be the end of me here.

My legs never slowed as I kept my eyes on the flashes of Layla's back. If I could just get Layla through the portal, I was sure all the other pieces would fall into place.

The stone tower appeared down the same trail as the poisonous apple tree. Two things I knew were not near each other. I ran by the massive tower, noting the side was still blown out from where Big Jimmy had crashed through and fallen to his death. Would his body lie at the base now? A disturbing image to throw me off my hunt? No. There was nothing there except the rapunzel flowers.

Layla stopped behind a large tree, and her pale face peeked from behind the trunk. *I'm coming.* No matter how many times she stopped to check if I was following, the distance between us remained the same. She never ventured too far from the trail, and I could keep up a steady jog without having to tramp through the bushes.

Small dome-shaped figures appeared between the trees, and I recognized them as headstones of the hidden cemetery. Of all the things I had seen on this run, the cemetery was by far the most distracting. My pace slowed.

I wanted to see if Scarlett May's name was etched on one of the markers. Layla's sinister laugh echoed through the forest. I looked up into the trees. The cemetery, the tower, the apple tree. I wasn't running through the forest; I was running through my memory. No matter how fast my legs carried me, I would not catch up to Layla until she was ready. Until *I* was ready.

What seemed to be an endless task, Layla playing hide-and-seek and me chasing a girl who didn't want to be caught, finally came to an end. I found her in a clearing, waiting for me. I slowed my jog to a walk and approached her carefully. I didn't want to spook her.

She looked around warily, as if she was frightened. But I knew that couldn't be true. She possessed just as much power as I did, if not more. She did not need to be afraid of me. And it worried me she might be afraid of something else. Something bigger than either of us.

Layla sized me up, as I did her. My heart hammered in my chest. She was only a few strides away, but I knew if I tried to grab her, I could not hold her long.

"I don't want to play anymore," she said through gritted teeth. "I'm done!" Her intense glower had me turning away and cowering, but she materialized in front of me, closing the small gap between us.

She was done? That was good news. I didn't want to play her games either. I searched her eyes, hoping to talk to the girl, but she looked . . . hostile. It put me on edge. She loathed me. But it didn't have to be this way. If only she knew I wanted to help her find peace. That I realized perhaps she'd been right all along, and I didn't belong in her world. I wanted to say something to make her understand, but she was such a flight risk, I didn't know how to start.

Her weight shifted back and forth as if she was getting ready to run. In the distance, a branch snapped, stealing my attention away. Walker's silhouette spun around on a ridge. He was looking for something. The fog surrounded him with somewhat of an ethereal glow. What was he doing out here? He cupped his hands around his mouth and called out, but I couldn't hear a single word.

"What have you done?" Layla demanded of me. She took a deranged swipe at me. Her hand passed through me like thin air. Her ghostly claws couldn't scathe me, and for that, I was grateful. She eyed Walker nervously and swiped at me again. She was almost helpless. I could see it in her eyes. For the first time, it seemed that I held the power between us. There was no reason for me to fear her. Not today, at least. Still, I didn't know what to do. Should I grab her? What would I do then? Clamp my hand around her tiny wrist and drag her to the state fair, searching for the red door?

"Please . . .," I muttered. *Come on . . . Do better than that.* I had to fake the confidence if it wasn't there naturally.

"Walker!" she yelled, trying to grab his attention. He ran his hands through his hair and called out in silence again.

What was happening? Why did she want Walker to see us? She never wanted him to see her. And why couldn't he hear us? And then I thought of the most important question—why was *she* afraid of *me*? Something was terribly off and yet familiar all the same. It was almost as if I had been here before.

Walker wandered aimlessly, weaving in and out of the trees, yelling my name silently. Layla and I watched as he came close enough that either of us could reach out and touch him. But his eyes were frightened as he passed by, and I didn't dare grab his arm. A chill ran down my spine. Had Layla and I become two of the same kind? Invisible? Forgotten? Undeserving, perhaps? Were we now both under Walker's curse?

I looked at Layla, and her brown eyes appeared to soften. She was hurting, just as I was. We seemed to recognize that pain in one another. I watched her face as the demarcations of her brows lightened and her eyes drooped with sadness. For the first time, Layla and I were in the same boat. We were both invisible to the outside world, both hurting, both trapped, and neither of us wanted it any longer.

My eyes watered with sympathy for this lonesome girl and all the pain she must have lived through. Walker passed by again, leaving nothing but a chill in his wake. I lifted a hand ever so slightly, touching the slight breeze as he passed by.

"You don't belong here," I said, my voice small and empathetic. She looked at me as if she could not hear me either. As if my lips moved in opposition to my words. The fog had blanketed more than just the forest. It muffled our hearing and drowned out our voices.

I searched for other ways to communicate. I patted my jacket, feeling for a pen or notepad. Could I manifest them?

Walker stiffened, and I could tell something had alarmed him, but I didn't know what. He took off running in the direction he'd come from, causing Layla to look more worried than before. I could tell she was about to run. I found what I was looking for just in time.

In my hands was the old worn book, *Waking Dreams*. The familiar sharp, penetrating pain of an oncoming headache pierced my head, and I winced. I had no time to wonder how I'd gotten the book. I scribbled down the message on a random page. *You don't belong here.*

I hoped it would be enough for her to realize that I wanted to help. She needed to know she could trust me. I tore the page from the weathered book, and several more pages came out with it. They swept into the air with a gust of wind and fluttered down to the ground.

"No!" I reached out.

Layla dropped to her knees, grasping at all the pages, desperately seeking a way to communicate.

"I can help you. I know how to get you home . . . if you let me," I said.

She never looked up. More like she couldn't see me anymore. She had the same distant gaze in her eyes that I'd seen in Noah, and eventually Walker.

Her brown eyes saw through me effortlessly. I watched as her trembling hands grasped at the pages, flipping them over and looking for anything that could help her communicate. I stepped closer, peering over her shoulder as the published print disappeared, leaving only my handwritten note.

"You don't belong here," she whispered.

"You don't!" I murmured over her shoulder. She paused for a moment, and I thought maybe she had heard me. Then she swiftly jumped to her feet and took off running in the direction that Walker had last been seen. In her absence, I found a mound of soil, sticks, and dried pine needles covering the extra pages that had fallen from the book. She'd buried them? Why?

As I stood alone, bewildered by her actions, I turned to the book that I had once coveted. But it was not the mysterious book that took my breath away; it was the crimson velvet of my sleeves. I shuddered as I looked down to find myself draped in a red cloak.

My hair lifted in curled locks, and a weird energy buzzed around me. The locks of hair danced above my shoulders like the snakes on Medusa's head. I *had* been here before, just not in this body.

Power surged through me. My skin buzzed with pure energy. I felt oddly unstable. Fluid-like. As if I could be swept away in a gust of wind. I felt strong, yet incapable. I couldn't make myself be seen or heard, but I was still mighty. Almost too big for my body. *Her* body.

I followed Layla through the forest, more determined than ever. This time, she didn't run, and she didn't look back to see if I was following her. Was *I* Layla now? Had I somehow changed spirits with Walker's past love? Was that the only way to set her free? To take her place in the invisible and forgotten realm in which she lived?

My insides fell hollow at the very thought. I asked for this, hadn't I? I asked for Walker to be happy. It was my one wish upon a shooting star. Of course, I wanted it to be with me. But I would sacrifice myself to give him Layla back—if that was truly what he wanted.

I watched Layla from behind, dusting her palms on the back of her jeans as she hesitated before joining Walker by the shore. I crested the ridge just in time to see them reunite, and it hurt more deeply than I could've ever imagined.

"Are you all right?" Walker ran up to her. I had no difficulty hearing him, now that I was out of the clearing with the weird energy buzzing in the air. He looked concerned for her well-being, rightly so, as she had been missing for decades. "What happened?" he asked, taking her hands in his. He examined the dirt that dusted her pale skin. I leaned against a tree and sucked in a quivering breath. I wiped away a fallen tear with the soft velvet of my sleeve. *So this was sacrifice . . .*

Broken clay pigeons were scattered across the tiny cove, and Walker's canoe was pulled on shore. I remembered this very well now. This was the day he'd taught me how to hone my magic.

Walker picked up a clay pigeon and tossed it into the air. Layla fired at it with a flick of her wrist, a natural at magic. Could he not see that he was with Layla? Did he think she was me? And was she going to pretend she was?

I had half a mind to step out from the elusive forest and unveil myself as the true Kinsley Wilde. I took a small step forward, but something stopped me. Walker laughed. He was happy.

"I don't deserve you," he said to her. I crouched forward, hanging on each spoken word.

"That's not true! Don't talk like that," Layla snapped. Walker's shoulders drooped.

"Did you see her?" He threw another chip of a clay.

"Yes." Layla broke the disk into tiny shards, and they rained down on the lake like hail.

"Did *she* see *you*?" he asked.

"Yes."

What was this? I inched forward.

"And?"

"Nothing. She doesn't get it."

Walker's shoulders slumped, and he seemed to curl in on himself. He was more defeated now than I had seen him in the past. "She doesn't know me like she thinks she does."

"Then show her!" Layla said, visibly stressed.

"I'm trying! She only sees what she wants to see. Nothing more!" Walker pressed the heels of his palms against his eyes.

"And what is that?" Layla checked behind her shoulder nervously, and I darted behind a tree, pulling the hood of the red cloak over my head. I felt every bit like a dirty secret hiding within the haunted forest.

"She wants me to be her protector. She wants me to be the good guy. But I'm not. And honestly, a part of me is afraid she'll find out. I don't know what to do anymore."

Walker threw a piece of clay angrily, and it exploded into tiny bits all on its own. I couldn't believe my eyes. He had his own magic! He *had* been holding out on me. But why?

"She wants the man of her dreams. Can you blame her?" Layla asked, her tone warm with compassion to counteract Walker's rising frustration.

"No. I guess not. It's her dream after all. She controls what she sees and what she doesn't." Layla nodded and placed a hand on his shoulder. "She just wants a hero. She wants to be loved for all that she is, but more importantly, all that she's not."

I grabbed my chest, right where my heart would be if I had one. This hurt more than a thousand knives in the back.

"Yeah. I think you're right."

Layla rubbed Walker's shoulder, and then her hand trailed down his back. My chest cinched tighter.

Why were they talking about me like this? How come he never told me he had been in contact with Layla all this time? Had I truly only seen the things I wanted? Surely, I never wanted a fire to rip through the cabin and scorch Scarlett May, turning her to ash in a pair of cowgirl boots.

If I could see all the horror in Baylor, then why couldn't I see the truth? It couldn't have been as scary as everything else I'd witnessed this summer. I watched intently, as if seeing for the first time the other side of the coin. A part of my world that I had unknowingly hidden from myself.

"Do you *truly* love me, Walker?" Layla asked, looking deep into his eyes. My mouth fell open.

"I have loved you for more lifetimes than you can remember . . ." Walker said in a husky voice. He melted at her side.

I definitely did not belong here!

"Then how do we get home? Because I'm losing hope."

"I know. I know."

"I'm scheduled to be home tomorrow," Layla shook her head, as if it were an impossible feat.

"I promise. I'll get you there." Walker bowed his head until his forehead met hers.

I had to get away. I didn't even know what I was fighting for anymore. I would find that door tomorrow, and I would run straight for it. Any world would be better than this. And nothing else mattered.

"And you won't be far behind me?" she asked.

"I promise. If you go, so will I," he said.

I took a step backward and tripped over the tail of the crimson cloak. It ripped off my back, and I took off running through the mysterious forest of memory, fearful that they had heard me stumble.

7

I ran through the forest as fast as my legs could take me. I ran through the rapunzel bushes and over the fallen trees. I ran aimlessly. Baylor was like a web spun just for me. Ensnaring me deep within its deadly trap. And I was stuck there now, not knowing which turn would set me free and which would entangle me more. I feared I'd never get out alive.

The part I couldn't bring myself to understand was that, in this scenario, I wasn't just a moth fighting for my life. I was also the spider, trying to end it. My wings were bound, and I was trapped in what could very well be a deadly nightmare. But wings aside, I also had short poisonous fangs, and I was eager to live a life full of magic, both dark and light. If I died now, it would be by the bite of my own dark side. My fault, and nobody else's.

The fog was so dense in the forest that all I could make out was white mist and varying shadows of gray and dark green. The moist air felt as if my lungs were coating with water, slowly dry drowning as I ran.

Which way? Did it even matter? I had followed Layla out to the ridge in what seemed to be a giant circle that was even more disorienting now as I ran away. I had fallen asleep in one place and woken up countless times in another place altogether. Sometimes even an entirely separate realm. The land of the living, the land of my past. I supposed it didn't matter which way I ran. I would wind up wherever my mind took me, regardless.

I recognized the tall stone tower just breaching my vision. I ran straight for it, hoping for answers. What would I find inside? What could I see from the window? And most importantly, would I find a red door? I was certainly ready for my escape. Would it be as simple as my willingness to depart? I doubted it.

I stopped several feet away, checking over my shoulder to make sure I hadn't been followed. When I confirmed the coast was clear, I approached the tower and placed my hand on the stone, feeling its warmth where cool had been expected. These were no normal stones that made up the disappearing tower.

I circled the base, looking for the hidden door. The door that hadn't been available the first time I'd seen the tower. I reached out to grab the corroded doorknob, my hand hesitating just above the metal. Though I felt ready to find the portal home, I was still afraid. In a split second of courage, I grasped the doorknob, ready to meet my fate.

The knob shook with anger. I couldn't pull my hand away. The whole door trembled, and the force exploded up the tower. Dust plumed at the base of the structure as it shook wildly out of control. I tried to pull back but couldn't free myself. My hand was locked in place, cemented by the choice I'd made to enter.

The tower began to crumble, top to bottom. The stones fell to the ground, and the door splintered into shards. I coughed as the dust enveloped me. I was finally able to pull my hand back to hide my face in the crook of my elbow, but the rusted doorknob came with me, still secured within my grasp.

My feet were covered in heavy stone, and it took several tries to pull them free. This wasn't my portal after all. This wasn't my chance to get back home. When the dust settled, there was no pile of collapsed rocks left behind. There was no evidence of the fairytale tower, but for a corroded door handle held tightly in my hand. I threw the old piece of metal as hard as I could and wiped orange rust off my skin. Was nothing safe from my destruction?

I walked down the trail, my head hanging. I was no longer in a hurry. I wasn't sure anything mattered anymore. No amount of effort ever seemed to be enough.

I kicked a pine cone as I walked down a winding trail. Why would Walker hide his magic from me? It could have been fun to learn together. I should have questioned how he knew how to teach me. I should have questioned a lot of things. But I was terribly naïve.

Layla had magic in her, too. That I knew from the shapeshifting, the disappearing acts, and our showdown at the balloon festival when she'd said I was going to ruin everything. *What did that even mean? What was I going to ruin?*

What did Walker mean when he said, *she only sees what she wants to see*?

So much of my reality was false. Make-believe. Was it even possible to see the truth under such circumstances as these?

I didn't know what to believe anymore. The brief conversation that I'd spied on had me spinning. Everything I thought I'd known this entire summer was flipped upside down and turned inside out in the few minutes I watched

Layla and Walker. I wanted so desperately to speak with Walker, but the *old* Walker. The Walker that I knew to be true. Not the stranger I had seen on the ridge who spoke of me like a blind idiot.

Did I still love him? I rubbed my forehead, kneading the tension that was building into a headache. My shoulders slumped in defeat. I wasn't sure the man of my dreams existed anymore. Maybe that's why they called him the Phantom of Baylor Lake; because he was delusion in disguise.

It was then that I noticed a gigantic red, glistening apple hanging just within my reach. There were a dozen of them. Twelve of the most sinfully alluring pieces of fruit I had ever seen. My mouth watered at the very sight. Was this it? Was this the way home? A bite of a poisonous apple? Sure, it would end my life here in Baylor. But would I go home, or would I be doomed to stay here and be on the invisible side of Walker's curse?

I reached up and touched the apple gently. It dropped almost willingly into my hand. The skin was bright red with small veins of burgundy. A sheen covered the apple like a coating of clear resin, and the most perfect stem sprouted from the small dip at the top. It seemed ironic that, though I held the most beautiful poisonous apple in my hand, it was my mouth that flooded with venom.

I wasn't sure what would happen to me if I took a deadly bite, but things couldn't keep going the way they had been. And I couldn't stop my mouth from opening.

An unknown force pulled at my hand, drawing the apple toward my mouth. I closed my eyes and felt the apple bump against my teeth. But as I bit down, expecting the sweetness to dance across my tongue and course through my veins, all I got was a mouthful of smoke. A hot, vile vapor filled my mouth. I shook my head, trying to escape the taste of rot and sulfur.

"No!" I shouted to the sky. This couldn't be happening!

I jumped to grab the next hanging apple. I bit into it, hungry, desperate. But just as my teeth touched the apple skin, the entire fruit bled into black vapor, and a putrid, rotten taste coated my mouth and tongue.

I spun around, spitting into the dirt. My stomach wrenching as I dry-heaved. With tears in my eyes, I watched the apple tree vanish.

"No!" I yelled again, but there was no one to hear.

I picked up a rock and threw it angrily. A blue vein of electricity ignited, lighting the base of the now invisible tree and branching out to the tips of each leaf. My tears stopped immediately; my anger replaced by curiosity. I wiped the wetness from my cheeks as I walked toward the tree, still invisible to the naked eye.

Slowly I reached my hands out, taking tiny blind steps until I found the tree trunk. As soon as my hands touched the bark, the same veins of electricity ignited, lighting up the tree once again. But this time, the energy seemed to eat away at the memory. My hands sank through the trunk, and there was no longer any evidence of the memorial we'd planted for Lainey.

How I missed Lainey now. I wished she was back at the cabin so I could talk to her. Pour my heart out. Even though she'd be afraid, I knew she would be there for me. But then I thought of Emma as I left her, scrubbing the floors of the cabin. She hadn't even looked at me. Had she been angry with me for getting her stuck in Baylor? Or had I been a ghost that she could no longer recognize? I wondered if that would have happened to Lainey, too.

I continued walking, the fog parting with my steps. I didn't stop for the cemetery when I saw the headstones, I just sighed and looked away. I could barely see them from the corner of my eye as they shook and crumbled to the ground. The world I created and lived in was evaporating. And pretty soon, so would I.

When I finally looked toward the graveyard, there was nothing there. There would be no more headstones marked with a terrible fate, and I would never get to see how I died. Though if I was taken right now, I guessed my headstone would read, *Taken an Outcast*. Because that's all I was anymore. I hung my head, kicking up dust as I moseyed down the trail until I finally stumbled home. I was somewhat surprised to see Noah still scratching his head, staring at the same pile of two-by-fours he'd dropped on the ground. Gunner barked at the same hole he had been digging in when I left. He shoved his nose inside, sniffing eagerly. Had time passed at all, or was that broken too?

The hole didn't appear to have deepened since I left. I patted my leg, but Gunner's eyes never so much as shifted from the hole. "Hey, buddy," I said. When nothing changed, I pet his wiry head. I stroked him gently until his head fell from beneath my hand and his nose pushed deep into the hole. I used to think being invisible would suit me, but now I knew it didn't. Everybody wanted to be seen to some extent.

Without the back deck, I had no way of getting to the collapsed patio door. I walked past Noah and headed to the front of the cabin. It appeared the cabin was frozen—not in time, but in a moment. A moment of desperation and destruction. The ash had not settled to the floor but still floated, as if it were never-ending. The air was still thick with smoke, and the same chill wafted in through the broken windows. It did not surprise me to see Emma where I had last seen her, her back hunched over a wash bucket as she scrubbed the same square foot of floor.

"Emma?" She sobbed quietly as she wrung out the black-stained towel. Her hands were red and raw. "Emma, can you hear me?"

I kneeled to see her eyes, and for just a moment she paused. My breath caught. *Please hear me.* My chest tightened with smoke. I reached my hand out, grabbed her shoulder, and squeezed. Emma let out a hoarse sob, as if she had been crying for hours, and her voice was wearing thin.

"Emma! Emma, wake up! It's me!" I shook her violently, but she just stared blankly. I knew she was in there. I knew it.

"Emma?" I watched intently as she continued to scrub the floor without so much as a look of confusion. Wherever Emma was now, it was far away from here.

I was trying to devise a plan to drag Emma out of the cabin when I heard voices outside. I peered out the misshapen door that overlooked the lake and saw Walker and Layla paddling to the dock. My heart thumped in my chest. Layla looked just like me. She was going to fool everyone.

Noah's head lifted, and he turned to watch the canoe approach as if he was waking from a stupor. Frightened, I spun to see Emma toss the rag into the bucket of water and wipe her hands across her jeans. They were waking up! I had to get out of here before they saw me!

I heard the bustling sound of laughter and something in the distance that reminded me of a video game I'd once played with my little brother. As I ran to the front door, I could hear the drone of the bees. The faintest, ghostly outline of Asher walked up the stairs, holding onto an invisible banister. My heartbeat floundered and tried desperately to find its rhythm.

I got the front door open and ran up the driveway, batting my hands at the rogue bees swooping down at me. Looking back at the cabin, I caught a glimpse of the pale outlines of Noah and Kai, dressed in layered clothing and throwing rocks at the hive nestled in the eaves. I ran for the woods, where I knew the shadows would hide me.

Of course, Asher and Kai had died long ago. I was no longer living a linear dream. My timelines were bending like origami creatures, and the entire summer's manifestations were folding in on themselves. The old was mixing with the new in impossible ways, and the dead were walking with the living. If I knew one thing, it was that I didn't want to stick around to see how it ended.

"Mom? Dad?" I yelled into the labyrinth of forest. My voice echoed, bouncing off the trees.

"Get me out of here! I want to go home! I want to go home!" I screamed.

I stopped to bellow out my last plea. "Please! Take me home!" My voice splintered into a million cries, and I prayed they were strong enough to be heard in the realms beyond this one.

8

My fists were balled as I screamed into the night, demanding that I be freed. The dense fog gave way to the dark of night, and a stillness came over the wilderness. The critters hid, and the leaves stilled. I thought of giving up. If I lay at the base of a boulder, nestled in brush and pine cones, would anybody ever find me? Or would I be lost forever?

I wondered if I would ever talk to Walker again, and guilt washed over me for trying to leave without saying goodbye. I rarely made promises, and I had no intention of breaking this one. There was still a part of me that needed him and hated the thought of running away. I had done it once before, and to my regret, I caused an entire plane to crash to smithereens. I killed people. A lot of them.

I knew I was capable of great things, but it seemed to only be for the dark. Not once had I made something so beautiful and life-changing here that I could say I was proud of myself. I thought that maybe falling in love would be the beautiful thing that made it all worth it. And it certainly would have been life-changing, had it not been fake.

But I'd been so gaslit by the Baylor phenomenon that I'd fallen in love with an idea, not a guy. I reminded myself that the entire manifestation of Walker St. James was fake, because believing that he was both real and lying to me was far too hurtful. I thought of all the warnings that Walker had given me. He tried to warn me, but it was no good. I ignored them all. And yet, there was still a small voice in my head that said to ignore them now, despite what I had seen. To love him fiercely for the person I knew him to be. The person he *could* be.

I sat down, leaning back against a fallen tree trunk, my head in my hands. It was one thing to be living in a nightmare, but an entirely different thing to fall in love with somebody who didn't exist. To be so willing to open up to a person you could only see half of. I only saw half of Walker. The other half had been with Layla.

I drew in the dirt with a twig, making small broken hearts and zigzags, just to wipe them clean. I willed my gran to visit. I tried to manifest a red door. The hospital. And eventually, after nothing worked, I settled for listening for my mother's distant song. When not even her melody would come to comfort me, hollowness spread throughout my chest, and my body numbed.

I waited on the forest floor for what felt like hours until something finally changed. A clatter sounded in the distance. Clanking and clatter of mass commotion. My back straightened as I turned my head like radar, trying to locate the direction of the living. A small light emanated from between the trees and flickered with shades of blue and green. Like a moth to the light, it drew me through the forest.

As I stepped out of the hidden woods into a secret clearing, carnival music sprang to life. The smell of buttered popcorn and livestock hung in the air. The loud drone of generators hummed near and far. I'd finally made it to the Summerfield State Fair. Or rather, the fair had finally made its way to me.

I lingered in the shadows, tucked between the forest and portable restrooms that skirted the fairground. I surveyed my surroundings, immediately searching for some type of portal to get me home. The only one I knew of came in the shape of a red door. But were there others? Perhaps a picture booth? Or a fortune teller?

Lights percolated on a massive Ferris wheel that seemed to arch over the entire fairgrounds like a radiant rainbow. I stared in awe as my stomach turned in on itself. It was difficult to see all the fair had to offer, but the Ferris wheel couldn't be missed. It stood four times taller than anything else in the clearing, and it matched the vision that had been burned into my memory from the first night I drowned. It was hard to pull my eyes away, as the ride both terrified and excited me. The sheer height of the wheel was enough to make me tremble. Adding my fear of heights to the terror of meeting my unknown fate, it would be next to impossible to take a seat on the ride.

I took a deep breath and stepped out of the shadows. A father walked by with a young boy sitting on his shoulders, and I stepped back to let them pass. A mixed group of pre-teens approached, and I lurched forward, zigzagging in and around the traffic. A girl passed on the arm of her boyfriend as she ate a cloud of pink cotton candy. And for just a moment, it made me miss Walker.

I ran my hands through my hair, determined to stay strong. I was looking for a red door, and I needed to focus. It was proving more difficult than I thought. I spun when I heard the screams. A group was riding the swings, there screams whirring by. A wave of terror washed over me, and I felt my heartbeat quicken at the perceived threat. This didn't feel like fun.

I hated these rides. There were so many people and so many lights. The quick pace of the music and the tinny high notes made me anxious. I felt the familiar crawl of a dull ache spread across the back of my head, and I knew I would be riddled with a migraine soon. I used the pain to propel me forward.

I walked quickly, surveying the crowds. My eyes bounced from face to face, hardly seeing the people passing by. There must've been thousands of them. I didn't recognize a single one until my sight fell upon Mr. Vandal. Our eyes met and locked. He'd been watching me. He averted his gaze and then checked back to see if I was still watching him. My step faltered at the sight of him, but I continued searching; he wasn't the one I was after.

I passed a petting zoo, weaving in and out of the small children lined up to get their hands on a dusty goat. I scanned the shadows behind the pen and peered through the lines of people. I searched the hidden corners of the grounds and searched in plain sight, but I could not find a way home. I finally made my way to the Ferris wheel, following the lights like the North Star.

I wished my gran were here to guide me—if only to tell me I was on the right track. To hold my hand in a moment of uncertainty. Just then, I remembered how Gran had told me to lean into my weakness. It wasn't something I was comfortable with, and I eyed the Ferris wheel with trepidation. Even though Gran wasn't with me now, the memory of her wisdom was almost as good as her presence. Screams, followed by laughter, erupted from the building next to me. It was a funhouse of mirrors. I winced. *Who liked these things?*

I saw the back of a guy who seemed familiar to me; tall, broad shoulders, and black hair. He reminded me of Kai. Before I knew it, I was in line, pushing through people and trying to catch up to the stranger. The guy disappeared into the funhouse as I got stuck in the crowd. A girl shoved me with her elbow and gave me a dirty scowl. It reminded me I was in a line full of people who had been waiting their turn. I shrank back and waited like everyone else while I drummed my hands against my thighs. Manners seemed so insignificant at a time like this, still I complied.

When it was finally my turn to enter the dark, strobed building, I parted from the crowd at the first available turn. "Kai!?" I called, but the carnival music was too loud and drowned out my voice.

I saw the crowd in front of me disappear around a dark corner, and I turned away, finding myself boxed into a small room of mirrors. I had never wanted to see so many versions of myself, but there I was, extrapolated by the dozens. I tried not to look too closely, for fear my subconscious would take over. The best thing for me now would be to have no reflection at all. I never imagined I would long for the days when I thought I was soulless, but here I was, having the opposite problem.

I convinced myself the girl in the mirror was not me. For she was too plain. Her skin was ashen and her hair frazzled. Her lips were oddly pale, and if I had to guess, I would say she looked cold, as if there were no warmth in her veins. I didn't want to know what it meant. I stumbled around in the dark, patting the mirrors and looking for an exit.

"Kai?" I called out again. It was silly of me to think he was here now, but I couldn't shake how familiar the stranger's stride was. The way his shirt clung to his shoulders, the way his hair lay.

"Kins?" a reply sounded through the walls. What was that? Could it really be him?

"Kai is that you?"

"It's me Kins! It's me!" he yelled. I was so excited, I nearly tripped over my own two feet. I fell through a doorway that opened up into a larger room.

"Where are you!?" I flinched at the sight of the reflections.

I'd thought the cold-blooded Kinsley was bad, but these reflections were far worse. Distorted. Elongated. My face could have been a match for a ghostly Halloween mask. My chin drooped to my knees, and my eyes looked as if they were melting from their sockets like molten lava. Beyond turning my stomach sour, the sight of my reflection did one other thing—it made me fear death.

How could I possibly have wanted to begin my afterlife? How could I have *wanted* to be a ghost? As I looked at my peculiar face in the fun-house mirror, I wanted nothing more than to live. To live a full and robust life. One with pink cheeks and pouty lips, a warm touch, and a beating heart. I yearned to be the flawed human girl who'd once mistakenly felt uncomfortable in her skin. Never again.

"I'm right here!" Kai yelled, pounding on the wall in the room next to mine. I saw the mirror shake, and I placed my hands on top of the warped reflection.

"Just stay there! I'll find you!"

The lights flickered and beamed an electric blue, making everything white appear to be glowing. A group of kids stumbled through the door, laughing and banging into the walls and mirrors. The black lights flickered on and off, and the music drowned out the surrounding screams. I hurried toward the direction the kids had funneled in from, and I found an exit that led to a narrow hall. My fingertips grazed the walls as I felt for the next opening into a room.

When I was sure I found the door that would lead to Kai, I opened it to face my reflections in three warped mirrors in a tiny room. Kai was nowhere to be found. "Kai?" I pounded on the mirrors, thinking maybe he was stuck somewhere in the walls. I had once been stuck inside the walls, too. I caught sight of my body scrunched like an accordion and my legs long and spindly. I frowned, slapping on the mirror. Where was he? Why couldn't I find him?

The glow of white pearly teeth appeared in the last mirror. A smile floated just behind my head. It stretched wide—far beyond what any natural mouth could do. It reminded me of the Cheshire Cat. It's just the effect of the funhouse mirror, I told myself. Nothing more. But I wasn't smiling.

Was there some other entity in the tiny room with me? I reached my arms out, touching two mirrors at once, and then the third. There was nobody in the room but me. I stepped closer to the mischievous smile and peered deeply into the reflection. My eyes morphed into the glowing eyes of a predator.

The big toothy grin elongated into fangs and dripped with sparkling venom. I gasped and stumbled back, slamming into the mirror behind me. A cackle boomed over the high-pitched trickle of music, and I tripped once again, falling into the narrow hallway.

I checked my hands in the flash of the strobing light and was relieved when I saw fingers instead of paws, nails instead of claws. I ran down the darkened hallway, much too fast for the low visibility, and I slammed into Noah's chest. "Kins?" he asked, seeming surprised to see me.

"Noah?" I was even more surprised to see him. And so . . . *alert*.

The last time I'd seen Noah, he'd been like a zombie waking from a century of sleep. And the ghost of his past had been gallivanting with Kai in the yard. If there were two of him, like there were seemingly two of me—no thanks to Layla—then which one was he? I wished I wasn't leery, but I didn't know who I could trust anymore. I took a step back and watched as his brows furrowed with confusion.

"What's wrong, Kins? Are you okay? Do you want to get out of here?" Noah placed his hands on either side of my arms, trying to comfort me, but I stiffened under his touch.

"Did you see Kai in here?" I asked, wanting desperately to get away from the distortion of the mirrors, yet not wanting to leave Kai behind. Again.

Noah's jaw hardened, causing the blue light to flex across his cheeks. I immediately regretted my words. Noah looked at me like I had said something incriminating. Was this a test? Had I failed?

"Kai? You saw Kai?"

A couple squeezed by, the guy's hand trailing behind to hold his date's hand. The girl's bright white shirt cast a glow on Noah's face, and I could see concern in his eyes. For a moment, I wanted to run, but Noah was all I had left. "No. But I thought I heard him."

"That's right." Noah nodded. "He *is* here. This way." He took my hand in his.

Something didn't seem right. His words were saying one thing, but his face was saying something entirely different. He led me against the flow of the crowd through the narrow hall. I pushed up against the wall to let people pass by. I didn't want to go deeper into the funhouse. I wanted to get out into the fresh air. It was my guilt that kept me searching for Kai.

Noah pulled me into a room that I had not seen before, though I was positive I had been in every room thus far. It was a small rectangular room with four mirrors surrounded by brightly colored chalk paintings that glowed in the black lights. Neon orange, yellow, green, and pink. I pulled my hand out of Noah's and rubbed my temple. My head was pounding.

"Well, where is he?" I asked, taking a step back from Noah.

Noah said nothing, but pointed to the first mirror. Hesitantly, I peered within. Just like Noah had said, there he was. It wasn't like seeing Kai behind a glass windowpane; it was more like looking into a magic mirror and barely making out a faint memory. But this wasn't a memory of something I had seen before. Kai hit the walls, calling my name.

"Kai!" I yelled. My hot breath clouded the center of the mirror. Kai spun around, seeing me for the first time. He ran up to me and placed his hands against mine. I desperately tried to feel for warmth, but there was nothing there. Nothing but the sadness and fear in his eyes.

"Get me out of here!"

My heart lurched. "What should we do?" I asked Noah in a panic. The way he stood there perplexed me. He seemed to be unaffected by Kai's plea. He motioned to the next mirror.

There was more? I bit my lip and looked at Kai, but couldn't bring my eyes to meet his. Slowly, following Noah's gesture, I stepped to the next mirror. My heart broke further when I saw my parents huddled together in a dark corner, crying.

I gasped. "No!" I pounded on the glass, trying to find a way in. "Why are you doing this?" I asked Noah.

He took a step back, beckoning me to follow. I shook my head. I couldn't bear to witness what was trapped in the next two mirrors. I couldn't handle what I had already seen. As it turned out, it didn't matter. It wasn't my choice. The mirrors rotated clockwise so that the third mirror was directly in front of me. This time, it was Layla.

At first, seeing the girl who had betrayed me was far easier than seeing my parents or Kai. I quite enjoyed seeing her in a box. My empathy for her had been squashed, and now there was an anger boiling inside. Oh, how I wished I had the wolf's reflection now. I wanted to let loose on her. But this was a funhouse mirror, and my retribution would have to wait.

I frowned at the girl and stepped forward to give her a mouthful of my most venomous words. She played me, and I would not take it. As soon as my shoes bumped the base of the mirror, our features aligned. Something odd happened. I jumped back, startled by what I'd seen. She and I looked eerily similar. How had I not noticed this before? I looked at Noah, shocked, and he crossed his arms over his chest and waited.

I took a deep breath and really took in Layla's appearance. She was every bit the gorgeous girl I had envied all summer long. Her hair was luscious and long, her lips were a beautiful red stain. Her skin was like porcelain, and it warmed her gorgeous brown eyes. I was drawn in, once again, and watched as our features aligned, not just similarly . . . but perfectly.

I had no way of telling if I was seeing my reflection or hers. "What is this? What kind of trick is this?" I asked.

"You only see what you want to see," she said, repeating Walker's words from the ridge.

"I want to see the truth!" I growled.

She smiled softly. My anger did nothing to her calm demeanor. But that only made me more furious. It was then that I noticed a green fleck in the bottom of her right eye.

"It's about time," she said, as if congratulating me on some unknown success.

Anger seized me. That was *my* green fleck! It was the only thing I had left of my late gran. How dare she steal it from me! I reached back and punched Layla square in the nose.

The mirror shattered, and my knuckles burst open and bled. "Ahh," I cried, cradling my hand to my chest.

"Wait!" Noah said, as I darted out of the room. "Wait, you haven't seen the last mirror!" I barreled through the crowd and slammed into the walls. Eventually, I found my way out of the funhouse.

What Noah didn't realize was that I had seen the fourth mirror. The red had been blinding. I knew it was the door I'd been searching for. But I also knew it was a trap. Layla wanted me to take her place, and I knew she'd convinced everybody else to help her. Perhaps, she'd even risen an army of my dead friends to do it. But I'd had a tiny taste of being invisible, and I didn't want to live like a joker in the shadows. A moth caught in a web.

9

The fairgrounds were crawling with people. The crowd had thickened, and the lines had tripled. I scurried through the crowd in a hurry. I pushed through a group of young teenage boys and skirted around a family, checking over my shoulder regularly. Not just for Layla, who was out to get me, but for my friends, too. Somehow, Layla had turned them against me. I imagined her coming back from the shooting lesson with Walker and talking to all of my friends, both dead and alive. Convincing them she was me, and that *I* was a traitor.

Well, I'd be the traitor then. I'd get home and leave them all here with her. Could I do that? I felt a sudden weight on my shoulders. I couldn't do that. No matter how betrayed I felt. At this point, I didn't have a plan. No way home, and nobody to trust. It was hard to follow my heart when the pieces lay scattered as so.

What could Layla have told my friends to make them turn on me? That I killed Trinity with my jealousy? That I killed Levi in a fit of rage? Drowned Ethan in my worry? Or perhaps she'd told them I'd been keeping them caged in Baylor for my benefit. Because I needed more time to fall in love with a stranger. And because I wasn't ready to go home, so neither could they.

Would she remind them I'd turned my back on them once? That I tried to catch a plane home and leave them all behind with a killer lurking in the woods? Or that I never trusted them and set up surveillance cameras to keep a watchful eye? The list went on and on. I couldn't blame her for thinking I was a monster that needed to be eradicated. Because all of those things were true. I'd been not just a terrible friend this summer, but a god-awful person. And now, my best of friends were out to capture me.

A warm hand grabbed my arm and yanked me into a tiny booth draped in a heavy curtain. I was staring straight into the eyes of a frantic old lady. Her hair was gray and frazzled, nearly a foot above her head in winding curls. She smelled like sage and wore a loose-fitting satin shift. There was a hunger behind her eyes as she pushed me down into a seat.

"Who are you?"

"My spirits have a message for you."

A small table rested between us, draped in velvet and covered in cards and flickering candles. "I think you have the wrong person," I said, standing in protest.

The fortune teller jumped to her feet and blocked the hidden exit. I eyed her suspiciously, then assessingly. I would not find Layla inside this tiny booth, but maybe I could find some answers.

"Be quick," was all I said. I sat back down, determined to be on my way soon enough.

The lady sat down, closed her eyes, and spread her arms. She tilted her head back and breathed deeply. Her hands trembled before she brought them together, rubbing them as if igniting a power within.

"I feel you're at a crossroads. You're up against a problem, and you need answers." She opened her eyes and peered at me for confirmation.

"Isn't everybody?"

She dropped her hands to the table, ignoring my snide comment, and started shuffling the cards. "So you're having a problem and you need my help? That's what I hear."

I rolled my eyes and sat back in my chair. My leg bounced as I eyed the surrounding curtain, trying to find the slit that I'd come in through.

"I'm hearing there is a love interest. But there's been some deceit. You want to know if you can trust him." My leg stilled as she shuffled her cards and the candles flickered.

Admittedly, this caught my attention, but I gave the same response out loud. "Doesn't everybody?"

The fortune teller appeared to be in some kind of trance. I didn't know if I could ask questions, because she certainly wasn't answering them. She shuffled the cards until one fell out of the deck. Face up. "What is that?" I blurted, more invested than I wanted to appear. These weren't normal playing cards. A wilted rose with a sword piercing the bud couldn't be good.

The fortune teller peeked at me briefly and then shuffled her cards again. "The deceit runs deep and true."

My breath quickened. I already knew this. "Tell me something I don't know."

A new card fell out, as if jumping from the deck to answer me.

"The Emperor!" I arched to see the card, but it meant little to me. A figure sitting in a chair. "Power, authority, and protection. You are being protected. It might not feel like it, but it's in your best interests."

"What's in my best interests?"

"There's more to it than meets the eye. Soon, the truth will reveal itself."

I huffed and sat back in my seat. This wasn't helping me at all.

"I'm hearing things are changing for you. Your path will soon be chosen, and those who have deceived you will stay behind. But not all deceit is evil. Some hide as protection. They will need your forgiveness."

"That sounds oddly generic," I said, with my arms folded across my chest.

Another card fell out of her deck, and I stretched my neck to see. She slapped the card down on the table, revealing a village littered with gold stars. "Wealth. Your hard work *will* pay off. There is great fortune coming your way."

"Okay. I'm done." I popped to my feet and pawed at the curtain surrounding her booth.

"You've chosen your path. It's a hard path, and few take it for this reason. The gold is at the end of the rainbow. But it's not wealth you seek, it's love."

The curtain parted, and a waft of popcorn air whooshed in. The fortune teller grabbed my hand on my way out, sending a shock straight up my arm. I tried to free myself, but her wild eyes caught me by surprise. They were unlike anything I'd seen before. One a deep brown, maybe black. And the other light. Like a wagon wheel, it had dark spokes spearing the center pupil.

"You don't belong here," she whispered. Entranced in her eyes, it was the first thing she'd said that really meant something to me. I yanked my arm away and stumbled through the curtain. The dim glow of the candles snuffed as the curtain fluttered into place. I disappeared into the bustling crowd.

I tried to convince myself she didn't know what she was talking about. She could have said those things to a hundred people, and they would all make sense in a hundred different ways. Everybody feels like they've been deceived to some extent. Everybody wants protection and love. Everybody hopes there will be a pot of gold at the end of their long, grueling journey. I wanted to believe it for myself, but I couldn't shake the eerie feeling I'd gotten when I stared into her wagon-wheel eye. She certainly had a message for me, and she wasn't the only one.

At first it was subtle, a mother staring at me as I wandered through the crowd. But the more I thought of the difficult path ahead, the more I feared I had chosen wrong, and the more I began to notice strangers with watchful eyes. I told myself that I was paranoid, but when I passed a set of triplets with ice cream dripping down their chins and six piercing eyes following my every move, I stopped to survey the grounds.

I turned slowly in a circle and looked at every single face around me. The background seemed to swirl as I turned, disorienting me. But the faces I saw were rock solid. Most of the strangers looked away as our eyes met, but a few glared back at me with vengeance. I didn't know what they had heard about me, but it was clear that word had spread in this tiny town.

My eyes rested on a man who was familiar to me, but I couldn't place. He was leaning against the back side of a booth. His face cast in the shadows with a single eye visible, trained on me. *Who was he?* Someone bumped me from behind. A large man passed by unapologetically. I whipped my head around just in time to see him checking over his shoulder. But this was no random behemoth of a man. This was Big Jimmy.

I took off running, but he was quick to turn on me. I glimpsed the man in the shadows as he lurched out and followed suit. As the full light cascaded down on the man, I immediately recognized him as the anesthesiologist from my surgery. He was the one who'd been able to see me when nobody else could, and he was after me now. It was a good old game of capture the flag. Only I was playing against a village, and they weren't playing at all. I feared my capture would mean sudden death.

I jumped and pushed through the crowd, accidentally knocking down a young boy. The few people who had been oblivious to me before were now watching. I felt eyes by the hundreds, and I swore they made me feel heavier, like I was carrying their judgment on my back. The more eyes that turned, the more I recognized, and the thicker the air became, making it hard to breathe.

The doctor caught my shoulder, causing my nails to sharpen in defense. I swiped a hand down his arm, leaving deep, open claw marks. He groaned and fell back, causing Big Jimmy to trip over him and creating a slight distraction.

My heart floundered when I saw Kimber in the crowd. Her eyes, like all the others, were set on me. Was she a friend or foe? I didn't know who I could trust, and I was just about done giving chances. I felt the crowd move in on me, and I continued to run, passing by my old friend.

As soon as I made the decision not to trust her, she turned and darted after me. It was three against one, but I knew this was just the beginning. Everybody was after me. The dead and the living. What did they want from me? My need for survival was stronger than ever, and I could feel the wolf's blood waking from its dormant state. It wouldn't be long before I turned bloodthirsty and decimated the crowd of thousands that had come to the Summerfield State Fair.

Kimber was incredibly fast. She whisked through the crowd nearly at the speed of light. My mouth turned dry and my lungs burned as I ran from her. I was giving it everything I had, and it still wasn't enough. She clobbered me from behind. Though she did not weigh enough to take me down, I still struggled to stay on my feet.

She wrapped her spindly arms around my neck, and I clawed at her to set me free. I knew the beast was rising inside me, but how shameful it would be to let it loose on somebody as frail as Kimber. She was no match for me as I was, let alone my grotesque wolf, who towered over every human here.

I threw her off me with ease, and she slid out into the dirt before me, causing a small brown cloud of dirt to mushroom around her. She wasn't so easily dissuaded, though, and she grappled to her feet with vengeance. Why was she so angry with me? What had she heard? Whatever had turned my friends against me was unjust. A downright lie.

We squared off. My heart pounded as if pumping three times the normal amount of blood. Or was it poison that coursed through me now? All I knew was that my hands were still covered in flesh and that my emotions were the most dangerous threat to cross in Baylor right now. Wolf or not, Kimber was putting herself in the crosshairs.

My anger raged. How dare she attack me like this. Had she expected I wouldn't fight back? Isn't that what anybody in their right mind would do?

"Get back to that door!" Kimber growled. She ran at me, a scream ripping from her lungs.

It took everything in my power not to turn her to dust. The fight was so unfair I tried to keep my emotions back; I knew they would end her life and I didn't want that. She grabbed me, then suddenly froze. A cold, pale blue crept up her fingers and spread up her arms.

"Go! H—" The pale blue covered her mouth, stealing her last words. I watched as her sky-blue eyes turned icy and opaque. Then she was a statue. An ice sculpture. Kimber stood strong, yet incredibly breakable. I breathed out in relief. It was better than death.

10

It was the first time I noticed the crowd had parted, leaving a wide berth around Kimber and me. Little kids pointed to the ice figurine, and mothers tried to hide their shock with hands cupped over their mouths. The entire crowd, as far as my eyes could see, was still as they watched me and my attacker. My heart continued to drum as I took in the stares of a thousand glimmering eyes.

The doctor and Big Jimmy barreled through the sea of stillness. I took off at once, my shoulder bumping into Kimber's statue. "No!"

I tried to catch her, but there was no time. She toppled over, and as if bursting from the inside out, ice spikes shot out like daggers. There was no sign of Kimber when I looked over my shoulder. I had thought that maybe when the statue broke, she'd be set free; but that wasn't the case. The crowd gasped and shielded their faces from the shards of ice raining down. The same thing had happened to Layla when I'd gotten mad, and she still came back to haunt me. I didn't kill Kimber . . . *I didn't*.

I fought through the crowd, the adrenaline coursing through my veins and turning the wolf's blood into a potent poison. These men were twice my size, and I needed all the help I could get. I didn't mind borrowing a little evil from my nightmares.

On instinct, I cast the same spell on the two full-grown men. Suddenly I was no longer being chased. I watched the color leach from the men as the frost crawled up their bodies, turning them to pale, delicate figurines, suspended in mid-chase.

What was happening? The anger rose inside me. The instinct to fight grew stronger than any other power I possessed. Even my compassion. I had once hated myself for overtly harming Big Jimmy. And now, I'd decimated three people in only minutes. I knew it was only the beginning, but nothing could stop me now.

I vaguely took in the innocent eyes around me, and I knew they would not last through the night. I both needed the beast inside to keep me alive and hated everything it symbolized. But there was no backing down, and there was no shutting it off. Not while I was being threatened.

More doctors emerged from the crowd, stepping forward to capture their flag. It was the very dream I'd had about a war, only in this version, I fought alone. "Kinsley!" I heard a familiar voice drown out the whispers. Innocent bystanders parted, making way for my new opponent. I stopped dead in my tracks. Because how could I run from my best friend? Lainey stood amid the parting crowd with Gunner by her side.

Lainey could almost pass for normal, apart from the pale green tint of her skin. It wasn't the same paleness that took over my arctic figurines, but more like a bruise that was still healing. Or rather, like she had been living underwater for far too long.

Gunner's mouth gaped open in a wide crocodile smile. Being reunited with his owner made him the happiest dog alive. And for a moment, I felt it too. As if everything was going to be all right. As if I could get through this difficult time if only I had somebody by my side. Lainey could be that person. She had always been my person.

In that moment of stillness, a group of men snatched me from behind. My arm tugged in one direction, and my waist was pulled to the next. I had never played football before, but my little brother had tackled me once, and I imagined this felt similar to being incapacitated by four or five muscular men on the field. I was being pulled in two.

I screamed, slashing at them with my claws, but to only minimal effect. My hand was still made of human flesh and my fingernails were barely sharpened. They were not the small daggers I had hoped for. Even though I slashed through their skin, I made only surface-level wounds. The men were unstoppable. They hoisted me up on their shoulders.

"Let me go!" I screamed.

The men marched on. *Where were they bringing me?* I wrestled as best I could, trying to get a look in the direction we were headed. All I could see was that we were heading toward the funhouse of mirrors. That's when it clicked for me; they were going to throw me through the portal since I wasn't going willingly.

I so wanted to go through that door, but I needed to do it on my own terms. With all the trickery at the state fair, I was paranoid it was a trap. That door probably led to a different realm. One I wouldn't be waking from. And it was so painfully obvious that Layla would take my place here in Baylor. She'd have no problem taking Walker from me, too. She'd already stolen my friends. Resurrected them and turn them against me. No, I couldn't allow them to force me through that portal.

Half dozen men easily moved through the parting crowd with me on their shoulders. The mob turned angry, yelling.

"Get her out of here!"

"She doesn't belong with us!"

"She's a devil in disguise!"

"That selfish wench! Shove her through the door, or she'll kill us all!"

The crowd rushed forward, pushing me off the men's shoulders and down a long line of angry hands. This differed greatly from crowd surfing at a concert, but only because this wasn't entertainment. Not for me, at least. Everybody else, though, seemed to be enjoying themselves.

"Red door! Red door! Red door!" the masses unified their chants.

I looked up, trying to find a moment of clarity and calmness in this dire moment of life and death. But the beautiful night sky I expected to see held something else. Something dark swirled above my head, reminding me of a baby's mobile tethered above their crib. The darkness whirled round and round. I stretched my eyes, trying to make sense of it. Abruptly, I understood.

"Levi..." I gasped. All the deaths that fell by my hands, or rather my thoughts, were back. Back with a vengeance.

Levi led a flock in a wide vortex above my head. He was the biggest crow of all, his wingspan twice that of the other birds. I grabbed at the hands of strangers and pushed them off me but fighting on my back left me at a disadvantage. I watched the birds funnel downward like a tornado. I was the eye of the storm.

"Red door! Red door! Red door!" a familiar voice chanted.

I craned my head, searching for a voice I had not heard for some time, but did now, clear as day. I looked over the many faces I recognized and the ones that seemed like generic filler. Somebody grabbed my cheek and bumped my head. A finger found its way into my mouth, and I bit down. Hard. All I wanted now was to go home.

A sense of homesickness spread throughout me. The feeling was far greater than any anger I felt toward the crowd or the situation. It was worse than the pain of deceit coming from the familiar voice, though I felt that too.

When I found the face that matched the voice I so wished wasn't here, it was the pinnacle of all my terrible feelings. A culmination, as everything rushed together and exploded. A volcano of horror, suffering, guilt, and regret burst out of me as my little brother stood with the angry mob, chanting for my demise.

The moment I saw his face, I finally unleashed the monster that lay caged inside.

"No!"

The hands that were passing me from one to the next immediately froze and dug into my backside unforgivingly. The vortex of angry crows froze in the sky, just before the first talons reached me. Everything was still. And everything was cold.

I fumbled around, knocking over several icy figurines as I fell to the ground. On my hands and knees, I stared up at the many pale faces around me. My brother's cheeks were dusted baby pink with anger. *How did he get here?*

Gunner's ears were pinned back in a way I'd never seen before. It took a special person to make a good dog turn vicious. *What was wrong with me?* I so wanted Lainey to be the one I could turn to, but even my best friend had turned on me. Gunner and my own brother too.

The crows now truly hung like a dark mobile, as if pinned to the sky with invisible strings. Cool gray wings scarcely contrasted the black night sky, with tiny pinholes of twinkling stars. It was an eerie place, and the shrill carnival music only made it worse. It gave me the horrifying feeling of being trapped inside a music box. A new fear added to an ever-growing list.

I weaved through the crowd, trying hard not to knock over the statues. Had the entire crowd turned to mannequins? Petrified icebergs? Breakable to the touch? A figurine fell as I tried to slide by, causing a domino effect and shattering several people in its wake. I gasped and stumbled back, stepping on the toe of another figure. I was able to catch this one; a young girl, frozen with her cotton candy.

Once out of the thick crowd, I weaved in and out of the stragglers that remained behind the angry mob. It looked as though they were still rushing toward the commotion, trying to see all that had happened while they were stuck in lines. These faces seemed calmer, though, and most of them had a bag of popcorn or a lollipop, some with giant stuffed bears on their backs. The farther I moved from the center of the mob, the less angry the faces appeared.

At the entry of the funhouse of mirrors, I looked again at the immobilized fairgoers. It was safer to enter now that it was entirely my decision. That door was the only way I knew how to get home. If I opened the door and saw myself lying on the hospital bed, it would be safe for me to walk through. On the other hand, if I opened the door and a nefarious black void wafted beyond, I would run. I simplified the decision in my mind.

I took a deep breath, reminding myself to be brave. To lean into my weakness. I entered the funhouse of flickering black lights and weaved through the narrow halls, retracing my steps. It was even scarier now that the funhouse was empty, and I was alone. I caught my reflection in a distorted mirror, and my heart nearly leapt into my throat. I reflexively jumped back and slammed against a wall, and then closed my eyes briefly to catch my breath. *You can do this...*

I found the room that Noah had brought me into. I stepped into the rectangular room with four mirrors surrounded by neon glowing colors. I could see the red glow emanating from the last mirror's reflection, and my hands tensed by my sides.

I took one single stride forward, aiming for the portal, but stopped dead in my tracks when I saw Kai's ghost. Even his spirit had turned to an ice sculpture. He was frozen in time, his fist coming down on the mirror, ice upon glass.

The second mirror contained my parents, caught in a moment of despair. My dad was frozen still as he wiped a tear from my mom's cheek.

I trailed my fingertips across the mirrors, and a chill came over me when I reached the third one and realized Layla was no longer trapped within. I stepped closer, expecting to see her. I searched within the reflection, but no matter which way the black light flickered, Layla had evaded the spell.

I gasped, whipping my head around, expecting to find her behind me. Her scrawny hands ready to push me through the door. But even though I felt as if I were being watched, I did not see her.

Unsettled and nervous, I moved to the fourth mirror, checking over my shoulder more often than I'd like to admit. Layla had been invisible to Walker all these years. Of course she was invisible to me now, in the shadows of a funhouse.

I positioned myself in front of the red door, and like the many times before, its gold knob enticed me in a way that I could not turn from. I reached for the doorknob, and my bloody knuckles scraped the mirror's surface, leaving marks of red behind.

What was this? I pawed at the doorknob, frantically searching for something to grab hold of, but it was just a two-dimensional reflection. I stepped closer. The door distorted before my eyes. The bottom half stretched long and thin, while the top scrunched into a stubby, wide version of itself.

I bit my lip, staring at the hoax and wishing it were my way home. Had I missed my chance? Was this my new life?

With the heels of my hands pressed into my eyes, I saw the pinwheel of electric lights in my thoughts. And just for a moment, I felt like I was drowning again. I sprang to life one last time. This was my last chance. I had come so far, and all I had to do now was check that Ferris wheel.

I made my way through the funhouse, completely riddled with the fear that another failure awaited me. That I would soar to new heights and cry into the night as I waited for change . . . and nothing would come.

Once in the open air, the arctic night delivered an invigorating breath into my lungs. I skirted around the frozen people and ducked underneath the low-flying crows. I saw many faces I recognized, both from this realm and from the other. I saw old classmates, teachers I'd liked, and teachers I hadn't. I even saw my brother's friends with angry scowls and small stones clasped in their hands, wound like pitchers. But as I passed the figurines by the hundreds, there was one face I continued to search for.

I didn't expect to see him here, but when I passed his pale skin, all the fight inside me dropped like a ton of bricks. The wolf turned dormant. Walker stood amid the angry crowd, encased in stillness, just like the rest. But unlike everybody else, he wasn't wearing an angry expression. His face was frozen in a mask of worry and sadness.

What have I done? More importantly, how do I undo it? I thought of him and Layla, and thought maybe it was for the best. He couldn't hurt inside there, could he? I trailed my finger across his battered brow. The ice was jagged and sharp there, and I knew his heart had been breaking as he'd come to the Summerfield State Fair.

I pulled my finger back, studying the water that dripped down my hand. Somehow, the jagged edge of his scar had been dulled by my touch. I stepped toe to toe with him, and I leaned in close. I promised him I wouldn't leave without saying goodbye, and this was me making good on that promise.

I closed my eyes, imagining the warmth of a farewell wish. It seemed I had little magic left after the volcano of emotions had spurted from me like a natural disaster, but I knew I had this one simple manifestation left in me. I opened my eyes to the warm glow of a single floating feather. It was the only thing left that still felt pure. Its heat sent a shiver down my spine, reminding me of just how cold I was. I leaned into Walker and kissed his cheek. It turned a deeper hue of pink beneath the melting ice.

"Goodbye, Walker," I whispered. I never thought I would say the words, and even though I felt unsure of who he was when I wasn't around. I was still very much in love with the Walker I knew.

I went to pull away, continue my mission, but my feet were locked in place. I nearly stumbled backward, grabbing hold of Walker's firm shoulders to keep me upright. My feet were covered in ice. Walker's shoes were less opaque, and beads of water streamed down his pants as he melted. The colors of his clothing were more prominent where the ice had thinned.

I forcefully jerked my foot back, hearing the tether snap between Walker and me. I loved him, but I no longer wanted to live a life in the shadows. And I no longer would settle for *half* of his heart. And while a month ago I may have chosen to be petrified if it meant being by his side, I had a clearer picture of reality now.

I'd heard my mother calling, and I knew the veil between her world and mine was thinning. And the closer I got to my past life, the further I grew from Walker and his. Plus, something was not right here. I didn't always know who I was in Baylor, and that scared me more than the depths of the haunted forest itself.

With nearly crippled feet and frozen shoes, I took off running for the Ferris wheel. A single thought now could change the course of my life forever.

As the Summerfield State Fair was still, its crowds made of etched glaciers, there was one thing that remained in motion. One massive thing that remained alive in a world otherwise dead. The Ferris wheel glowed with its antique lights. Colored bulbs rotated on the wheel high into the sky. It seemed as I hobbled toward my destiny that an invisible threshold had been crossed. There was no turning back now, and I would soon find out what waited for me.

11

"Ten minutes!"

Who said that? Was it Layla? Everybody else was frozen. Though, by the sight of Walker, I knew the ice was melting. Soon, the angry mob would be alive to hunt again. Ten minutes sounded fairly accurate.

I had an odd sensation of running through a dense patch of air, a barrier set to slow me down just as a timer had begun. I waded through the thickness, keeping my eyes trained on the Ferris wheel. I felt like my spirit had detached from my body and was struggling to stay with me. As if somehow, it was getting caught in the invisible web I worked to get through.

My head scorched with the pain of a migraine, and I worried I might pass out before reaching the finish line. This was one race I couldn't afford not to win. Even though I continued to run, I couldn't feel my feet, as they were bound in icy shoes and frozen solid. The closer I got to the Ferris wheel, the stranger I felt in my skin.

Was I waking up? I hoped this wasn't what being alive felt like.

"Nine minutes. Don't be late," the voice called. I was fairly certain it was Layla. I heard the call both in my head and in the thick air surrounding me. I tried to hobble quicker, causing me to trip over my impairment. My spirit lagged before boomeranging back into my body, and for just a moment, I felt hollow.

Stay with me. We can do this . . .

I scrambled to my feet, powerless against Layla's magic. The more I saw to be true, the less power I had to change the surrounding reality. I pushed myself forward, my heart racing against time.

As I stood at the base of the Ferris wheel, it looked even taller than from afar when it towered over the fairgrounds. Old, rusted metal framework held the massive ride together. It couldn't be safe. But then again, neither was being lost in a coma.

I opened the safety gate and approached the moving cars, only it didn't slow down for me to get in. I grabbed hold of the next car, and it sped up, pulling my arm with it. I let go, my hand burning from trying to stop the momentum of the massive machine. I wiped my hands on the back of my jeans.

The control panel was nothing short of an antique. Sun-bleached buttons dotted the board, and the remnants of labels were barely visible. There was a single lever to the right of the panel that looked like it belonged in an old stick-shift truck. My palms itched as I debated which to try first. Some buttons had a pale pinkness to them, and I assumed that one day, when the ride had been shiny and new, these buttons were once red. Red was universal for stop, right? I pushed the first pink button and watched the Ferris wheel for signs of slowing.

"Eight minutes. You're not going to make it."

In a wave of panic, I pushed all the buttons that appeared to have once been red. I monitored the wheel as it continued making revolutions, hoping it would slow. It was then that I noticed, in the very top car, a single person. Long, dark brown hair cascaded down from the girl's face as she watched me struggle with the control panel.

"Time is ticking," she yelled down.

I knew it was. With every passing minute, it was harder, my task growing insurmountable. "I don't know how to make it stop!" I yelled back.

I looked up, surprised that the girl was still in the very top car, even though the ride had continued to rotate. The ghost of Layla floated between the many cars that passed by, always remaining at the very top of the wheel, as far as possible from the ground.

"What are you going to do? You only have eight minutes..."

"I know! I know! Stop it!" I yelled, grabbing at my head. If she was trying to make me crack, she was succeeding.

I grabbed the lever and tried to pull it with all my weight, but the metal had corroded, and it would not budge. I looked up at Layla one last time, and I knew what I had to do. But a voice inside begged to differ. *I can't climb that! I'll fall!*

"I can't! I can't do it!" I cried out. Half-frozen crows fell from the sky. I was running out of time.

Layla encouraged me in the same way Walker would have. In the same way I imagined Lainey would. Or rather, the way I hoped she would. It could have been the biggest hoax of all, but I couldn't think of it now. I had just shy of eight minutes left, and I needed to climb a monumental wheel of terror.

"Start slow. Climb up the frame in the center," Layla yelled.

I tried one last time to capture a car in desperation, but as it swooshed by, I realized this was about conquering my fear and nothing else. It wasn't about the mechanics of the old antique ride. It wasn't about being smart enough to figure out how to make the wheel stop. It was simpler than all those things put together.

This was my ultimate nightmare, and I had to do it alone. I'd been petrified of heights my entire life; I couldn't think of a worse scenario than what I was facing now. My stomach swirled as I gripped the first metal bar. My ice shoes clinked as I stepped on the beam, and the lack of traction made my foot slide. I was only one step from the ground, and I clung to the cold metal for dear life. *Impossible . . .*

"One step at a time!" Layla yelled.

I didn't dare look up. My eyes watered as I reached for the next rung. My feet clattered with every step I braved. My hands became sweaty and just as slippery as my foothold. But Layla drove me forward. *"Just don't think about it,"* I breathed to myself.

Instead, I thought of how my greatest insecurity had become a strength. Maybe I wasn't the best student. And maybe I hadn't made this the very best summer, the way I wished I had, but I'd done some remarkable things. I'd frozen time. I'd turned human flesh to ice. And I had survived a lot of dark days and nights. I was more capable than I gave myself credit for. And I could do this. I could do this . . . as long as I didn't look down.

But nothing was easy in Baylor. A simple thought was all it took. It was all it *ever* took. I looked down. I don't know why I did it. It just happened, as if I was trying to torture myself. My breath turned shallow, my head woozy with disorientation. I could feel my spirit trying to leave my body again.

"I can't do this!" I whimpered, teetering between self-encouragement and self-sabotage like a pendulum.

"Seven minutes. Do you want to go home?"

What kind of question was that? "Well, I'm not staying here! Did you think I would take your place? I'm not giving up that easily!" I stepped to the next rung.

"Answer the question!"

"Yes! Of course!"

I made it halfway. All the spokes met in a single disc. The intricate design came together in corrosion and rust. I eyed a bolt that had unscrewed itself and was ready to fall out from its tethered hole. I didn't want to know how high I had climbed, or rather, how far away the ground was. The very thought made me sick. I moved myself to the next beam and watched the bolt fall out and ricochet off a nearby cable.

"Then why can't you see? Why can't you see this is just a dream?"

"I can! I do!" I had known I was dreaming for quite some time now. Of course, it was heartbreaking in the beginning, when I hadn't understood. But I knew it now.

"But you've never turned lucid. You've never gained full control and awareness."

"And why do you think that is? You stole the damn book from me!" I yelled, climbing a little faster now.

Layla laughed, reminiscent of a witch's cackle. "This isn't about the book, and you know it. *Waking Dreams* was just another obstacle you put before yourself. You've known you were dreaming, and yet, you've chosen to spend your time chasing your dreams and running from your nightmares. Why can't you just open your eyes the way I have? Why do *I* have to be the logical one?" Layla argued.

What did she mean, why couldn't I open my eyes? They were open. I saw the sheer height that I had climbed all too well. And I could see all the lives I'd turned to statues below. They were so small from up here, but I could still tell they were mostly done thawing. I closed my eyes and shuddered. If anything, I was seeing too much.

"You're the furthest thing from logic! You are absolutely crazy! All you do is hide in the woods and run from the very few people who have ever tried to help you! Do you want my help to cross over? Because my patience is running thin, and I have half a mind to throw you off this wheel!" I shouted. At least she was distracting me from thinking about how high I'd climbed.

Layla's laughter rumbled in the sky like thunder. Her ghost was everywhere. It was somehow tied to the atmosphere and living in the very molecules that held this realm together. She was a force I could not reckon with.

"You think *I'm* the crazy one?" Another rumble of thunder boomed across the sky, causing the last of the crows to drop, and the metal rod to vibrate within my grasp.

"Nobody in their right mind laughs like that!" It was true. The only characters that cackled like that were villains. The characters that had fallen on poor luck. The ones that had a tango with a dramatic trauma of sorts, and their only way of survival meant leaving their wherewithal behind. And to continue living a life with half a heart and a darkened mind. What was Layla's trauma? Was it that her soon-to-be fiancé accidentally took her life? It would certainly be enough to turn her into a villain.

"Look again Kinsley. Everything you've seen here in Baylor has been a lie.

Most of the conversations you've had have been misconstrued, what you believed you *deserved* to hear."

Why would I believe I deserved *this*? To be haunted by Layla and the ghost of my best friend, the dark dimensions of the woods, and water? I *knew* I deserved better than this! But did I deserve Walker's love? Well, I would never be as pretty as Layla. That was just a simple fact. And they'd had a bond, long before I ever entered the picture. She was just trying to confuse me. I began to look down, but caught myself and averted my gaze. *Stay focused . . .*

"Why have you been hiding from Walker? He loves you more than anything in this world, and you've been hiding from him for decades! *You* don't deserve *him!*"

"You're so far off the mark, I pity you . . . Four minutes." Her tone was flat. I had finally struck a chord.

I had four minutes left, and I thought I could make it. I had already climbed three-quarters of the wheel, and I was gaining momentum. Nothing drove me quite the same as Layla did.

"Let me ask you this," Layla continued. "You know how Gran has been reading us fairy tales?"

Us? I didn't answer. My gran was none of her business. How did she even know that?

"Yeah. You know what I'm talking about. But what I can't understand is, why have you played along? Why did you allow yourself to succumb to the wolf?"

"I didn't! That beast took over—"

"Because you let it!"

"What was I supposed to do?" I argued.

"Tell yourself you're dreaming. And wake up!"

"That's not how it works," I said, shaking my head, refusing to believe I could have woken at any moment. I grabbed the next rung with a sweaty hand.

"Oh my gosh, Kinsley! You're exhausting! You are so stuck in your own head you can't even see what has been so blatantly obvious!" Layla was looking out over the fairgrounds when she paused. "Oh look, they're all melted now. Better hurry. Three minutes," she said.

I launched myself up to the next rung. My arms were shaking, and I was exhausted. I didn't dare look down.

"Let me ask you this; why do you think you're wearing glass slippers right now?" she continued, sounding bored.

I frowned and tried to wiggle my toes, but couldn't. Ice encased my feet, not glass. But that was only because the spell I cast on Walker had leached from him to me. But could there be another reason? Suddenly my feet weren't so cold. "I—" I began.

"It's just another fairy tale! If you believe it to be true like you had for all the others, then what do you think will happen next?" Layla laughed, and her roar shook the cables. *Don't fall. Don't fall.*

A single slipper loosened and fell from my foot. I was too afraid to look down, but I heard it fall, chiming off the metal rods for what seemed like an eternity. If Layla was telling the truth, and I had just lost a glass slipper, then I supposed my prince would find it next.

I closed my eyes, wanting to see if Walker was my prince, but I was far too afraid. I felt the vibrations in the metalwork and heard the angry mob below. I knew they had found me, and I didn't doubt they were faster climbers than me.

Layla peeked over the edge of the car, gauging my progress. "Don't you see? You've been imagining it all. But instead of controlling it, you let *it* control *you*. It's just a dream, Kinsley. And it's time to wake up."

"You're right! It's just a dream! You're not real!" I climbed quicker, using the better grip from my freed foot and the fear of the mob to propel me upward. Once I climbed to the top, I'd vanquish Layla, and I'd be set free.

A thread of lightning danced across the sky as Layla laughed out loud. I grabbed the rim of the Ferris wheel. I finally made it. Now, I just had to get into the car.

"One minute..." she breathed.

I pulled myself up with weak, trembling arms, and her brown eyes met mine. I grabbed hold of the car with what little strength I had left. My moist hand slipped on the wide rim of the car. "No—"

My wail was cut off when Layla grabbed my hand. My body went rigid. For a moment, I thought she would peel my fingers back and let me fall. Just as I had threatened her minutes earlier. Instead, she helped pull me up.

I collapsed at the bottom of the car, thankful to be in something more substantial than the outside of the metal framework, where falling would mean certain death. My arms quivered and quaked. For the first time, Layla rotated with the other cars and we started our descent.

I didn't take my eyes off her as I found the seat behind me. As the ride rounded, several wet strangers tried to swipe at the car as it passed by. I held on tight to the edge of the bench and found that sitting across from Layla was even more intimidating than the mob *and* the climb put together.

"You still don't get it?" She peered at me, her head cocked to the side. "I'm just as real as you are."

"You're a ghost!" I snapped, shaking my head.

"I'm *you* . . ."

12

I stared into Layla's brown eyes, not comprehending her words. *I'm you.* It was a meeting of two single words that combined like oil and water. They never quite mixed to make something new. I waited for it to click, for it to make sense, but it didn't. Looking into her eyes was like looking into the funhouse mirror. Only, this one wasn't distorted. Her face reflected the same impatient stare I knew mine had. We both cocked our heads to the side, waiting for something that did not come.

"We're *all* . . ." Layla lifted her hand to motion to the angry mob that waited at the base of the ride and the handful of people who were crazy enough to start climbing. "You."

The wheel was now mid-rotation, and we were nearly at ground level. I turned to assess the strangers, whom Layla had indicated were different parts of me, but all I could see was Walker. He was as real as anything, and he watched me with sorrow-filled eyes, a glass slipper dangling forlornly from his hand.

"And him? He's just a figment of my imagination?" I asked, not wanting to know the actual answer.

When Layla fell silent, I pulled my eyes from Walker to read her face. She looked like she was being pulled in opposite directions. It's exactly how I felt, and I wondered if that was another mirrored effect. As our car neared the ground, I dodged the angry, open hands. Their hands still pale and icy. Nobody grabbed at Layla, though, and she sat patiently until we climbed out of their reach again. My heartbeat raced as I was on the verge of collapse.

Layla looked at her watch, and a crease deepened between her brows. I recognized that watch; I wore it regularly. Though I hadn't packed it for my trip to Baylor. The wheel continued to ascend, but as we lifted into the sky, I worried my heart was being left behind. Layla checked her watch again, and her face filled with worry as she peered over the car to watch Walker shrink away. I turned to watch him, too.

Walker's face fell as he checked the time on his own wrist. I knew I was seconds away from meeting my fate, whatever it may be. Whatever was supposed to happen on this Ferris wheel, it was bigger than just me. It would most likely affect Layla and Walker too. Possibly the whole crowd.

"Wait. What do you mean, *you're me*?" The uncoupled words finally mixed, making a small sentence that both made sense and didn't. If she was me, then was *I* the crazy one? I tried to wrap my head around the idea.

The Ferris wheel sped up the moment the thought clicked in my mind. I remained focused as best I could, but I was afraid. Layla's eyes grew wide as she flickered in and out of my reality. One moment there, then not. As if she disappeared into thin air, only to reappear as a true translucent ghost. Her image glitched as the fairgrounds turned to a blur.

I could see the back of the bench straight through Layla's chest and the distortion of distant lights behind her eyes. Just as her energy pulsed, so did the feeling of my soul leaving my body. My breath was stolen as she wavered back and forth, somewhere between my body and the seat across from me. I looked at my hands, trying to ground myself and make sense of the quivering sensation of being whole one second and split into pieces the next.

The Ferris wheel accelerated more than I thought possible, and we reached the top just as we were falling to the bottom. It spun so fast that all I could do was grab hold of my seat and pray I didn't get thrown off. We spun round and round, the sky blurring with the ground in a mixture of black and brown.

My soul flickered in and out, and my head pulverized with pain I had never endured before. My heartbeat raced and lifted into my throat. I knew I could not take this torture much longer. My teeth were chattering, and my grip was slipping off the rim of the car.

If this is a dream, all I must do is, *wake up*!

For a fraction of a second, Layla sat across from me. Her body fully fleshed and her eyes piercing. She leapt across the car and into my body. A bolt of electricity hammered into my chest. My heart was ground zero of a massive earthquake that shook me to my core. The voltage branched out into my limbs, like fingers of electricity, and seized me.

The momentum of the impact swept me from my seat. The remaining glass slipper shattered on a nearby beam as I flew from the car. I had an overwhelming feeling of free falling, but I was not afraid. And I was no longer in pain.

The blur of colored light bulbs swirled around me, dancing in kaleidoscopic fractals as I fell. It was beautiful. It was calming. And then it was red.

I had been so worried about doing the right thing, it felt like pure relief to fall. Because I knew I was no longer in control. My part was done now, and it was up to fate to finish, one way or another.

I closed my eyes and spread my arms wide, feeling the wind that did nothing to slow me. I couldn't tell the difference between falling and flying. I felt light as a bird, soaring through the night sky.

I had a vague understanding that Layla was a part of me now. That she lived somewhere inside of me. Whether it was my head or my heart, I did not know. But I felt more whole falling to my death, than I had living my summer of dreams.

I continued to fall. My hair whipped wildly in my face, my cheeks were flaccid, and my stomach was in a perpetual state of freefall. Yet, somehow, some way, it was euphoric. Was it because I embodied the ghost of Layla? I never truly liked her. And I had only wanted to help her for my gran, and then later, Walker. But from the moment she and I became one, I found the good in her. I found the side of me I had been missing all along.

I felt terrible that she'd been lost in the woods all summer long. Invisible. If I was in the cabin with all of our friends, then had *she* truly been an outcast? Just . . . alone? Had she spent her time with Walker when he and I were apart? Would I have her memory of that now?

I tried to think, but my mind was racing far too fast for me to latch on to one thought alone. At the beginning of summer, I hunted Layla for sport. Was it my manifestation that kept her on the run? It was sad to think that Layla had tried to get my attention, and I'd mostly spent my time hiding from her. I treated her like a dirty little secret and kept her in the shadows. If only I had known then what I did now. But she did. She knew we were one and the same. Why had she disappeared, then? Why didn't she shake me awake? Make me see?

I thought of her worried expression while she looked at her watch. Then, I thought of Walker's same expression, his same concern for the time. Maybe time played more of a barrier than I'd realized. Maybe I couldn't go home until I was ready. Until the very minute when I was healed just enough to return.

Layla said that all I had to do was wake up. Could she wake? Or had she stayed here, not wanting to leave without me? My heart opened for the girl. The part of me that wouldn't give up on myself.

But what if Layla had gone home without me? Would I have woken up in the hospital a completely different person? A version of myself nobody recognized? I could almost hear the chatter now... "*She hasn't been the same since her accident.*"

A wash of gratitude came over me as I began to love the girl that I'd spent the summer loathing. She must have sacrificed so much, and I never even realized it. I wondered if I would've been better off if she went home without me. I shook the thought from my head. I had learned to accept my faults and deficits while in Baylor, and I was done wishing them away. I was the whole me now: beautiful, competent, deserving, and insecure. Sometimes, even a little dark and twisted.

If Layla and I had reunited earlier in the summer, I might have been happier. Maybe I would have actually swung from the stars. Or had the tea party underwater with Lainey as a mermaid. And after I'd drowned in the lake, maybe I wouldn't have felt so alone.

My mind raced in a million different directions at once as I continued to fall through the never-ending atmosphere. The red door swirled all around me, trying to catch me. Were Noah and Trinity just manifestations of my insecurity? Would Walker have loved me sooner if I were whole? Would I have come home sooner? Or would I have made Baylor so magnificent that I'd never want to leave?

I was pulled through the mouth of the portal and swallowed whole. There was nothing but black as far as I could see. I knew this place. This was the void where I sometimes saw Gran. *Our* Gran. I was so used to thinking of Layla as a separate entity that it was now difficult to think of myself as singular.

I felt as though I had fallen from a distant star and was drifting through the galaxy. My hair continued to lash at my face as if in a dark vortex or windstorm. I searched for signs of life, holding my hair back from my eyes, but I couldn't see into the darkness. I fought back a feeling of disassociation. It was far too easy to be nobody, and nothing in the void. And I knew if I succumbed to that oblivion, I'd be forgotten; lost forever.

I was weightless. I couldn't see; I couldn't smell. And the silence was somehow deep and remote, like it spanned throughout space and time. Because I had been living for months with only half a spirit, my body felt full in an unfamiliar way.

"There you are, dear. I'm so proud of you." Gran materialized from nowhere. Her green eyes were magnificent, like shards of pale peridot light and dark emerald shadows. Her skin was flawless—nearly pearlescent. And a radiant glow emanated from within her that instantly soothed me. The feeling in my chest slowed, and eventually equalized, like an elevator slowing for its exit. I stepped forward to meet my beloved gran.

"Where am I? What's happening?" I asked, disoriented still. There were a million questions tumbling in my head, but where and what seemed to be the foundation to begin with. Everything else was subjective, maybe even theoretical. I was sure questions would riddle me for the rest of my years, so I'd take what I could now and here.

"You're going home, dear. You're almost there now," Gran said, taking my hand in hers. Her touch soothed me. For a split second, all motion ceased, and it was just us. Her emerald eyes to my small emerald fleck.

But a moment was all I had before the feeling in my chest reversed with a vengeance. Could I fall in reverse? The sensation began rising from my core. A strong lifting of something inside of me. My soul was on the move, and my body struggled to keep up. My mind, body, and spirit were not used to being united. They fought like triplets.

I grasped Gran's feeble hands in mine. "Will I ever see you again?" I suddenly feared this would be the last I would ever see of her. And there was no time for a proper goodbye. How do you even put such a feeling into words? There were none. None that I was aware of.

Gran smiled warmly and shook our hands. "It's time, dear. It's time."

"Gran? Gran!" I called in a moment of panic. My hand slipped from hers. As if my soul were being siphoned into another dimension, somewhere above where I visited now, I felt the sucking and pulling as I journeyed into the unknown.

Everything went dark in the absence of Gran's glow, but there was a new light quickly approaching. The darkness turned to swatches of orange and gray that danced behind my eyelids. My body was heavier than normal. Like my cavities had been filled with cement.

My toe twitched. It reminded me that my feet were free. A thin fabric brushed against my toes. A sheet? Was I in bed? Had this all been a dream, like so many I had before? Would I open my eyes to see the window overlooking Baylor Lake? Would I roll over into my pillow and scream a muffled cry? A call for help that nobody would answer?

My thumb spasmed, and I felt the hints of a sheet beneath it as well. Suddenly, my eyes became restless, and my heavy lids broke apart. I squinted as a bright light assaulted me, and my eyes fell shut instantaneously. It was only a small sliver of vision, not enough to tell which realm I was in.

I tried again. It took an immense amount of energy to open my eyes. There was a splash of white that trailed down the center of my vision. Dots of pink and a faded pale turquoise. I wasn't sure where I was, but it wasn't the cabin. My eyes fluttered as I tried to keep them open long enough to make sense of where I was. But this tiny task was nearly impossible. I had to try something different.

I lifted my hand ever so slightly before it fell heavily upon my chest. *I can do this. I can do this.*

I opened my eyes again, feeling a rush of dizziness. The room was set into motion. I felt sick. The splash of white was a bed with bland white sheets. The twin peaks at the end of the tiny bed were my feet. And the faded pinks and blues turned out to be the wallpaper in the hospital room.

My hand twitched one more time as I took a deep, labored breath. I knew vaguely that something was in my mouth, but I didn't care. I was too tired to care. *I made it. I made it home.* Then, as if the opening of my eyelids for the first time in months had been a marathon, sleep took hold of me, and I could finally rest peacefully.

13

A gentle voice hummed in the background. "Hey . . ."

My eyelids flickered, but that was about all I could do.

"Hey," somebody else replied quietly.

"Is she going to be waking up soon?" the voice whispered.

"I think so. That's the plan, at least. They're pushing the medicine now. The doctor said it could take quite a while and to just be patient. I don't know."

I recognized one of those voices. At least I thought I did. I thought it was my mom, speaking in a hushed tone. The same tone I'd heard growing up, when she spoke to my dad and didn't want us kids to hear. The same tone she spoke in when she thought I was sleeping and didn't want to wake me. But this time was different. This time I was awake, only I couldn't open my eyes. I couldn't become fully alert no matter how hard I tried. The sleep was still calling.

"It's all going to work out. You know that. You need to trust, Dad." This voice was familiar too, although I couldn't place it. Not yet.

"Brooklyn swears up and down that everything will be okay. But I don't know how much of it I believe. She's always had these premonitions. When is it real, and when is it just fortune telling?" Mom asked.

"Don't give me that! You know it's real. She predicted my success, and you can't deny that, now can you?"

There was a long pause before a small stent of snickering. I thought I could place the voice now, because only siblings would bicker and boast like that. The other voice must be Aunt Nora. She and my mother teased each other often, and it made sense that she would come here today. Had they planned for me to wake up today? Had everybody known I was waking up on this particular day? I thought back to Walker, checking his watch. How did everybody know except me? It seemed unfair. Like they had purposely kept me in the dark.

I tried to show them I was awake now, but all I could do was twitch a knuckle. It felt like a big sign, as if I had been waving a white flag of surrender over my head. But the small tension building in my knuckle was not the grand gesture I had wanted to make, and nobody noticed. I tried to hang on to each word, but sleep was calling me, and it was so tempting. *Just one more nap?*

"You know it's true. Do you know how many millions I just collected for my client? And they were willing to *pay* in settlement, too. I told them, *I don't settle.*"

"I know. You're very good at what you do."

"You can say that again . . ."

The voices quieted, and the darkness felt like a lullaby, rocking me back to sleep. When they finally spoke again, I startled and again tried to open my eyes. I looked to the left and then the right, but it did little while my eyelids were out of commission.

"Did you hear anything about the boy next door?"

"Actually . . ." Nora said, in what I thought might be a mischievous tone. But I couldn't trust myself to pick up on the nuances and reflections of a muffled voice when I had been unconscious for so long. Heck, I was half unconscious now. Who were they talking about?

"What is that? No! You didn't! Nora, tell me you didn't . . ." Aww, there she was. Perhaps it was the tone I knew best from my mom. Somebody was about to get in trouble, though I couldn't imagine why.

There was a long pause in which I tried to speak. Make my presence known. I flexed my jaw and pursed my lips. *What was this*? Rubber? What was in my mouth? I couldn't feel my lips pressed together, but they had pressed against something foreign. I moved my tongue around, trying to identify the object. But even my tongue was lethargic and wouldn't cooperate the way I wanted. *Come on! Just work!*

"It is him!" Nora said.

"It is?" My mom sounded surprised.

Who was what? What was happening?

"Yeah."

"Why would they do that?"

"Oh, they don't care. They're a hospital. They take in the sick and wounded. They don't consider personal preferences for your next-door neighbor . . . Oh! Wow! It says they had to put a metal plate in his head and partially down the side of his face . . . something . . . to reconstruct his cheekbone."

What was that? They put a metal plate in *my face*? I wanted to cry out. Pull all the metal from my body and rip out whatever was stuffed in my mouth. The only problem was, I was far too weak. Even opening my eyes was a challenge now. There was no way I could communicate that I didn't want to be a cyborg for the rest of my life. Half human, half robot . . . I only wanted to be me.

"Yikes," Mom exclaimed.

"Yeah. It sounds like he got the worst of it."

"So, have you found the toxicology report? Is it in there?"

"I'm still looking. Hold on," Nora sounded like she was on the verge of something big. A dog catching the first scent of its prey.

"Hey. Hey. Hey," my mom hurried a hushed warning.

"Good morning, Nora. How are you?" It probably didn't look like much, as I felt no movement cross my face, but I felt like crying when I heard Dad's voice.

"Good morning. I'm well. Big day, huh?"

"Yeah." A heavy sigh followed, and I imagined my dad's brows momentarily bunching together before releasing. Though I couldn't see anything except the darkness I had grown so accustomed to.

"Hey, what's that?" he asked.

"Oh, it's nothing," Nora said.

"Well, it's not nothing. It turns out the boy next door *is* the one that caused her accident." I was listening, but I couldn't quite focus. Something about the boy who had nearly killed me, recovering in the very next room. It made me uncomfortable. Or was that the catheter? Either way, I was more vulnerable than I could withstand.

"Really? Geez, I don't think he's going to live," Dad said.

"What makes you say that?" my aunt asked.

"Well, I heard them talking in the hall on several occasions. It didn't seem favorable, I'll say that much. How did you find out it was him?"

"Ugh, she stole the dang file!" Mom complained.

I don't know why this made me happy, but it did. I always knew my aunt to get what she wanted, and often she would cross into what she called *the gray area* to get it. The gray area was her favorite place to operate, and she spent time there frequently. But it always seemed to benefit her. She was a wealthy attorney, and she was thriving in her own right. Nobody had the confidence and air that Aunt Nora had, and sometimes she had to earn that with a little mischievous behavior.

"Well, he can't die! I'll have a hard time suing him if he's dead!" Nora snapped.

"I'm sure everything will work out . . ." my mom said, her voice becoming somewhat distant.

Had she not noticed that I'd been trying to alert them I was awake? That I was sending smoke signals with twitches and lazy tongue movements? I listened to the pause in the conversation and tried my hardest to lift my hand. I was so aggravated with myself for not being able to do the things I deemed simple. I tried to open my eyes, but they would only crease, letting in a small sliver of light. The blurry figures moved around the room every so often. When one approached me, I tried to smile, but I couldn't with the thing shoved in my mouth. I wanted to scream out loud, "I'm here. I'm here," but I could only think about it. And unlike when I was in Baylor, my thoughts wouldn't get me very far.

I felt the warm touch of somebody's hand caress mine. The velvet touch was unlike anything I'd felt all summer long, and it did wonders to soothe me. I tried to squeeze my hand in response. My eyes gave a small flutter, and I attempted to make a sound with no such luck.

"Is she waking up?" Dad asked. This was it. This was my chance. A small stint of silence followed as I tried to make a sound, any sound. But my mouth was as dry as the Sahara Desert and my throat scorched by a thousand suns.

A small whimper came from Mom. I hoped they saw something in me.

"Kins, can you hear me?" Mom murmured.

I pinched my thumb and forefinger together, squeezing her hand. It felt more like a twitch than anything else, but she recognized it as the monumental victory it was, and that was all that mattered.

"Oh my god, Kins! Doctor! Get the doctor!" Mom flew into hysterics. I could hear the commotion spread across the room, and I tried to open my eyes to see what was happening. The excitement felt like a jolt of adrenaline, temporarily helping me fight the drowsiness.

I felt the bed give on either side of me, and another warm pair of hands caressed the side of my face. It took up more real estate than my mother's hands would have, and I melted into my dad's rough hand. "Kinsley, oh god, I love you so much! I love you so much!" Dad sniffled. I might have cried too if I wasn't fighting the sedation.

"She's waking up! We need to get a doctor in here!" Nora yelled distantly.

It all seemed to happen so quickly, and the amount of effort it took from me was astronomical. I felt the sleep pulling me back toward the darkness, as if the void had staked a claim on my soul, and it was time to report back. But I knew I had to make a show of my awareness, if only for a moment. I had to let them know I was in here. That I had made it. And that I was going to live.

"Has she made any signs of waking?" an unfamiliar voice asked. I felt a hand pat around my neck and chest and something cold press against my bare skin. My eyes fluttered open to see a face I'd never seen before. I groaned in a soundless protest.

"Yes. I saw her eyes move," Dad said.

"She opened them!" Nora corrected.

"She grabbed my hand!" Mom insisted.

I wanted to smile, but that would be far too much effort. It was a bit of a stretch; I hadn't reached over and grabbed her hand. I managed a small pinch. But in her defense, that spasm had meant just as much as me reaching out for a hug. And she knew that.

I sensed the doctor moving around the room, pressing and pulling, checking equipment. I tracked the sounds and tried to flutter my eyes as often as possible. But the one sensation I couldn't comprehend was feeling he had wedged my feet back in the glass slippers. Why would he do such a thing? What a terrible thing to do to a girl recovering from an accident. I tried to squirm. I tried to protest. I didn't like how my feet were unable to move.

My lids parted, followed by several faint blinks. I focused on the doctor standing at the foot of my bed, massaging my feet as he spoke medical jargon. Far too complicated for my injured brain to understand. Instead, I narrowed my gaze on my feet. It highly irritated me that my perception didn't match reality. My mind struggled with the view of a gentle massage, as if the doctor had only been trying to increase circulation, and the feeling that he had slipped my feet into quick-drying cement. Why couldn't I understand this? Why couldn't I put my imagination to rest? I feared some delusional part of my dreaming mind was flipped on like a light switch and would never turn off, even in my waking hours.

How long had this been happening? And how long would it continue? My aggravation with the doctor and the stimulation grew into frustration and worry. What if I never changed? What if my mind was messed up from the accident, and I would never be the person I used to be? I would never fully be able to appreciate the Kinsley I once loathed but had fought so hard to become. I felt the anxiety begin in my chest and spread through my limbs.

"She's awake!" Dad rushed to my side.

"My baby!" Mom cried.

The doctor came to my side, shining a flashlight in my eyes. How rude. The assaults continued from this man. I tried to groan. I tried to shake my head loose from his grip, but all I managed was a blink. I had every bit of mind to slap that flashlight out of his hands and yell, *Stop messing with me!* When he peeled my eyelids open and shined his light at me again, I tried to fight back.

Success! Well, almost. I'd lifted my hand off my chest. It wasn't what I imagined, but still, everybody celebrated, including me. *I did it!*

"Hello there, Kinsley. I'm just checking your vitals. How are you feeling, dear?" the doctor asked.

Seriously? Did he think I had enough strength to rip this thing out of my mouth and have a conversation with him? I blinked, because that was about all I could do. He continued to ask me questions, and I finally understood it was with the expectation I wouldn't answer. It must have been a habit in his line of work. He turned to my parents and explained the protocol. I didn't listen.

I was falling back to sleep when I felt somebody reaching into my mouth, grabbing a handful of my lungs, and pulling them up through my trachea and out my mouth. I was sure I had thrown up something vital, something I couldn't live without. But when I opened my eyes in shock, I saw a long clear tube that in no way resembled my organs. My mouth closed, and my teeth rest heavily against each other. I moved my tongue sluggishly in my mouth. I wanted to ask for a glass of water, but that was too advanced. My mouth was so parched, I was sure I hadn't had a drink in years. How long had I been in this coma? Did they not give me water the entire time?

Something stabbed my lips, and this time I felt a frown crease my forehead. That was an improvement, at least. It was good to show my emotions. It meant more communication. But why were they stabbing me, and why were they pulling things out of my body? It was a difficult process to endure, and I wished I had fallen back to sleep when the room was quiet. They certainly wouldn't let me sleep now.

I forced my eyes open and focused on what was right in front of me. A glass of water with a straw bent to my lips. I should have been more grateful, but I didn't have it in me. I puckered my lips and took in the smallest sip of liquid gold. My mouth moistened, but it wasn't enough to undo the months of damage. The trickle went down the side of my throat in a narrow stream, leaving most of it achingly dry. I puckered my lips again, the only way I knew how to ask for another sip, and took in more. Though it was not enough, I was satisfied with the work I'd done.

The small sips of water felt like an awakening. My eyes fully opened and I took in the room for the first time. Several blurry figures stood around my bed, watching and waiting for my response. It sure felt like a lot of pressure for somebody so weak. I didn't want to disappoint them, or myself. And if I was being honest, I was still confused. My mind was still playing tricks on me.

I strained my sight until Mom became a single human being, her two figures merging slowly under my double vision. Dad enveloped her in a hug, and I took in his kind eyes. It appeared Nora had left, and I wondered if I'd fallen asleep during the process at one point or another.

When my eyes landed on somebody I couldn't recognize, I feared that I should have known her. Her presence made me somewhat leery, and I eyed her suspiciously. What if I had lost my memory? What if she was my best friend, and I didn't even know it? But that wasn't even the confusing part. The part that really rattled me was how Gran could be here. I thought she had died *before* my accident.

Now, I wondered if the whole thing had been a premonition. Was she going to die? Was it my job to tell Grandpa Green? To tell Gran? Had I become some guide that helped spirits move on to the afterlife, and the summer in Baylor was the start of my training? I eyed her just as warily as I eyed the stranger, but her green eyes glimmered with warmth, regardless of my conspiracy theory.

"Mphh." An airy sound passed through my lips as I tried to speak. I searched the eyes of my mom and dad for signs that they understood.

"It's okay, baby. You don't need to say anything. We're here." Mom rubbed my hand. I moistened my lips and tried again, but it wasn't easy.

"Mm. Mom," I uttered. It was breathy, but I think she understood. She leaned down and hugged me tight. I took in her scent. Her normal perfume was just a hint on her skin now. I focused, really taking her in. She looked unkempt. As if she had been sleeping in the same clothes for weeks. As if her hair wasn't washed, just scraped back into the low ponytail that lay flat against her neck. I felt terrible for what I had put her through.

"Dad," I said, a little clearer this time. Dad broke down crying as he grabbed my hand and pressed it against his cheek. I tried to moisten my mouth, which seemed to be the key to speaking coherently.

Gran, who was still smiling brightly at me, patiently waited her turn. She sat down on the edge of my bed. "Gran..." I said, looking into her eyes. I reached out with a weak, trembling hand. She smiled with confidence, unlike my parents, who were an utter mess. It was good. Comforting. I needed somebody to be strong for me.

Uttering those three simple words was as hard as running a marathon, both physically and mentally. It was taxing, and I was exhausted from the effort. Gran rubbed my leg, and I smiled at her to show my gratitude. But when I glanced back to my parents, all I saw was a worried look, shared between them.

Mom's mouth parted as if she contemplated speaking, but she couldn't seem to find the words. Dad gave a small shake of his head. I must have said something wrong.

As I fought back the sleepy hold the drugs had on me, I spied my bedside table. A book my family had been passing down from generation to generation lay open as if mid read. It was the old book of fairy tales Gran had read to me as a child. She'd memorized many of the stories and recited them to me over the telephone on the occasions when the book had been left at my house by accident. They were fond memories, but they made me feel somewhat anxious now. A bookmark lay across a page with a beautiful watercolor drawing. A princess climbing into a round pumpkin carriage, decorated in colorful sparkling lights. I closed my eyes and let sleep take over me like a thief in the night.

14

I had a faint memory of reaching up into my hairline and getting scolded like a child near a hot stove. A peek in a hand-held mirror. And a scraggly, gaunt girl looking back at me. She had purple shadows under her gaunt eyes and a shaved section of her head. But I'd grown suspicious when seeing a reflection in the mirror. I didn't know who she was, but I think they said it was me.

I slept a lot. I wasn't sure how many days and nights had lapsed. It was probably a side effect of the medication. Something that dripped through my IV. I did some toe wiggling though, and I was proud of myself when I passed the test. I wasn't so happy about leveling up to leg lifting. Lifting my legs was like lifting a spoon through nearly set Jell-O. My feet seemed to rise, but the flesh and muscle of my leg lay stubbornly on the bed.

Today was the best I'd felt yet. I still woke groggy, but it took less time to become alert. I recalled waking only once in the night. I longed for Walker to be by my side, but once I gained some consciousness and realized I was in the hospital, I just let the ache in my heart pull me back to sleep. It wasn't the same sleep I'd been in all summer long. I didn't return to an alternate existence when my mind drifted. It was quite the opposite, really. Nothing happened at all.

One of the first faces I woke to this morning was my little brother's. Conrad came to visit, and I was excited to see him in his true form. The last memory I had of him was one I wished would soon be forgotten. The smile that spread across his face reminded me I'd done right by coming home. Now, I couldn't imagine all the pain I would have brought to my family if I had stayed in Baylor. And it was difficult to forgive myself for having that as my plan for so very long.

"You *are* awake!" Con announced.

I smiled lazily and cleared my throat. "Hey there." Con came crashing into me with a big hug, and suddenly words didn't seem to matter anymore. There was nothing I could say that he hadn't already said for both of us with this loving gesture. He trembled as he grabbed me tight. At thirteen years old, he was as tall as I was, but much stronger. "It's okay. I'm okay." I promised. My throat and mouth were properly hydrated, and speaking was easier now.

"I thought you were going to die!" he choked.

"Conrad!" Mom scolded.

"What?"

"It's okay. I did too." I admitted. Of course, I wouldn't admit all of it. Nobody needed to know the extent of my nightmare.

"You did? Do you remember it?" Con asked, as he pulled back and sat with one leg stretched across my bed.

"Do I remember what?"

"Con. Please. She needs to rest," Mom said.

"What? She literally did nothing *but* sleep!" he protested, his voice cracking as he fought to become a man in a boy's body.

Mom sighed, and Dad rubbed her back. "Honey, it's okay. We have all the time in the world to talk about what happened, and you don't need to go over all of it right now."

"It's okay. Really. Do I remember what?" I asked. It was always like Mom to be overprotective, but I couldn't see how burying everything inside was going to help protect me now. I had already gone through months of damage. Months of being caught in a nightmare, ensnared in a web. If anything, not talking about it would probably do worse damage.

"Do you remember the crash?"

I took a deep breath and looked around the room. My eyes settled on Gran as she sat quietly in the corner of the room. So quietly, in fact, I hadn't realized she was there. I would have to ask my mom how she was doing when she wasn't present. Con's eyes followed my gaze before looking back at me impatiently.

I went over all the facts I'd known about the accident in my head. The car flew off an overpass of sorts. I was wearing a yellow blouse. There was another car that remained on top of the overpass. It was nighttime. The windows had shattered.

I thought long and hard about what it all meant. And I soon realized that most, if not all, of these memories were from seeing the accident from an outsider's perspective. My memories solely came as nightmares that had haunted me while I lay helpless in a coma. And because of that, I supposed I had no actual memory of the accident. I wasn't entirely sure where I was headed that night or why. I didn't even know if it had been my birthday, or if that was something I had made up in my head.

"I think I wore my yellow shirt?"

Mom beamed, encouraging me to continue.

"I think it was, maybe, my birthday?" I asked again, uncertain.

"Yes. It was your eighteenth birthday, and you were heading out to meet your friends," Dad said, and then added in a quiet voice, "You never came home . . ." I could see that he was trying to be strong for me, but his entire frame looked like it was ready to crumble. A strong man brought to the verge of breaking.

"I'm . . . I'm sorry. I didn't—"

"No! Don't you do that. This was *not* your fault! Do you understand? This was *not* your fault," Mom enforced.

"You—" Dad paused to take in a long quivering breath. "You were hit. The guy didn't even stop at the red light. We think he was intoxicated. Somebody said they saw that same car at the bar earlier in the night. You did everything right, so please don't blame yourself. We're just happy you're all right."

I looked into Mom's and Dad's eyes and went with it. Maybe the accident wasn't my fault. It's not like I could recall it myself, so I would have to take their word for it.

"What else do you remember?" Con prodded.

"Well, I remember a lot, actually. I dreamed about you," I said in a teasing voice.

"You did!?"

"I sure did. And I turned you to ice!" I said, twirling my finger around like a witch's wand.

"Wow, really?"

"Heck yeah! I had powers. You wouldn't believe the things I did this summer!"

The laughter in the room faded, and their eyes turned wary, flickering in unspoken concern among themselves. I had the sense I'd said something wrong again. It didn't look like anybody wanted to say the words out loud, but I wouldn't let it slide this time. They were all thinking *something*.

"What is it? What did I say?" I asked Con. He turned to my parents, so I too looked at them for answers. They silently debated, and I turned my questioning eyes to Gran. She slowly pointed to a calendar on the wall, indicating I would find my answers if I looked hard enough.

I had seen calendars countless times this summer, but this one was different. It was real. I'd grown accustomed to seeing only thirteen days in the month, but this one had a full month. I counted thirteen days crossed off in red marker. Honestly, I was just happy it wasn't written with blood. I bit my bottom lip and let it roll between my teeth, somewhere on the verge of fidgeting and finding pain to distract me from finding the answer on the wall. There was something about this calendar, something odd that I couldn't quite put my finger on. *May*? Had I been in a coma for nearly a year?

"How long was I in the coma for?" I asked, suddenly fearful.

"Thirteen days. Thirteen long, terrible days."

That made little sense. I looked back at the calendar. May? But that would mean that summer hadn't even begun yet. Had the entire two months I imagined in Baylor happened in just thirteen days in the real world? Had time slowed so much that I had experienced an entire summer before it had ever started?

"Only thirteen days?"

"Did you think it was more or less?" Dad asked.

"I . . . I thought I was gone all summer."

A nurse came to check on me, but she did little to interrupt our conversation. I let her move about as my family and I talked.

"Oh, heavens no! Not that long."

"Wait? Did you really dream?" Con asked.

"Um, yeah. I did. You wouldn't believe the things I saw."

The nurse stiffened by my side. "You remember having dreams while you were in the coma?" she asked.

"I know. It's probably impossible or something," I shrugged.

"Well, yes. That's what they'll tell you. But if I'm being honest," she lowered her voice and checked behind her shoulder for listening ears. "I hear all sorts of stories about dreams and out-of-body experiences while people are on the operating table, under anesthesia, in comas, you name it. I believe it," she said with a wink.

I grinned, feeling validated for the first time since waking. Like maybe I hadn't been as lost as I once believed.

"Are you going to tell us, or what?" Con interrupted my thoughts.

I laughed. His impatience used to drive me up the wall, but now it seemed endearing. "What do you want to know?"

"Everything, of course. Start from the beginning, and don't leave out a single thing." He settled in, leaning his back against the foot of my bed where a pillow had been stashed. My parents laughed, and the nurse went about her work checking the machines and readjusting sticky things on my chest.

"Well, it's a long story, but here goes. I went to Baylor Lake for the summer with a group of friends."

It was just the beginning and already my mom was interrupting. "Fascinating! You've been planning that trip all year long with Lainey and Emma. You must have dreamed about it because that's what you were looking forward to doing after high school graduation!"

"Graduation?" I looked back at the calendar. The dates were a little foggy, but I knew that May was early for the summer break, and I had been in a coma for far less time than I had imagined. "Has that happened yet?"

"It's next month, dear."

My thoughts raced. How could I have spent my entire summer celebrating my high school graduation when it hadn't even happened yet? I thought back to my memories of graduation, and I couldn't pull up a single detail other than my gown and cap hanging from the windowsill in my bedroom.

"Yeah. I guess I was looking forward to celebrating," I murmured. Dad squeezed Mom's shoulder as they waited for me to continue. It was hard for them to see my confusion, and I knew they felt sorry for me. I would have to try to hide it better next time. I didn't want them to worry any more than they already had.

"We went to Baylor Lake and stayed at Uncle Tanner's cabin all summer long. It was going to be the best summer I ever had. Until something terrible happened. Trinity died . . ." I lost myself for a moment in the memory of her body washing up on shore.

I really should have spared the details for my little brother's sake, but it was one of the first memories I had, and it just slipped out. I obviously wasn't going to tell them I had drowned right after my car accident. That would only make them feel more helpless. Right then and there, I decided not to tell them I once thought I was dead, either.

Mom's face turned pale, and Dad's forehead creased with worry. I realized I couldn't really tell them much of the story at all. I should keep all the horror locked up in a little box that nobody would ever find. It wasn't going to do anything but worry my parents anyway.

"Who's Trinity?" Con asked. He was eager to find out the rest of the story, as if it were no more than an old ghost story. That's how it was beginning to feel to me too.

I waved my hand toward my parents and then realized they were waiting for the answer, too. It's not like Trinity and I had been the best of friends. I tried to think if she had ever come to the house. That's when I caught sight of the cards sitting on the bedside table. I became sidetracked and picked up the ones closest to me to read. Mom handed me the rest.

I had a beautiful card from Lainey, talking about how she was so sorry we wouldn't have the summer we planned before she headed off for college. I had another card from Emma, talking about how she would help me through recovery, and how we could watch endless movies together while I lay in bed and rested. I flipped through a few letters and cards from my family; Nora, Grandpa. But that was it. No letter from Trinity, no card from Noah. I thought back to all my friends and how I'd questioned their friendship over the summer. Maybe they weren't as good of friends as I'd thought they were.

"Did Lainey visit?"

"Yes, Lainey and Emma have been by every couple of days." There was no mention of anybody else, and I wondered why. It hurt. It brought me back to the night I'd drowned and nobody cared. Nobody noticed. It was one of the reasons I didn't want to come back to this life. Because I was tired of being invisible.

Con nudged me with his foot. "Oh, sorry. She's nobody. Just a friend from school. Anyway, we had a wonderful summer, really. We entered the bass tournament." I tried to find something positive to say.

"No way!" Dad exclaimed. He loved the tournament and looked forward to it each summer.

"Yeah. And Emma snuck a store-bought salmon onto the boat and pretended she caught it!" I laughed. It was a genuine laugh but clouded with confusion and an anxious energy. I was still a little cautious of how much to say, and I worried I didn't quite have a grasp on reality yet.

"What? There's no salmon in that lake!" Dad chuckled.

"Yeah, I know! It was so funny. I wish you were there. Um, let me think. We went to the Baylor Parade, and one of my friends got into a fight with Snow White's seven dwarves!!"

"Really?" Mom asked, nervously eyeing the book of fairy tales on the bedside table.

"Yeah. And I threw a ton of parties too. Sorry, not sorry." The laughter boomed. And for the first time, I realized there were several nurses and doctors crowded in the tiny room listening to my stories. The entire room was electric with excitement, and for a moment, everything felt right.

"We may have broken a few things," I frowned. She shrugged lightheartedly, and everyone laughed.

"What happened next?"

"Well, I met this boy," I said coyly. My brother was already bored, but the nurses drew closer. "His name was Walker, and he was so handsome! He took me for a ride in his canoe for the Fourth of July, and all the fireworks froze in time, just like streamers glittering down from the sky. It may have been a date." I shrugged.

Mom and Dad stiffened, and I could tell I'd said something wrong again. But with the audience I had in front of me now, I couldn't ask. I made a mental note to circle back when we were alone.

"We could reach out and grab the fireworks, and they fizzled in the palms of our hands. And this one time, I swam to the bottom of the lake where . . . Mermaids lived!"

It wasn't entirely honest, but after talking about how Trinity died, I wasn't going to give them anything else to harp on. And Lainey had looked majestic under the water occasionally. I remembered the way her hair floated in the dark water and danced around her freckled face. She was, at times, beautiful. This was the only side of the story that Con needed to know. That any of them needed to know. And I would take the rest to my grave.

"Could you breathe underwater?"

"No. But only because I didn't *need* to breathe at all."

"Could you fly?"

"No. But I *did* jump off a cliff. And fall off the Summerfield State Fair Ferris wheel!" I said enthusiastically.

"No way! Were you scared?"

I pretended to think it over. "Actually, it was pretty cool."

"What was the coolest thing you did?"

"Hmmm . . ." I tapped my finger on my chin. I looked to Gran to help jog my memory. "That's a hard question. I turned into a wolf at one point, and I think that was the best. I had claws and fangs, and I was gigantic! I stood on two feet and walked like a human. I even had the strength of a dozen men. But I could also control lightning and thunder with my thoughts, and I could manipulate bees and make movies come to life! Oh, and I could stop time, and walk on water, so it's a toss-up, I guess." Everyone erupted in gasps and laughter.

The room was packed with nurses and doctors, and I could barely see Gran sitting in the corner. "But now that I think of it, the best part of all was when Gran read me fairy tales from a rocking chair, by the light of a wood-burning fire," I said, smiling at her warmly. She smiled fondly and put her hand over her heart.

The room parted to follow my gaze, but something wasn't right. Several nurses shuddered. One doctor looked to have caught a chill as he ran his hand up and down his arm. A wary look passed between my family members and the medical personnel as the room fell eerily quiet. Embarrassment washed over me, but I didn't know why.

"Okay. I think that's enough for one day. Kinsley should get her rest," Mom announced. She ushered everyone out.

The nurses parted as my brother blurted out, "Do you really think she saw Gran's ghost?" Mom sucked in a breath and smacked Con's shoulder.

I watched all the blue scrubs funnel out the door, whispering among themselves. As the room emptied, I stared at the lonesome seat where my gran had sat moments prior.

15

The next several days I dealt with what my parents quietly described as withdrawal, but I knew more accurately as ignoring. I mentally checked out on things I couldn't care less about, but more importantly, the things I specifically didn't want to know. Like my craniotomy. Like the fun fact that they'd removed a portion of my skull so that my brain could swell outside of my head. What person in their right mind could possibly want to know the details of that? I had already witnessed the operation when I'd been stuck within the walls of the cabin. I didn't need to hear the medical jargon too.

I tried not to touch the shaved part of my head, because I'd rather pretend it never happened. But sometimes, when nobody was looking, I'd reach into my hair and feel the sharp points of the stitches. It made me feel like a modern Frankenstein. A product of science. Like two girls, Kinsley and Layla, had been stitched together to make one whole person. Because I'd never been enough to stand on my own.

I thought of Layla often. How I hadn't truly seen her during my time in Baylor, but seemingly she was actually a very important part of me. A part I hadn't recognized in myself and hadn't come to accept. Now, when I had a positive outlook on something insignificant or produced a wicked laugh at one of my brother's jokes, I would think of her. I hadn't realized how much my laugh sounded like a witch's cackle until now. Or had that been the rasp in my voice from having a breathing tube in my throat for thirteen days?

The week passed in a blur of check-ins with more doctors than I could count and a multitude of tests. Most of the doctors told me the same thing. I barely lived. Apparently, I only had a fifteen percent chance of survival. And even then, I wasn't expected to make a full recovery. Whatever that meant. They told me I was a miracle, but I didn't believe any of it. By and large, I knew it all boiled down to fate. *Something* had brought me back home, and it wasn't a statistic.

I had a lot of work ahead of me. I had a ton of recovery still to face, and it would be anything but easy. I wasn't looking forward to the challenge, and I often wished I were back in Baylor. I wished that my recovery was as simple as a thought that manifested before my eyes. That it was nothing more than something I could conjure in the cool mist. And sometimes Baylor seemed to be the lesser evil of the two realities. Though having a full recovery from a brain injury was going to be an uphill battle, sometimes I felt capable of that challenge. Most times I did not.

The staff was supportive, though, and they reassured my parents and me that my recovery was moving along faster than expected. Time seemed to crawl by, though, and I couldn't imagine taking things any slower. The more I was awake, the more I pretended not to be. And on several occasions, I rested while listening in on conversations I shouldn't have. Talk of my expected recovery. The pursuit of a possible lawsuit. How much money Nora thought she could pull from the kid who hit me, and whether he was drunk.

I heard them talking about what they called my hallucinations. Apparently, that's what Gran was. The doctor said it wasn't uncommon for somebody in my position to have hallucinations after a coma. And if somebody was hallucinating, it would make sense that they would choose to see a loved one who had passed on. The doctor said they see it all the time in the hospital. Gran made fewer and fewer appearances after I heard that conversation, and I figured they were right. Maybe I had only seen her because I wanted her comfort. And maybe she was the last manifestation I would ever have.

But there was one more conversation I heard and knew I shouldn't have. It was very hush-hush about the kid who was fighting for his life on the opposite side of the wall. When I was in the ICU, I thought about him often. I wondered if he was trapped in a nightmare like I was. And some nights, I fought the urge to sneak over and hold his hand. Other nights, I wanted to unplug him for all that he'd done to me.

At some point in my stay, maybe a week after waking, my time in the intensive care unit came to an end. I got moved to the lower level of the hospital for recovery. The nurses made a big show of it, clapping and lining the hall to the elevator. I tried to appear pleased with my progress, but all I really wanted to do was get a better look into the room next to mine. I could barely make out movement through the slats of the blinds. From what I could see, the kid had visitors.

The following week in recovery went by a little slower. Perhaps because I was awake for most of it. I'd taken several assisted walks throughout the days and was allowed outside for some fresh air. Both Lainey and Emma visited me, but one of the best surprises of all was seeing Gunner. Lainey snuck him in, and none were the wiser because Gunner was wearing his special vest that said he was working. When he jumped on my bed and gave me kisses, all my worry melted away.

It was when the kisses stopped that I realized how uncomfortable Lainey was. She kept looking at the side of my head, and I knew she was afraid that Gunner would hurt me. I reassured her I was all right, but it didn't seem to help. I still had black circles under my eyes, gaunt cheeks, and if my hair was lying just right, you could see where the hair was shaved. It was going to take time for everyone to realize I wasn't as fragile as they thought. Thankfully, I could avoid all the reminders in the mirror. Lainey and Emma weren't so lucky.

Every single night, I went to sleep trying to get back to Baylor. I imagined the fair. The cabin. Sitting in Walker's canoe. But when sleep took over, the lights were out. The curtain had closed, and the magic show was over. The summer I spent in Baylor was gone, and I worried that it might be lost forever.

The night before I was to be discharged, I snuck out of my room. Walking was still difficult, and I felt unstable all by my lonesome. But I knew if I dragged my hand alongside the wall, I'd draw even more attention to myself, and I didn't want that. Luckily, I found an abandoned wheelchair and made a quick escape into the elevator. I pushed the button for the ICU floor and nervously played with my robe until the doors slid open.

I tightened my grip around the thin tires of the wheelchair as I peered around the corner. The hall was dim, but I still recognized a nurse working in the distance. I waited patiently until her desk was clear and then rolled myself as quickly as I could through the corridor of the ICU to the next hallway. I stopped at the room just before the one I'd been in.

Behind that door was the kid who almost took my life. A part of me wondered if it would bring me closure if I just snuck in and laid my eyes on him. If I looked at him and realized that he was only human. That he was hurt, too. Maybe then I wouldn't be so angry. Maybe I wouldn't feel like this terrible thing had happened to me, but rather, it happened to *us*.

I wheeled to a nearby corner and ditched the wheelchair. I stood up slowly and shakily and walked close to the wall. I didn't have long before the nurse came back to her desk, so I hobbled as quickly as my weakened legs could take me. Someone in a pair of scrubs came around the corner, and I turned the doorknob without a second thought and swiftly vanished from the hall.

Once in the dark room, I felt a sense of relief. I could probably stay here for a good amount of time without being caught. I didn't recall getting more than one or two checks in the night when I'd been in the ICU. I briefly wondered what they would do if they caught me here, but I was going home tomorrow, so I didn't care how awkward it might be. This was important, I told myself, as I thought of my empty bed and the possibility of a nurse coming to check on me. Would they sound an alarm? Code something? I hoped not.

In the dark, I grabbed the edge of the boy's bed and patted my way up to him. By the light of the monitors, he wasn't as young as I'd originally thought. From the outline of his body under the sheets, he didn't look like a boy at all. My parents had made him out to be a newly licensed driver. But he was probably older than me. It was hard to tell with how swollen his face was. His entire head was shaved, and a line of puckered stitches was carved down the side of his face. He looked to be in awful shape.

I listened to the rhythmic beat of his monitor, and I felt oddly at peace in his room.

I had anticipated the possibility of wanting to grab the pillow from behind his head and smother him for all he'd done to me. And I was fully prepared to drag myself out of his room, if that were the case. Because I knew that death was permanent in this realm. But I didn't get that urge, and I quietly thanked Layla for that.

A simple thought here wasn't enough to create something on its own, and there would be no conjuring in the hospital tonight. I wouldn't turn into a dark witch here, and the machine keeping him alive wouldn't malfunction, just because I thought about it. Which I did . . . several times.

As I stared at his closed eyelids, I wondered if he was dreaming. Did he remember more of the accident than I did? He obviously had the other half of the memory that I was missing. Would I ever pass him on the street? Would I know who he was? Or would he not be as lucky as to walk out of here?

I gazed oddly at his face. I thought this would be more of a monumental moment for me to sneak into his room and see him lying here, so helpless. But it wasn't all that I hoped it to be. It was just me, staring at another patient in the dark. Just me, watching a stranger sleep. Whoever he was, he wasn't in this room. Just like I had been far, far away, this guy was too.

Was he fighting to get back home like I had? Or had he made his choice to stay like I once wanted? That didn't sit well with me, and I frowned down at him. I didn't like the idea that he might escape this place by choice. If I had to go through recovery, he should, too.

I leaned over him, doing for him what Gran had done for me. "Come back. You must come back," I said, my voice still raspy.

I watched his motionless face, waiting for signs that he heard me. But there was no response. I recalled the book of fairy tales by my bedside and my mom singing to me when I was deep in sleep. I'd heard those things. They'd seeped into my subconscious and fed into my dreams. I hoped my words would do the same for him. I hoped they would be a beacon of light in an otherwise dark and twisted realm.

I didn't like the guy, and I was still angry with him for what he'd done to me—accident or not—but I needed him to pull through. I couldn't be the only survivor of the accident. Not that misery loves company, but rather misery loves hope. He was worse off than I was, and if he lived, then maybe I really had a chance at having a full recovery. Mentally and physically.

I decided my work here was done. There was nothing for me here, beyond satisfying my curiosity. But when my hands caught on his chart in the dark, a rush of mischievous delight coursed through my veins. Maybe there was something here for me? My Aunt Nora would be proud. I picked up the chart and squinted as I tried to read the tiny black print. The room was dark, and there were far too many words on the page for me to know where to begin.

A door closed nearby, and I feared they were doing midnight rounds. I hurried to place the folder back and scurried to the door. I cracked it open just as Cyndi, the nurse who had taken care of me in the ICU, emerged from the neighboring room. I panicked and my limbs froze, rendering me useless. The door opened and pushed me into a small dark corner between the curtain and the door. I held my breath as the nurse flipped on a set of dim lights. The door swung shut, exposing me. It was only a matter of time before she turned and saw me. I didn't move an inch, and I wished now, more than ever, I had the power of manifestation.

"Walker, Walker, Walker. How are you doing this fine night? Is that pillow bothering you? Let me fix that," the nurse said as she moved about.

I couldn't believe my ears. In fact, I didn't. Did she say *Walker*? I felt faint. My knees grew weak, and my hands felt cold and tingly. The edges of my vision grew dark as I took a step out from behind the curtain.

"Did . . ."

Cyndi threw her hands in the air and yelled, alerting the other staff to my presence. It was the last thing I remembered before dropping to the floor. Unfortunately, I wasn't out long enough to avoid the discomfort of getting caught. I was sprawled on the floor when I regained consciousness. The security guard reached me before any other nurses or doctors. Cyndi calmed everyone down once she recognized me.

"I know her. She was my patient last week. They moved her downstairs. I'm not sure what she's doing up here. Maybe she got lost? Her room used to be next door," Cyndi said.

"Did she show any signs of aggression toward you?" the security guard asked. His boots were so close to my face, I could smell the rubber soles.

"Oh, heavens no. She just scared me, that's all. The poor thing took a step out and went down. I can't imagine how she got up here?"

"Okay. As long as you're all right, I'll get a wheelchair and escort her downstairs."

"Thanks, Charlie. I'll call a nurse to come meet you."

I sprang to life, grabbing Cyndi's arm as she passed by. "Did you say Walker?" Cyndi searched my frantic eyes, trying to make sense of my words. Then she patted my hand and freed her arm.

"It's okay, Kinsley. Mr. Charlie is going to take you back to your room now."

"But—"

"Shhh, you go get some rest."

"But, Cyndi! Cyndi!" my voice cracked.

The door closed behind Cyndi, and Charlie helped me into a wheelchair, adjusting my feet on the footrests. He spun me around so that he could back up through the door. My eyes fixed on the patient lying in the hospital bed. Was it really Walker? It couldn't be. Walker was a ghost. He didn't live in my world. He couldn't . . .

My eyes lingered on the stranger named Walker until the door shut rather too quickly between us. As we passed his window, I tried to look through the slats of the blinds, but I couldn't see past the darkness.

I turned, looking over my shoulder, somewhat panicked, and saw Cyndi on the phone. "Cyndi?" I waved my arm overhead. She barely lifted her gaze.

"Cyndi!" I called louder. She wiggled her fingers in my direction, dismissing me again. My heart pounded in my chest and my thoughts raced.

It took forever to get to my room, but after some initial misinformation from the staff, Nurse Martina got me settled back in bed. She shook her head, making tsking sounds as she lifted the bed rails. But she knew it wasn't an accident and that I hadn't fallen out of bed.

"What did you do, Miss Wilde? Roll out of bed and sleepwalk back to your old room? Or were you sneaking up to that boy's room on purpose?"

"Do you know whose room I was in? A patient named Walker?" I pled for answers.

"No dear. I don't have patients in the ICU." Martina peered through thick false lashes and thought for a moment. "Do you know the boy? Is that why you were in there? Oh, honey, he'd better be a cute one if you went through all that trouble."

"Well, no, I don't know him. But—" Martina's forehead creased as she turned away. I panicked. I didn't want to be left alone. My thoughts were far too loud for solitude.

"He hit me!" I blurted out. Martina froze, and then reengaged.

"He *hit* you? That boy is in a coma."

"No. I mean yes, but not like that. His car hit my car. That's how we both wound up in the hospital."

"Oh!" Martina waited for me to continue.

"This is going to sound weird . . ." I tangled my fingers together as Martina sat on the edge of my bed. I could tell that she was into weird by the way she leaned in, yearning for more. She reminded me of Emma, and I smiled fondly.

"Oh, honey, there's nothing you can say that I haven't already heard. I've been working in this hospital for thirty-two years now, and I've heard a lot of weird in my day. Let's give it a go," she said, waving a hand as an invitation for me to continue.

"Well, okay. I had dreams when I was in my coma. You might have heard," I said with a shrug. She nodded, and I felt my cheeks heat. I waited for her to tell me it was impossible, but she barely batted an eye. She was used to this kind of thing, and I relaxed for the first time that night. "And in my dreams, there was a boy named Walker."

Martina pondered this.

"Don't you think it's weird that the boy next door, the very one who crashed into me, is also named *Walker*? I swear, I've never met another Walker in my life. It's not a very common name."

I hadn't realized when I'd done it, but at some point, I'd reached out and grabbed Martina's hand, pleading for it to be true. For the love of my life to be real, and not a phantom, trapped in a dream I could never return to.

Martina thought long and hard, and I waited with bated breath, but her words weren't what I hoped to hear. "Ohhh, I see now. While it's true, some people dream in a coma, it's more likely that you heard his name from the paramedics and staff at the hospital, and that's how his name entered your dream."

A blanket of defeat draped over my shoulders, and I hunched over. I would have given anything for it to be true, for Walker to be real. Now that I knew Layla was a part of me, I understood that Walker hadn't been deceitful like I once thought. He loved me. All of me. No matter where the bits and pieces of my soul scampered off to.

"Have you ever had a dream that it was raining, and when you woke up, the rain was so loud on your roof that it entered your dream?"

I shook my head, unable to look at her without tearing up.

"Hmm. Have you ever had a dream that you had to pee, and when you woke up, you *really* had to pee?"

"Yeah . . ." I admitted.

"It's like that. Only more complicated."

"But I had all sorts of dreams! My friends were there! And this girl named Layla Barns was lost, but then we found her!"

"Layla Barns?" Martina sat back with a gaping smile. I frowned, and she broke into rolling laughter.

"Oh, honey. This is exactly what I'm saying. They've been showing reruns of *Starlet* all month! Layla Barns has been playing nonstop on the television."

"Huh?"

"Yeah! The new season is coming out soon, and they're playing reruns. It's a promotion or something. *Starlet*, seasons one through eight. I've seen it fifty times this month. But we all know and love Layla. And since she's been on TVs throughout the hospital, it only makes sense that you've heard her name several dozen times. I know I have. These things have a way of seeping into your subconscious, honey. Heck, I've probably dreamed of Layla Barns at this point!" Martina rolled her eyes. "Don't think another thing of it. Mystery solved." Martina stood and dusted her hands as if she had a hard day's work, when all she really did was crush my soul.

"The main character in *Starlet* is Layla Barns?" I asked, though I already knew the answer. If you would've asked me when I was ten years old what my favorite show was, I would have said *Starlet*. Layla was so popular that I once had a poster of her on my wall. I even dressed up as her for Halloween that year. No wonder I felt inferior to her. She was my childhood idol.

"Huh. She kind of looks like you, now that I think of it. Get some rest. And stay in bed!" Martina turned out the light, leaving me alone in the dark. My thoughts clamored in my head.

If Layla Barns was just a character on a TV playing in the background, then likely, Walker was just the name of the patient next door. Or perhaps we did share an ambulance ride together. I had plucked his name from someone's mouth and given it to the guy of my dreams. A character I had made up all on my own. And just like Layla had never been a real person, neither had Walker.

16

After a summer in Baylor and two weeks in the hospital, I thought I would be happier to go home. The thirteen days I'd spent in Baylor had seemed like an eternity, and the two weeks following passed in a blur of confusion, disappointment, and drugs. I got used to sleeping with all the noises throughout the night, and I worried my house would be too quiet.

Martina was one of my favorite nurses, even if she didn't believe in all that I wanted her to. But what I loved most about her was her willingness to keep me company when she should have been working. Most of the other staff avoided talking to me about my experience as if it were taboo. As if they believed in science but witnessed the unexplainable way too often while working in the hospital. But Martina asked questions, and I appreciated that. I tried not to talk about it with my family as openly as I did my favorite nurse, because I knew it worried them. And my parents had enough on their plates.

Was I excited about going home? Not really. Home was not my little house in Clover anymore. Home was the cabin, and I knew I wouldn't be returning there again. Not in my dreams, at least. I tried to imagine the day I'd go back to the cabin in real life, but I couldn't picture it.

I wasn't exactly excited to leave the hospital, either. While there was a part of me that yearned for normalcy, there was another part that didn't want to leave the stranger named Walker behind. I still had mixed feelings about him, but the part that ate at me the most was, *what if?* What if he *was* my Walker? I thought back to the time he'd said we were more alike than I knew. I wondered if he'd been trying to tell me that he, too, was alive and dreaming. Though every time I thought about it, I'd shake my head. *Impossible.* Even *I* didn't believe it.

With all the headaches, confusion, and muscle atrophy came anger. I didn't like to admit it, but I was growing angry with Walker. Not the one I'd fallen for, but the one who'd hit me. The one who lay unconscious in the hospital. I didn't deserve what happened to me on the night of my birthday, and I knew I'd be dealing with the consequences of the accident for far too long. In all honesty, I wasn't sure I'd ever recover from the psychological damage I'd undergone. If it was just a dream, why hadn't I forgotten it already?

Martina helped Dad load me into the back seat of our car. She gave me a quick hug goodbye. "It was a pleasure taking care of you, honey. Don't come back now, you hear?" she said with a wink.

"I won't. Promise."

Dad shut the door, and my parents spoke to the nurse for a few minutes longer. I ran my hands across the seat and relished the leather smell. It wasn't the best smell in the world, and it was far from new, but it wasn't the hospital, and I loved that. My eyes wandered through the parking lot and settled on a few people coming and going from the hospital. A wave of melancholy crept up on me.

"Ready to go home?" Mom asked, as she got into the car.

I forced a smile and nodded. I only wished I felt whole and happy. But leaving the hospital was like leaving something behind. I knew I was taking Layla with me, but I was leaving Walker there. Or at least, my idea of him. Every time I tried to find the truth somewhere inside of me, all I found were more questions.

A tear pricked the corner of my eye as we pulled out of the parking lot, and a very serious part of me wondered if I would ever be happy again. I knew the road to recovery was going to be a long one, but I hadn't expected it to be mental, too. I was an idiot for thinking I only had to deal with physical pain. What lay ahead now was a whole lot worse than any pain I could ever bear, and it would run deep, scarring me from the inside out.

"What's that, Mom?" I asked, pointing to a bag in her hand. I hadn't noticed it before, and it appeared she was trying to hide it.

"Oh. It's nothing." Dad pulled his eyes from the road to look warily at her. It only stoked my curiosity more.

"Well, it doesn't look like *nothing*." For a moment, I watched the distress pass between them.

"It's just a bag of your clothing, from the accident. Your cell phone, jewelry . . . We're going to dispose of it when we get home. We didn't want to upset you," Dad said, checking my reflection in the rearview mirror. He took my mom's hand across the center console, like they were lending each other strength.

I sighed heavily and looked out the window. My favorite yellow top was in that bag. But they were right to throw it away. I'd never wear it again. In fact, I'd probably never wear yellow again. Was this how superstitions were born?

"I'm getting a new phone, right?"

"Yes. We'll get you a new phone. We just want you to recover first."

Conrad greeted us in the driveway when we got home. He helped me walk inside and supported me when our dog, Roxie, leapt against my leg. She usually had a sweet disposition, but today, I was greeted with a rambunctious jumble of black fur and white paws. She was overly excited to see me, and it brought a smile to my face. "Hi, girl! I missed you too!" I said, scratching the top of her head as she stretched up my leg. It was always nice to be missed.

"She wasn't the only one who missed you," Dad said, as he kissed my forehead. I smiled up at him. Even though it was genuine, it was also a distraction. I caught sight of Mom tossing the bag of my bloodied belongings in the trash beneath the sink.

"Is it okay if I just lie down in my room?" I asked. It seemed like a lot of pressure, just being home. And even though they probably weren't, I felt like my family was watching me. Judging me. Analyzing my behavior and wondering if I would ever be normal again. I wasn't sure I would be.

"Of course. I'll help you upstairs," Mom said.

Once we reached my bedroom, she hovered in the doorway.

"I'm okay, Mom. I just need to rest." I began to close my door, and Roxie ran through the small crack before it shut.

"I love you."

"I love you too, Mom."

I took in my room for a moment and sighed in relief. My graduation gown was no longer hanging in the window. Would I ever be able to wear it? I fought with myself internally, mentally separating the memory that I had already graduated with the fact that I hadn't. Like two sides of the same coin, they both seemed to exist in one reality or another.

My bed was freshly made, and I grappled with the memory of Walker and me clinging to one another the last time I had thought I was in my bedroom. But it was just another fake memory. Another moment that felt as real as this one now, but wasn't. I saw no real distinction to separate fact from fiction, other than the timing. The summer was as fake as a spray tan. Separating these memories were difficult and would be time consuming.

Roxie jumped onto my bed and curled into a little black ball at the foot of the bed. I wanted to join her, but caught myself looking out my window at Noah's house. Just a few doors down was the guy I'd crushed on for the last couple of years. I wondered what he was up to now and what he'd heard about my accident. It made me sick to my stomach thinking about all the kids at school talking about it like some hot gossip. There were probably many rumors floating around. I suddenly understood why my parents weren't eager to replace my broken phone. I guess ignorance was bliss.

I slipped into a light trance as I stared out my window. I was beginning to feel the comfort of being home, and it made me sleepy. I found myself swept into a daydream about returning to school, and it seemed almost natural when I saw Gran's reflection in the window beside my own. My heart warmed under her gentle gaze, and I finally found the peace I'd been looking for since leaving the hospital. It seemed as if I would survive this mess, if only Gran stayed by my side. I begged for it to be true, though somewhere in the back of my mind, I knew it wasn't.

"Welcome home, dear," a faint voice said, somewhere between my ears. My eyes strained as I pulled back from my daydream and fixed them on Gran's reflection. What was this? How was I seeing her? Did I really hear her speak? Would I have to report this hallucination to my parents?

I didn't want to scare Gran away. If it was truly her ghost visiting me from the other side, I knew what I did next would be crucial. If I looked away from her reflection too quickly, she would likely disappear. But if I remained calm, acted as if it was no big deal, and turned my head ever so slowly, she might just stay. I swallowed a rising lump in my throat and slowly moved my gaze from her reflection to the woman standing next to me.

Gran smiled crookedly, just as she'd done before. Only this time she was in my bedroom, and I knew she was dead. My eyes grew dry, but I was afraid to blink her away. "Is that you?" I whispered, barely audible.

"Dear, who else would I be?" She laughed, and this time I swore I heard her distant voice brush against my ear. Was I hearing this outside of my head? Did that make me crazy? I couldn't deal with the dry eyes any longer. I blinked repeatedly. But no matter how many times I closed my eyes, Gran was still standing before me when I opened them again. Her green eyes still shining bright and pure.

"But, Gran, how?"

"Your mind is still somewhat flexible, dear. You haven't fully recovered, and because of that lack of rigidness, you are able to see what most cannot."

"Are you dead? Really, truly, gone?" I asked, unable to tell from looking at her.

"Am I?" Gran looked down at her own body. Her eyes came back to me as she smiled, and I took it as an invitation to look her over. She was a real, live ghost. My eyes trailed from the deep creases around her eyes down to her liver-spotted hands. "How can I be *truly* gone if I'm also here?"

"Are you really here, I mean?" I whispered, suddenly afraid my family might hear me speaking to myself. What would they think?

"I am, if you want me to be. But if I'm scaring you, dear, I'll go," she said, motioning toward the door, although I imagined she meant it figuratively. She wasn't really going to walk out the door. Would she? Would Con see her too?

"No!" I blurted, and then reminded myself to lower my voice. I looked back at Roxie, who had sat up at the edge of my bed. Her head was cocked to the side with one ear perked up and the other folded over. Did she see Gran too? Or was she just perplexed by me talking to myself?

"Don't go. Please. I need you. Will you stay with me?" I pled quietly.

"Of course, dear. I'll stay as long as you need me to."

I nodded and stepped away cautiously, checking over my shoulder multiple times to make sure she was keeping her promise. I crawled into my bed and pulled the covers up to my chin. Roxie cuddled up next to me, resting her head on my arm.

A lazy yawn escaped me, and my eyes fell to half-mast. It was midafternoon, maybe three or four o'clock, but the time didn't matter much. After spending so long in Baylor, I wondered if time would ever matter again.

Even though I had been haunted by my own insecurities in Baylor, I had glimpses of my strengths. But my true reality was quite sad. I had no genuine pride in myself. Very few friends. And I had often felt like a ghost myself, walking in the halls of my high school. So, if I had to teeter on the edge of psychosis and allow myself to believe my gran was near, then that's what I would do. I saw no other choice. I couldn't do this alone.

"Gran, you're going to be here a very long time. You might as well get settled in."

"All right, dear." Gran snuggled next to me on the bed, and goose bumps covered my arms as I realized the bed hadn't dipped under her weight.

Before, I had struggled to distinguish fact from fiction. I'd been consumed with trying to decipher what was real and what was not. But as Gran lay next to me reciting old fairy tales, I could no longer fight my phantom reality, nor did I *want* to. Because even though I knew she wasn't real, in my heart of hearts, I knew she was the only thing that would keep me going. And if my heart loved her that much, then she was real enough.

17

It was dark and cold, and something in the air spoke of familiarity. Feelings of déjà vu coursed through my veins. A small light flickered in the distance, and I was under the overpass again. It was the scene of my accident, and it appeared as though I was early. I shivered, looking for Gran.

In slow motion, headlights grew bigger and brighter. There was a screeching that I hadn't heard in times before. Tires? Tires skidding on asphalt? A loud crash shook me to my core. I instinctively shielded my head and cowered.

The four-door sedan soared through the sky as I uncoiled. Parts of the guardrail chased after it, in a race that none wanted to win. I was pretty sure this memory would be etched into my mind forever. A continuous loop to play through my head on nights I felt anxious, tired, or stressed. A feed that would play while I slept for years to come, shaping the very person I would grow to be.

I spotted the yellow top against the window, and I hurt for the girl trapped in the car. Out of all the times I'd seen this crash, I never once felt what it was like to be me, trapped within. I had no memory of being struck, or of the fear I'd felt from the impending crash, though I was positive I'd been terrified. If I didn't have the scars to prove it happened, I might have thought it was another fake memory of the long-lost summer that never was.

But for reasons beyond me, I remembered standing under the overpass. Remembered the way the windows shattered and the glass danced through the starry night sky. How each tiny shard of glass captured the reflection of the headlights and sparkled like diamonds, cutting through the night that almost took my life. And I'll never forget how there was nobody there to save me. How desolate and quiet it had been after the cars had settled.

The sedan scrunched like an accordion and fell onto its roof. I let the debris finish falling before I stepped out of the shadows. Then I walked to the wreckage, singing Mom's lullaby to keep me company. "My heart blooms . . . Blooms for you . . . Wildflowers because of you . . ." My trembling voice filled the silence in the dead of the night, but it brought little to no comfort.

There was a mass of dark hair pressed against the broken window. I was thankful that my face was covered. Some things didn't need to be seen. The bright yellow fabric faded as I peered curiously into the window. It was the brightest color in this dreadful nightmare, and it was being leeched before my eyes. I watched it turn from a bright poppy yellow to a dreary gray. And just as the last bit of yellow disappeared inside the wreckage, it reappeared on me.

I wore a satin shift dress, as dark as the night sky. But at the very bottom of the hem, a splash of hope ignited. Yellow seeped up the dress like a sponge, and before I knew it, my entire shift was as bright as the sun on a warm, summer day. My hair curled and wound around my shoulders, and my pale, cold skin warmed. A new life breathed inside of me.

I took a step back, trying to examine the changes that had taken place, and I nearly stepped on my broken cell phone. I stared in awe at the single glass slipper on my foot. I wiggled my free toes against the asphalt. Was I dreaming again? Was I finally the princess?

I tried to get a better look at the car perched above the overpass. From what I remembered, it was some time before the ambulance would arrive. It was far in the distance that a shadow figure stood by the other wrecked car. I had seen this before, and I remembered how it frightened me.

If I was dreaming, my fears could very well be conjured at any moment. But unlike before, I knew I wouldn't die, no matter how bad the nightmare got. I owed it to myself to find out what I could about the guy who'd hit me. I placed one foot in front of the other, trembling as I grew closer to the dark shadow. The last thing I wanted to do was walk right into the hands of the Grim Reaper himself. But I had to know who caused this accident, and I had to look for clues as to why. I'd probably never get this chance again.

Although the figure didn't move as I hobbled on one heel and one bare foot up the desolate off-ramp, I still felt as if it were watching me, turning its head ever so slightly. I had an odd sensation in my chest, as if a magnet was pulling me forward, even when I was afraid. As if I was under a spell, drawing near the shadowed figure.

I tiptoed around the back of the vehicle and met the figure in front of the headlights. It was a man. Or perhaps a ghost or dreamer. I could tell that his soul was wounded by the deep sadness I felt as I grew near, and I was no longer afraid he had come to steal my life. But I was worried about the guy inside the car. The one named Walker. Because he was on death row at the hospital, and maybe this man was here for him.

"Excuse me?" I asked softly. What was I doing? Would I protest? Argue for his life? The figure did not move.

"Excuse me, sir?" His back remained still and rigid as he peered down at the wrecked car.

A life for a life? No . . . I couldn't do that to my family. I only just got home.

I took a step back and peered into the driver's seat of the deformed car. My heart stopped as I saw Walker, bloodied and unconscious. This was not *just* the Walker who had hit me, but the guy of my dreams. The guy I had fallen in love with. The one I had spent a summer at Baylor Lake with, paddling across the lake and fighting demons in the haunted forest with. I had dreamed of this guy for two months straight, and he was *real.*

He wasn't a ghost. He never was. I stumbled back, my single glass slipper clattering on the road.

The shadow turned. Walker wore a navy blue, slim fitting suit, and he was holding my glass slipper between his white-gloved hands. His golden eyes pierced the night and emanated a deep sorrow that I would never forget as long as I lived.

Was this another one of Gran's fairy tales? Had she been reading to me before I fell asleep? I took a step back, my bare foot falling over sharp glass.

"Don't hurt yourself," Walker said. He crossed the short distance between us and kneeled down, sliding the glass slipper over my bare foot. I quickly glanced at the car, seeing his body slumped over in the driver's seat. He returned my foot to the ground, his fingers lingering on my ankle. I shifted my weight onto the other heel and stood a little taller.

"I don't understand." I looked into his eyes as he rose to full height. His gloves were soft under my forearms as I rested my hands on his chest. This was no dream. This was just like being in Baylor.

"We are more alike than you think." His brows knitted as he tilted his head to the side. I'd heard that before.

There was something in the way he spoke. Something in the way his voice sounded. It was different. Or maybe I was receiving it differently. Maybe, because I wasn't under the influence of the propofol any longer, everything was clearer. As if an invisible filter had been lifted.

"What do you mean? Is that you over there? Did you hit me?" I asked.

Walker's mouth fell open. He began to look at the car, but stopped. He couldn't bear it. "I tried to tell you."

"When?!" I nearly shouted. I must have been more upset than I realized. But I couldn't think of a single time he'd tried to tell me.

"I tried to tell you everything, Wilde. I tried to *show* you everything. But you only saw what you wanted to see. I'm *not* the man you think I am," he said in a broken voice. I had heard him say that before too, only it wasn't said to me. He'd said it to Layla. It didn't count.

I trembled. The warmth from my transformation was over, and this was no ball. The night was chilly, and the secrets were drifting freely in the air. Walker slipped off his jacket and wrapped it around my shoulders. I eyed the suspenders over his white button-down shirt. At least he was a gentleman. Could I fault him for telling only one of me? Or was it I who hadn't wanted to listen?

"Then who are you?" I had nothing left to lose, and a life without answers felt like the worst torture now.

Walker sighed. "Well, for starters, I'm that guy," he said, pointing to the figure with blood running down his face, unconscious over his steering wheel.

I peered through the windshield, and my heart broke for Walker. It was one thing seeing myself in the wreck, but it was an entirely different thing seeing him. I felt detached from my body as it lay broken in the car. I couldn't feel the pain or remember the fear. It was sad to see, and I wanted to help myself, but it didn't feel . . . *real*. But as I looked at Walker's lifeless body, I felt oddly protective.

"Is that . . . Is that what happened here?" I asked, as I gently ran my fingers across the scar on his eyebrow.

Walker nodded. It was the first time I felt like I truly understood. All this time, I'd imagined his guilt had been for taking Layla's life. And now I knew. I was Layla.

I trailed my hands down his suspenders. How could I have been so blind? How had I lived an entire summer under a sun of lies?

There was really only one question that burned in me now, and it was the question I was most afraid to ask. "Are you going to make it?" I fixed my eyes on a tiny pearl button in the middle of his chest.

Walker took my hand in his and wrapped one arm around my waist, pulling me close. He took a step out to the side, and I followed ungracefully. Before I knew it, we were slow dancing in the glow of his headlights. I rested my head on his chest, and I swore I could smell his cologne. It reminded me of the very first night I met him. When I had feared for my life. Now, I only feared for his.

The silence grew into an answer I didn't want to hear. I'd just found him, and I wasn't able to keep him. This really was a curse.

"What else did you try to tell me?" I was open now. I'd taken off my armor, and I was ready to hear the truth. All the ugly truth, and all the beautiful poison.

"I tried to tell you I fell in love with you. That I loved you from the very start. That you and I were meant to find each other. I tried to tell you I would have married you, if only given a second chance."

I lifted my head from Walker's chest and I tried to read the pain in his eyes. "But you said Layla—"

"You *heard* Layla. You were so afraid of getting hurt, you pretended I was in love with another girl. Hell Wilde, you were so afraid of being somebody wonderful that you cast that girl into the shadows. You have to understand that you are *everything* to me. All the good, and all the bad."

"How? How do you know?" How was he so sure of himself? I'd never been sure of myself.

"My heart knows you. It always has."

Somewhere, far, far in the distance, I heard a siren. My breath quickened, as I knew our time was running out. "And I don't deserve you," Walker whispered, dipping his forehead to mine.

"What do you mean?" I asked, pulling out of his hands. This sounded like a goodbye. A goodbye that I couldn't bear.

Walker winced. His forehead began to bleed profusely. He reached up, staining the tips of his white gloves. I tried to cover it with my hands, but I didn't know how to help. He writhed in pain and dropped to one knee.

"Walker!" I kneeled down next to him, searching for a way to help him.

The ambulance pulled up to Walker's car first. The lights shined brightly upon us, but nobody could see the two star-crossed lovers caught in the rays of light. The paramedics hurried to assess the accident.

"Help!"

A paramedic crouched by the vehicle.

"Help him!" I yelled, trembling in the thin dress and glass slippers. I begged and pleaded as Walker crumbled into my arms. But we were *nothing* in their world. Not sound nor sight. Not even a prayer.

The poppy yellow of my dress faded to white, camouflaging me even further in the light of the high beams. I shielded my eyes with a bloodstained hand. Walker's full weight collapsed on top of me as I continued to plea, my cries useless. An intense light brightened all around us until I couldn't see anything at all.

Walker wasn't just a manifestation. Nor was he a ghost. He was real, and he was stuck in another world. A world that was quickly coming to an end.

18

I watched the steering wheel as Mom drove me to physical therapy. I wondered what it would feel like in the palms of my hands, as Mom babbled about my missing homework and other responsibilities I couldn't care less about. Nothing seemed to matter anymore. Deep down, I knew she felt it, too.

"That reminds me. I need to drive you down to pick up your last check from the art gallery. They won't release it to me, and it's only good for six months."

"Really? It's probably only fifty dollars." I shrugged.

"I know. But we should do it soon, if not today. I heard they were going out of business. Tammy said she heard Mr. and Mrs. Vandal have been laundering money through the art gallery, and they're currently being audited. You don't need to be wrapped up in that mess."

Mr. and Mrs. Vandal? Laundering money? They were always a little weird. I thought little of it. "Yeah. It's probably true," I said absentmindedly.

We arrived at physical therapy, and Mom walked me inside. My eyes wandered over the colorful mats and resistance bands as she checked me in. This was my new reality. Three times a week, I would be lifting medicine balls, stretching hot pink bands around my ankles, and doing anything else my therapist thought would build back the strength I'd lost while in the coma. The regimen started slowly but grew in difficulty. Sometimes, it was downright agonizing. But when I wanted to give up, I'd see Gran's reflection stretched in a full-length mirror, and it gave me the motivation I needed to continue.

It was with great apprehension that I lowered my hands to the steering wheel, determined to drive myself to the art gallery. I wrapped each finger around the leather, and I held on through the emotional roller coaster I was riding.

My breath caught in my throat, and I had to remind myself to breathe. Each breath was more shallow than the next, and the more I tried to calm down, the worse it got. It was the first time I'd sat behind the wheel of a car since my birthday, and it was terrifying.

It was an amazing thing how my body remembered something my mind couldn't. How physically afraid I was, even though I had blocked the accident from my memory. My hands seemed locked around the steering wheel, and my muscles were clenched tightly. It took some time before I could lean back and sink into the seat. I was afraid I would never be comfortable driving again. What if I became so afraid, I hyperventilated and blacked out? What happened when you passed out behind the wheel? I guess I already knew.

Part of a healthy adult life is independence. I thought I'd gotten that when I moved to Baylor, but I was wrong. It appeared my independence had been stripped from me, and I was moving backward in life. In many more ways than driving. I couldn't bear to live my life alone. I wasn't stable enough. I wasn't strong enough. And the pressure to do so made it harder to try. And the longer I waited, the more fear grew.

If I could pick up my check from the art gallery by myself, I'd claim a small piece of my independence back. The only problem was, I was sitting in a parked car inside my garage, and I was fighting a full-blown panic attack. The garage door hadn't even opened yet, and I could almost see the ambulance arrive.

My eyes fixed on the dashboard, but I wasn't really seeing it. There was an image on the edge of my memory, and it was trying to break through. Something about how the stereo was playing my favorite song and how the night was dark and desolate. I could see it now, just as if I were there.

There were no cars on the road as I turned off the highway. My light was green as I drove up the off-ramp toward the intersection. The headlights came out of nowhere, blinding me. The car headed straight for me. I remembered lifting my hands off the wheel to shield my face, but I had no concept of what the impact and lack of control would do to me.

Suddenly, the back of the garage door came back into my sights. That was it. That was all I could remember. Exiting on the off-ramp and headlights blinding me. Was the rest of the memory also locked somewhere inside? The part where I skidded off the overpass and crashed below?

I didn't want to remember from behind the wheel. What if, when I finally remembered, I was driving? What if my eyes were hijacked, and the memory played while I was driving sixty-five down the highway?

A face appeared at my window, and I nearly jumped out of my seat, my hands unlocking from the steering wheel for the first time. Mom knocked on the window again. Her face hung with concern. I was ashamed, not only for trying to be independent, but for failing at it.

"What are you doing? You can't drive," Mom said.

"Obviously. I wasn't." Because I would if I could. Because I would've been gone if I had the courage. If I wasn't damaged.

Mom's face softened, and she walked around the car and got into the passenger seat. She sat silently with me, waiting for me to crack. It didn't take long.

"Am I ever going to drive again?" My voice was shaky with pent-up emotion.

"Of course you will, in time." In time. In time. Everything took time. What if I didn't want to wait any longer?

"I remembered." I pulled my clammy hands from the leather and wiped them on my jeans. "I remembered the green light, and turning into the intersection. There were no cars on the road that night. It was late. His car came out of nowhere."

Mom sniffled, tapping a tear from the corner of her eye with a trembling hand. "What's wrong?"

"It's nothing," she whispered.

"Mom, it's not nothing. Tell me."

"I always told myself it was better you didn't remember. Because what I went through, watching you struggle to survive, I could never forget. And it haunts me. I'm so worried that your memories will come flooding back and haunt you like mine have haunted me."

I thought about what she'd said. I wasn't worried about remembering the accident. Only not being able to control when the memory took hold of me.

I had been tortured for an entire summer. I had forged friendships based on life-and-death situations and the need for family in a time of solitude. I had fallen in love and chosen to spend my eternity living a life of make-believe. I'd turned into a monster, and my deepest fears were those that were caused by my hands, my thoughts, and my worry. When I'd woken up, all those relationships I nurtured were fake. They simply never happened. I had thought I felt alone in Baylor, but that was nothing like the loneliness that had followed me into this world.

As I watched my mom wipe the tears from her eyes, it sank in just how depressed I really was. From the look on her face, my biggest fears should have been flashbacks of the accident. From the conversations we'd had, my biggest obstacle should have been physical therapy. But what I was dealing with was so much darker. And I never wanted her to know.

I looked into the rearview mirror when I felt somebody's eyes on me. There sat Gran, quietly watching us. I had been conjuring my dead grandmother because I was too afraid to be alone. It was that bad.

My thoughts were unstable. I couldn't tell the dreams from reality, and I had to constantly remind myself that the time I'd spent in Baylor didn't exist. It felt as though all my friends had turned their backs on me. As if I was going through a dozen breakups all at once. But the truth was, we were never friends at all.

I took my mom's hand in mine. "You don't have to worry about that, Mom." She didn't. But I wasn't being entirely honest, either. I looked back into the rearview mirror and caught Gran's eyes—a disapproving shade of forest green. "Honestly, I haven't been dreaming much at all."

"Really? You had so many dreams while you were in the hospital. Have they stopped?"

"Yeah. Pretty much." I tried to make my tone lighthearted, and it seemed to work. Mom appeared more relaxed. But Gran was frowning.

I'd only had one dream. And it wasn't even a dream, per se. At least, I told myself it was more than that. It felt like more. So much so, I'd tried to get back to the void on several occasions. I tried to see Walker again and again. Night after night. But nothing worked. As soon as I fell asleep, that was it. The darkness took over, and I couldn't remember a single thing come morning.

"What do you think about talking to somebody?" Mom asked.

"What do you mean?"

"Like a therapist."

"I don't need a therapist, Mom," I said, feeling slightly offended.

I knew I was in awful shape. I didn't need anyone else knowing it. And I was afraid that if I told somebody, out loud, what was actually going on in my head, it would somehow become more real. More dangerous. And I would be labeled for the rest of my life as somebody who'd had an accident and never fully recovered. But if I just kept it to myself, I thought I could hide the severity. And perhaps, one day, have a better chance at a normal life.

"I'm worried about you. I think it would help. You don't have to talk about anything you don't want to. You could just talk about, I don't know, your dreams, if you wanted." Mom's voice hitched, and it caught my attention.

"I could talk about my dreams?"

"Oh yeah. Maybe a therapist could help you figure out why you had the dreams you did. And see if there's any meaning to them. You know, sometimes dreams mean something."

"Yeah. I think you're right. Maybe," I said. I wasn't interested in doing a deep dive into my feelings of inadequacy, but talking about my dreams seemed like it might be nice. I kept it all inside because I didn't want my family to worry. And I knew my friends would never understand.

I suddenly became excited about the thought of offloading all my baggage, and hope grew that maybe a therapist could help me unravel the mystery that was Walker. Who knows, maybe they've seen this before? Maybe they could hypnotize me and help me get back to him?

"I'll make you an appointment?"

I nodded.

"In the meantime, I can drive you to the art gallery."

"Thanks, Mom, but if you don't mind, I was going to see if Lainey could take me."

An hour later, I got into Lainey's car and smelled the sweet aroma of vanilla. It was the thing I loved most about riding in her car. She always had air fresheners that smelled divine. Especially after the summer sun had baked the scent into the upholstery.

"Thanks for the ride," I said, picking up a soda from the center console. She always brought me a drink when she drove. It was one of the sweet quirks I adored about her. I was really going to miss her when she moved away for college.

"Anytime!"

"Anytime . . . For the next two weeks," I amended.

"For the next two weeks, anytime. After that, you're on your own," Lainey laughed. I did too, but it wouldn't be funny when she left.

Emma was leaving too, but not until the end of summer, and even then, she wouldn't be far. Lainey was moving clear across the country, and I would only see her if she came back to visit her family for the holidays.

"I just have to pick up my check from the art gallery. My mom said they were under investigation for laundering money." I sipped my soda, and the bubbles tickled my nose.

"Oh, wow. I should've brought Gunner!" Lainey frowned.

"Where is he?" I glanced into the backseat.

"My mom has him."

"Are you going to take him with you when you move?"

"Yeah. My mom jumped through a bunch of hoops so I could have him with me."

"That's good. Maybe I'll have to come visit and take him on walks while you're in class," I laughed. Lainey didn't know the extent of the relationship Gunner and I had built in my head, but I liked to think Gunner remembered.

"You'll be too busy with classes of your own," Lainey said, looking at me sharply from the corner of her eye. Like any best friend would, she knew something had gone unsaid.

"Actually, I've decided to take some time off before going to college. I don't think I want to do art history, anyway."

"Really? What are you going to do then?" This rattled Lainey to her core. She had been so regimented with her credits, aligning classes like they were pieces on the chessboard of life. Each move was a step in climbing the ladder to success. She was calculated and always in control. The thought of me not knowing my future was enough to give her anxiety.

"Honestly, I don't even know. I really want to write movies, but I just worry it would be an uphill battle."

"Maybe taking a little time off won't be so bad. You've certainly been through enough. I'm sure your family would love to take care of you for another year while you get back on your feet."

"I'm sure they would. It's right here on the left," I said, pointing into a parking lot.

"This is where the drug deals go down?" Lainey joked.

"This is it!"

Lainey parked, and we walked quietly into the art gallery. I was surprised to see most of the paintings had been taken down. The walls were stark white, making the hallway appear elongated.

The door closed behind us, the echo reverberating through the empty building. Mr. Vandal came out from the back room dragging a large, heavy box. My stomach grew nervous, and I took a sip of my soda anxiously.

When it was clear that my old boss hadn't seen us, I forced myself to speak up. "Good morning, Mr. Vandal. How are you?"

"Oh! Kinsley, you're back!" he said, as if he hadn't expected me.

"Yeah, my mom said I needed to come and pick up a check?" I scratched the back of my head. It was so awkward asking for money, even if I earned it.

"Oh! That's right! Mrs. Vandal is in the back room. I believe she has your check. Um, it's good to see you. Glad you're all right," he said curtly. He continued to drag his box across the glossed concrete floor. Lainey followed me into the back room.

"Good morning," I said, knocking on the door as I walked in. Mrs. Vandal flinched and immediately clicked out of several windows on her computer until she came to a blank blue desktop. She hurried to cover up stacks of paper on her desk with manila folders, while Lainey and I stood awkwardly staring at the walls. There was something odd going on here, but I already knew that.

"Good morning! Sorry, it's such a mess. Your mom said you were trying to pick up your check. I have that. One minute. I know I left it here somewhere . . ."

She turned her back to us momentarily while she rifled through a cabinet. Lainey shot me a quick glance that confirmed my suspicions. I pursed my lips and waited for the check to be handed over so we could get out of there.

"Here it is."

The white envelope found my hand.

"Thanks," I said, lingering while Mrs. Vandal continued cleaning her desk.

Her cheeks were flushed, and she barely looked me in the eye. That was it? It seemed like a weird way to part with an employee, but then again, I hadn't worked there very long, and I had no other jobs to compare it to.

Lainey grabbed my arm, beckoning me to leave. I couldn't help but take a deep breath as I left her office. I hadn't realized I'd been holding it in her presence. I felt a weight ease from my shoulders with every step we took closer to the exit.

Mr. Vandal was dragging a new box as we approached the door. Something shifted inside of me. The axis of dream and reality shifted, and for a slight moment in time, Mr. Vandal wasn't dragging a box, but a black body bag. The glossed concrete floor was flourishing with lush flowerbeds and a pair of rose shears hidden in the grass.

"Kinsley!" Lainey hissed.

I snapped out of it. The light came flooding in, and the body bag morphed back into a cardboard box once again. Lainey was staring at me with bright red cheeks that almost camouflaged her freckles. "Are you okay?"

I opened my mouth, but nothing came out. I was still adjusting to the light when two men dressed in black and covered in tattoos entered the gallery. A shiver ran down my back, and I had a deep sense of trouble in the pit of my stomach.

Lainey took hold of my wrist and pulled me past the men. They barely spared us a glance and then locked the door behind us.

We rushed to her car, whispering and peeking over our shoulders. "What was that? You just froze in there!"

"I'm sorry. I don't know what happened," I said, checking over my shoulder again.

"Those guys did not look like they were buying art!"

"No. They didn't."

19

I sat in the waiting room twiddling my thumbs. Mom was on the other side of the wall giving my new therapist the rundown on all I'd been through and sharing areas of concern with her. I knew it would not be good. I'd heard her speaking earlier to Aunt Nora over the phone. What had started as a conversation about the lawsuit had ended with Mom's worry about my mental health. Apparently, I hadn't been as sneaky as I thought, and Mom heard me talking to Gran in my bedroom. She told my aunt that I must be having hallucinations. I was beyond mortified. If the therapist brought it up, I planned to deny it.

I rifled through countless magazines, flipping the pages so quickly that my eyes never fully landed on the images inside. It felt like an eternity before Mom finally emerged. "She seems really nice. She's ready for you. I'll be waiting right here."

I stood nervously and scowled at her as I walked by. I placed my hand on the doorknob but didn't turn it. "Mom? Would you mind waiting in the car?" I wasn't planning on saying anything to the therapist, but if I did, the last thing I wanted to worry about was whether she could hear me through the walls.

"Sure. I can do that." Mom smiled softly and then headed down the hall. I watched her disappear before I opened the door and greeted my new therapist.

A woman in her late sixties or so waited patiently for me. She had a short blonde bob cut that was losing its vibrancy. Her natural gray was seeping through the thin golden tone and turning her hair ashy and distinguished. She had angular rimmed glasses and a petite body that appeared even smaller behind her large, ornate desk. She beckoned me forward with a wave, motioning to one of the seats before her.

"Good afternoon, Kinsley. It's nice to meet you. My name is Dr. Shelton."

I took a seat. The chair was stiff, and I could tell this session would drag on forever.

"I'm so sorry to hear about your accident. Your mother tells me you had quite the recovery story. I'm glad to see you're doing well. But just like with any traumatic event, it's nice to talk about these things. Are you open to that?"

I stared at her crisp white collar and the silver cross pendant necklace that lay just below her clavicle. "I'm not really sure I *need* to talk about it. Honestly, I only came to make my mom happy. She seems quite stressed about my recovery, and I want to make it as easy on her as possible."

"That's very thoughtful of you. How do you think your mother is doing with all of this?"

"Oh, not well. She lost her mom recently. My gran. And soon after that, I had my accident. It was just three days later. She's had a really rough couple of months. I think she's trying to be strong for me, but I worry about her. She might need this more than I do." I laughed nervously.

I looked at the framed photos of Dr. Shelton and her family in her bookcase. One black-and-white photo was of a beautiful lady covered in deep-set wrinkles and bearing a wide toothless smile. Something inside of me softened at the idea of talking to the doctor. It looked like she was close to her family as well, and I assumed she could understand my worry.

"I'm sorry to hear you lost your grandmother. I recently lost my mother as well. It sounds like you love your mom very much. And I don't doubt she's trying to be strong for you. Parents often try to hold up that facade. And after a while, it becomes more difficult to manage. But it sounds like you're doing the same thing for her. Which actually is probably causing her to be more worried. Do you think it would help if you two talked about it? Maybe you can lean on each other?"

"I don't know. I don't think she wants to talk about Gran."

"Why is that?"

"She hasn't said anything about her death, really. And I've just . . . been following her lead, I guess."

"Do you want to talk about it now?"

I thought about it. I picked and pulled at a slight snag on my nail, causing my fingernail to splinter into thin layers. I looked around the room for Gran, and I suddenly understood fully that I was using her as a crutch. My heartbeat drummed in my chest. It was too personal. "I don't think so?"

"That's all right. You don't have to talk about anything if you don't want to."

"Okay."

"It takes time. One of the best ways to heal from grief is simply letting time pass by. It's a slow and difficult path, and sometimes it doesn't feel linear. But I promise, one day you'll be able to look back and remember your gran and smile. Maybe you will even want to share some stories about her. But until then, let's talk about something else. I hear you had quite the adventure while in the hospital. Your mother tells me you had dreams while in your coma? And you remember them?"

"I did!" I sat up a little straighter.

"Fascinating. What was that like?" Dr. Shelton scribbled into her notebook.

"Um . . . Is this confidential?"

"It's absolutely confidential, unless I feel that your safety is at risk. At that point, I'd be obligated to advocate for your safety and health."

"But we're just talking about dreams, right? That's safe?" I asked, nodding my head, though I was still uncertain.

"Yes. That seems safe."

"Okay. I did have dreams. They were . . . oddly realistic."

Dr. Shelton adjusted her glasses on the bridge of her nose. "How so?"

"In how I'm still having trouble identifying what's real and what's not."

"Oh dear! That sounds troublesome. Can you tell me more?"

I sighed and looked around the room for something to ground myself with. My eyes fell upon Gran, sitting in the seat next to me. Her hands folded in her lap as she waited patiently to hear my story. I closed my eyes momentarily and told myself it was just that; a story, a fairy tale. Just like Gran had told me time and time again.

"It all started with a summer vacation to a lake house with a group of friends." I remembered Gran standing on the dock in the dim light, watching us play in the water. But I didn't say that.

"It was kind of an odd thing, because I had a mission to find this girl named Layla. She was a character from an old campfire ghost story. Supposedly, she had been a victim of a crime. I had to help her. But finding her was difficult at first."

"A crime? What kind of crime?"

"Well, it was a killer-on-the-loose kind of story. The guy had tried to kill her, but I guess she got away. She needed my help. Everybody told me so, but I didn't know why."

"A killer? Do you like murder mysteries? Are you a horror fan?"

"No. Not particularly."

Dr. Shelton wrote more notes, and I glanced at Gran warily. The silence grew louder until I had the urge to fill it with my voice.

"The girl was weird, though. Layla. It felt like she didn't want to be found. Like she needed help, but wasn't ready to accept it. There were hints of her here and there, but she was quite elusive at first. On the occasions that I found her, she ran from me. One time, I even caught her. I wrapped my arms around her, but before we fell to the ground, she disappeared." I bent some of my fingers backward and examined all the red creases in my palm.

"Why do you think she didn't want to be found?"

"I think she was just a piece of me. A piece of me I didn't recognize as my own. In the end, she told me that she and I were the same person." It sounded awfully weird coming out of my mouth.

"And what did you think of that?"

"I couldn't believe it. I'd looked at her like she was, I don't know, better than me?" I bit my lip, uncertain of how I was coming across to the therapist. "I know it sounds weird, but I kind of admired her. It felt like she was a better version of me and that I could never be like her. She was happy and free-spirited, or at least that's how she appeared in the beginning."

"Are *you* happy?" Dr. Shelton tilted her head to the side, and I felt a strong burn in the back of my throat as if I wanted to cry. Was I happy? I didn't know how to answer that. I still didn't feel whole. I accepted Layla in my dream, but ever since I woke, it was like I'd lost her again.

"I . . . I felt empty in my dream. I felt invisible. Inadequate. It was so bad that sometimes when I looked in the mirror, I had no reflection at all. Like I had no soul." My chest tightened. I glanced over at Gran for comfort. She nodded her head, and I knew I was doing good by her.

"Do you feel inadequate?"

It was hard to admit something like that to a doctor who obviously had her life together. She was smart, driven, and from the pictures on her bookshelves, she was well loved. And me? I didn't know who I was. "I guess so."

"If you had to tell me a reason for your inadequacy, off the top of your head, what could you come up with?"

"For starters . . . I'm dyslexic. I don't read well. It's something everybody can do, and I always felt, I don't know, behind? I mean, I get good grades. B's most of the time. But it's an unbelievable amount of work. It's a struggle every single night. My friend Emma, she reads a couple of books a week. She loves it. I've always wanted to be like that. I've always wanted to escape this world and fall into another, but I can't. I just read the same line over and over again. I stumble on the words and skip lines. My eyes become unfocused, and it's hard to decode the symbols on the page. It's something everybody takes for granted. I think I've used it as a measuring stick of sorts. I never quite add up."

Dr. Shelton took off her glasses and held them in her hand while she spoke. "Well, struggling in school when all of your peers seem to find it easy can take quite a hit on your confidence. It's important that you know it doesn't mean you're inadequate."

"So I've been told." I forced a grin. She cleaned her glasses with a thin cloth she took from her desk and then delicately slipped them back on as she gathered her thoughts.

"Did you know that being dyslexic isn't *all* bad? Neurodivergent minds just work a little differently than neurotypicals. And sometimes there are even perks, like having a greater chance of being gifted in unique areas like engineering, industrial and graphic designs, architecture, and construction. They are also known to be fantastic at 3D spatial reasoning, imagination, art, and creativity," Dr. Shelton said, tapping her pen on the rim of her notepad.

"Really?" It sounded a like what Emma and Walker had tried to tell me in my dream. "Like maybe my disadvantage is also a strength?"

"Yes! Yes! Exactly! If I had to guess, it might have something to do with why your dreams seemed so real. With all of that creativity and imagination, the ability to visualize and conceptualize life in 3D imagery, it's no wonder you're having a difficult time telling the difference between memories and dreams."

I chewed on my lip as I thought about it. Maybe therapy wasn't such a bad idea after all. I scanned the book spines on her bookshelf and sat up a little taller.

"You know, you don't have to read. They're plenty of books on audio that you could listen to. Have you ever tried that?"

I shook my head.

"Your mom tells me you're not excited about art history anymore. What is it you want to do?"

"I never really wanted to sell paintings. I just seemed to be naturally good at it. What I really want to do is screen write. I want to create movies like the ones I see in my head." I felt the heat creep into my cheeks. Admitting a dream of mine was embarrassing. It was nothing more than a pipe dream, and I knew I should try to be more realistic. "But I know that's a lot of writing and reading." I shrugged, feeling defeated at the mere thought of it all.

"They're tons of dyslexic screenwriters out there. Authors too! If you have the gift of creativity, don't waste it in the face of hard work." Dr. Shelton's voice took on a more authoritative tone. Don't waste it in the face of hard work, I thought . . .

"Really?"

"Certainly. I think you should try it. Plus, Kinsley, you've been getting decent grades in school. You've learned to be hardworking and persistent from a young age. Being dyslexic has given you the gift of grit and drive. You've been training for this your whole life!"

"Ha, I guess you're right." I felt somewhat proud of myself. Maybe she was on to something. Maybe, just like in my dreams, all my insecurities started with something that wasn't all *that* bad. Maybe it would take me longer than anybody else to write a movie, and maybe it would be two or three times harder. But the more I thought about it, the more I thought it was worth it. Because I'd rather be bad at something I loved, than good at something I hated.

"Yeah. It's just like my gran told me, lean into the darkness."

"Your gran used to tell you that?" Dr. Shelton asked. I caught my slip, then pursed my lips. This time, I waited out the silence. She would not trick me into talking about Gran. I fought back the need to check on the ghost next to me. I didn't need to give her any reasons to dig deeper.

"Well, it sounds like one of your reasons for inadequacy might come down to perspective. I know it's hard, dear, and I'm not trying to take away any of the hardship that you've dealt with in school, but if you can learn to embrace it, I think it will help build your self-confidence."

"Yeah. Maybe," I agreed.

"So, you said you found this girl. Layla, was it? What happened next?" She flipped to a clean page, ready to make more notes.

"Well . . . She kind of fell into me," I said, uncertain of how else to say it. "It was like her soul adhered to mine, and we became one." The embarrassment climbed to new levels as Dr. Shelton wrote fiercely on her fresh piece of paper. I prayed nobody would ever lay eyes on that notebook of hers.

"And how did you feel about that?"

"At first I didn't like it, because I was jealous of her. But in the end, I felt more whole. Like I was a full person instead of this empty creature. I don't know how else to explain it."

"That sounds . . . wonderful. Maybe you could take her health and happiness and fully embody it?"

"I wish . . ." I said, exhaling a big breath. "It doesn't feel like I will ever become healthy again. I just don't understand it," I ranted.

"I felt lost before. Like I was caught in a web of complex thoughts and feelings inside my dream. But in reality, I was just lying in a tiny hospital bed. I wasn't lost at all. And now that I'm back home—or rather, awake—I feel more lost than ever. My memories are a mixed bag. Some are real and precious. Some are nightmares. Hollow reflections and split personalities. If I'm being honest, I don't fully recognize myself when I look in the mirror. If I'm not the girl that I was this summer, then who am I?"

I guess there was a lot bottled up inside me, because it all came exploding out. And to think, I wasn't even going to talk to her . . .

"Well, I would imagine you are the girl you were *before* your accident. Don't you think?"

"No. I don't. Because that girl was going to college for art history. And I'm not. That girl was content being insecure, and I'm not. I want to be this bigger, brighter, and better version of myself, just like Layla, yet I don't know how to get there." I ran my hands through my hair and closed my eyes.

"I'm physically weak, and I'm mentally drained. I can't even get behind the wheel of a car! I'm a completely different person than I was three months ago." I opened my eyes to see Dr. Shelton looking at her watch, and I had to remind myself that no matter how much I opened up to her, she was still paid by the hour.

"It looks like our time is up for today." She scribbled down a few notes before closing her notebook and folding her hands across her desk.

Time's up? But how was I supposed to feel right again? Did she have the answers or not? I stood up as Gran faded away.

"Kinsley, I think it's possible that you are in a period of growth. You're right. You're *not* the girl you were before the accident. But it sounds like you're stronger already. Remember, healing takes time. I'll see you next week." I nodded and then turned around and walked out of Dr. Shelton's office feeling unsettled.

20

On the morning of my high school graduation, I lay in bed scratching behind Roxie's ears and staring at my open closet. I was beyond intimidated to return to high school. I didn't know how to face all my peers after an accident that almost took my life and caused so many rumors to spread far and wide. I knew people would be staring and whispering as I walked by, which was terrifying.

I had given up on my independent studies weeks ago. I had two classes that I needed to pass in order to graduate high school in my last semester, but my grades had dropped because I had missed so much work. In one of my classes, the final exam was worth fifty percent of my grade. I had every intention of catching up from the comfort of my bed, but every time I tried to work on my laptop, my brain parted like the Red Sea. My mind would wander, and I would daydream about faraway lands.

Why did homework matter anyway? It seemed like a silly thing when I was fighting for my life not too long ago. When I was trying to decide whether to live, or live beyond. And now, my entire general education hinged on a single test. I couldn't make myself concentrate any more than I could make myself care. I didn't know if it was because of my brain injury or if it was a new perspective I'd been given after the accident. Maybe I was just giving up.

One of my teachers graciously waived everything he'd given in class from the day of my accident. He was willing to give me the B I had earned at the beginning of class. But my other teacher wouldn't bend the rules. She wouldn't bend the rules in the least. And for that reason, and my failures to comply with independent studies, I would not be graduating with my friends. I would never wear the graduation gown that had hung in my window for weeks. I would never hang a picture of my graduation day in my bedroom or throw my cap high in the air. The accident had taken yet another thing from me.

There was a knock on my bedroom door, but I didn't answer. I knew Mom would walk in after a moment anyway. When she did, I didn't bother to look. I didn't want her to see the redness in my eyes.

"Are you okay?" she asked, as she sat down on my bed next to me. My eyes betrayed me by glancing at my graduation gown, which I had pulled out of the closet and hung on the door just to torture myself.

"Oh, honey . . ." Mom caught sight of the gown.

"It's fine," I lied with a shrug.

"You will just have to make up that one credit. You can do it this summer and graduate in time for college. I promise, in the grand scheme of things, this will not matter." Mom reached forward and stroked Roxie.

"I don't want to go to college anymore."

Mom sighed, but she didn't seem overly surprised.

"What? I don't. You know how I feel about art history. And I don't want to spend the rest of my life doing something that I don't love." I folded my arms over my chest.

"But you're so good at it."

"So?"

"You know, it wouldn't hurt to put off college for that year we spoke about and take time to recuperate. Doesn't that sound nice? I'm telling you, I think it would be really beneficial. And if going to a different college is something you want to do, you'll need time to look into it and apply."

"Yeah. Maybe that's what I'll do."

Mom ran her hand down my head. "You should start getting ready. We don't want to be late."

"Do I *have* to go?" I asked, even though I knew the answer.

"You don't have to go, dear. But it would be a nice thing to do, to show Lainey and Emma some support. Plus, you haven't been out of the house except for therapy. And I worry about you. I think it might be good for you to see everybody, even if it's just for a little while. If you're feeling overwhelmed, we'll leave early, okay?" Mom rose to her feet.

"Promise?"

"Just say the word, and we'll go," Mom smiled on her way out.

I eyed my graduation gown with a frown. What was I supposed to wear now? I rummaged through my closet for what seemed like an eternity. I refused to wear anything with a spot of yellow, and given that it had been my favorite color before the accident, I had many sundresses with yellow accents.

I ended up wearing a blue skirt and a mismatched top. I curled my long, dark locks to give body to the shaved portion of my head that often caught my attention in the mirror. Nobody could see the shaved spot unless I ran my hands through my hair, which I never did on that side. I tossed my heels aside and slipped on my sneakers. I was steady on my feet now, but I didn't want to torture myself as I walked on the field.

Walking onto school grounds made my palms sweat. I swore everybody was looking at me, even though I trained my eyes on the ground. My mom kept a protective hand under my arm, and I pulled away when I heard the first whisper. Mom eyed me suspiciously, so I gave her a quick shake of my head. She knew.

It was hard to sit behind the sea of navy-blue gowns and not join them in celebration. I had worked so incredibly hard, and an accident had stolen my chance to walk in my high school graduation. It was as if some unknown force had doomed me from the very start. If dyslexia didn't hold me back, the car accident certainly would. It wasn't fair, but it was life.

I sat with all the parents and family members who had come to celebrate their graduating student. It wasn't until the ceremony started that I felt the social pressure ease. These parents didn't know me, and they certainly weren't talking about me. Though I instinctively turned around when I heard a whisper. My eyes landed on Gran sitting a row behind us. She smiled and waved her pamphlet at me with a giggle. I turned back around, feeling more confident in myself, and finally engaged in the ceremony.

I shielded my face with the pamphlet containing all the graduating seniors' names, trying to get relief from the blistering sun. I watched student after student who, presumably, had coasted through high school receive their diploma. But with each name called, my open wounds grew deeper. I should be up there, I thought.

"You should be up there," Mom whispered in my ear.

I sighed. Should be, but wasn't. I counted the heads in the upcoming row and waited for Emma and Lainey to be called. When their names were announced, I clapped hysterically, and Mom took several pictures at my request. I spotted Lainey's parents and Gunner several rows ahead, and I wondered if Gunner would feel like we had a connection, or if he would ignore me like he had on my last day at the lake.

When the ceremony was over, I wanted to say the words that would bring me home, but I fought them back. I would not jump on a plane home and run from my friends when times got tough. I'd made that mistake once in Baylor, and I died regretting it. Never again. I would stay, and I was going to be the best friend I could be, no matter how afraid I was to face my classmates. I could do it, as long as Gran was nearby. I checked on her often, and she was always there, somewhere within the crowd.

I trudged through the blue gowns, careful not to step on the hats strewn across the grass field. The excitement was electric, but my jinx cut through it like a hot knife. The misfortune seemed to float around me, guiding students out of my path. Had I been cursed like Walker?

I caught Emma's eye, and she came bounding over to me with open arms and a huge smile. She nearly knocked me over with a monstrous bear hug, and I couldn't help but giggle on the outside. On the inside, I was very aware of just how different we'd become.

"Congratulations, Emma! You did it!"

"Thank you! I wish you were up there with us!"

"Girls! Girls! Squeeze in for a picture," Emma's mom said, waving us together.

"Wait for Lainey!"

"Lainey!"

Lainey found us easily enough. We wrapped our arms around each other, oblivious to the cameras snapping a mile a minute.

"I'm so proud of you guys," I said with tears in my eyes. I *was* happy for them, but I was also feeling left behind. It took little to draw tears from my best friends. We all laughed at each other as we tried to keep the mascara from running down our cheeks.

Gran stood silently by her lonesome, always an arm's length away. No matter how hard I tried to be present, I couldn't fully get there. Gran was a gigantic white elephant that only I could see. She both fulfilled something inside me and stripped it away, all at the same time. Her presence made me feel like Layla was alive in me. And that I was every bit the beautiful, capable girl I'd once thought of as my childhood idol. But she was also a dreadful reminder of how much tragedy had recently occurred. On days like today, I put on a brave face, and none were the wiser.

Emma and Lainey fell silent as they spied the large group of popular kids gather to take epic photos. I, too, got sucked in and watched them longingly. Asher swept Kimber up in his arms, and she thrust her graduation cap high in the air as she hollered. I wished I had a picture of myself like that. Unfortunately, my boyfriend was a phantom, and I didn't graduate.

Trinity looked like a model, with her long black hair and striking hazel eyes. Even from this distance, it seemed like her eyes were a portal to a witch's brew; if you looked for too long, a spell might befall you. Most of the guys in our high school spent too much time looking into her eyes, and they were all under her spell, as were we.

Trinity didn't even have to smile, just a smirk from the corner of her mouth, and she was drop-dead gorgeous. Most of the girls hated her for it, and she only had a couple of real friends. It took a seriously confident girl to be friends with someone so stunning, and most of us weren't up for the challenge.

Scarlett May had white and yellow plumeria flowers pinned to the side of her short, beach-blonde hair. Although she wasn't in cowgirl boots, she wore a pair of sky-high shorts underneath her gown and a pair of stilettos that made her legs look twice as long. Levi grabbed Scarlett May's leg like a guitar in a big show for the camera.

"I bet her stilettos are sinking into the grass. Why would she even wear those?" Lainey asked.

"Because she can," I muttered. Her stilettos were impractical, I'd admit, but she obviously liked them, and they looked amazing on her. I thought back to the night she and I had bonded under shooting stars, and I wondered if she had a real live Sampson of her own. I wanted that for her. A pang of sadness ached in my chest. I missed Scarlett May. I missed the person I thought she might be. But then I had to remind myself, I never really knew her at all. Just like Kimber and Trinity, I only knew the assumptions I'd come up with in my head, and those were based on jealousy and rumors.

Kai wrapped his arms around Ethan and Noah, and the three boys yelled and hollered as their parents clicked dozens of photos. The three of us had been watching the group grow up throughout high school. And instead of moving on with our own lives, we wished we had theirs. The funny part was, we didn't even know them. We'd only seen pictures on our phones every Friday night and heard rumors on Monday morning.

"Oh my god. Is he coming over here?" Lainey whispered, gripping my hand tightly. Noah and his mom were walking toward us. My friends were aware of my long-standing crush on Noah, and it seemed like everyone else knew too. It was all we ever talked about.

A wave of nausea washed over me as I wondered how I felt about Noah now, and if I really wanted to speak to him with part of my head shaved, no matter if he could see it or not. I still knew it was there.

"Clara, it's so good to see you. I'm sorry we missed you when we dropped off the casserole," Noah's mom said as she hugged my mom. Noah stood awkwardly by her side.

"Congratulations," I said meekly.

"Yeah, you too," Noah said, before quickly trying to redirect his comment to Lainey and Emma. Of course, there was nothing to congratulate me about on this hot summer day.

"I mean—"

"It's okay," I said, cutting him off.

"How are you feeling?" he asked.

"I'm doing better. Thanks for asking," I said, trying to clear the tension in my throat. The truth was, Noah and I had spoken little since we were younger. We barely spoke at all, and that was part of the reason I'd watched him and his friends move on while I stayed behind.

As Noah rose to rule our high school, I retreated into the shadows. He became loud and confident, while I became quiet and uncertain. He excelled as a double star athlete while I struggled with my homework at the kitchen table. He had girlfriends, and I watched from my window.

While he partied, Emma, Lainey, and I would wonder what it would be like to be at those parties. Somewhere along the way, I had missed an invisible fork in the road that separated Noah and me. He excelled, and I was too afraid.

Lainey and Emma were the same way, though for different reasons. Emma preferred to live in the world of literature rather than the real world. I understood that more now than ever. Meanwhile, Lainey wanted something that Kimber and Scarlett May had, that intangible thing that we all wanted, but she was too anxious to chance failure. Lainey would rather put her effort into building a career with a predictable outcome than take any kind of risk. As a result, the three of us had huddled together at lunch under the shade of a giant tree telling stories we'd heard whispered around the classroom.

"Are you girls coming to the after-party?" Noah's mom asked us. Noah's cheeks flushed.

"After-party?" Emma asked.

"Yeah, come on over. We're just having some of Noah's friends over before they leave for the lake. Nothing big, just loads of pizza," she smiled.

"If you're around, stop by," Noah shrugged. I froze. Was this a pity invite? Everything inside me stopped. But that wasn't the case for Emma, though I wish it had been.

"We'll be there!" Emma exclaimed, gripping my pinkie finger so tightly I thought it might fall off.

"We will?" Lainey asked.

"We will!" Emma insisted, giving her a stern look.

I couldn't believe what was happening. Graduation day had just become a nightmare. My stomach churned with anxiety at the thought of walking into the lion's den. I hoped Gran would be there.

"Are you sure that's a good idea?" I asked quietly.

"It'll be fun!" Emma said, choosing to not pick up on my hesitation. I wasn't sure about the *fun*, but it was too late to back out now.

21

Emma, Lainey, and I exchanged heated glances at one other on the way home. Though Mom seemed pleased I had friends coming over, we hadn't expected to be joining her across the street for Noah's graduation party. Mom would have been devastated if she had the slightest clue what I'd actually dreamed about in my coma and how this was going to mess with my head. It would probably take months to unwind the knot in therapy. And had I known that keeping secrets from my mom was going to leave me so vulnerable, I never would have done that either.

The three of us tromped upstairs to make a plan behind closed doors. Lainey balanced on one foot while unbuckling her heels, and Emma carefully placed her graduation cap on my desk, deep in thought. "What was that all about?" I asked Emma, my pitch much too high to hide my true emotion.

"What? You know you wanted to go! I saw the way you looked at Noah!"

"You mean, *you* wanted to see Levi!" Emma's eyes rolled back in her head, and Lainey sighed. The room fell quiet as we all worried about how we would get through the next couple of hours.

"Guys, we can't go. It's going to be so incredibly awkward. Let's just not show up," Lainey pled. I nodded. It was a solid option. The *only* option, as far as I was concerned.

"No! We're graduates now. All of that awkwardness of who's who is behind us now. Come on. We can do this. It's not a big deal," Emma quipped, though the crease between her eyes told me she was bluffing. She was just as scared as Lainey and I were, if not more. Her eyes turned watery as she waited for our answers.

I looked to Lainey and shrugged. "I guess we can eat some pizza . . ."

"Yes! Oh my god. We're doing this! It literally took until the very last day of school to get invited to one of their parties, but it still counts!" Emma rambled as she fixed a smudge of eyeliner under her eye in the mirror. I caught my reflection looking back at me. My eyes were dull, and I struggled to recognize myself. Who was I among this family of misfits, if we were strangers?

"We got invited by Noah's mom. That doesn't even remotely count," Lainey said. It was true. It didn't count.

I thought back to the time that Noah and I had shared an English class earlier in the year. He and I had been stealing glances at one another, but I always told myself otherwise. I remembered the time his mom was out of town and his dad was on a business trip. He was planning on throwing a big party, and he invited me. It seemed like no big deal as he nodded to a group in English class, myself included, and said to stop by.

But come lunch hour, I knew that if I told Lainey and Emma, there would be no backing out. At the last minute, I chose not to tell them about the invitation. I ended up watching the party from my window that night. Curled on my window seat, underneath a blanket, I fell asleep with my forehead pressed against the windowpane. I'd regretted my decision all night long, and I promised myself if I ever had an opportunity to be bold, I'd take it.

"Girls! Are you ready?" Mom called from downstairs. We hadn't even had time to freshen up.

The girls and I shared a look of panic before I called out, "Coming!"

Mom led our small group with a bowl of hot cheese dip, and I dragged behind with the bag of chips. Several cars were parked along the curb, and a few more were showing up as we approached the house. I'd been inside this house a hundred times before, but not in recent years.

Noah's mom greeted us at the door. She gave me a big hug and whispered in my ear, "I'm so glad you came." It seemed she meant something more than she was letting on, and I wished for just a moment that nothing had gotten in the way of my relationship with her son. She was a sweet woman with a kind disposition.

Asher and Kimber squeezed past us in the entryway. Kimber's eyes trailed behind her, and Asher's brows furrowed at the sight of us. My stomach sank immediately. We didn't belong here. It was a closed party for their group of friends. I saw the same recognition in Emma's eyes as she folded her arms tightly across her waist.

"Come on in, girls. There's plenty of pizza in the kitchen. Help yourself to a drink. I think everybody's outside."

I took the first step. Lainey and Emma were quick to follow. The three of us loaded our plates with pizza, taking as long as we possibly could before joining everybody outside. I picked the pepperoni off my pizza and then pretended to search the kitchen for napkins. As if I didn't know my way around.

Trinity appeared out of thin air. I could feel Emma and Lainey stiffen, though nobody was more uncomfortable than me. I was the only one who was wondering if Trinity and I had actually thrown everybody's clothes off the dock during the naked cheetah races. But that belonged in the summer that never was. It didn't happen, I reminded myself. I used it to my advantage, anyway. Pretend as if it were real. As if I belonged. It was then that I saw Gran wander through the back yard, passing by the kitchen windows. I relaxed immediately.

"Hey, Trinity. Congratulations on graduation. I love your dress. Where did you get it?" I asked.

"Thank you. Um, I didn't see you up there. Did you graduate?" Her hazel eyes burned through me like lasers. My palms turned sweaty, and I quickly remembered that she and I had never been friends for a reason.

"I didn't."

"Mrs. Black wouldn't allow one credit to slide! She *should* have been up there with us," Lainey said in my defense.

"Oh. Well, a credit *is* a credit." *Ouch.*

Trinity reached for a plate beside me. "I didn't realize you were friends of Noah's?" Trinity's voice was like a snake in the grass. I wasn't sure where she was going with her questioning, but I knew the ending would bite.

"Actually, Noah and I have been friends for a long time. We grew up together. And I live down the street." It wasn't exactly a fib, it was true. Though I never would have claimed to be his friend under other circumstances.

"Then why have you never hung out with us?" Her voice was bitter and taunting. It was no wonder she'd been the first to go in my dream.

"I . . . I don't know—"

"Weren't you in a coma or something?"

Emma gasped.

"Didn't you used to lie in elementary school and say you were in a kid's swimsuit commercial?" Lainey snapped. With Trinity momentarily silenced, Lainey grabbed my wrist and yanked me out of the kitchen and into the back yard.

"Why is she *so* mean?" Lainey asked.

"I can't believe you said that!" Emma said. It was unlike Lainey to stand up to anyone. She didn't have a mean bone in her body.

Even with Lainey's comeback, I knew Trinity had gotten to me. Trinity obviously didn't care that I'd recently been fighting for my life. So why did I care what she had to say? It was easy to shrug off in the moment as I looked into the back yard full of living characters from my summer. But I knew when I was alone at night, with nothing to distract me, I would think about what it felt like to be struck by Trinity's venom.

Kai tossed a football at Noah just as he turned to see us, and the football struck his shoulder. Lainey, Emma, and I took a seat far away from the crowd, sitting on a stone wall on the outskirts of the yard. All the patio furniture had been taken, which made us appear to be even more out of place than we already were.

Noah nodded his head, and I gave him a quick smile in return. He picked up the football and threw it back with no remorse. Nobody else noticed us.

"Why are we even here?" Lainey asked Emma. "Are you planning on talking to Levi? Because we could've just stared at him through Kinsley's window if all you wanted was a view." Lainey was so far out of her comfort zone, she was turning snappy in a way I'd never seen. I understood, though, because I was on edge too. We all were.

"You guys, I just wanted to end high school on a good note. Plus, I finished a series this morning, and I'm not sure what to read next."

I groaned through a mouth full of pizza.

"I didn't want to be afraid of them anymore, because you know what's going to happen? History is going to repeat itself in college, and I don't want that. We could've gone to any of their parties if we wanted to. It's not like they hand delivered invitations with a wax seal or anything. I'm sure half the people showed up without an invitation. That could have been us. But it wasn't," Emma said.

"Because we didn't *want* it to be," Lainey complained.

"That's what we've always said. But is it really true?" Emma tossed the crust down on her plate.

"You're right Emma. We should have gone. But we're here now, thanks to you. And honestly, I think it reconfirms the fact that we never really wanted to be here. These aren't our people. You guys are my people," I said.

"You're my people too."

"I'm going to miss you guys," Lainey said.

"But just for the record, we never would have known that these weren't our people if we hadn't come. And now we can stop guessing, right?" Emma asked.

I nodded. It had been difficult spending all of those semesters in high school just wondering, what if we did this, or what if we'd said that? Emma was right. If we would have just gotten to know these people, we would have stopped wondering. And we probably would have moved on to find better friends.

"Kinsley! Come sit over here!" Ethan gestured to three seats at the table. Trinity, Mason, and Levi had just gotten up, leaving the seats empty. A little taken aback, we left our spots on the ledge for prime seating in Noah's back yard.

"Hey, I heard they didn't let you graduate. That's shitty. Sorry about that," Ethan said as I sat down. Unlike Trinity, I could feel the sincerity in his voice.

"They didn't let you graduate?" Kimber asked.

"Um, no. I had quite a bit of missing work from being out of school the last month."

"That's bullshit!" Scarlett May hissed. I smiled. Once upon a time, she and I were friends. And I thought I might have seen a glimmer of why.

"It is!" Emma agreed.

"So, all of that was true, huh? You were really in a coma?" Scarlett May asked.

"You can't ask that!" Kimber snapped. The table fell quiet, and everybody's eyes landed on me. It appeared they were all curious, and I didn't mind sharing.

"There were that many rumors?" I asked.

"Yeah." Ethan's tone was matter-of-fact.

"I heard you died," Scarlett May said through gritted teeth.

"Scarlett May!" Kimber barked.

"What? It's true! She asked!"

"It's okay. Really," I said. "I don't really remember any of it. The accident, I mean. I have a good idea of what happened, but it doesn't feel like an actual memory, if that makes sense. I was in a coma for a couple of weeks. Thirteen days, to be exact." I lightly traced the rim of my red plastic cup as I spoke.

"Wow. What was that like?" Ethan asked. It was weird to be having a conversation with these people. I wanted to tell him, you would know, because you were there. But I constantly had to retrace my thoughts and remind myself that they didn't know me at all. And what I knew of them most likely wasn't true either. Apart from Trinity, that is. I think I had her spot on.

"What do you think she's going to say, Ethan? She basically slept for two weeks," Scarlett May said.

"Actually, I dreamed. A lot." Out of the corner of my eye, I saw Lainey look to Emma. I don't know why I said it. I hadn't spoken about it since leaving the hospital. And this certainly wasn't therapy.

"No way! That must have been so trippy!" Kimber said, leaning in. I smiled and nodded. It absolutely captivated them. And at that moment, I couldn't remember why I was so afraid to come here.

"You have *no* idea."

"Do you remember any of your dreams?"

It was the moment of truth. Was I going to tell them? Was I going to say that I had spent two months with them? I couldn't. I would sound like a stalker, or worse. "I remember some of them. They were weird, though." I shrugged.

"How so?" Kimber asked.

"Do you really want to know?"

"Um, yeah!" Scarlett May blurted.

"Yeah, I don't know anybody that's been in a coma before," Ethan said.

"I can see that. It's weird because I can remember the dreams like they were yesterday." I glanced at Emma and made a split-second decision that I hoped I wouldn't regret. "Have you ever heard of a place called Baylor Lake?"

I had known all along that Scarlett May had been planning a big summer trip there after graduation with all of her friends, including Noah. It was a weird coincidence that my uncle had a cabin at the same lake. That's when we'd come up with the idea that the three of us would go to my cabin for the summer. It was the perfect place to make memories. We planned to hit all the local events: the Summerfield State Fair, the Baylor Bass Tournament, the Baylor Parade. And we may or may not have hoped to run into Noah and Levi while visiting.

And somewhere in the back of my mind, I had imagined that our small group of three would join theirs. And the one thing we all had in common—that we were brand new at being adults—would have united us into some type of family. An unruly and most likely dysfunctional family, but a family, nonetheless. We would argue over bonfires, crash the golf cart, and who knows, maybe even fall in love.

It was supposed to be the best summer of our lives, and the memories would be ours to cherish forever. But the whole thing seemed stupid now.

"Are you serious? I have a place in Baylor Lake. We're all going there right now!" Scarlett May checked her watch, and I caught sight of Emma's ruby cheeks.

"No way!" It was my turn to get Emma back for making us come to this party. "Same with us! I have a cabin there too! Well, my uncle does."

"Wait, what?" Lainey coughed. The toe of my sneaker met her shin.

"No way!" Scarlett May echoed.

"We should hang out! We're going up in a couple of days and staying most of summer. Will you be at the Water's Edge Concert?" I asked.

"Yeah! I already have my cowgirl boots packed. This is going to be so much fun!" To my surprise, she was sincere. It made me wish I was too. But I had absolutely no plans to go to Baylor Lake. I would cancel last minute and say that I couldn't escape because of my physical therapy. Everybody would understand. But most importantly, Lainey and Emma would still go and get a chance at the summer we'd planned all senior year.

"All-night parties, a little fishing, barbecue. Damn, I can't wait!" Ethan's eyes twinkled with hope. Lainey wore a look I hadn't seen on her face for a long time. I recognized it as equally excited and terrified.

The rest of the group gathered around the table. It seemed the party was wrapping up, and they had a flight to catch. "Hey Noah, did you know that Kinsley and her friends were going up to Baylor Lake this summer?" Ethan asked.

"What? I didn't know that!" Noah exclaimed.

My insides screamed. A couple of months ago, it would've been a dream come true to be sitting at this table and be invited to hang out in Baylor. But as I sat here today, I no longer had feelings for Noah. All because he'd done something in a dream that I hadn't forgiven him for. It was ridiculous. I knew that. But it didn't change the way I felt. Plus, I kept comparing him to somebody else. Or rather, the *idea* of somebody else.

"Yeah! Apparently her uncle has a place on the lake, and the three of them are going in a few days. We're going to hang out at the Water's Edge Concert next weekend! Hey Kinsley, do you have cowgirl boots? Because I have an extra pair, and they're already packed if you need them," Scarlett May offered.

"I'd love that. I actually needed to find some. Thank you," I said. She had no idea how much that really meant to me. I was touched beyond words, because even in my wildest dreams, Scarlett May had barely warmed up to me.

"Well, it's time to hit the road. Our plane leaves in two hours," Kai said. The group started to break apart, just as Trinity opened her mouth for revenge.

"Didn't you have a part of your head removed or something?"

Everybody froze. Trinity's tone had cut through the commotion and rung like a gong. Everyone's eyes flickered between her and me. Not even Lainey could find the right words now.

I'd suppressed a particular side of myself for a very long time, but drew strength upon that side of me now. I slowly ran my hand down the side of my head and lifted my hair to reveal a scar that was puckered and ugly. I said nothing.

Gasps erupted around the table, and my stomach plummeted. They could accept me or not, but I was done hiding.

"Gross . . ." Trinity murmured.

"No way! That's bad ass!" Kai argued.

"Wow! That's so cool!" Ethan said, leaning over to get a closer look. I dropped my hair and looked around at the crowd as they stared with wide eyes. I didn't know which rumors I'd just confirmed, but they were shocked.

"I wish I had a battle scar!" Kimber said to Asher.

"She's such a tough chick!" Mason said, as he headed for the door.

Out of everybody here, *Mason* was calling *me* tough? *Kimber* was wishing for something *I* had?

Trinity snarled and broke away. The group departed and made their way into the house. As I pushed my chair out, I shared a look of shock with both Emma and Lainey. This was not what we had expected from coming here. It was so much better.

Noah hung back from the group, walking by my side. "Don't mind Trinity. She's just jealous the entire school knows your name. You're kind of famous now, like it or not."

"Leave it to her to be jealous of something so terrible."

"Right. So, are you really going to Baylor this summer?"

"Yeah. We've been planning it all year. Such a coincidence."

"Maybe we'll hang out?"

A bolt of heat trailed down my back as we made our way to the entry. I wasn't sure if my old self was coming alive or if I was just completely uncomfortable with the whole situation. I loathed lying. "Yeah, I'd love that. I'll text you our address so you guys can come by," I said, with no phone and no intentions to actually follow through.

"Promise?"

I smiled as Ethan slapped Noah's back and ushered him out the front door. The cars were already packed and waiting. Noah's mom squeezed by to find her son for a hug before he left for the airport.

"I guess we'll see you girls up there then! Have a safe flight," Kimber said, waving goodbye. The three of us waved as the multiple cars pulled away from the curb. We stood in his driveway until the last of them vanished from sight.

"And they're off," my mom said.

Noah's mom wiped a tear from her eye as we stared down the empty street. "It's okay, Mrs. Hampton. You raised a good son. He's going to be all right."

By the end of the night, with Mom's help, we had not only secured two plane tickets, but a spot for Gunner as well. The girls were excited to have the summer they thought they'd lost out on, but they were ashamed to show it. Luckily, I wasn't ready for Baylor anytime soon.

22

Gran and I sat side by side, staring at the back of the garage door. Mom's car was parked, my hands were wrapped tightly around the steering wheel, and I was acutely aware of the seconds ticking by. My therapy appointment was starting soon, but I was frozen. I'd convinced my mom that I could drive myself into town. But I may have been exaggerating. I hadn't driven since the accident, and she knew that. We all knew that.

Gran was biting her fingernails in the passenger seat. It wasn't the vote of confidence I was hoping for. Of course, I would drive again. But when would I be brave enough to do it? I told myself I was brave enough now. With Lainey and Emma off to Baylor Lake, the least I could do was drive myself to therapy. It was a few short miles away, and I didn't have to take the highway to get there. It was easy. It was daylight. And I had Gran riding shotgun. What more could I ask for?

"I just need music." I shrugged, turning on the stereo.

"Or will that distract you?" Gran asked.

I turned off the stereo.

"I just need to go. I need to stop overthinking and go." I quickly hit the garage door button and threw the car into drive.

"Not now! Wait for the door to open!" Gran arched her back to see over the dashboard. She braced herself with spread arms, holding onto the door and the back of my seat with white knuckles.

I slowly lowered my forehead to the steering wheel. "I *can't* do it."

"Yes, you *can*."

"I'm never going to drive again." I put the car in park.

"You're going to drive *today*!" Gran said, slapping at the gearshift. It was a sad sight to see Gran try to make use of her hands. It was probably the only thing I felt more deeply about than my failed driving attempt. I wasn't about to let her fumble in such an inadequate way. I placed my hand on the gearshift, and she held her ghostly hand on mine. With her cool touch over my hand, we put the car in drive together.

"I'm going to drive today . . ."

I saw the garage door swing open, and Mom appeared. She leaned against the doorway and folded her arms over her chest as she watched me struggle. She was coming to give me a ride. She had probably been counting down the minutes on the other side of the door, just waiting for me to freeze up. I wouldn't allow it. I opened my window and Gran disappeared into the oblivion.

"I'm going! I'm going! I can be there in seven minutes."

"You don't need to rush, honey. But your appointment is going to be starting soon. How about I drive you there and you drive back?"

"No, Mom, I've got this. I'm going right now!" I took my foot off the brake and eased onto the gas. Mom hid her worry behind a hand that covered half her face. I forced a smile and a small wave before rolling down the driveway. I made a wide turn at the mailbox and drove excruciatingly slow down our street.

"She gone?"

Gran's voice was faint. She was crouching low to hide from the window. I smiled. She didn't need to hide from Mom, of course. Nobody could see her but me. There was nothing better than an invisible grandmother hiding from her own daughter.

"She's gone," I said, laughing.

"Well, don't look at me! Keep your eyes on the road! You're driving!"

"I'm driving! Hey, it's not so bad. I don't know why I waited so long," I said, pulling up to my first stop sign. Gran's eyes were round and full of wonder. She couldn't have been happier to see me break free, and I loved her for it.

But by the time I came to my first light and saw dozens of cars, I knew why I'd waited so long. The cars made me anxious. The intersection was busy, and everybody drove too fast. Somebody honked at me for waiting too long after the light had turned green. But all my anxiety melted when Gran turned around and gave them the finger.

I stand corrected; there's nothing better than a feeble old grandmother with a threatening middle finger and a scowl that nobody could see. Gran knew every bomb in my path and every way to defuse them. She was absolutely my guardian angel, and I didn't know how I could live without her.

I pulled into the parking lot with two minutes to spare. I wasn't even late. I grabbed my bag and opened the door but had the sense that I was leaving something behind. I went to rummage through my bag to see if I had my keys, something I hadn't carried with me in a long time. Instead, I found something I wasn't looking for.

An envelope with "Kinsley" penned across the front was nestled in my bag. How had I not seen this before? Gran's handwriting was elegantly written on the envelope. I looked at Gran in my passenger seat, who appeared dimmer than before.

"What's this?" I asked. I glanced around to make sure nobody had heard my belligerent self-talk.

"I wrote a few letters in the weeks before my departure. Grandpa stopped by the other day to see you, but you were in physical therapy. He'd been holding onto this letter for a special time, but I convinced him there's no better time than now."

"You wrote me a letter?" I looked down at her handwriting. It was so real, so tangible, that it made her ghost less true. This letter I held in my hands was from my *real* Gran. Not the one sitting in my car that I had conjured. And certainly not the one I had dreamed about while being under sedation in the hospital.

I sat back down in my car and closed the door. "You're going to be late, dear . . ."

I shook my head. Nothing mattered but this. Carefully, I opened the letter. It was a beautiful one-page letter. Her handwriting was something I could never get back. I ran my fingers over the indentations of her script on the page. I somehow felt closer to her in that moment than I did with her ghost by my side.

My Dearest Kinsley,

I have had the joy of watching you grow into the young woman you are today. You were my first grandchild, and you brought so much happiness into my life. I am so sorry that I won't be able to be there to see all the special moments in your life, but I hope that, in some small way, you will always carry a piece of me with you.

Just because my time on this earth is coming to an end, it doesn't mean my love for you will ever fade. I will always cherish the special bond we share, no matter how far apart we may be. You are my granddaughter, and nothing will ever change that.

I know it's hard to say goodbye, but please promise me you will remember all the happy times we had together. It can be difficult to miss someone so much and still be able to hold on to the good memories, but when you think of me, I want you to find happiness. I know you are stronger than you realize.

And one more thing, I want you to take care of your grandpa. I know that seeing him will remind you of how much you miss me, but please try to be there for him. He will be all alone in our house, sitting in the rocking chair on the front porch, staring at the sunset each evening with a cup of tea and a book, but he won't be able to read. Please encourage him to continue to get out of the house and see you, your brother, and your mom and aunt. Play poker with him and cheat wildly—he loves that.

Life can be exciting, and you'll be going off to college soon, but please remember that nothing is more important than the relationships you have with the people you love. Don't leave them behind. And never be afraid of love—regret can be worse than a broken heart.

I love you, my dear. Until we meet again,

Gran

A tear fell onto the page and splattered on her signature. The blue ink immediately spread. I folded the letter with shaky hands and tucked it back into its envelope before my tears could ruin the keepsake further. I sniffled, running my arm underneath my wet nose. Gran looked up at me with hazy, loving eyes. Her figure was dimmer, even more transparent than before. I gave her a little nod, still unable to speak. My throat was swollen, and I was working overtime to keep the tears back. I had an entire therapy session to get through, and I couldn't come in late *and* sobbing.

Gran and I walked side by side into the building. Her words sank deeply, where they would find a forever home. *You are stronger than you realize.* I thought about all I'd endured. Every struggle. I had been through a lot. But my strength was only a byproduct of my survival. I wasn't sure I could take credit for that.

I sat in Dr. Shelton's office frozen, in a daze. Gran sat in the open seat next to me.

"How are you doing today, Kinsley?"

"Good," I lied.

"Last time we spoke, you were taking on a different persona. I believe you called her Layla. Have you put any thought into that since our last session?"

I stared at the wood grain on the arms of my chair. I didn't answer her. All I could think about was the letter from Gran.

After an uncomfortable amount of time, Dr. Shelton asked a different question. "Your mother told me your dreams took on the life of fairy tales. Which fairy tale did you resonate with most?"

"The next story in the book was Cinderella. And I'm fairly certain I would have dreamed about that next. However, if I choose a fairy tale that resonated with me, I think it would be Beauty and the Beast."

"What do you mean, you would have dreamed of Cinderella next?"

"I mean, if I stayed in the coma, somebody would have read that fairy tale, and its elements would have created the next several weeks of my summer."

"Interesting. What resonates with you? Why do you think of Beauty and the Beast?" she asked, as she pushed her glasses up the bridge of her nose.

I chewed on my lip, not wanting to say his name aloud. I hated how the fresh wave of pain hit every time I said or thought it. "W . . . Walker said he was cursed. Which would make you think he would be the Beast. But I'm not so sure. I think *I* was the cursed one. Every time I looked in the mirror, I'd see a homely girl, or worse, nothing at all. I had trouble recognizing myself. Hence, I would've been the Beast."

"If you're the Beast, than who's Beauty?" Dr. Shelton scribbled down a note on our hypothetical conversation. I couldn't imagine it was noteworthy.

"Walker." I thought of his deeply etched dimples, his lustrous golden eyes. Of course, he was Beauty.

Dr. Shelton tapped her pen across her lips. "Have you considered that, perhaps, Layla was Beauty? And you were the Beast. Opposite sides of the same coin?"

I ran my hand through my hair and traced the scar along the length of my head. I was definitely the Beast, but could I also be Beauty? "How is that possible?"

"It's possible that Layla, as a part of you, was the person you've always wished to be but never allowed yourself to become. Perhaps your dyslexia hindered your confidence, casting you into a self-fulfilling prophecy. Putting a wedge between your current poor self-image and your future ideal self. A wedge so massive, so incapable of bridging, that you felt as though you could be none other than two entirely different people."

Dr. Shelton paused, and I thought about what she had said. There was a part of me I loathed, but was very comfortable with. And there was also a part of me, very much outside my comfort zone, that I strived to be. And no matter how detrimental, comfort was easy. It was definitely possible that Layla was Beauty.

"And perhaps, when your grandmother died, your two personas grew even further apart. The grief set you back from reaching Layla, that happy, healthy girl. And now, when you feel hurt and lonely, when you don't understand life and why things have happened to you, you look at Layla, so far in the distance, and think you might never reach her."

How true it was. I hung my head.

"But it doesn't have to be that way. As soon as you see yourself for all that you are, you can bridge that gap. You can be both Beauty and the Beast. You can wear your grief and insecurities, all while living a happy and fulfilling life. There *is* room for both of you."

I shrugged and looked down at the carpet, my eyes catching the faintest outline of Gran. I thought about how I'd been my own worst enemy. How I became my own monster. In a world where I had the power to give myself anything I wanted, I gave myself a broken heart. I could have had a smile, but I chose fangs. Why? Because I wasn't ready to own my shortcomings, and now, my grief?

"I'm stronger than I realize . . ." I repeated the words from Gran's letter as I began to believe them. Maybe struggle had found me, but that didn't mean my strength wasn't earned.

"You're right. Most likely, you'll never know just how capable you are. Most people will never realize their full capability."

I gazed at the ornate detail of her wooden desk, my eyes unfocused, my mind far away. "I've been avoiding my grandpa. I didn't even realize it," I admitted.

"Oh? And why is that?" Pen met paper with quick deliberate strokes.

"Because why would I want to go to his house when all I smell is my gran? Why would I want to visit when all I see are her belongings? What if I see her shoes, and I think she'll never wear them again? What if I see her books and think she'll never read them again? There are too many reminders that she's not here, and I don't know how to deal with it." I closed my eyes for a moment, squelching the burn. "Does that make me a terrible person? A terrible granddaughter?"

"Avoidance can be a common side effect of grieving. But the first step is acknowledging it. Which it seems like you've done here today."

"I don't want to push my mom and grandpa away just because I'm afraid of the pain. They're hurting too. And all I've done is make it worse."

"To be fair, Kinsley, they may be pulling back themselves. It's easy to isolate when we're in pain. What are some ways you think you could help change that?"

"I think I should talk to my mom. I think I should let her know that I'm stronger than I look. That she can talk to me. Lean on me."

"Yes, we talked about this a little last time. About you taking on a better version of yourself. Are you ready for that?"

"I've been through a lot. I can handle this too." It was the first time I truly believed it.

"What about visiting your grandpa? Do you think that would help?" Dr. Shelton put down her pen and clasped her hands.

I thought about walking into my grandparents' home. It was a custom home Grandpa had built in a beautiful clearing, high on the bluffs of a mountain top. It was the most peaceful, serene home I had ever been to. But somewhere along the way of cars and boys, I'd stopped going. Gran was right;

life became too busy with meaningless things, and I would never get that time back. It seemed the longer I waited, the harder it would be to visit.

"I think it's going to be difficult," I said, meeting her gaze for the first time today. I could still see Gran out of the corner of my eye, though barely.

"You're not wrong about that. It absolutely will be difficult. There's nothing about the grieving process that isn't. But remember, time heals everything. And it *will* get easier. Don't rush yourself. It could take years, and that's okay, too."

Slowly, I dropped my gaze from the doctor to my lap. I interlocked my hands and twisted my fingers. I found a smudge of dirt under my pinky nail and worked diligently to clean it out. I was stronger than I knew. And I was going to face the fact that I'd lost my gran. I was going to ask my grandpa for stories about her and play cards with him again. I would find new and creative ways to cheat and win. I smirked.

The first thing I was going to do when I got home was give Mom a hug. I was going to ask her how she was doing, because in all honesty, I hadn't. I hadn't asked her once how she was holding up from the death of her mother.

I had been so wrapped up in my own feelings, and then the accident happened. I hadn't even realized everybody around me was going through tough times of their own. And now that I thought about it, I was the only one who'd had extra time with Gran. I'd spent a full summer with her. I'd been able to call her on the telephone and chat with her in my bedroom months beyond her death. Until this moment, I hadn't realized how *lucky* I was.

I felt that way now. Lucky. Lucky to have had her in my life, even though I felt our time was too short.

It was in that exact moment that the ghost beside me glimmered. Just like a thought taking flight in Baylor, the fresh perspective grew wings of its own and changed reality before my eyes. I turned to meet Gran's disappearing emerald eyes. They sparkled like precious stones and spoke of quiet joys. Before I knew it, the chair beside me was empty, and I knew I wouldn't be seeing my gran again.

I had finally reached the moment where I was strong enough to stand on my own. I'd just never realized what that meant. Gran had to go back to wherever she belonged and leave me behind. Since the accident, her world and mine had collided in a mixture of natural and supernatural, and it was in this exact moment that our two worlds parted. I would be lying if I said the fear hadn't crept back in. But this time, I knew I was strong enough to handle it on my own.

23

All I saw was the gray sky, full of storm clouds. The air was thicker than normal. My fingertips trailed in the frigid water as my arm hung lazily over the edge of the canoe. I swirled my hand back and forth through the rippling water. Where was I? My back was stiff, as if I'd been lying here a while. I lifted my head from the belly of the boat and peered out.

Sitting in the middle of a lake, in a canoe with no paddles, I recognized the shoreline as Baylor Lake. My heartbeat spiked. Panic took over. I ripped my hand from the evil waters and cradled it against my chest. Why was I back here? I didn't want to be back here.

I thought my dreams had ended. I tried on countless occasions to get back to the void and to find Walker. But ever since he slid the missing glass slipper on my foot, I hadn't been able to get back to him. But this was no false reality. I was back in Baylor, and I didn't know why, or for how long.

I rubbed the goosebumps on my arms, trying to pinpoint which direction the cabin was. I couldn't tell the time of day, as the sun was hidden deep behind the clouds. I only hoped I could get out before nightfall.

It didn't matter that I knew where my monsters had spawned from. They were still just as terrifying. And I didn't want to spend my time fighting between the jaws of a beast when I had a job to do. I needed to find Walker. And I needed him to come home with me.

I took a deep breath and plunged my hand into the cold water. I cupped the water and pushed it behind me. Hard and fast, I dug through the lake. But I tired quickly and found the canoe was moving in circles. It was useless. I was stuck in the middle of the lake, and time was ticking. *Think. Think, Kinsley.*

Would manifestation work? Now that I was completely aware I was lucid dreaming, would any of my old tricks work? I closed my eyes and tried to warm my wet hand between my legs. I thought of the cabin. I imagined the canoe gliding up to the dock and Walker waiting for me on the back porch.

I opened my eyes when I felt the canoe bump against shore. I was surprised to find I wasn't at our dock, but a small cove I didn't recognize. Warily, I stepped out of the canoe and into the shadows of the forest. I tromped through blackberry bushes and scraped my legs on thorns until a small trail appeared, winding through the dense trees. I hurried along in search of help.

"Walker?" I called out.

At first, I thought I saw a person in the woods, but as I looked closer, I could see it was a full-length mirror leaning against a pine tree. A girl I used to know stared back at me. And as I'd been somewhat traumatized from the funhouse and the many hours searching for my soul in empty mirrors, I hurried into a jog down the trail.

Tiny hairs on my arms rose, and I knew the quicker I got out of the forest, the better. Things in Baylor had changed since the last time I was here. Small, decorative mirrors hung like Christmas ornaments from the trees, causing multiple pairs of brown eyes to watch me as I crossed the forest floor. I sucked in a deep breath as one dropped and shattered on the path. Woodland critters scampered into the shrubs. I had to remind myself to be brave, that I was stronger now.

After making eye contact with my reflection a handful of jarring times, I realized the eyes weren't always the same. Sometimes they were bleak, empty eyes, and other times they were mysterious and prevailing. I was certain now that somebody was watching me.

I spun in a slow circle as my eyes studied the depths of the forest. There were clumps of purple rapunzel flowers, a noisy crow jumping from one branch to the next, and a trail of black smoke in the distance.

"Layla?" I called out, hoping the mysterious eyes belonged to her.

A loud crash sent me leaping forward as I covered my head. A large mirror broke just feet behind me. I looked up into the treetops where several giant mirrors perched between branches. How did they get up there? And why?

The crow hopped about, causing branches to bow under its weight. When the next mirror hurtled down, I jumped out of the way with a yelp. The clatter echoed throughout the forest, and the trail was littered with broken glass. I had to be very careful if I didn't want the sky itself to break. I knew it could.

I walked on, trying to remain calm and collected. At first, I thought a reflection from the gray sky had peeked down through the leaves and ricocheted off the fractals of broken glass that lay on the trail. The slight movement of dancing light illuminated the forest floor. But as my eyes found the sharp fragments of glass beneath my feet, I saw something I wasn't expecting.

There, in a triangular piece of broken mirror, I saw Walker pulling me from the lake. I kneeled down, watching the memory play out before me. My shaking wet body fell helplessly into the canoe. Starlight lit my face from a perspective I'd never seen before. And Walker's mysterious and warm eyes shifted from wonder to . . .

"What the hell were you doing all the way out here? We must be miles from the nearest shore." I could barely hear his voice floating somewhere near and yet far at the same time.

I scanned the hundreds of mirrors, all reflecting distinct memories, throughout the forest. And that's when I could hear them. I could hear them all.

"We get to stay here all summer?" Kimber asked in awe.

My head snapped in the opposite direction, and I rose to a crouching position. A TV newscaster spoke, sending chills down my spine. "147 people died Thursday night on flight 351 to Clover. Caught in the storm, the plane came crashing down in the middle of Grand and Fifth, demolishing the historical bank here in Charlee City."

"No!"

I reached out, eager to find the memory and smash it. Stop it from ever happening in the first place. But I froze in my tracks when I heard a small, frightened voice, more familiar than the rest.

"What happens if I don't go home?"

"You mean if you stay here?" Gran asked, her tone worried and faint.

"Yeah, if I stay." I felt the heartbreak and all the uncertainty that had plagued me over the summer. I searched for the memory, but it was lost in a sea of voices. I walked in circles, trying to find it.

"And you won't be far after?" Layla asked. I took a few steps off the path before finding the vision in a massive mirror that was lying on the ground, slightly hidden behind a rock. Layla was speaking with Walker, and I was peeking out from behind the trees. Eavesdropping on a conversation that would change the course of my entire life.

"I promise. If you go, so will I," he said.

I watched myself trip over the crimson cloak. Both Walker and Layla whipped their heads around, peering into the forest. But I was long gone, the cloak left behind in a cloud of dust.

He'd told her he would follow her home. Why didn't he?

My mom's song drifted in the distant air. "My heart blooms. Blooms for you. Wildflowers because of you." Her song clashed with the other voices, pleading for my attention. I closed my eyes.

"I'm not going to spend eternity rotting in my own guilty conscience!"

"Secrets? Secrets are for the living. What do you need to hide in your afterlife?"

"Just read it!" . . . "I can't! I don't want to!"

"Everything you've ever thought or felt has a home. A place to live in a dark, forgotten corner of your mind."

A voice yelled from above. "Wake up!" Lainey hissed. I looked up just in time to see a pair of desperate yellow eyes reaching out from the haunted water. I screamed as the mirror crashed down, breaking on my shoulder and slicing open my arm.

Voices surfaced near and far. A different dimension. A different time. All flooding back into a single moment. I tightened my fists and blocked everything out the best I could. The desperate voices, the regrets, the burn of my open wound. There was only one reflection I needed to see now.

"Layla!" I cried. I waited for her reply, but nothing came. Movement flickered like an ancient TV screen, but I saw stillness in her eyes. An old Victorian mirror swayed gently from a low-hanging branch, and a pair of deep brown eyes met mine with a knowing gaze.

I crossed the path of broken glass, reached out, and took the decorative mirror in my hand. I stared into Layla's eyes as my breathing slowed. "Layla . . ." I whispered. I watched her ruby lips move in unison with my plea for help.

This time, I saw myself in her. Everything I had ever needed to get through this nightmare was hiding in plain sight. I was capable of finding Walker and bringing him home.

I nodded into the mirror and let it go. It spun fiercely on its cord, causing a small glimmer of light to flicker throughout the forest, until it was wound so tightly the light stopped, illuminating a path I hadn't seen before.

I worried there wasn't much time left and took off running toward what I hoped would be Walker. The strung mirror unwound itself, throwing flashes of light wildly throughout the forest. Mirrors dropped near and far, and shattering glass exploded like grenades on a battlefield.

It's only a dream. Lean into the darkness. Gran's words echoed in my mind. I hoped I would make her proud, wherever she was.

I ran until I broke free from the web of memories. The cabin sat peacefully in the clearing. Then, I saw Walker's canoe, floating like a burning barge in the middle of Rock Creek Cove. A trail of black smoke signaled high in the sky eliciting fright and panic.

"Walker!" I screamed, as I barreled down the hill.

He couldn't die. I wouldn't let him.

"Walker!"

I ran straight into the water and dove when the surface met my thighs. The flames were shrinking. The canoe snapped in half, both ends tipping up as the center began to sink. I floundered, searching wildly for a body I couldn't bear to see.

I ducked under the water, kicking hard to catch the sinking wreckage. I knew I could hold an infinite breath when I was in Baylor, but something seemed different. My lungs spasmed, and despite my best efforts, I needed air. I was living now, and the thought of running out of air frightened me. I didn't want to die.

I surfaced and took a gulp of air, then dived deeper, but no matter how many times I tried, I couldn't reach the canoe. Air bubbles nipped at the surface as I cried.

Had he ended his life? Was it so miserable here without companionship? Had I been too late?

I remembered the spontaneous fires in the trees, the campfire chairs, and even the clouds. Had the poison finally rolled through Baylor, sweeping away all the lives left behind?

I swallowed water on my way back to shore, crying and coughing uncontrollably.

"Wilde?"

I climbed out of the lake on hands and knees. Silt covered my legs, and blood ran from the wound on my arm. Standing where the back patio door would have been—if it hadn't caught fire—was a silhouette.

"Walker?" I took a muddy step. He cocked his head and slung a black washcloth over his shoulder. "Walker!" I screamed.

He was alive! He was lonely, and most likely heartbroken, but he was alive!

I couldn't imagine what living in Baylor would be like had I done it alone. My friends were the only things that kept me sane, and I hung on to that sanity by a thread.

I ran up the hill, slipping on wet grass under muddy shoes. The deck was missing, and the backside of the cabin was a sorry sight. Black char covered the collapsing doorframe and surrounded the broken windows. The cabin appeared not only abandoned, but haunted. And Walker was glum enough to be the ghost that lived there.

Walker jumped to the ground in the staircase's absence. I ran straight into his arms, crashing into him. I cried on his shoulder, unable to get the words out.

"You're shaking like a leaf."

"I thought . . . I thought you were . . ."

"What's going on Wilde? Why are you here?" Walker pulled back. He seemed more confused than anything else.

"I thought you were dead." That single word crushed me, and I crumbled before him.

"What? No! I'm right here. I'm right here." He cradled me in his arms.

I sank back against his chest, trembling involuntarily at the very thought of losing him. "I saw the canoe."

"Everything's burning. It has been for some time now. The canoe and dock went this morning. It looks like I'll be staying here. Let's go inside," he said, shifting his arm around my waist.

"You don't have to stay here. Come home with me." My voice quivered, and I realized I was more afraid now, as I waited for his reply, than I ever would have been fighting my nightmares in the fog-dense forest.

"That world's not meant for me . . ."

"Yes, it is. What are you talking about?"

"Wilde, I don't belong there anymore." He shook his head, and the lights went out in his eyes. "This is my home now."

I followed him through the front door, and it shocked me to see the cabin was exactly how I had left it. Exactly.

It was suffocating. Flakes of black ash were still settling in the air, as if the fire had just happened. The walls were charred black and crusted over. The smell of smoke made it difficult to breathe.

Immediately, I looked to the corner where I had seen Scarlett May's cowgirl boots peeking from within a mountain of embers and ash. The pile remained, but I was relieved to find that her boots were gone. I had to remind myself that she was back home. Or rather, on the other side of the lake now. Yes, she was in Baylor, but she wasn't in this Baylor.

"I've got some cleaning up to do, but hey, I've got time." The look on his face seemed pained. He seemed lonelier than ever before, and that was saying a lot for Walker.

"You can't live here. It's inhabitable. It's . . . a nightmare," I whispered. It was my nightmare.

Walker's eyes flickered with recognition. It almost seemed like he had forgotten he was in a dream. Forgotten that he had a family to get back to. I remembered how easy it was to succumb to the darkness. When the light seemed so far away, so unobtainable, I'd convinced myself I didn't want it any longer. I feared that if I didn't get out in time, I might be swallowed up by the night and lost forever. I had to focus.

"You have a family. You have a life. You're in a hospital, and everybody is rooting for you. You need to come back!"

"You don't know that." Walker hung his head and walked into the kitchen, avoiding eye contact with me. What had happened to him in the time I'd been gone? Time moved slower in dreams. Exactly how long had he felt abandoned? Long enough to lose feelings for me?

"Yes, I do! Because I was in the room next door. I spent a week listening to your monitors through the thin walls of the hospital. Listening to your friends come and go. Listening to your mother cry when visiting hours were over. I had to hear your little sister try to comfort your mother in a way that no child should ever have to do! I know this because I was there!"

Tears clouded my eyes as I pointed an angry finger at his chest. I felt so very alone in the hospital. And even though my family was often present, nobody knew what I was going through. But Walker would have, if only he'd chosen to fight.

Walker pulled the dirty black towel from his shoulder and kneeled in front of a small wet spot on the kitchen floor. He dipped the rag into a bucket of black water, wrung it out, and plopped it onto the floor. And then, mindlessly, he began scrubbing.

It reminded me of Emma when I'd last seen her in Baylor. She had been scrubbing the same soiled spot, trying to clean the soot stain from the floor. It never came clean, and she never gave up. Something inside of her had gone dim. Dormant. The lights had gone out, just like I saw in Walker's eyes now. I'm certain that she would have spent eternity trying to clean the same square foot of the kitchen floor if I hadn't climbed that Ferris wheel.

"Walker?" My voice was but a whisper.

He said nothing.

"What about your family?"

He scrubbed vigorously. His muscles bulged from his arm, and veins popped across the back of his hand. Had he not heard me?

"Is this because of the curse? Because you don't think you can find love? Well, I'm right here! You found it! You just have to come get it!" I spread my arms open, wishing he'd claim his prize.

His back stilled for just a moment, but I could tell he'd given up on that thought long ago.

I did the only thing I could think of. I crossed into the kitchen and pulled a dish towel from a blackened drawer. Then I kneeled beside him and submerged my towel in the dirty water. I wrung it out with two hands as I caught Walker's eyes unwillingly shift back and forth. Fighting between caring just enough and being too numb to care at all.

"What are you doing?" he asked, his voice grave. Somewhere inside, he wanted to come home. I guided him the only way I knew how. And in this twisted realm, dark psychology was my best bet.

"I'm cleaning." I slopped the wet towel down on the black floor and started to scrub.

"Don't bullshit me, Wilde! What are you doing?" I flinched. I'd never seen Walker this angry before, but at least the fire was back in his eyes, and for that, I was thankful.

"If you stay . . . I stay," I said, glaring at him.

"You belong with the living!"

"Don't test me! You know what I'm capable of!" I said through gritted teeth.

"I will not let you ruin your life because of me!"

A minute passed with no words spoken. I briefly wondered how I'd possibly get him home. Even if he agreed. I didn't have a plan beyond this fight, and I didn't know where the next red door would be.

His eyes narrowed. "Don't test me," he countered. "You have no idea what I'm capable of . . ."

"If you had magic, then why didn't you use it?"

"Because! I could have killed you. I did kill you. I made a promise when the paramedics pulled you from the car. I stood on the overpass, and I made a deal with the devil. If we owed a life, it would be mine." Walker beat his chest.

"You what?"

I searched his eyes, looking for the smallest sliver of hope. I saw nothing.

"You cursed yourself?" A tidal wave built inside me. How were we going to fight this? "But you said you were going to come back! You were supposed to follow us . . ."

"I'm a monster. A killer. It's in my blood." Walker shook his head. Though his confession was raw, it couldn't be real. A place like this could take a sound mind and twist it till it broke. And he was very much broken.

"Did any part of you want me to stay?"

Walker threw his rag into the bucket, and water splattered the floor. "Loving you was the hardest fight I ever fought. And I lost. I hated myself for it. I begged Layla to take you home. But you were so stubborn! You sabotaged yourself at every turn!"

He covered his face with his hand. "And the longer I spent with you, the more I wanted to believe that I was the guy you dreamed of."

I took his wrist and pulled his hand from his face. "You are!"

"I killed you!" he yelled.

I dropped his wrist and leapt backward. My heart pounded. "It was an accident," I insisted.

"Don't you see? I'm no good for you." Walker's golden eyes turned watery and red. "I belong here . . ." He gestured to a fluttering flake of ash.

Walker wasn't a murderer. He wasn't the Baylor Butcher, and he wasn't his father. He was just a guy who'd had an accident. A guy whose life changed forever in a split second.

"Your curse is my curse. If you don't come home, I'm the one who will never love again." I threw my rag on top of his and placed my hands on my hips.

Walker shook his head painfully. It wasn't what he wanted. And I could tell he'd never considered that if he punished himself, he'd punish me as well. If he wanted me to be happy, he'd have to forgive himself first.

"Come home with me."

A single tear spilled from Walker's eye. He quickly averted his gaze and tightened his fists. "I'm sorry, but I can't. Keep your promise, Wilde. Say goodbye."

The ground moved under my feet, and I nearly stumbled backward. Walker and I both slid toward the opening where the patio door used to be. A wide-open red door called to me. I felt my soul flutter as if getting sucked into the vortex just beyond the portal.

Walker was using his magic, and I feared it would be the spell that broke us. "Walker! No! Don't!" I continued to slide backward as if on some invisible conveyor belt. My hair rose from my back as the wind became stronger.

I lunged forward in one last attempt to save Walker from himself. I grabbed hold of his flannel collar and pulled him to me. I pressed my lips against his in the most passionate kiss I'd ever had. I kissed him like my life depended on it. And this time, I didn't hide behind the guise of a wolf to do it.

I clung to him. My shirt beat against my back. My hair lashed violently. The vortex pulled and pulled. When I tripped backward, we were sucked through the door. The shackles of the curse broke and fell away as we plunged through the clouds. I felt Walker grin into our kiss.

24

Dawn was breaking outside my window, and the night sky lightened to a hazy purple. My chest rose and fell quickly as I brought my fingertips to trace my lips. I could have sworn they were still warm from Walker's kiss. A smile spread under my touch. *I did it.* I brought him home. I leapt out of bed, slipped my feet into my sneakers, and grabbed a hooded sweatshirt to pull over my head as I ran out of my bedroom.

I tried to be quiet, as my parents were still sleeping, but my enthusiasm was thunderous as I ran down the stairs. I grabbed the keys from beneath the never-shrinking pile of unopened mail on the kitchen table, and I ran into the garage. I didn't hesitate to start the ignition or pull out of the driveway. Driving no longer scared me.

My mind raced as I drove to the hospital. Was he already awake? Was he just waking now? Would my face be the first he'd see since the accident? I pulled into the parking lot and scurried into the hospital.

I slipped past the check-in desk and made my way to the elevator. I drummed my hands on my legs until the door glided open. How would he respond? Would he remember me? My pajama pants and messy hair kept the questions at bay in the ICU. I must have fit in with all the other visitors who looked like they hadn't slept in days. Knowing my way around the hospital helped too.

My sweaty hand nearly slipped off the doorknob. But I couldn't take the time to prepare myself or I'd get caught in the hall. I wasn't sure what I'd say, or how I'd say it. I only knew that I had to get to him. I opened the door and hurried inside. My heart sank as my eyes fell upon his empty bed.

What? Was I too late? Had they moved him to a different room? I grabbed his chart but froze when I heard the toilet flush. I pressed the clipboard against my chest and took a deep breath. I turned to face Walker for the first time in real life.

"Well, it isn't much," a grumpy man said as he shuffled toward me. He reached out and handed me a cylinder of warm amber liquid. The stars vanished in my eyes, and the heat from my cheeks turned cold. I realized not only was this man *not* Walker, but that I was holding his chart . . . and urine sample. He turned for bed, his robe parted and exposed a labyrinth of dark curly hair on his upper back. The toilet seat was still lifted as the restroom door swung shut. "Don't be scared. It isn't gonna bite."

I ran out. I discarded the man's file in a slot by his door, then ran to the nurse's desk, the sample still pinched between my fingers.

"Excuse me?" I asked. "Do you know where Walker went? He was in that room before." I hooked a thumb over my shoulder.

"Are you related to the patient?" the young nurse asked.

"Yes," I lied.

"You mean Lance? He is downstairs in room 24. Is he your father?" The nurse typed on her keyboard, glancing at me only briefly when I faltered.

"Lance?" I stuttered, trying to come up with a believable lie when I saw Martina.

"Martina!" I called out, slamming my free hand down on the counter.

It took a moment for her to recognize me, but when she did, her face lit up. "Hey Kinsley! What are you doing back here? Is everything okay?"

"Yeah. Everything's going well. I was just checking on Walker St. James?" I pointed to his old room. "Do you know where they moved him?"

Martina tilted her head and leaned in close. "Now you know I'm not supposed to tell you other patient's personal information."

"I know. I know," I pled.

"I can't tell you much . . ." she hesitated.

"Anything! Anything you can tell me! I'd be so grateful."

"He's not here. He hasn't been for a long time. His mother took him to a new hospital, and I don't know which one, so don't ask me!" She pointed her finger at me, silencing my next question before it arose. "Now, don't tell anybody I told you that much. You hear?"

"I understand. But—"

"No buts!"

"But why did he get moved?"

Martina's face fell and her shoulders slumped. One corner of her mouth lifted as she said, "I don't know. Something about this hospital not giving him what he needs. Now it's time to go back to wherever you came from." She put her hands on my shoulders and spun me around.

"Thank you," I whispered over my shoulder.

"Don't thank me. I did nothing." She gave me a knowing stare.

"Wait!" I spun around.

"Now, I told you—" I handed Martina the urine sample and left without another word.

After stopping in a restroom and washing my hands under hot, soapy water, I drove home. I couldn't imagine Walker waking up in a hospital without me. I remembered how confused I'd been when I woke up. I knew he needed me. I wasn't sure where I would find the answers. The world suddenly seemed so large, and I was too small. I reminded myself that he'd found me once on the road, and I had found him once in a dream. I hoped that fate would bring us together for a third and final time.

Mom was upset when I got home. Something about me taking the car without asking. But I was eighteen now. Not exactly graduated, but almost. Still, I didn't fight with her. I didn't have the energy. She and I had been talking a lot more recently, opening up about Gran and things. I didn't want to ruin our newfound trust with a battle over independence.

Mom slammed her phone down on the table and rubbed her temples. "I'm sorry. I'll let you know next time. I just, I couldn't sleep, and the sun was almost up. I wanted to go for a drive and listen to music. That's all." Normally I was an honest person, but one small lie led to many.

She waved her hand dismissively. "That was a message from your Uncle Tanner. Apparently, there was a noise complaint last night at the cabin. Do you know anything about that?"

"A noise complaint?"

"They said there was a party, and they had to call the sheriff to shut it down at nearly two in the morning."

Lainey and Emma threw a party? I couldn't imagine such a thing. I mean, I certainly could imagine throwing a party at the cabin; I had done it several times in my dreams. But Lainey and Emma? In real life? Not possible.

I poured Mom a cup of hot coffee after the machine beeped. Her face softened when I put it down in front of her. "I'll call Uncle Tanner today and apologize. And I'm going to call Lainey and Emma right now to get to the bottom of it," I said.

"Thank you." She took a sip of coffee and then stared blankly out the window. I slipped away to call my friends.

It surprised me when Lainey picked up. She was typically an early bird, but if they had a party last night, I would have figured she'd sleep in. I was wrong.

"Hello? Kinsley?" Lainey whispered into the phone.

"Hey, it's me. Why are you up so early?" I asked as I settled in my bed, still in my pajamas from the hospital run.

"Gunner won't stop barking. He doesn't want to be inside, but he can't stop barking outside. Your neighbors are going to be so pissed." I heard the door open and slam shut. Gunner's bark sounded like an alarm in the distance.

"What is he barking at?"

"I don't know. Something in the water. A duck maybe? It's too foggy to tell."

I had the clearest memory of Gunner barking at the end of the dock. It made me uneasy to think anything, anything at all, was similar now. "Where's Emma?"

"Gunner! Gunner!" Lainey hissed.

"Where's Emma?" I repeated sternly.

"Oh my god, Kins. Your parents are going to kill me. He's dug holes all over the lawn!"

"Lainey!" I snapped. "Where. Is. Emma?"

"What!? She's sleeping. What's the big deal? Come on, Gunner. Come on."

"Are you sure?"

"Yeah, I'm sure. Where else would she be?" Lainey's breath was uneven and labored, and I could hear Gunner grunting in the background.

"Go check! Check right now!" I had felt helpless before, but sitting at home in my pajamas was a new low.

"I'm going. God Kinsley, you're scaring me." I listened to the door swing open on a creaky hinge. Gunner's toenails pranced on the kitchen floor and footfalls thumped up the steps. I held my breath, waiting for confirmation that Emma was okay and hadn't sunk to the bottom of Rock Creek Cove. When Lainey sighed in relief, I did too.

"She's sleeping! Like everybody else is doing at six a.m. What was all that about? I just tracked mud through the house. You have no idea how much cleaning I have to do today."

I closed my eyes and tried to relax. I had to remind myself that their trip was not the same one I'd taken. It wasn't the summer from hell. It was their graduation celebration. It was everything it was supposed to be, minus me. Nothing more. Nothing less.

"Well, I have an idea. I heard the neighbors called the sheriff on you guys. Did you throw a party last night?" I asked with a chuckle. The thought was so unlikely, it seemed ridiculous to even ask.

It took too long for Lainey to answer, so I pressed the phone closer to my ear. Did she really throw a party?

"About that—"

"Oh my god! You threw a party!"

My Lainey threw a party. How I wished I were there. I tried to imagine such a thing, but when I did, my smile died. I saw a red door in the hall beckoning me. Luring me. At first, I felt like I'd missed out, but now I felt like I'd dodged a bullet.

"I'm so, so sorry. I didn't plan it. I tried to stop it for like two hours! They just kept coming!"

"It's okay. I'm not mad. I'm a little shocked is all. I can't believe *you* threw a party. Was it fun? Wait, tell me nobody broke my pottery . . ."

Lainey laughed. "I don't think anything was broken. And yes. It was so much fun!" she squealed. I snuggled up in bed, ready to hear all the stories. It was the perfect distraction from losing Walker.

"Tell me everything! Who was there?"

"Okay. So we met up with the group after running into them in town. We didn't even try; it just happened organically. Scarlett May was asking where you were. I mean, they all were. But she, especially, seemed sad that you weren't here. They asked where the house was, and we told them. We thought nothing of it when they said they might stop by. When they showed up, we were mid-movie, and Emma had a face mask on!"

"No!" I gasped.

"Yes! When they knocked on the front door, she bolted upstairs and sent Gunner into a panic!"

I threw myself onto a stack of pillows and covered my face with secondhand embarrassment.

"I opened the door, surprised to see everybody. Noah held up chocolate, marshmallows, and graham crackers, hoping for an invite in. I could tell it crushed him you weren't here. But before I could get any words out, Mason pushed through the crowd with a case of beer on his shoulder, and everybody just followed him inside. At first, I was really stressed, but then the boys made a fire out by the shore. It was actually really fun, Kinsley! I'm so sad you missed it."

"Don't worry about me. I visited my grandpa. He plays a mean game of Go Fish. So, did you toast marshmallows?"

"Yes. We sat around the fire toasting marshmallows and telling scary ghost stories. It was the best. Even Emma told one! But then we heard this creak in the woods. It totally freaked me out. I was actually terrified, but everybody else just laughed. That part was embarrassing," Lainey rambled.

I could hear her voice turn dismissive, but I *knew* that sound in the woods. I knew it was more than a settling branch or a nocturnal critter. There were predators out there, invisible to the naked eye. Invisible to the vulnerable likes of Lainey and Emma. My chest tightened to think the summer was repeating itself.

"You have to trust your instincts, Lainey. Don't go into those woods alone! They're dangerous!" Goosebumps prickled my arms.

Lainey laughed. "No, no, no. It was just Scarlett May's friends. Apparently, she's friends with a couple of the locals, and everybody is super connected here. She invited a couple of people last night, and when they heard us telling ghost stories, they snuck up on us. It broke the ice, and we all laughed pretty hard. We even have an inside joke about it. Can you believe I have an inside joke with Kimber and Asher? Like, what is this world we live in?" I could hear her smile through the phone.

I believed it, and then some. The more she talked, the more my summer came to life. I'd been working diligently to make sure my dreams were contained. Placed in a neat box that I could shut the lid on, and padlock for good measure. I needed my dreams to be silenced, because when they were free, they spread throughout all my memories, making it difficult to tell where the fiction ended and the truth began.

All the work I'd done to tame my nightmares were diminishing now that stories of Baylor were hot off the press. Of course, they weren't having the summer I had, but there were similarities. Something as little as the dog barking, or a blanket of fog over the lake. It all had meaning to me.

Lainey and I talked a little more that morning. But the more details I received, the more I grew anxious. I lost count of the number of times Lainey told me I was scaring her with my *cryptic* warnings. Finally, I had to get off the phone.

The first thing I did after hanging up was grab a notebook off my desk and start jotting down the things she'd told me. I separated them from the similar things I had dreamed. Over the next couple of weeks, that list became pages and pages long.

Lainey and Emma ended up staying three full weeks in Baylor. It wasn't the whole summer, but it was a great start. They had more stories to tell when they got back than they'd had their entire high school career combined. I couldn't have been happier for them. Emma had even spent some time alone with Levi. Enough time in fact that she was no longer attracted to him. I told her it was probably for the better.

Both Emma and Lainey found something in Baylor that had been lost to them. A sense of belonging, a sense of connection. And as it turns out, Baylor was a magical place after all. Because I had found something in those woods too. I found a girl named Layla. I found not only acceptance there, but pride too. It only took me months of therapy and one special ghost to realize it.

Emma and I saw Lainey off to college that summer, and I was able to concentrate enough to finish my GED. I graduated high school, and when the certificate showed up in the mailbox, I celebrated.

I eventually finished physical therapy and began exercising regularly. I got a job at a small bookstore, a place I never thought I'd enjoy. But I learned a lot about story, and I even began to write my first screenplay. Several pages in, I crumpled it into a ball and threw it in the trash. The only story I wanted to tell was that of a haunted cabin in a remote forest. Once I gave in, the story flowed effortlessly. It changed in new and fascinating ways. It became my new guilty pleasure. And as I wrote my story, I began to silence the summer that never was. I could finally put a lock on that box and throw away the skeleton key.

The only setbacks I had were when Aunt Nora updated me on the pending lawsuit. It was my only real connection to Walker. I knew I'd see him again, and that kept me from fully healing.

Everything inside me screamed to let him go. Open my heart to somebody else. Somebody real. Somebody living outside of a fantasy. Because even though Walker had been real, the time we'd spent together was not. I didn't know him. And he didn't know me. Still, it would take a great deal of time to get over my idea of him.

I couldn't help but compare the few boys I dated to Walker. And soon, that became a recurring conversation with Dr. Shelton. She helped me realize I was afraid of putting myself out there and getting my heart broken. That's the reason I compared my dates to a fictional guy. She reminded me over and over, and the more times I heard it, the more I believed it.

One year later, I'd forgotten what Walker looked like. I tried to picture his face in my mind, but I couldn't quite remember if he had dimples or not. I thought maybe he had. I couldn't remember what shape his lips were, or what shade of pink they were. And I thought his eyes might have been hazel, but I couldn't remember them either. His hair was dark; I was certain of that, and I was pretty sure he had a scar on his forehead. Other than that, Walker became a symbol of perfectionism. An invisible marker that I used to compare and measure against. A shadow of a man that I wanted to love, but was too afraid to.

25

A little more than a year after the accident, I had grown very comfortable with what I used to call Layla. Now, it was just me. I was attending college locally. I chose the same college Gran and Grandpa Green had attended, and sometimes, when the sky was gray and glum, I'd see her.

Not the Gran I'd known, but a younger version. A student, walking between classes. I'd watch from underneath a large oak tree, my knees bent, and my back curled against the trunk. Gran was beautiful and vibrant, but most of all, she was mysterious. She'd disappear into the crowd, and I'd never be able to hold on to her for very long.

Lainey was thriving, but Emma had moved back home. She didn't like the university and quit after her first year. She enrolled with me, and we moved out together into a small studio apartment. I visited Grandpa often, and I got quite good at playing cards. Sometimes I'd join him and a couple of his retired police academy friends to play poker. And when I did, I cheated.

My Aunt Nora kept me updated on the pending lawsuit. Not long after she officially filed suit, we were shocked to find out that Walker's attorney had filed a cross-complaint, alleging that *I* had caused the accident.

At first, I was outraged, but my aunt described to me how both witnesses had diagnosed brain injuries. My testimony wasn't very credible, and neither was his. To top that off, both our vehicles' black boxes were destroyed, and ironically, the police report had come back with little to no information as to what had happened. All either of us knew for sure was that we'd incurred an astonishing amount of medical debt.

Nora called the lawsuit an outright brawl. She said that if we wound up in trial, it would not only be outrageously expensive, but stressful too. She didn't want that for me or my parents, and neither did I. As a family, we agreed to mediate before incurring more cost, and Nora was confident that she could get a favorable settlement in a single day.

For the better part of the year, my dreams had completely stopped. I thought I'd be sad about that, but as my mind quieted and my life fell into step, I couldn't be more grateful. In the weeks leading up to the mediation, I was happy to be past the idea of Walker. And just like any normal dream, I could no longer remember him or the time we'd spent together. On the day of mediation, the only thing I was certain of was his name.

I knew I'd been in an accident, that I'd spent two weeks in the hospital and months thereafter recovering both mentally and physically. And I remembered having twisted dreams and struggling with them after I woke. It had been a dark time in my life, but one I found necessary to get where I was today. I had a lot of growth come from that accident, and as painful as it was, I wouldn't trade it for the world.

I finally moved past my nightmares. Past the insecurities. I grew to love myself. I even learned to grieve for my gran instead of burying it deep inside. All my relationships had strengthened in one way or another, and I was currently in the process of getting an agent for my screenplay. Which had turned out nothing like what I had truly experienced, though I couldn't fully remember why. I had notes about what was real and what wasn't scribbled down everywhere. But when I read them now, they hardly made sense. The summer that never was had vanished, just as it should. The last piece holding me back was the lawsuit. And soon, that would be over too.

Aunt Nora honked outside in the early morning. I clutched a hot mocha to my chest as I walked to her car. I faked a smile as we pulled out of the driveway and took a deep breath as we began the drive to downtown Decord City.

"Are you okay?" Aunt Nora asked.

"Yeah."

"You don't need to be nervous. This is standard practice."

Maybe for an attorney. But this was a lot more to me than settling my case and putting the accident past me. This was more than money and the opportunity that came with it. Deep down, I knew I'd face my last demon today. I had to confront a man whom I'd never met yet was responsible for shaping the very person I'd become. "I'm not nervous."

Aunt Nora raised a brow.

"Okay. Just a little bit."

"Let's go over what you should expect in there. I don't want you to be intimidated by the process, okay?"

"Okay."

"First, this is *not* a trial. There won't be a judge or jury. We're privately agreeing to see a third party who specializes in trying to reach settlements and get people to agree on terms. He is called a mediator. And actually, I've worked with him many times before. Jon Walon. He's a friend of mine and will give it to us straight."

"That's good."

"Yes. He's very good at what he does."

"So, am I going to tell everyone what I remember? Because I remember some of the accident, but not all of it. And what if I'm wrong? What if—"

"No. It won't be like that. In fact, it's just going to be us in our own private conference room all day. From sunup to sundown if necessary. Most of our time will be spent waiting. You won't even see, or talk to the other side, if you don't want to."

"Wait, what?" I didn't have to see Walker? All this time I'd been so nervous to look into his eyes, and now I might not even see him?

"The mediation will take place in separate, private rooms. Sometimes we get together, but that's only if everybody wants to. I don't even know if Rushbrooke's client is going to be there. Sometimes, when the insurance company is involved, they just leave it up to their attorney to deal with mediation, and the client doesn't even show."

"Who's Rushbrooke?" I cracked my knuckles, trying to anticipate what lay ahead.

"The boy from the accident, St. James, his auto insurance company is on the hook for this, so they appointed their own attorney. And he's a real ass." Nora pulled onto the highway, and the acceleration threw me back into my seat.

"But, Walker, he might not be there?" I asked, my mouth running dry.

"He might not be."

I sighed. All this stress for nothing? "Wait. Then did I have to come?" Could I have let my aunt fight my last battle for me?

"Technically . . . no. You are not required to attend."

"Aunt Nora!"

"But how are you supposed to become a lawyer if you don't fall in love with the process?"

"I'm not becoming a lawyer!" my voice climbed. Aunt Nora chuckled, and I groaned.

"I just wanted to spend the day with you, my dear. It's not often I have such a wonderful client."

"And it's not often I have such a *sneaky* attorney. Oh wait, it is."

"Hey, you want a sneaky attorney. Trust me. I will fight dirty. I'll fight tooth and nail for you, and you know it." She pointed her oval red nail at me.

"I know. I'm just anxious."

"You don't have to be. Promise."

I turned on the music and looked out my window. The thought of not seeing Walker eased my mind. Nora promised this would be a painless day. Boring conversations and subpar lunch. She hoped we would walk away with the settlement and the promised cash would be coming my way. I hoped for closure.

When we got to the business park and I climbed out of Aunt Nora's fancy car, I scanned the parking lot for a face I had only seen in my dreams.

I was even more nervous when we entered the building. I had passed several men in suits, both young and old. I trained my eyes on the floor before me. A tightly woven navy-blue carpet with orange and tan diamonds.

"Ms. Faye, I thought I'd be seeing you today." A middle-aged man in a burgundy sweater smiled fondly at my aunt. My heart thumped in my chest as I looked at the surrounding suits, wondering which one was Walker. Wondering if he was around the corner or if I'd bump into him in the halls.

"Jon Walon! Meet my favorite niece. This is Kinsley Wilde. She's my client today."

"Oh boy! This is going to be some mediation," he said with promise. I hoped it wouldn't be. I wanted to skip the negotiation, sign the papers, and leave. I didn't care what they said. But Aunt Nora wouldn't allow it. She was determined to make me *whole*.

Mr. Walon escorted us to the conference room where one other gentleman waited. "Kinsley, this is Robert Brown. He is your other attorney, appointed by your auto insurance, and he will be helping us today."

"It's nice to meet you, Ms. Wilde." Robert shook my hand and I smiled. I didn't know I would have two attorneys. It all seemed a bit much. I took my place at a large oval table, and my two attorneys sat by my side. Across from us, the mediator placed his belongings.

"Kinsley, is this your first time in mediation?" Mr. Walon asked.

"Yes."

"It's important for you to understand everything that you discuss with me in here is a hundred percent confidential between us. I will share nothing you say with the other side unless you allow me to do that. There is no right or wrong in here, and nobody is judging you. Please speak up and ask questions. It's going to be a long day, okay?" Walon peered at me from behind his glasses.

"Okay."

"Okay, let's start—"

"I have a question," I blurted.

Mr. Walon smiled. "Go on then."

"Is the . . ." I leaned over to Aunt Nora and whispered. *"What do you call him? Defendant?"*

"Correct. St. James is the defendant," she said.

I cleared my throat and tried again. "Is the defendant here today?"

"Yes. St. James is here. His personal attorney, Bradly Barratt, is here. And his insurance attorney, Rushbrooke, is running late." Walon rolled his eyes, and I felt the same annoyance ripple down my side of the table. "But he'll be here too. They're down the hall in their own private conference room. I'll go back and forth between the two rooms for as long as it takes to get this case settled on terms that you are comfortable with."

"What if it doesn't get settled today?" I asked. The last thing I wanted was to drag this out.

"Well, that's up to you guys. You may demand more written discovery, take depositions, request another day in mediation, or decide to go to trial and let a jury decide your fate. But it's in everybody's best interests to settle. So, we're going to work real hard to do that. Okay?"

"Okay. I'm ready to start."

Walon nodded, and the negotiation began. I glanced over my shoulder at the floor-to-ceiling glass wall. It didn't feel very private. I tried my best to engage but was terribly distracted. Over the next several hours, a few things became more apparent than the rest.

Walker and his attorneys were relentless. They didn't come here to defend Walker's case; they came here to fight. Their demands were in excess of all my insurance policies combined. I was terrified, but Aunt Nora rose to the challenge. In fact, she welcomed it. The more allegations they came at us with, the dirtier the fight became, and the more money Nora demanded they pay.

"I'm telling you, Walon, he's got a killer in his blood! His father was a drunk and killed a family in an accident of his own! The apple doesn't fall far from the tree!" Aunt Nora seethed.

"Now, Nora, you know we can't use that."

"Tell him! Tell him she had a craniotomy. *Two weeks* in a coma, *two weeks* in the hospital, *four months* in physical therapy, and a *lifetime* of psychotherapy. You tell him he *stole* her eighteenth birthday, *stole* her graduation, and caused hallucinations for *months; maybe for the rest of her life*!" Aunt Nora leaned over the oval table and prodded her red nail into the open air.

"No! Don't tell him that!"

She whipped her head around and stared at me in surprise. "Why?"

"Because that's embarrassing," I complained.

Nora sat down and called for a break. It was past noon, and it felt like we were in a worse spot than when we started. I excused myself to the restroom, where I planned to hide for the rest of eternity.

26

Needing a break, I walked down the hall and made my way to the restroom. I peeked through the glass windows at all the meetings going on and wondered if they were having as bad a day as I was. But when I came to the last conference room near the restroom, my steps slowed and time stilled.

An attractive guy in a white collared shirt sat at an oval table. Two men were caught in a quarrel, but he paid them no attention. He sat with fire blazing in his eyes as he spun a gold ring on top of the conference table. I knew without a shadow of a doubt it was Walker.

He had dark hair. A shadow on his unshaven face. And there was a scar running from his eyebrow to the corner of his eye. I knew from reading his chart that there was a metal plate beneath the skin of his cheek.

He looked nothing like what I remembered, yet something about him was oddly familiar. I knew exactly how he felt in that moment. Angry, robbed, frustrated, and utterly exhausted with it all. I felt that way too. And as I watched him through the glass, compassion softened all my rough edges. I didn't want to fight any more.

His eyes ticked upward, locking on mine. I stiffened at once; a deer caught in headlights. I spun around and bumped into a gentleman who was coming out of the restroom. I faltered and then barreled into the women's room. I leaned against the cold tile wall and hid my face in my trembling hands. Seeing Walker brought up a mixture of emotions that I couldn't possibly understand.

Whether he was *my* Walker or the defendant, I didn't know. But the one obvious thing was, my body remembered something my mind didn't want to.

My head was swimming, my skin flushed. I wrapped my hair into a bun and lifted it from the nape of my neck.

Memories began to flood back like a tidal wave. Eyes like spun honey. Cotton candy and stone towers. I took slow, steady breaths, and I reminded myself that I was strong and capable.

I spent so long in the restroom, pacing back and forth, that my aunt came to find me. "Kinsley? What's going on? You've been in here for twenty minutes. Lunch is almost over."

"I'm not hungry."

"Are you sure? Are you feeling all right?"

"Yeah," I said, but my strained voice betrayed me. As soon as Aunt Nora recognized it, I broke down in tears and fell into her arms.

"What's wrong, dear? It's okay."

"It's all so much!"

Aunt Nora let me cry, but only for a moment. "Are you saying you don't want to become an attorney?" she asked.

"Are you serious? This is the worst day of my life!" I laughed, wiping away my tears.

"Really? Because I'm loving it." She had my mother's smile.

"That's because you find pleasure in my pain," I teased.

"And don't you forget it. Now come on. We have to finish this thing. I can feel it. They're going to break soon. Time tests everything."

"Impossible."

I peeked inside the conference room as we passed by. Only one attorney sat at the oval table. Walker was gone. "That's Rushbrooke. He's the attorney causing all the problems today."

Rushbrooke had thinning hair, a bulbous nose, and a red, pitted face.

"He looks mean."

"He's the worst."

As we approached our conference room, Walker and Mr. Barratt were heading back from the lunch area and were caught in an intense discussion. Before our eyes could meet again, I ducked into our room and turned away from the open glass wall. I felt his eyes on my back as their footfalls passed by.

"Very interesting." Aunt Nora rose a brow.

I waited for the second half of the day to begin with a bouncing foot that wouldn't quit and wandering eyes. But as mediation continued, we were informed that the fight had taken a drastic turn, and nobody knew why.

"Well, you're never going to believe it," Walon said.

Aunt Nora and Mr. Brown leaned forward, and I followed their lead, preparing for bad news. "St. James and Attorney Bradley Barratt have demanded that his insurance pay policy limits. I wish I could take credit for this, but in all honesty, I had nothing to do with it."

"Why?" Brown asked. It was the first thing he'd said all day, but we were all thinking it.

Walon spread his open hands and shook his head. The room fell silent as we passed around our confusion. "If I've learned anything in my thirty-nine years of mediation, it's that you don't question a good thing, and you don't argue when you're winning. You see, reality is not just what you make of it—it's also what you dare to dream, and what you are willing to fight for."

"That's why you're the best, Walon," Aunt Nora said, her light tone triumphant.

"I could say the same about you, Ms. Faye."

The mood in our room shifted considerably as we waited for the draft settlement papers to come in. When Walon came back with a proposal, Aunt Nora got her pen ready. She began reading, her finger moving along the words at lightning speed. But then she came to a screeching halt.

"What is it?"

"What is this?" Aunt Nora seethed. I tried to look, but there were about a thousand words on that page. I had to be patient.

"You can't blame him for trying," Walon said with pink cheeks.

"Yes, I can! There's no way in hell I'm signing this. And she won't either!"

"Okay. Okay. Does she want to counter?"

"No counter! This is unacceptable!"

"What is he asking for?" Brown asked. I waited for somebody to tell me what was happening, but it was clear that Aunt Nora was too angry, and Brown was still in the dark.

"Kinsley, one term of the settlement is that you agree to allow St. James to take you to dinner tonight, immediately after mediation."

"What!?"

"He's requesting your company at the steakhouse. I hear it's quite good."

"Can he do that?" I asked, my cheeks heating with embarrassment.

"No!" Aunt Nora snapped.

"Actually, nothing's off the table in mediation. He's allowed to ask for whatever terms he wants. You'd be surprised at what comes across this table."

"She won't do it! We'll walk out of here right now!" Aunt Nora stood, the chair jumping behind her.

"Wait!"

The room grew silent as everybody's eyes fell upon me. My heart thumped in my chest and my throat constricted. "I'll do it."

"Kinsley, no." Aunt Nora shook her head.

"It's okay. It might help me get . . . *closure*. Maybe he wants to apologize,"

I said. Aunt Nora slowly sat down, and Walon waited patiently. "But I have a counter."

"Yes ma'am. What would you like to counter?"

"I'll go to dinner . . . but I'm driving."

Brown and Walon broke into laughter. Aunt Nora moaned, hiding her face with her hand, and sinking further into her seat. "Your mother's going to kill me," she said beneath her breath.

"Well, you won't have to do that. It's directly across the street," Walon said.

It took several hours for the final version of the settlement agreement to be drawn up. They awarded me one million from the auto insurance policy, an extra two million from Walker's umbrella insurance policy, and of course, one dinner. I signed on the dotted line, and I knew my life was about to change yet again.

I was a completely different person than I was when I'd gotten into my car on my eighteenth birthday. And whether the time I'd spent falling for Walker was real or not, this contract was between me and a complete stranger. I had no expectations, but I did have hopes of putting the past behind me, getting answers to a few burning questions, and finally moving forward.

While we waited for signatures, I compiled a mental list of things I wanted to ask Walker. I wanted to know what he remembered of the accident. I wanted to align my story with his and finally get a full picture of the accident that had nearly stolen my life. I told myself, beyond that, nothing else mattered. But I knew it was a lie. I was curious about him. About his father, his family, what he'd gone through to recover. And I would be lying if I said there wasn't a piece of me, somewhere inside that dark forgotten corner of my mind, that was aching to know: what did he remember about me?

"I'll wait for you. I'll even eat at the same restaurant to keep an eye on you. And I'll drive you home," Aunt Nora insisted.

"It's okay. I really don't mind. I can call a taxi."

"Kinsley, your mother is going to be *so* mad!"

"Once she hears you got policy limits, I doubt she's going to ask how I got home, where I ate dinner, or who with." Aunt Nora drummed her fingers on the table. It took some time, but she agreed. I *was* legally an adult, after all.

It was dark when we left the conference room. Everyone signed the settlement agreement, and the lawsuit was over. Brown and Walon bantered lightly with my aunt as we walked to the elevator. I stood in the back against the padded wall. The doors began to close as Rushbrooke approached and slammed into the buttons. The doors opened and Brown glanced sideways at Aunt Nora.

My breath hitched as Walker and his two attorneys entered our tightly packed elevator. His amber eyes met mine, and I studied the scar that sliced through his eyebrow. His deep-set dimples were visible in his clenched jaw. He was wildly handsome, and he hadn't taken his eyes off me. I thought I might pass out, hit my head and be rushed to the hospital for a new journey to begin again.

Walker pushed his way to the back of the elevator and stood right by my side. Aunt Nora gave me a quick, protective glance. I nodded to let her know I was okay, but I was pretty sure everybody in the elevator could hear the galloping of my heart that said otherwise.

I didn't know this man, but I wanted to. Something inside me was drawn to him, and I didn't know if it was his good looks or the idea that dreams do come true. I only hoped that this pull was not caused by a curse, awakened in a distant, far-off land.

The elevator doors closed, and the cabin jerked as we began our descent. I caught a reflection in the steel doors through the tightly packed bodies in the elevator. A girl with dark chestnut hair, brown eyes, and ruby lips stared back at me. A reflection of a girl I both knew and loved. Standing beside me was not a stranger, but somebody I had known for much longer than my conscious mind would allow me to remember.

Walker was so close, I could feel the heat from his skin radiating against the back of my hand. Against all will, my pinky finger sought his. Our flesh touched as I trained my eyes forward, unblinking. Walker wrapped his pinky finger around mine in a small, but monumental gesture.

I froze with bated breath. His finger intertwined with mine for what felt like lifetimes, past and present. Reuniting with Walker brought with it more than just his memory. Within the steel reflection, only our two souls existed. No Aunt Nora. No Mediator Walon. And no lawsuit. No matter which direction I looked, there was only us, standing in an eternal void. A creeping mist enveloped us in its ghostly embrace.

Before I could react, the elevator shuddered to a stop, and the phantom mist dispelled. The lights brightened, and a cheery bell rang, announcing we'd reached our final destination. I cleared my throat and tried to catch my breath. Walker's hand slipped away from mine as he and his two attorneys exited the elevator.

Aunt Nora checked with me one last time as she ushered me out of the elevator and through the lobby. Once outside in the brisk evening air, I said goodbye to my aunt and thanked her for all she'd done for me. Then Walker and I watched as our attorneys ducked into their cars. We stood silently on the curb as they drove off, parting ways.

Walker placed his hand on the small of my back, as if he'd done it a million times before. We crossed the street, stealing glances at each other and merging in with the crowd. All the black suits hurried on their important business, but Walker and I took our time.

As we approached the steakhouse, I couldn't help but notice the magnificent, ornamental red doors. Three times taller than any regular door, these truly looked like they belonged in a fairy tale. I paused in front of the steakhouse, taking it all in. A moment too precious for me to forget.

Among the bustling crowd, Walker and I stood side-by-side, marveling at the steakhouse store front. Slowly, he turned to me, leaned down and stole my breath away. "I know you," he whispered in my ear.

"Welcome!" the doorkeeper interrupted in a husky voice. He pulled on the golden handles and opened the luxurious red doors, grand enough to be a real-life portal. And as we stepped inside, I knew that a life I couldn't have imagined in my wildest dreams was about to begin.

The End

Epilogue

I always wanted a scar. Nothing revolting. Just a gash. Something that said I was dangerous . . . or that I could be. I wanted to be mysterious. I got that, and so much more.

Etched into the side of my head was more than just a battle wound. It was a reminder of the pain and suffering it took to become the person I am today. And the gold band on my thumb reminded me of all the unpredictable and enchanting ways our lives could take shape. You see, reality is not just what you make of it—it's also what you dare to dream, and what you are willing to fight for.

Seven years after the accident, I sat in a movie theater on opening night of my first movie. As opening credits illuminated the big screen, Walker pried my white-knuckled hand from the arm rest and together, we took a deep breath and welcomed yet another twist in our remarkable story.

THE END
WITH LOVE,
Laura C. Reden

www.ingramcontent.com/pod-product-compliance
Lightning Source LLC
Chambersburg PA
CBHW020721310726
48979CB00004B/1011

* 9 7 8 1 9 5 4 5 8 7 3 6 6 *